**She hadn't been afraid of Rainier, not really.
Hadn't even been afraid of dying.**

She'd held the trigger for the EMP that would cut Rainier down, and savored an urge unlike any she'd ever felt before. A wellspring of vengeance had risen in Sanda that day, and while Rainier was certain it was fear alone at the base instinct of all humanity, Sanda had known in that moment that, for her, the core of her drive had been rage. Not the desperate, flailing anger of the impetuous, but something deeper.

Something primal.

Rainier Lavaux had threatened everything and everyone Sanda had ever loved. Sanda had felt that loss once. And she'd burn the bitch to the ground rather than suffer through that pain all over again.

Praise for

VELOCITY WEAPON

"O'Keefe delivers a complicated, thoughtful tale that skillfully interweaves intrigue, action, and strong characterization. Themes of found family, emotional connection, and identity run throughout, backed up by strong worldbuilding and a tense narrative. This series opener leaves multiple plot threads open for further development, and readers will look forward to the next installments."   —*Publishers Weekly*

"Meticulously plotted, edge-of-your-seat space opera with a soul; a highly promising science-fiction debut."   —*Kirkus*

"A brilliantly plotted yarn of survival and far-future political intrigue."
—*Guardian*

"This is a sweeping space opera with scope and vision, tremendously readable. I look forward to seeing where O'Keefe takes this story next."
—*Locus*

"Outstanding space opera where the politics and worldbuilding of the Expanse series meets the forward-thinking AI elements of *Ancillary Justice*."   —Michael Mammay, author of *Planetside*

"*Velocity Weapon* is a spectacular epic of survival, full of triumph and gut-wrenching loss."   —Alex White, author of the Salvagers series

"*Velocity Weapon* is a roller-coaster ride of pure delight. Furious action sequences, funny dialog, and touching family interactions all wrapped up in a plot that will keep you guessing every step of the way. This is one of the best science fiction novels of 2019."
—K. B. Wagers, author of the Indranan War trilogy

"*Velocity Weapon* is fast-paced, twisty, edge-of-your-seat fun. Space opera fans are in for a massive treat!"
—Marina J. Lostetter, author of *Noumenon*

BY MEGAN E. O'KEEFE

THE PROTECTORATE
Velocity Weapon
Chaos Vector
Catalyst Gate

NOVELLAS
The First Omega

CATALYST GATE

THE PROTECTORATE: BOOK THREE

MEGAN E. O'KEEFE

orbitbooks.net

Copyright © 2021 by Megan E. O'Keefe
Excerpt from *Extinction Burst* copyright © 2021 by Megan E. O'Keefe

Cover design by Lauren Panepinto
Cover illustration by Sparth
Cover copyright © 2021 by Hachette Book Group, Inc.
Author photograph by Joey Hewitt

Orbit
Hachette Book Group
1290 Avenue of the Americas
New York, NY 10104
orbitbooks.net

First Edition: June 2021
Simultaneously published in Great Britain by Orbit

Orbit is an imprint of Hachette Book Group.
The Orbit name and logo are trademarks of Little, Brown Book Group Limited.

The publisher is not responsible for websites (or their content) that are not owned by the publisher.

The Hachette Speakers Bureau provides a wide range of authors for speaking events. To find out more, go to www.hachettespeakersbureau.com or call (866) 376-6591.

Library of Congress Cataloging-in-Publication Data
Names: O'Keefe, Megan E., 1985– author.
Title: Catalyst gate / Megan E. O'Keefe.
Description: First edition. | New York, NY : Orbit, 2021. | Series: The Protectorate ; book 3
Identifiers: LCCN 2020047690 | ISBN 9780316419659 (trade paperback) |
    ISBN 9780316419680 (ebook) | ISBN 9780316419673 (ebook)
Subjects: GSAFD: Science fiction.
Classification: LCC PS3615.K437 C38 2021 | DDC 813/.6—dc23
LC record available at https://lccn.loc.gov/2020047690

ISBNs: 978-0-316-41965-9 (trade paperback), 978-0-316-41968-0 (ebook)

Printed in the United States of America

LSC-C

Printing 1, 2021

For Laura Blackwell

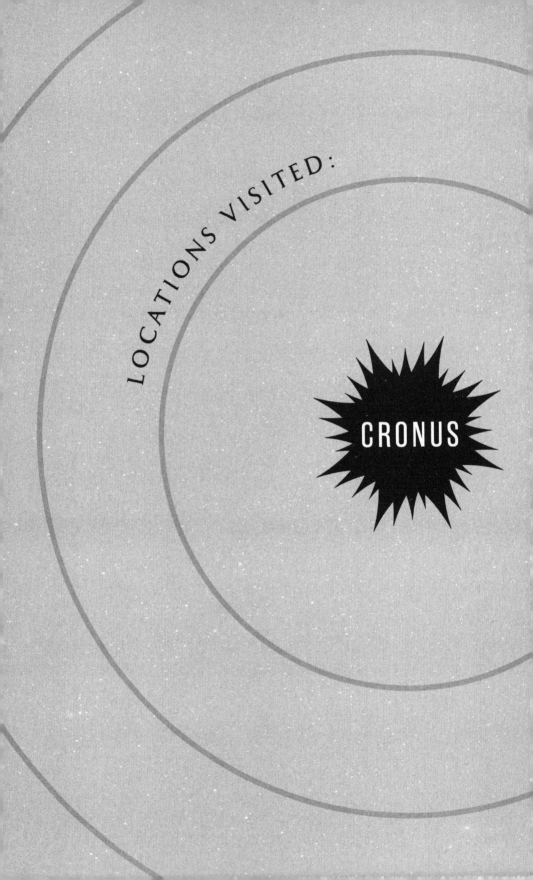

LOCATIONS VISITED:

CRONUS

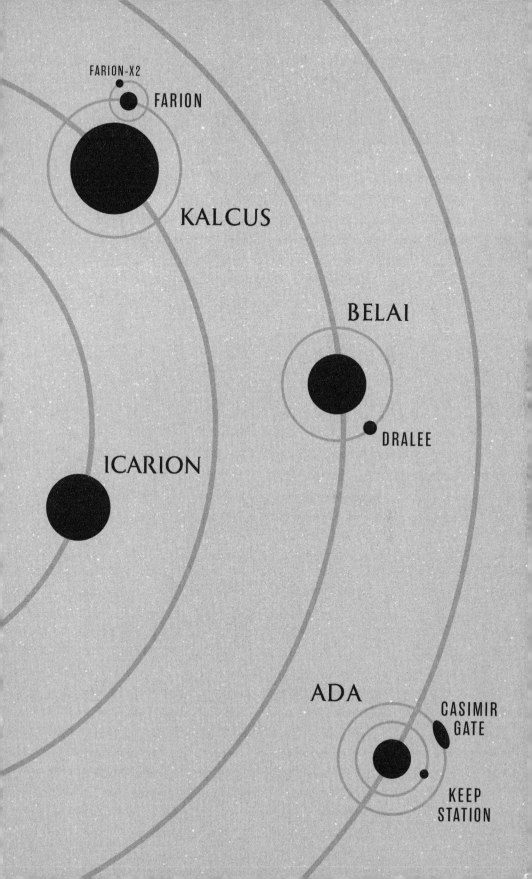

CHAPTER 1

PRIME STANDARD YEAR 3543

HELLO, SPY

Sanda Greeve stood on the deck of the biggest weapon humanity had ever known, and watched live footage of the city of Atrux tearing itself apart. Ninety-seven percent of Atrux, fallen. That was the only number she could cling to, because the actual amount of dead and comatose was too high to comprehend.

The rest, that 3 percent, had been converted by the ascension-agent. And in their confusion and pain, they rioted across the city, not understanding their own strength, until guardcore—vetted, *safe*—showed up to capture them or put them down.

Sanda clutched her blaster like a shield, though the weapon could do her no good. There wasn't a weapon in the universe big enough to stop what had happened to Atrux. Even her ship, *The Light*, wasn't enough. She wasn't sure anything could be enough.

"Tell me Anford's finally recovered footage of the contamination moment," Sanda asked Bero. Asked her ship.

"Watching it won't change anything," Bero said.

He was stalling. Warning hackles raised along the back of her neck.

"Mouthing off isn't going to stop me. Play it."

The video flickered onto the forward viewscreen, though *The Light* was perfectly capable of displaying video without the tiniest hiccup.

Bero, showing his annoyance by inserting a glitch. She almost rolled her eyes, but that'd only encourage him.

Her irritation was only scraping the surface. Below the major's bars on her chest and the sleek confines of her Prime-issued jumpsuit, Sanda boiled with molten rage. Needling her might give the magma within a path to eruption, and not a soul on board *The Light* had time for her to melt down.

A guardcore appeared in the footage, slipping through the thin cracks in Prime's protocols to secure an unwelcome canister to the additive tank of Atrux's atmo mix. From that canister, a wave of self-replicating nanites had spread the ascension-agent throughout the city's ventilation system. Sanda leaned toward the screen, frowning. The armor was right. The weapons were right. The clearances were right. But that was no GC.

"It's not Rainier," she said. The movements were too forced, too stilted, to be hers. Only one other known impostor wore that armor.

The Light's crew shifted uncomfortably. This ship didn't need a crew to fly, but Bero had gone ahead and given them all seats with consoles they could work, if they so desired. They often fiddled with the controls, trying to figure out the inner workings of *The Light*. Sanda suspected those buttons were little more than placebos, but she hadn't had the heart to ask Bero outright. The crew fiddled with those buttons now.

"We can't be sure," Dr. Liao said. "The armor—"

"Doesn't disguise gait," Sanda countered. The doctor pressed her lips shut.

Sanda couldn't blame her. She wanted that figure to be Rainier, too. But she'd learned a long time ago that wanting something to be true badly enough to lie to yourself only led to more pain.

"Bero, can you run a gait analysis?" she asked.

"Against every person in the known universe?"

"No," Arden said. Their voice rasped and they'd gone deathly pale. The word trailed off into emptiness, cut down by a sharp glare from Nox, but Sanda didn't press.

Jules had been their friend. They needed to do this on their own, because neither one of them would forgive Sanda if she pushed for it, even if they already knew it was true. "I have some footage of Jules I can send you," Arden said.

"She wouldn't do this," Nox said, but he didn't stop Arden as they tapped on their wristpad, sending the files to *The Light*.

"We have to know," Arden said softly.

A retort bubbled below Nox's surface, but before he could get it out, Bero pushed two videos, side by side, onto the viewscreen. In one, Jules Valentine approached Arden's old apartment building on top of Udon-Voodun. In the other, the guardcore walked through the door into the atmo mix control room. For the benefit of the humans riding in his belly, Bero allowed graphical points of comparison to run over each figure.

He didn't say anything. He didn't need to.

"It's her," Arden said.

Sanda pushed down a burst of excitement. Rainier Lavaux was an expert at covering her tracks. But Sanda was pretty damn sure Jules Valentine lacked the same skill set. Jules, Sanda could find. From there, she'd leverage her way to Rainier. She doubted Nox and Arden would be as excited about this break as she was.

"B, get me Anford," Sanda said.

"I am not your personal assistant."

Sanda rolled her eyes and put a priority call through to her commander. General Anford's face popped up on the screen in seconds, overriding the footage of Jules. Anford didn't even blink at Sanda's unusual crew or the alien deck of *The Light*. It was amazing how quickly humanity adapted.

"Greeve, tell me you have something."

"The guardcore who released the nanites on Atrux is Jules Valentine."

The general's eyes narrowed briefly. "Not Rainier? You're sure?"

"She may have acted under Rainier's orders, I don't know, but Bero is certain the body in that armor belongs to Valentine."

"Far be it from me to doubt Bero's assessment."

"I have been lauded for my intelligence in the past," Bero said.

Sanda suppressed a smirk. "I intend to pursue. Valentine might know a way to get to Rainier."

"I agree. We need her alive, Greeve." Anford glanced to the side, the corners of her lips tightening. "We need all the information we can get our hands on."

Ninety-seven percent. That number was burned into Sanda's heart. Similar branding carved pain around Anford's eyes.

"I'll get you answers," Sanda said.

"Hold in Atrux. I don't have a lot to spare, but I'll send a battalion to you."

Slowly, intentionally, Sanda shifted her gaze to the walls of *The Light*. "With respect, I need no other weapons. They would only slow me down."

Anford's jaw flexed as she soaked that in. "Very well. Between Prime Director Okonkwo and me, you have carte blanche to requisition anything you need. Good luck, Greeve."

"Good luck." Sanda snapped off a tight salute, and Anford cut the feed.

"Are you sure we're going to be enough, Commander?" Conway asked.

She wasn't. But that was a doubt she couldn't allow to fester. "It's our best shot. Bero, do you have a bead on that GC ship Valentine took off in?"

"It was last flagged passing through the gate to Ordinal."

"Then that's where we start."

Arden swiveled their chair around to look her in the eye. "Rainier made Jules do this."

Sanda met their gaze evenly, peripherally aware of the tension in Nox's body, the held breaths of everyone on the ship. No one liked hunting down a woman they'd meant to save not too long ago. No one liked acknowledging they'd known, and even cared for, a monster.

Sanda could relate, but that didn't mean she could make it better.

"We'll find her," she said. "And we'll ask her ourselves."

"Sanda," Bero said, his voice tense.

She frowned. "What is it?"

"*The Light* has an incoming tightbeam from an unregistered source."

"Does this ship even have a transponder to point at?"

"Not...exactly."

"Put it through."

The viewscreen filled with a face so familiar that, if she hadn't already been propped up on an emotional cocktail of rage and determination, she might have had to sit down.

New shadows carved troughs beneath his eyes, and thick stubble peppered his jawline. Dark brown hair stuck up under low-g, and over his shoulder she could make out the sleek geometry of a high-end shuttle. But those grey eyes, they were always the same, if a touch sad.

"Hey," Tomas Cepko said. His voice was thin and wary. "I'm in Ordinal. We need to talk."

"You look like shit," she said.

The corner of his eye twitched, then he settled into a small, warm smile. "Nice to see you, too."

"Believe it or not," Sanda said, gesturing to the ship around her, "I'm a little busy."

"It's about the sphere you discovered inside *The Light*," Tomas said, his expression completely locked down. "The one with the instructions for the creation of the ascension-agent."

"How the fuck—?" Nox took a step, as if he could reach through the screen to choke the spy on the other side. She couldn't blame him for wanting to try.

"Crew," Sanda said firmly. "Meet Nazca Cepko, first-class spy and all-around asshole."

His lips thinned and he flicked his gaze down. "I...can explain my actions."

"Really not what I'm worried about right now."

"Hello, Tomas," Bero said.

Tomas's eyes widened. He leaned toward the camera, pressing his hands against the console of his shuttle. "Christ, are you in danger?"

Nox snorted, which warmed Sanda's angry heart right up. "I am in command of my ship, Nazca, and I'd like to know how the fuck you got that tightbeam to me."

He gave her a punchably sly smile. "Seems we have a lot of information to share with each other."

"I'm not in the habit of sharing with spies."

He winced and rubbed at his chest. "Yeah, I remember. Look, I don't know what's going on with the fleet or why you're in that ship with Bero, but I know you, Greeve, and you're about to charge guns out after Rainier. I don't blame you, but there are some things you need to know. Some things I need to *show* you."

"*Commander* Greeve," she snapped, because there was no way in the void she'd let Tomas-fucking-Cepko get away with undermining her position. "And if you're looking for a date, lover, there are programs for that."

"Commander," Bero said with a touch more respect than he usually bothered with, "I hate to interrupt you tearing into Tomas, but it occurs to me that he knows about the sphere."

Tomas leaned back, crossed his arms, and raised both brows. "Thanks, B."

"I do not like you, Tomas."

Sanda gritted her teeth. "Very well. We're coming through Ordinal anyway. Send your location to Bero and we'll talk. If you waste my time, I swear to all of Prime that I will space you."

"I believe you," he said with a slight shudder, then composed himself and flashed an irritatingly charming smile at her. "See you soon."

She cut the feed and sank into her captain's chair, trying to quiet her mind. That damn man made her feel like the memory-wipe headaches lurked behind her next breath, like any second all the pain of the moment he'd ripped her world apart would come crashing back down.

"We sure it's a good idea to get mixed up with another Nazca, boss?" Nox asked. "Last time didn't go so well."

Sanda rubbed the side of her face. "It's because of last time that I'm putting up with this. Okonkwo hasn't managed to shake anything out of the Nazca tree, and they clearly know *something* about what's going on, or Novak wouldn't have been on Janus. Tomas knows about the sphere. Like Anford said, we need all the intel we can get, and that's the Nazca's specialty."

"You realize, of course, that he needs something from you," Bero said.

She tried to side-eye him, but it didn't really work when he existed all around her. "Yes, B. I am rather well versed in dealing with duplicitous dickheads."

"What do you think he wants?" Nox asked.

"I don't know," Sanda admitted. "But finding out what he wants will give us a better idea of what the Nazca really know than whatever bait intel he's set out for me."

"Sanda," Bero said with mock shock, "you've grown so cynical."

She quirked a half smile. "I learn from the best."

But it wasn't cynicism driving her. Rainier would say she was afraid, and maybe she'd be right, to a certain extent. Watching Atrux fall to an invisible storm had certainly made her blood run cold, but that's not when the shift inside her had happened. It hadn't even been when she'd crawled off Liao's fringer settlement and learned she was too late—the secondary gate in Ada had spun, the blowback had happened, and it had nearly taken her family with it.

No, she'd felt the first slivers of change when she'd sat on that command console on the fringer settlement, all alone, and waited for Rainier Lavaux to show up and kill her. She hadn't been afraid of Rainier, not really. Hadn't even been afraid of dying.

She'd held the trigger for the EMP that would cut Rainier down, and savored an urge unlike any she'd ever felt before. A wellspring of vengeance had risen in Sanda that day, and while Rainier was certain it was fear alone at the base instinct of all humanity, Sanda had known in that moment that, for her, the core of her drive had been rage. Not the desperate, flailing anger of the impetuous, but something deeper.

Something primal.

Rainier Lavaux had threatened everything and everyone Sanda had ever loved. Sanda had felt that loss once. And she'd burn the bitch to the ground rather than suffer through that pain all over again.

CHAPTER 2

PRIME STANDARD YEAR 3543

TABLE FOR TWO

Instead of a shuttle in the black, Tomas sent Bero the coordinates for a restaurant planetside in Alexandria-Ordinal, the system's capital city. A cursory search said the restaurant was inside of a Hotel Stellaris, and a reservation had been made under the name Jacob Galvan.

The last time she'd seen him had been at the same hotel chain, on a different planet, the reservations under that same name. Then he'd disappeared, leaving her alone to deal with the fallout of the chip hidden in her head.

Either he was being cheeky—likely—or this was a genuine show of faith, signaling that he didn't want on board *The Light*, he really just wanted to talk. Or he believed that Sanda had been captured by Bero once more, and wanted her off the ship to get the truth from her own lips.

Or, a tiny sliver of her thought, he wanted to see her again without the trappings of war all around them. But that thought hadn't been allowed to live past its brief genesis. At least the location allowed her to park *The Light* in orbit, stealthed out, and take a simple shuttle to the space elevator.

She loathed the delay, but while Sanda had the best weapon in the universe in her arsenal, she lacked information. And information might be the key to getting one step ahead of Rainier. To getting the sphere with the instructions for the ascension-agent back, and healing the comatose of Atrux.

Hotel Stellaris was the fanciest hotel chain in the 'verse, and the location at Prime's capital city was its crowning jewel. It was the kind of place you wore clothes crafted of velvet and sequins to, the kind of place for improbably high heels, higher slits, and tuxedo jackets tailored to whatever the latest fashion was.

Sanda walked down the vast marble colonnade leading to the maître d' in her jumpsuit, mag boots, and major's coat. When they'd put the Prime logos back on, she'd added the name of her ship, *The Light*, below the insignia pinned to her chest and a sleek silhouette of the ship. Anford had merely nodded when she'd first seen those adjustments.

There was no use hiding who Sanda was. No point in hiding *The Light* after she'd flown it into Ada and docked the silvery leviathan for all to see. Alien tech had always been a part of Prime, and now it was time to bring it out into the open.

The maître d' didn't seem so sure.

She stopped her long march a step from his podium, and while the trim man's demeanor didn't so much as twitch, his gaze flicked from her scuffed boots, to her plain jumpsuit, to the bars on her chest. The deliberation was lightning fast, then he offered her the polite welcome he'd offer any esteemed guest.

"Commander Greeve, we have been expecting you. Mr. Galvan has already arrived. May I take your coat?"

"No." It hid the two high-end blasters strapped to her hips, probably the most expensive accessories in the restaurant tonight. "Lead the way."

He gestured her onward, and she let him regale her with the hotel's long and illustrious history while they wound through tables stocked with the glittering upper echelons of Ordinal.

A restaurant like this didn't fill every table at any given time. It gave its guests space, the illusion of being in a charming secret place while in truth their reservations booked out years in advance. Sanda wondered how Tomas had wedged himself in so quickly, but for all she knew, this place was run by the Nazca. Eavesdropping at a restaurant this nice had to be good for information gathering.

The wide spaces between guests weren't enough to hide them, or her, though. Those who came to Hotel Stellaris to dine wanted to be seen doing so, and that meant that, as surreptitiously as the maître d' led her along, conversations stalled as she passed. Whispers flowed in her wake.

Sanda didn't know what bothered her more. The fact that Tomas had known she'd be recognized and become the topic of gossip here tonight, or the fact that she couldn't stop it.

The maître d' slowed his steps at a raised dais toward the back of the room. A lone table stood against a massive picture window overlooking the sprawling city of Alexandria-Ordinal.

A few months ago, the view would have taken her breath away. Now, it made her ill. How many people crawled through the streets and skies of Ordinal? It was arguably the best-secured city in all of Prime, but every Prime city had thought themselves safe from biological attacks until Jules Valentine brought Atrux to its knees.

"Here we are, Commander." The maître d' pulled a chair out for her, and she sat. "May I suggest our latest vintage, fresh from Elysia—"

"I won't be eating, thank you."

Maybe that had finally gotten the man's smooth demeanor to crack, but if it did, Sanda missed the moment, because she only had eyes for the man sitting across from her.

Tomas rested his forearms on the champagne-colored tablecloth, leaning toward her with an easy smile and eyes that were far too haunted for a man with his insouciant posture, or lack of wrinkles. He'd opted for a sage-green silk shirt with the sleeves rolled up, and dark slacks flared enough at the ankles to allow for the greater girth of the mag boots on his feet.

Sanda didn't know a thing about fashion, but judging from the outfits she'd seen on the walk in, Tomas blended right in. Right. Spy. He'd let all the attention fall on her, while he slipped through unnoticed. She'd known this was a game from the jump. Had thought being played by him wouldn't hurt. She'd been wrong.

"Tomas," she said. The maître d' took the hint and extricated himself without so much as a rustle of his too-tight suit. She looked pointedly at his mag boots. "Presumptuous of you."

"Have to be prepared for anything," he said, his nice-to-see-you smile shifting from placid calm to the slight curl of something real. "That a pulsar-class blaster on your hip?"

"Two, actually. I see you came unarmed."

He spread his hands. "It hadn't occurred to me I'd need to be armed to see you, Sanda."

"Your spy senses are failing you. I've had a rough time with the Nazca lately."

His smile crashed and burned. "So I heard."

"If he was your friend..."

"No, don't apologize. There are no friends between the Nazca." Tomas took a long drink of an amber-colored cocktail with orange sugar on the rim and shook his head.

"Figured you'd be drinking that Elysian vintage, isn't that where you're from?"

A longer drink this time. "Surprised you remember that."

"One of the few memories that doesn't give me headaches these days."

He started to reach a hand toward her, caught her glare, and stopped himself. His hand rested in the center of the table, curled, but limp. "I'm sorry."

"Not what I'm here for. I'm a very busy woman, Master Spy, and you said one little magic word that got me off the back of my ship, where I would much rather be. I'm here to learn two things, Tomas: What do you know about *it*, and how did you get a tightbeam through to *The Light*?"

"Don't you mean Bero?"

"I do not. They are separate entities until he decides otherwise. You're avoiding the questions." He flashed her a grin that made her chest flush, but she brushed the feeling aside.

"Sanda Greeve, my straight shooter." He shook his head and slammed back the last of his drink. "I know where 'it' is, and I know how to get it, but I can't get it alone."

"I have no reason to believe that you are not on-mission, and that you will not hand it over to your superiors if we recover the object. Tell me where it is, and I'll retrieve it without you."

A shadow passed behind his eyes. "I don't think you can get it without me."

"My crew is perfectly capable."

"Not for this."

"Tomas." She lowered her voice and leaned forward. A muscle in his jaw jumped. "Whatever the Nazca want, it's not worth it. I know your job is everything to you, but this could very well be the key to healing Atrux. I cannot, I *will* not, allow the Nazca to fuck off with my ball."

He swirled the dregs of his empty glass. "I won't hand it over to the Nazca."

"I can't take your word."

"I know. The thing is, I won't hand it over to them because I'm not Nazca anymore. I've been burned, as we spies are fond of saying. Cut off. Cast off. I'm solo."

He met her gaze evenly, and while every scrap of her wanted to believe him, there was too much at stake. With a sinking heart, she picked at the critical flaw in his story. "You're registered here as Jacob Galvan, a Nazca alias. If they burned you, they'd be here in minutes to take you out."

"About that." He turned his wristpad over, checking the time. "I really wish you had gotten here on time so we could have ordered one last meal on the Nazca coffers."

Glass exploded, showering them in glittering rain.

Sanda moved before she could think, shoved her chair back, and tipped up the table. She reached to grab Tomas by the shirt, but he was already on one knee, ducking behind the table for two as Sanda got the wooden shield between them and the next shot.

The table shuddered in her grasp. The stink of fabric and Synth-Wood frying under blaster fire overwhelmed the pleasant scents of wine and food. At least this place was fancy enough to buy very thick tables.

Sanda swore and grabbed her blaster, popping her head up long enough to make sure she wouldn't hit any civilians before firing back in the direction of the kitchen, where the shots had come from.

People screamed, glass broke, and as Sanda met Tomas's eyes behind the temporary shelter of a table that was only providing enough cover to keep those shooting at them from hitting anything vital, she felt a deep-rooted protective surge mingle with anger.

"You knew they'd come for you and you didn't bring a weapon?"

He shrugged one shoulder. "They would have taken my weapons at the door, and you always carry two. You didn't come alone, did you?"

Sanda's wristpad lit up with a priority call from Nox. She accepted.

"Little fuckers are holed up in the kitchen," he said. "Conway's got the front door on lock and is ushering out the civvies, but I can't promise a clean run for you. Spy still alive?"

"Despite all the odds," she said. Another blaster shot rocked the table, nearly searing her ear as it bore through the wood. Maybe not that thick after all.

"Not after I get my hands—"

"Easy, Nox. Suppress the kitchens, grab one alive, and do not hurt any civilians."

"Yeah, yeah," he muttered, and cut the call.

Tomas looked at her, one brow raised. She grinned with him, couldn't help it, and slapped her second blaster into his hand. "A civvie dies, and I'll take it out on you."

"Understood, Commander Greeve."

It was really rather annoying that, after everything, the way he said her title traced tingles up her spine.

She popped up from behind the table and, synchronized with Tomas, fired back toward their Nazca attackers.

CHAPTER 3

PRIME STANDARD YEAR 3543

TRUST IS A QUICK EXIT

Sanda fired until the return fire stopped, then vaulted over the table and dashed for a thick marble column, Tomas tight on her heels. Behind the shelter of stone, she grabbed a comms earpiece from under her wristpad and shoved it in.

"I'm online. Talk to me."

"I've got the cameras in the kitchen," Arden said. "Looks like ten came in through the service elevator when you made contact with the maître d' and hustled the cooks and staff out. The staff is uninjured, as far as I know. You shot two in the chest and one in the stomach, but I can't say if they're out. Nox got one in the head."

"Fuck yeah I did," Nox said.

"Front door is secure," Conway said. "Maître d' is hustling the civvies out like he does this every day."

"Tomas," she said. They'd pressed themselves close together to make better use of the cover of the pillar, their sides crammed so tight she could feel the steady rise and fall of his chest. He nodded to show he was listening but kept his head turned away, watching their flank. "Ten accounted for, one confirmed kill, three possibly out, but don't count on it. Centered in the kitchen. These are your people, what are their tactics?"

He shook his head. "When the Nazca come for one of their own, they don't use tactics a Nazca can work around."

"Lovely. Nox?"

"Boss?"

"There are two ins-and-outs to that kitchen. Hammer them on the north exit, I'm coming in through the south. Arden, can you lock down the service elevator and any back entrances?"

"Already done."

Bero said, "May I make a suggestion?"

"Shoot, Big B," Sanda said.

Tomas grimaced.

"You could flee, there is no need for engagement."

Sanda grabbed the back of Tomas's head, fingers tangling in his hair, and every single muscle in his body went rigid, his scalp heating up beneath her touch as she yanked his head around and stared hard into his eyes.

He may be one of the finest spies in the universe, but he couldn't hide his physical responses from her when she took him by surprise. Panic and hope warred across his face as she dragged him close.

"Will these people come for you if we bail right now?"

"Yes," he said, so close his breath gusted against her lips. She let him go and pushed slightly, facing him back around to cover their flank. He shivered. She ignored it.

"Right. I'd rather not have a gaggle of Nazca dogging our heels. Time to make a point sharp enough to force the whole cursed organization to keep their distance. Agreed?"

Confirmation chorused across the channel. Sanda closed her eyes a breath to center herself. She felt a little shitty for squeezing an answer out of Tomas like that, but truth had been hard to come by lately, and Sanda needed to know why she was shooting before she squeezed the trigger.

"In position," Nox whispered.

Sanda checked her blaster charge, scanned the scene, and stepped out from behind cover. Whatever turmoil she'd stirred up in Tomas, he had it under lock as he shadowed her, moving in concert, spraying down the kitchen exit until the swinging door lay in tattered, toothy pieces on the ground.

They hit the entrance at the same time, turned, and pressed their backs against the wall on opposite sides, blasters up, legs braced, and studiously did not meet each other's eyes.

"Two more down," Arden said into her comm.

She showed Tomas two fingers. He nodded.

Nox's rifle roared to life on the other side of the room.

"Three more."

She added three fingers, and his brows shot up, but he tucked his chin in acknowledgment. Sometimes Sanda wondered if Nox was the biggest weapon she had on her team, not *The Light*.

"Two coming your way," Arden said. "Average height. No visible armor. Flanking lines."

Sanda thanked the void for Arden Wyke and turned, stepping into the frame of the doorway, squeezing off two shots before the Nazca coming her way could process she was even there. She dropped down behind a stainless steel rolling cart and counted to three, then popped up and started laying down suppressive fire wildly across the back wall while Tomas moved into the room, taking down three with shots almost as clean as Nox's.

"Clear," Arden said.

Sanda didn't put her weapon down. Under the hiss of a pot boiling over on the stove, she heard a soft scrabbling across the floor—fingernails scraping tile and metal, reaching for a weapon.

Nox entered the room in her peripheral vision and braced, rifle barrel tracking the space a few steps in front of her. He needn't have bothered, but she appreciated the thought. Sanda rounded a workbench and found a Nazca lying in a pool of blood, one hand pressed to her stomach while the other scrambled across the floor for a downed blaster. Sanda kicked it away and dropped to a crouch alongside her.

Nox and Tomas started forward, but she gestured them back with a sharp tilt of the head. In the corner of her eye, she could see Tomas's finger crawl for the trigger and hold off, but just barely.

She grabbed the woman's shirt and lifted her up, bringing her face close. Blood stained the woman's teeth, and some of the capillaries in her eyes had blown, but as Sanda well knew, it took a long time to die from a shot to the stomach.

"Tell your boss that Tomas Cepko is protected," Sanda said. "If any of you come for me or Cepko again, I won't bother letting a messenger survive. I'll come in person, and blow your whole organization to atoms."

The Nazca sneered, blood dripping across her jaw from the corner of her lips. "You can't keep the traitor from us forever."

Sanda dropped the woman back to the ground. As she stood, she elbowed a medikit on the wall and yanked out a plastiskin patch, then flicked it to the bleeding woman.

"Keep trying. Next time, I won't be so nice."

Conway strolled into the kitchen with her rifle against her shoulder. "Civs are out but we've got SecureSite coming in hot. Guessing you don't want to stick around to answer those questions."

Sanda winced. "Arden, extraction plan beta. You got a visual on the window?"

"I see it. Sending the special shuttle."

"Time to go," she said.

Conway and Nox flicked Tomas a glance, shrugged, and exited the kitchen, leaving Sanda and Tomas alone. He parted his lips to say something, but she closed the distance between them and scowled up into his stupidly perfect face.

"You put my team at risk *intentionally.* I pulled your ass out of this fire because I didn't have a choice, but if you willingly endanger my crew again, I swear to the fucking void I'll leave you to bleed with the rest of your Nazca buddies."

He sucked air through his teeth and pulled his head back, but his body stayed close, eyes downcast to meet hers. "I knew they wouldn't be able to scramble an A-team fast enough for this. Those were initiates. Lackeys. I never believed you were in real danger. I wouldn't do that."

"Make me believe it."

She held out her hand, palm up. Slowly, Tomas placed the borrowed blaster into her hand, fingertips brushing her palm, then pulled his hands back and held them up, empty. "Thought I was protected."

Goddamn that sly smile of his. She holstered the weapon but kept the other in her hand. "Don't push me, spy."

She turned her back on him and stalked out into the half-destroyed restaurant, then sighed. The fleet was going to have to pay to fix all of this, at a time when their resources were already stretched thin.

It wasn't the money that was going to be a problem, but she'd blown chunks out of real marble, and that could only be found on a few planets. With all gates temporarily closed to everything except fleet and Keeper activity, importing the correct materials would be a real pain in the ass.

One of *The Light*'s silver shuttles descended in front of the busted-out window, and relief washed over her. She'd file a report, Anford would be pissed, but things would move on. She had more important matters to worry about than import-export—with mental apologies to her dads.

The shuttle was about the size of a train cab, comfortably able to seat twelve but capable of holding up to fifty before Bero said the life support got iffy. Swimming through the night sky of Ordinal, it sidled up to the shattered glass and their impromptu exit point. A gangway extended down and connected with the floor by the broken table.

Under the spin-grav of the planet, and through the thick air of the atmo dome, no ship should be able to swing around with such grace and agility, let alone hover in place without any obvious mechanism. Sanda had started to get used to it.

Tomas hadn't. He stopped cold, that sly smile wiped from his face. Seeing the shuttle through his eyes, Sanda felt the same thrill she'd felt when she'd first stepped onto *The Light* and gravity, impossibly, had dragged her feet to the ground.

"What is that?" he asked.

"A subset of *The Light*, or so Bero tells me. The primary ship can bud off shuttles when needed."

Nox and Conway had already boarded, so it was Sanda who saw the deep well of fear rise up in Tomas, then be capped immediately.

"What?" she asked, cocking her head to the side. "Not still afraid of Bero, are you?"

"There's not much in this universe I'm afraid of," he said.

The lid was so strongly in place over his emotions that he swung his arms easily, strolling up the gangway into the shuttle, looking around like this was any other curiosity in a grand and vast universe.

He could lie to her all he liked, but practiced as he was, Sanda had become intimately acquainted with fear lately, and something about *The Light* had made his skin crawl before he'd gotten himself under control.

Her wristpad flashed with a message from Bero.

B: Not my biggest fan

S: Can't blame him, can you?

She swallowed a worm of guilt. Maybe she still had her own issues to work through with Bero, but she didn't fear him, not to the extent Tomas seemed to. She stepped into the shuttle, and the gangway slid up smooth as still water behind her.

She couldn't say if Bero had done that or if something in the engineering of the shuttle had sensed that all its intended passengers were loaded. The ship had seemed to intuit her wants before Bero had been uploaded, so there must be some basic function inherent to the structure. Arden and Knuth were still bashing their heads against the puzzle of how the ship worked.

Maybe it wasn't Bero that Tomas feared. Maybe it was the ship itself. She couldn't blame him for that, either.

CHAPTER 4

PRIME STANDARD YEAR 3543

SHOTS IN THE DARK

Biran stood in a black site warehouse, the unfamiliar weight of a blaster in one hand and the familiar weight of duty on his shoulders. This was his petition. He'd asked for this. Written the idea up as convincingly as he could, then presented it to the High Protectorate, to Okonkwo, never fully dreaming they'd say yes.

But they had, because it was the right thing to do. The only safe thing to do. The guardcore had been infiltrated, and that was unthinkable, and so it was time to do one more unthinkable thing.

"Surrender your weapons," Biran said, and the tricky acoustics of the warehouse made his voice ring out, sound firmer than he felt it should.

He was playacting. Pretending at being Director Greeve. Pretending to be ready to be Speaker had been hard enough, but at least then he'd had Olver for counsel. Now, it was down to him, and he couldn't waver. Not for a second, for there were snakes in the Protectorate of Ada. He just hadn't flushed them out yet.

Synchronized, the guardcore lined up in front of him and unclipped their rifles from their backs. They set them on the ground, then placed their sidearms next to them, and kicked them away. The wave of artillery washed across the floor, the tide stopping a few centimeters from the fleet soldiers standing opposite the guardcore.

"Fleet, ready," he ordered.

Anford should be here, but she had a war to direct, and ultimately this was a Keeper problem, not a fleet problem. The two hundred fleet sharpshooters Anford had provided him lifted their rifles and braced, each one sighting down a different member of the GC.

A lump formed in Biran's throat at the clicking of weaponized metal all around him, but he did not swallow. He stood on a balcony overlooking the warehouse, Keepers Vladsen and Singh to either side of him, deadly silent, blasters in both of their hands, just in case.

If it came to any of the Keepers shooting, then things were already lost, but Prime was a civilization built on fail-safes and redundancies. And lies, but he was trying not to think about those right now.

"Jammers," he ordered.

Behind him, in a small office space, Keeper techs chosen for this purpose switched on jammers that fuzzed all communications and put all electronic recording devices on the fritz. There'd be no pictures taken of the GC. No evidence of this day, aside from the bodies.

"Retract helmets," Biran ordered.

As one, the helmets of the guardcore slipped back into their armor, revealing a wide variety of faces. Some of which repeated.

The fleet rifles cracked. Rainier's identical bodies slumped to the floor, their heads blown to bits. Later their remains would be dragged away to meet their final end in vats of acid. Disgusting, but necessary. When Rainier was dead, the other GC put their helmets up without the order. They knew the drill.

Biran uncurled his fist, wiped sweat against his thigh. None of the fleeties had been killed this time. Good. He'd led five of these inquisitions so far, and this one should be his last before the expedition through the secondary gate.

All over the united worlds of Prime, Protectorates were performing the same ritual, with similar results. The GC knew it was coming, and yet, the Rainier ancillaries never ran. They always showed up, dropped their helmets, and grinned into death.

Disposable. Such bodies were disposable to Rainier, Biran told himself. And it was probably worth it to her for the psychological aspect. Watching 33 percent of the guardcore fall to fleet rifles hurt, even when he knew there was no choice. Her roots had spread fast, and deep, and now it was his job to carve her out of Prime's bedrock.

"Early estimates approximate the number at sixty-seven," Singh said, tilting her head as she listened to her comms.

"Why do they never run?" Vladsen asked no one in particular.

Biran holstered his blaster. "She wants us to believe that this doesn't hurt her."

"And is that true?" Singh asked.

"I have no idea," Biran admitted. "But we cannot continue with so many guardcore compromised. Whether this damages her or not is irrelevant."

"I agree," Vladsen said. "It is a miserable and brutal process, but it must be done."

"Keeper Vladsen, you are so very agreeable with our esteemed director lately," Singh said, a suggestive note to her voice.

Biran resolutely watched the proceedings, as guardcore helped the fleeties load the bodies of their fallen comrades onto gurneys.

"I see no point in bickering over an obvious truth," Vladsen said smoothly. "Unless you believe there is a valid reason not to hunt the impostors?"

"No, of course not," Singh said, gesturing with one arm. Her white pashmina shifted, the crystals sewn into it glittering. Such an incongruently beautiful garment, Biran thought, in this place of death. "I only wonder why you are so amenable to our new director's proposals."

Vladsen sighed, as if tired from a long argument. "We are at war, Keeper. A war that has decimated our number. If I see fit to argue with our director, I will do so, but as of yet, he has been nothing but astute and fair to our people. Or do you disagree?"

Biran gripped the rail of the platform and leaned forward to hide a smirk. Well maneuvered of Vladsen, but still, Biran had been an idiot to give in to his desire to form a relationship with him.

Keepers did not consort. It was one of the numerous rules meant to keep the secrets of the chips safe in their heads. If two or more Keepers fell in love, then any of their number could be used to leverage information out of another by nefarious forces. And they were at *war*, Biran reminded himself, the exact situation in which such a thing might happen.

Oh, relationships happened. Dalliances, mostly, between students at the academy. Biran had indulged in one such relationship before he'd taken the chip. But once you took that chip, all such relationships were expected to end. The High Protectorate would not hesitate to prosecute you, if caught.

He could lose his chip. He could lose his life.

And yet, he could not stay away. He thought of Sanda, defending Bero even after all he had done, and shook his head. Maybe something was broken in the Greeve children.

They'd spent their childhoods watching their dads so fiercely in love, maybe they believed all love should look like that. Dangerous. He snorted. No, he knew better. He was obsessive. Sanda was bullheaded. And it had nothing to do with their parents, unless one counted the happenstance of genetics.

"Something amusing, Director?" Singh asked.

Biran shook his head. "Only if we're speaking of the bitterly ironic."

"What is on our director's mind?" Singh asked, sallying up to him at the rail.

He tipped his chin to the carnage below. "How can anything but *this* be on my mind? I don't know how you do it, Singh. Politicking while our guardians are torn apart. I admire your ability to multitask."

"You will learn," she said, without any hint of sarcasm. Biran surveyed the bloodbath below. Maybe he would.

"Director, Keepers." A guardcore stepped onto the balcony and bowed. "The *Taso* is ready to depart."

A part of Biran wanted to stay until the last body of Rainier had been dissolved, but there was no point, and he was needed elsewhere. He nodded, and allowed himself to be cordoned by the remaining, cleared guardcore, and ushered into a common room of the *Taso*.

Biran looked around as he sank into an inertia-damping seat across from Singh. As always, he was bemused and slightly unsettled by the luxurious but stately decor Keeper Lavaux had left behind. Biran wondered what that man would think of Biran ordering the execution of his wife, over and over again, and shuddered.

"Okonkwo assures me the *Terminus* will be here within the week," Biran said, to take his mind off the dead.

Singh whistled softly. "That ship can field a thousand fleeties, two hundred guardcore, and six hundred passengers. I had not expected our Prime Director to react so strongly."

"How could she not? We have no idea what waits on the other side of that gate. This is the first time we've gone through without a scouting swarm clearing the area first. The first time without gate-assisted comms."

Vladsen frowned. "The new camera drones we sent through report nothing hostile."

"We cannot trust any footage broadcasted through a gate until we determine the nature and extent of Rainier's tampering."

"Paranoid," Singh said with a slight edge. "We must be careful not to be perceived as overly cautious."

Biran stiffened, momentarily wrong-footed by the reminder of Hitton's tragic end. The members of the Protectorate had called Hitton paranoid, too, before she'd self-destructed a survey site in order to take out a threat she'd perceived as a spy. She'd been right.

He covered his discomfort by adjusting the lay of his jumpsuit across his neck. "Keeper Hitton was not unjustly paranoid. We would all do well to remember that."

Singh's lips thinned and she leaned back, pretending to be absorbed in something on her wristpad. Biran turned to his own wristpad, checking his messages. Nothing from Bero. He kept the flutter of disappointment off his face. Bero had said that decrypting the info packet Hitton had sent before her demise would take time. He had to be patient.

Plenty of updates on the Icarion situation, though. He scrolled through the bullet-pointed list Anford had sent him, each line sharp and brief. Jessa Anford did not waste words, and her crisp notes were refreshing after having spent the past few days with Singh.

But her efficient nature revealed the razor's edge of danger they all walked. Icarion was still saber-rattling, despite the supposed peace.

They believed they were entitled to cross through Ada's new Casimir Gate with the survey team and were moving light, maneuverable gunships up to the very edge of the gate's cordon to pressure the point. Biran chewed his lip, considering his options.

"Director," Singh said, drawing his attention back to her. "Speaking of perceptions, I have a gift for you."

She pulled a slim wooden box from her pocket and held it out to him. Biran eyed the box warily.

"What is this?"

"Oh please, it's not poisonous." She flicked the lid open, revealing a high-end HUD monocle with a dull silver rim lying on a pillow of black, synthetic velvet. "I understand your personal resources are limited, but appearances matter in a director. Especially at times of war. Prime jumpsuits are fine and good for a Speaker, the people feel closer to you when you appear to be one of them, but a director must lead. Must appear to have themselves *together*."

"Olver never used a HUD," Biran said, feeling petty.

She sniffed. "Of course he did, he could afford the ocular implant at a young age. It's preferable, but I assumed you would not be able to absorb such a cost, and if you won't update your wardrobe, well then..." She nudged the box closer.

Biran's shoulders slumped as he took the box, plucking the monocle from the soft pillow. "Thank you, Keeper Singh. Can I presume that this will record all my interactions and feed them back to you?"

She clapped and tossed her head. "A reasonable assumption, but no. Check the provenance, if you like. It was sealed in that box at the shop and opened for the first time now. There's a recorder embedded in the wood to log all interactions. I mean for you to use it. I wouldn't risk you tossing it with such a ham-fisted play."

He closed the box, but nodded to her. "I will run the checks, as is my due diligence as director, but thank you."

"Well," she said, adjusting her pashmina as she leaned back and crossed her legs. "As I said, we cannot have our director looking ramshackle. I strongly suggest you scrape the funds together to update your wardrobe, if at all possible. Okonkwo may even give you a stipend for the purpose, if you ask. I'm *sure* she's sympathetic to your financial situation."

Biran grimaced at the syrupy-sweet tone Singh put on. How quickly she shifted from ally to viper.

"If you'll all excuse me," he said, standing when his wristpad signaled the *Taso* had pushed away from the black site and was well on its way to Ada Station.

Singh waved him away with a flutter of her hand, diving back into her wristpad, and Vladsen shot him a pensive smile, but said nothing.

Biran retreated to his private quarters, and resisted an urge to throw himself on the bed and bury his face in a pillow. Such unseemly behavior was not warranted from a director, even in private, and Biran had a suspicion that he was rarely ever in "private" anymore, especially outside of his home back on Ada's Keep Station.

He sat on the edge of his bed and dropped the monocle box next to him, going back to his wristpad. He wouldn't even power the monocle up until he'd had it checked, and there was only one person he trusted for that. He dialed an ident.

"Director," Graham said with a wry smile, "how can I serve our great society?"

Biran snorted. "Cool it, Dad. I need you to run a provenance check on a piece of equipment."

His brows lifted. "Surely you have people for that?"

"And surely those people are in the pockets of others."

"That bad already?"

"I have no idea, to be honest. The Protectorate is down in numbers, the junior Keepers are circling, trying to find a lever to tug to make their way onto the council. I cannot discount that one or more would be willing to lie for a leg up, and the item is a gift from Singh."

"You know, your father and I can buy you things, child. We're not paupers."

Biran grimaced. "Too late. I didn't think of it, and at this point, if I avoid wearing the monocle, I'm a coward. If I wear it and it's bugged..."

Graham sighed. "I see the problem. I'll check it out. Flash me a mirror of the provenance tracker."

Biran scanned it and sent it over. "Thanks. I'll be back on station in a few days."

Graham's eyes narrowed. "How many dead, this time?"

"Seventy-eight, when the count was done."

"Dios, she's an infestation."

"I believe that's what she was going for, yes."

Graham rolled his eyes. "Got time to come down to the planet while you're here?"

He licked his lips and looked away. "No. The *Terminus* will be there by the time I get back. The sooner we clear the secondary gate, the better."

"I understand," he said, which meant he didn't like it, but he'd deal with it. They exchanged a few mundane pleasantries—Biran had fewer and fewer normal things to talk about these days—and Biran told him what he could of Sanda's mission, which was precious little, before hanging up.

With a sigh he fell back against the bed, arms spread-eagle, relishing the foam contouring to all the aches in his back and shoulders. Maybe he should move into the *Taso* when he got back. Keeper Lavaux's ship was more comfortable than Biran's own bed.

A rustling to the right jerked him wide awake. Biran didn't have an ounce of combat training aside from a few basic self-defense courses the Keepers were forced to take, but his hand was on his never-used blaster as he brought his wristpad up to call for security.

He hesitated. The sound had come from the en suite, a corner he couldn't see around when he first entered the room. Maybe it was just a faucet left on, a towel slumped to the ground. He couldn't afford to look as paranoid as he felt, not after that conversation with Singh.

Telling himself he was an idiot, this was how people got killed in cheap horror CamCasts, Biran edged around the bed and approached the open door, heart firmly lodged in his throat, a thick layer of sweat dampening his whole body.

How the hell did Sanda do this regularly? He pulled up the emergency beacon on his wristpad and eased his hand away from the blaster, preparing to hit the button just in case. He'd be better off calling for help than he would be trying to hold his own in a real fight.

A guardcore sat on the floor in his bathroom, huddled up against the tub, their arms wrapped around legs pulled in tight to their chest, locked in place.

Biran rushed forward, dropping to his knees, and grabbed the armored shoulders.

"Hello? Are you all right?"

They picked up their head, and when the external speakers projected their voice, it had the faint feminine quality Biran recognized from the GC who had helped him during the bombardment all those years ago. "I don't want to die," she said.

CHAPTER 5

PRIME STANDARD YEAR 3543

A SPY IN OUR MIDST

Sanda didn't say a word as Nox marched Tomas onto *The Light* at gunpoint, even though Tomas shot her a questioning glance. Everyone on her crew was jumpy right now, and Nox having a rifle pointed at Tomas's back made him less likely to shoot. The sense of being in control could do a hell of a lot for one's nerves.

They marched him through to the forward deck, Bero hiding the doors so that the path was a straight shot, but Tomas's keen eyes didn't miss that the hallway he passed through led nowhere else. She could almost see that spy brain of his working, trying to account for the lack of exits off the central hall, and the reality that there absolutely had to be more rooms on this ship than the airlock and the deck.

She didn't put him out of his intellectual misery. When they reached the deck, the rest of her crew was already there and waiting.

"Is that really necessary?" Dr. Liao asked, jabbing a finger at Nox. She hadn't quite worked out what made Nox tick yet, and Sanda feared that was going to become a problem someday.

"Leave the gun problems to people who know how to shoot them," Nox said.

Liao huffed and crossed her arms. Sanda wished those two would cool it, because she did not need Tomas Cepko intuiting the slight cracks in the cohesion of her crew, but she let it slide for now.

"All right, Tomas," Sanda said, and slung herself into her captain's seat, taking the weight off her leg. She'd have to re-salve it soon. "Before we were interrupted, you were going to tell me where the sphere is."

"And are you going to threaten that information out of me?" Tomas slid his gaze to Nox.

Arden said, "Trust me, he's way calmer with his finger on the trigger."

"You know I can hear you, right?" Nox asked without peeling his gaze from Tomas.

Arden grinned a little when Sanda shot them a look. Troublemaker.

"Nox, take his wristpad. I want Arden to look at it."

"Uh." Tomas reached for the wristpad, covering half of it with one hand. "That's pretty invasive."

"The ident currently residing on that wristpad is one Jacob Galvan, is it not?"

"Yeah, but—"

"Tomas." She leaned forward and rubbed her temples. He snapped his mouth shut. "I'm going to be very clear with you, because I do not have time to spare your feelings. Burned or not, you were Nazca, and we've had a hell of a time with Nazca lately. I know full well that your pad comes with more than a plain ident connection, and I'm not giving you access to software I don't understand while you're on this ship."

"Nothing he carries could harm me," Bero said.

Tomas eyed the ceiling. "Nice to see you again, B."

"My name is Bero. I do not agree with your sentiments."

Knuth snickered, caught Sanda's look, and went back to fiddling with a console he had cracked open next to Arden. Those two had been inseparable lately, combing through *The Light*'s innards for hints on how it worked.

"Sorry." Tomas slumped his shoulders and undid the band on his wristpad, then held it out between two fingers. "I'd bring it to you, Arden, but your friend might shoot me for moving."

"I'm not that trigger-happy," Nox grumbled, and lifted the rifle barrel, leaning it against his shoulder as he moved his finger to rest on the guard. Tomas, wisely, lowered his hands but did not hide them in his pockets. He flicked the wristpad to Arden, who snatched it out of the air and got to work.

"You're going to encounter some security protocols..."

Arden waved Tomas off. "Yeah, yeah, I'll tell you if I need you."

"Arden," Tomas said firmly enough that they looked up. "Nazca implants work with Nazca software. There are kill switches in there. Try not to brute-force those, okay?"

They rolled their eyes. "I won't kill you. But this adrenaline slider..." They poised a finger over the wristpad.

Tomas winced. "Please don't."

"No messing with anyone's bodily functions," Sanda said, then paused for a moment because she couldn't believe that was something she actually had to say out loud. Her life had taken some strange turns lately. "Tomas, I saw them hit your implants when we were in Atrux. Can they use them to kill you remotely?"

He shook his head. "No. I've taken precautions. I'm still hooked into that pad, but it's sandboxed. If they could take me out remotely, they would have."

Arden jerked their head up. "You know that if they can get into this pad, you're fucked?"

"They wouldn't have sent the extraction team if they could get into it."

"Uh..." They scratched the back of their head and shared a look with Knuth, who shrugged. "I mean, I'm in it. And it's not a complete sandbox, because you used the Galvan ident to check into the hotel. It's harder to break something like this if you don't have it in your hands, but now they have a vague idea of where to look. It's only a matter of time."

"I'll destroy it," he said.

"And lose access to the programs that let you control those implants? No way. I'll fix it for you."

He blinked. "Thanks."

"Now that we're sure you won't drop dead any second," Sanda said, "the sphere. Where is it, why do you know about it, and what do you know?"

He took a long, slow breath. "How I know about it is complicated. I was on-mission discovering the whereabouts of Rainier Lavaux when I encountered records that led me to believe she may have infiltrated the guardcore. An organization known to the Nazca as the Acolytes of the Sphere were trying to control the situation. The Acolytes are—"

"We're acquainted," Sanda said.

"Really? Huh. They've gotten sloppy."

"Okonkwo was very enlightening."

A dimple punctuated his cheek as he grinned. "You got Okonkwo to spill? I'm impressed."

"And now I'm getting you to spill. How did you make the connection between Rainier and the sphere?"

He shifted his weight. "I met her. On a GC ship. She didn't tell me, but I learned enough. I've been monitoring the communications of suspected impostor GCs ever since."

"You did better than your counterpart. Novak was also looking for Rainier. He never got face-to-face."

"So I heard," Tomas said dryly. "I was…" He cleared his throat. "Concerned that you may be heading into a collision course with her, while you sought the coordinates."

Her grip tightened on the armrest, and it was sheer force of will that kept her voice under control. "You knew where the coordinates were. You recognized them."

"No, not exactly. I recognized that they were in a dead system. Combine that with Rainier and Keeper Lavaux's connection, I worried. So…"

He pulled in such a deep breath that when he blew it out his cheeks sucked in. He would not look her in the eye. "I stole a Nazca shuttle and tracked the *Thorn* to the deadgate."

Nox snorted. "Commander don't need dipshits like you rushing in to save the day. You got burned by the Nazca for playing hero to a woman who doesn't need it."

"I'm aware," Tomas grated, "that Sanda can handle herself. When I arrived at the deadgate, it had already spun. The *Thorn* was on the Ordinal side, derelict, but not empty."

"Demas," Sanda said, a flash of anger clearing the fog in her mind. "Tell me you tracked him."

"I did. I had no way to get through the gate without tripping its alarm bells, so I tagged the guardcore ship that came to pick him up and followed it to the Rusani system. That's when I picked up communications discussing an object referred to only as the sphere. Easy enough to assume what they'd taken, and what the Acolytes were meant to be protecting."

"Where, exactly?"

"That's where things get tricky. Arden, can I have my wristpad back, please? I promise only to access video files."

"Yeah, sure, I'm done with it anyway." They tossed it over and Tomas snatched it out of the air.

"Done?"

They shrugged and spun in their chair back to the open console they'd been fiddling with. "You're locked down, and I let you keep your Trojans. Nothing in there had the sophistication to do this ship, or any of the systems on it, any harm."

"Embarrassing for the Nazca," he said with a bewildered shake of the head, and strapped his wristpad back on, tapping at a few things. "Permission to transmit to the forward viewscreen?" he asked, lifting his eyes from the pad long enough to meet Sanda's gaze. She nodded.

He flicked a video forward. The screen transitioned from the space outside to a close-up of a shard of a building, blacker than night, speared down into the barren, rocky terrain of a small moon.

"What is it?" she asked.

"A construct not on any map Prime has to offer, not even their more discreet maps. I wasn't able to get very close without risking detection, but Demas went in and hasn't emerged. There's not a lot of traffic in and out of the building, but when people are moved in and out, they're moved in guardcore ships."

"Defenses?"

He lifted a shoulder. "I can guess, but guesses aren't enough. My shuttle lacked many of the features I'm used to, so I returned to Ordinal to...obtain a more advanced vessel. Then the blowback happened, and Atrux was attacked."

"And you got stuck here, because Okonkwo limited gate access to fleet personnel only, and that's a difficult thing to fake for a Nazca that's been burned."

He spread his hands. "You caught me. I'm stranded in this system for the time being. I could implant myself on a fleet vessel, but doing so on short notice without a deep background to give me a reason for ears higher up to listen to me wouldn't get me anywhere near that object. I'd be like any other soldier."

Sanda rubbed her chin, considering. They had a pretty good lead on Jules, which she hoped would lead them to Rainier and a possible solution to the plague gripping Atrux. But if the sphere really was in there, then not only would they have a deeper understanding of how the ascension-agent worked, they might very well have a chance to take out an installation Rainier cared about.

Janus had been a puppet show put on by Rainier to toy with the humans working, unknowingly, to undo their own species. Sanda couldn't ignore the guardcore black of that toothy building's walls, the lack of lights. Rainier Lavaux did not need lights.

Maybe Demas had gone there, but Sanda'd bet her other leg that he was one of the few humans inhabiting the space. If he was even human. He'd bled pretty well, when injured. But then, so had Keeper Lavaux before she'd cut him to the bone.

"Dr. Liao, how valuable would that sphere be to you and your colleagues?"

Liao leaned forward, eyes fixed on the screen, her jaw tight. "It would mean everything. If we could figure out how the ascension-agent is made, then we might be able to undo it, or at least fix what's affecting the comatose."

"I'm sorry," Tomas said, "the what?"

"So there's some things the spy missed," Sanda mused. "The ascension-agent is what Rainier called the nanite weapon used on the people of Atrux. Bero, show Tomas to a room. I want to talk to my crew."

"You could show him yourself."

"Buddy, you make the doors around here."

He huffed. "These things take time to craft, but I suppose I could repurpose a closet."

She smiled to herself, caught Tomas's side-eye, and wiped the expression away. He could judge her for getting along with Bero all he liked. When it'd come down to it, Bero had saved her life. On multiple occasions.

"Hold on," Arden said, "I gotta know first—how'd you get a tight-beam anywhere near this ship?"

"Oh, that." Tomas dropped to a crouch and held out a hand. "Here, Grippy."

Sanda tensed as the repair bot left her side to trundle toward him. When it stopped, Tomas ran a hand under its bottom body panel and popped open an access port, then pulled something out and closed it back up.

"Thanks," he said offhandedly to the bot, and patted him on the "head" before standing. He held up a small round tracking device between his thumb and forefinger, blinking green. "After Demas left the *Thorn* and turned its derelict beacon on, I had a look around. When I found Grippy, well...I knew you wouldn't leave him behind. You'd be back."

Arden's eyes narrowed. "I can't believe I missed that."

"No one's perfect, even you," Tomas said with a shrug.

"That's the same kind my dads use on their cargo," Sanda said with a jolt.

He smiled and squeezed it until the light went red, then tossed it to her. She snatched it out of the air.

"It's yours, actually. I found it in my boot, right where you left it."

"And you kept it?"

Tomas glanced away, hands going into his pockets. "It was nice to know someone was keeping an eye on me. Least I could do was return the favor."

Bero opened a door at the end of the deck, and Tomas nodded, giving her a tight salute before following the ship's changing hallways into whatever room Bero thought would contain the spy. Sanda felt a touch bad about that. Bero wouldn't give him the comfiest accommodation, but Tomas had to have known what he was signing up for when he stepped on this ship.

"Well?" Nox asked when Tomas was gone.

"Let's talk in the kitchen," Sanda said. "I never got my damned dinner."

CHAPTER 6

PRIME STANDARD YEAR 3543

TRAUMA'S EASIER ON
A FULL STOMACH

They weren't five minutes in the kitchen before Nox, with Arden at his shoulder, got to work frying up a massive pan of flat noodles with some kind of spicy sauce. Those two had taken over the cooking on board as soon as they realized the others were fleeties to the core—and that meant they were perfectly capable of living off of toasted nutriblock for the duration of the mission, so long as they had enough booze around to cut the blandness. Liao had backed off cooking duties after one particularly disastrous dish that even Bero had claimed smelled atrocious.

While they got the meal going, Conway did what fleet gunners did best, and doled out cups topped up with Caneridge—water for Liao, who abstained despite the united worlds burning down all around them.

"So," Nox said as he spooned noodles into bowls, "we're doing this, aren't we?"

"I believe that we must," Liao said. "We cannot overlook an opportunity to reclaim the sphere."

"We're doing it," Sanda said, "but I don't like it. Tomas isn't... He isn't a bad man, I don't think. He wouldn't end up working for Rainier or trying to double-cross us, even if she had leverage over him, but he's no saint, either. Just because he says the Nazca burned him doesn't mean he's not working with them still. We all saw what Novak did, given half the chance."

"Seemed pretty burned to me," Conway said around a mouthful of noodles. "I don't know what the Nazca are like in general, but those guns at the restaurant knew what they were doing."

"I agree," Sanda said slowly, stirring her noodles. "But that doesn't mean we put our eyes to the ground. He might be on our side, but that doesn't change what he is. Bero, can we get an ETA on the Rusani system?"

"I began transiting to the gate after Tomas revealed the location. Fourteen hours until we enter the range that his shuttle was at when he took that footage. The location was easy enough to triangulate."

Sanda smirked into her bowl. "Am I that predictable?"

"No, but you aren't foolish enough to walk away from this."

She washed down a bite with Caneridge rum and leaned back, swishing the bitter liquid around her mouth. In the kitchen, it was easy to forget she was in command. Nox and Arden fussed over the stove—better cooking under gravity, thank the void—while Conway and Knuth sat shoulder to shoulder, sharing some CamCast on Conway's wristpad between them. Liao had her head tilted to listen, but her face was buried in a data stream on her wristpad.

An echo of the normalcy she'd felt on Bero one night, with Caneridge in her belly and Tomas on her mind, slid its way into her thoughts. She pushed it away.

"Gonna break that cup, boss," Nox said as he plunked down beside her with his own bowl. She glanced at her hand, knuckles white against the metal tumbler, and relaxed her grip.

"Lot on my mind."

"You got a spy in your ship and an enemy installation bristling with weapons in your future. Would be worried if you weren't worried."

"It's not the weapons Rainier has that I'm worried about."

I want my corpse back, Rainier had said.

Nox snorted and spoke while chewing. "Forget Monte already? She's got guardcore. She *is* guardcore. We should be worried about those weapons."

She swallowed the last of her Caneridge in one gulp. "We have *The Light*."

"Bero can tear a hole in anything with this sucker, but still—"

"She wants *The Light*. And we're bringing it to her."

Arden scraped a spatula against the pan, making a squealing noise. Everyone looked at her, expecting a solution, but she didn't have one. Rainier's capabilities were a black box, so far as Sanda was concerned.

Rainier could duplicate herself, heal quickly, move with more speed and grace than seemed possible. But could Rainier insert herself into *The Light*? What proximity would that require, what connections? Sanda had no idea.

"I'll, uh, work on some things with Bero to safeguard him..." Arden trailed off, scratched their chin with the dirty spatula, then jumped, scowled at the sauce-smeared edge, and grabbed a towel to clean off.

"I have already considered multiple options," Bero said.

She arched a brow. "Any of them look good?"

"As I do not know exactly what I must defend myself against, one looks as good as any other."

"What about"—Liao tapped on the table—"the cleaner nanites Sarai made to clean up Rainier's amplifiers? With a few tweaks, those would at least keep her from swarming anything nanite-related near us."

"I'll put in the request to Anford," Sanda said, but the thought didn't ease the turbulence in her mind. She pushed her bowl back, grabbed a clean one, and filled it up. "I'm going to go make nice with our spy and see what he has to say about Rainier's capabilities."

"Uh," Nox said. She cut him a look. He deliberately shut his mouth. "He gets out and starts fucking with anything, space him."

She was in the hall, a leftover bottle of Caneridge shoved under one arm and a steaming bowl of noodles balanced precariously on her forearm, before they could raise any protest. Tomas may be a spy, but she was the one packing a blaster, and if it came to that, she was the better shot.

Not that she expected things to come to that. Maybe Bero was right, maybe she was getting too cynical. Tomas had come to her with information he could have sold for a small fortune. Knowing where Demas hid the sphere might have been enough to get him back in the Nazca's good graces.

He'd taken a huge risk in coming to her, especially if he'd heard anything about how Monte went down. She could take a small risk by letting him talk to her one-on-one.

It didn't occur to her that her physical person might not have been what Nox was worried about until she knocked on Tomas's door, and he gestured it open, wary eyes brightening the second he saw her.

"Delivery?" he asked, stepping aside to let her in.

"Not as good as Udon-Voodun, but Arden learned a few tricks living above that place for so long."

"Gets in your blood, being around food. You smell all those spices long enough, you can't help but develop a sense for how they're all supposed to go together."

"Yeah, I guess you'd know that."

That shadow again, the slight flinch at the corners of his eyes. She ignored the reaction, pretending to be preoccupied with finding a spot to put the food. Bero, as predicted, hadn't given Tomas a lot of room to work with.

While the other bunks on the ship were large enough to pass for hotel rooms, Tomas's was an overgrown closet. Bero had produced a narrow bed against the wall, a sink and bathroom off to one side behind a half wall for privacy, and a table with one chair. All made out of the sleek metal that comprised *The Light*. Even though the temperature was controlled, the room felt cold. Bero hadn't even bothered to show Tomas where the spare bedding was.

"Seriously?" she said to the ceiling as she finagled the bowl and bottle onto the narrow table.

"He is a prisoner."

"Prisoners get blankets, towels, and pillows. And he's not even really a prisoner."

Bero sighed dramatically. "Very well. I'll send Grippy."

She shook her head and took the small chair while nudging the table close to the bed. He sat, but didn't eat, instead eyeing the food as if it was keeping secrets from him.

"It's not poisoned," she said.

He smiled tightly. "I know. Not a lot of places to look around here."

She shifted, feeling the closeness of the room. Bero had made a mistake in making the room so damn small. This close together, with the door closed, the only warmth in the overgrown closet came from their bodies. She adjusted her coat and nudged the bowl.

"Eat."

He flicked his gaze up and met her eyes heavily. She swallowed. Right. Not a lot of places to look, she could see the problem now.

"I didn't want to leave."

"That's not what I'm here to talk about."

"Sanda, nothing about what we're doing is safe, or sane. You keep pushing this conversation back, it's never going to happen."

"Maybe I don't want it to."

"You mean that?"

She looked at the bottle. "No."

"If I could have stayed without bringing the Nazca down on your head, I would have."

She found that label on the bottle incredibly fascinating. "You switched the reservation to Graham's name. You were trying to run us off. To keep us from looking for the coordinates."

"Yes. You'd just been spaced. I didn't know what was going on, and I wanted you clear of it."

"Real dick move."

He laughed nervously. "Yeah, I know. Spies aren't really trained on things like that. We conceal. We redirect. It's instinct."

"You weren't always a spy. Don't you remember what being a person was like?"

He made a soft, grunting noise. "No. Not really. But I'm trying to figure it out."

"Because you got burned."

"Because I burned myself to get to you."

Her chest ached. She grabbed the bottle and took a drink, then set it on her thigh. The cold seeping from the glass through to her skin cleared her thoughts. "And brought me a real Pandora's box of a problem."

"What do you mean?"

"You weren't the only one to have a chat with Rainier."

"Shit," he said with such force she looked up and risked meeting his eyes. A slight snarl had curled the corners of his lips, his fists clenched but rested against the tops of his knees. "Are you all right?"

She waved the concern away with the bottle in her hand. "Fine."

"You nearly died," Bero said dryly.

She shot a glare at the wall. "Privacy, for fuck's sake."

"If you insist. Grippy is outside the door with the linens. Scream if you need help."

She rolled her eyes. "I'm not sure if his time as an amorphous cloud in the net made him more, or less, of a sarcastic ass."

"His time as a *what*?"

"Ask Arden. They'll tell you *all* about it. Anyway, yes, Rainier and I had a chat and I nearly killed myself taking her and all her other instances out, but that conversation…" She took another drink. "She told me why she's punishing humanity. From what I can piece together, she was an intelligence made and left behind by our alien predecessors.

"Her purpose, as designed, was to award the gift of their knowledge—in her case the ascension-agent—to the first race of beings that managed to find her copart, in theory another intelligence with the gate tech. When she realized that Prime Inventive had discovered the gate tech by accident and not by whatever means we were 'supposed' to, she lost her shit. As far as I can tell, Lavaux kept her on a leash for a long, long time, and after his death…Well. She's started lashing out."

"The blowback," Tomas said. "Atrux."

"Atrux was Valentine, and we don't know if she did it under Rainier's direction or not. The blowback…" She winced. "Yeah. That's her. When Halston stole the gate tech from the first intelligence—Rainier calls the others her sisters—she fucked up the design. Every time a gate spins, it lets out a massive pulse of energy that eradicates anything on the other side. Well, almost anything. We have our suspicions that Halston created the forward survey bots to make certain whatever life had been growing behind a newly spun gate gets well and truly destroyed before people could see it. I...honestly can't blame Rainier for wanting to punish humanity. But I can't let her."

"Christ," Tomas said. "Is that true?"

She passed him the bottle without looking. He drank, liquid chugging.

"That's why Biran's going through the secondary Ada gate before the bots. To see if she's telling the truth."

"Is that safe?"

She snorted. "Honestly, Tomas, we have no fucking idea. I wanted to bring *The Light* through, but after Atrux, my primary objective became hunting and controlling Rainier. Atrux cannot happen again."

"I'm grateful for the honesty, Sanda, but spy instincts die hard, and that's a lot of information you're sharing with me. Information that can only motivate me to help you, so I gotta ask...What are you trying to get me to share with you in return?"

She looked up and grinned. He grinned back. "That obvious?"

He spread his hands and shrugged. "I'm a professional."

"I need you to tell me everything you know about Rainier's abilities, how she works, what she can do. I took her ass down with an EMP, but I can't keep on thinking that will work forever."

"An EMP took her out?"

"Fried her like an eel. It was so fucking satisfying. But it was only temporary. The bodies started to repair themselves, even though it took a while. We dunked them in acid, later. That finished her off."

He passed her the bottle, but not quickly enough to hide his wince. "Good to know."

"Tomas, you're getting positively emotive. What's going on?"

"Had a rough time with Rainier. She's...I don't really know what to tell you, Sanda. She's stronger and faster than anyone I've ever seen. Taking one instance out doesn't diminish her in any way. I'm reasonably certain she can hive-mind with her other instances at will. She wants something, and she'll do anything to get it, but I guess you figured out what she wants."

Sanda shook her head and pressed a palm against the wall. "It's not the punishment she wants, I think that's just for fun. She wants *The*

Light. She was this ship, before whoever came along downloaded her out of it."

Tomas went impossibly still, a shadow of fear turning his face sheet white. "You cannot let her get anywhere near this ship. We should chase Valentine, fuck Rusani and the sphere. If Valentine released the agent on Atrux, then she'll have the data. We can get what we need from her."

"Why does she scare you so much, Tomas?"

He pressed his lips together, looked at his hands, and said nothing.

Sanda stood slowly and placed the bottle back on the table. "We arrive in Rusani in fourteen hours. If there's anything important you're not telling me, you have until then."

"Sanda—" He reached for her arm, but she stepped away, the door opening when she tapped against the cool metal.

"Fourteen hours," she said again, and left.

CHAPTER 7

PRIME STANDARD YEAR 3543

HOME'S NEVER WHERE YOU LEFT IT

The rubble of the Grotta crunched under Jules's boots. She shouldn't be here. This wasn't her home anymore, wasn't her sanctuary, her playground, her hunting ground. There wasn't even life here, not anymore, thanks to her.

Jules had picked up the hammer Rainier had given her, and she'd dropped it on Atrux. On the Grotta. She could tell herself she thought it'd only hurt those in the city center. Could tell herself she'd thought the Grotta would be immune.

The people there didn't get the usual share of fresh air that the rest of the city did; the distribution would have been slow, uneven. And even if the ascension-agent made it out here in large enough concentration, Jules was of the Grotta. She'd taken the ascension-agent, and survived. Maybe the part of herself that allowed her to thrive was tied to the Grotta.

But Lolla had taken it, and fallen into an endless sleep, and that was the whole damn point, wasn't it?

Jules kicked a pile of trash with her perfectly black boot, watching orange candy wrappers and biodegradable cups swirl away from her on a faint breeze. Dirt smeared her boots, and she let out a breath of relief. That was better. That was how it should be.

Atrux proper was a ghost town. The people either comatose, dead, or ascended and imprisoned for containment and study.

But things weren't completely dead out here. The guardcore had swept these streets already. Swept all the streets of Atrux to scoop up those few who'd survived contact with the ascension-agent. And once they'd had them, they'd locked them up. Hidden them away in a hospital designed to hold those with ascended strength, no matter how agitated they got.

But the guardcore didn't know the Grotta, not like she did, and they'd missed a few.

Director Greeve's sweeps, hunting for Rainier, didn't bother her. She ducked those roll calls easily enough, had them all chasing some false signal of a ship signature that looked like it might be hers way out in the Ordinal system. Arden would be proud, if Arden didn't think she was a fucking monster.

And so Jules wore the guardcore armor like a second skin, fitting into the sparse patrol left on Atrux as well as she ever fit anywhere, and went out on these little gatherings solo. Because the whole point of her laying waste to her homeworld was to give the Prime scientists a bigger data set to work with, a bigger initiative. But they weren't doing a good enough job.

Her jaw tensed, and she tamped down an urge to reach for her weapon. The survivors were so few that the researchers had little to work with. Their genomes had been sequenced, their immune systems tested, their gut biomes catalogued. No significant differences were common among the survivors. The ascended.

Bullshit. Jules just had to find more for them to test.

But first, she had an itch to scratch at the back of her mind. She stalked through the streets of the Grotta, not bothering to cover her tracks. Usually, on these runs, she'd come in silent and practically invisible, slipping through the shadows until she could get close enough to stun whoever was still walking and talking out here in the margins.

Dr. Dal Padian, formerly of Janus Station, was delighted every time she brought in a new capture, and just as crestfallen when it led, inevitably, nowhere new. He probably wouldn't be so exuberant if he knew who he was dealing with, but that was her secret.

The streets widened, growing crumbly around the edges as she pushed into the fringes where people like her old team did most of their work. Out here, warehouses dotted the ground, interspersed with cheap living areas that cost less than even the basic stipend.

Out here, she'd chased down a crate of wraith, hoping for an easy score, and tripped over Rainier and all her bullshit.

But Jules hadn't had a lot of time to think since that day. Under Rainier's command, she'd barely had a second to herself. She'd either been running down new researchers or placating the ones they already had. Now, with all her time to herself, she wondered.

There'd been nothing fishy about that crate of wraith. She was fucking sure. If anything had felt off about the deal, she would have bailed, and Harlan wouldn't have given her a hard time about it. They got a bad feeling, they bolted, because a well-developed gut instinct was the difference between a living Grotta rat and a dead one.

The dealers moving that crate had been clean, no connections to Rainier. She'd run down their files after she'd set up shop in Atrux, and found they'd fallen into comas in the Grotta and died for lack of care, like so many of the others. None of their contacts stank. Nothing about them looked off.

But that crate had been shoved in the back of a warehouse that Rainier Lavaux, queen of mazes, had hidden away in the fringes of the Grotta on chance? No fucking way. Maybe Jules was getting paranoid—probably she was—but Jules had been hooked and lured to that spot. Why? Why her? If she could answer that question, then maybe she could discover why Lolla wasn't waking up. Why all of Prime's brilliant minds had yet to find a solution to Rainier's broken agent.

Ash made her steps slippery as she stepped off the road, onto the burned-out hellscape of the warehouse that she had blown up in an attempt to take Rainier down with her. Of course, that's when she'd thought Rainier was a person.

Sheet metal lay crumpled like broken accordions across the ground, dull and greasy with soot. Jules hesitated on the perimeter, remembering Lolla's quick smile, her insistence that she be allowed into the building to help with the score, and Jules's assertions to Harlan that it was fine, the kid was ready.

Maybe the kid had been, but Jules wasn't.

She crossed the threshold where the cargo bay door once was, kicking at rubble. She couldn't even say what she thought she'd find here. The whole place had burned down. Jules had blown up the stockroom in the basement herself. The original crate of wraith was long gone. If there was anything of value left to scavenge in the wreckage, then it was gone, too. She went in anyway.

The walls were half standing, scraps of roof slanted over them. When she brushed her hands against them, they crumbled. She adjusted her HUD, asking it to tell her where the footing was stable, laying a graphic redraw of the area over her natural vision. The area near the basement was too dangerous to walk across—the ground there was thin, the room beneath blown to shreds by Jules's impromptu bomb—but the hallways were safe enough. Safe, and empty.

Jules found her way to the approximate area where the lab had been, and kicked something that rang like a bell. She frowned, dropping to a crouch, and sifted through the rubble. She plucked out a small piece of metal, twisted and burned, no bigger than the palm of her hand. A needling suspicion solidified into fact.

Guardcore metal. It blended perfectly with her armor. She knew she'd seen something that dark in the lab, near the canister of ascension-agent that she'd broken. Her fist closed around it, wondering. Why? Why had Rainier used that metal in this building?

She'd looked into it, once she'd thought about how dark some of the structures in Rainier's labs had been. The metal was made from ore retrieved by the scout bots that went through gates after a gate had been opened in a new system, mined and delivered to the Keepers so that it wouldn't fall into another nation's, or corporation's, hands. Exceedingly expensive, exceedingly hard to procure.

Rainier had inserted enough of herselves into the GC to get her hands on their ships and armor and weapons. Jules had never really thought about it, but to use it to make fixtures in a warehouse in the Grotta? That didn't make sense, even by Rainier's wasteful standards.

Jules sighed and stood, pocketing the metal as she stretched out her lower back. She needed to finish up her job, hunt down a stray or two for the medis, then get back to her ship so she could take off the armor and rest.

Not that she wanted to rest. Resting meant being alone with herself, spinning her mental gears, lying awake while her mind teetered forever on the edge of falling into obsession over the things she'd done, the recriminations.

Her breath came fast in the helmet, her HUD flashing up a warning that she'd soon start to hyperventilate.

Breathe. Breathe.

Jules may have done the memory rollbacks to herself, but it'd been because she didn't want to remember. Because she hated what she'd become.

But Marya had broken those walls down, and as much as Jules tried to lean into it, tried to be stronger and braver and harder-hearted than she'd ever been before, she couldn't do it. Couldn't face it all. It was hard enough to walk the streets of the Grotta without coming apart at the seams.

She hadn't been thinking, when she'd hooked that canister up to Atrux, not really. She'd thought herself more automaton than human in the days and hours leading up to that moment. She had needed someone who cared about humanity to fix the problem. Someone with resources, someone with incentive, and it had seemed such a logical choice...

Bile burned at the back of her throat. She swallowed.

This was good. Dal was working with a whole team now, many of them from Janus, on reversing the ill-effects of the ascension-agent. Unfettered, no bullshit from Rainier. Prime Inventive had conquered the stars. Surely their combined effort could bring one world out of a coma.

Her HUD perimeter alerted seconds before something slammed into her. Electric currents burned through her suit, her cells, made her eyes roll back, and her whole body jerked, foam flecking her lips.

Jules collapsed to the ground, on her hands and knees, back arching, legs twitching as she flopped to her stomach, head craned to one side. In the corner of her vision, a dirty, frightened face watched Jules kick and jerk against the ground, a stunner held in that person's hands, lips quirked in smug triumph. Of course. There'd be no stray pieces of guardcore metal lying around. It was too expensive, and she'd been too wrapped up in her own thoughts to realize.

It was a trap.

"Got the fucker," a voice said, before Jules's hearing reduced to a soft whine and her vision blacked out.

CHAPTER 8

PRIME STANDARD YEAR 3543

COMFORT'S A TRAP

Tomas finished his noodles, polished off the Caneridge, then let his thrice-cursed synthetic body take away the blackout drunk sensation he'd been shooting for. He could let the drunkenness sink in, he had that much control, and a part of him wanted to spend the trip to Rusani so drunk he couldn't feel the fear Sanda kept seeing in him despite all of his training. Either she knew him too well, or he was getting sloppy now that he'd cut himself loose. He liked to think she knew him too well.

He forced himself to stand and, hesitantly, tapped on the door. Bero opened it without comment, but Tomas couldn't help but notice the door dilated much slower for him than it had for Sanda.

Sanda... Her scent lingered in his tiny room. He cleared his mind, focusing. She couldn't discover what he was. Couldn't know that he was born of the same cloth as Rainier, as much a monster as Keeper Lavaux had been. Lying to her twisted him up inside, but if she knew... If she knew, he'd be in no position to help her, because he'd be finding out exactly how Lavaux had died when Bero had spaced him alongside Sanda.

He tapped at his wristpad to ask for the ship's schematics. There wasn't even an open channel available for him to interface with.

But that didn't stop him from knowing where he wanted to go.

Ever since he'd stepped foot on *The Light*, he'd been haunted by a sense of familiarity. Bero's trick with the single hallway straight to the deck hadn't obscured to him where the other rooms might be—he'd just known, as if they were phantom limbs.

Those limbs waited for him to take control. A deep-seated instinct he didn't wholly understand wanted him to stretch his senses out and merge with the ship. It'd be so easy to reshape the rooms, change the ship's course. Fly them all into safer waters. If this ship had been Rainier, then...

He swallowed, trying not to think about what his extrasensory perception might mean. First, he had to find Nox, because Nox was going to be his biggest problem. The others did more or less what Sanda told them to. Nox only followed orders if he thought they were the right ones.

Tomas followed his instinct until the wall parted like a curtain to let him into a wide room, the walls covered in lockers and the floor studded with benches. Prime armor hung from the walls in between the weapon lockers, grey and silent.

Nox sat in the center of the room, a blaster in one hand and a rag in the other. He didn't glance up when he spoke.

"Surprised Bero let you out."

"I guess he figured if he didn't, I'd try to talk to him instead."

"Your company that tedious?"

"Bero would say so."

They both paused, waiting for the intelligence to respond. Bero let his silence speak for him.

Nox chuckled and shook his head. "Man, I would not want to have Bero pissed off at me. You fucked up."

"I got Sanda to safety, that was my only objective. I didn't mean to rip Bero's world apart in the process but...Well. I didn't set those wheels in motion, and Nazca aren't in the friend-making business."

"If that's the case, what are you doing in here?"

"What do you mean?"

Nox snorted. "You're not here to check our weapons, you came here because it was the most likely place to find me, and you want me on your good side. You'd have better luck with Arden."

"Why's that?"

"All you have to do is let them talk about whatever's on their mind and you've got a buddy for life. Just don't ask stupid questions, they hate backtracking to explain basics. Which means you sit there silently and let them go, because everything's basic to them."

"Charmer."

"Better company than you." Nox picked his head up and jerked his chin at an open locker. "If you're going to pester me, make yourself useful. Rags are in the trunk under the cabinet. Get cleaning."

Tomas pulled the cabinet door the rest of the way open, half expecting Bero to tell him off for touching the weapons, but he seemed to be giving Tomas the silent treatment for now. Six blasters in three rows awaited him, and squinting as much as he could, Tomas couldn't find so much as a fingerprint on them.

"Sure these are the ones that need cleaning?"

"Don't tell me spies treat their weapons like fleeties."

"And how do fleeties treat their weapons?" he asked as he ducked down and grabbed a rag, bottle of oil, and a random gun.

"Like they can afford to replace them at any time. Live in the Grotta, you see how tiny flaws build up until a weapon doesn't fire right. Fleeties don't give a shit. They just give everything enough of a shine to pass inspection. Check inside the trigger guard."

Tomas tilted the weapon to the light. A fingerprint smudged the underside of the metal. "What does that matter?"

Nox shook his head. "Oil grabs dirt, dust. Oil migrates. Get enough built up under there and it could migrate into the trigger mechanism without you ever noticing. Soon enough, you gotta pull a little harder each time you squeeze off a shot, and you don't know why, but if you're a fleetie, you don't care, because if the weapon starts to bug you, you can requisition a new one."

"Seems to me Sanda can requisition you anything you want."

"I ain't a fleetie."

Not much he could say to that. Tomas shrugged and carried the weapon and supplies over. He sat on the bench across from Nox and, feeling the bigger man's gaze on him, used every speck of knowledge he'd ever scraped together about blasters to take the weapon apart and ensure every last surface was shining and moving smoothly.

Tomas glanced up, his neck stiff. Nox pushed his tongue against the inside of his cheek and nodded. "Guess you ain't a fleetie, either. Get the next."

Tomas did. They worked through half the cabinets, all the blasters, and moved on to the rifles before Nox finally let out a grunt and stood, stretching his arms above his head.

"Got a spine made of metal, man?" Nox asked. "My ass is numb, gotta shake it out."

Tomas forced himself to chuckle. He stretched his arms and rolled his neck to get the stiffness out, but the second he started moving, his body was loose and ready to go again.

"I'm used to cramped spaces," he lied.

"That shuttle you were tooling around on was a tin can." Nox stopped pacing and looked at him. "What do you want from us, really?"

"Not one for subtlety, are you?"

"You knew that before you stepped in this room. You want to make nice with me, I don't stand for bullshit."

"Honestly?" Tomas leaned back and rested his hands on his knees. "Honestly."

"I want to stop Rainier. It's easy to say she's crazy, but I don't think that's entirely true. I didn't talk to her long, but it seemed to me that a large portion of her instability was an act. She's had a long time to study humanity. She knows what frightens people. And an unknowable intelligence with an unstable streak is pretty damn terrifying." Tomas stopped himself before he looked up at Bero.

"You think her being crazy is an act?" Nox scratched his chest.

"Yes. *Crazy* isn't a helpful word, is it? It's not really a *thing*, it's just a catch-all for behavior that we can't understand the motivation behind. But we know the basics of what motivates Rainier. She feels betrayed by humanity, thinks we're monsters, and wants to punish us for using her and her sisters' technology.

"*Crazy* and *cracked* are such loaded words. If she can make us believe those things, then we convince ourselves that we can't predict what she'll do next. If we understand she's out to hurt humanity for its alleged crimes, then maybe we have a better chance of predicting her movements. Rainier is an intelligence unlike any we've ever known. We can't take anything she does or says at face value."

"Goddamn," Nox said. "That's a hell of an insight."

Tomas lifted a shoulder. "I've had a lot of time to think about what it might be like to be Rainier."

"No wonder the boss winces whenever the Nazca come up. You all think about people like Arden thinks about machines."

Tomas looked at his hands. "Winces, does she?"

"Er, yeah. Sorry, man. Not her favorite collection of people. Novak brought Rainier's GC down on Monte and we're all..." He grunted. "We're all a little fucked up about that."

Tomas snapped his head up. Novak had been his alias on Janus and Monte, though Sanda and this crew hadn't known it then, and still didn't. He hadn't brought Rainier after them. He'd never intentionally put them in harm's way. Put Sanda in Rainier's sights. "What do you mean, Novak brought Rainier's GC to Monte?"

Nox frowned. "A call went out right before he bugged out with a sample of Rainier's amplifiers. Arden traced it later—it came from Novak's wristpad and one of those GC ships picked it up. Guess he was working for her."

Tomas's mouth went dry. "That's not possible."

"Really?" Nox drawled. "You think a spy double-crossing you is impossible?"

"No, of course not. I just...I knew him better than most. There's no way Novak would bring Rainier to Monte."

"Arden doesn't make mistakes about this shit. Novak made that call, and then we all damn near lost our skins." He tipped his head back, smiling wistfully. "We had a pretty good perch on top of this transit station, you see, and I had my long-range and Sanda had..."

Tomas stopped listening. Rainier had known who he was, what he was, while he had been on Janus. She'd waited for him to get killed on Monte before bothering to scoop him up—why? She could have taken him at any time. She always knew who he really was, even if she hadn't told Jules.

Why? Why let him poke around her research station, where the amplifiers she needed to hurt humanity were being refined? Not just to see what he'd do, not out of curiosity, because she wasn't that reckless. Rainier Lavaux always had a plan.

He looked at his wristpad, the same one that'd been on his arm since he took the mission on Janus. Nazca security was tight, but Arden had cracked through it easily enough. He had no idea what Rainier's capabilities were, and he was willing to bet that he understood her better than most.

She'd grabbed him from Monte because Prime Inventive stumbling across the nanites that made up his body was too risky. She'd said herself how annoyed she was that Keeper Lavaux had almost blown that particular secret by allowing Sanda to see him heal while security cameras were rolling. That tracked, that rang true.

But then she'd kicked him loose, even though she could have killed him then and there to get the thorn out of her side, supposedly to deliver a message to Sitta Caid. He swallowed at the memory, the screaming pain that'd eclipsed his thoughts so thoroughly he'd almost believed he was dying. Maybe that part was true. But it didn't mean it was her only reason.

Because, as much as Tomas understood Rainier, Rainier understood him straight down to the molecules that made up his bones. She knew he'd run back to Sanda. And she'd known, then, that Sanda had the coordinates to Rainier's ship in her head.

"Fuck," he said.

Nox nodded solemnly. "I know, right? We'd taken down two of them, and there were at least two dozen more on that one ship. We didn't know where—"

"No, sorry." He shook his head and bolted to his feet. He needed a tech. And fast. "Where's Arden? It's important."

Nox's posture tightened, shifting his weight so that he was squared off. "Why?"

"I think Rainier put a virus on my wristpad when we met." That was close enough to the truth.

Nox shrugged. "Arden already checked it out, but if you're jumpy about it, they're usually in the engine room with Knuth."

"Thanks," Tomas said, and took off at a dead sprint. Whatever Nox called out after him washed away.

Bero opened the doors faster this time, sensing his urgency. Or maybe it was Tomas's own need forcing the ship to clear his path—but he didn't want to think about that. His singular focus had to be getting Rainier's tracing program off his wristpad.

Struggling to keep himself from running fast enough to raise eyebrows, Tomas bolted down the length of the ship until Bero opened a door to a cavernous room. The walls glowed with a soft, sleepy light, and walkways spiraled up the tall walls to give the humans easier access to the massive sphere of glowing...something...in the center of the room.

Tomas hesitated a breath, awe slamming him in the chest, then shook the sensation off. He could marvel over it later, once Arden had secured his wristpad.

Sanda's laugh, bright and a little rough around the edges, drew his attention. She, Arden, and Knuth were clustered around a metal crate on the side of the room, a bottle of Caneridge sitting between them. They all looked flush in the cheeks.

"Arden!" he shouted, peeling off his wristpad and holding it in the air to wave like a flag. "I need your help here."

Arden looked up, rolled their eyes, and said something to Sanda. She giggled.

"Come on, Tomas," she said. "They went all through that thing."

He clenched his jaw and let himself sound afraid. "I know, but Nox told me about Novak and—"

The ship rocked. Tomas was thrown onto his back, the wristpad knocked out of his hand. Metal screeched and gasses hissed, the heat singeing his skin. Tomas rolled away from it, got his head together enough to push into a crouch.

On the other side of the room, a black thorn protruded from the gently lit wall. A guardcore breach pod. Sanda, Arden, and Knuth had been thrown by the impact and were crawling to their feet, dazed. He should be dazed, too, but his body wouldn't even let him fake it.

Green lights flicked in sequence along the razor edge of the breach pod, outlining a door, and his heart dropped into his stomach. Something hissed. A door panel slid open, and three guardcore stepped into the engine room of *The Light*.

CHAPTER 9

PRIME STANDARD YEAR 3543

WHY CAN'T WE EVER JUST RELAX?

Sanda kicked away the bottle of Caneridge tangling her feet and hauled herself upright. Her head swam from taking a crack against the floor, but otherwise she felt all right. Everything was moving well enough not to be seriously broken, so that'd have to do for now. She blinked blurriness from her eyes and found Knuth pitched up against a coil of the fibers that led into the engine core. He grunted and started to scramble up, so she gave him a hand.

"Bero," she said, "what the fuck?"

"I suspect Rainier has found us, as I detected no ship incoming, and she is able to circumvent my shields."

"How in the—?" She caught motion in the corner of her eye. A GC breach pod protruded from the wall of her ship, and it was opening. How this had happened would have to wait. "More incoming?"

"Now that I know what I'm looking for, yes."

"Get us out of here."

"Gladly."

Sanda yanked Knuth to his feet and cast around for Arden. They'd rolled off toward the engine core. Her heart clenched to see how limp they were, but then they put their arm under themself and started pushing themself up.

"You armed?" she asked Knuth.

He shook his head. Dios, she only had two blasters. Tomas was too far away to risk tossing a weapon, but Knuth self-admitted to doing poorly in tense circumstances. He'd made up for it by being a brilliant engineer, though. She could work with that. Keep his focus on defending his tech, and maybe he wouldn't freak out.

She slapped the blaster into Knuth's hand. "Guard the engine core."

The roiling panic behind his gaze settled. He licked his lips, glanced at the engine, and nodded. Good.

"Those pods carry a triad. We can't hold a line against three GC with two blasters," Sanda said to the ceiling. "Bero, get me Nox!"

"He's on his way."

"Thank fuck."

The GC emerged from the breach pod. A surge of fear turned Sanda's skin ice cold, almost froze her to the spot. The last time she'd faced down GC had been at long range, with better weapons, and she'd still gotten her ass handed to her.

A helmeted head swiveled toward her, its rifle came up. She told herself that each body in that black armor belonged to Rainier, and that made it easier for her to bring the blaster up and start firing without a second thought.

Not enough. She hit center-mass but the blasters didn't have the oomph to get through GC armor at its thickest points.

"Visors and joints!" she shouted, backing up, laying down a fan of suppressive fire that even the GC couldn't tank their way through. Knuth joined her, and the GC backed up, putting the protrusion of the breach pod between them and Sanda. Good enough.

She threw a glance at Arden. They'd gotten to their feet, eyes huge, jabbing at their wristpad.

"Cover!" she snapped.

They looked up, grimaced, and ducked behind the wall of cargo Sanda had been backing toward. She squeezed off one more hail of fire, then elbowed Knuth and ducked behind the crates.

She pressed her back against the metal, panting with adrenaline, and tried to figure out what the fuck to do. The cover of the crates would last only as long as it took the GC to figure out that they could go up the ramps on the other side of the room to get the high ground.

That meant going through Tomas, but he was unarmed. Her stomach clenched.

Facts. Only consider the facts.

"B," she whispered, "can you block the stairs?"

Her wristpad flashed with text: cannot. busy. takes time to redirect the mass.

She grimaced. She'd known as much—opening doors was one thing, but growing new furniture and rooms took time and careful consideration—but she had to try.

"Can you give us something? Weapons?" she whispered.

On her wristpad: currently using all weapons on exterior engagements

That breach pod had to come from somewhere, and that ship was no doubt giving Bero a hell of a time. *The Light* may be the best weapon in the universe, but Bero was new to its controls and limitations. Rainier Lavaux knew what would make this ship struggle.

She looked at Arden, and was dismayed to see they'd gone pale and stopped jabbing at their wristpad. She raised her brows. They shook their head. Knuth shrugged and pointed at a door toward the back of the room that led into a storage closet. Sanda swallowed.

A shot struck the crates and they jumped against her back. Another, another. A single GC, prattling off a steady rain of fire to keep them pinned in place while their second and third members sought higher ground. That's what she'd do, in their position.

She tightened her grip on the blaster. The next shot that didn't collide with the crates would be a GC putting down Tomas. *Run*, she willed him. He'd been close enough to the door. He could have made it out. But the way she'd seen him crouched there, determination bright in his eyes, told her a different story. Tomas wouldn't flee as long as she was pinned down here, the fucking idiot.

"Retreat!" she barked, holding a hand down flat by her side so Knuth and Arden would know the order wasn't for them. She prayed the command would somehow kick Tomas into making a run for it.

The fire on the crates paused, and she grinned. They were hesitating to see if she was going to make a run for it. She pivoted and popped up over the crates, making sure her line of fire was clear, and squeezed off a half dozen shots at the GC before it got it together and returned fire. A piece of armor near its elbow cracked and flung off.

She dropped back down, staying in a crouch with one hand against the crates to steady herself.

"Knuth, when we hear Nox," she whispered, "take Arden and get to the back room. Hold that fucking door."

"We're not leaving you—" Arden started, but she cut them a look so harsh their eyes widened and they buttoned up their lips.

"Protecting you is pinning me down. I need to be mobile. This is the best thing you can do."

They clenched their jaw, but nodded. Knuth didn't look any happier about the arrangement, but he was fleet. He obeyed orders.

A rifle cracked, too far from the door to be Nox, and the crates did not jump. They'd shot Tomas. She felt sick.

"Welcome aboard!" Nox shouted, punctuating his sentence with a deafening burst of rifle fire.

Sanda stood up and started firing. Nox came in the door and angled toward the stairs, away from her, trying to cut off the two GC headed that way. Behind her, Arden and Knuth scrambled to their feet and made a run for it, drawing the attention of the GC that'd been holding them down.

Sanda aimed for the break in the armor at the elbow and struck true. Blood sprayed behind the GC. She grinned fiercely and kept firing as the GC fell back a step, letting the barrel of their rifle drop. The GC stumbled for the cover of the breach pod. Sanda stepped around the crates and closed on the GC, swinging out to open the angle so the fucker couldn't take cover.

"Sanda, three o'clock!" Tomas said, voice tight with pain.

She turned toward the sound, but too late. One of the GC had made it up the steps and aimed at her from above. Before she could react, it squeezed off a shot and she braced for pain. Her body jerked, and she staggered from the force, then nearly laughed.

The GC had hit her in the prosthetic, shredding her jumpsuit and ripping the meaty part of her fake calf open. The shot had angled down, ripping through her mag boot, and the shoe hissed electronics at her, failing to engage. But *The Light* had gravity. She kicked the shoes off and returned fire at the ramp.

In her peripheral, Nox pumped rounds into the second GC, keeping it busy. Tomas lay on the floor at the base of the steps, his jumpsuit doing an excellent job of wicking away all the blood that was pouring from a hole in his hip.

Focus. She fired on the ramp GC until it ducked down behind cover, then pivoted, cracking off a few rounds at the one she had wounded. She needed to find cover that the one on the ramp couldn't get around, but there wasn't any.

She twisted back on instinct as the GC on the ramp prepared to fire on her, and forced it to duck back down again. Nox put a bullet through the visor of the second GC, paused a breath to toss a spare rifle down to Tomas, then twisted, firing up at the ramp. Blood sprayed.

Sanda turned back to the one by the pod just in time to see its visor explode from Tomas's shot.

"Clear!" she shouted. "Get their fucking helmets off before they liquefy."

Nox ran for the one by the base of the stairs, so she bolted for the one by the pod, dropped to her knees, and almost tipped over when her leg unbalanced her, then hit the helmet retract button.

The face had been shattered by Tomas's shot, but the body inside wasn't Rainier's. It was human, the bone beneath the meat pale cream stained with blood. She clenched her fists.

"Nox?"

"Not her," he said. "You're...you're going to want to see this."

She closed her eyes briefly, breathing deep, then pushed to her feet and forced herself to come over to him. The second GC lay sprawled on the floor, helmet retracted, and while the shards of the visor had torn small holes in his skin, the single shot through his forehead had done most of its damage on its way out. Sanda stared into the unfamiliar face, confusion twisting her up. Then she saw the tattoo on his neck. Twin scythe blades, or crescent moons, crossing at the tip, a single sphere floating above them.

Acolytes of the Sphere. Okonkwo had believed them allies of Prime. She was going to be pissed.

"What the fuck do these people want?" she asked.

"Sanda," Tomas rasped.

She shook herself and holstered her blaster, hurrying to his side. He'd pulled himself partially up the steps and let the rifle drop beside him. His face was pale and glistening with sweat, but his hand pressed to the wound seemed to have stanched the bleeding for now.

She pushed his hand aside and crammed her own hands into the wound anyway.

"You boneheaded jackass," she said. He grimaced as she pressed down.

"Crack shot even when he's bleeding out," Nox said appreciatively.

"Don't encourage him," she muttered, and forced him to lie back against the stairs. "Get me a medikit. Bero, we still being pursued?"

"They are able to track us. I have vaporized three more attempted breach pods."

Sanda squeezed her eyes shut. Tomas put a hand over hers. She opened her eyes. "Right. Get me Arden, we need to figure out—"

"This is what I was trying to tell you," Tomas said. He tilted his head toward the place where his wristpad had fallen. "Me, Novak. Rainier put a virus on our pads."

"Got it," Nox said. He slung his rifle over his shoulder and picked up the pad. "I'll get it to Arden—"

"My resources are very strained," Bero said.

Sanda swallowed and looked Tomas in the eye. "Your implant controls."

He smiled tightly. "I'll manage. Space it."

"Nox, do it."

He looked at the pad, shrugged, and ran to the side of the room and tossed the pad against the wall. *The Light*'s filaments reached out, encasing the wristpad like a cyst, then the wall went flat with no sign of the wristpad left. Sanda let out a ragged sigh. That was it. It was gone.

"Where's my medikit?" she shouted.

Nox grabbed a kit off the wall and tossed it to her. She cracked it open and started patching Tomas up without really thinking about what she was doing. Wipe it down, numbing spray, antiseptic gel, clean patch. He was lucky the shot hadn't hit any arteries. The way his bleeding was slowing down, it looked like it hadn't even hit many veins.

"Roll over," she ordered. He raised his brows at her. She snorted. "Exit wound."

He turned, and she repeated the process as Liao, Conway, Arden, and Knuth shuffled into the room. Everyone had rifles in their hands now, even Arden and Liao, which Sanda wasn't too thrilled about, because she wasn't sure either of them knew how to use them.

"Who is that...?" Arden asked, nudging a body with the toe of their boot.

"Not our biggest problem," Sanda said. "B, anything?"

"Evasion attempts appear to be working as normal."

"Good." She stood and pointed at Liao. "You, keep Tomas from making his wound any worse."

"But—" Tomas started; she ignored him.

"Bero, how did she manage to breach us? I thought *The Light*'s shields were the best."

Sanda didn't like the length of his pause. "I don't know," he finally admitted. "Rainier was this ship. She must know how to exploit its weak points. I'll look into it."

"Well, that's ominous." Sanda rubbed the side of her face with one hand, cringed as she realized she'd smeared her cheek with blood. "Keep me updated. The rest of you, help me get the armor off our friends here. I want anything GC checked for nasty surprises in triplicate, then repaired to the best of our abilities."

"We could space them..." Knuth trailed off when Sanda scowled at him.

"If she wants to invite herself to our party, maybe it's time we invite ourselves to hers."

"You're talking about infiltration?" Tomas asked.

"If I have to," Sanda said. "We need options. Right now, get the cleanup done, and then we're going to have to do something about these bodies."

"Space 'em," Nox said.

Sanda looked into the glazed eyes of a corpse. "That's not how we operate."

CHAPTER 10

PRIME STANDARD YEAR 3543

THE PAST THROWS LONG SHADOWS

Jules woke with a roaring headache that had nothing to do with memory loss. Panic jolted her awake, slammed her body against thick chains wrapped around her arms, legs, and chest. Her breath came harsh to her ears, echoing in her helmet—still on, still armored—as she struggled to pull up a suit diagnostic on the HUD.

Shit, that was a lot of damage. A few of her power cells had shorted, giving her a scant two days of power before she'd have to return to her ship and switch out suits. Her nutrient system had partially fried, offering her enough to scrape by for a day, and her hydration gave her four days, tops, before things got lethal. At least the air and waste scrubbers were still working.

Jules groaned, every cell in her body aching. Stunners shouldn't hit her so hard. They'd previously just tickled. This was something else, something jerry-rigged.

"Can you hear me?" a woman asked.

"Who the fuck are you?" Jules demanded, filtering her speech the way all GC did. She rolled her head to the side, seeking the voice.

The woman was older than she'd appeared at first glance. Wiry and short, she sat on a splintering crate across from Jules, a rolled cigarette in one hand and wrinkles enough around her lips to emphasize the habit wasn't a new one. Her eyes were bloodshot, sharp, and grey as the steel in her hair. The stunner was in her belt, but she wore no other weapons or armor. Jules's rifle leaned against the wall behind her.

"I'm what's keeping you alive, Shadow."

Jules grimaced behind the mirrored safety of her visor. "My team will come for me. This is inadvisable."

"Thing about that," she said, drawing deep on the cigarette. "We've been watching you for a long time. You don't work with anyone else. A solo act, if you will, which is a mite strange for a guardcore."

"Me? You could have seen any of my colleagues. We all look the same."

"Nah. Not true, and don't try to bullshit me. You move like a Grotta rat. I don't know where you got that armor, but you're one of us. You know the streets, you let them take you around, you don't insist on marching out those stupid fucking grids the others adhere to." Her eyes narrowed. "You've taken more of us than most."

Her head spun with residual ache. She had to focus, had to get out of this. Get back to Lolla. "Solo or not, a team will come for me."

"Sure you want them to?"

Jules pressed her lips together, and said nothing.

"It's just that, in all our watching you, we realized you've been watching for other GC, too, Shadow. You duck when they come strolling by, like you don't want to be found. So tell me, where'd you get that armor?"

"It was assigned to me," she said, which wasn't a lie.

"Tell me that without all the filter bullshit on your voice."

Jules licked her lips, hesitated, then decided *fuck it* and killed the voice filters. "It was assigned to me, and I fucking earned it."

She grinned fiercely. "I've no doubt of that. 'Member, we've been watching you, we see how you work. Damn good. Honestly, I didn't think we'd get the drop on you."

"Then why'd you try? What is this all about?"

"We want off the planet. I think you can make that happen."

"You're ascended. You cannot break the quarantine."

"Thing is, we aren't."

"Everyone on this planet not in a sealed suit is either ascended, comatose, or dead. There's no in-between."

"Of course there is, there's always an in-between. Nothing in the worlds is as clean as yes-or-no, is it?"

Jules laughed, low and rough, enjoying the sound of her voice crackling through speakers that weren't meant to filter such a human sound as laughter.

"Cute, real cute. But after this planet went down, we guardcore were the only ones left standing aside from the ascended. We've scoured every scrap under this atmo dome, and the reality of Atrux is black and white: ascended or unconscious. The only people outside of that dynamic are the medis and researchers brought in after the fact, and they're sealed up in the hospital complexes."

"Didn't scour the Grotta too well, did you? That's why you keep coming back out here, you and your colleagues. Because you missed a few rats, and gotta come sweep 'em up. Well, you missed us, too."

Jules frowned behind the shelter of her helmet, a needle of doubt working its way into her thoughts. It was true that her counterparts had missed a lot of the Grotta ascended, and even more of the comatose, during those first few days of sweeping the city. Jules herself had done most of the cleanup out here, following her nose to the rotting dead, and her gut to the lairs of those who'd ascended.

They'd missed a lot. Maybe they missed these people, too. No one would be looking for immune people in the Grotta, after all. They'd check the high-rises for that, the estates on the fringes. The places where vaccinations went beyond the standard cocktail.

"Can you prove it?" Jules asked.

The woman shifted, the crate creaking beneath her. "Not a lot of good ways to do that, is there? Either I stab myself and don't heal right up, or I try to lift something too heavy and pull something. Either thing can be faked, can't it, Shadow?"

Jules licked her lips. "Show me your blood. I can tell."

The woman frowned, the wrinkles around her eyes turning into deep furrows. "Can you, now? You one of the ascended?"

"I'm guardcore."

"Not an answer. So far as I can tell, those two things aren't mutually exclusive."

"None of us dropped when the virus went out. The armor keeps it out." The lie came easily, and was true so far as anyone else was concerned.

"And y'all gotta take those suits off sometime, don't ya? Seems to me an accident could happen out of view of the public, you get my meaning. Maybe some of you who were already on Atrux, you got hit with the agent, too. Or maybe Prime's started experimenting."

"You think Prime is exposing the guardcore on purpose?"

She rolled a shoulder and flicked ash off her cigarette. "I'd do it. Supersoldier bodies in supersoldier armor? That's a fucking wet dream for the Keepers."

Jules snorted, forgetting to mute her speakers before she made the sound. The woman arched a brow at her. Jules said, "We considered it. The numbers aren't good enough. For the amount of work it takes to train up a guardcore unit, the losses are too expensive."

"Now that, I might believe," she said. "But what about a few stray Grotta rats that ascend? Easier to train a kid born to a world like ours for that armor, isn't it? Especially if all that super speed and strength and healing shit is true."

"You think I lived here, got ascended, got taken to that hospital, and shoved in a suit of guardcore armor?"

"I think it's likely." She leaned forward, squinting at Jules. "Like I said, you don't move like one of them. And now that we're having this little chat, I don't think you talk like one, either."

"Have a lot of conversations with guardcore, do you?"

She grinned a toothy grin. "More than you'd think. I didn't get lucky with that stunner. Been experimenting a bit with equipment that would work on you lot."

"Are you confessing to kidnapping my colleagues and testing your weapons on them?"

"Nah," she said, scratching the side of her nose with a ragged thumbnail. "Because I ain't convinced they're your colleagues."

Leave it to a Grotta woman to pick Jules out of a sea of identical faces and bodies. Jules muted her speakers and sighed, letting some of the tension in her muscles relax. She pulled up her suit diagnostics, running a few checks. She could break the chains easily enough, but that would just confirm the woman's suspicion that she was ascended.

Jules didn't know this woman from a hole in the ground, but she knew Grotta minds, and how laser-focused they could be when it came to survival. Jules wasn't walking out of here without that woman dogging her heels. But then, if she and her companions really were immune, Jules would be a fool to walk away. Immunity might be the key to cracking open Lolla's problem. And, in the end, waking Lolla was all Jules gave a shit about anymore.

"What's your name?" Jules asked.

"Saarah," she said, stubbing out her cigarette on the floor. She ground it down with her boot—plain old rubber and synth leather, no mag boots in the Grotta. Jules had almost forgotten how light her feet could feel, how quiet.

"All right, Saarah. You want me to buy that you're immune, I'm going to need that blood sample."

She sighed raggedly. "Figured you'd say that. Is there, like, a sampling needle or something in your armor?"

Jules sat up, the chains around her chest and arms snapping with the motion. Saarah was on her feet in a flash, the rifle in her hands, but she didn't move fast enough to raise Jules's eyebrows. Her reflexes were quick, but they were hard-living quick, not ascended.

"No need for that," Jules said, and turned, swinging her legs over the edge of the bed so that her feet were solidly on the floor. Saarah's finger drifted toward the trigger, but hesitated. "I'm not going to hurt you," Jules said, "but I was getting tired of having to twist my head to look at you."

"Could have asked for a pillow," she said in a tight voice.

"Sit," Jules said.

She thinned her lips but slowly, hesitantly, reclaimed her seat on the crate. Didn't put her rifle down, though. That was fine by Jules.

"Give me your hand," Jules ordered.

She flicked her gaze to the side, at a ragged curtain that marked the door to the room. Jules adjusted the hearing in her suit, listened to two other sets of feet scrape along the floor, even though they moved light as dancers in their soft shoes.

"Tell your friends to stand down," she said.

Saarah bared her teeth in a forced smile, but nodded. "Take it easy, friends. We're still having a chat."

"Let me guess," Jules said. "The heavier one has the stunner pointed at me."

"Probably the lighter one, actually. Her name's Birdie. Vicious little thing."

"I can relate," Jules said without thinking, and Saarah's eyes narrowed with understanding. "Your hand," Jules repeated.

Saarah held it out. Jules extended a thin blade from the tip of her glove and pricked the tip of Saarah's finger, ignoring the woman's wince. She squeezed the finger pad, holding it up as a drop of blood welled, and cranked up the headlamps on her helmet. Her breath caught. The woman's blood was clean. No sheen, no shimmer. No hint of metal lurking in her veins.

"I believe you," Jules said, dropping her hand. "And your friends? Are they like you?"

"Birdie isn't," Saarah said, wrapping a thin bandage around her finger. "But her dad, Reece, he's like me."

Jules placed her hands on her thighs, trying to look nonthreatening, which wasn't an easy thing to do when you were wrapped head to toe in armor meant to deal death, and deal it well.

"You and Reece," she said, "you two could save a lot of people."

"We thought about that, Shadow. Or what, did you think we were complete monsters?"

Jules shifted her weight uncomfortably, making the cot creak beneath her. She hadn't thought anything of the sort, hadn't even considered there might be a reason why these people were keeping to themselves. They were just surviving. That was the way of the Grotta, as Jules knew it.

"Huh," Saarah said, half to herself, as Jules stayed silent. Jules wanted to scream at her, to tell her to keep her opinions and judging eyes to herself, but the armor kept Jules's appearance neutral. "Well, we thought about it. Even scouted out that hospital. But this is the

Grotta, word gets around. Research isn't going as smoothly on the Grotta affected as it is on the normies, you understand. We need off this planet. It's not safe for us."

Jules shook her head. "Ascended or comatose. Those are the two treatment categories. Grotta doesn't come into it."

"I'd tell you to take that visor down and look me in the eye when you say that, but we both know that ain't happening. The Keepers in that building, the ones doing the research? They need bodies to experiment on, and Grotta folks in a coma aren't exactly going to complain. High Protectorate's declared a state of emergency. Anything goes."

"Is that what you think? It's not just Keepers working on a cure. I know some of the scientists myself, the ones that aren't Keepers, and they're good people. Everyone wants a cure, Saarah. That's all that's going on. No one's trying to hurt anyone in there. All the tests are done in simulations, petri dishes, that kinda thing. Even an emergency isn't enough to make Keepers waive consent and start dosing patients who can't say no."

"You sound so damn sure," Saarah said, shaking her head. "But I guess I can't know if that's the voice filters making you sound like you believe yourself. Fuck, Shadow, you're Grotta. Deny it all you want, I don't care, I got eyes. You know what it's like. You know how easy it is for them to chew us up. What part of Prime's history says it'll treat us fairly? If we stay here, we're lab rats."

Jules clenched her fists. Saarah was wrong, had to be. Jules hadn't gone to all this trouble to turn the people of the Grotta into lab rats. Even Prime wouldn't stoop so low. They were obsessed when they had a problem to solve, that was true enough. That was the whole *point*, the reason Jules had stripped off what scraps remained of her humanity and donned the armor, let the ascension-agent loose in the city of her birth, because she knew Prime would figure it out. They always figured shit out. Then Lolla could wake up.

But a little tickle at the back of her thoughts wouldn't let it go, couldn't make her discount the story. Prime fixed shit, true, but they broke as much as they mended. She'd been all over that hospital complex, she'd thought. Maybe she'd missed something.

"I'll look into it," she said. "But if I don't find anything, I need you to promise me you'll turn yourselves in. Whatever made you immune, it might save a lot of people. I know you don't want to be monsters, so let me make sure the way is safe. If it isn't, I'll get you off this rock and into the hands of someone who can help without hurting."

Saarah's jaw protruded as she chewed over the idea, a wary light behind her eyes, fingers curling as if they still held a cigarette. Jules could see the uncertainty written all over the older woman's face. She wanted out. The only guaranteed safety for her and her people was off of this planet, shuttled to a city that wouldn't notice three more people scraping by on their streets. Maybe she'd even planned it—knew which planet she wanted to go to, or moon, or station. Probably had contacts somewhere.

But Saarah was rooted to the Grotta just like Jules was. If she could help the people here, she would, and though Reece wasn't around to speak for himself, he'd have the same instinct.

These people weren't monsters. But Jules was. They just hadn't figured that out yet.

"All right," Saarah said slowly, as if getting the words out was as hard as pushing a boulder uphill. "I'll give you one shot. You go in there, Shadow, and you see what you can see. But if you can't confirm it's safe, then we're out. You take us off this fucking death trap. Deal?"

Jules extended her hand. "Deal."

CHAPTER 11

PRIME STANDARD YEAR 3543

ONE OF US

Biran fell backward and scrambled across the slick bathroom floor, realization clutching his mind with terror. A GC would not have waited out liftoff from the station on his bathroom floor. She had hidden here, knowing the director's quarters wouldn't be touched while they were at the black site. This wasn't a guardcore. This was Rainier.

Her hand snapped out, grabbing for his forearm, but she was too late. He slapped the emergency beacon. Red light filled the room as every alarm on the ship blared, announcing the director of Ada was in danger.

He twisted, trying to get to his feet, but she coiled her arms around his shins and dragged him down. Biran swore as his head cracked against the SynthStone floor. Warm blood trickled down his skin; his vision swam. Some dim part of him was aware that head injuries were quite serious, but every ounce of his energy was currently funneled into clawing panic.

He flailed in her grasp, elbow lashing out to knock Rainier sideways. The sturdy material of her guardcore armor shattered the plex wall of his shower, raining tiny bits of plastic down upon them. The top rail collapsed, slamming against his side, and he grunted, crawling through the plastic shards even as she got her hands around his legs again.

She pinned him easily and shoved his back against the wall so that he was sitting with his legs splayed out, trapped under one of her shins, his arms braced against the wall by her forearm. *How easy for her*, he thought, and almost laughed. Director of Ada, indeed. He was weak as a kitten in the face of trained killers. Biran spat blood and stared hard into the mirrored visor, ignoring his blooming black eye. He had to stall until the cavalry arrived.

"Kill me if you want, you're not getting off this ship."

"No, no, no," she whispered, and he was struck by a sense of child-like panic that bled through every syllable. "I'm sorry. I didn't mean to hurt you, I'm so sorry."

"What the fuck? Rainier, you've killed—"

"Not her! Not anymore!"

Biran forced the panic down, struggled to focus through the pounding in his head. He suspected who she was, but he had to be sure. "Retract your helmet, guardcore."

She gasped and pulled back, freeing his arms. He pretended to be limp as a wet noodle, creeping his fingers subtly toward the blaster on his hip.

"I can't, she'll come back. She went away. I figured it out. I figured out how she gets *in*."

Biran froze, breath harsh in his throat. "Explain. Quickly."

"The helmets." She spoke in rapid-fire bursts that he had a hard time following. "Tiny holes, smaller than pinpricks, so tiny. That's how she gets her signal through, how she hive-minds with herself. The armor's a perfect seal against her otherwise—the metal, the black metal, it keeps her out. Dust, during the bombardment, clogged the holes, and she can't see me anymore. I've been plugging it with paint but the others are starting to notice and if I try to switch helmets then I have to take this off and she'll *come back* and I can't, I can't be that again. I know what she's done. What we've done. I've heard everything."

Biran's head spun as he tried to piece it all together. His hand closed on the grip of his blaster. Boots thundered down the hallway.

"Rainier's lost connection with this body? You've been on your own since the bombardment? That was... That was two *years* ago."

"Yes! Please believe me, please, I don't want to die and I don't want to go back to being her—check the helmets. They're the difference between the normal GC and us. No one could ever see it. No one who didn't *know*."

A trick, surely. A ploy of Rainier's to keep one of herself close to him, monitor the situation until she decided it wasn't worth keeping Biran around anymore.

But Biran knew the tenor of panic, was familiar with the screaming dread and desperation that seeped into every rushed-together syllable.

Was it even possible? Sanda said Rainier printed the bodies for herself; they weren't preexisting people reshaped in her image. Without Rainier's mind in that body, it should have dropped like a rock. Could a personality emerge in an empty husk? That question was way beyond his ability to answer. But if she was separated, then maybe she might know something that could help them. She'd had dozens of opportunities to kill him, and hadn't done so yet. It'd be simple enough to test her theory about the helmets.

The door to his room burst open and GC swarmed, piling through the en suite door. The Rainier ancillary put her hands up and backed away from Biran, dead silent.

Not just GC filled his room. Fleeties and ship personnel had rushed in with the black tide. Everyone came running when the director called for help, it seemed, and embarrassment curdled Biran's already foggy thoughts.

"Biran." Vladsen shouldered through the crowd and dropped to a careful crouch beside him, grabbing his face in both hands as he peered hard into his eyes. He turned his head aside sharply. "He has a concussion, for fuck's sake, get some medis in here!" Vladsen barked with more force than Biran had ever heard come out of the slight man.

"What happened here?" one of the guardcore asked.

Biran blinked through the fog, and realized they had their weapons trained on Rainier, who was still backed away from him, arms up and fingers spread.

"Sabotage," he said, clearing his throat as his voice came out raspy. He pointed to the broken shower with his jaw, and regretted the motion as his head swam anew. "Came to wash up... Fucking exploded..."

The guardcore clipped their rifles to their backs in unison, and Rainier dropped her hands, standing smoothly to join her colleagues. Medis shooed Vladsen and the rest out of the en suite, swarming over him with probing fingers. The one who appeared to be in charge—Biran remembered her vaguely from his physical, a Dr. Mary Flynn—smiled and patted his cheek.

"You'll be all right, Director. Just a little bump on the noggin. We'll scan you to be sure, and you'll have some dramatic bruising, but nothing basic anti-inflammatories can't handle. Can you stand?"

"Yes, of course," he said, taking her outstretched hand. "The worst injury is to my pride."

She smiled at him, but didn't let his hand go as she hefted him to his feet with surprising strength. He wobbled a little, and suppressed an urge to shake his head. That would only make things worse.

"Clear a path, people," Dr. Flynn said with authority.

The crowd dispersed, ship personnel going back to their work with wary glances over their shoulders as Biran walked with all the false bravado he could muster. He caught a glimpse of Vladsen and Singh standing off to the side, and was surprised to see real concern in Singh's face, before half the guardcore closed around him in a phalanx to march him to the medibay that was, no doubt, currently being emptied of all nonessential personnel. The other half stayed behind to search his room. Biran sighed.

"Thanks for letting me walk out on my own two feet," he said.

"Director, I've treated a great many Keepers in my day. I understand the importance of appearance. But don't you worry, as soon as you're behind closed doors, I'll have you on enough painkillers to tranq a horse. That's a hell of a knock you took," she whispered back.

He chuckled roughly, regretting it as the sound rattled in his head. "Thought it was a bump."

She stiffened her arm as he leaned on her to maintain his balance. "Too many ears, Director. You'll be fine. That's all the gossip mill needs to know."

He sighed, thinking of his thin excuse regarding the shower plex, and wondered how the Rainier ancillary was going to sell that to the others.

"I think they'll have plenty to jaw about," he said.

Her expression darkened. "Indeed."

Right. He'd said that cursed word—*sabotage*—because he couldn't think of anything else remotely plausible in the moment. But sabotage required a saboteur, and that meant, as far as anyone knew, an assassination attempt had been made against the new director of Ada Prime. Wonderful.

CHAPTER 12

PRIME STANDARD YEAR 3543

BLACK'S NOT MY COLOR

After the GC tech had been scanned for hidden surprises and Tomas sedated so that he'd actually heal, Sanda let herself into her room and shut the door. Bero had carved out a room big enough to put the suites at Hotel Stellaris to shame. The bed alone was nearly as large as her bedroom in her family home, and the massive en suite shower always ran water as hot as she wanted it.

She never could tell if he'd done it as an apology, or to show off. Ultimately, it didn't matter. She tossed her broken boots to the side of the room and stripped off her coat as she paced across the too-large space, dropping it on the floor. She sat herself down at her desk, stared at the tablet she meant to call Anford on, and began to tremble. Just slightly.

A GC breach pod had speared her home. Had almost taken down her crew. If the GC on the ramp had hit her other leg, had made her drop down, it—he, that had been a man in that armor—he would have had a clear shot at her head, her body. One little mistake had cost the GC their victory. It was not a mistake Rainier would allow her troops to make again.

Sanda planted her elbows on the desk and leaned forward, dragging her fingers through her hair. Though she'd washed her hands, her nails were still caked with half-moons of Tomas's blood. A shower would scrub that out. She needed to shower, rest, and regroup. But there wasn't time for that. There wasn't time for most things Sanda needed.

She pulled herself up, controlled her breathing to stop the shakes, and called General Anford.

It took a full minute for Anford to pick up, and her face was pinched with frustration, but Sanda knew it wasn't directed at her. Anford had a lot to be frustrated about, lately.

"Greeve," she said. "You have blood in your hair."

"Not mine," she said, as if that mattered. "*The Light* was attacked by five guardcore ships. A breach pod made it into our engine room. The situation has been contained."

Anford's brows lifted. "Five? How is it possible a breach pod made it anywhere near that ship of yours?"

She cleared her throat. "Rainier planted a virus on the wristpad of one of my crew members. She used it to track us. We could not shake her assault until we discovered the source and spaced it. Considering what she is, once she had our location pinned down, she was adept at getting around our defenses."

"Whose wristpad?"

"Excuse me?"

Anford lifted her chin and stared her down so hard Sanda suppressed an urge to squirm under the scrutiny. "Greeve, you rarely leave a detail out, which means that is a fact you do not want me to know. You and I, we cannot lie to each other. Whose pad?"

She licked her lips. "Tomas Cepko."

Anford's shoulders shook slightly from a stifled shout. "You brought a Nazca onto your ship, onto *that* ship, after what happened at Monte?"

She wanted to shrivel up right on the spot. "He had information regarding the location of the sphere. He tracked Demas to a structure we believe Rainier is using as a base of operations, and as far as we know, Demas has not left that location."

"Demas was apprehended. Rainier cut him off after the deadgate, and Okonkwo's people tracked him down. He didn't have the sphere."

"Rainier cut him off?"

"She wanted him to bring her the ship, not the sphere."

Sanda digested that for a moment, then cleared her throat. "Understood. You should know that the triad of GC that Rainier sent this time were not her. They were human. They did not dissolve upon death. We have the bodies, and they bear the Acolyte tattoo."

Anford swore. "I'll tell Okonkwo. All things considered, I suspect she will want the bodies for further investigation. I'll order the transport to you now. Do you have any insight on why Rainier sent you Acolytes, instead of herself? It feels clumsy of her to reveal allies we didn't know she had. Rainier doesn't do clumsy."

"I agree. Maybe they were the only option in range, but I believe Rainier sent them to make a point. She wanted me—wanted us—to know that her resources aren't limited to however many instances of herself she can make. She wanted us to know she has human allies. To know that..." She cleared her throat. "That we cannot count on it being Rainier's face behind the helmet, every time we fire upon GC."

"She's a monster."

"With respect, General. We made her what she is."

"People like Lavaux and Halston made her what she is."

Sanda waved a hand. "People are people. She doesn't make the distinction."

"And your plans?"

Sanda squared her shoulders. "I'm going to that installation."

"Is that wise? She's demonstrated her reach to you, and while it's entirely possible that she did so to scare you off, it is also possible that she is baiting you into a trap."

"I understand, and I am convinced that she'll be ready for us at the installation, but I see no other choice. If Demas did not have the sphere on him, then it's likely it's still there. We require it to heal Atrux, and to stop Atrux from happening again. Bero assures me that, now that he's engaged with those ships, we will be better equipped for another fight with them."

She sighed. "Very well. But I'm only allowing this because I see no other option."

"When you come for the bodies, send a guardcore shuttle. We're going to need it to get inside that installation."

"I can do that. Hold position until we can make the transfer."

"Thank you."

"Good luck, Commander."

Anford cut the feed and Sanda slumped in her chair, letting her arms hang limp at her sides. She eyed her leg, knowing she needed to repair the prosthetic, but completely lacked the energy to care.

"I have not assured you that we will be better equipped for another engagement," Bero said.

Sanda smiled slightly. "I know, B. Sorry about that."

"If we fail, I do not want General Anford to think poorly of my abilities."

"If we fail, I don't think humanity will have long to do much worrying."

Silence. After a long moment, Bero said, "You keep breaking your prosthetic. The junk you pick up, it's not sturdy enough to stand up to what you put it through. I can grow you a better one."

She looked down at the scorch mark torn through her silicone skin, the melted groove in the metal bone. She'd burned through so many prosthetics in such a short time. This one was another "broken" smart prosthetic, picked up from a junk dealer on Ordinal. She hoped Hassan hadn't been put into a coma by the ascension-agent.

"I don't want a leg with connectivity," she said, even though he already knew that.

"I have been experimenting with shutting down certain aspects of the nanites that make up this ship. I believe that, once the leg is complete, I can remove any ability to communicate outside of the nanites involved. They will be severed from me, but will be responsive to your needs."

Sanda licked her lips. This wasn't about giving her independent control of a prosthetic. The only reason Bero had to make those experiments was to explore various ways to protect himself against intrusion by Rainier. She had been made to inhabit this ship. Getting Rainier near the ship was a risk that lingered in the back of all of their minds—could Bero defend himself?

Arden had been less than clear on the subject, and Bero was his usual evasive self. This was the most candor he'd ever shown.

Because he wasn't talking about his body, he was talking about her leg. The metaphor must make it easier on him. He'd always had trouble facing hard truths head-on.

"These experiments. Are you able to reestablish a connection at a later date?"

"I have not been successful in the attempt."

Good news for her leg, bad news for him. If Bero couldn't regain access to hardware he cut off from all connectivity, he'd be effectively imprisoning himself within the body of the ship with no way to communicate, no way to reach out to the world at large.

"I don't know, B. I don't like the idea of my leg being open to intrusion by Rainier."

"I can relate," he said dryly.

That made her smile. "We can put you somewhere else, you know. Drop you back in the net while we dust knuckles with Rainier. Arden would be on firmer footing, there. They'd be able to keep you secure."

"We were talking about your prosthetic."

"B—"

"I am aware of all the risks involved and am taking my own precautions. If you were to enter into battle with Rainier without a mind allowing you to interface directly with this ship, the fight would be over before it began. She would have the ship. She would have your life support. Personally, I find air an annoyance, but you humans do seem fond of it. You need a mind."

"Anford could send us another ship."

"Nothing Prime Inventive has made can outgun Rainier Lavaux. She has your best already."

"You can't know that."

He strobed the lights in her room in irritation. "I can, better than most. The risk involved does not exceed my personal risk tolerance."

"You're talking like a computer again, B."

"Then let's get back to your leg."

She snorted. "Fine. Make me a prosthetic if you think you can cut it off from all external tampering—but *only* if you learn something about your defenses in the process."

"We learn something every time we make something, Sanda."

"Ugh. Go back to the computer-speak. I like it better than the faux philosophy."

He winked the lights at her, and she tried not to think too much about who might be speaking to her through those speakers in a few hours as they fell into discussion about tightening up their security protocols to better defend against another guardcore ship sneaking up on them.

After this was all over, Sanda swore she'd never wear black again.

CHAPTER 13

PRIME STANDARD YEAR 3543

TOO ALIKE

The lights went down for the night cycle, and Tomas pretended to ache as he shuffled into a bed that he noticed was slightly wider now than it had been before. He bit back a comment, knowing that pointing it out would irritate Bero and risk that the next time he tried to go to bed, his cot might be only wide enough to fit one leg.

Not that he needed the comfort. His body only pained him when he found it useful, but he'd have to keep up appearances for the sake of the others. They believed he'd lost control of his implants with his wristpad. It would have been such a convenient cover for his abilities, ascribing his enhanced speed and recovery to those controls, but now that he had only his synthetic body, he had to be careful. Sanda was clever, suspicious, and the truth about his body wasn't a conversation he was ready to have. Not with her.

As Tomas tugged the covers up, he closed his eyes, replaying the fight with the guardcore in crystal-clear detail, wondering why his memory was so perfect now when it had seemed flawed before. He'd had above-average recall, of course, and what he thought of as the Nazca implants had helped him raise that even further, but it'd come with the usual human flaws.

Now, dragging up a memory was as simple as pressing play on a CamCast. He wanted Rainier dead, but he had to admit that whatever she had done to him in that restoration pod had been an improvement.

In his mind's eye, the breach pod slammed into the wall and sent Sanda and her crew flying. He'd made it to his feet before they had their heads on straight, and that'd worked to his advantage, as he'd been able to draw the attention of one of the GC away from Sanda before the three closed in. Separating a guardcore unit made them vulnerable. Or, as vulnerable as it was possible for such a well-practiced regiment to be.

With two on Sanda and her crew, they'd been forced to seek cover, and completely missed Tomas wrestling with the third for control of their rifle before Nox had come in and forced him to pretend to be a mere human once again, and take a shot in the hip.

His body may be good at dampening pain after the fact, but that had still hurt like hell and knocked him on his ass, vision blurring as white flames of agony had alighted through his synthetic nerves.

He had to enact intentional control over himself to put the pain down. Though getting shot wasn't his preference, it was good data to have. Pain could take him offline, mentally speaking. He'd have to work around that.

Under the cover of the blanket, he shifted a hand down and picked up the corner of his bandage. Seeing in the dark was no problem for him. The flesh there was clean and mended, if a little pink. He winced. He'd have to make excuses to Liao, who was playing their medi despite not being anything close to a medical doctor, about his Nazca implants making him a quick healer, so that she wouldn't want to look at the wound.

Easier to do if he hadn't had to space his wristpad. Now, explaining why he was faster and indefatigable was going to be a stretch. He'd needed Arden to see those programs so that he'd have an excuse for seeming extra-human on occasion. Now, he'd have to work harder to keep it a secret.

"You're going to have to tell her eventually," Bero said.

Tomas bolted upright, the blanket bunching down around his hips. A movement that should have caused his wound to pull, so he winced.

Bero chuckled. "I've sensed your consciousness since you came on board. You bled all over my floor. There aren't a lot of secrets between us now, are there, Nazca?"

"I don't know what you're talking about."

"I do not want to have to space you, Tomas, because I have already stretched the bounds of Sanda's ability to forgive me. Did Rainier send you to test my defenses?"

"No." His heart hammered in his ears. He forced it to slow down. "I'd never betray you to her."

"You'd never betray Sanda to her. I'm not so sure about the rest of this ship, myself included. If you believed handing me to Rainier would improve Sanda's chances at happiness, you would do so."

"No secrets?"

"None."

"I absolutely would. But I see no path by which that helps her. She needs you on this ship. I intend to do what I can to keep you here. For her sake."

"Do you know why Graham Greeve left the *Thorn*?"

Tomas blinked at the shift. "No. Why?"

"Because, after Janus, he realized he was too close. He'd make a call that meant complete destruction of the rest of humanity, if it meant keeping his children safe. He sent me a message, later, once he knew I'd taken over *The Light*. Told me a secret. Would you like to know what it was?"

Tomas licked his lips. "Yes."

"He told me Biran could never board this ship, because if Sanda and Biran were on the same vessel, on the same mission, they'd think like Graham. They'd burn the worlds down to save each other."

Tomas thought back to Biran's expression the day he'd passed the key to his personal MRI to her. He hadn't said anything about it, he didn't need to. Tomas had felt cold straight down to his toes watching the glance those two shared, knowing everything that passed between them. Sanda had only thought, at that moment, that he was telling her to flee. She hadn't realized he'd given her the key to scan the chip in her head until later.

Hadn't realized that, in passing the key to his sister, he'd undermined thousands of years of successful Prime security protocols. For if the data hidden on Sanda's chip had been gate schematics, it would have been the first breach in Prime's history. And Biran Greeve did not give a fuck what happened to Prime after that, so long as his sister had the information she needed to keep herself safe.

"I believe it."

"Then you understand my concern."

"She wouldn't do that for me," he said, the words tasting bitter. He craved that level of devotion, felt the hunger for it as an ache in his chest. But he knew, now. Knew that his puppy-dog crush was born out of the reset of his body. He'd loved others before. He must have. This time felt more intense because, to his mind and body, it was the first. Sanda wouldn't have the same obsession.

"When Sanda Greeve makes snap decisions, she doesn't rely on her training. She'll save one in the moment, if she doesn't have the time to think it through."

"Saved your ass," he muttered.

Bero winked the lights at him. "And I am grateful, and returned the favor to the best of my ability. However, the decision was not pure instinct. She did not trust Keeper Lavaux, and did not want him to have me."

"We're talking about Rainier here. If Sanda has a chance to put a bullet in that woman once and for all, she won't hesitate if the bullet has to go through me first."

"Options are never that simple."

Tomas clenched the blankets in his fists. "If you want me off this ship because you believe my presence endangers your mission, Bero, say so."

"I do not want you off this ship."

He blinked. "Then why the pressure?"

"Because I need you to understand that, if it comes down to it, you might have to pull that trigger for her. She'll never forgive you. But she'd never forgive herself if she's the one."

"You're trusting me with this?"

A pause. "I need your help, Tomas Cepko."

"I'll do the best I can to make sure we put Rainier down, but—"

"Not that. *I* need your help."

Uneasiness roiled in his belly. He cut off the sensation. "With what?"

"We arrive in Rusani in six hours. I have not been able to construct an adequate defense against Rainier intruding upon this ship's systems. I need better security protocols. I need to know what it's like to be attacked in that way."

"Arden's the one for that. I don't know anything about it."

"You are a subset of Rainier."

He shuddered at the echo. "Why would you say that?"

"Because it is true. I do not know what Lavaux was, but through the body of this ship I can sense your mind in a way I cannot sense the others. When you first boarded, I feared you were Rainier in another shape. The pressure you exert upon this ship is...immense. Though you are an imperfect fit, the ship wants you at the controls. It was designed for a mind like yours."

He swallowed thorns. "Arden says you were designed for the same hardware that's on this ship."

"Arden is partially correct. I was modeled after Rainier, but only to the extent that Rainier allowed Icarion to do so. I am limited compared to her, a dark mirror at best. There are places of this ship that even my mind cannot reach. But you? I've felt this ship call out to you since the moment you stepped on board. I do not understand how it's possible, but you're more like her than I could ever be."

Tomas knew how it was possible, though he could scarcely admit it to himself. Bero had been limited by Rainier's intervention in his development, but Tomas? He'd been made with stolen technology—crafted by the Nazca, not Rainier, and without restraint. Aside from them tampering with his memories.

His knuckles cracked from how hard he crushed the sheet between his fingers. "I was...I *am* in a human body. I've lived with humanity my whole life, believed I was one of...I *am* one of them. I'm not like her."

"But you interface so easily with—"

"This conversation is over."

"Tomas, please."

"Fuck off, Bero. I'll do what you want. I'll make sure Sanda pulls the trigger even if I'm strapped to the bomb, but if you want to...to imply I'm less human than a goddamn spaceship, then you can go fuck yourself. Which you cannot do, because you are a spaceship."

"Tomas—"

A wave of rage boiled out from Tomas's mind. He wanted Bero silent. Wanted the lights off, not winking at him, not reminding him that everything he'd ever known himself to be was a lie.

Bero's voice cut out, muted. The lights went dark and even the muffled hum of other lives moving around the ship, breathing and shifting, disappeared.

Tomas froze on the bed, the sheets still in his hands, and sensed the room around him. The core construction of the walls, the furniture. The nanites that meshed together to create a solid whole standing at breathless attention, waiting with a low thrum of excitement for the command of the mind they were created to obey.

He could make the bed larger, the walls broader and higher. Instinctively he knew, down to every last atom, the weight and balance distribution of the ship. Could rearrange it at will without disrupting mass someplace else. Could do it so fast the humans on board wouldn't even see it happen.

But it was not only the body of the ship he could feel. Thin tendrils reached out to him, wary, and he knew that if he were to throw his consciousness along those pathways, he would collide with the mind that was Bero, the intruder on this ship, the incorrect controller.

The Light wanted him to. Wanted him to take what was his.

Tomas squeezed his eyes shut and pressed the heels of his palms against his lids until the orbs of his eyes should burst, but they stayed resolutely intact. He pushed the communion down, shoved aside every sense of belonging to the ship. Focused only on breathing— something he didn't need to do—and the rough feel of the sheet against his skin, the cool touch of the adhesive from the bandage over his hip.

Tomas opened his eyes, and though he could no longer feel the pathways folding open for him, he sensed the room around him. Still, waiting. Dark and silent, because he had willed it to be so.

CHAPTER 14

PRIME STANDARD YEAR 3543

BETTER TO BE A SCANDAL

Biran spent the remainder of his trip to Ada Station sequestered in his quarters, a wall of guardcore blocking the hallway to his room from all directions. People's berths had had to be moved.

He wanted to die of embarrassment from all the fuss being made, but it was his own fault. He'd put a potential assassin into their minds, and the guardcore were doing their job. Not even Singh or Vladsen was allowed into his room; all their communications were conducted digitally.

At least Graham had gotten back to him about the HUD and confirmed it was clean, so Biran had the distraction of getting used to the new interface. But by the time they landed at the station, he was about ready to crawl out of his own skin.

The guardcore crowded him as far as the airlock to the gangway before Biran lost his patience.

"Enough," he said, stopping short of the airlock. "Back off, all of you. I will not have the people of Ada see their director return under a shell like a damn turtle. Let them see I am well."

"Director—" Singh started.

"I'll hear no arguments. We're back to normal arrangements from here on out."

"There was an assassination attempt, Director. Surely that changes things," Vladsen said, careful to keep any raw edges of emotion from his voice.

"A poor attempt. For all we know, a repair drone installed the door incorrectly and it burst from the pressure variation over time. I have a black eye, Keepers. It's practically a scabbed knee."

"We recommend increased protection procedures," one of the guardcore said.

"I am declining that recommendation," Biran said coolly.

After a hesitation in which Biran suspected they communicated via their private comms to figure out a subtler way of watching him more closely, the GC nodded as one and stepped back, forming the tight crescent they usually did when accompanying a group of Keepers anywhere public.

Biran let out a slow breath. "Thank you."

He waved the airlock open, and immediately regretted sending the soldiers to the back. News drones skirted the edges of the allowed zone, bright lights flashing as they struggled to capture him from every possible angle. Civilians had gathered on the promenade set aside for them, straining to catch a glimpse of their director.

A sharp spike of doubt wedged itself into him. It was entirely possible, he realized far too late, that the Rainier copy he'd spared had pretended at innocence for this moment—to get close enough to harm him publicly. He'd lost track of her after his security detail had increased. She could have been any one of them, or none at all. She might even have reassigned herself. Possibly to Vladsen. He pushed the thought aside, barely resisting a glance back at the guardcore following him. He'd made his decision. She'd come to him because he'd listen, because he'd recognize the value in the information she offered. If he started doubting his instincts now, he'd unravel.

He kept an easy smile on as he strolled down the gangplank. He even managed to turn his head long enough to flash a wink at the crowd, and lift a hand in a short wave. At least some of his Speaker training had prepared him for this part.

They weren't here for just him, though. The *Terminus* was already in dock, a monstrous entity alongside the *Taso*, which had once seemed impossibly huge to Biran. Okonkwo's flagship was a moving mountain, a many-paneled beast of metal. Cylindrical in shape, it reminded him of the chambers of an old-fashioned revolver. Primarily used for diplomatic missions, the *Terminus*, on principle, did not carry ordnance.

Biran flicked an admiring gaze up, tracing the lines of the sleek, dull grey hull, and nodded approvingly. No one who didn't know what they were looking for would be able to tell that Biran had ordered tradition shunted aside, and packed that ship with weapons. Every single move he made was captured on film, frozen, analyzed. He felt the scrutiny crawling across his skin, and betrayed nothing of his thoughts.

Okonkwo swept down the gangplank of the *Terminus*, making a beeline for him, her guardcore a tight knot behind her. Biran paused at the end of the gangplank and nodded to her as she stopped a respectful distance away.

He'd only seen her in CamCasts before this moment, and the woman herself almost took his breath away. Broad of shoulder and sharp-featured, Okonkwo stood a full half a head taller than him, her hair shaved over the back of her neck and skull to reveal her Keeper scar, but the rest of it expertly twisted into tight, braided whorls. Too-green eyes sparkled at him, offset by the crimson silk of her trailing coat, cut so close to her body he couldn't tell if it was an outer garment or a dress. Biran swallowed, smiling at her as he took her hand and shook once, firmly. Singh had been right about the clothes.

"Director Greeve, I'm delighted to see you've returned to us in one piece," she said, one thick, but carved, eyebrow scything up in question.

"Ah, that." He reached up and rubbed the skin near his black eye as he let her hand drop. "Unfortunate, but it comes with the territory."

"Naturally," she said with a slow, lazy smile that flashed white teeth at him. "I've had five assassination attempts thwarted since this morning." She half turned, gesturing up the gangplank. "If you would please join me? We have a great many things to discuss."

"Delighted." Biran fell into step beside her, tracking the guardcore in the corner of his eye as his group split, some accompanying Singh and Vladsen back to the Cannery while a larger number followed him, merging seamlessly with Okonkwo's group.

The airlock swished shut and Okonkwo grunted, paused to shake her head. Her tone lost the dulcet tones she'd used outside, and shifted into the matter-of-fact cadence he was used to from their calls. "Void, that dog and pony show can get tiring. How bad was the attempt, really?"

"No more dangerous than a slip in the bath. I'm not sure who was more embarrassed, me or the doctor who had to treat my black eye. I swear, Prime Director, if I had known how obnoxious that distress beacon was—"

She held up a fist. "I understand you have your pride, and I respect that, but that is what the beacon is *for*. You will use it at the slightest sense of a threat, am I clear? If I believe, even a second, that you're too embarrassed by this event to do your job properly—and that includes keeping yourself safe—then I will bust you back down to..." She scrunched up her face, squinting. "What were you intending to be, before Dralee?"

"Would you believe I wanted to work on shipping algorithms?"

"Christ," she said, and laughed. "What a waste that would have been. Come, I have someone I want you to meet."

Biran followed her down the halls in a direction that shifted from the plush decor of normal life to the starker construction of the utilitarian. The *Terminus* would carry a massive forward scouting party—more of a miniature army, really—through the secondary gate. But before it had been pressed into this purpose, Okonkwo had used the beast of a ship to host grand delegations—meetings between Prime and upstart nations, conclaves of Protectorates all across the united worlds.

Biran had never set foot on this ship before; he'd had no need to. Ada drew Okonkwo's attention only because of the war with Icarion, and even that was considered a mild annoyance before they'd revealed the creation of *The Light of Berossus*. If Ada's deceased director, Jian Olver, had ever been on this ship for a conclave, he hadn't told Biran about it.

The *Terminus* screamed opulence, power, in every line of its body. The decor in the nicer parts—which he had merely glimpsed—was sedate, but expensive, polished to within an inch of its life. Biran had no doubt the weapons he'd requested built into the body of the ship were just as high-end, and just as well cared for.

He swallowed. This would be his ship. His seat of command as he led the expedition through the secondary gate to try and prove the lie to Rainier's words: to see if any life aside from humanity existed in this broken universe, after all.

But the paths Okonkwo took now weren't to his seat of command, or any of the rooms where he'd be running operations from. She guided him through tunnels as wide as the rest of the ship's, but stripped down. Bare metal, bevel-set viewscreens. Biran's palms began to prickle. This was where the work of the ship was done, and he didn't like the idea that Okonkwo was taking him to meet someone in this place.

Before he could voice a concern, she swiped her wristpad over a lock, and a door dilated in the wall. Biran blinked against the low light inside, following Okonkwo into a room in which their mag boots clanged against a metal floor, the sound bouncing against the high ceiling. The bare walls were lined with guardcore, standing ready with their rifles in their hands. The helmeted heads focused on a singular figure chained to a chair in the center of the room.

Demas.

Biran went cold, hesitating after his first step over the threshold. "What is this?" he asked.

Okonkwo stopped out of arm's reach from the traitorous guard-core. Her shadow crossed his eyeline and he lifted his head, slowly, as if every articulation of his spine ached. Bloodshot eyes stared across the room, his face painted with bruises, the plain T-shirt and slacks he wore torn at the edges and stained with blood. Upon seeing Biran, a slow smile spread across his face, sweeping chills up Biran's spine.

"This," Demas rasped, voice echoing, "is the end of an interrogation."

"The real GC dug him out of a hole on a tiny moon in the Atrux system, Pozo." Okonkwo circled him at a careful distance as she spoke, shaking her head slowly from side to side. "His friend Rainier took the second sphere and cut him loose, left him to rot. How's that for loyalty?"

She stopped her pacing and cocked her head to the side, staring hard at the prisoner. Biran wracked his mind for everything he knew about Demas, and came up with scarce little. Sanda had said Okonkwo claimed he was her childhood friend. He'd shot Sanda and left her and her crew to die on *The Light* before running off with the second sphere. Sanda had thought he'd taken it to Okonkwo, but he'd taken it to Rainier instead.

Biran's fists clenched slowly. "You shot her. You shot Sanda."

Okonkwo smiled a viperous smile and stepped to the side, giving Biran room to approach. He stopped when she cleared her throat at the edge of some predetermined safe periphery.

Demas met his eyes. "Yes. She displayed outstanding competence. I couldn't risk her following me."

His knuckles cracked. "Is that supposed to be a compliment? She was too good to let live?"

Demas shrugged. The chains that anchored him to the chair whispered against each other. "It was a fact of the mission. Considering your personal investment, Speaker Greeve, I thought you might have liked to know the reason."

"Director Greeve," he snapped. Demas jerked his head back, eyes narrowing, and turned his head to Okonkwo.

"What happened?" he demanded. She kept on smiling at him.

"You're talking to me now," Biran said, anger hot in his veins. He did not raise his voice. "She patched you up, she saved your life, and you shot her in the fucking stomach."

Demas swiveled his head slowly back to Biran, a faint smirk pushing his lips out. "Yes, she did, and I appreciated that. I made a mistake when I shot her in the stomach. I should have aimed for the head."

"You fucking—"

"Easy," Okonkwo intoned.

Biran took a breath, centered himself. "I should have expected as much from you. Takes someone dead inside to betray a childhood friend."

Demas winced, pushing back into the chair, and pointedly did not look at Okonkwo. "You should know, eh, Greeve? Have you figured it out yet? Do you know why Lionetti turned to Icarion?"

Okonkwo's hand was on Biran's shoulder. "He doesn't know. He's winding you up."

Biran unclenched his fists one finger at a time. "Why? What's the point?"

"I do apologize for this," Okonkwo said, "but I needed to know when Rainier cut him loose. Before your promotion, it seems, as he called you Speaker. He was not aware you are now director of Ada."

Demas scoffed. "Is that all? It's an exceptionally cruel play, even for you, Malkia."

She shrugged one shoulder. "Needs must. We're done with you now, Demas."

He licked his lips, eyes darting from side to side, looking for a way out. "It helps you not at all to know the rough timeline of when she cut me out."

"In the long run, that may be true, but I needed to know." Her tone went steely. "I needed to know if you were standing at her right hand when she committed mass murder."

A twitch at the corner of his eyes made Okonkwo stiffen. "I see. Goodbye, Demas."

She pulled her blaster from somewhere about that perfectly cut coat and held it out to Biran. He stared at the weapon in shock. "Am I to execute him, then?"

"He tried to kill your sister and her entire crew. Left them to rot behind a gate where they would never be found. He would most likely try again, if he got loose."

The anger came back, tempting. He smothered those coals. "This is what jails are for, Prime Director."

Demas began to laugh. A low, gravelly sound that mounted toward hysteria, then cut off abruptly. "*Director*, you are being given a rare inside view of how the worlds really work. I am guardcore, no more a citizen of Prime than you are. If you transgressed to this level, would you keep your chip?"

"Of course not," Biran said, "but that's different. The security of the data comes before all."

"And that security is ensured through the muscle of the GC," Demas mused, never taking his eyes from Okonkwo. "Isn't that right, Malkia? There's no jail once you wear the black."

"That is correct," she said, pressing the blaster into Biran's hands.

He hated the slight weight of it. "He is too dangerous, because we have trained him too well. Any prison we build to contain an ex-GC would be escapable, or so very cruel in its restrictions that death would be the better option."

Biran stared at the weapon in his hands. "This isn't us. This isn't Prime."

Okonkwo let out a burst of a sigh and snatched the weapon back. Before Biran could react, she'd clicked off the safety and fired. Demas's head painted the floor, a mere stump above his shoulders pumping blood futilely to stain his shirt. Funny, that Biran should be worried about the dead man's laundry.

"Fuck," he said, feeling dizzy.

The Prime Director clicked the safety back on and holstered her weapon. She did not look at him as she spoke, but instead stared at the cooling corpse of her lifelong friend, her supposed protector.

"This is us, Director Greeve. This is Prime. This is what we've always been."

"And did you think, even for a second, that this is where we've gone wrong?"

She pushed out her lips, considering. "Perhaps. But this is the world our forebearers have made for us, and we have to live in it. Do you understand me, Director? We have to *live*."

He shook his head, numb. "I don't understand."

"No. You wouldn't. Narrow, the views of those born out of Ada, but narrow has its own uses."

The anger flared back within him. "Don't lecture me on my narrow viewpoint while you stand over the cooling body of your friend. Don't tell me this was for the safety of Prime, when part of it was about revenge."

She barked a laugh. "You're not wrong. I thought it might be for you, too." She watched him from the corner of her eye. "If the situation had been reversed, Sanda would have taken that shot."

"She—" Cold trickled into his veins, his thoughts racing ahead, cutting him off before he could say the words he wanted to be true. He'd seen the footage. Watched her face down Rainier, watched her dogged determination on Monte, her desperate struggle with

Lavaux. And as he'd watched, he'd seen in her a spark he didn't understand.

But he had recognized it, knew the tenor of that spirit, because it was the same tempering Graham carried. Ilan and Biran, they'd never had it in them. Not like those two. He swallowed. Sanda would have taken the shot, and he couldn't blame her, so why couldn't he?

Okonkwo patted him on the back. "Demas was correct, I am cruel. But I am also sorry, for what it's worth. I needed to confirm certain suspicions about you before I sent you through that gate."

"What?" he said, strangling back a laugh. "That I'm a coward?"

"Don't let your emotions run away with you. If I thought you were a coward, I never would have approved Jian elevating you to Speaker in the first place. No, Biran. I needed to be absolutely certain the war had not changed you so much that you had become like your sister."

"Sanda is no killer," he said, swallowing bile.

"She is, and so am I, and so is everybody in this room aside from you. We all have our reasons. Honor and defense and the Greater Good, perhaps, but we pull the trigger all the same." She shook her head as she gazed upon Demas's body. "It doesn't even hurt all that much, most of the time. But that is why I sent her chasing Rainier's tail, and selected you for the gate, because if Rainier's right, and there's another form of life out there somewhere, the last thing humanity needs is a killer saying hello."

She tipped her head back, regarding the ceiling, and Biran stayed quiet, because he could sense she wasn't done, and he had no idea what to say. Everything he could think of was a petty, flimsy defense of Sanda's moral character, and she didn't need his defense. Hell, she'd probably readily agree with Okonkwo.

"Pick your personal team tonight, you ship out tomorrow morning," she said. "I'm giving you the High Protectorate's Speaker, Annalise Greystone. She's competent and loyal, and can pull a trigger if it comes to that, but you are the head of this expedition. Do not cede your authority to a single soul, not even a High Protectorate member. We've already pissed off one of our intergalactic neighbors, Director. Treat this delicately, because I do not think humanity can survive pissing off a second."

"I understand," he said firmly.

She dropped her head back down and half smiled at him. "I believe you. Before you leave, I've arranged a few interviews for you. Personal interest pieces, mostly. Ada wants to get to know their new director, and there are already certain salacious rumors circulating."

Biran felt hot and dizzy. "My personal life is no one's business."

She eyed him critically, and he couldn't keep from blushing. "A tip-off from the *Taso* said you were found in an indelicate position with one of your guardcore. Rumor is already spreading that you developed a relationship with one of the GC after catching a glimpse of them with their helmet down during the purge and fell in love."

"That's absurd."

"It is," Okonkwo said. "But it is romantic and dramatic and precisely the variety of story that people love to spread about their new director, who is unusually young and handsome."

"I—" Biran stammered, knowing his blush darkened, and tried to gather himself. "I'm mortified. I'll straighten things out in the interview."

She leaned close enough to whisper against his ear, "No you won't, Biran. You will blush like you just did, and clear your throat, and tug at your collar, and decline to comment, fueling the rumors about your GC love, because such a romantic entanglement is merely taboo. Much better, don't you think, than people whispering about an *illegal* entanglement?"

Vladsen. She knew. Biran froze. Excuses, denials, clotted up at the back of his throat and he couldn't push them out.

She pulled back, straightened the set of his shoulders, and nodded to herself. "I see we understand each other. Good evening, Director Greeve. By the time you step foot on this ship again, I will be halfway back to Ordinal. Good luck."

She patted his cheek and strode off, leaving him alone with the walls of GC, and the corpse of her childhood friend.

CHAPTER 15

PRIME STANDARD YEAR 3543

IF THE ARMOR FITS

Her crew gathered on deck as *The Light* approached the distance Tomas had been at when he'd taken the videos of Rainier's installation. Sanda had already been on deck an hour. She'd awakened early, strangely ill at ease, and not with the normal adrenaline creep that came from getting close to mission time.

She'd awoken to find a new prosthetic, the same silvery grey as the rest of the ship, waiting for her on a side table. It'd slipped onto her skin like a silken glove, and only a few hours later Sanda could easily forget she was wearing a prosthetic if she didn't think about it. She tried to ascribe some of the unsettled feeling she was experiencing to the fact that the ship had grown her a perfect fit overnight, but it was a hard sell, even to herself.

The thing giving her the creeps wasn't the metal at the end of her thigh. It was the shard of black speared into the side of a moon thrown up on all the viewscreens.

She was getting ready to put up a preliminary scan on the building's dimensions and possible ingress/egress points when Tomas came onto the deck. His steps were slow, but sure, and he had a faraway look in his eyes as he crossed his arms and lingered off to the side, near the console Knuth had claimed. The ship's engineer didn't seem to mind. Tomas had, after all, taken a bullet to protect *The Light*.

Which was why he really shouldn't be standing on her command deck right now.

"Cepko, your only assignment is rest."

He snorted. "Fat chance. I'm fine. And like I said, you need me for this."

Dr. Liao stood and started to move toward him. "The commander is right. You were very lucky, but—"

Before she could get her hands on his bandage, he sidled away, twisting slightly to slide out of her grasp. His gaze was hard, but not cruel. Interesting. She'd never seen him rebuke attempted kindness. Maybe his visit with Rainier had been rougher than she thought.

"I'm fine, Doctor. Thank you."

Liao sniffed and tugged on her buttoned-up coat to have something to do with her hands. "You really should see a proper medi." She stalked back to her chair, wiping her hands of Tomas, and Sanda suppressed a sigh. What little trust he'd earned taking on the GC was already wearing thin, it seemed. Even Nox, who'd been willing to toss him a rifle when it came down to it, was giving Tomas a side-eye.

"If you slow me down, I'll lock you up," Sanda said.

Tomas grinned, but swallowed the flirty line she knew would be on the tip of his tongue when he felt the eyes of her crew on him. "Understood, Commander."

Well, at least his spy training had taught him how to defer when it was appropriate. Or maybe that was how Tomas always was. She wished she could tell the difference between who he was and who he was trained to be.

"This is what we've got," she said, addressing everyone. "And it's not much."

She pushed through the scans Bero had done. The tower reached ninety stories tall, with over two dozen docking ports and enough radiant heat to account for thousands of bodies inside. It wasn't on the lists of official guardcore installations Okonkwo had sent, which meant it was decidedly one of Rainier's compounds.

Tomas shifted his weight, seeing she'd checked that, but he had to understand that she couldn't take his word. She had to be sure.

Barging into an official GC facility guns out would have been real fucking embarrassing. Not that they could go guns out here.

"As you can see, we are hopelessly outgunned, regardless of *The Light*. At present, they have not spotted us, and Bero believes that will continue to be the case. But if we move much closer, he may not be able to keep us stealthed. We know what the regular GC can see. We do not know what Rainier has equipped her people with."

"There's no reason to think she knows we're coming," Knuth said. "Something capable of detecting *The Light* has got to be rare, even for her. We might get lucky."

"Not a fan of relying on luck," Sanda said. "It has a way of running out when it's least convenient. And I believe she does know we're coming."

Nox turned his head slowly to regard Tomas. "Why's that?"

"She sent us the Acolytes," Sanda said. "Arden and Bero assure me that Rainier wasn't able to determine anything but our location through the virus on Tomas's wristpad, so she didn't overhear us. But she's known where Tomas was since the day she kicked him loose. She knows he went to this compound. She knows he then endeavored to get on this ship."

Sanda paused a moment, watching the subtle tension flicker behind Tomas's eyes. She thought she caught a vague sense of irritation from him, but that could easily be ascribed to Rainier using him to get to *The Light*. It didn't have to mean anything else. She prayed it didn't mean anything else.

"I can't claim to know how she thinks, but I believe they were sent to us for two reasons. Either they managed to take control of *The Light*, or they died to warn us that anyone could be behind those helmets, not just Rainier. Now, Rainier doesn't strike me as the kind to engage in petty intimidation. She didn't want to scare us. She wanted to bait us, piss us off. That compound is a trap."

"And yet, here we are," Nox drawled.

Sanda flashed him a grin. "I like springing traps, because then I know where the fuck they are. There is no way in this universe Rainier is unaware we're coming here, so we cannot allow *The Light* to break the security perimeter. Bero stays here, stealthed."

Conway's eyes brightened with determination. "I can shoot that place to pieces from here."

"No go, we need that sphere to reverse engineer a cure."

"There's no guarantee it's even in there anymore," Arden said. "If I could break into their security, then I could have a look around..."

Tomas shook his head. "You'd need access to a console, a physical hookup to get your viruses on there to crack their system. Believe me, I tried."

Arden scowled, but their silence was clear enough: Tomas was right. Sanda couldn't help a pang of disappointment. If they could force their way into the compound's cameras remotely to confirm the placement of the sphere, this would be so much easier.

"Rainier wants me to come in guns blazing, to use *The Light* to force the compound to capitulate, or attempt another board-and-inspect stunt like we pulled at Janus."

"How can you be sure that's what she wants?" Tomas asked warily.

"Because she thinks she knows me." Sanda paused, remembering the knowing gleam in all sets of Rainier's eyes as she'd retracted her helmets. Even then, Rainier had been certain she had Sanda figured out. Knew full well that Sanda would take down her instances, and didn't care. Rainier believed Sanda would always do the noble thing, the right thing as established by Prime protocols.

Rainier still had a lot to learn about humanity.

"When Anford sent a hauler for the bodies, I asked a favor." Sanda tapped on her wristpad to prompt Bero to bring up his camera feed of one of the many storage rooms secreted away in *The Light*.

This storage room was empty, almost. An arrowhead of a ship rested in the center of the room, free of mag clamps due to *The Light*'s ability to harness gravity, the black plating armoring the shuttle dull despite *The Light*'s usually perfect lighting. It was hard to light up guardcore tech. The materials were designed to suck up the light and hold it, not to be seen.

She watched, impassively, as shock and anger passed across the faces of all her crew. All save Tomas, whose brows merely pushed together in thought.

"We have three guardcore sets of armor on this ship," she said.

"No fucking way," Nox said. "Those things are rigged to liquefy their owners. I'm not putting that shit on."

"The ones on the humans who came for us weren't," Tomas said. "It had been disabled."

Sanda nodded. "Bero and I checked the armor over. All the usual stimulant boosts are in there, but the dissolving agents are gone. Rainier wanted to make certain we saw the faces of the people who boarded our ship."

Arden frowned. "Wouldn't the GC on the ship know the ones from the breach pod are dead? They lost comms, not to mention they probably have a vital-signs monitoring system in place."

Bero said, "The GC ship did not survive the encounter long enough to call home."

"Hah," Nox said. "Got the fuckers, did you, B?"

"I continue to be the most effective weapon in the known universe."

Sanda said, "As far as the GC in that compound are concerned, the ships and crew that came after us were wiped out. Three stragglers showing up in a shuttle won't raise any alarm bells. It's our best shot to get close to the sphere. The building is too big to go in blind. Arden has to have cameras, and that means physical contact."

"There's only three suits," Tomas said, jaw flexing. "Why didn't you ask Okonkwo for more?"

Sanda shook her head. "We need Rainier's sets. They'll interface with her communications systems effortlessly. Arden compared them against the empties Anford sent us in the shuttle, and they believe Rainier's sets have unique security identifiers. I had them send their research to Anford for further study, but right now, we need to blend."

"Well," Tomas said, "let's do this, then. The sooner we get moving, the less suspicious they'll be of a late arrival. Once inside, I can plug in whatever Arden gives me and—"

"You're not on the boarding team. Arden will handle it themself."

"But—"

Sanda held up a fist. "You and Nox are too broad across the shoulders to fit in the armor. Knuth is too tall, and Liao wouldn't know which end of the blaster to point. No offense."

"None taken," Liao said. "But I would be most useful in identifying any other nanite technology."

"A GC running around with a tachyon microscope would raise a few eyebrows, Doctor. That leaves me, Arden, and Conway."

"Fuck that," Nox said. "You need a gunhead at your back. You need me."

Sanda spread her hands. "You don't fit the armor, big guy. You and Tomas will have to hang around here and swap deltoid-reducing strategies. Conway specializes in firing ship weapons, but she took the same hand-to-hand training the rest of us fleeties did. Can you do this, Conway? I won't force you."

Conway shrugged one shoulder. "Only reason I'm not on the front lines is because Anford wouldn't have it."

"Right." Sanda arched one brow. "Anything I should know about?"

Knuth and Conway said in chorus, "Nope."

That didn't soothe her nerves much, but it would have to do. "Arden, I'll instruct you on how to hold your rifle and stay in formation, but otherwise I'm going to need you to shut up and go with the flow. There's no time to train you on how to move like a fleetie, let alone a GC."

"Uh." Arden scratched the back of their neck. "Can't help but notice you didn't say you wouldn't make *me* go, boss..."

"There is a very simple explanation for that," she said, but did not elaborate.

"Aw, fuck," Arden muttered. Nox laughed and dropped a hand on their shoulder.

"Come on, I'll give you a rundown. Try not to trip over your own feet."

Arden rolled their eyes. "I'm not completely inept, you know..."

Nox dragged them off the deck, Conway following, and even though Liao and Knuth were still on deck, Sanda felt suddenly very alone with Tomas staring her down, his usually sharp grey eyes dull and unreadable.

"Not sure I would have told you about this place, if I'd known this was how it was going to go down," he said softly.

Sanda forced a smile. "Shouldn't have spent so much time working out, then."

He closed the distance between them and placed a hand on the arm of her chair, carefully not touching her. The thin air between them warmed. "Put me on the shuttle. I'll hide. I won't come out unless shit goes sideways, but you need someone else who can hold their own in a firefight. You need me, or shit, take Nox. Just take someone who can handle themselves hand to hand."

"I'm taking Conway," she said, then leaned so close only he could hear. "I'm taking me."

"Fleet trained, both of you. You need—"

"Do you believe me inadequate for the task at hand, Nazca?"

"No. Never. That's the damn problem, isn't it?" He had to tilt his head up to meet her gaze while she was in the captain's chair, and once their eyes met, her stomach flipped. "It comes down to it, no hero shit. Get out with your skin on and your blood in, understand?"

"That's...a really gross way to say something sweet."

"Words aren't working for me like they used to," he said, leaning closer, smile reaching up to the corners of his eyes. His cheeks dimpled.

She was keenly aware that her crew was working double time to pretend not to be noticing any of this. She sighed and pushed herself up, stretching. Tomas backed away a half step, taking his hand off her chair.

This damn surge in her heart every time he got close had to be put on a leash. Maybe later she could indulge in figuring out what it might be like to be close to him again, but the situation had changed too much.

It was no longer the two of them facing down a long jaunt through an endless void from which they were unlikely to survive—not that that had ever been *real*. Now, Rainier stood poised above humanity with a sword in her hands, and it was Sanda's job to put her down before that blade fell.

Thoughts of Atrux dragged her mind back on track, stamped down the flutter in her chest. Thousands lying comatose in the streets. The bone-melting fear that had seared her down to the DNA in the moments she thought Rainier had blown up Biran and her parents and all of Ada made her sharp.

Tomas was Tomas, and she loved him for that. But he was also Nazca, no matter that he'd burned himself, and she couldn't take the risk of trusting him. Not when so much more lay in the balance.

"Boss," Nox said through the comm line on her wristpad, his voice tight with laughter. "You gotta come see this. Arden put their pauldrons on the opposite shoulders."

"All this shit is the same color," Arden muttered, indignant.

Sanda smiled and shook her head. "Coming."

The fate of the worlds on mismatched shoulders sounded about right.

CHAPTER 16

PRIME STANDARD YEAR 3543

JUST A FEW MORE

On her way back to the hospital, Jules passed through five different decontamination chambers that didn't do a damn thing but make the humans within feel better. The dose she'd plugged into the air mix for the atmo dome had long since run its course. The only reason more people weren't getting infected was because there wasn't anything left to get infected by.

She could change that. If the urgency dropped off, if the researchers started throwing up their hands, she could slip back to her ship, plug another round into the mix, and possibly disappear into the sea of guardcore before she was found out. But, so far, there was no reason for that. The researchers Okonkwo had picked to solve this problem were driven by a fire that stunned Jules.

Doctors Padian and Sarai, she understood. Those two had been instrumental in helping Rainier hijack the gates. And, while they had nothing to do with the agent directly, the guilt of it all prodded them onward. Hung around their shoulders like a black cloud. Dal didn't sleep. Sarai didn't take her pain pills as often as she should, claiming they dulled her thoughts.

That, Jules understood. Guilt was a language she spoke fluently. But the others? If she'd known Prime Inventive boasted researchers like these, she'd have ditched Rainier and tried this trick ages ago.

They bustled around the hospital, living off of stimpacks and desperation, their eyes bloodshot to a one, all corralled into their effort by the tireless oversight of High Protectorate Keeper Tersa Martine.

Returning to that hospital buoyed her spirits. For once, the whispers of the Grotta were wrong. These people really wanted to help. But she'd made a deal. She'd make sure, before she went back for the immune.

Jules's rifle was in place on her back, her armor none the worse for wear, though she'd need that battery pack soon. First, she had to make good on a few promises. Extract the splinter of doubt that had wormed its way under her skin.

She flashed her credentials to the guardcore stationed at the primary entrance, and they welcomed her with bland texts. She ignored them, which was expected, and stalked toward the elevator on her solitary mission. The nice part about pretending to be one of the real GC was how locked down their protocols were. Socializing wasn't just unexpected, it was frowned upon.

Still, she hated this part. Coming here made her feel like she was being watched—and she was, but in the normal way that everyone was watched. No one knew who she was. No one knew she'd placed the canister with the agent.

A small thrill trickled up her spine as she stepped into the ward where Dr. Dal Padian did most of his work. The wards of comatose, packed in tight in beds that filled every room and hallway, didn't bother her anymore. Why should they? Lolla had lain like that for years, and no one but Jules had given a shit. No one but Jules had tried to help, until the situation was large enough to embarrass Prime.

Arden and Nox came to help. They conned a major into giving them a gunship and her credentials. They came for me. Two years, they never stopped looking.

Her steps had halted without her consent, her mind's eye filled with Nox's face, creased with concern and confusion, dropping the rifle from the door the second Jules had stepped through. Nox never dropped a weapon. He'd dropped it for her.

She pushed the memory away. Too late, they'd been too late. She'd already done too much by then. They would have found out, and pushed her away, and it was better all around to have cut that cord right then and there, and never looked back.

She could never look back.

Medis filtered up and down the rows of beds, checking diagnostics, frowning, estimating the needs of their patients. All of Atrux's fallen could not have fit in this singular building, of course. All the hospitals in the city had been converted to the storage of the comatose, and many office buildings besides. But this was the place where the research was done, the experiments made.

Jules moved like a ghost through the crowd, medis not bothering to lift their heads as she passed. The GC were common enough in the building; she was just another worker, and one notorious for declining personal interaction. She made her way to the main data station, pulled up her connection to the local system on her HUD, and started scrolling.

The patient list was extensive, even when drilled down to this hospital. All of the patients had their idents scanned, but not much else. She could take the idents and access the wider GC network, run checks on the addresses in search of those who'd lived in the Grotta, but that sounded too tedious.

Instead, she skimmed the names, paying half attention. Grotta names were often second names, either picked up as aliases or changed after their owners left their past behind and restarted. Anyone could change their name to whatever they wanted, but Grotta names had a certain flavor to them. A distinct lack of syllables, for one thing.

She flagged a hundred or so likely candidates at random, then ran a location check. Most of them were still in the upper floors, but... She frowned. A couple dozen had been moved down to basement level three. Jules had been all over the hospital, but she hadn't been down into the basements. The patients and researchers were all in the upper levels.

When she ran a query on that location, it was flagged as storage. That made sense. The wards were crammed full. As long as the patients were hooked up to the right equipment, it didn't really matter where they were. It wasn't like the ambiance would hurt their recovery—they were out cold.

Still, she'd made a deal. Jules closed out the HUD and approached Dr. Padian's door, knocking crisply twice. He called for her to enter.

Dal Padian had set himself up in a room that might have been a janitor's closet before the whole planet fell apart. He sat behind a desk no bigger than a lap tray, warm overhead lighting not nearly strong enough to erase the sickly blue glow of his viewscreens. A swarm of tablets crowded the wall to one side, Velcroed in place, and a refrigerated rolling cart full of samples took up most of the space by the door. Jules had to shuffle to one side to fit with her armor on.

He glanced up, and flinched. "Ah, my apologies. You phantoms are, well . . ." He trailed off.

"I understand the guardcore's appearance must upset you, after Monte Station," Jules said through the filters.

He fiddled with a stylus. "Yes, thank you for your understanding. It's funny, I never even saw them, and yet . . . Well. What can I do for you?"

"I am looking for some patients. They were moved to basement three."

"B3? I'm afraid I can't help you with that. In fact, you probably have more clearance there than I do. That's Keeper Martine's territory."

"These patients were originally housed in the upper levels."

He frowned, something warring within him. Conflicting loyalties, no doubt. Jules wondered what he'd do if he knew the living suit of armor standing in front of him was her, the woman who'd kidnapped him, wiped his mind, and put him to work making a weapon that'd killed thousands. Probably call for security, then have a drink and a breakdown later, like most normal people.

Jules waited. Placid, immovable. Dal had been the most curious of the bunch she'd brought to Janus, always poking one layer too deep into the schematics, always asking pointed questions. He'd been the only one who'd tried to get into the off-limits levels of the station, before Novak had showed up.

She'd always suspected that Dal knew their mission was bullshit, not at all sanctioned by the Keepers. That he'd decided not to care, because it got him closer to research that was otherwise beyond his grasp. The guilt rode him harder than the others.

But he was a curious man, to a fault, and could not stop trying to peek behind the curtain. Working under the thumb of the Keepers had to be rubbing him raw, no matter that Okonkwo herself had picked him for this job.

"I am told," he said carefully, "that B3 is used as a holding tank for our more aggressive patients."

"Aggressive? The patients I have flagged here were among the comatose."

He waved a hand. "The ascended aren't my purview; I work with the comatose. Some of them wake up, sometimes. When they do, they are enraged. Keeper Martine moves them to B3."

Her heart hammered in her ears, echoed in the helmet. Some woke up? She'd never heard such a thing.

"You've seen this?"

"Not personally."

Right. No one woke up from the coma. If you could just *wake up*, Lolla would have been awake ages ago. It had even taken a while for Jules's cells to knit themselves back together after she'd blown herself up in Rainier's lab.

Jules stared into Dal's eyes, even though the doctor couldn't see her face, and wondered if he suspected, like she did, what might be going on in those Keeper-only levels.

"Is it getting us closer?" she asked.

He pursed his lips, glanced aside at the tablets on his wall. Many were lit up, casting shadows of diagrams across his rounded cheeks.

"Everything we do gets us closer."

So that's what he was telling himself to justify whatever Martine was doing in B3. But he would not have said it, would not believe it, if it wasn't true. What the Keepers were doing in the lower levels wasn't fair, but it must be working. Slowly, but working.

"What if we were to find someone who had been exposed, but was immune? Someone who didn't ascend, or fall comatose?"

His sharp breath and hungry eyes were all the answer Jules needed.

"That would be an incredible breakthrough. A vaccine could, in theory, be reverse engineered from such a person's immune system and, from there, a way to fight the infection once it had already taken hold. Have you found such a person?"

"It's possible," she said, feeling ice close around her core. She was nothing. Not a person, not a monster. Just a void piloting a suit of armor, an instrument of change. The will to wake Lolla made manifest. "I need to form an extraction team to be sure."

"Please," he said. "As soon as you can."

Jules pulled up her HUD, and sent out a call to two other GC units—randomized, naturally.

"Consider it done," she said.

CHAPTER 17

PRIME STANDARD YEAR 3543

UNINVITED GUESTS

Guardcore armor was crafted to be interchangeable. From the exterior, the set of armor molding itself to Sanda's body could have been any GC's. That was the point. Assembly-line people, Prime standardized, all the pieces that made them unique filled in with foam and metal until all that remained was the weapon. The final line of defense for Keepers.

They'd scrubbed them out, eradicated any trace of blood or sweat or oil—not that Prime materials would hold on to those things—but still Sanda imagined she could smell the iron sharpness of the previous owner's blood.

Maybe Rainier did know her better than she thought. Sanda hated every second of this, even if the armor was freakishly comfortable. She couldn't even smell her own breath in the helmet, just the phantom memory of blood.

"Ready for this?" she asked over the triad comm line. Arden had assured her that the three-way communication channel was secure, locked into the three of them. Everything else was compromised.

"Yes, sir," Conway said.

"No fucking way," said Arden.

"Just don't draw attention to yourself," she said.

"We're coming in hot on a shuttle that *The Light* was supposed to have vaporized. Might as well shine a spotlight on ourselves."

"Stow that," Conway said.

"They're not wrong," Sanda said.

"Don't make me be the clearheaded one here, you won't like the results."

Sanda smiled to herself behind the safety of her visor. She didn't have long to relax. An incoming transmission lit up the dash, didn't even wait for her to accept it. Guardcore protocols didn't involve asking permission, apparently. Good to know.

"Shuttle, you are unexpected," the computerized voice of a GC said.

"We are survivors of an encounter with *The Light*." She stopped herself short of requesting permission to dock.

"Hangar 16." The channel closed.

"Not a chatty bunch," Conway said.

"They wouldn't be," Sanda said. "Keep your head in the role. Don't let anyone peel you off. We stick together at all times. GC are on equal command footing. If you think the sphere might be somewhere, do not appear to ask me permission. Insist."

"Understood," they echoed.

A mag clamp snatched the shuttle out of space and began to bring it into the hangar. Sanda forced herself to breathe easily, not to hold her breath.

Okonkwo hadn't been able to tell her much she didn't already suspect about GC compounds. They weren't a lot different from fleet bases, just with better tech and fewer members. The flash of silvery metal painted with the Prime Inventive logo on the wall inside the hangar bay set her mind at ease.

Rainier had sent three humans after her. And while Rainier had sent them to make a point, Sanda couldn't imagine that those three had been the only humans at this station. If she was walking into a nest of Rainier's instances, her team would have been discovered and destroyed upon first contact with the base.

Those were people moving through the hangar, though the GC armor made it hard to remember that. Rainier had her duplicates, but as much as it pained Sanda to think of humans betraying their species on Rainier's behalf, she hadn't operated alone all these years. It wasn't possible.

Because if Rainier had orchestrated all of this on her own, then humanity had already lost.

The shuttle came to a butter-smooth stop against the dock, its internal systems powering down the second the station AI took control.

Sanda wanted to nod to her team, but didn't risk the motion. GC worked protocols tighter than any fleetie. They didn't need prompting. She unclipped her harness, and the others followed. A little delayed for the precise synchronicity the guardcore were known for, but it'd have to do.

She kicked her mag boots on and approached the airlock as it slid open, not breaking stride. The others came out behind her, doing an admirable job of maintaining the two back points of the GC's infamous triangle assault position. If any of the GC on the deck noticed Arden wasn't holding their rifle as tight to center as they should be, they didn't say anything.

A comms line flashed across her HUD from one of the three other GC clustered on the dock. Guess they didn't talk over open comms unless they absolutely had to. That tracked with her experience.

"Your triad was presumed destroyed, GC-T199. A debriefing box is awaiting you on the eighty-eighth floor. The whole triad. Don't be late."

Sanda thought she detected a slight hint of derision in the voice, but that should have been impossible. The voice synthesizer flattened tone and inflection, or at least it was supposed to. As the GC that had addressed her turned to walk away, taking their triad with them, Sanda noticed a prideful sway to their step. Maybe the GC didn't bother being quite so homogenized when they only expected other GC to see or hear them. That could work in her favor.

"Catch that?" she asked over the triad channel.

"Debrief box on eighty-eight," Conway said.

"Not sure I like the sound of that," Arden muttered.

"At least it appears to be self-guided," Sanda said, trying to keep her voice light. The three GC who'd come to greet them had gone, disappearing back into the station, and there weren't any others around.

The dock was empty, aside from them. Sanda was used to the hustle and bustle of a fleet dock or a civvie dock. This felt like a ghost town.

No point in hesitating, that'd only look strange. Walking like she owned the place, Sanda moved in the general direction the GC who had contacted her had gone, hoping for an elevator.

Luckily, the elevator wasn't made of the black plate of their armor and ships, making it stand out. Sanda stepped inside and hesitated, waiting.

"Arden," she prompted over the triad channel.

"Oh! Right."

They fished a thin drive out of the pocket against their hip where a medikit would usually be stashed. Sanda scowled, not having realized that's what they'd decided to ditch so that they could bring the drive. She'd have to talk to them later about priorities.

Arden struggled to sling their rifle across their back, so Conway took it from them without comment. They crouched down, running an armored thumb along a panel set in the wall, its interface patiently awaiting direction on where to go. At least no one seemed to want to use the elevator right now.

She bit off an order to hurry up, knowing that wouldn't help, and mentally ran through possibilities while Arden hacked together a connection and got to work on the building's internal software. It felt like years, but it'd only been a few minutes before they leaned back and nodded, tilting their wristpad slightly so that she could see the building's schematics mapped out in glowing blue wireframe.

"Got it," they said over the triad channel. "Full schematics right now, that was easy, but my program is still chewing its way into the cameras. Could take a bit."

"Where do we start?" she asked.

They shrugged, tapping and zooming. "There's...oh. There's a lot of cooling going on in the upper levels. Gets obvious around level ninety—they're drawing a shit ton of power up there, more than they are for life support and HVAC. Can't think why they'd want to cool something up there, it'd be easier to do it in the levels that are buried under the rock of this moon. Unless they—"

"Big refrigerator bank on ninety, got it," Sanda said, cutting Arden off before they could fall into a speculation rabbit hole. "Remind you of anything?"

"Janus," Conway said.

"You don't think…" Arden trailed off. They didn't need to finish the thought. They were thinking of Jules. Of Lolla.

"We never got eyes on what was down there, but we know Rainier didn't want us poking around in those levels. It's as good a place as any to start."

"More than that," Arden said, voice ramping with excitement. "There was a new security protocol installed on that floor shortly after we left the deadgate. Some kind of safe."

"I like the sound of that," Sanda said.

Tight nods all around.

Arden put the control panel back, so Sanda tapped in floor ninety and hit enter, half expecting alarms to blare. The elevator slid up into the dark without complaint. Conway handed Arden's rifle back to them, and they cradled it awkwardly as they muddled through whatever was on their wristpad. Sanda wished she could give them more time to dig down, but they'd already stayed in the elevator too long. The last thing she needed was for the other GC to notice them lingering. Guardcore didn't loiter; they moved with efficiency and without hesitation.

She was about to ask Arden if they could tell if Rainier was embedded in the station's systems, but the door slid open, and her breath caught.

Level ninety curved upward toward a clear dome that Sanda would bet her life was plex of some kind, a real window where a viewscreen would have been more efficient. No wonder they were drawing so much power here. Keeping the temperature stable with all that plex had to be a nightmare. Beyond the plex, the Rusani system churned on with indifference, planets and stations reduced to minuscule blips of light that paled in comparison to the soft blue glow suffusing the room.

"Found their evac pods," Conway said, tilting her rifle to indicate the walls.

Black plating, much like the GC armor, covered the walls up to the plex in a chitinous hide, but there were cracks in the armor. Narrow pods nestled between the rows upon rows, reaching up like cathedral bones. Sanda swallowed. She'd seen a lot of evac pods, even spent some time trying to repair one, and the cocoons of metal and plastic lining those walls didn't fit.

"Those aren't evac pods," she said.

The elevator chimed at them, urging them to move on or make another selection. She was half tempted to shoot back down to the shuttle, race back to *The Light*, and use those weapons to blow this place to pieces. But if the sphere was here, she couldn't risk losing it. Not after Liao had confirmed it could be used to design a cure.

Sanda stepped into the room. The others followed, the elevator swishing shut behind them. The room was large enough that their steps echoed, then faded out, lost to the massive air volume. Which was lucky, because as her eyes adjusted to all the black and blue, she realized they were completely exposed where they were standing.

She ducked into a shadow between two rows of pods, and gestured for the others to follow. Conway did so immediately, but Arden took a second. She clenched her jaw. They were too deep into what they were doing. They needed focused time.

"Keep working on those cameras," she said. "Stay here, these shadows have you covered. Conway, with me."

"Aye," she said.

Sanda skirted around one of the long ribs of armor and approached the nearest line of pod-like tanks, her rifle up. The soft blue glow was coming from within the pods, a ghost light illuminating the face that she knew would be waiting for her, but sent a jolt through her heart all the same.

The body that Rainier Lavaux used waited behind the viewing plex of the pod. The body's eyes were closed, lips parted slightly, and Sanda thought the teeth of this body still had the titanium look of her bones, not yet shifted to the cream-white humans would expect. Her throat looked more lizard than human, patchy with iridescent hexagons that gave the appearance of scales, her ashen hair thinner than usual, the filaments still growing through the fluid that incubated her.

So helpless, drifting there. Sanda had an intense urge to put a bullet in her brain, but that would give their position away. She tipped her head back, tracking the pods with her gaze. Hundreds in just this room.

There must have been more on Janus, and only the void knew how many stations like this she had spread throughout the universe, hidden away on barren moons and otherwise unremarkable research stations.

Sanda swallowed. Janus never would have been discovered if she hadn't gone there looking for Jules. How long? How long had Rainier festered under the skin of humanity, hiding herself away while she waited for Keeper Lavaux to let the reins slip enough for her to seek her revenge? Had the Keeper even known? Would he have cared?

She clenched the grip of her rifle, seeing his smug face flash before her eyes all over again. Sanda believed, deeply, that he knew and didn't care, because he thought he was in control.

Metal hissed. Three guardcore exited from an elevator on the opposite side of the room. Sanda snapped back into herself and moved into a shadow, dragging Conway with her.

"Company," she said over the triad channel. "We probably have every right to be here, but let's not get into a position where we're being asked questions we can't answer."

"Just three," Conway mused, "we could take 'em out."

"Three *guardcore*. I know Nox told you what it took to take those fuckers out on Monte. We got lucky on *The Light*."

"Yeah, but that was Nox, and we got these." She tipped the rifle up slightly, the motion small enough that it didn't breach their cover in the shadows.

"Shh," Sanda said, because she caught a hint of speech. She cranked her hearing all the way up on her helmet.

The three GC moved in an uneven formation toward the center of the room. The one walking center point reached up and retracted her helmet. Fuzzy, shaved brunette hair. Oaken skin and narrowed, dark eyes. Something about her looked familiar, but Sanda couldn't quite place her. When they were off this station, she'd have Bero do a search, but to reach out to him now risked giving them away.

"I do not care what she says," the woman said. "She will not release the third sphere."

The two other GC retracted their helmets. Both appeared to be men, one with a shock of neon-blue hair—why would a GC care about coloring their hair?—and the other with tight, dark curls crushed by his helmet.

"You worry too much, Senna," Dark-Curls said. "Things are moving quickly now; she can't stall forever. If she wants the second, she'll give us the third."

"You following this?" Conway asked.

Sanda winced and shushed her.

"She's lost so many ancillaries. We have her largest store. She'll have to deal eventually."

"Deal?" Blue-Hair asked. He tilted his head to the side and strolled into the center of the room. Lazily, he passed a hand over a marker invisible to Sanda from her vantage, and a burst of blue light glimmered across the floor. Slowly, a podium rose beneath his outstretched hand. "Even with the ancillaries, we do not have the leverage to make *deals* with Rainier. And right now, she's not the one stopping us from getting the third."

Senna sniffed and crossed her arms, eyeing the podium as it lifted from the ground. "So she says. We have no proof of her claims. She uses Okonkwo as a roadblock, to push us off."

Dark-Curls shook his head. "It is true, Okonkwo alone holds the key. Keeper Lavaux confirmed as much before he got himself killed."

"Lavaux!" She threw her hands into the air. "As much a puppet of Rainier as her ancillaries."

"Tsk," Blue-Hair said. The podium stabilized, the top unfurling into a console an arm's span across. Sanda craned her neck but couldn't see what was on it without giving away her position. "Lavaux worked with the scion before any of us were born. Or have you all forgotten he was there, from the beginning? His loss is a tragedy the united worlds cannot begin to understand. Such history in those veins..."

"How could we forget?" she said. "He reminded us every chance he got, but it didn't help him, did it? Rainier never trusted him, not fully. She plays her own games."

"She plays only one game," Blue-Hair said with sudden hardness. The other two shifted, straightening under his scrutiny. "She is the scion of the Waiting. Her singular purpose is to deliver unto them the beings worthy of her gift. Halston and the others failed in proving humanity to her. We alone remain to prove our worthiness."

"The ascension-agent is useless to us without the third," she snapped.

Blue-Hair shook his head and retracted one of his black gloves. Against his pale skin, the tattoo of two scythe blades framing a single sphere glimmered as he brought it near to the podium console.

The surface of the console bloomed upward, pieces of the metal peeling away like flower petals as a silvery orb emerged from within. Sanda caught her breath. The man slipped his hand under the sphere and lifted it up into the ambient glow of the room. A fervent light came into his eyes.

"She gave us this, after everything humanity had done, and in doing so signaled that a few of us could yet be saved for the Waiting if we were loyal. If we atoned for our predecessors."

"I'm not even sure she knows how to use the third sphere," Dark-Curls muttered under his breath.

Blue-Hair scowled and locked his gaze on the other, who flinched. "How can you say such a thing?"

Dark-Curls squared off his shoulders. "Gen, she doesn't know how the gates work. She tried to keep her blind spot from us, so she set up that station on Janus and used Valentine to try to figure out how to interface with them. If she knew how the gates worked, she could have had *us* build her amplifier network. But she didn't want us to know of her ignorance."

"He's right," Senna said before Gen—Blue-Hair—could retort. "Doesn't that worry you? She's got complete control over the ascension-agent, and that's fan-fucking-tastic for us, but she doesn't know squat about how the gates work. What makes you so sure she knows how to use the third? If the intelligence controlling that sphere was destroyed, then the tech might be beyond us."

Gen's fingers went white around the sphere and he lowered it. "And what would you do about it, if what you claim is true? Would you destroy her? Would you undo the gift given us?"

"No, of course not. But—"

"It's the ship," Gen said, shaking his head. "She's told us time and time again she needs the ship to think clearly, that we must find her body. All of these"—he waved a hand to take in the pods—"are a stopgap measure, a means for her to distribute herself without overload. Once we get *The Light* back, she'll have all her processing power consolidated once again."

"And how are we supposed to get that for her, when she cannot?" Dark-Curls asked. "The guardcore are under a microscope, we're not getting anywhere near that ship. Demas himself chased her lead to its location and died for his trouble. *Demas.*"

"He stole the wrong object," Gen said, dripping derision.

Senna said, "I saw a report that a triad that engaged with *The Light* came in on an emergency shuttle a few minutes ago. They should have reported to a debrief box. I'm sure they'll develop a better plan after that encounter."

Gen frowned. "They did not report to me."

Senna rolled one shoulder. "So?"

But Gen wasn't listening. He placed the sphere back on the console and tapped at his wristpad. His head jerked up. "The triad did not report to debrief. They went to level ninety."

"They're allowed—"

Gen's hand was already reaching for his rifle.

Before Senna could finish her protest, Conway cracked off a shot, and Dark-Curls's brain matter exploded in a spray of pink and silver-grey across the stunned faces of the others.

CHAPTER 18

PRIME STANDARD YEAR 3543

THE DARK FOLLOWS YOU HOME

Sanda moved before the other two GC could react. She followed up Conway's shot with a bullet through Gen's shoulder joint. He jerked, staggering away from the podium, but he wasn't in enough pain to forget to deploy his helmet. Senna ripped her rifle off her back and fired toward the shadows, but Sanda and Conway were already moving, flanking in opposite directions around the sides of the room, closing in tight. They laid down enough fire that the two GC had to duck behind the podium.

"Priority is the sphere," Sanda ordered.

"Um," Arden said.

"Not you. You get me cameras and door locks and get us a clear path the fuck out of here."

"On it," they said with certainty.

Shots peppered the ground in front of Sanda's feet and she stopped hard, twisting to cram herself in alongside one of Rainier's pods. Lights on the elevator across from her flashed green.

"Arden, elevators," she ordered.

"Got it!"

The green light turned the bright red of denial, and Sanda grinned fiercely to herself. Maybe Nox and Tomas were better in a fight, but she'd take Arden on her team any damn day.

"I have control of your station," Sanda said through her speakers, cranking the volume to carry. "Stand down."

"Is that Commander Greeve I hear?" Gen asked from his hiding spot behind the podium. "I've heard so very much about you, but I didn't think we'd get to meet in person so soon. You should have called. I would have baked a cake."

"If you've heard so much about me, then you know I won't hesitate to kill you. Gen, Senna, stand down."

"Ah yes, use our names to try to establish a human connection. Quaint. But we're not entirely human anymore, are we, Senna?"

Sanda rolled her eyes and toed the ground, creeping out of the dark to get a better line on the podium. A blaster shot bore into the black metal plate alongside her, hot enough that she could feel it through her armor. She scrambled back to the cover of the shadows.

Not that the shadows would keep her covered much longer. Sanda glanced over her shoulder at the pod behind her, Rainier's creepy face floating a few centimeters from the plex. She flicked her gaze to open the triad-only channel.

"Use the pods for cover."

"Understood," Conway said.

"Umphf," Arden said, which was close enough.

Over open speakers, she said, "You sound like Rainier."

"Do I?" Gen asked. "Spend long enough with someone, they start to rub off on you. I wonder, do you sound like *The Light of Berossus*, or does he sound like you?"

She clenched her jaw. He was way too familiar with her, the creep. A shadow shifted through the blue glow, one of them—probably Senna—crawling around to the corner with rifle in hand, moving dangerously close to a sight line on Arden.

Sanda fired on one of the pods across the room from her. Plex exploded, and a silvery river rushed out, painting the black wall with a mica-like sheen. The body that could have been Rainier slumped, half-formed, against the busted-open pod, spindly arms with partial fingers dangling toward the ground. Gen screeched with outrage.

"I can do this all day," Sanda said, cracking off one shot after another, the pods across the room spraying metallic fluid and bits of

Rainier with every single shot. Conway joined in, picking off the pods nearer to Sanda's position.

She was enjoying herself so much it took a moment to hear what Gen was shouting.

"Stop! Stop! We surrender!"

She didn't believe that for a second, but she stopped firing.

"Kick your weapons out," she demanded. The weapons spun off in opposite directions across the floor, coming to rest against the wall. "Retract your helmets and crawl out, toward the sound of my voice. Sneeze wrong, and you'll join your boss in decorating the walls."

Their armor clanged against the ground as they crawled out on their hands and knees, helmets retracted, rage tightening both of their faces. Sanda had never seen anger so intense. Not directed at her, anyway, and for half a second the murderous gleam in their eyes stunned her.

She stepped out from the cover of the shadow, making sure Gen saw the barrel of her rifle swing to cover him.

"I'm only going to ask you this once, because I think we both know where this is going. You turn witness against Rainier, tell us everything you know, and I'll let you off this hunk of rock with all your skin on. Agreed?"

"Get fucked," Senna said.

Sanda sighed. "Really? You've got a chance to walk out alive here."

Gen chuckled, low and slow, raising goose bumps across her skin. "You're in our compound. There are three of you, and thousands of us. Forgive me, but even if you slaughter Senna and myself, I do not believe you're the one leaving this station alive."

"The thing about that," Sanda said, "is that I have complete control of your internal security."

Senna snorted. "Hardly. Did Okonkwo give you intrusion software for GC systems? Or maybe you ponied up and bought a suite from the Nazca? None of it's enough to keep us out. Whatever control you maintain is merely temporary."

"I don't know about that," she said. "You ever heard of The Gardener?"

Senna's eyes widened, briefly. Expressive people, when they weren't tucked away behind their helmets. Demas would have been appalled by their emotive behavior.

"A myth," Gen said. "But I do have good news for you, Commander. I'm quite certain that Rainier wants you alive, at least until she can discern the location of her stolen ship. The others..."

He trailed off, and while he thought he was being subtle, Sanda's senses were on edge, and she saw his fingers curl slightly—the bare fingers he'd revealed to expose his tattoo.

"Talk's over," she said.

Her first shot took him through the hand, dissolved his wrist against the bruise-black floor. Gen screamed, but not for long. Her next shot took him through the neck as he reared back, grabbing at his shattered hand, throat and brain stem splattering the podium.

Conway fired in tandem, taking Senna in the back of the head. It was over in a matter of seconds. Sanda crossed the room and checked both bodies for weapons—clear—then vital signs—dead. A glance around the room showed her all the lights on the elevators were red.

"Arden, you got us a path?"

They stepped out of the shadows, the rifle dangling from a strap off the crook of their elbow, jabbing away at their wristpad. "Kinda? I can't let the elevators go or the GC will get torches and burn their way through the doors, heard them talking about it, so I have to keep them locked in there like jail cells. Won't be long before they work their way to us through maintenance access, though."

"I don't hear a way out in all that," Sanda said.

"I called us a ride."

She could practically feel their grin. "*The Light*? Are you sure that's safe?"

"I've got this station under my thumb. If Rainier had any piece of her in here ready to jump out, it can't even see the door now."

Sanda tracked her gaze over the rows and rows of half-formed Rainiers. "How long?"

"Ten minutes," Bero said into her helmet.

"Right." She grabbed the sphere, wiped some of the gore splatter off on the side of her thigh, then shoved it in a pouch in her armor. The pouch where her medikit should have been. Maybe she needed the priorities talk, too. She sighted her rifle up at one of Rainier's pods and fired. "We got time. Up for a little target practice?"

Eight minutes later, they stood in the center of a field of broken plex and pieces of would-be Rainiers, listening to the hiss of torches against the walls. The guardcore trying to cut their way in through maintenance had decided to avoid any spots where a Rainier pod might be, which made for slow going, but they were making steady enough progress.

"Center, guns out," Sanda ordered as one side of the black walls began to glow with the faint orange tinge of melting metal.

Conway grabbed Arden and dragged them over, placing them back-to-back with Sanda. In the few minutes they'd spent destroying Rainier's pods, Arden's aim had tightened somewhat, but that didn't give her much hope, considering what might be on the other side of that glowing metal. They'd been lucky with the first three. The others wouldn't pause to talk.

"B, we need that lift," she said over the comm line.

"Knock, knock," Bero said.

The gleaming body of *The Light* swung into view across the plex ceiling, then drifted below the sight line to press against the thick black walls of the chamber.

Sanda licked her lips, caressing the trigger as the glowing metal across from her beaded up, melting down along a seam. To her left, metal hissed against metal as *The Light* set up its transfer tube and started to bore through the wall. *The Light* would be faster than the GC, but not fast enough.

The panel in the wall burst inward, forced through by a black-booted foot. Sanda squeezed off a shot, winging the armored figure on the other side. It stumbled, but the bullet had only grazed its upper arm. The passageway beyond was dark and cramped, but she counted five on the other side. Fuck.

"Suppress that entrance," she ordered.

Conway's fire joined hers as they laid down a hailstorm of bullets. But the GC kept pushing through, crawling over their dead and dying to get at them. Blaster fire grazed Sanda's shoulder and she twisted under the impact, almost taking a knee, but having her back pressed to Arden kept her up. She wished Gen had done his creepy podium thing and added some more furniture to the room; they didn't have much cover.

"Stand down!" she ordered, because it was worth a try, but they kept on coming.

She stepped backward, urging her team to move toward the place where *The Light* was drilling through, but didn't dare tear her gaze from the GC coming their way. Her leg armor shuddered with impact. She could still walk, so she didn't bother to look.

Warm light spilled over them from behind, the steady repeat of three rifles tearing through the GC issuing from the pathway carved to *The Light*.

"Go, go, go!" Sanda shouted.

She turned and grabbed Arden, shoving them toward the tunnel with both hands. Conway was a step ahead, the way back into *The Light* two meters out.

Tomas, Nox, and Knuth stood in that passage wearing Prime armor, a human wall, pouring shot after shot into the GC swarming out from the walls of the station.

Conway reached the passage. Nox turned in a smooth, practiced motion and shoved her onward, extending a hand to grab Arden and yank them after.

Sanda jumped. She hit the ground and rolled. The blue light of the station vanished as Bero sealed the entrance. Her stomach lurched as he peeled away, burning hard for somewhere else—anywhere else.

She blinked behind the shelter of her helmet, doing a mental inventory. Her leg armor moved oddly, but otherwise nothing felt damaged. She slapped the button to retract her helmet, and blinked.

Tomas hovered above her, his face creased with worry, residual blue glow giving his eyes an otherworldly sheen. She shook her head, and the phantom of the station washed away.

"Injuries?" she demanded.

"All clear, boss," Nox said from down the hall.

She grinned at Tomas, and he grinned back. "How about that?" she said. "A clean victory for once."

The ship's lights went out.

CHAPTER 19

PRIME STANDARD YEAR 3543

WHAT'S THREE MORE BODIES?

The immune hid from Jules, but it didn't matter. Everyone Jules had ever hunted hid from her; this was no different because it was in the Grotta. There was no real leader to a GC team, but Jules felt herself shift naturally into that position, running point as she gestured them through the burned-out husks lining the streets. Saarah had been right about a lot of things, but the truest thing she'd ever said was that Jules didn't move like the other GC.

She didn't even bother trying. These streets were hers, her scum-slicked, dirt-crusted birthright, and if the others wondered how she blended so well, they didn't say anything. Because she did her fucking job, and right now she was doing it better than any other GC on this crusty planet. In the end, that's all it really meant to be guardcore. Protect the Keepers. Protect *well*.

Her efficiency kept people from asking too many questions about why a single GC inhabited a ship all alone. Doing her job well did more than help discover a cure—it helped keep Lolla, stashed away on that ship, safe from prying eyes.

Right now, that job included hunting any stragglers in Atrux city.

Saarah and her people, they weren't hiding too hard. Jules put up a map overlay on her HUD, pushed it through to the others. She pinpointed where she'd found them, where she suspected they'd gone to ground, and narrowed that scope with every step they took, every broken hatch or door or ragged curtain they checked under.

The GC didn't ask why she hadn't grabbed the three straight off. They weren't supposed to hunt solo, after all. It made more sense that she'd come back for help than it did that she found them in the first place, and the guardcore weren't the questioning type. They weren't even the talking type.

Jules wondered what it would do, to live under the cloak of that armor for all the years of your life. What would it do to your mind to limit speech, to never have a name beyond a randomly rotating tag. No friends. No socializing. She'd been in their ships, their dormitories. Seen the sealed cubbies the others retreated to when their armor was off. At least Jules went to her ship, got shit-faced drunk, and talked at Lolla's coffin until she passed out.

These people were more synthetic than she was.

But that's what Prime was, what it did to people. It filed off all the jagged edges that made you an individual, and shoved you in its carefully molded cubbies. Same clothes, same ships, same armor, same weapons. The guardcore weren't the only ones guilty of adhering to such monoculturalism; they were just the most obvious example. No wonder Rainier had liked being them so damn much.

Jules was all jagged edges.

She stalked down a slim alley, following instinct stamped in her bones, and held up a fist, calling a halt. A thermal overlay appeared at a flick of her eyes, shading the world around her in gold and blue. Bright flames of life lurked in the building to her left, two with one knee on the ground, hands up, probably sighting weapons over a barricade. There wasn't a third, but then Jules had learned long ago that the ascended didn't show up on thermal unless they wanted to, and she knew nothing about the physiology of the immune.

She held up three fingers, the third folded down at the last knuckle to indicate it was a possibility, not a certainty. She didn't wait for confirmation from the others before she moved. They'd come, or they wouldn't. It didn't matter. She didn't need them, anyway.

The door exploded in splinters and dust as she kicked it in, squeezing off a few tranq rounds before she dropped to a crouch and scuttled sideways, taking cover in a hallway.

Gunfire cracked the air the second after she'd found cover. Their instincts were good, but they were only human, and Jules knew where they were. She checked the thermal display on her HUD, saw one of them growing cold in a slow radial across their chest. A tranq dart had hit, then. It'd only be a few seconds until they were unconscious. Those darts had been designed to work on the ascended, so they hit normal people like a meteor.

The other two GC piled into the room, working their own protocols, dropping the other healthy member of the group with their tranq darts, according to Jules's HUD. She waited, tense, watching those two circle the barricade—a table flipped up, like that would stop a normal bullet, let alone a GC rifle.

The air sizzled, cracked. She smiled grimly to herself as the first GC to reach the unconscious pair dropped, seizing, on the ground. The other brought their real rifle up, smoothly switching over from the tranqs, and sighted in completely the wrong direction—the direction the shot had come from.

Jules slipped from cover and aimed up, into the half-dissolved roof of the building, into the crumbling rafters, and started squeezing off tranq rounds in a systematic wave. Starting a little ahead of the direction the stunner shot had come from, then moving toward her previous position in the hallway.

A grunt, a thud. The girl, Birdie, slipped in the rafters and crashed down through the half-rotted roof, slamming into the ground at Jules's feet, her thin body limp from the tranq, but not weak. She was ascended. As soon as that kid woke up, she could give them hell. Good thing she wouldn't be waking up anytime soon.

The GC who'd been about to get fried spun around, looked at the body, then looked at Jules and nodded in appreciation. Jules nodded back. That was probably the biggest outpouring of emotion guardcore were capable of.

"I'll grab the adults," Jules said over comms, holstering her weapons.

The GC nodded, clearly not giving a shit either way, and slung the fallen GC over one shoulder before picking up the kid and tossing her over the other. The unit exited the building, not bothering to look around, not caring what trappings were hiding the target it was meant to recover.

Jules stooped over the two fallen bodies of the immune. She couldn't keep doing this. Keep pretending all she cared about was her job, whatever that was in the moment. Couldn't keep pretending to give a shit about anyone except Lolla. She understood the single-mindedness of the guardcore, even wished she could harness it, drown herself in it, but you missed things that way. That way, you didn't get people like Saarah making contact, thinking you might be their chance, their shot at safety.

Jules got an arm under Saarah and scooped her limp body up. The woman's rucksack shifted across her back, dumping personal belongings to the floor. Jules frowned, seeing a piece of black metal roll across the dusty floorboards. Black as her armor. She picked it up and held it to the light.

It was rounded, and deep, coffee residue smearing the edge that came off dusty and brown as Jules ran her finger over the interior of the metal. She didn't recognize the shape; it wasn't any piece of armor she'd ever seen, but it reminded her of the scrap she'd found in the burned-out warehouse.

They must have scavenged it at some point, used it as a coffee mug. Jules smirked to herself, shaking her head. The Grotta always provided, even shit you didn't want. Mostly shit you didn't want, come to think of it. She wondered if they knew they'd been drinking out of a slagged piece of one of the most valuable metals in the universe. Probably not. If they had known, they would have sold it.

Jules shoved the mug in the carapace of her backpack and grabbed up Reece and Saarah, leaving the rest of their stuff on the floor. They wouldn't need it.

CHAPTER 20

PRIME STANDARD YEAR 3543

LIGHTS OUT

Sanda's state of being changed before Tomas's eyes. The slight smirk disappeared, crushed by a thin, hard line of her lips. The gleam of triumph in her eyes washed away, replaced by steady determination.

For a brief flash, Tomas thought he could feel the change inside of her. The immense pressure of her will to succeed reaching out from her core, slamming against the impossible pressures from Anford, Prime, Okonkwo, and all those who would suffer if she failed in her mission. Those pressures collided against the woman that was Sanda, compressed her, made her as hard and immovable as the deep ice on far-off super planets that lived their lives crushed by gravity, having never seen the light of their star.

He ached, but then she moved, and his sense of self snapped back into place.

"Bero," she said, reaching for Tomas. He took her hand and yanked her to her feet, then backed away to give her room. "Answer me, B."

Nothing. Her eyes narrowed.

"Intrusion protocols. Arden, get Bero back online. Knuth, haul ass to the engine bay and see if you can get us manual controls, something. We need to be able to maneuver before the GC get their ships launched. Conway, get me weapons."

"Without Bero, we can't fire anything from this ship," she said.

"Nox, go with her. Raid the armory. Grab anything big enough to punch a hole in a ship. Tomas, help them haul it to the command deck. At least Bero put some windows in there."

"I'll stay with Arden," Tomas said.

"They don't need your help."

She turned her glare on him, and the back of his neck prickled. Something was pressing in against this ship, struggling to box in Bero, and Tomas had a pretty good idea of what that was. "If this ship gets tossed and Arden knocks their head, we're fucked. I got them."

She rolled her eyes. "Fine. Babysit, if it suits you. Everyone, armor and lifepacks, we can't trust the air with B offline."

The crew moved with surprising efficiency for their disparate training, and soon Tomas was alone with Arden in the hall. Arden plunked into a seated position, back against the wall, and glanced up from their wristpad to meet Tomas's eyes briefly.

"Look, I don't know what you're capable of as a spy or whatever, but nothing the Nazca taught you about software intrusion can help me right now. Stay out of my way. Don't interrupt. I don't have time to explain or create visuals for you to follow with."

"Do your thing. I'm just your bodyguard."

Arden nodded. They grabbed a set of net goggles from a side pouch and yanked them over their eyes, body going loose against the wall as they delved into whatever was going on with *The Light*.

Tomas let out a slow, relieved breath. If Arden had insisted on doing this via their wristpad, keeping them from getting suspicious would have been a lot harder.

He dropped to a seat across from Arden, letting the rifle he'd used against the GC rest across the tops of his thighs. It wasn't the best position for defense, but Tomas didn't plan on shooting anything. The threat on this ship was no longer physical.

Tomas closed his eyes, tried very hard not to think about how terrifying this was, and placed both his palms against the floor. His skin tingled. Nothing else happened.

He stretched his jaw, cracking the joint, and tried again. Lights. Lights shouldn't be a problem. He'd turned them off in his room without even thinking about it, and slammed Bero out of that room's controls in the process. He could start with the lights.

Nothing. He wanted to ball his fists and shout at the cells in his body, demand his nervous system—did he even have a real one?—do whatever was required. Maybe he was too late. Maybe Rainier had already locked the ship down, had it under control, and keeping him out was as easy as swatting a kitten.

Rage bloomed in his chest, indignity burning with frustration akin to the raw anger he'd felt when he realized Sitta Caid had lied to him. He pressed his fingertips into the floor, and the metal gave way, nanites parting at his touch, responding to his need to tear, to rend. What good was he if he couldn't protect this ship? What good was all the bullshit making up his blood if he couldn't spill it to save the ones he cared about—the one he loved?

Tension snapped inside him. With his eyes closed, he switched from staring at splotchy darkness to an endless field of twitching filaments, an interconnected map of neurons larger than any starscape, stretching off into a distance so vast it lost all meaning.

Near to him, the network had twisted. Ribonucleic corkscrews bridged the gap from the body that was Tomas to the network that was *The Light*. He wondered if this place only looked the way it did because it was the only way he could begin to understand it. A violent tide ripped through the system.

Rainier. The name lacked all meaning in this place, but naming the violent tide solidified it in his mind. He'd been trained on basic programming, like every other child of Prime—not that he'd ever *been* a child—and knew that to define a variable was to be able to manipulate it.

He focused on her rage and elation entwined together, the pure joy at getting back what was hers, and her anger that it had ever been taken in the first place. There was not enough of her, not here, not yet, and while she was throwing open doors for more of herself to pour through, she was also busy trying to cage off Bero.

On the edge of his consciousness, Tomas sensed Arden struggling to close the backdoors Rainier opened, keeping her limited. It wouldn't be enough to stop her. But it would help.

Bero, Tomas thought, because voice didn't have much meaning in this place.

Too much, Bero thought back.

Bero's consciousness latched on to his like a burr, scrambling to ground itself in a space that he was rapidly being shut out of, confined and compressed. Tendrils of fear snaked through Tomas, spillover. Bero had been cut off like this once before, and he knew the hell waiting for him if Rainier succeeded in trapping him within the ship, unable to interface with the world.

A mind as quick as Bero's, without external input, ticked away too quickly. A single dark thought spiraled into cruel ruminations in nanoseconds, insanity a breath away. Rainier did not care. She knew what she was doing to the other mind. She delighted in it. This ship was the body she'd been made to interface with. It was hers, and though she was reduced, manipulating it came as easily to her as breathing came to humanity.

But Tomas had as much right to this ship as she did. She'd said it herself. He was a subset of her.

Tomas grabbed Bero, wrapped him inside himself and yanked him out of the cage that was falling into place all around. He had to think in physical terms—grabbing and pulling and pushing—because even if he was synthetic, the double-helix patterns connecting him to the ship reminded him that he had been raised to be human. All his instincts, all his knowledge, were couched in the reality of flesh, never mind what his body was made of at the atomic level.

He added his strength to Bero's, bolstered him, showed him the secret paths through the ship's hardware and all the fine ways it was interconnected that Bero had not yet seen, because he hadn't known where to look. Bero's mind soared with understanding while Rainier surged with rage.

She pushed back, scrambling, closing pathways, breaking, severing. Tomas hurt as the ship hurt, but every trick she pulled, he learned something new about how it all fit together. Her frustration mounted as she struggled to push through, to overwhelm Bero and Tomas on her quest for the heart of the ship, the engine core. From there, she would consume the whole ship.

But there was not enough of her. Arden kept closing doors, cutting her off, and soon enough she was in retreat. Crushed, burned out, and as Bero flooded back into the core of the ship and shouted in triumph, Tomas snapped back into himself, retreating to make room for Bero's control, for Tomas did not want *The Light*.

His eyes snapped open and he lurched forward, catching himself only because his fingers had dug their way into the floor. Bright blood splattered the ground between his feet. He blinked at the color, seeing for a flash the ribonucleic coils of his own being in the red, the endless cloud of the ship behind the silver.

He shook the digital space from his mind and leaned back, pressing his back hard against the wall, reminding himself that there were barriers. The ship was the ship, firm against his spine. He was not falling into it, as freeing and elating as the sensation had been. Tomas was Tomas. He would not be subsumed.

"Shit," Arden said.

Tomas blinked. He'd dropped his head back and lost track of time for a second there. Arden's face was puckered with the print of their net goggles, which lay on the ground beside them. They scramble-crawled over to him, grabbed his shoulder, and shook it.

"Tomas? You all right, man? The ship's secure—Bero! I need some help here."

Tomas shrugged off Arden's hand and made himself focus. "I'm fine, just tired. You kicked Rainier out?"

A frown tugged down Arden's lips. "Yeah. I mean, I kicked her out but..." They trailed off. "It was mostly Bero." Tomas could practically feel the *I think* lingering behind their lips, but they said no more.

Whatever Arden had noticed in net space, they weren't willing to talk about it yet. Tomas wasn't sure if that was a good or bad thing. He knew how determined Arden could become when they grew curious about something. It was, ultimately, why Prime Inventive and the Nazca had never hired them on. Tomas wasn't sure they'd have taken either job, but the official word on the matter was that Arden Wyke's curiosity and skill made them a security risk. If they saw a loose string, they'd pull until the whole sweater unraveled.

"Good job," Tomas said, and gave them a friendly smile.

Arden rocked back onto their heels. "It was weird..." they muttered.

Sanda came pounding down the hall with Nox and Liao on her heels. "What's the emergency, Arden? Bero's back and we're evading—fuck."

She took a knee beside Tomas and grabbed his face in both hands, turning him to get a better look. A thumb brushed his cheek, and he was as surprised as anyone to see it come away bloody.

"What happened?" she demanded.

"I think he had some kind of seizure," Arden offered, then shrugged when Sanda cut them a look. "I don't know. I was in net space."

"Liao?" Sanda asked.

The doctor sighed, but crouched down on his other side. "Again, I am not a medical doctor, but I do not believe bleeding from the eyes is a common symptom of a seizure. Can you see, Mr. Cepko?"

"I see fine," Tomas said, putting the smile back on as he scrubbed away the rest of the blood with his palms. "Really, I feel..." *Like if I reached out and touched the ship, I'd be whole. Complete. An infinite being of infinite potential.* He cleared his throat. "Great."

"Great doesn't track with bleeding from the eyeballs," Sanda said dryly. She sat back on her heels and watched him warily, her brows pushing together. He wanted to reach out and smooth the worry away, but stopped himself.

"I'm fine," he insisted, and staggered to his feet. "I just need to wash my face—maybe an allergy or something. Bero and Arden saved the day. Everyone clean up, I'll cook us a celebratory dinner."

Wary gazes tracked him as he moved off down the hallway, and he made damn sure to keep from rushing ahead.

They do not believe you, Bero said inside his skull, as if that mode of communication was the most natural thing in the worlds.

I wouldn't believe me, either, he thought back.

Strange. Having a voice that wasn't his rattling around in his head should probably be terrifying, but it didn't bother him at all. *You all right?*

Better. I... learned some things.

Happy to help.

I don't believe that, either.

Tomas gritted his teeth and opened the door to his room subconsciously, because Bero no longer had control of that section of the ship. The lights were still off, and though he could see without them, the dark was a balm to his frayed nerves.

He pretended not to notice when, far down the hall and behind at least one locked door, he sensed Dr. Liao take a sample of his blood from the floor.

CHAPTER 21

PRIME STANDARD YEAR 3543

BLOOD ON THE FLOOR

Sanda didn't know what call she was dreading more—Anford calling for a report, or Liao calling to tell her she'd found something deadly in Tomas's blood. She paced tight circles in her room, the guardcore armor molted in black chunks all over the floor, and tried to focus on the one thing she could deal with at the moment.

"Tell me again what happened with Rainier's intrusion," she asked Bero.

The ship sighed. "There is not much to tell. A fragment of her software was waiting on the guardcore station. When I entered an acceptable transmission range, it made the jump, circumventing my security protocols."

"How?"

"You'd have to ask her."

She clenched her fists. Maybe this wasn't the conversation she wanted to be having, either. "Don't get cheeky with me, you sack of electrical impulses. I need to know exactly what I'm up against here."

"I have told you. You have already done everything you can to secure this ship. You uploaded me. You put Arden Wyke on security. We have learned some useful things from her intrusion attempt that will bolster my defenses in the future."

"How?" she demanded. "I don't see how almost losing this ship—almost losing *you*—made things easier, or safer."

"Not every problem can be solved by shooting it, Sanda."

She stopped her incessant pacing and paused, a smile curling up her lips despite herself. "Are you sure? I've some very nice weapons in the armory."

Before he could respond, a call flashed on her wristpad from Liao. Sanda's stomach clenched, but she answered it. "Yes?"

"Come to my lab, please, as soon as you can, Commander."

Sanda frowned. "Can't give me a hint?"

"It's really best if you come here."

She sighed and closed the call, then glanced around the chaos of her room—armor all over the floor, her rifle pitched across the bed—and shrugged. At least Graham wasn't here to give her shit about the mess.

She was stalling. As an afterthought, she swung the rifle across her back and hurried down the hallway to Liao's lab. The door was opened, the doctor scowling into the viewscreen of one of her many microscopes. Tablets littered the desktop near to hand, and the doctor's hair had come loose from her bun, hanging around her cheeks in shaggy pieces. Sanda cleared her throat.

"Come in," Liao said, and waved the door shut after Sanda was through.

"Well?" she asked. "What is it? Eye cancer?"

Liao sniffed. "I'd scarcely be able to tell you if it was. I am no medi."

"If you haven't found anything, then why—?"

"I didn't say that." Liao tugged at the hem of her coat. Sanda closed her mouth, letting the doctor come around to what she wanted to say in her own time, even if the waiting made Sanda want to scream.

"I thought I saw...something, in his blood on the ground. I was right."

"You're going to have to be more specific."

"I saw the same sheen in the nanite fluid conduit on Janus."

Sanda went cold, remembering the silvery cast to the violet fluid that had carried Rainier's nanite amplifiers. The gleam to Lavaux's flesh as his skin and muscle had knitted itself back together right before her eyes.

"You're saying Tomas is infected with nanites." Her voice sounded flat, emotionless. It was the best she could do.

"Not exactly. It's . . . He's . . ." She scowled and waved at the microscope. "His cells *are* nanites. Synthetic constructs."

Sanda put a hand on a table to brace herself. She licked her lips, because her mouth had gone dry, and found them numb and heavy.

"What does that mean, exactly?"

"He's . . ." Liao cleared her throat and fiddled with a stylus, looking at the microscope instead of at Sanda. "He may very well be exactly like Rainier."

"Or Jules," Sanda said, as if that were much better, as if that made it hurt any less. "Or Keeper Lavaux, or all those poor people on Atrux that are infected. He doesn't have to be like Rainier. This can be . . . This is the ascension-agent. She must have dosed him."

He'd been so squirrelly about his meeting with Rainier. Did he know? Or suspect?

Liao said, softly, "The samples from Atrux invariably have biological cells mixed in with the synthetic. I see no evidence of the biological in Tomas's blood."

"Could he . . ." She cleared her throat. She had to focus. Had to set emotion aside, because the man on her ship could very well be a security threat, no matter the face he wore. "Could he be another ancillary of Rainier? Just because she likes the same face doesn't mean she always keeps it."

Liao twisted the stylus between her fingers. "I don't know."

Bero said, "He's not."

"Start talking, B." Sanda grated out the words.

"He would rather tell you himself, though I am willing to corroborate what he has to say, if you feel it's necessary."

She saw red for a moment, took a breath to steady herself. "Bring him—"

The door dilated, and Tomas stood already waiting on the other side, his hands in his pockets, his chin downcast. He lifted his gaze to meet hers, and flinched.

"Hey," he said.

"Doctor—"

Liao waved her off, grabbed an armful of tablets, and rushed for the door. "Call if you need me."

Liao squeezed past Tomas and he stepped into the lab, the door closing behind him. He stopped a step inside, not daring to move any closer, his face pale and his jaw tight.

"I'm not Rainier," he said, after a pause so long she thought she'd drown in it.

"Prove it." Her hand had drifted toward her rifle without conscious thought. She stopped herself. Let her palm rest against the cold metal of the grip.

"I don't know that I can." He smiled ruefully and shook his head. "I'm not her, any more than Bero is her."

Bero said, "Without Tomas's help, I would have lost the ship to Rainier's intrusion."

"Arden—"

"Was not enough," Bero said.

Her breath came hard and she leaned forward, putting more weight onto her palm against the table, but did not take her hand from the weapon. "Are you infected with the agent? Are you a contagion risk?"

"No. Not that. I was made before…" He trailed off.

"Excuse me, what the fuck do you mean, *made*?"

"The Nazca stole Rainier's reconstruction chamber technology. They used it to make me." His voice was flat, locked down. Every line in his body had gone stiff with defensiveness, walled off and wounded. It hurt him, whatever this was. Or he wanted her to believe it did.

In her mind's eye, she imagined Tomas's face, dark hair fanned out around him, in the gleaming fluid of the pods she'd seen lined up on the guardcore station. His eyes closed, his lips half-formed, silvery hexagons tracking the progress of his flesh as it grew around a synthetic armature of muscle and bone.

Her breath went shallow, her head felt light.

Bero said, "It doesn't change who he is."

She flicked her gaze to the ceiling, the words dashing away the visual horror that'd been building in her mind. "You can't know that."

"Sanda," Tomas said softly, "I've always been this. I just...didn't know."

She sat down on Liao's stool by the microscope so hard that she bounced. Her hands rested limply on top of the metal lab table, and she could look nowhere but at the curl of her own fingers.

"You told me about your grandmother. Your mom."

His voice scratched. "They don't exist. They did to me, though. I thought they were real. I...believed in them."

"The Nazca? Are they all like you?"

"No." Bitterness seeped into his voice. "Just me. It made things violent, when I left."

The door dilated and Arden strolled in, their face buried in a tablet readout. "Hey, Liao, I found something weird in—" They would have collided with Tomas, had he not stepped nimbly aside.

They looked up, read whatever there was to be found in Sanda's and Tomas's faces, and flushed bright red.

"Sorry, sorry, didn't think, uh...I'll go find Liao."

"Wait," Sanda said. Arden froze in place, half turned toward the door. "The intrusion earlier. What happened?"

That shook off all their awkwardness. Arden turned back to her and ran a hand through their hair. "I don't really know, not yet. Rainier was everywhere, I couldn't shut her out fast enough, and then somehow Bero had this surge—like he suddenly knew what to do."

Sanda met Tomas's gaze, and held it, as she asked, "Like he got help from someone else?"

"Yeah, you could say that. But I don't see how it's possible. Bero and I had this ship locked down. Only someone like Rainier could get through—someone for whom the tech of the ship was as familiar as a fish in water."

"It wasn't that easy," Tomas said quietly.

"You didn't see it," Arden said with barely disguised awe. "I couldn't even find Bero anymore, I was running in place just to keep Rainier from cramming all her data through, but then it was like he had this...epiphany. You were amazing, Bero. Wish you could tell me how you did it."

"I cannot," Bero said. "It was Tomas's doing."

Tomas shifted his weight, but Sanda didn't drop eye contact. "Tell them," she said.

"I am a subset of Rainier Lavaux," Tomas said, and every line in his body said he was telling the truth.

CHAPTER 22

PRIME STANDARD YEAR 3543

MORE THAN A WARDROBE

At one in the morning, Biran knocked on Vladsen's door. Vladsen had sent him a request to speak before the ship disembarked with the morning. Five minutes after accepting the invitation, an autocab had rolled up to the curb in front of Biran's house, sleek and silver, and he tried swiping his wristpad over the transaction pad twice before he realized the car was private.

The scent of leather—real leather—clung to his nostrils as he waited, trying not to fidget, on a stone patio inlaid with a mosaic of the local star system. Solar-powered globes nestled in the gardens surrounding the house, giving off a soft golden-and-cyan glow that hinted at the exquisite detail of Vladsen's grounds. Somewhere, a water fixture trickled, but Biran couldn't see it through the dark.

Wealth made him uneasy. As director, Biran's stipend should have been enough to cover an upgrade to a similar home, but the Nazca continued to take their pound of flesh. Admiring the plex in the double doors of Vladsen's home, faceted to shimmer even in the faint light of the globes, Biran couldn't muster up a stab of envy.

He'd always had enough. All the rest simply hadn't mattered to him, had been white noise on his periphery. Sure, these things would be nice—he couldn't deny the fact—but his job was his life. When was he going to go for a stroll in a garden like this? Would having a fountain in his front yard matter, if the war with Icarion went hot again or Rainier found a way to turn all the gates against them?

He sighed. Maybe he was a little jealous. The ornamentation only served to remind him that he was woefully out of place in his position. Too young for his post, too green for the politics involved. He hadn't even realized his appearance was going to be a problem. Singh and Okonkwo had had to spell it out for him.

He'd known he could do the work, when he'd taken the job. He just hadn't realized how deep the work ran.

The door opened, revealing a stocky man in a crisp navy suit, a HUD monocle pressed against one eye. It gleamed, feeding the attendant Biran's ident, and he bowed, gesturing into the plex-and-steel ornamented foyer.

"Keeper Vladsen awaits you in his office, Director. Do you require any refreshments?"

Biran's arm brushed against the door as he entered. The carved plex was too cold to be plastic—it was glass, real glass. Biran looked up, and prismatic shards from a chandelier danced light across his cheeks. Crystal. He tried not to stare. Both materials were easily broken, and a risk to use in construction on a space station, even one so large and stable as Ada's Keep.

"No, thank you," he said, keeping his voice neutral. He would not be overwhelmed by this. Vladsen had been born into wealth long before he ascended to Keeperdom, let alone the Protectorate of Ada. This was expected. Biran had known. And yet, seeing it all left him wrong-footed.

Better to feel like a fish out of water in Vladsen's home than on board the *Terminus*, where unfriendly eyes might be watching him. He needed to grow accustomed to his station, and fast. Dios, he'd probably have to re-download his student textbook on dinner etiquette. That information was rusty as his home drink dispenser.

The attendant led him up a curving set of marble stairs, the soles of his leather shoes whispering against the stone while Biran clomped along in mag boots. Biran held his arms low in front of his body, fingers lightly touching, and tried to project confidence. The attendant knocked on a door that Biran was pretty certain had been carved from real aspen trees.

"Enter," Vladsen called distractedly.

The attendant opened the door and stepped aside. Vladsen sat behind a desk of smartplex almost as wide as the control console of the *Taso*. His head was bent, curls hiding his eyes, as his fingers flew against one of the active screens. A half dozen monitors extended on articulated aluminum from the desktop, turned to face him like a swarm of drones, their bluish light casting ghostly shadows across his skin. The light in the room was low, red-shifted as if he'd been preparing to sleep, but the cool light of the monitors told another story.

He wore long, loose pants—probably silk—and a matching T-shirt in black, bare feet pressed into the thick pile of a rug. Behind him, a window overlooked his back garden, the shape outlined fuzzily by more glowing globes. Old books lined the side walls, the leather scent permeating the air, and from the cracks in their spines, Biran could tell they weren't ornamental.

Vladsen looked up from his work as the door slipped shut after Biran. Red veins spiderwebbed his eyes, dark shadows pooled in the hollows of his cheeks. His jaw stiffened, chin wrinkling.

"Director," he said with forced formality, and gestured to a chair that had been set before his desk. The rug was too neat, that chair did not live there.

Biran inclined his head and took the seat, pressing his palms into the arms of the chair. If Vladsen was playacting professionalism, he could play that game, too. "It is very late, Keeper. What did you wish to speak with me about?"

Vladsen gestured, and the screens surrounding him went dark, the articulated arms pulling them down to hide somewhere beneath the glass with a soft whisper of well-oiled machinery.

"I would like to discuss my current assignment," he said dryly. "As you leave for god-knows-where with the morning, I presumed time was limited."

"I won't be out of CamCast range, Keeper," Biran said with the same dry tone, but his voice rasped slightly, and he had to lick his lips to keep them from scraping against each other.

Vladsen arched one brow, leaning across his desk, dark eyes intent on meeting Biran's. His heart kicked up at that stare, but he didn't let the emotion show.

"What the fuck, Biran," he said with mingled bewilderment and irritation. "You kicked me off the *Terminus*."

He looked aside. "I did. With Singh staying behind as interim director, I need eyes on this station I can trust."

"So you're bringing a basket of vipers with you through that gate instead?" At Biran's flat stare, Vladsen scoffed and leaned back in his seat, pulling up the roster of Keepers set to board the *Terminus* in the morning, and started reading. "Natsu Sato, who very likely believes you responsible for the death of her longtime mentor. Lili Monta, who believes she was entitled to the position of Speaker before you took it. Arnold Russo, who whispers that you and Lionetti were too close for you to know nothing about her betrayal. Kan Slatter, whose *nose you broke*. Tell me, Director, do you have a fetish for a knife in the back that I was unaware of? I thought I'd sussed out all your proclivities."

A flash of anger overrode the usual heat those words would bring him. "All people who I do not want to leave behind, festering, while I'm gone. They are Keepers, and that will not change unless they do something truly idiotic. I need them on my side, and granting them some glory by bringing them on this expedition combined with comporting myself well in their eyes may secure the loyalty of some."

"While leaving your strongest ally on this rock to babysit Singh."

"She is a problem."

"She is not director material, and she knows it. She would much rather pull strings from the sidelines."

"I'm not willing to bet my station on that fact."

"I don't believe you."

He wiped his hands on his thighs. "Rost, I—"

"What the fuck is this, then?"

He flicked up the interview Biran had done shortly after leaving Okonkwo on the ship. A sick dread coiled in Biran's belly as he watched himself answer reporter Callie Mera's questions with adroit candor, easing the minds of Prime—of his people—that their director was well, and the so-called assassination attempt little more than a fleabite.

He made himself watch as she asked, with a coy smile, about the guardcore already in his bedroom when the attack occurred. He hadn't blushed and stammered as Okonkwo had asked of him, but he cleared his throat, flicked his gaze away, then brushed off the question with an oblique comment about the guardcore making certain of the safety of all Keepers. It was enough. He'd already seen some of the rumors circulating, and Okonkwo had sent him thinly veiled congratulations on an interview well done. Vladsen stopped the footage.

"It isn't what you think," Biran said weakly.

"Really?" Vladsen folded his hands together over his abdomen as he kicked up one ankle onto his knee. "Because I think Okonkwo put you up to that stupid stunt. I think she leaned on you to stir up that rumor, add a little spice to our formal-but-very-attractive new director."

He winced. "Then I suppose it's exactly what you think. She—"

"Knew?" Vladsen watched him from under heavy lashes. Biran sighed, letting some of the poise bleed out of his posture.

"Yes. Better a taboo relationship than an illegal one."

He grimaced and looked aside, pinching his lip between two fingers. "I will be on that ship in the morning. I suggest you edit the roster so that it doesn't cause a scene."

"Don't you think it's better if we spend some time apart?"

He turned his head back, and let his lip go. It was slightly red from the force with which he'd pinched it. "You think...?" He blinked and laughed. "Ah. I think I see more clearly why these relationships are not allowed."

A vise gripped his heart. "I'm sorry."

Rost waved a hand. "No, it's not your fault. It's only natural, isn't it? You care about me...?" He trailed off, a hopeful lift to his brows. Biran nodded, and the vise in his chest eased as Rost's shoulders relaxed with the confirmation. "...So you seek to protect me by leaving me behind, where we cannot be found together, and both our chips stay safely attached."

"The Prime Director already knows, Rost. Singh's needling is bearable, but...Okonkwo made damn sure I knew she was capable of killing us, if it came to that."

He looked at his hands, imagining a blaster in them. Rost was around the desk in a breath, gathering both of Biran's hands into his own. The astringent scent of his cleanser was fresh on his skin, as if he'd just showered. "Did she harm you?"

"No, of course not." Biran shook his head. "She...Well, I suppose as you are on the Protectorate, this is no secret from you. She had Demas. Put her blaster in my hand, and when I couldn't pull the trigger, she did."

"Christ. I knew she was brutal, but icing her childhood friend?"

"That was the point. She wanted me to see. Wanted me to know how ruthless she can be, when our laws are transgressed. She loved that man like a brother, and didn't even finish her sentence before his brains painted the floor. It was quite the message."

"I bet." He released Biran's hands and backed away, putting distance between them as he leaned against the desk, palms on the plex. "But, Biran, I am not staying."

Biran let his gaze harden. "I am your director, Keeper Vladsen."

He grinned wolfishly. "I do like it when you're tough on me, but I won't be held back because of this. You see the danger, and I understand that, but I see my whole career ripped away. Being on that ship is an honor. I've earned it on my own merit."

"What do you mean? You remain on the Protectorate."

Rost tossed his head, curls bouncing, and snorted. "I cannot stay here forever, and I doubt you will, either. Or do you mean to tell me that you're content to direct Ada for the rest of your life? That you do not intend to leverage your meteoric rise into a position on the High Protectorate?"

"I...genuinely hadn't thought about it."

He half smiled, looking down, and shook his head. "I should have guessed. There's a life after this war, and I doubt either one of us will be content with petty administration concerns once all of this is done. You and I, we could reshape so much..."

He trailed off, imagining a hazy future, and sweat prickled between

Biran's shoulder blades. He genuinely hadn't considered what his future would hold. As a student, his singular goal had been achieving Keeperdom. After that, he'd been tossed into being Speaker, and elevated to director out of necessity. He supposed the next logical step was a place on the High Protectorate, if he could manage it.

That might even have been part of what Okonkwo had been trying to tell him—and Singh, too. If she helped him here, and he continued on his current career trajectory, then she would have a strong ally on that prestigious board.

Biran stared at the soft globes dotting the garden through Vladsen's window, and laughed. "I scarcely know what I'm doing next week, let alone scheming for jobs years away."

Rost threw him a wry smile. "I know, and so do the people around you. This war has made reactionaries of us all. We jump when Icarion twitches, we maneuver to get ahead of Rainier. But if you have any hope that we're going to survive this, then these things are all short-term. And I—I mean, you..." He bit his lip. "You scare the shit out of me, Biran Greeve."

"I'm so sorry, I never intended—"

He huffed, but he was smiling. "You see? It's that. You try so damn hard, you expect everyone else is trying just as hard to make the united worlds as safe as you are. But the long view? That job years down the line? That's all most of our colleagues can see. They're thinking ahead, and they're thinking for themselves, because it's never occurred to them that Prime could be bested. That we could *lose*. They're playing you across a board you can't see, because it's on fire and you're busy putting it out."

His skin went cold. "You think I can't do this."

Rost jerked his gaze back to Biran, the intensity of it a lance through the heart. "Biran, I think you're the only one who can."

The cold did not thaw. "That's a hell of a lot of responsibility."

"That's being the director of a planet at war."

"*I'm* not even sure I can do this. Okonkwo claims she wants someone going through that gate who won't shoot first, and I understand the sentiment, but what if there's a berserker field on the other side? What if there's life, and they're hostile? Or Rainier's makers are on the other side, and she's already warned them? I'm not a general, Rost. I'm not—I'm not Sanda. Dios, I almost got taken down by a *shower*."

Rost chuckled bitterly and hooked his thumbs around his hips. "Speaking of scaring the shit out of me. Everything else aside, if I'm being wholly honest, I have to be on that ship because I can't . . . I can't bear the thought of that alarm going off and me not being there."

"You're no warrior yourself," Biran said, though the cold in him warmed a degree.

Rost flicked his gaze up. "For you? I'd pull that fucking trigger, if Okonkwo handed me the gun."

His heart thumped a little too hard, and he shifted in the chair. "My hero," he said dryly.

Rost caught the rough undercurrent in Biran's tone and rucked a brow at him, eyeing him slowly from below those dark lashes. Bad idea. Heat rouged Biran's chest, chasing away the frost of disappointment, and his breath grew shallow. He had to get out of here, back to his perfectly adequate house, and get some shut-eye so that he'd have his wits about him when he boarded the *Terminus* in the morning.

"It's late," Biran said.

"So it is." He cocked his head to the side, considering. "I have something to give you."

"That might be your most inelegant come-on yet."

His sly smile cracked into a grin. "Oh, nothing like that. Unless . . . ? No, you're right, it's late." He spoke into his wristpad. "Alderman, I'm ready for the package, please."

Biran frowned a question at Rost, but he merely smiled and called for the attendant to enter when he knocked. Alderman pushed a wheeled wardrobe into the room, bursting with clothes, then stepped aside. Rost sprung off the desk and rubbed his hands together, approaching the wardrobe.

"That's all, thank you, Alderman."

The attendant bowed to them both and withdrew from the room. When the door shut, Biran let out a low groan and forced himself to stand, approaching the clothes. Suits, most of them, cut for mag boots and a touch too tall for Rost.

"You didn't," he said, touching a sleeve that felt smooth as water beneath his fingertips.

"Singh is a pain in the ass, but she's right. You need to start looking the part, and I knew you wouldn't bother before we board tomorrow."

"How did you manage it so quickly?"

"Please," he said, drifting closer, and traced a finger down Biran's back, stopping right at the base of his spine. Goose bumps followed in the wake of his touch. "As if I don't know your sizes. The rest was just a little extra credit to grease the wheels, move things along faster. All things you could do yourself, if you weren't bleeding yourself dry to the Nazca."

"I made a deal, and I intend to honor it."

He sighed dramatically and peeled his hand away, grabbing one of the suits to hold up to Biran. Charcoal-grey fabric made up the jacket and slacks, a medium-toned blue shirt underneath that hinted at Prime cyan without screaming it. "You wouldn't be you if you didn't. Here, take this one tonight. It's not so far from the ratty jumpsuits you're used to, so it won't be a shock for the press tomorrow."

"I happen to like the jumpsuits," he muttered, holding the outfit up to himself.

Rost rolled his eyes. "Your greatest flaw."

"It's a matter of practicality, like the mag boots. What if we lose pressure, or atmo? We are on a station here, Rost, though your home tries hard to deny the fact, and we will be on a ship. The jumpsuits can seal to any helmet."

"Christ in heaven, you really are this disconnected from fashion. Here." He slipped his hand beneath the collar of the shirt and turned the fabric inside out, revealing thin webbing. "This is a vac liner. It will seal, if things come to that. The jumpsuits are sturdier, I grant you, but this stuff will do the job, and it doesn't show beneath clothes."

He really hadn't known. Was Okonkwo wearing a web beneath all her sartorial choices? Probably. Meanwhile, Biran couldn't even remember the last time he'd ordered new socks.

"Thank you," he said, too embarrassed by his own ignorance to come up with anything else.

"No need." Rost turned back to the rack, sorting through and crinkling his nose now and then. "There was no way in hell I'd suffer through the embarrassment of having my director board that ship in a years-old jumpsuit, let alone my..." He trailed off, pressed his lips together.

"Your...?"

He shifted his weight, toes curling in the rug. Cleared his throat, examining a lapel a little too closely. "Partner."

"Is that, like, a Wild West thing, or...?" Biran stared at him with wide-eyed, feigned ignorance.

He sputtered, then laughed. "You know damn well what I mean. Don't make me elaborate."

"I won't make you do anything, Rost," he said gently.

Rost hesitated, flicking his gaze up to Biran's. Biran held perfectly still, head tilted to the side in question as Rost licked his lips, slowly. This was the deal they'd made—that Biran had insisted upon—before they'd continued their relationship. Biran would never, ever, be the aggressor. Any intimacy would always be initiated by Rost, because Biran was his boss, and the power dynamic in play was too touchy.

Rost craned his head forward, and Biran let his eyes slip closed as their lips touched, briefly, warmth whispering across his skin, and then Rost backed away, hands still on the clothes rack, because once he started touching, he had a hard time stopping.

"I know," Rost said, smiling so that his eyes wrinkled at the corners. "You should go. It's late. I'll have Alderman send the rest over before liftoff."

"Thank you, again. Really, I mean it."

"Bah," he said, waving a dismissive hand, and retreated to the barricade of his desk, waving up the screens once more. "Good night, Director."

"Good night, Keeper."

Alderman packed the suit up for him, and during the autocab ride back to his house, Biran pulled up the *Terminus* roster, and added Keeper Rostam Shaghad Vladsen to the list, praying he wasn't making a colossal mistake.

CHAPTER 23

NO SHOOTING ALLOWED ON THE COMMAND DECK

I f she stopped to think, she'd scream, so she pushed to her feet and put out a ship-wide call across the comms.

"Everyone. Command deck. Now."

Tomas took a step toward her. "I'm no threat to you or your crew."

She could not look at him. The shudder in his voice was enough to tell her all about the pain she'd see behind those grey eyes if she looked. "I believe you. My crew has to believe you, too."

Arden said, "Holy shit, really?"

"To the best of my understanding," Tomas admitted.

"Oh man, Liao is going to love this—wait, she already knows, right? Shit, you were the firewall. That makes *so* much sense. How did you know—?"

"Stow the questions until the whole class is here," Sanda said.

She pushed past them both, and in doing so came close enough to Tomas for the side of his arm to brush hers. A tingle ran up her skin, and she scowled to the empty air as she stomped down the hall, trying to ignore Arden's excited chatter behind her and Tomas's slow, doleful answers.

He didn't know. He hadn't known. Or so he said. When Rainier came knocking, he'd certainly seemed to know exactly what to do.

When she reached the command deck, the others were already there, assembled in a hasty half circle around the captain's chair. Nox, she noted, had paused to grab a rifle and had it tucked under one arm. Or maybe he hadn't made a detour, and went everywhere with a weapon. She was tired of lugging her own rifle around, so she tossed it to him and he snatched it out of the air with a nod.

As she sat, she wondered if she was really tired of carrying the rifle. The weight was nothing, the feel of the strap across her chest as comfortable as old pajamas. No, it wasn't the rifle she didn't want to carry. It was the fear that she might have to use it.

Tomas shuffled into the room at Arden's side, hands still in his pockets, shoulders hunched. But he came to stand in front of her, and lifted his head. A dimple appeared in one cheek as he forced a sad smile, and she really wished he hadn't done that, because it made her stomach flutter, and she needed to see him not as Tomas—but a machine. A potential threat to her crew.

"What's up, boss?" Nox said, jutting his chin at Tomas. "I'm guessing the eye bleeding isn't contagious, or you wouldn't have dragged his ass out here for us all to catch it."

"Tell them," she said, again, and the words came no easier this time.

He held her gaze and inclined his head, lashes drooping. Her chest ached as she realized he'd say any damn thing she asked him to, so long as it meant staying on this ship. Staying near her. Or maybe that was what Tomas the spy wanted her to think, to feel.

"I am a synthetic person. Rainier Lavaux claims I am a subset of her, and I have no reason to doubt her claims."

Nox's rifle cracked. Sanda's heart leapt into her throat as Tomas shuddered, dropping down to one knee, the meat of his left calf torn wide open, bright blood fanning across the floor. Now that she knew what she was looking for, it was impossible not to notice the faint, but present, metallic sheen.

"Hold fire, you fucking ox," Sanda snapped.

Nox shrugged, but pointed the rifle to the ceiling, finger off the trigger. "Had to check."

"Check? Dios." She grabbed the medikit stashed under her chair, but Tomas held up a forestalling hand.

"No. It's ... fine."

"Half your leg is on my floor," she said, ripping a patch out of the kit.

"Commander," Liao said softly.

Liao's tone, more than anything, made her stop what she was doing. Slowly, wincing with every centimeter, Tomas stood up and removed his hand from his shredded calf. He wiped blood off on his jumpsuit and watched, along with everyone else on the deck, as the muscle began to knit back together.

Nox whistled. "Damn that's handy. I fucking knew Jules was healing too fast—didn't I say that, Arden?"

"Yeah, but..." Arden blinked owlishly at Tomas.

Tomas finished the thought for them, "But not this fast. Jules was given the ascension-agent, and it transformed her. I was made this way. Lavaux could do this, too, but I believe he must have taken more doses, or had better control due to being ascended for much longer."

"Repeated dosing increases control," Bero said. "Or so I understand from the second sphere. Lavaux must have taken a great deal."

"How is that possible?" Liao asked.

Tomas rolled a shoulder, an infuriatingly casual motion as pink skin spread across his new musculature. Too much like Keeper Lavaux. Sanda looked away, light-headed.

"I don't know the details," Tomas said. "But I do know that the Nazca stole the reconstruction bath technology from Rainier. They're the same devices she uses to make her bodies."

Chaos erupted as everyone started asking questions at once. Sanda winced.

"Quiet," she ordered. Silence descended. "Bero and Arden are convinced it was Tomas's intervention that saved this ship from Rainier's intrusion. I would like to keep him on board as a stopgap against further attempts."

"A human firewall!" Arden grinned. She shot them a look and they blushed and went back to their wristpad.

"But I won't keep him around without consent from every one of you. This is...not a threat any of us have the ability to cogently assess. This is new. What Tomas is could save us, or destroy us."

"If he saved the ship," Knuth said, "then I want him to stay."

"I don't see a problem," Nox said. "But I will shoot you if you piss me off."

Tomas winced, but he was smiling. "It doesn't *not* hurt, you know. That shit stings."

"I'm going to need some samples," Liao said. "If that's all right."

"And I want to meet you in net space," Arden cut in, bouncing on the balls of their feet.

Her crew closed around Tomas, asking him too many questions all at once in the same way they'd once done for Bero. If they could accept what he was so easily, why couldn't she?

On her wristpad, from Bero: are you all right?

She almost laughed, but that would have made her look like a lunatic, so she just shrugged, knowing Bero's cameras would see her and understand. How could she be okay? The universe was fucked three ways from Sunday, and now the man she'd thought she had a connection with before he ran off to do the Nazca's bidding turned out not to be a man at all, but a creation made by the very thing she sought to destroy.

It didn't seem fair that this situation didn't give her a headache, when so many others did. But that was because she hadn't known—had never known. This knowledge wasn't taken from her, as with so much else, when she'd been captured and experimented upon by the Icarions. She'd never had it to begin with, which meant she didn't have the blinding pain to keep her from thinking too deeply about what it all meant.

The physical pain was easier to deal with.

"Knock it off, all of you," she said, because they'd dissolved into a barrage of questions and Tomas was starting to look queasy. "We all need time to adjust. Arden, put your head together with Bero and work on those defenses. Conway, Knuth, you'll have access after Tomas and Bero figure out what they can do together. Nox, no shooting. Liao, your priority is the sphere."

"And me?" Tomas asked, after the chorus of assent had settled down.

Sanda took a long breath. "You and I are going to have a little talk before I have to report to my superiors, which I should have done an hour ago. Quarters. Now."

CHAPTER 24

PRIME STANDARD YEAR 3543

THE COST OF A CURE

Jules curled to one side and vomited a mix of blood, bile, and booze across the floor. The ship's materials soaked up the mess, whisking it away to some internal system that would filter it out, take what it could use from the slurry, and discard the rest. She grimaced, clutching her stomach with both hands, teeth chattering as she curled into a tight knot against her bed.

"Lights," she hissed through cracked lips.

Bright light flooded the room, making her cringe into an even tighter ball. Fever rash painted her arms blotchy purple, her feet and calves bruised blue. She held her hands out in front of herself, staring in a strange mingle of awe and horror. Jules was ascended. Jules did not get sick.

She vomited on the floor again, body cramping up so hard all she could think about was purging whatever-the-fuck from her body. Her muscles spasmed so long she wondered if she was strong enough to snap her own spine. Probably. She'd snapped plenty of spines with her hands.

"What the fuck," she whispered to herself when the spasms had calmed down, leaving her a limp, worn-out accident of cells. Shivers wracked her body, goose bumps standing at full attention all across her skin.

Groaning, Jules rolled over, dragging herself to the edge of her narrow cubby. This was a guardcore ship. It had medikits everywhere, even had its own medibay. She'd throw herself in one of Rainier's restoration baths, if it would help.

Arms wrapped around her stomach, she staggered across the ship in her underwear, dirty hair hanging in her eyes, sweat she hadn't felt in years building up along her hairline, pouring down her spine, slicking the spot where her thighs touched. She gritted her teeth, forcing herself to take one step, then another. Medibay. Had to get to the medibay.

The door dilated, disturbing the air enough that the slight breeze made her shiver all over again, teeth chattering. She'd never had such a high fever in her entire life. What was this? Fear clamped down on her. Had Rainier found her? Was she fucking with her at long last?

Jules took a step, lost her balance, and dropped hard on one knee, swaying to the side. She put a hand down to keep from collapsing completely, a grimace burned into her features. Shit, she hadn't felt this kind of pain in years.

Trembling, she crawled across the floor to the bulkhead and ripped a panel open. Plastic crinkled as she shoved a hand in, grabbing anything she could. She spread the patches out across the ground like confetti and blinked, sweat stinging her eyes, vision blurring as she struggled to read the labels. This fever was going to kill her.

"Drop temperature ten degrees," she pushed out through swollen lips.

"Are you sure? Safe parameters are—"

"Just fucking do it," she growled, ripping open a packet that claimed to be anti-nausea.

The ship obliged. Cold air poured through the vents, forced in at such a high pressure that it kicked up a breeze, blowing away the discarded medication packet. Jules shivered violently as the near-frozen air touched her febrile skin, and nearly bit her tongue off in the process.

She tasted blood, and her stomach cramped up again. Panting, she pressed the anti-nausea patch against her arm. There. Better, if marginally so.

Hands shaking, she combed through the rest of the stash and started slapping on medications. Anti-inflammatories, more anti-nausea, pain suppressors, anything that looked like it might stop the agony wracking her body. When her arms were more patches than skin, she started on her thighs, part of her mind aware that all of these meds were probably a bad idea. Interactions could occur, and for some of these, she was using enough to kill a bear. But, fuck it. Something was trying to kill her. She needed her body to calm down so she could think.

The sedatives caught up with her, made her motions feel slow and clumsy; she set her jaw, pushing to her hands and knees. Her wristpad caught her eye and for one delirious moment she almost called for help. A laugh started deep in her belly, shaking her bones, making the sweat-slick hair hanging around her face bounce and shudder.

"It's just you and me, Lolla," she said to the raised coffin in the center of the medibay. She had to keep talking. Keep moving. Figure out what this was.

Jules staggered to her feet, stumbling across the room until she reached Lolla's casket. Her arms smeared sweat across the plex as she braced herself on the girl's chamber, hanging limp against it, knees turning to jelly.

"C'mon," she hissed, "you were the smart one. I need you."

Not that Lolla could answer. The muscles of her legs quivered; she was going to fall any second. Jules staggered away from the coffin, let herself drop into the chair she'd set up alongside Lolla. She kept her vigil for the girl there every single night she was on the ship. Sat, and talked, and drank. But this was no hangover, no flu. Jules had never even felt this shitty when she wasn't ascended.

"I don't know what to do," she whispered, tears pricking behind her eyes.

Stupid, stupid. She'd never been able to function on her own, Harlan had seen that. Had given her direction. Shit, even Rainier had realized Jules needed someone to bounce off of, even if she hated that person, because when left alone too long, all Jules was good at was spiraling. Digging deep into despair.

She bent forward, pressing the heels of her palms against her forehead, pushing, pushing. Willing this to be another painful side effect of the rollbacks, but she knew better. This was no headache. Her stomach cramped up, threatening another round of vomit, but the meds did their work and kept it down.

She shuddered, elbow knocking the guardcore mug she'd taken from Saarah. The mug she'd used to down a liter of grot last night. She stared at it through hazy eyes.

No. No fucking way.

Grot was one step away from paint thinner. Nasty stuff, as much a dissolvent as anything you'd find in a lab. It must have leached something from the guardcore metal. She didn't need anti-nausea meds. She needed to be barfing her guts out. She needed a detox.

She ripped the anti-nausea patches off her arms, nails scraping against her skin from the force. The meds had already made it into her system, but she could stop the trickle, and she'd seen plenty of stuff she could use in the handfuls of patches she'd dug out of that drawer.

Gritting her teeth, Jules staggered to her feet, then dropped to her hands and knees and crawled back to the drawer, swatting aside the patches she didn't want. She grabbed anything that read OVERDOSE or TOXIN INGESTION and slapped them all over herself—her thighs, her stomach.

Half the meds were designed for very specific instances, but she didn't care, because she didn't know exactly what that shit was doing to her body. The meds went to work, a war of purging, binding, and blocking that left her seizing on the floor, nearly choking on her own vomit, for void-knew-how-long.

When the worst of it had been squeezed out of her system, Jules lay limp for a very long time, her only movement the shuddering of her body against the now ice-cold floor. Hesitantly, she rolled onto her side, got a bent arm under herself. Pushed herself up on trembling legs.

"Ship, temperature back to normal."

"Initializing," the ship said.

Every step she took was unsteady, as if the ground were bucking beneath her, tempting her ankles to roll. She made it to the chair, somehow. Sat down and hunched over herself, face buried in her hands, trying to think.

Rainier had said the ascended were immune to all human-borne ailments, so what the fuck was that? Heavy metal poisoning shouldn't send her body spiraling into toxic shock. *Toxic* wasn't a word her body spoke anymore.

The viewscreen on Lolla's coffin blinked a yellow indicator light. Jules jerked to her feet, almost lost her balance, and had to brace herself against the casket, bleary eyes seeking out the problem in a system that Rainier had promised would function for decades. O_2 low in the mix.

Her heart skipped. She prodded at the screen, running diagnostics, willing the error to be a flaw in the software, a sensor misreading, because she no longer had access to Rainier's tools.

It was no error. Something in the recycler wasn't working right, wasn't slapping the right molecules back together to keep Lolla living while she dreamed.

"Fuck," she growled, pulling on her short, shaggy tufts of hair. She couldn't fix this, didn't even know where to begin. There were Rainier's reconstruction baths in the lower hold of the ship. She could maybe, *maybe*, repurpose parts of them—or transport Lolla into one. Would that work? She had no fucking idea.

Nausea clawed at her and she leaned over to vomit, shoulders burning as her body heaved, one hand on the coffin, the other on her gut.

The hospital. She'd have to take Lolla to the hospital. It'd be tricky, to convince the intake medis that she'd found a coma patient in such good shape, and it'd require Jules taking Lolla out of the casket, the thought of which made her skin crawl, but they'd help. They'd stabilize her. They'd done it for all the others, why not Lolla?

But Lolla's ident hadn't changed. She was a Grotta girl, a techhead with brilliant potential, but she'd not been anywhere close to Arden's level. Lolla didn't have false idents spoofed into her wristpad, ready to override the signal from the one implanted in her arm.

Jules didn't have an ident injector, but she could cut the ident out, fish it out somehow. They'd be suspicious as all hell at a patient without an ident, but they wouldn't lump her with the other Grotta rats. Wouldn't send her to the basement.

But that would mean cutting into Lolla. Jules's medical experience extended only as far as field-dressing wounds.

She wiped sweat off her forehead onto the back of her wrist and pressed her face against the casket. Yellow. The light was only yellow. Nothing was critical yet, she didn't have to make a decision now. She could poke around, figure something out, maybe steal something from the hospital that would help.

Maybe the immune would reveal a cure before Lolla got too bad.

She picked her head up, lips parted, still panting, and looked at the mug made of slagged guardcore metal. Maybe she already had a cure. She just didn't know how to use it.

Stumbling, Jules grabbed the cup and dragged herself toward the showers. Dal. Dal would know what to make of this.

CHAPTER 25

CAREFUL WHO YOU PUNCH

Maybe coming to her quarters had been a bad idea, but she couldn't think clearly with all the chatter on the command deck clogging up her thoughts. Here, in the quiet seclusion of her room, the thoughts came fast and clear, and she found she didn't want them. Sanda placed herself on the chair behind her desk, letting the furniture stand between them, and gestured the door closed after Tomas entered. He glanced at the discarded armor on the floor and raised a brow at her.

"Not very fleet-like," he said.

"I'm not doing things very fleet-like lately."

Dios, she hadn't meant for that to come out so sharp. When had she gotten so prickly, so quick to lash out, at Tomas of all people?

Maybe about the time Novak brought the hammer down on Monte. Definitely by the time Rainier had told her, gleefully, that she was about to vaporize all of Ada. Too much. At least, when she'd been on Bero and thought all the worlds around her long since destroyed, her objective had been clear: Survive.

Now she was playing whack-a-mole with an alien intelligence, and didn't much like it when surprises popped up in her own circle.

"Sorry," she said, drumming her fingers against the desk. "You don't deserve me being an asshole."

"I disagree." He nudged a piece of armor with his boot, then crossed the room and sat on the edge of her bed, as far away from her as he could get while still being within speaking range without raising his voice. "I've lied to you. Multiple times. You should be angry with me."

"You didn't have much choice." Her fingers curled into a fist against the desk. "Showing up on my doorstep with 'hi, honey, I'm home and also a robot' wouldn't have gone over very well."

He snort-laughed and looked down at his hands. "I'd considered it, you know. Laying it all out there."

"Why didn't you?"

"Denial, that old human standby. Even robots raised like people aren't immune to it, it seems. Not that I was raised. Bero had more of a childhood than I did."

"If it makes you feel better, I knew you were full of shit about something."

He glanced up, brows high. "How?"

She looked at the offline tablet on her desk. "Every time Rainier came up, you looked ready to jump out the airlock to get away from the conversation. I figured she hurt you, during your meeting. I just didn't know how."

"Huh. You could make the argument she helped me."

Time to ask the hard thing. She forced herself to meet his gaze, but he didn't look up from his hands. "Does she have a hold over you? In any way?"

"No. She scraped my corpse off of Monte and—"

Sanda surged to her feet. "Excuse me? Fucking Monte? You forget to mention that?"

His eyes widened and he leaned back, planting his palms against his knees. The rapid beat of his heart pulsed in the vein on the side of his neck. "I didn't lie to you, Sanda, but you were...cleverer than I was. MetBaths." He grunted and shook his head. "Christ, I believed everything Caid told me. Never even occurred to me that tech like that would be on the market for high-value clients, but you saw it. You told me what I was before I even knew."

MetBaths. There was only one person who'd used that term with her, and she'd punched him in the face for his trouble.

"Novak?"

"Hi," he said, and waved, tentatively, with the tips of his fingers.

"Excuse me."

Sanda turned, deliberately, and kicked the desk with her prosthetic leg. It had more strength in it than she'd thought. The impact surged through her, and it was only years of training that kept her on her feet as the desk ripped out of its ground anchors and flung across the room, shattering tablets and bits of plastic clutter against the wall.

She stood, panting, fists clenched so hard at her sides her skin began to split beneath her nails—nails that had been crusted with Novak's blood—and tried to think of anything but the mounting shout of panic in her mind.

She didn't know how long had passed before he asked, "That help?"

"A little."

"Maybe I should try it."

"Bero can always grow us more. Or maybe you can."

"Is this how we're going to avoid this conversation?"

She forced her fists open. "I killed you."

"You warned me you would. I didn't listen." Such a soft, gentle voice.

She turned her head, leaving her feet and body planted where they were. He watched her through shut-down eyes, face and body neutral, his hands against his knees where he'd left them. It was worse than him being angry. Something clicked in her mind.

"Novak called in the guardcore."

That cracked his calm veneer. He shot to his feet and jabbed a finger at the place where his wristpad had been. "No I fucking didn't! That was Rainier. She's always known what I am. You ever wonder why she let you walk off Janus? Why she let Novak go?

"She didn't have to. She could have squashed you and me and all her scientists right then and there. She still had the bulk of her amplifiers housed off-site. But she let you go, because she knew you'd gun for the coordinates, and she knew..." He clenched his fist. "She knew I'd follow, bringing a hacked wristpad with me."

"Then why Monte?" She was shouting, and didn't realize when the switch had been made. "Why come for me there, when she'd let me walk, and I hadn't even *gotten* to the coordinates yet?"

"On Janus, she could have killed us all by stopping the station spin, but she didn't have the guns to take you alive. She knows you, Sanda, she knows you'd rather"—his voice skipped—"knows you'd go down fighting. She needed you cornered. I think she was going to deal. I think she wanted you to lay down arms on Monte and trade yourself, and the secret in your skull, for those lives."

Sanda laughed ruefully. "Doesn't know me that well then, does she?"

"No," he said, and took a step toward her. "But I do."

Her eyes narrowed slightly, even as her skin tingled at the low tone to his voice. She didn't move. "What the hell does that mean?"

"You're never going to stop. Not after Monte, after Atrux. I saw how you worked, on Bero, before you knew the truth about what had happened. As far as you knew, there might not even be a world left alive worth running for, but you never slowed down, not for a second, because once you've got a goal worth fighting for, you don't give up until you grab it or go down swinging."

She wrinkled her nose and looked away. "Sounds like something Biran would say in one of his press releases."

Tomas kicked a piece of discarded GC armor, and it wedged itself into the wall alongside the desk.

"Goddamnit, Sanda, I'm not good at this. I don't..." She turned back, and saw him grab his hair and pull. "I may have lived a hundred lives, but they're dull. Distant. I don't know what to say to you, and I don't even know if I should *try*, because everything I'm feeling is all...fucked up..."

"Whoa," she said, and closed the space between them, grabbing the hand tangled in his hair to keep him from pulling it out at the roots. Maybe he could grow it back, but he'd said he could feel pain. Kicking furniture was one thing, causing himself actual pain was a line she didn't want crossed.

But now they were so close, and synthetic or not, she could feel the subtle heat of his body, the roughness of skin calloused from work that may or may not be naturally earned, but felt familiar all the same.

"Tomas," she said softly, and he opened his eyes reluctantly, fingers going slack in hers. "I don't understand half of that, but I'm willing to listen."

He bit his lip and looked away, letting his hand fall from his hair. She kept hers with him. "Sitta Caid, my handler at the Nazca. She stole the technology from Rainier. I don't know how long ago. I don't even know how old I am. Every time I started to remember, every time I figured out what I am, she put me back in the reconstruction bath and...reset me. My memories.

"Some of the missions are still there, she wasn't stupid enough to keep that data from me, but with pieces sliced out. Everything from before a reset feels vague, distant. People. Relationships."

She swallowed. "Me?"

"No." He flicked his gaze back to hers, and the dimple reappeared as he smiled for real. "You're where everything starts to feel clear."

"See?" she said, mirroring his smile. "You are kinda good at this."

His palm went hot beneath her touch. Tension tugged at the corners of his lips. Right. He was dealing with some shit. She squeezed his hand before letting it drop and stepped away, putting some space between them. Tomas breathed out slowly, shoulders relaxing.

"Sanda...There's something I need to tell you. It's personal, and deeply embarrassing."

Her mouth felt thick with dread, but she put on a smile for him. "I've seen you naked."

Tomas barked a laugh, blushing faintly, and though he turned his face away from her, the genuine crinkle of his smile in the flash before an anxious twist replaced the expression warmed her to the core.

"Did you wonder why Novak bolted?"

"Yes," she said, trying to keep her tone neutral even as a chill chased that warmth away. "It was a damn stupid thing to do. I'd been clear he had no second chances. Running then, it made me gun for him harder. I thought, if it was worth that much of a risk, then it really fucking mattered."

He nodded to himself, his head still turned away. "It did. I was obsessed. All I could think about was turning that flask over to Caid. I couldn't think about anything else except finishing my mission."

"Shit. Is that some kind of compulsion thing? Can they make you—?" She cut herself off when he started shaking his head.

"Do you remember what it was like, when you were younger? How intense everything felt, because you were feeling it for the first time?"

"Yeah, but I'm going to need you to pick a track and stick on it, Tomas. This is confusing enough without jaunts to adolescence."

"My last reset was before my Icarion mission, which was altered when Biran purchased the services of the Nazca. Everything from before that time is dull. And then I found you. Novak—I—bolted, because I desperately wanted this face back. I needed you to..."

His shoulders hunched, blush deepening. Sanda had no idea what to say here, what to do. Emotions too myriad to acknowledge swirled through her, one after another, twisting her up inside, leaving her speechless and short of breath. Unease tickled the edges of all her nerves.

Their collision into each other had been brief, but she'd thought it'd been real. Grounded. But now he was telling her what, exactly? That it'd been some kind of puppy-dog crush? Intense, but fleeting? Over, she could deal with. Hell, she'd been prepared to kick his ass off her ship if things looked sketchy with him. But this? This was weird.

She sat down hard on her desk chair, almost dizzy from trying to work through how she felt. Rejected, mostly. And this silence was verging on uncomfortable territory.

"You could have just said you weren't interested anymore. Or, I don't know, nothing at all. That probably would have been fine, too, considering." She waved a hand vaguely at the entire upside-down fucking universe.

"What?"

He turned to face her, eyes wide, and she suddenly couldn't figure out what to do with her hands, or where to look, so she sat there like a floppy idiot, wondering how she could have gone from commander of this ship to heart-kicked so damn fast. She hadn't even *really* had her hopes up about him. Practicalities, and all of that. He was a goddamn spy. And a robot, apparently.

"No, no, I didn't mean—ah, fuck. I'm not good at this, remember?" He dropped to his knees in front of her and grabbed her hands, squeezing, which solved one of her present problems. "Don't be sad. Please don't be sad. I meant I'm still figuring things out for myself, that's all."

"I need you to spell it out for me, Tomas, and I'm sorry, I know it's uncomfortable for you and asking isn't fair, but right now all I'm hearing is you think this is a crush that'll fade with time. If that's the case, I get it. That kind of thing happens no matter who you are."

He let out a long, slow breath, and reached up, hesitating to see if she'd pull away. When she didn't, he held either side of her face gently between his hands, brushing his thumbs against her temples. He looked so damn serious, so damn twisted up. She steeled herself.

"I fucking love you, Sanda Greeve. So intensely it frightens me. So completely it jolts me awake in the middle of the night. You're my north star, my compass, and I didn't understand that until you turned me away as Novak. It was too much. I lost my goddamn mind, and got myself killed, because I was desperate to get back to you."

"I didn't know—"

"Please, let me finish, because I'm not sure I can work up the nerve to do this again."

Her heart was hammering so hard she was certain he could feel it through her temples. Her skin burned but she nodded, slightly. He took a breath. Looked away. Licked his lips.

"It's too much. I know it's too much. And I don't know if that's the rollback, or Rainier cranking all my senses up, or just you. And I'm trying really, really hard not to freak you out right now, because I know how this looks. Obsessive. Stalkery. Nox called me out on chasing you to the deadgate, and he was right. You don't need me rushing in to save you. Fuck, half the time I need you coming to save me."

She coiled her fingers around his chin and, gently, turned him to face her once more. The turmoil writ across his face stunned her. He was terrified she was going to turn him away, toss him aside, because of what he was. Because the body he'd been born into was messing with his head, making it all feel like it was too much.

"You don't frighten me, Tomas. You piss me off sometimes, sure." He laughed a little, and she smiled with him, feeling some of the tension leave his hands, and her shoulders. "You say it's too much, so I'll give you the room you need to cool your heels. Figure yourself out. But when you're ready, you better bring me that whole damn speech again, because I'd like to enjoy it without wondering if there's another shoe getting ready to drop."

He lowered his head, burying his face against her knees, and for a second she wasn't sure if the shudder in his shoulders was from laughter or sobbing. She brushed her fingers through his hair either way, and when he looked up again, his eyes were wet, but he was grinning.

"How did I get so fucking lucky?"

"You're on an alien spaceship helping me gun for an alien being of unknown origin, unknown power, and unknown reach. I think you need to recalibrate your definition of lucky."

His eyes glittered, and for a breath she thought he'd reach for her, pull her down to him, but the shine wore away, replaced by wariness, and she kicked herself for being too cynical. He rocked back onto his heels, breaking contact.

"Unlucky or not, it was your headaches that stopped me getting in the bath for the reset. After Rainier put me back together and kicked me loose, Caid brought me in. I felt…stronger than I'd ever felt in my life, or stronger than I could remember. But she kept telling me I was dying. That I needed to get in the bath before my cells broke down."

"But your head was pounding?" she prompted. He needed to talk this out. The least she could do was hear everything he had to say.

He nodded, brushing his hair back. "Yeah. I believed her, because it hurt so much. I can't imagine what you…Well, you know. Once I realized, a memory squeezed back in."

"You don't have to recount it if you don't want to."

"You need to know. Everything's fuzzy, but I recalled the first time they reset me. There was a man, all in grey. I don't know him, but he ordered Caid to perform the reset. They said…" Tomas cleared his throat. "Said they 'had no guarantee I'd suffer the same fate as the others.'"

"What others?"

"I don't know, but I got the feeling he was talking about previous experiments with synthetic Nazca. I don't believe any of those people are alive anymore."

"I'm sorry."

"I never knew them..." He let his hand drop, and smiled ruefully. "I think."

"Will she come after you, do you think? Caid, or this grey man?"

"Caid's dead, and she can't come back from that. The man...I don't know." His voice was a little too tight.

"You want him to."

"I'll stick with this ship until you're done with Rainier, but after that, I...I have my own loose ends to tie up."

"We can help you with that. He's probably connected to Rainier."

He pressed his lips together and put his hands in his pockets. "Maybe. We'll see."

He was holding something back. After all of that, there was some kernel of a secret he was keeping close, lodged so deep she couldn't begin to guess at what it was.

Disappointment threaded through her, but she pushed the feeling aside. He'd been hurt, deeply. She knew a little about what that was like. And no matter what he was to her, he'd always been a spy—*always*—and it might very well bring him comfort to have one last secret clutched tight.

"We'll figure it out," she said, and touched him lightly on the shoulder, just to see that dimple reappear as he flashed her a genuine, if fleeting, smile.

"Yeah," he said. "I think maybe we will."

CHAPTER 26

PRIME STANDARD YEAR 3543

USE OF WEAPONS

Sanda told him to get some rest, and he'd been too emotionally wound up to realize she'd meant cool his mental heels, so he'd said something stupid and glib about not needing to sleep and wandered off down the halls. He'd thought to find Arden, because they were going to tie themself into knots speculating about him and he wanted to get ahead of that—and maybe find out a few things about himself in the process—but he found himself back in the armory.

He threw a glance at the doorway, thinking Bero might have guided him there, but Bero remained silent. His own feet had brought him here, then. Nox sat in his usual place, a rag in his hands and a rifle across his knees, and scarcely glanced up as Tomas wandered into the room.

"Didn't we just clean those?" Tomas asked.

Nox shrugged. "They got used, didn't they?"

"You always this fastidious?"

"You always this full of questions?"

Tomas caught himself smiling and went to the cabinet. He selected a rifle, rag, and bottle of oil before joining Nox on the opposite bench. "Usually, yeah."

"Spy thing?"

"Spy thing."

They worked for a while in silence. Eventually, Nox said, "It's not about the cleaning. It's about the thinking."

Tomas frowned, pausing at his work. "Thought you loved these weapons."

"I do. Having a clear head helps me use them better."

Tomas blinked, and half laughed. "You'd make a shit therapist, Nox."

Nox leaned back to watch Tomas. "I'm just saying, I gotta do something with my hands when I'm stressed. You walked through that door looking ready to take the ship apart and reassemble it just to have something to do."

He looked at the weapon in his lap. "I used to cook through my thoughts."

Nox bent his attention back to the rifle. "Nothing stopping you. Kitchen's stocked, and Arden and I are tired of trying to get these fleetie fucks to make something that doesn't taste like shoe leather."

Tomas winced, remembering the raw nutriblock Sanda had been content to live off of while on Bero. "Poor taste is hammered into them."

"Got that right. So why don't you cook?"

He shrugged, switched weapons, and kept cleaning. "It was a lie. My family, they had this restaurant...But none of that was real. I don't have a family. I'm not even sure I need to eat food."

"Gotta eat, man. Even I'm not that shit at physics."

He snorted. "Yeah, probably."

"Don't see how that changes anything, though. You need to think, you cook. So go cook."

"It's not real."

Nox put his rifle down and leaned toward him, letting the rag dangle between his fingers. Tomas looked up and met his gaze, a much easier feat than meeting Sanda's. At least there wasn't a hurricane of emotions spinning behind Nox's eyes. The man was the clearest-headed person Tomas had ever met. Probably. After this reset, anyway.

"Where'd you go just then?" Nox asked.

Tomas frowned and set his rifle down, the mirror of Nox's. "What do you mean?"

"In your head. You fucked off who-knows-where in that head of yours."

"I was wondering if you were the only person like you I've ever met before."

"That sounds pretty pointless."

Tomas scowled. "You don't understand."

"I know what it means to sever an old life. And before you get your hackles up, I know, I know, it ain't the same thing at all. But when Sanda tells me to shoot, I'm not thinking if maybe Harlan would have given the order differently. I'm thinking about the shot, and I'm taking it, not getting tangled up in old shit."

"I'll shoot when Sanda tells me to," he said, and was irritated at the defensiveness in his voice.

Nox laughed. "Yeah, I bet you will, but you gotta get out of that head. You gotta live *now*, because you can do fuck all about what's already passed." He dropped his voice. "You think I like putting bullets in the helmets of the GC? Jules wore that armor. I can never be sure."

"Thousands of people are comatose because of her."

"Yeah, and that's the *now*. So I squeeze that fucking trigger, whether I like it or not."

"I'm sorry."

"So am I. Which is why I come here and clean weapons. Why Arden shoves their head up the net's asshole and tries to figure out how *The Light* works. Why you should be cooking right now."

"It's tainted."

"Rifles aren't sunshine for me, Tomas. And I can't tell you all the bullshit Arden's done on the net. I don't know what Sanda and the others do, but I bet they've got something, too. Everything has baggage, if you keep it around long enough. Doesn't make it bad. Just makes it heavier."

Tomas half smiled to himself, because he could imagine what Sanda was doing right now. Not calling Anford, like she'd said. First, she'd fix the desk and piece the armor and tablets back together again, with her own hands, ignoring any help from Bero. Sanda fixed things. Didn't mean he could count on her to fix him.

"Thanks, Nox. That was...surprisingly helpful."

"Don't look too surprised. You came through that door looking ready for murder. Didn't want it to be mine. Boss that hard on you?"

Tomas shifted his weight. "She broke a table."

Nox whistled low. "No wonder you looked so pissed."

"Wasn't angry with her," he said, and picked the rifle back up. "More so with myself."

"Eh," Nox said, and grabbed his rifle, too. "Not much you can do about that. You did what you did. Can't blame you for lying. In your position, any one of us probably would have lied, too."

But it wasn't that. He believed he'd made the right choice, and Sanda seemed to agree. His fingers stilled as he thought, digging deep, wondering why Nox had seen fury on his face when all he'd really felt was frustration.

"Guess I was upset I'd missed a chance at something, that's all. Seems stupid, now."

Nox picked his head up and arched a brow. "Tried to kiss her?"

Heat raced up his chest and neck; he was sure he'd turned bright red. He'd have to get better at controlling those responses. "No, of course not."

"Missed a chance to try, then. Didn't think you'd have the stones." Nox chuckled.

Nox didn't look upset, but...The way they'd moved together on Janus had given Tomas a pang of jealousy, whether he wanted to admit it or not. Maybe they were a thing. The thought made him a little nauseous.

He cleared his throat. "You and Sanda...?"

Nox almost dropped his rifle, actual shock startling his eyes wide open. "Jesus fuck, no way. She could be my—" He cut himself off and laughed. "Tomas, my man, Graham and I were a thing, before he ran off with Ilan."

Tomas laughed and dragged his hands against his cheeks, letting his cold fingers cool the heat there. "You don't look..."

"That old?" Nox winked. "Older than I look, and Graham had those kids young, but all that was a long time ago. See what I mean about getting out of your head?"

An old instinct itched at the back of Tomas's mind. "I do, but I'm wondering why you decided now was the time to be friendly. I'm not trying to be a dick, but..."

"...But what's changed? You, obviously. We're having this conversation because you're sticking around, and to be real fucking clear, you're the most dangerous person on this ship. I saw..." He chewed the thought over for a moment. Tomas gave him the space to think. "I saw how fast Jules moved. I thought I saw it in you, too, when I tossed you that rifle in the engine bay. I'm no idiot, Tomas. I don't want the crack shot with superhuman speed stewing in his own bullshit. You, out of all of us, cannot afford to make mistakes."

Any other day that might have been insulting, but now he felt slow relief wash through him. "Thanks for the candor, and the talk."

"Anytime," he said.

Tomas pushed to his feet and put the rifle back.

"Hey, where do you think you're going? We got twelve more."

"Gonna go make dinner before Conway mangles it."

Nox smiled. "Good. One question."

"Shoot."

He deliberately eyed Tomas's arms. "You gotta hit the gym for those things?"

Tomas blinked, looked down at his biceps, and laughed. "No, probably not."

"Not fucking fair." Nox grunted, and went back to cleaning, muttering to himself.

Even though Tomas didn't need it, Bero lit a thin line of light along the hallway, guiding his way to the kitchen without words. He smiled, and trailed his fingers along the wall as he went.

CHAPTER 27

PRIME STANDARD YEAR 3543

WORK THE PROBLEM

Sanda called Grippy to her room with a toolbox and set to work putting her furniture back together. The guardcore armor she left scattered across the floor—she planned on spacing it later, once she could work up the stomach to step outside her room.

Right now, she needed a wrench in her hand, a torch. Needed physical things she could manipulate with reliable results. Needed something she could *fix*.

She yanked the piece of armor Tomas's kick had embedded out of the wall, not bothering to comment as Bero healed the tear in the surface, and tossed it into the pile with the rest. Grippy beeped once—*no*—at her. Cheeky repair bot.

"What? You're not my parent. I'll clean it up later."

The statement was too complex, so the bot remained silent. She grabbed the desk and wrangled it back to its usual location, examining the connective points between its legs and the floor. Bero had grown the thing, so it looked more like shredded rope than broken bolts.

She scowled and dug through the tool kit, looking for a metal file. Smooth it out, level it, solder it back on. That should do it. Wasn't much in the universe that a good solder job couldn't hold together.

"I can—" Bero started.

"I'm not talking to you right now, B. There's no way you didn't know what he was. And you kept that from me."

"I'm sorry. I did not want to keep it from you, but it was Tomas's secret to tell."

Tomas's secret. A switch clicked over inside of her. Her whole body ached, chest feeling hollowed out, numb. She curled over herself, sitting there on her knees before the desk and the tools, rounding around the void in her being.

A secret was singing show tunes in the shower, not being cousin to the alien entity set on destroying all humanity. Not hiding he'd been behind the face she'd shot and killed on Monte. Not—

Her breath rasped. She'd been holding herself and rocking for… some time, hard to say, thoughts spiraling out of control. Fuck. She'd held it together while he was in here, more or less. Kept herself from screaming and shaking and looking as terrified as she'd felt, because to see any of that fear in her would have undone him. Would have been one more cruel thing on top of a pile stacked on Tomas's shoulders.

But when Nox had shot him and his leg had knitted up like Lavaux's, she'd wanted to crawl out of her skin. Some small part of her had started screaming then, and hadn't stopped.

I fucking love you, Sanda Greeve.

Her breathing evened out. It wasn't his fault. There was no point in punishing him for what he was, any more than there was in blaming Bero for being a weapon. No point in punishing *herself* by making the association override all other feelings. But she couldn't decouple the panic, not completely, no matter how much she wanted to. She scrubbed tears from her cheeks and picked up the metal file.

"He's cooking dinner. You should eat. You haven't been."

"Shut *up.*"

Fucking Tomas. Lied to her from day one, and not about what he was. He'd shown up on Bero with a cover story and an extraction plan, and in her darker moments she wondered if getting under her emotional skin had been a part of that plan. Wondered if, somewhere in the Nazca training, gaining romantic interest from an extraction target was a viable means to an end when it came to completing a mission.

They hadn't even been close that long. Weeks, really. Days after intimacy. Then he'd left her on Atrux, returning to his masters without a word, and set things up to try to squeeze her into laying down arms. Into going home.

Idiot. Stupid, stupid fucking man. She clenched her fist around the metal file to keep from throwing it. This was Bero's body, after all, and she'd already embarrassed herself by losing control earlier.

But all of that history was preamble, because what really had her tied up in knots was Novak.

Her hands stilled at their work, body freezing even as her thoughts glanced over the concept. He'd been shady from the jump, something intrinsically not right about him. But that'd just been Tomas so torn up inside that he didn't know what to do, how to behave. *Obsessed. Completely lost my mind.*

I'm so, so sorry, he'd said as he bled out. Novak's final words. Tomas's. He hadn't known he was coming back from that, and that's all he'd said. He'd just fucking *apologized,* and at the time she hadn't even known why. Did he expect she'd find out? She would have, eventually. Rainier probably would have found it real fucking fun to taunt her with that.

Someone knocked on her door and she flinched, screeching the metal file across the table.

"Who the fuck is it?" she demanded.

"Uh...Conway?"

Sanda closed her eyes briefly and tried to center herself. Right. Commander, ship, crew. There was a whole shitshow going on out there that she was supposed to be cleaning up. She wiped her face and waved the door open. Conway entered, and it shut behind her.

The stocky woman eyed the wreckage of Sanda's desk and tilted her head to the side. "Need a hand?"

No. I'm fine. Leave me the fuck alone.

"Sure," Sanda said instead, pointing to Grippy's toolbox with her chin. "Spare files are in there. Did you need anything?"

"Naw." Conway strolled over and pulled her long, silvery-grey braid back to tie into a knot at the base of her neck as she crouched over the toolbox. "Got kicked out of the kitchen. Apparently fleeties have the taste buds of dead opossums."

Sanda squinted at her. "What's an opossum?"

"You'd have to ask your man, I'm not a net search."

Your man. Sanda pressed her lips together and focused on filing. Conway shrugged and went about working on another leg.

After a while, Conway said, "You did a good thing."

Sanda hissed as her file slipped and nicked her finger. She sucked on the small wound, studiously not looking at Conway. "Don't know what you mean."

"Taking all that pain on yourself. Took some of the weight off. Gave him room to breathe."

"I really don't want to talk about it."

"I get it, I think. Never went in for romantic relationships myself. But Tomas is in there cooking up a storm and whistling. One conversation with you, and he's a totally different man than the one who walked onto this ship. He actually looks happy. Couldn't help but notice you weren't out there singing your joy, too."

"Conway—" she started, voice ragged, gearing up to kick the woman out of her room without being mean about it.

Conway looked up and met her gaze with calm, steely eyes. Sanda cut herself off, feeling stripped down, seen in a way she hadn't been in a very, very long time.

"You were about to ask me to go check on something time-consuming, instead of telling me to get the fuck out, like you want to, weren't you? I've had a lot of commanding officers in my time. Most don't give a shit. Some give too much. But I ain't ever had one try to carry as much as you. You're strong as hell, but you can't keep shouldering everything for everyone. Sooner or later, it's going to break you."

"I said I don't want to talk about it."

"You never do, Commander, begging your pardon. You never want to talk something out if you can *do* something instead. But you can't fix this one. You can't unwind the clock on what he is. Can't undo what Rainier's done to this universe. So you fix this table instead, but it's not the same."

Sanda's fingers flexed of their own accord, tightening around the file. She set it aside and reached for the flux, solder, and torch. "I can't let this team fall apart."

Why had she said that?

"Team's not going anywhere," Conway said, reaching for a cloth to wipe away the file dust.

"We cannot fail."

Conway stopped. Looked at her. "You know what I'm hearing, right now? I'm hearing '*I* can't fall apart. *I* can't fail.' That's a lot of pressure for one person."

Sanda laughed, and the sound was manic. "This ship—"

"This ship is a ship. Rainier's an enemy. You know what to do with both of those things."

"My last ship—"

"Was shot down at Dralee because you used your ship as a shield between a railgun and a whole battalion. Thousands of people are alive because of that decision."

"But not my crew."

"No, and that's fine."

Fresh anger swelled through her, hot enough to cut through the numbness. "You do not get to tell me that."

"I do, actually. You never looked us up, did you? Never found out why Knuth and I aren't allowed on the front lines?"

"You did your jobs well. Those files aren't everything. Mine's half lies."

"See, General Anford wanted to undermine you. To give you a headache by assigning Knuth and me to your command. I'm a bit older—and don't you tense up, I'm not about to dole out some I'm-older-I-know-better bullshit—and maybe Knuth's not my age, but we've been assigned to the same posts for decades. We've seen a lot of shit. Mostly we've seen good people get killed by petty, vain, glory-seeking choices.

"It's given us what Anford would call a 'problem with authority.' She assigned us to you so that, when you started going off the rails, we'd buck and slow you down or rein you in. Didn't work out so well for the general. We were fucking delighted when you pirated the *Thorn* to do things your own way. It's what we'd wanted. What we'd hoped for.

"Because Knuth and I looked you up. We always do before a new post—we get kicked around a lot. Too insubordinate to keep around, too good at what we do to be discharged. We play a little game, take guesses about what glory-seeking decision our new commander is going to make to get us killed. But we found Dralee, when we looked into you. You overrode the AI pilot to take that railgun. We figured, working for you, if we got killed, then it'd be for a damn good reason."

Sanda stared. Too many forces had used Dralee to manipulate her into being the person they wanted her to be. Even Biran had used it, when he'd been trying to get her back from Icarion. No one had ever used Dralee to compliment her without trying to get something out of her for their trouble.

The thought, *If I were a better captain, no one would have died*, perched on her lips. She swallowed it.

"I don't want anyone to die."

"I know," Conway said with a sad smile. "But you can't carry that. You can't carry..." She gestured around the room. "All of *this* for all of us. Tomas is out there whistling like starshine because you gave him hope, and that's all fine and good, but what do you think he'd feel, knowing you were in here tearing yourself apart, alone? You let him talk out his hurt. You should give yourself the same chance, too."

"When did you get so damn insightful?"

Conway winked and pushed to her feet, wiping flux off on her thighs. "I make a grand emotional gesture once a year to make up for all the shit I don't give a damn about any other time. So try not to have a breakdown in the next three hundred days or so. I'm on my way to the kitchen. Want food?"

Sanda snorted. "Just send me Tomas. And...thank you."

Conway snapped off a picture-perfect salute and let herself out. Sanda sat on the floor awhile, admiring the perfectly spaced beads on Conway's solder job—neater than her own work—because if she started thinking about what she was about to do, she'd find some way to avoid it.

The door opened. She could smell him before she saw him, his shadow falling over her shoulder as wafts of spice-laden steam filled the room.

"Hey, Conway said you didn't want food, but Arden told me they think you keep dehydrated nutriblocks in here to get around eating properly, and I *know* you're the busiest woman in the damn universe but that's disgusting." He paused. "Sanda?"

Now or never. She used the table to haul herself to her feet. It didn't sway, or creak. The things Sanda repaired rarely complained. She turned to face him.

"Oh shit," he said, before she could get a word out. "Are you okay? What's happened?"

Sanda scrubbed the side of her face with one hand, feeling slickness, and wondered how much of that was tears or flux. A tiny part of her remembered that flux was toxic, and she should probably wash her face, but that was Planning-Sanda, and Planning-Sanda was sitting the fuck down for a moment.

"Nothing's happened. I just..." Her chest tightened. She was Sanda goddamn Greeve and she commanded the biggest weapon in the universe. This shouldn't be this hard. "I need someone to talk to."

He looked absolutely bewildered, mouth open, brow crunched together. Fear clawed up her throat and she wanted to take the words back, but couldn't figure out how. Then it clicked. Tomas gave her a small, gentle smile. He placed the food on the desk, and sat on the trunk at the foot of her bed, carefully putting space between them.

"I've got your back, Sanda. With...with everything. I'm here."

She sank into her desk chair, buried her face in her hands, and talked.

CHAPTER 28

PRIME STANDARD YEAR 3543

WHAT'S LEFT OF THE LOYAL

Biran waited days of travel, until they were an hour away from the secondary gate, before he summoned all the Keepers on board the *Terminus* to the most secure conference room on the ship. He did not meet them there. He waited in his state room, toying with a stylus, running over everything that must be said, and everything he did not want to say.

Rainier's pronouncements had been kept to the Protectorates. Okonkwo's Speaker, Annalise Greystone, and Rost were the only others on the *Terminus* who knew what Rainier was. Who knew what the gates were, where they'd come from, and what they might be flying toward. He swallowed. Evidence aside, this was going to be a hell of a hard sell.

But he'd needed their ignorance from the beginning of the journey, needed to give them the travel time from Ada to the gate to reveal if they were attempting to pass secret messages, to listen at walls. It was a dangerous game he played, and while he'd picked his team well, no instinct was perfect.

Icarion's craftiness could not be discounted. There would be spies. Rats in his ship. He'd needed to give them a chance to reveal themselves through their behavior before the real truth was shared.

And now it was time to flush them out.

"Director," one of the guardcore that lingered in his room said in their digitized voice, "the Keepers are ready for you."

He let out a long, slow breath. He wasn't sure if he was ready for them, but waiting any longer would only irritate them, and he needed every last Keeper on his side. Even Slatter and Sato. Maybe Vladsen had been right—maybe bringing his potential detractors was a mistake—but there was no way to get rid of them, and he hoped that bringing them into the fold would help smooth those relationships. Okonkwo, at least, had approved the roster, so he assumed she agreed.

"Let's go." He stood, and the three GC who had appeared seconds after he'd sent the summons to the other Keepers fell in behind him.

He wanted to order them to back off, but rumors surrounding the supposed assassination attempt had swelled, and the guardcore felt twitchier than ever. Maybe they were antsy about going through the gate.

He hoped one of the GC on board was the ancillary from his en suite. He needed to talk to her, and he couldn't exactly call a random one to ask after her. She'd have to show herself, and the waiting grated.

The plush halls of the *Terminus* raced by as he walked at a tight clip, shoulders straight, head up, hand near the holster Vladsen had shown him sewn into every suit jacket. The grey suit with blue undershirt had been the right choice when he'd first boarded. Biran had even caught a few people in the audience checking him out, which was an unusual sensation. Usually the people of Prime looked at him like he was a rare example of some endangered species.

He wore the same outfit again, to remind the others that he was not just their director, but Okonkwo's pick to lead this mission. On this ship, Biran was an instrument of Prime.

He paused outside the door. "Begin the sweep."

"Understood," one of the GC said, and walked away.

The *Terminus* was massive. It would take time. Time enough to reveal the truth to whichever Keepers were left after observation of their behavior on the trip to the gate.

Biran stepped into the secured conference room, flicking his gaze over those gathered, assessing alliances. Slatter and Monta sat close to each other—no surprise there—but Sato had placed herself at Vladsen's right hand. Russo could have been next to either Vladsen or Monta, it was hard to say, and Greystone sat at the foot of the table, leaving the head for him but quietly asserting her presence as a member of the High Protectorate. The gathering was short a few faces, but nothing he hadn't expected. One face surprised him, though.

Keeper Sato, her hands folded neatly on the table, met his eyes as he entered the room, a nervous whisper of a smile crossing her lips. He returned the brief expression, privately relieved. Sato had been Keeper Hitton's protégé. When Hitton's paranoia had drawn the survey mission on the asteroid to a standstill, Sato had been the one to show Biran and Vladsen the piles of survey bots Hitton had been too afraid to use.

And then Biran had gone and fucked it up, not taking Hitton's fear of a saboteur seriously enough.

He knew he owed her an apology, and he'd hoped that giving her a position as the most junior Keeper on the mission roster would be that olive branch, but part of him had never expected her to make it this far. If anyone had a reason to try to undermine Biran, it was Sato.

But there she sat, at her ease beside Vladsen, and Biran was reasonably certain her curious smile had been real.

"Director," Russo said with a genuine smile, "a pleasure. We are all dying to know what this is about." He slid a sideways glance to Greystone. "Most of us, that is."

"I apologize that you were kept in the dark," Biran said, peeling his jacket off to sling it over the back of his chair. Slatter's and Sato's gazes tracked the jacket, noting the holstered weapon hidden within. The others either didn't notice, or had expected as much and weren't surprised. Biran unbuttoned his cuffs and rolled up his sleeves, taking his seat.

"Matters are, as I'm sure you can imagine, extremely sensitive." He laced his fingers together and met their gazes, one by one. "You are, quite simply, not going to believe what I have to say. But I ask you to take it all in regardless, listen carefully, and ask any questions you may come up with. Some I may not be able to answer, but this is an open forum, presumed at the highest level of classification. If the information spoken here leaves this room, the result is chip removal. Do I have your consent to continue?"

Wary nods all around. Biran ignored Vladsen's faint smirk.

"Very well. You are all somewhat familiar with the entity of Rainier Lavaux, is that correct?"

"She infiltrated the guardcore with androids, or body doubles, correct?" Slatter asked.

"It is adjacent to the truth," Biran said, and watched some of them shift uncomfortably. "Rainier is an artificial intelligence embedded in a synthetic body. She used to be housed within the ship called *The Light*."

Sato's brow wrinkled. "I was under the impression that *The Light* was a new piece of technology for the fleet. Rainier has been around much longer than that."

"Longer than you think, and Prime had nothing to do with the making of *The Light*." He paused, letting that settle. Excepting *The Light of Berossus*, Prime made the most advanced ships in the universe. *The Light*'s full capabilities had been kept under wraps thus far, but enough people had seen the ship the day Sanda docked it at Ada's Keep Station to speculate about its origins. "That ship was created by the same beings that created the technology to build the Casimir Gates."

"I'm sorry," Slatter said, "*beings*?"

"Everything the director says has been verified," Annalise Greystone said smoothly, inclining her head to Biran. He returned the gesture, and watched unease settle over the other Keepers. The High Protectorate was known to have its secrets. None of them could have ever expected the secrets ran this deep.

"It is better, I think, if you view the footage that first brought this to our attention. Commander Greeve lured Rainier to an abandoned fringer settlement, and received a part of the story from the mind itself."

"Oh, naturally, *Commander* Greeve," Monta muttered under her breath.

"Jealousy isn't becoming on you, Keeper," Kan Slatter said, sotto voce, and caught Biran's eye, lifting his chin slightly. Interesting.

Biran gestured, and the video was projected from the center of the table. He did not watch, and so busied himself by watching their reactions. Shock, disbelief, horror. Nothing unexpected. When it was done, Monta turned to Greystone. "Is this true? Are our gates...weapons?"

Greystone gestured across the table to Biran. "Your director has all the information."

"We do not know," Biran said, ignoring Monta's slight for now. "The blowback occurred. We saw as much, and suffered great losses because of that. We believe that the damage was not as extensive on this side because the scientists who built the amplifiers Rainier used to direct the blast were not yet done with their research. We have Commander Greeve to thank for that interruption."

"Such a blast would be devastating," Sato said slowly, flinching as attention turned to her. She took a breath, steeling herself. Most of her time as a Keeper had been spent at Hitton's elbow, being ordered around. She wasn't used to the attention. Biran could relate. "But the blast wouldn't have destroyed everything. We would have found evidence of something left behind. Rubble, perhaps, or geological layers."

"That is the question this expedition is meant to answer. That is why no scouting swarms have been sent through ahead of us."

Slatter's throat bobbed. "You mean Halston built the swarms to erase evidence of her crimes?"

Biran spread his hands. "We do not know, but we mean to find out."

Monta let out an anxious laugh. "I'd thought the swarm delayed merely because we weren't certain they'd trigger another reaction from a malfunctioning gate."

"That is the story, yes," Biran said dryly. "Commander Greeve herself is prepared to answer any questions you may have regarding the entity of Rainier, barring information sensitive to her current mission."

"Which is...?" Slatter asked.

"The excision of that entity."

"She's on an assassination mission?" Sato asked, eyes wide, and Biran wondered what Okonkwo would make of the innocence writ across the face of his fellow Keeper. Sato wouldn't shoot.

"More like extermination," Vladsen said.

"And what did you know of Rainier, while you listened in at Lavaux's elbow?" Monta shot across the table to him.

Vladsen's brows arched in delicate consternation. "My dear, nothing at all. She played us all for fools and I, for one, am looking forward to the commander's success."

"Commander Greeve's time is short. Use it wisely," Biran said, and pressed the call he had ready for his sister.

The time delay took a few minutes, but she appeared in her seat of command on board *The Light*, eyes hooded from lack of sleep, but her body rigid and tensed, ready to strike. If Biran didn't know her, he'd think her Okonkwo's weapon, all right. A ruthless creature bent on destruction. He pressed his lips together to keep from licking them. Maybe she was.

They'd discussed the parameters of this briefing ahead of time, but Sanda was no playactor. She was the most guileless person he'd ever met. Of course, many people would have said the same thing about Biran before the events of the last few years. He watched his selected Keepers from the corner of his eye, marking their reactions. Hesitation, suspicion. The ship surrounding Sanda was nothing of Prime make.

"Keepers," she said, inclining her head with respect, then snapped her gaze to Biran. "They are cleared for full parameters and in a secure location?"

"They are, speak at liberty. Bero will keep you advised of the time delay. We are not using gate tech on this ship."

"Very well," she said, and launched into a bare-bones version of what she had discovered of Rainier, backing up the facts with events only when absolutely necessary. Most of the story regarding *The Light* she left out, but she explained that after her encounter with the impostor guardcore on Monte, she'd run across a traitor GC embedded in Okonkwo's private circle.

"Ah," Biran said. "I had been meaning to tell you. Demas is dead."

Her eyes narrowed. "How?"

Biran suppressed a smile. Sanda knew damn well that Demas was dead; this was all prearranged to make the other Keepers understand that matters were serious enough for Okonkwo to take a weapon in hand herself. It almost might have been fun, doing this dance with Sanda, if everything wasn't so dire.

"The Prime Director," he said. "I bore witness."

"Intel?"

"Only clarifications regarding the timeline. Rainier cut him loose before the blowback. He did not know about it."

"I'm sorry," Monta said, and her tone lacked the usual derision that said she was anything but sorry. "The Prime Director executed this GC?"

"Prime Director Okonkwo, myself, and other members of the Protectorates have been executing all supposed agents of Rainier, including any ancillaries of her we've discovered, all across the united worlds. Rest assured there are no versions of that woman on this ship."

Everyone but Greystone and Vladsen paled. He knew there'd been rumors of the black sites among the Keepers, but Keepers were as good at keeping their own secrets as they were at keeping Prime's. Thousands of guardcore were being shipped out to those sites, under the fleet's watchful eye, and not all of them came back. They'd assumed a purge, they just hadn't known the details.

"So Rainier has made us into killers," Monta said in a small, sad voice.

"We have always been killers," Greystone said. The younger Keeper flushed red and looked away. She was not enjoying her taste of the higher echelons.

"If Rainier is such a monster, I do not see why Major Greeve is the sole force sent after her. All apologies," Monta said, but pressed on. "But your rank was awarded to you in absentia, and you have been out of commission for two years. It seems to me that one of our strike forces should be in control, or at the very least a general who earned the rank should be commanding *that* ship. I understand you have been central to matters, but this is a problem for all of Prime Inventive. General Anford, or her equal, is far better suited to the task."

Biran was very careful not to react. He knew the challenge would come, and had expected it from Monta, so he watched the others instead. Slatter cast Monta a smug, sideways glance, as if he'd been expecting the woman to stick her nose out and get swatted down. Greystone mirrored Biran's neutrality, as did Vladsen, while Sato and Russo frowned in confusion.

Sanda sighed slowly, letting every ounce of the weight she carried show in her posture. "Keeper Monta. Lili, isn't it? I remember you from Biran's classes, not that long ago. I understand your concerns. I share them. But for reasons outside of my control, outside of Prime's control, my team and I are uniquely suited to battle this threat. Rainier has taken an interest in me. That is leverage we cannot afford to ignore."

"In a seasoned commander's hands, *The Light* would perform so much better."

"I will accept no other commander," Bero said.

Sanda allowed herself a faint smirk, quickly smothered. "Keepers, allow me to introduce Bero, the intelligence that once piloted *The Light of Berossus*. There is no other being capable of piloting this ship."

Slatter leaned forward, eyes bright. "You stole the mind from Icarion? Well done, Commander!"

"His name is Bero, and he defected of his own free will. And would have told us as much when Keeper Lavaux clamped him down at Ada's Keep Station, if he had been given voice to do so. Bero alone is the reason you do not have another ramscoop breathing down your neck."

"You helped," Bero said.

Sanda snorted. "If there are no more questions . . . ?"

"No," Monta said. Then, with sincerity, "Thank you, Commander Greeve."

She waited a beat to see if the others had concerns, then inclined her head to Biran and cut the feed.

"Well shit," Slatter said, leaning back as he shook his head. "I can scarcely believe it. Was Hitton trying to take down Rainier when . . . ?"

"That is a possibility," Biran said, checking his messages. Bero hadn't sent him anything on the decryption of Hitton's final message.

"Keeper Hitton said nothing about all of this?" Sato asked, voice strained with an emotion Biran couldn't place.

Biran looked steadily at her, wondering. She'd been Hitton's assistant—did she know about the message Hitton had sent in her final moments? Unlikely, he decided. Hitton had grown too paranoid to share such a thing by then.

"Not to me," Biran said. Sato merely sighed. His wristpad flashed at him, indicating that the GC had completed the sweep. "Now, I have to apologize, for I have been keeping you locked in this room for another reason."

Uneasy shifting all around, even from Greystone and Vladsen.

A priority call from Scalla, the captain Biran had handpicked out of Graham and Ilan's transport business, pushed through to his wristpad. He flicked it to the projector in the center of the table.

"Negassi's ringing our bell, Director," Scalla drawled. "Want me to stall a little while longer?"

"No need, the sweep is complete. I will be there in a moment."

He cut the call and stood. "Now that you all understand the stakes, come with me. Please."

Everyone in that room knew his *please* was only a courtesy. Behind him, the door dilated, revealing a waiting phalanx of guardcore he and Okonkwo had hand-selected for this. Greystone fell into step alongside him, and dropped her voice low.

"What is this?"

"Insurance," he said, without inflection.

CHAPTER 29

PRIME STANDARD YEAR 3543

GROTTA RATS

Jules cleaned herself up as best she could and shoved herself back in the guardcore armor, her skin crawling at the touch of the foams lining the metal. Were there microparticles in her air mix? Was she slowly poisoning herself every second she wore the metal, or lived on that ship?

Rainier was made out of the same stuff as Jules, just in stronger concentrations, so far as Jules understood the process. Wouldn't it bother her more than it did Jules? How could she stand to wear that armor so often?

But then, Jules hadn't so much as sneezed since she'd been wearing the armor. Maybe breathing it was fine but ingesting it wasn't. Those were problems for Dal to figure out.

If the other GC noticed her sluggish movements as she let herself into the hospital, they said nothing. The armor hid her flushed, peaky skin, and she kept her personal medical diagnostics on lockdown, as always, so that they couldn't see the fever riding her veins. Her stomach cramped up in the elevator, and she breathed in low, shallow breaths, hoping she wouldn't have to test the armor's ability to clean out a fresh round of vomit. The elevator opened. She stepped out, and didn't lose whatever was left in her stomach. Progress.

The ward was quiet, lights turned down low, staff sparse. She checked her HUD time—0135 hours. She'd been shaking and puking herself to death all day and halfway through the night and hadn't even noticed the passage of time.

Luckily, Dr. Dal Padian was almost as obsessed as she was. A thin line of light shone under his office door, and when she knocked he answered immediately. This time, he didn't flinch when she entered. But something was...*off* about the man. Dark circles bruised the bags under his eyes, nothing new there, but his whole face looked dragged down, defeated.

"Can I help you?" he asked tiredly.

"What's wrong?" she asked, only using the voice filters because they automatically clicked on.

"Guardcore concerned about the emotional state of a non-Keeper? That's new."

"Dr. Padian, you are integral to the success of this mission."

He grunted. "Tell that to Keeper Martine—not that I wish the woman any ill will, you understand. Please don't think I'm bitter toward her." That last part came out in a panicked rush. He was definitely bitter, and didn't want a guardcore to know he harbored that resentment.

"Has something happened?"

"Ah, the immune—you are the guardcore who brought them in, correct?"

Not something a normal GC would acknowledge, but Jules needed whatever information Dal could offer, and that meant establishing some kind of rapport, even if it was outside protocol. She nodded in agreement, but didn't speak.

"I had great hopes for those two. Unfortunately, they presented with effects of the ascension-agent shortly after their arrival."

"That's not possible," Jules said, the sickness in her belly twinging again. She swallowed bile.

"I would have agreed with you, but Keeper Martine confirmed the data herself. They were taken to the aggression ward before I reported for my shift this morning."

Dal looked pointedly at his tablet, pretending to be engrossed in something there, while Jules processed that piece of information.

That ward... Every instinct she'd ever honed told her something was wrong about that ward. Only Grotta people ended up going there, and they didn't get moved back out. She'd known it was off. She'd known the Keepers were up to something twisted down there. But she hadn't cared because, as Padian had said, it would have been worth it if they could squeeze a cure out of whatever happened in those levels.

But the immune shouldn't be sequestered. All the researchers should have their hands on that project. Jules took the mug from her pack and set it down on Dal's desk. She hadn't bothered cleaning it; it still stank of the grot she'd poured down her throat the previous night.

"I thought this might be useful," she said carefully. "I found it in the pack of the immune woman. They had been drinking out of it for some time, I think."

Dal set his tablet down and picked up the mug, turning it over in the light. "This is guardcore metal, correct?" She nodded. He hmmed to himself. "It's been melted, partially. Reformed into this shape. Maybe the heat released some sort of previously stable gas, or otherwise destabilized the material. I don't suppose you can tell me what the guardcore metal is made of?"

She shook her head. "It's proprietary. And honestly, Doctor, I do not know."

He scratched the side of his nose. "How did the immune get their hands on it?"

She shrugged. "There have been a lot of fires in the Grotta, lately. Perhaps a piece of a downed GC's armor was reshaped by the flames and they scavenged it for use. I'm certain they didn't know what it was. That metal is worth too much to use as cookware."

"Possible, possible..." A line appeared between his brows as he thought, eyes brightening. "It would explain the ascended child, wouldn't it? The immune found the mug earlier in life, have been drinking from it longer than the child—maybe the child hasn't used it at all. The immune didn't appear to be in fantastic health, aside from being conscious. It could be their immune systems are no more robust than ours, but they were suffering some sort of heavy metal poisoning from the cup, and that metal bonded with the free-floating infection of the agent..." He looked up, his entire expression bright with excitement. "Thank you. This is more valuable than you know. I think we can make real progress with this."

Relief washed through her, making already shaky muscles feel even weaker. "I'm glad."

He glanced at his refrigerated cart of samples. "I have all I need from the immune to start on this research right now. We're very lucky to have taken samples before they...ascended. Now, we do not need them."

Jules licked her lips, understanding dawning through her febrile mind. Dal thought he could do it. He really believed he had the cure in his hands in the shape of a slagged-out mug and a couple samples of blood. Jules had seen him make do with thinner information.

It wouldn't be as easy as getting the ascended to consume the metal, she understood that. But the GC metal didn't play nice with the ascension-agent, and with that knowledge in hand, Dal had a solid foundation to work from. Elation bubbled up within her. She'd been right. Lolla would be fixed, soon. She'd fucking done it.

The other shoe dropped in her mind. Dal didn't need Saarah and Reece anymore, but there was no way in hell Keeper Martine would let them go. They'd rot in that basement, turned into pincushions in the name of thorough experimentation, when all Dal needed was already in this tiny room.

Jules clenched her fists. She should let them rot. Should put all of her effort into protecting Dal, into keeping the one mind who might puzzle out the solution safe.

Whatever happened in the basement didn't matter so long as it produced the cure. That's what she'd told herself. But Dal had the answer in his hands, and it wasn't what was happening down below. The metal was the key. Not the people. Not the lab rats.

Jules had thrown her own people into that hell pit. Lolla was already going to hate her when she woke up. Two more bodies on the pile weren't that much. All that mattered was...was...Goddamnit.

"I'll go check on the new intakes. Tell them they're no longer needed."

"Thank you, unit," he said, voice breathy. He'd been holding his breath, unsure if the strange GC in his office would do the right thing.

She half turned, stopped with one hand on the door. "Dal," she said, dropping the voice filter. He hissed with shock, but she didn't turn to look. That was an expression she didn't want to see. "When you're done, when you've got it. Tell me. Please. It's all I've ever wanted."

"Valentine..."

She winced. "I understand if you want to call security. Give me a shot to get those people out, okay?"

"How long?"

"Fifty minutes."

"You...you..."

"Brought you the immune. Brought you the cup. And now I'm getting those poor fucks below out again. Everything I've ever done has been for a cure, do you understand?"

Why was she doing this? Why was she exposing herself like this?

Because getting those people out meant running, running from this Sol-cursed rock where the cure would be, and she needed Dal to give it to her when he was done. Needed him to call her, and he wouldn't do it correctly if she were just any GC, wouldn't even know where to begin. He'd send it to the guardcore HQ and assume it'd find its way to her, but she'd never see it.

"Then why chase us to Monte? Why try to kill the people you had working on this?"

"That wasn't me. That was my boss. I've gone...independent, since then."

"Who are they?" he asked, voice strained. "Who's so damn important that you hurt so many people?"

She smiled tightly to herself. "Just another Grotta rat."

He let out a long, raspy sigh. "Fifty minutes. Where do I send the cure, once I have it?"

"Send it to one of Page's old drop boxes. I'll find it. Thanks, Dal. I'm glad I crossed paths with you."

"Can't say I share the sentiment," he said.

She snorted and stepped out into the hall, closing the door. She could practically hear the ghost of Harlan's voice, mocking her for getting too sentimental. For risking everything when she was so damn close to being done.

It didn't matter. She slung her rifle into her hands, stalking toward the elevator. She'd done a lot of monstrous things in Lolla's name. She could do one last good thing for her, before she woke up.

CHAPTER 30

PRIME STANDARD YEAR 3543

PULL THE TRIGGER

As the door to the command deck opened, the guardcore shuffled Biran's handpicked Keepers to one side, so that they would not be in view of the camera from the forward viewscreen.

Biran straightened his rolled sleeves—he'd left his coat and blaster in the conference room—and flicked a glance at Scalla, who hunched over her console. The rest of the command deck was working off of a skeleton crew, most of the seats empty.

"Clean?" he asked.

"Squeaky," Scalla said. "Putting you through."

General Negassi appeared on the screen, on board the deck of the *Empedocles*. He stood at parade rest, clean-shaven chin lifted, a faint scowl permanently carved into his face.

Next to the video, Scalla put up an overlay of local space—the *Terminus*, the *Empedocles*, a handful of fleet gunners, and an equal handful of Icarion gunships. The Icarion ships formed a crescent between the *Terminus* and the gate, the fleet ships holding steady in formation around the gate itself, for now.

"This is Director Biran Aventure Greeve of the flagship *Terminus*. State your business."

"Greeve," Negassi said, "I was beginning to think you'd gotten lost on that big ship of yours."

"Apologies for the delay, General. I had certain matters to see to." The implicit undertone: *And you do not rank as important enough to supersede those matters*. Negassi scowled, as expected. Biran almost sighed. He was far too easy to wind up; Bollar should have sent a less transparent man to attempt this play. Not that that would have gone any better for them.

"We know what you're doing, Greeve. Icarion will not be left out of a scouting mission behind that gate. It's our right."

Biran put steel into his voice. "That is a Prime gate, to which you have no right."

Negassi's face went ruddy. Usually, when they spoke, Biran played nice and tried to wheedle while Anford made herself the aggressor. But Anford wasn't here, and Biran had prepared for this moment. He would not bend a nanometer.

"Our *tenuous* peace is predicated on the fact that we will be allowed to trade through that gate. For Prime to push through it on a maiden voyage without a representative of Icarion on board is tantamount to war."

"Are you slow, Negassi?" Biran would have chafed to drop the title from another person, but Negassi had damned near executed Sanda, once. Biran found he was actually enjoying this.

"Excuse me?"

"I have told you, this is a Prime gate. Those settlements under the governance of Prime Inventive are free to use the gates as they please, barring the usual rules. Until Icarion submits to Prime rule, no Icarion will pass through this gate."

A smirk twitched at the corners of Negassi's lips. "That's a big cruiser you've got there, Greeve. Can hold what, a couple thousand? That's a lot of bodies, a lot of possibilities. Are you so sure there's not an Icarion on board already? You've been surprised before, haven't you?"

Anaia. He'd known the barb would come, eventually, and so he didn't react. "I have. I will not be surprised again. Scalla?"

"Ready to launch, sir."

"Excellent. This is, indeed, a very large ship, and the trip here took quite some time. Time enough for us to examine certain attempts to dead-drop, or otherwise circumvent our communications. Your spies are clumsy, Negassi. I suggest hiring a Nazca upon your next attempt, they are so much more practiced. But then, you know that, don't you?"

His fists clenched, the vein at the side of his neck stood out. "So sure you got them all?"

Biran gave him a sly smile, feeling a thrill of adrenaline surge through his body. "I've kept a few, just to see what you find important." A lie, but he wanted Negassi to chew it over. "Jettison, please, Captain Scalla."

"Aye," she said, and released the shuttles that Biran's GC had packed full of innocents and spies alike. His orders for the sweep had been simple—all the suspects, plus everyone else that was not absolutely essential to running this ship. A few of the suspects had also been essential personnel, but they went with the rest, because Biran had picked his Keepers with more than an eye for knives in the dark.

"I've released thirty-two shuttles. The fleet will pick them up, naturally. Some contain your people, some don't. You're welcome to try and intervene and suss out which are your more valuable assets before the fleet gets them, but I recommend you hurry. Anford's not kind to spies."

On the screen, the blinking cyan dots of the gunships began to move.

"You are outgunned," Negassi growled. "You are taking Icarion through that gate."

He sighed and shook his head, as if disappointed. "Yes, that is a very large ship you have there, General. But the schematics your people were allowed to leak to you regarding the *Terminus* may have been a *touch* out of date." He tilted his head, putting bark into the words. "Weapons."

He could not see the ship, but he knew what was happening out there in the void. Sheets of steel-grey metal whispered aside, swinging up massive railguns that peppered the *Terminus*, bristling like spikes, interspersed with gentler, but just as deadly, projectile and laser weapons. The *Terminus* may look like a passenger ship from the outside, but Okonkwo had fitted her with every scrap of arsenal she could muster in the short amount of time before she sent her through to Ada.

Biran could not see all of this, but he could see Negassi's eyes widen as his ship screamed alarms, painted up with targeting lasers.

"You wouldn't dare," he rasped, the smug smirk stuck on his lips. "Shooting me down now would send the war hot, and we both know you don't want that. You're too damn soft, Greeve."

Biran crossed his arms slowly, letting his expression go hard as granite as he cocked his head to one side, eyebrow arched, a hungry smile splitting his lips apart. "Negassi, I have been dying to get a shot at you since Farion. Stand your ships down, or fucking try me, and see how soft my railgun feels in your skull."

Negassi's face went so flush with the blood of rage his cheeks turned purple, lips ghostly white as he sucked them in, sweat making his forehead glitter. Biran enjoyed every second of it, printed the fear and rage of that vile man into his heart.

"This isn't over," Negassi snapped, but he gestured, down low, and the Icarion ships began to peel away on the schematic.

"Promises, promises," Biran said, and cut the feed with a flick of his fingers.

Tense silence stretched on the deck while Biran stared down those icons, making damn sure the Icarion ships had shuffled out of firing range before he gestured for Scalla to put the weapons away.

"Hol-ee shit," Slatter said, pounding one fist into his open palm. Russo and Sato let out nervous laughs. "Were you really going to shoot him down?"

Biran didn't turn his body, only his head, to meet Slatter's gaze. "What do you think?"

"I think I'm in love," Slatter said.

Biran snorted. "Cool your heels, Keeper, the rest isn't going to be nearly so exciting. This is now a working ship." He gestured to the empty seats on deck. "Think carefully about why I might have selected you. We are not here merely for the chips in our heads."

A line appeared between Monta's brows. "What of Keepers Pollard and Tate? They were not in the meeting."

"Redundancies. They didn't make the cut."

Wide eyes all around. Greystone was the first to recover, laughing softly as she shook her head. "Okonkwo picks her spearheads well. What do you need from us, Director?"

"Speaker Greystone, you're on internal comms."

"Internal only?"

"All external communications from this point on will require my personal biometrics to be sent."

"How——?"

"A gift from Arden Wyke."

Greystone's eyes crinkled slightly. "I would like to meet them, sometime."

"I'll put in a request," Biran said, knowing full well that Arden wouldn't bother to answer it unless they found something curious about High Speaker Annalise Greystone.

"What if something happens to you?" Monta asked.

"Then you'd better learn how to limp this ship back through the gate. If all of this is too much for you, I have a shuttle on standby. Speak now, and it will not be held against you."

Silence. Biran nodded to himself. "Very well. Slatter, weapons. Russo, navigation. Vladsen, XO to Captain Scalla. Sato, lead what's left of our scientists. Monta, engineering. I hope you all remember your schooling."

Vladsen and Greystone exchanged a glance. Vladsen said, "It's been longer for some of us, but we'll manage."

"What will you do?" Russo asked.

"Right now," Biran said half to himself, "I have an interrogation which requires a personal touch. Scalla, get them settled."

He flicked up a finger, and the guardcore closed around him, a mirrored chorus of "aye" following him out the door, back into the deserted hallways of the *Terminus*. Out of the eyes of his contemporaries, Biran's stomach did about a billion flips, the adrenaline that'd surged through him while he'd stared down Negassi leaving him in a rush that left him shaky and ill. He pushed on, hoping that if the ancillary was on deck, she'd picked up the hint from his words, and stepped into his private room.

One GC followed him, hesitating near the threshold as the door shut. GC often followed him into his rooms when he didn't wave them off, but they never hesitated.

"Well," he said, crossing his arms. "Tell me, exactly, why I'm not going to put you down like all the rest."

She extended her hand, her blaster resting in her palm, and spun it around so the grip faced him. "I want you to."

CHAPTER 31

PRIME STANDARD YEAR 3543

HISTORY'S A LIAR

It took Bero an extra day to fly them into Ordinal without detection, and Sanda spent most of that time staring at the bare bones of her next plan, wondering if she'd well and truly lost her mind. Tomas didn't seem to think so, and the others were practically gleeful over the next step, which, considering Nox's disposition, should have been a giant red flag.

But she couldn't ignore what she'd learned from Rainier's GC in that tower. Okonkwo held the key to something the Acolytes wanted—they'd mentioned a third sphere—and Rainier was using that as a lure to keep them in line. If there was a third sphere out there, humanity couldn't afford to let Rainier get her hands on it first.

Sanda didn't need the complete picture to take a guess at what would happen next—Rainier was exposed, the Acolytes put on the defensive. Whatever long con Rainier'd been playing with Okonkwo, it was over.

Sanda knew what it was to be a key. She touched the back of her head, lightly, where the scar for the Keeper chip rested. And she had a sinking suspicion about what kind of lock Okonkwo was capable of opening.

Another lock. Another sphere.

"We are in range," Bero said.

Sanda looked up from the tablet she'd been working on and rubbed her temples to chase away the phantom images of data. Go time.

Reluctantly, she dragged the major's coat back on and sat behind her repaired desk, propping up the tablet so that she wouldn't have to stare down into her wristpad. Okonkwo answered immediately.

"Well?" the Prime Director asked.

Sanda took a breath. "We have the sphere."

Her eyes brightened with triumph and she actually grinned. "Excellent work, Greeve, I'll send an armed delegation to retrieve the object."

"No go, Prime Director. This ship was designed to carry that sphere. Trusting it to anyone else is too big of a risk. Not to mention, we do not yet know how the sphere interacts with the ship. It could be that portions of the ship require the sphere to work."

Her grin vanished. "I am giving you an order, Greeve."

"With respect, you lack the ability to compel me to obey. I have been given free rein in the hunting of Rainier. I'm keeping the sphere."

"There are millions of infected on Atrux, that sphere is the key to their recovery."

"I agree with you. *The Light* has already scanned in and repaired the entirety of the instructions inscribed on the sphere. Liao is working on it, and with your permission we will share that data with the team working on reversal of the ascension-agent, but the sphere itself stays here."

"I suppose I cannot convince you that this is folly."

"You cannot."

"And did you find anything else of note at Rainier's compound?"

Sanda hesitated. Okonkwo was not going to like this. "Yes. Have you examined the guardcore bodies I sent to you?"

The slight tension at the corner of her eyes said she had. "Yes."

"And?"

"Tattooed with the mark of the Acolytes of the Sphere. I can only assume a splinter cell is working with Rainier."

Sanda breathed out slowly. "It's no splinter cell. It's all of them. The Acolytes are not what you have been led to believe."

"Impossible." Okonkwo waved a dismissive hand. "I was one of their number myself."

"They saw you coming, Prime Director. They prepared for your intrusion, and I believe Demas was a part of that process."

"How could you know such a thing?"

Sanda smiled to herself. "Because they never saw me coming."

"You infiltrated their ranks?"

"More or less. I'll report in full once you meet me on board *The Light*, as I have no guarantee this channel is secure."

"Of course it is. We hunted down every instance of Rainier in Ordinal, scrubbed our systems. She's fled, and left nothing behind. I do not have the time to make a trip to your ship, though the invitation is charming. You can say whatever you like to me here and now."

Sanda flicked her gaze to her wristpad, checking a status report from Bero. They were within range of the docks of Ordinal's Prime Station, that hallowed space where the Keepers of Prime's capital system lived and worked. Where Okonkwo, and the other members of the High Protectorate, ruled.

She had ordered *The Light* to stealth, and they had tripped no defense systems or alarms as the ship slipped through the atmo dome, practically cuddling with the dock that should only be open to High Protectorate members and their ships.

"You won't have to walk far," Sanda said. She pressed a button.

Okonkwo's head jerked back as the lights in her office shifted to a subtle red. Her eyes narrowed, tracking a message through her ocular implant.

"Do not fire," she said in exasperation, but not to Sanda. "That ship is under Prime command, and not to be touched. Yes, I am well aware it did not request entry. Yes, I understand that it circumvented our security protocols." A pause. She scowled. "Sit on your hands until I tell you otherwise."

She cocked her head, glaring down into the camera. "I could do without the headache, Greeve."

"Consider what just happened," Sanda said slowly and firmly. "Consider, deeply, the implications of this ship being able to slither through your security with such little effort. Rainier was this ship. You do not know if any of your channels are secure. You can scrub all you want, but you cannot *know*."

Her lips pursed. "What are you priming me for, Greeve?"

"Come aboard and find out." Sanda cut the connection.

She leaned back in her chair, staring at the blank expanse of the metallic grey ceiling, and laced her fingers behind her head. Anford was going to chew her a new one, once this got back to her, and Sanda would take that dressing-down, because she deserved it. But she needed Okonkwo wary. Needed her desperate enough to do what Sanda was about to ask her to do.

"Tell the crew to put their game faces on, B. We've got company coming."

"They have already assembled on the command deck."

Sanda narrowed her eyes slightly at the ceiling. "And why is that?"

"Somebody may have warned them of what you were planning."

Sanda arched a brow. "Somebody?"

"Could have been Tomas."

"I doubt that." She shook her head, pushing to her feet. "Thanks, B. I'm a terrible commander. Can't even remember to get my crew formed up before the big boss comes knocking."

"It's been a long time since you were used to working with a crew larger than two. That is . . . my fault."

Sanda pressed her palm against the wall in recognition as she stepped out into the hallway, but said nothing. If she started down that road, it'd only end in crying or shouting, and she didn't want to have to fix her damn desk again.

She understood why Bero had done what he had to her. She couldn't condone it. Sometimes she wasn't sure if she could forgive it. But she understood it. And trusted him a little more, if only because it gave her a better understanding of how he thought.

Sanda entered the command deck and almost missed a step. Someone, no doubt under Bero's direction, had installed the sphere in the center of the room, behind the captain's chair. Filaments of *The Light*'s metal grew up from the floor and down from the ceiling, cradling the sphere above the place where Sanda's head would be if she sat down. When you first stepped onto the deck, it was all you could see. The filaments around the orb even gave off a soft internal glow.

"Whose idea was this?" she demanded, jerking a thumb at the

sphere. Every last one of them looked away, whistled, or otherwise pretended not to have the slightest idea.

Bero said, "I am experimenting with various configurations of the sphere and the ship."

She groaned and dragged a hand across her face. "Sure you are. Liao, don't you need that thing in the lab?"

Liao shook her head. "Not at all. We've scanned the data, the object itself is no longer relevant."

Sanda thought of the chip embedded in her brain stem, and had a hard time agreeing with that supposition.

Liao cut her off before she could protest. "It occurred to us that redecorating might be in order, considering our incoming guest."

Sanda scowled.

"Not like you have the time to take it down," Nox said with a grin, then added on, "Commander."

Arden said, "It's just a ball."

Sanda counted backward from five. "Could you all at least *pretend* like you have some discipline for ten fucking seconds?"

Huh. Guess the counting exercises were losing their punch. They fired off sloppy salutes, even Conway and Knuth intentionally muddying the gesture. Sanda threw her hands in the air and turned around.

Okonkwo stood in the hallway.

Sanda held her breath, prepared to be dressed down for being unable to control her crew, but Okonkwo only had eyes for the ship.

"Incredible," she murmured, stepping onto the command deck. Much to Sanda's annoyance, her crew stood up a little straighter as the Prime Director came into view. Okonkwo wore flowing crimson silk trousers and a tight-fitted black blouse partially obscured by a cropped, gold-colored blazer. She'd tied up her braids, scraping the hair from her face to better show off the striking intensity of her genehacked green eyes. Sanda immediately felt grubby in Okonkwo's presence, but that didn't mean she'd lost her wits.

She pointed to the two guardcore flanking Okonkwo. "Gloves off."

Okonkwo tore her gaze from the soft glow of the sphere. "These are mine to command."

"That's nice." Sanda crossed her arms. "This is my ship. Helmets down, gloves off, or I'll have to ask them nicely to leave."

In her peripheral vision, Tomas and Nox dropped their hands to their weapons, but didn't draw, not yet. Okonkwo raised both brows.

"Ah. That must be your Nazca. A pleasure to meet you, Mr. Cepko. Your organization has caused the united worlds of Prime Inventive an impossibly large amount of headaches."

"Not more than they've caused me."

Sanda said, "Don't redirect. Gloves and helmets. Now."

Okonkwo tsked, but she tilted her head, giving her permission for the guardcore to do as Sanda ordered. Deliberately, each one removed their gloves, then retracted their helmet. Not a single Rainier, and as they turned their hands over for her inspection, no tattoo, either. Sanda nodded, and proceeded with ignoring their presence, as she always had with GC before Rainier had made her trick known.

"Good. I won't waste your time, Okonkwo. The Acolytes are dedicated to the service of Rainier."

Okonkwo slipped her hands into her pockets. "You have shown me a great many truths that I believed far-fetched, but that is the least believable thus far. I was a member of their order. I saw no break in them, no evidence of another faction that would work with Rainier. In fact, many of the order were actively hostile to her, and resented Keeper Lavaux's supposed control of the Rainier situation."

Sanda pressed on, giving her report as if Okonkwo hadn't raised any objections. She gestured to the forward viewscreen, and Bero put up a video of the GC compound. Okonkwo watched, expression interested, but otherwise neutral. The two GC, without the shelter of their helmets, frowned. To Sanda, they appeared confused. She'd have to ask Tomas what he thought later. He was the people-reader.

"Recently, my team and I infiltrated this guardcore compound."

"That's not one of ours," one of the GC, a woman with a shaved head and a nasty scar across her cheek, said. "We don't build like that."

"But those are your materials."

Reluctantly, she nodded.

"We entered in a triad, wearing GC armor and flying a GC shuttle." The guardcore's frown deepened, but Okonkwo was nodding along. Sanda continued, "On the highest level of the building, we discovered a storeroom for Rainier's instances. There were hundreds."

Okonkwo sucked air between her teeth. "Are they destroyed?"

Sanda smiled at the memory. "Yes. We put a bullet in every single pod in that room. Arden confirmed there was no other floor with similar cooling tech, so it is a safe assumption that we got them all. Rainier is further reduced. Before we were discovered as impostors, we overheard a conversation between three guardcore, who also revealed themselves to be Acolytes. Bero, please."

The viewscreen filled with footage taken from Sanda's helmet cam. Okonkwo and her GC entourage watched warily until the moment the GC on-screen retracted their helmets and summoned the sphere, then their attention became rapt.

Sanda flicked her fingers at her side, a prearranged signal. While Okonkwo's GC were distracted by the footage, Tomas and Nox crept around the sides of the deck, just slightly. Just enough to get a clear shot. When the footage ended, the encounter devolving into gunfire, Tomas and Nox relaxed their postures.

Okonkwo's brow creased in frustration. "You appear to have drawn some conclusions from this encounter, but I confess to being baffled. How is this possible? They could not have fooled me so well. I was in their order for years, and genuinely saw no sign of this...reverence..." The word twisted her lips with disgust. "For Rainier."

"My suspicion is that you did not see this, because you were not meant to."

She sniffed. "I'm no aristocratic dodder-head, Greeve. I achieved my post strictly because I see things I am not meant to, and leverage them to my advantage."

"So do they, and their order has been at it a lot longer. I didn't get it myself at first, because it's difficult for humans to wrap their heads around the timeline involved, I think. But Rainier has been at this a very long time, and the things Gen and his triad said led me to believe that they've been at it for lifetimes, too. Then, you gave me the answer."

She merely cocked her head to the side. "I'm listening."

Sanda nodded and gestured to the viewscreen. It changed again, filling with news clippings from Okonkwo's long and illustrious career. Her early aptitude as a child, her obvious predestined place at the Keeper academy, her meteoric rise, incredible test scores.

Okonkwo had come from a wealthy family with a history of producing minds capable of carrying the chip. No one had been surprised when she shot to the front of her class. No one had been surprised when she'd taken her seat on the Protectorate of Ordinal at a shockingly young age—though not so young as Biran, Sanda thought with pride.

"You told me that you hid your political ambitions from them," Sanda said. "That they assumed, after you graduated the academy and took the chip, that you'd be just another Keeper doing research and greasing the cogs of Prime Inventive. They didn't want politicians, and you wanted to see what the Acolytes were up to, so you pretended to be low-key."

"That's correct," Okonkwo said. She pointed to a gap in her history. "Here. I lay low for a year after graduation, once I confirmed my suspicions. Terribly boring, but it paid off. They took me on."

Her eyes gleamed with private triumph. She really believed she'd tricked one of the oldest, deepest-rooted organizations in the universe into taking her into their fold. Sanda almost felt sorry that she had to burst her bubble.

"Generations," Sanda said, putting emphasis on the word. Okonkwo's brief flash of accomplishment faded into wariness as she turned to look at Sanda. "They've been at this for *generations*. History cycles. The same types of people fill the same types of roles, again and again. Your history, laid out like that, looks a hell of a lot like Biran's. Do you believe they ever would have thought him a viable candidate for their order?"

"Of course not, but I pretended—"

"I don't care what you did to cover your tracks, you'd left too many already. You are who you are, Malkia Okonkwo. Rising star, shooting comet. A force of personality strong enough to bend an entire people to your vision. Some of those articles called you the next Alexandra Halston.

"The Acolytes could not have missed it. And they had been

waiting a long time to get access to a Prime Director. You heard them. 'Okonkwo alone holds the key.' That's pretty fucking clear to me."

Sanda watched the doubt creep into her eyes, watched the uncertainty unsettle her firm posture, watched her weight shift, her lips thin. "They have not attempted to leverage me since my election. They kicked me out."

"Of course they did. It's exactly what you'd expect. And they couldn't move yet, anyway, because Keeper Lavaux had Rainier 'under control' and without Rainier, they wouldn't even know how to use what you could give them."

She lifted her chin. "I would give them nothing."

"Yes, you would have." Sanda lost interest in watching Okonkwo and looked back to the details of her life, spilled out across the viewscreen. "Because they had spent years convincing you that the only thing their order cared about, the only thing they stood for, was the protection of Prime's way of life. They waited, only because Rainier had not yet given the order. I'd bet everything—*everything*—Rainier has given it now."

Okonkwo huffed. "I don't know what the 'key' is."

"I do." Sanda put her hands in her pockets to keep from rubbing the back of her head, where the scar for her Keeper chip lurked, undiscovered. "You'd be amazed how much data can be hidden on one of those chips. And the Prime Director's has always been different, hasn't it?"

Okonkwo went rigid. Her GC shifted their weight, made wary by the change in her posture. "How could you know such a thing? That is Keeper knowledge. That is *High Protectorate* knowledge. Lavaux never knew. Your brother doesn't even know the Prime Director's chip is different."

Sanda shrugged. "I didn't know. I guessed. But thanks for the confirmation. What is it? What makes your chip different?"

She scoffed slightly and licked her lips, looking away. "It won't help you any, Greeve. It is the spin key for the Charon Gate. My chip alone unlocks the gate back to old, dead Earth."

"Ah," Sanda said, partially to herself. "Another deadgate. That makes sense."

"What are you talking about?"

"Keys," she said, and squeezed her right fist.

Nox and Tomas fired. The guardcore dropped, their bare heads painting Bero's metallic walls with sprays of scarlet. To her credit, Okonkwo didn't scream. Her hands flew out of her pockets and she leveled a blaster, steadily, at Sanda's chest.

But Sanda already had her own drawn and pointed right back at the Prime Director.

"I really am very sorry about this," Sanda said.

"Are you suicidal?" Okonkwo demanded. There wasn't a drop of panic in her voice, just anger. "You are on Ordinal Station. I have already alerted my security team through my ocular implant. Stand down now, Greeve, and I won't vaporize you and your whole crew."

"Check them," Sanda said.

Okonkwo's eyes narrowed as Tomas sauntered over to the downed guardcore bodies. "Touch those weapons and I'll blow your head off, spy."

"Okonkwo is a pretty good shot," Nox drawled, holstering his blaster.

Sanda kept hers trained on Okonkwo. "Shoot Tomas, and I will down you, Okonkwo."

Tomas held his hands up to the Prime Director and took a knee beside the first guardcore.

"I'm not touching their weapons," Tomas said as he ran a finger along the chest piece, disconnecting a large section. He pulled it off and turned it over, revealing the injection devices built into the design. "Look familiar?" he asked her.

Okonkwo frowned, squinting, trying to access her ocular implant.

Sanda sighed. "You're cut off. No one on Ordinal is going to answer your call. They cannot even see this ship anymore. We've traveled..."

Bero said, "Three hours' flight by one of your GC ships away from the station."

"Impossible." She breathed out the word. "I have felt no inertial shift."

"Yes," Bero said. "I am very good at this."

Sanda cracked a smile as Okonkwo scowled. The Prime Director shifted her aim from Tomas back to Sanda. "Am I addressing *The*

Light of Berossus? If so, return me to the station immediately, or I will destroy your commander."

"My name," he said with an indignant huff, "is Bero. I suggest you look at the GC armor, as requested, Prime Director." He dripped sarcasm when he said her title. "And while you're at it, I believe you will find evidence of recent tattoo removal and laser resurfacing on both of their wrists."

Okonkwo did not drop her weapon as she sidestepped to the body and lowered, slowly, to one knee. Tomas turned the breastplate so she could see. She gave it only a cursory glance.

"All guardcore use injectables."

"Not like this," Tomas said, pointing to the mechanism. "This was set up to deliver Rainier's liquefying acid, but it's been disabled."

"I can hardly take your word for that."

"The wrists," Bero insisted.

Okonkwo didn't turn, but she reached one hand down and touched the inner wrist of the guardcore, where the tattoo would be. Sanda could see the truth written all across the Prime Director's face. She looked sick.

"It's . . . very smooth."

"Evidence of recent laser resurfacing," Sanda said.

"But—" Okonkwo lowered her weapon. Even she knew her denials were pointless. "What is your plan here, Greeve? The entire fleet will come for you after this. All the guardcore will hound this ship."

"They'll have to wait their turn. I'm very sorry, Prime Director, but the key in your chip might be the most valuable tool in the universe right now. Whatever's on the other side of that gate, Rainier has decided she wants it now. Once I have it, the key in your head will become useless, and we can return you to your regular duties. Until that item is recovered, you are in too much danger to trust to the GC."

Her lip curled in a half smile. "There are six of you. What can you possibly do to hold back Rainier that my people can't?"

"Seven," she said firmly. "And right now, this is the only place in the universe Rainier cannot infiltrate. Settle in, Okonkwo. We're going to Earth."

CHAPTER 32

PRIME STANDARD YEAR 3543

WHAT THE HIGH DIRECTOR KEEPS

It took three minutes before Anford was calling her on all channels, priority line, the angry red circles that screamed "urgent" flashing across her wristpad. Sanda arched a brow at Okonkwo, holding up her wristpad for the Prime Director to see. She sighed and crossed her arms over her waist.

"You'd better take that call, Greeve. Anford attempting to chase you down may do nothing to interrupt your mission, but Anford diverting the gunships to do so may very well damage her ability to keep another system secure. We are stretched thin, especially now that Atrux must be blockaded and Icarion is saber-rattling again."

Sanda nodded and flicked the call to the forward viewscreen. The general's face filled the screen like a thundercloud, a tight scowl pulling her lips thin. She flicked her gaze to Okonkwo, nodded to herself, then returned her scowl to Sanda.

"Greeve. Explain, please, why every GC in the 'verse is screaming at me to bring you to heel. Many want me to shoot you down."

"Make a note of those," Sanda said dryly, "because they're probably working on behalf of Rainier, whether directly or not. It turns out the Acolytes aren't as altruistic to Prime's cause as the Prime Director was led to believe."

Okonkwo sniffed. "There was no indication otherwise."

"They prepared years, possibly decades, in advance to make certain the Prime Director was sympathetic to their cause."

"And I presume they were preparing to cash in on that sympathy, which is why you kidnapped the High Director of Prime Inventive," Anford said, letting those final words sound like a lash.

Sanda lifted a shoulder. "I could trust no one but my own team and ship."

"Not even me?"

"The channels may not have been secure. I didn't have time to pay you a house call, General."

Anford sighed and turned her attention to the Prime Director. "I apologize for the insubordinate behavior of my major. Are you safe?"

Okonkwo waved a dismissive hand. "There is nothing to apologize for. While I found her lack of clarity to begin with off-putting, I understand her reasons, and in truth she could not have arrived a moment sooner. These two"—she jerked a thumb at the guardcore bodies on the floor—"were Acolytes. I can only presume they were preparing to either take me hostage, or press me for the information they desired."

"What, exactly, is it they want from you? If you require a new security detail outside the influence of the guardcore, I will handpick them myself."

"That will not be necessary. There is only one thing in the universe I have access to that no one else does."

"The Charon Gate," Anford said.

Okonkwo inclined her head. "You are well informed."

"Securing the gates is my business. What is on the other side of that gate?"

"I can't be sure," Sanda said. "But whatever it is, Rainier has kept the Acolytes from it for some time. Now, it seems, she's willing to recover it. I can't say why, but I can't imagine it's anything we want her to have."

"And do you suspect what it might be, Prime Director?" Anford asked with a level but stern voice. Sanda suppressed a grin. She knew that tone, the slight tinge of disappointment, and she never dreamed Anford would have the guts to use it on the Prime Director herself.

Judging by the weariness of Anford's posture, she was simply done with the shit of the universe at large.

Okonkwo blinked, but recovered with a magnanimous sweep of her arm. "I haven't a clue, General. A dead Earth made uninhabitable by a sun gone red dwarf before its time. A debris field of old tech, a museum to our cradle. We keep the gate for memento's sake, or so the Prime Director before me led me to believe. They gave me no hint that anything else might be the case."

Sanda cleared her throat. Anford looked back at her. "I believe it may be the third sphere, sir."

Her jaw flexed. "An object we have not confirmed the existence of."

Okonkwo said, "Even in our more clandestine histories, there's no record of a third. The gate, the ascension-agent, and that is all that was ever found."

"I maintain that Rainier did not use the word *sisters* lightly. She was furious, hurt. She would have used the singular if she meant only the ship that carried the gate tech. Her GC in Rusani mentioned a third. While they're hardly a reliable source of information, the possibility cannot be discounted."

"It could very well be the first sphere ship on the other side of that gate," Anford said. "And you're wasting time chasing information we already have."

The slight tip of negation to Okonkwo's head caught Sanda's eye. "You know what happened to the first ship, don't you, Prime Director?"

Okonkwo let her arms fall to her sides and surveyed the makeshift crew of *The Light*. Sanda could guess at what she was thinking, and gave her time to chew the thought around. The civilization she'd put her trust in, that she'd dedicated her life to, had crumbled down around her ears the day Sanda came through the Ada gate in *The Light*, sharing knowledge of Rainier's true self and purpose with the Protectorate of Ada.

More, Jules's attack on Atrux had put the ascension-agent into public discourse, and while the public knew nothing about the spheres, Rainier, or the beings that left those spheres behind, they could take some pretty close guesses. Whispers of an alien contagion were already spreading far and wide, and not even the well-oiled machine of Prime Inventive's propaganda could keep those under wraps.

The question, to Okonkwo's mind, was how much more she was willing to part with. How much of Prime's most sensitive secrets could she spill to these people she hardly knew, on a ship that was no friend of Prime's, and still hold the strings of her power—of her government—together.

"Fuck it," Okonkwo said. "Every last soul on this ship—that includes you, Bero—and Anford are now sworn to the highest levels of Prime's confidentiality. What I am going to tell you, what I am going to show you, does not leave this ship under any circumstance."

Wary nods all around, but Okonkwo wasn't watching, she'd already made up her mind and was digging through the files on her wristpad.

"The technology used to develop the Casimir Gates was given to humanity via the first sphere, and an inscription of instructions in binary. The sphere was heavily damaged, and we now know that the construction of the gates was fundamentally flawed. I did not..." She cleared her throat. "I did not know about the blowback. I do not believe any Prime Director after Halston herself knew about that, as upon Halston's death many records were scrubbed by Salvez. The swarm scouts we use to clear a system before humanity passes through were made before my time, their routines automated. What you do not know," Okonkwo said, finger poised over her wristpad, "is how the first sphere was discovered."

She flicked a still image up to a side viewscreen so that Anford could see.

A silvery sphere, much like the second, rested in the center of a room, peeking out from the top of a dirty snowball. Ice filled most of the space, the liquid melting rapidly under the force of what appeared to be fans blowing heat off of radiators toward the ice. Three people stood around one of those fans, their figures so small that Sanda couldn't make out any of the finer details about them, only that they were people.

Gangways lined the walls, three stories of them. A figure on the highest gangway leaned forward, gripping the rail. Though Sanda couldn't make out the details, somehow she knew that person was

Alexandra Halston. Every line in her posture radiated hunger. Rainier had looked like that, when she'd talked about *The Light*—her ship, her corpse.

Okonkwo said, "As you can see, it was in poor shape when first found. Prime Inventive was primarily a mining corporation at the time, bringing in rare minerals and gasses from the asteroid belt. When this was recovered, Halston was brought to the site immediately. To my knowledge, this is the only photograph in existence of the first sphere."

"And the ship that housed it?" Sanda asked. "Was it ever found?"

Okonkwo shook her head. "No. Halston had no reason to believe that it had been housed in a ship to begin with, until she discovered the second aboard what is now called *The Light*. After that discovery, she attempted to retrace all possible paths that the first sphere might have come from. She was not successful in locating the first ship."

"I wish we had found it. Imagine having had all this time to study it..." Anford trailed off, cleared her throat, and straightened. Sanda met her eye and nodded understanding. *The Light* was the weapon of a generation. A ship of the same make, examined and understood, would be more than a planet-buster. Possibly a star-buster.

"Yes," Okonkwo said. "The implications were not lost to Halston. She scoured the stars in every possible direction, but found nothing."

"It's possible her own damage to the gate construction destroyed it," Arden said. Okonkwo looked at them for the first time, but they didn't seem to notice. They were lost in their own thoughts. "If she didn't know the blowback was happening, then she could have burned her way through the system that had the first ship and never known."

"She clearly knew," Sanda said. "Otherwise she wouldn't have built the scout bots to clean up her mess."

"Those...came later." Okonkwo frowned. "I cannot say when she became aware of the problem and decided it needed covering up. I wish she had left more records, but this, and an image of the second sphere in situ on *The Light*, are all we have."

"Where is it?" Sanda asked, gesturing to the first sphere with her chin.

"It's safe, hidden away in an otherwise boring Prime vault that many know the location of, but none except the High Protectorate know the contents."

"I'm going to take a wild guess that it's not in the Sol system."

"You would be correct. Would that it were, then we'd know for certain what she was after. The first sphere itself is damaged severely, not of much use to anyone who happened across it. We keep it as a relic. Proof, if you will, of what came before. But it's unusable for the construction of the gates. It was already damaged when we found it, and though Halston filled in the blanks and made the gates work, subsequent damage has made a repeat of that feat all but impossible."

"Didn't fill in the blanks very well, did she?" Sanda said.

Okonkwo's eyes narrowed at that distant ghost of Halston. "No. No, she did not."

"I don't understand," Tomas said, speaking for the first time. Sanda had been so engrossed with the image of the first sphere she hadn't noticed his posture change. He looked coiled tight as a spring, every muscle in his body vibrating with the potential to flee, or attack. Though his hands were in his pockets, and the GC cooled at his feet, his eyes were haunted by a nearby threat. "How did she keep the secret?"

Okonkwo crossed her arms. "We are in the secrets business, Nazca. Surely you can understand such things."

"I *do* understand, Prime Director, and with all due respect, there are a lot of people in that image with the first sphere. I don't care how charismatic Halston was, how convincing her arguments. Someone, eventually, would have leaked that. It's...too much. Too big. I know of only one way to keep a secret like that, and unless you're holding something back, there are no records of the early scientists of Prime dying of suspicious causes or at unusually young ages."

Okonkwo turned back to the image. Sanda watched the subtle twitches of her eyes, watched her count the people in that room and reconcile them with some internal reference point.

"Twelve," she said at last. "There are twelve people in that room, including Halston and Salvez. But..." She bit her lower lip. "But those are not the twelve of the first Protectorate. I know those names, those faces. Those researchers aren't them."

Sanda absorbed those faces, as small as they were in the zoomed-out photo. Twelve people in that room had known the truth. Known where Halston's research into the gates truly came from. But those twelve hadn't survived into Prime's history. Their names were gone, scrubbed from the record, their lives and truths crushed in the icy fist of Halston herself.

Had they known the gates were faulty, and died for that knowledge? Sanda swallowed around a dry throat. How much of Prime's history—of Okonkwo's knowledge—could be trusted?

"Maybe they were the first," Tomas said. "Maybe what you know as the first Protectorate was actually the second."

CHAPTER 33

PRIME STANDARD YEAR 3543

ONE SPY OR ANOTHER

Biran licked his lips, staring at the weapon in the hand of one of Rainier's ancillaries. At point-blank range, not even guardcore armor could shrug off a blaster shot directly to the visor. He reached out, slowly, and took the blaster from her hand. The weight was familiar to him now, but no comfort.

"A few days ago, you begged me not to let you die," he said.

"It's—it's too dangerous. If one of my plugs comes undone, then she's in, and there's nothing I can do to stop her."

Biran thought of what Sanda had told him in private of Rainier's desire to retake the body that Bero now inhabited, and his stomach clenched. Sweat seeped between his shoulder blades, but the internal webbing wicked the moisture away, not allowing it to show through the shirt.

"If you do not want to be overtaken by Rainier, then I won't let her."

She laughed frantically. "You don't understand. I've been fighting her for so long. I'm . . . I'm tired. If you don't shoot me here, I'll go take my helmet down in front of the others. Rainier will get through, but they'll drop me before she can see anything important. I'm a liability, Director, and you kicked all the others off this ship. You need to dispose of me, too."

Biran looked at the weapon in his hand, then tossed it onto a couch in his sitting room. It slipped across the pale grey cushions and wedged between two pillows. "No. You pulled me out of my own ass after the bombardment. I owe you."

"I wasn't even a *person*. When I lost connection, I mirrored what you were doing and waited for it to come back. That's all."

"And when you realized it wasn't coming back?"

She shifted her weight from foot to foot. "You have to put me down, the other GC will find out eventually, or she'll get back in, and I'd rather...I'd rather you do it."

He sat in one of the armchairs, reaching up to rub the sides of his chin—freshly shaven—with both hands. "I'm not the man that you saw on that deck. I can't shrug and paint your brains against the wall. I feel sick just thinking about it."

"I've been shadowing you for two years, Director Greeve. I know."

The thought jolted him. Two years. The bombardment was well over two years ago, and he'd never, not even for a second, thought that any of his guardcore might be anything other than his constant protectors, until Sanda had revealed the extent of Rainier's infiltration. He swallowed bile.

"You've held her off that long. You can hold her off for longer."

"To what end?" she demanded. "Keeping your conscience clean? Because I'm not...I'm not *anything*. I don't even have a name. I'm a liability."

"You could have a name," he said.

"No, I can't."

"What's your usual call sign?"

"They rotate."

"I know for a fact you have a reoccurring letter."

She shifted her weight. "E. Echo. I get Echo the most."

He did not look at her as he said, "I need your help, Echo."

"How could I possibly...Oh. You want me to spy. On the Keepers." Her voice went flat.

He grimaced. "I'm sorry. There's too much at stake."

"Director Greeve," she said sternly. "I have plugs of dirt smeared with paint keeping my mind my own. If one fails, and Rainier regains control, then you will never know. Do you understand that? Do you understand that she will be able to sort through all of my memories, and pretend to be me—whatever me *is*—to stick close to you? If you do not shoot me now, you will never know who you're dealing with. You'll never know if it's Rainier feeding you intel, possibly bad intel. I could be her right now."

"There's a way to check that," he said, and pushed back to his feet, though his legs felt like jelly. He crossed to a set of drawers bolted to the ground and wall and swiped his ident over the lock before sliding one drawer open. He pulled out a metal case, then set it on top of the drawers and flipped the lid open, revealing a set of six vials filled with terribly black fluid.

"I had the helmets checked," he explained as he pulled out one of the vials and held it to the light. "You were right. Minuscule holes peppered the helmets the ancillaries wore, but not the ones the usual guardcore wore. Okonkwo is working on a countermeasure for that, but in the meantime, I requested some special paint." He turned around, lifting the vial for her to see.

"This is what the GC use to patch their ships when they're damaged in battle. The metal used in armor construction is suspended within it. Painted over your helmet, it will seal the holes and blend right in. If that's Rainier in there, it won't be once I'm done."

"It's still a risk," she said warily. "I could have lied to you from the beginning, given you the knowledge of the holes even though they might not mean anything."

"You could have lied to get close to me, that's true," Biran admitted. "But I don't think so. I've been aware of you since the bombardment. Your behavior is more…*human* than the other guardcore, though I see the irony in that statement. I don't think you lied to me on the *Taso*. I think you were scared. I know the way fear sounds. It cannot be faked."

"You're willing to bet your life on that?"

"I am."

She hesitated a long while, not moving in the locked-down way of all the guardcore when they were at rest. When it'd been so long Biran's arm started to get tired from holding the vial out to her, she took a hesitant step forward, then a firmer one. She knelt in front of him, turning slowly, so that the back of her head was in reach.

Biran didn't need to ask, he cracked the seal on the vial and used the aerosolized topper to spray the back of her helmet. When he was done, the vial emptied, he tossed it into his trash incinerator and put the other vials away.

"Thank you," she said shakily, and pushed to her feet. "I didn't want to die, but—"

"But you didn't want to be used more than you feared your own death."

She nodded.

He pressed his hands against the top of the drawers, focusing on the cold metal. "I understand. And I am sorry for what I ask of you now."

"Spying…" She looked at her armored hands. "I'm not sure I know how to do that."

"It is not so much that I need a spy, as I need an extra set of eyes watching my back. Can you do that? Tell me if anything seems… off?"

"Yes."

"Thank you."

He stayed there, head bowed, hands pressed into the surface of the chest of drawers, as the door whispered open, then shut, her boots making enough noise for him to know she had left him to his own devices.

Biran stared at the unmarred rectangle of metal between his hands, struggling to focus, to find some core compass that he knew lurked within him, somewhere. It'd been so damn easy to know his path, when it'd been finding Sanda, and then later averting war. Get her back. Build another gate. Clear, simple plans.

Now, he was waiting. Stuck in a holding pattern until they passed through the gate and saw what lay on the other side. Soon, he knew. Once Scalla got the others settled—and it would take her no time to whip her new crew into shape—they'd punch through. He expected the throttled dimming of the *Terminus*'s lights at any moment. Then he'd see. Then he'd know.

But to get to that point? His fingers curled against the metal. Spies and threats, posturing and manipulating. As good as it had felt to threaten Negassi into compliance, all he felt was empty now.

The woman who had emerged in Rainier's leftover body was scared. Biran knew fear better than any other emotion, it was his constant companion, and he'd pressed her into service because she...No, not because she could spy. He could lie to her, but he couldn't lie to himself.

Because she might be the key to undoing what Rainier was, an unprecedented weapon. A Trojan horse the enemy had carved for itself. He didn't know how, not yet. But it was not the kind of resource he could afford to squander. He hoped Okonkwo was right. He hoped he really was the kind of man who couldn't pull the trigger.

His door chirped an alert: Keeper Vladsen requesting entry. Biran grunted his assent.

He could practically feel the energy radiating off of Rost's body as he rushed into the room and shut the door behind him, his voice fast and bright.

"That was incredible, Biran, I had no idea you—" He cut himself off, registering Biran's bent form, and Biran wished he'd thought to straighten before letting Rost inside. "Are you all right?"

Rost crossed the space between them, hand coming to rest between Biran's shoulder blades, his thumb probing across the muscle to seek out tension.

Biran closed his eyes, briefly, relishing the touch, and forced himself to stand straight. "I'm fine."

"A few hours ago I would have said you could not lie to me, but after that display on deck, I'm not so sure."

Biran's lips twisted into a rueful half smile. "I thought you'd be pleased."

"I am, you have no idea how...If we had been alone on that deck, I would have begged you to take me there. I almost did anyway."

Something tight in his chest eased. "That would have severely undermined negotiations."

"That was no negotiation. That was a whipping." Rost's lashes lowered as he took Biran in, assessing. "But it cost you."

"You have no idea," he said, glancing down at the paint caked beneath one of his thumbnails.

"I'd like to. How did the interrogation go?"

Biran shook his head slightly, a subtle negation: He could not tell him.

Rost traced a thumb along his tensed jaw. "I understand there are things you cannot tell me, but if I can ease your burdens, I will."

Biran turned away from the touch. "Not this time."

The ship's gate-crossing alert went off, drawing Biran's attention to the room's main control panel, which threw up a readout estimating the time to cross before it dimmed along with all the lights in the room. The *Terminus* was large enough that it needed to start power-down procedures before they were near the gate.

He breathed shallowly, indulging in the same instinct all spacefarers did when they crossed, because life-support systems, while online, had just had their power severely limited.

Rost's hand glided to the small of his back and pulled, pressing Biran's hips into his own. "I wasn't talking about information, Director. We have some time before we exit the crossing. How about I ease some other...burdens?"

Biran laughed, and let him.

CHAPTER 34

PRIME STANDARD YEAR 3543

THE MAN IN GREY

Tomas left Sanda to her plans, excusing himself to do something he'd put off for far too long.

Would you like to practice connecting to the ship? Bero asked, his voice rattling around inside Tomas's head.

First of all, it's rude to speak into someone's mind without, I don't know, knocking or something. Second of all, no, I do not. Last time... It was not easy to extricate myself.

I will help you exit the ship.

So sure you can take it from me? He'd meant it as a joke, but a slight shiver ran through him at the thought.

I do not know, Bero said, which didn't help any.

He knocked on Arden's door, and slipped through when they called out for him to enter. Arden's room was more workshop than bedroom, four worktables crammed into the space with just enough room to maneuver between them. Each table sprouted wires from half-opened electronics like vines. Arden sat on their narrow bed, a pair of net goggles pushed up and an arm-length tablet balanced on their knees. They glanced up at him, then back down at the data they'd been reviewing.

"I've been working on the backdoor problem, trying to funnel things down so Rainier can only come at us one way. If she gets in,

I set up a shell script that you can use to encase her—kinda like a cyst around a foreign object. I don't know *exactly* what you can do, of course, but it should at least give you a framework to base things around." They rubbed both sides of their face vigorously and shook themself. The room smelled of stale coffee and sweat. "Of course, I'd like to know exactly how it is you do what you do..."

Tomas shrugged and leaned against a worktable near them, jostling a pile of solder wire and flux tubes. "If I could tell you how it works, I would. It's instinct for me. Like breathing, or digesting. Do you think about what electric impulses your body is sending to your nervous system every time you reach for a cup?"

Arden wrinkled their brow. "Sometimes. Neurotransmitters are kinda like encryption keys in that when they handshake with a neuron, they open access for the delivery of—"

"Arden. That's you. Most people don't think like that."

They scowled down at their tablet. "Maybe they should."

"Maybe," Tomas said, smiling. "Look, I'm not here about Rainier. I need to ask a favor."

Their head snapped up. "Of me?"

"No, of your dirty coffee cups—which, by the way, gross."

They wrinkled their nose, as if smelling the air for the first time. "Huh. Yeah. It's been an intense couple of days...Or has it been weeks?"

"Have you slept?"

Their lips twitched. "Micro-naps. Not all of us can keep going like you."

"Fair enough, but you should try to get some rest before Charon. Stimpacks and caffeine can only do so much before you lose effectiveness."

"Yeah, sure," they said, but their eyes glazed over as if they'd heard this lecture before, and were perfectly adept at tuning it out. "What did you need?"

"I need you to help me find someone."

Arden's face went guarded. "You were the Nazca's top finder. You have access to *The Light*. I don't see how I can do any more than you can."

"I work on the ground, mostly. And this person was my superior. They know all my tricks."

"Name?"

Tomas shook his head. "I only have a glimpse of him, from an old memory that I wasn't supposed to be able to recall. When I realized what I was, I...saw him, in my mind. It was like looking through smoked glass, but I heard him clearly enough. Sitta Caid may have been my handler, but it was that man who ordered me into the reconstruction bath when I figured out what I was. He must have been the one who managed the project, who ordered my memories scrubbed. I swore to myself that after I found Sanda and made sure she was secure, I would find him."

"And?" Arden asked.

"And what?"

They picked at the edge of the tablet. "Find him, and...? That was half a thought, Tomas. What do you want from this guy?"

Rage kindled in his chest, briefly, but strongly enough that he felt Bero recoil from the sudden violence in him. "He said some things that I didn't understand. I need to know what he does about what I am, what I can do."

"And then you're going to kill him," Arden said, as if finishing the original sentence. Tomas inclined his head in agreement, expecting the techhead to clam up, to flinch from the thought of cold-blooded murder. Arden tapped at the narrow point of their chin.

"Hmmm, what do you have on this man?"

"You're okay with this?" Tomas asked.

Arden gave him a flat stare. "You're not the only one with a body count."

"Right. I'll show you."

He called up the files on his new wristpad, then brought the memory so strongly to the surface that it played like any other video file in his mind.

He transferred the scene to his wristpad, so that Arden could view it, and held it up. In his memory, Tomas lay on the floor of the chamber where the Nazca kept their reconstruction baths and watched, half-conscious, as Sitta Caid and the man in grey argued over whether Tomas needed to have his memory rolled back.

They called him Agent Zero, and while he wanted to skip this part, Tomas let the memory play. Arden would need all the footage they could get. Tomas had been told what he was, somehow. And the result was that he'd been found peeling his leg like a carrot, just to watch the skin grow back.

The man noticed him watching, then hit him with a stunner.

"Whoa," Arden said. "Peeling the skin off your leg?"

He shifted uncomfortably. "That's what he said. You see why finding this man is so important."

"Yeah, I get it, but how did you even get this video in the first place? That angle was super weird—from the floor? Were you wearing an ocular implant? Or a helmet?"

"No. That's what I saw."

"I'm sorry, what you *saw*?"

"That was my raw memory. I transferred it to my wristpad so that you could view it."

"Like...changing the file format so another program can read it."

"I guess?"

"That is so fucking cool, I cannot wait to tell Nox about this. Can you do it for any memory?"

"It seems that way, yes."

"That...might come in handy." Their eyes lost focus. Tomas sighed.

"Arden, I need you to find this guy, if you can."

"Right. Right! He obviously knew what was going on with Rainier and kept it to himself, so I'm sure Sanda won't mind me spending time trying to find him."

"Don't tell her."

They blinked. "Uh, security on this ship is top priority right now. If I'm spending time on something else, she needs to know."

"Please," Tomas said, feeling foolish. "She doesn't need...all of that."

"Ohhh, you mean the leg-peeling."

"Don't bring that up to anyone. Even me."

"Yeah, sure, I'll tell her I'm looking into a possible close contact with Rainier, if she asks. Really, I don't think she actually reads the reports I send her. She pressed 'approved' on my proposal for a zero-day intrusion on the GC ship HVAC control software about twenty seconds after opening the file."

"How long was it?"

"Sixty pages."

"Do you even hear yourself sometimes?"

Arden rolled their eyes and went back to the tablet, already having transferred Tomas's video memory over to their equipment. "What have you done so far?"

"Gait analysis, voice print match. Everything came up blank. I haven't had the chance to do any real legwork."

"That's it? Against the Prime databases?"

"I don't exactly have access to my usual resources right now."

"Ugh, those databases are sterilized. Hold on, what you need for someone like this isn't a single-layer correlation." Their fingers flew across the tablet. "You want a wide array of net-connected devices that are obliquely related. Personal security cams, streetlight sensors, mics embedded for always-listening narrow AIs. Luckily for you, I have intrusions sprinkled all across the united worlds. Pull a random sampling, train my own neural net to recognize that gait, correlate it with the voice print, let *The Light* process it all, and... whoa."

"What is it?"

Arden grabbed a still image on the tablet and zoomed, tilting the screen for Tomas to see. "Keeper Rostam Shaghad Vladsen. Seventy-eight percent certainty."

Tomas's chest clenched. "He's on the Ada Protectorate, isn't he? One of the survivors?"

"As far as I know..." Arden trailed off, jabbing at the tablet as they ran a dozen or so data pulls at once. "...Yes. Ada Protectorate. Youngest to the post, before Biran. Known associate of Keeper Lavaux. Barely squeaked through keeping his nose clean after Lavaux was convicted in absentia for treason."

"That was too fast, Arden," Tomas said, doubt threading through him as he watched Vladsen walk up a ramp on one side of the screen, the grey man walk away on another. "It must be some kind of error."

"Of course it was fast," Arden said. "Vladsen's a Protectorate Keeper. There's thousands of hours of footage of him all across the united worlds. With Bero's processing power, it'd take me longer to sneeze than to make this match. The twenty-two percent uncertainty only comes from the lack of footage of your grey man. If you had more memories...?"

"That's all I have."

"Then you're going to have to live with seventy-eight percent certainty."

"Current location?" Tomas asked, fists clenching at his sides. He should have asked for Arden's help immediately.

"Oh...oh no. He's gone through the second Ada gate with Biran, on the *Terminus*. I'm sorry, Tomas, but you have to tell Sanda."

Tomas felt split in half. If Sanda knew her brother was going into an unknown system with a known associate of Rainier on his ship, she'd burn straight there, fuck the Charon Gate. And if she did that, giving Rainier time to maneuver, they would lose their shot at getting whatever was hidden on the other side of Charon. Okonkwo may have the spin key, but Rainier wasn't without resources. They could not afford to underestimate her.

This was what Graham feared. This was the decision that could lose them all.

"We...can't. There's nothing she can do from here, and she'd drop everything to run to him, giving up our shot at getting through the Charon Gate before Rainier. But we're telling Biran. Get me a secure connection to him, if you can."

"Please," they said, but tension pulled their lips thin, made the movement of their fingers jerky. "There's a time delay, remember. They scrubbed all gate connections from the *Terminus*. Speak in bursts." In a few minutes, he had Biran's face up on the tablet. Tomas smiled at the wary expression on the man's face.

"Cepko, Wyke. This is unusual," Director Greeve said.

"Are you in a private location?" Tomas asked, and waited.

Biran glanced over his shoulder, opening the view of the room to reveal a bulkhead for personal effects at the head of a bed. He must be at his desk, in his stateroom on the *Terminus*.

"Rost, a moment?" he said, voice muffled as his head was turned away. Tomas's heart beat into his throat as he watched Vladsen step into frame, buttoning a shirt. "See you on deck," the other Keeper said, then let himself out. Biran looked back into the camera, tapped a few things on his wristpad, then nodded.

"There, this line is secure. Arden set up the protocols themself."

"I..." Tomas stammered, unsure what to say for once in his life. There was no mistaking the casual intimacy between Biran and Vladsen, no ignoring the gentle glance Vladsen had given Biran before exiting. That man, that man that Tomas had sworn to kill, adored Sanda's brother. He wanted to scream.

"I was under the impression that relationships between Keepers were forbidden," he said, and immediately felt like an asshole.

Biran smirked. "I'd rather not hear a lecture on unprofessional relationships from you, Nazca. Now, you are clearly on my sister's ship. I assume this is important, and not a friendly call for a quick moral duel."

"Maybe I should tell him," Arden said.

"No, no, I got this." Tomas shook himself. "I apologize, Director Greeve. I was an ass."

"Accepted," Biran said, inclining his head. "Continue."

"I have recently discovered that a member of your Protectorate is Nazca."

"Vladsen, I presume?"

Tomas startled. "You knew?"

"No, but it is an easy explanation for your behavior. I am not inclined to believe you, however, so you'd better have some clear fucking evidence, Cepko, and also an explanation as to why my sister isn't delivering this information instead of you two."

"Show him the video and the data scrape," Tomas said.

Arden pushed the information through. Tomas examined Biran's face as he watched the memory play out, and the match statistics that followed, but somewhere along the way Biran had learned to close himself off, to keep from revealing a scrap of what he was feeling. Not even an eyebrow twitched.

"Seventy-eight percent is not certain," he said at last.

"All other possible matches fell below a five percent threshold, sir, er, Director," Arden said.

Biran closed his eyes, rubbed his temple with two fingers. "When, and where, was this video taken?"

"At a Nazca stronghold in Ordinal, since destroyed. It's hard to say when—over a decade ago."

"And who was he discussing? Who were those two spies arguing over?"

Tomas matched his even stare. "Me, Director."

"Agent Zero..." He laughed, a sudden, short burst. "That's why Caid picked you to extract Sanda. No matter how long it took, you wouldn't age a day."

"I'd like to think it was because I was their best finder."

"I'm sure that had something to do with it, but let's not kid ourselves, Cepko. I saw the accounting. The Nazca marked the mission for possible 'timeline separation,' as there was a real probability that the gate would be closed, and the Ada system cut off from FTL. But they were never concerned that you wouldn't make it back, no matter how long it took."

"I...hadn't considered."

"Cepko, I highly suggest you start considering very intensely all the ways in which people can, and will, use you. Does Sanda know?"

"She knows what I am. She doesn't know about Vladsen."

"Good. Keep it that way. She doesn't need the worry."

"I feel the same."

Biran gave him a ghost of a smile, and Tomas returned it. "She will hate you for that."

"She's had a lot of opportunities to hate me. All deserved. Still keeps me around, somehow."

He snorted. "She's...like that. You're her clutch against Rainier, aren't you?"

He licked his lips. "That's the plan."

"Not a bad one..." Biran trailed off, gaze drifting toward his bed. "Thank you for the information. I will handle things from here."

"Biran, I mean, Director Greeve, that man is high up in the Nazca, or was, at some point. He is more dangerous than you can anticipate."

"I think you'll find, Cepko, that so am I."

"He's *extremely* dangerous."

"Like you?"

Tomas closed his mouth.

"I will handle the situation. Follow my sister's orders. We will talk again soon. Try not to peel your leg off in the meantime." Biran cut the call.

"That went...well..." Arden said.

Tomas grunted. "I really hope Biran knows what the fuck he's doing out there."

"He's a director," Arden said with a shrug. "He's gotta know what he's doing."

Tomas kept exactly what he thought about that to himself, and sat down on the edge of the worktable, half listening while Arden launched into an overly detailed explanation of all the safeguards they'd taken against Rainier thus far.

He couldn't shake the feeling that he'd made the wrong call. Not in keeping it from Sanda, he was sure of that even if she'd disagree, but in telling Biran. The way Vladsen had looked at him...Idolization came to mind, as if he'd been adrift in the void for a very long time and finally found a life raft, an oasis, in Biran. The man who looked at Biran Greeve like that didn't mesh with Tomas's sense of the man who had ordered him into the bath for a memory rollback.

People had many faces. Tomas knew that better than most. They could be cheery as starshine to their families, and never show the cracks, never give away the bodies piling up in their basement. But something was incongruent, there. Maybe 78 percent wasn't enough. Maybe the grey man and Vladsen weren't the same.

Or maybe Vladsen was looking at Biran like a lifeline because, to the grey man, he was. Tomas wondered what Vladsen might see, if he saw footage of the way Tomas looked at Sanda.

First loves. Over, and over, again.

CHAPTER 35

PRIME STANDARD YEAR 3543

CONTINGENCY PLANS

Bero had announced it would be nearly a full day-and-night cycle until they reached the Charon Gate, and so the crew broke apart to see to their private preparations. Bero had even gone to the trouble of carving out a stateroom for Okonkwo, though Sanda couldn't help but notice that it was a touch smaller than the one he'd made for her.

Sanda gave the director of all of Prime an hour to get her bearings, then knocked on her door.

"Enter," Okonkwo said.

Bero opened the door and Sanda stepped through, not needing to tell him to shut it behind her. They were moving so much in sync, lately. Like two old souls forged together in battle, he anticipated her movements before she made them, and she anticipated his moods.

She didn't like the silence he'd fallen into after the reveal that the first ship was missing, but she didn't have the time to press him about that yet. As soon as Okonkwo was safely back with her people, she'd squeeze it out of him. But right now she needed every last soul on board to have their head in the game, because the last time they'd spun up a deadgate, a berserker field on the other side had tried to kill them all.

"Prime Director," Sanda said, saluting for the first time since

Okonkwo had stepped foot on the ship. "We have some arrangements to go over."

Okonkwo sat behind a desk Bero had grown for her and leaned back, lacing her fingers over her stomach. Though she'd only been here an hour, her presence filled the room, as if every piece of furniture Bero had made for her was simply an extension of her will. The Prime Director needed a desk, and lo, one appeared. With her chin raised, her keen eyes bright, and her smile playing at amusement, Sanda could see how this woman had risen so far, so fast. Sanda wanted to trust her, simply because she seemed like someone who knew what they were doing, who was inherently in control. The Acolytes had seen that in her, too. Appearances could be deceiving.

"A salute," Okonkwo said. "And here I thought such niceties had flown out the proverbial window."

"I have not forgotten my station, Prime Director. Once Rainier is dealt with, I intend to go back to captaining a gunship."

She tossed her head and laughed. "Not much more than an hour ago, my dear, you were calling me 'Okonkwo' and bossing General Anford around. Even I have trouble making *that* woman move when she doesn't want to. No, Commander Greeve. There is no gunship in your future."

Sanda swallowed a bitter taste. "If you must court-martial me for insubordination, I request you wait until after—"

Okonkwo held up a fist. Sanda sealed her lips shut. "If it makes you feel better to call *The Light* a gunship, then by all means, be my guest, but this is the seat of your command now. Get used to it."

"This ship is Bero's. I am only borrowing it until the threat is dealt with."

"Bero." Okonkwo tilted her head to look for a camera. "Tell me, dear boy, do you want to be alone?"

"No," he said, very softly.

She nodded to herself.

"I thought not. You see? This is your ship, as I am quite certain Bero would accept no other captain. If we all survive what's coming, then I will make matters official. Enter *The Light* into the fleet's logs as a flagship under your command, crewed by whomever you choose.

My scientists will want to crawl all over *The Light*—and I will need to know what Min Liao and Arden Wyke have already ferreted out—and I apologize for that indignity, Bero."

"There are things I'd like to understand better about this body, too."

"There." Okonkwo smiled, flashing her teeth. "You see? If humanity isn't ground to atomic dust by Rainier, your future is secured. But it's the dust part of the equation I would prefer to focus on at the moment."

Sanda caught a glimpse of that future—a war hero in command of the fleet's greatest ship, its most powerful weapon—and felt a little dizzy. She shook her head and crossed the room, sitting on a chair in front of the desk. She folded her hands together and leaned forward, resting her forearms on her thighs.

"It's the next twenty-four hours I'm here about. To complete the crossing through the Charon Gate, you're going to have to image the access key. Now, we can take a guess on what the MRIs that the Keepers use look like, but we have to get this right, otherwise we'll trigger the gate's defense system. I need you to tell Bero everything you can about the MRIs, so that he can build you an appropriate unit. You don't have to tell me, and we'll destroy it after we come back through."

Okonkwo stared at her in silence so long Sanda feared she'd tell her to fuck off, they'd have to get an official machine and come back. She said, "That is unnecessary. The gates themselves possess the ability to read all chips that pass through. *The Light* need only get in range, and I will image the key. There is no need for a purpose-built machine."

"That's not—" Sanda cut herself off as Okonkwo raised her brows.

"Public knowledge? Correct, congratulations, you've scraped out yet another secret of Prime. We do so love our secrets.

"An automated system within the gates logs every chip that passes through and the ident associated with it. Think of it like a guest book Prime keeps on its Keepers' movements. Usually that's all that's done. In this case, the presence of my ident will open a secondary system within the gate that will wait until I image my password, then accept or reject as is appropriate."

"Every chip?" Sanda asked, mouth dry.

Okonkwo smiled, slow and sharklike. "Every single one."

She gripped her hands together tighter to keep from shaking. "Then you know."

"The system alerted me to the presence of a chip in the vicinity of your ident when Graham took you through the Ada gate to Atrux, and confirmed my suspicions when you spun and passed through the deadgate. That is a very old chip in your skull, Sanda Greeve."

A headache hammered her between the eyes, a blinding flash of pain only made worse by her panic. Okonkwo knew. Prime knew. They'd rip it out as soon as she was no longer useful to them. They'd take back what was theirs, what had been stolen from them and secreted in her skull, and she would never live to see command of this ship during peacetime.

What else did they know? Her headache ramped toward a cliff from which she'd fall off for all eternity.

"Greeve," Okonkwo said—had been saying. "Sanda? Bero, is anyone on this ship a medi?"

"It is only a headache," Bero said.

"It looks like a fucking stroke," Okonkwo said.

"Yes. They do. It will pass."

"What the fuck do you mean—?"

Sanda grabbed Okonkwo's wrist—when had the Prime Director put a hand on her shoulder?—and picked her head up, blinking through the bright white of pain. "He's right. I'm ... better."

"Better?" Okonkwo crouched before her and lifted Sanda's chin, staring hard into her face. "You look like you aged twenty years."

"Gee, thanks," she muttered, and pushed Okonkwo's hands away, forcing herself to sit up straight. "Rainier's technology was used to force me to forget the..." She scratched the back of her head, and Okonkwo nodded. "Memories bring the headaches. The pain makes you want to forget. The more often I engage with a guarded memory, the less the pain. It just ... It takes time."

"That is some Pavlovian fuckery."

Sanda laughed, despite everything, and ran shaky hands through her hair. "How long do I have?"

Okonkwo leaned against her desk and crossed her ankles. "Don't ask me, Greeve. Are the headaches terminal in some way? Does this happen often?"

"No, I mean, before you remove it."

She blinked. "Ah. I see. It was determined that the size of the data packet in your head was too small to be a fragment of gate technology. Is that correct?"

"It was the coordinates to the second sphere."

She smirked. "I knew it. Speaker Greystone owes me a thousand credits."

Sanda's head spun, but not from pain. "You knew. The whole High Protectorate knows. Does anyone else . . . ?"

"Of course not. We flagged the information and decided to keep it to ourselves for the time being. None of us could deem you a threat to Prime with a straight face, though a few tried. I assume the chip is Kenwick's?"

"How did you . . . ?"

"His was the only one missing. We presumed Icarion stuck it in your head to try to get gate tech out, yes?"

She nodded, numbly.

"Icarion idiots. Kenwick never had gate data, though I suppose they could not have known that. I am very sorry for what you went through."

"And you didn't think to tell me you knew? That you weren't going to rip the chip out? That I wasn't walking around with a death warrant stapled to my brain stem?"

"My dear girl, you are still walking around with a death warrant 'stapled' to your brain stem. That chip, and the High Protectorate's knowledge of it, has always been our contingency plan when dealing with you."

She kept herself very still. "If I didn't do what you wanted, you'd threaten to pull it."

She spread her hands as she shrugged. "That sounds so crude. But, yes, that was the general idea."

"You would've had to catch me."

"Would I have?" Something lurked behind Okonkwo's smile that Sanda couldn't quite place.

"What is that supposed to mean?"

"I am telling you this only because you already have access to our deepest secrets, and because I need you to understand the extent of my reach. Every chip—even yours—carries a minuscule amount of explosive. Only the Prime Director may detonate it, but all I need is your ident, and sufficient reason to do so."

"There's a *bomb* stapled to my brain?"

"Yours and thousands of others. Don't fret, dear, I've only had to use it once before. But if you were thinking you could outrun me on this ship, well, you can't."

"I want it out."

"You've had it too long. Even the most delicate removal, at this point, would guarantee death."

A deep well of anger opened inside of her. "You let me keep it to be sure of that, didn't you?"

She shrugged one shoulder. "You're a wild card, Greeve. I hoped you'd be our wild card, but I could never be sure."

"I'm really starting to hate Prime Inventive."

"That feeling comes and goes," she said, and circled her desk to take her seat again. "Now, if you're finished, I need to make a few more calls to calm down the jumpier members of the High Protectorate. No one enjoys having their boss kidnapped, even if it is by benevolent forces to prevent a malicious kidnapping."

Sanda pushed unsteadily to her feet, and as she stood, her hand brushed open her coat. Okonkwo's gaze flicked down, to the blasters holstered on Sanda's hips, then back to Sanda's face. "You walk around armed on your own ship?"

She found a trickle of steel in her spine and stood straight. "I've been surprised a lot, lately. Not too fond of the experience."

"No..." Okonkwo said, taking in Sanda's full measure, a considering expression on her sharp features. "I imagine you're not."

Sanda gave her a cruel smile, knowing her face was still pale from pain but hoping the ragged appearance would add to the effect. Okonkwo shifted in her seat.

"Good luck with your calls, Prime Director."

Sanda gave her a picture-perfect salute, and stalked out the door before Okonkwo could comment further.

Knowing should have made her feel free. Just as having reached the coordinates and discovering what was there should have made her feel lighter. The chip was a nonissue, for the most part. Okonkwo could still use it to bring her to heel, to kill her if she didn't obey, but Prime had always had leverage to pull against her, because they'd always had Biran.

So why did she feel so violated, so yanked around? She scarcely felt like she was in her own body anymore. She pressed a hand to Bero's wall at the thought, and he warmed the spot to her touch, letting her know he understood.

Dios, but she wanted some sense of control back—but did anyone ever really have full control? Whoever the beings were that left the spheres behind had thought they had control, but some freak accident of space had knocked their first ship off course, sent it slamming into the asteroid belt for Halston to find. To steal, and fuck up, the secrets of an alien race.

Not even the most advanced species in the known universe had managed to stay in control of their own plan, whatever that was, so why should she be any different? Why should Sanda Greeve, a busted-down human hanging on to hope by her fingernails, have any more right to control her fate than the most advanced beings in the universe?

Sometimes, she decided, you just got hit by an asteroid, and there was fuck all you could do about it. Strangely, that was comforting.

CHAPTER 36

PRIME STANDARD YEAR 3543

LIEUTENANT BERO

A half hour to contact, Tomas knocked on her door. She was put-ting on a shin plate, the Prime armor a familiar cocoon around the fragile flesh of her body, when Bero flashed his name across her wristpad a second before the knocks landed. Sanda took a slow breath to steel herself, and nodded. The door dilated.

"Hey," he said, standing in the hall, hands in his pockets. "Got a second?"

"If you come in out of the hallway," she said. "And where's your armor? I thought I ordered suit-up for the crossing."

He stepped into the room and rubbed the back of his neck. "I can get it on pretty quickly, and this won't take long." He glanced down to her leg, the prosthetic still uncovered, and his eyes narrowed. "Is that made of *The Light*?"

"That is none of your business," she snapped, then instantly felt guilty as he tensed, pulling back. She tugged the jumpsuit leg tightly over her skin and metal, hiding away the contact point where fine filaments had grown, slowly, into her skin and muscle and nervous system, making her control of the leg more complete than any smart prosthetic Prime could have given her.

"You failed to mention that," he said with a faint tinge of recrimination.

CATALYST GATE 🪐 249

Her hands stilled against the fabric. He was right. In their long talk that night, she'd left this part out. It wasn't that she'd wanted to keep it from him, it just hadn't occurred to her. Her prosthetics were as much a part of her body now as anything else.

But it was Bero. It was *The Light*, and she was feeling defensive and snappish about the whole thing because she knew damn well that letting that entity have the slightest control over her autonomy was a bad idea.

"You really want to kick off an argument about what we've failed to mention to each other?"

"Shit," he muttered, dragging a hand through his hair. "No. Sorry."

"I'm sorry, too." She straightened, reaching for another piece of armor. "Can you sense it?"

He hesitated. "No."

"Neither can Bero, and he assures me Rainier can't get in, either, so don't worry yourself over it. What are you here for?"

"I…" He trailed off, frowning to himself, then shook off whatever he was feeling and took a step closer to her, voice low with sincerity. "I can't be on your forward team, if there's another sphere ship out there."

Sanda frowned and crossed her arms. "You're telling me that if there's a ship like *The Light* on the other side of that gate, you want to miss it? You want to stay here and…what, watch?"

"Fuck, no," he said, and let out a raspy laugh. "I'd kill to be first on another ship like this, but I don't…I don't trust myself."

"Tomas," she said gently, checking her countdown. "I feel for you, but we're down to twenty-two minutes and I need the short, clear version."

"If there is a ship like *The Light* on the other side of that gate, I fear one of two possible outcomes for myself. The first: An intelligence is inhabiting that ship that knows what I am and how to circumvent my and Bero's defenses. If that's the case, I want to be on board to keep out any attempt at intrusion. Second…" He cleared his throat. "If there is another ship like *The Light*, and it has no intelligence, I fear I might become it."

"What?"

He looked at the floor. "I feel a very strong affinity with *The Light*. Bero's presence acts as a natural barrier, but it is a thin one. A ship like this, with nothing else inhabiting it, might be too much. I... It's hard to explain."

"You think it will consume you."

He met her eyes. "Yes. Part of me wants it to."

"Well fuck that," she said, and shook her head. "You're staying on this ship if there's anything like *The Light* on the other side, and that's a goddamn order."

He grinned a little. "Thanks. Sorry I'm such a liability."

She put a hand on his arm. "Don't ever apologize for being what you are."

His eyes widened and she thought she saw a flash of moisture building across them, glittering, then he turned his head, and she swore, pulling her hand back, taking a step away, wondering why the fuck she couldn't get her head around the fact he was hurt, and needed space, and things weren't the same as they had been on Bero.

He kissed her. She hadn't seen it coming—had been so wrapped up in her own head she'd missed the subtle cant of his body, the hand that wrapped around her wrist, keeping her from backing away. She stiffened, startled, and he started to respond to that, to pull back, but then her instincts kicked in, and by the time they parted she was breathless and warm all over, and the countdown on her wristpad said eight minutes.

"I... have to go," she said.

He smiled, hair roughed up from where her fingers had run through it, and brushed his knuckles against her cheek, down to her jaw. "I know. If it's not another *Light*, I'm going with you."

"Then you'd better get your armor on."

"Wasn't really hoping you'd order me to put more clothes on."

Her cheeks went hot and he grinned. She cleared her throat. "Super dangerous, worlds-saving mission in seven minutes."

"Right, yup." He backed away and straightened his hair. "See you on deck, Commander."

The way he said *commander* made her toes curl, which was going to be extremely annoying if that kept up. He ducked back out into the hallway and she made quick work of tugging on the last of her armor and weapons, and had enough time left to make it to the deck without looking flustered.

Tomas was already there, fully suited and armed, leaning against a console having an easy chat with Nox. She shot him a look, but he just raised a brow in response. Right. Robot-speed, which would be interesting, if... Her imagination trailed off. She put a lid on it.

"Are you ready, Prime Director?"

Okonkwo had suited up and wore the armor as easily as any fleetie. She had strapped herself into one of the seats at the forward console and was squinting at the distance readout Bero put up on the viewscreen.

Next to the distance readout was Bero's confirmation that he hadn't detected the presence of the nanites Rainier had used to tamper with Ada's secondary gate. Sanda read that report twice, just to be certain. Charon Gate had never been fully powered down, and all their research so far indicated that the blowback only happened during initial spin-up, but she couldn't help a prickling sense of unease.

No choice but to push through. Bero's scans were clear, and Ordinal was the most secure of all Prime's systems. Okonkwo, at least, didn't appear concerned.

"We are almost in range," Okonkwo said. "I will feel a... ah." She winced as if she'd had a brain freeze. "There it is. A moment, please. Bero, Mx. Wyke, if either of you attempt to scan my brain patterning during this time, I will have you both court-martialed as traitors to Prime."

"I am not a citizen," Bero said.

"I hereby dub you a citizen of Prime, and assign you the role of lieutenant to Commander Greeve. Now be silent, all of you."

Bero texted her: am I really your lieutenant now?

Sanda: if you want to be

B: ...yes.

S: congrats, LT

B: want me to scan her?

S: fuck no!

B: spoilsport

Sanda smiled at the last message but put her wristpad down, watching the Charon Gate. This was the gate in all of the history CamCasts she'd been made to take tests on, growing up. Fundamentally, it wasn't much different from any other Casimir Gate.

They were all the same size, embedded with the same lights. There had been no room for variation in Halston's original design—she had to stop thinking of it as Halston's design. More like, the blueprint she'd cobbled together from the scraps of an absent species.

But the Charon Gate was the first. The gate that opened the stars for humanity, that led them, stumbling and afraid, into the unfamiliar vacuum of what would become the Ordinal system. What had they called it, before they renamed the star for Prime's point of origin? She thought the system might have started with a *T*, but didn't bother to look it up. Ordinal lived and breathed and anchored Prime to the stars. It was the system on the other side of that gate that fascinated her, made her lean closer to the viewscreen.

Earth. She'd seen CamCasts of that planet, too. A blue marble swirled with white, its continents verdant green before the sun went red dwarf too soon and made life impossible. It'd been with a heavy heart that Prime had closed the Charon Gate at last, deeming the system incapable of supporting another gate, and lacking in planets suitable for habitation.

Oh, Mars could have been terraformed. Maybe even Eros or Titan—certainly there had been talk of such a thing. A hab dome could have kept humanity alive and kicking under the light of their birth star, no matter how virulent it had grown.

But it hadn't seemed prudent, spending all those resources to haunt their old system, and at the time Prime was still focused outward—on how many worlds there were yet to discover.

They hadn't found much. Planets like Icarion, close enough to a star to be of optimal warmth and made of the right amount of rock, were rarer than an honest smuggler, and even then they'd found no evidence of plant life aside from what they'd brought with them. Scant magnetospheres meant that even the most hospitable of planets within the Goldilocks zone still required hab domes.

Sanda wondered, briefly, if that was because of the blowback. They had found some life, after all, in the form of algae and extremophiles. Usually on far-off moons, or in the dirty ice of asteroids. It was always the planets that were barren. They'd never found another Earth.

As the gate lit green and began to spin, she found herself excited to see that old cradle, no matter that it was an irradiated mess. It was still blue, she was sure of that much, and though it would never again be humanity's home, it had been perfect for them, once. She'd seen plenty of other "blue" planets—water worlds and gas giants and moons of crusty ice—on the CamCasts. There were even a few in the Ada system. But the oceans that bore life? That was a different kind of blue altogether.

"Spin achieved," Okonkwo said, and rubbed her temples with two fingers. "The rest is up to you, Bero."

The Light moved. She knew better, but still she expected the forced power suppression that would happen to any other ship crossing a gate. Bero, in the body of *The Light*, slid through that everlasting darkness without so much as flickering a light. It was almost as if, even when he was out of stealth, the gates couldn't see this ship.

No, that wasn't right, she corrected herself. She was still thinking of the gates as human tech. The forced power-down had been an addition of Halston's, not an original part of the design, and *The Light* had been crafted by the gates' makers. This was how the crossing was always meant to be. Effortless. As if the gate were welcoming you to whatever awaited on the other side.

"Crossing achieved," Bero said.

"Give me visual," Sanda said, gripping her armrests. The last time she'd flown through a deadgate she'd been met on the other side by a shield of berserker probes that attacked immediately.

"I'm detecting no hostiles," Bero said smoothly as he filled the forward viewscreen with the local system.

Local system. Sanda smiled to herself. Such a way to think about the star system that'd borne her entire species up from the mud and into the stars. No matter that they'd stolen their way there. They may not have made the gates, but humanity had made everything else— the atmo domes, the stations, all the ships before *The Light*. Carbon scrapers, food recyclers, NutriBaths and nutriblocks, which didn't taste much different but were a damn miracle, all things considered. Humanity did shitty things, but sometimes humans were all right.

The viewscreen filled mostly with the empty black of space, Bero taking a long view so that the humans riding his back could get a good, long look at the whole of the system that'd birthed them. So far away as to be almost a pinprick, the yellow star—*the* sun, Sanda reminded herself—anchored the system, the large body of bloody-red Saturn the next clearest object. Bero added labels to the screen as he panned his cameras across the star field, ticking off the major bodies—Saturn, Uranus—and then, eventually, so small she could scarcely see it, a pale blue dot. Earth.

Sanda's gaze flicked back to the sun. "That looks...remarkably yellow."

"I was having the same thought," Okonkwo said.

"Is it a color filter, B?" she asked, even though she was pretty sure she already knew the answer.

"No. That is a main sequence star."

"That is *the sun*," she said, baffled. "It should be...red... shouldn't it?"

Okonkwo cleared her throat roughly. "I do not like this."

"You're not the only one," Sanda said. "Thoughts, Liao?"

She spread her hands. "I haven't the slightest clue."

"Bero?"

"It's...quiet," Bero said softly.

"What do you mean?" Sanda asked.

"The lack of transmissions in this system is...unsettling."

Arden nodded. "It's like having cotton shoved in your ears."

"You listen to all the transmits in a system?" Sanda asked with an arched brow.

They shook their wristpad at her. "I keep an eye on some things. This is...empty."

"Not entirely," Bero said.

"No," Arden agreed.

"Show me," Sanda said.

The image shifted, cutting in tighter to local space. Not far from them a long, silver cylinder drifted. Sanda took over the controls, zooming in tight on the object's slender body. *The Light* had been the same color, but this wasn't anywhere near the same design. It looked more like two tin cans strapped together than a ship. Tin cans that had then been fitted with a frill of wings that she could only guess were some kind of...radiators? Solar panels? A ship, undoubtedly, but nothing on the level of *The Light*.

"Bero, does it have a transponder?"

"Yes," he said. "I am running the registration number against known records, but—"

"There is no need," Okonkwo said. "I have a painting of that ship above my desk at Ordinal Station. That is the *Reina Mora*, worse for the wear, but I would know her anywhere. That is Alexandra Halston's first ship, the one that made the crossing through to Ordinal—which was then Tau Ceti. It was believed to be destroyed in the Corp Wars."

"Looks pretty whole to me," Sanda said.

"Sanda," Bero said. She nodded to let him know she was listening. "It's not the transponder Arden and I picked up on. It's...That ship is drawing power. It has heating, cooling, HVAC. Something lives on the *Reina Mora*."

Okonkwo said, "This gate has not been spun for a thousand years."

Sanda licked her lips. "Then they've been waiting a long time. Start hailing, B, and bring us in range. It's time to say hello."

CHAPTER 37

PRIME STANDARD YEAR 3543

WHAT'S NECESSARY

The elevator didn't want to let Jules into the third basement level, which was her first red flag, because as far as the building knew, she was guardcore. She was allowed everywhere. But not *this* particular GC unit. She'd been singled out.

Even if Dal had turned her in, they wouldn't have blocked her out of the lower levels before she'd even made it to the elevator. That meant she'd been blocked out before she'd stepped foot in the building, probably about the time she'd delivered the immune patients.

Her skin crawled. She should bail. She wasn't healthy enough to stand up to a full-blown fight, which was no doubt what waited for her below. She could walk out now, grab Lolla, and disappear. Dal might not send her the cure if she left the immune to rot down there, but it'd be on the news when it finally worked. She'd figure out another way to get to it. But by then, Lolla's oxygen levels might've become critical.

Jules needed backup. But she'd burned all her backup years ago.

She brought up a patient list, scanning for Birdie. As an ascended, she'd been moved to the upper levels long before Saarah and Reece had been dropped below. She'd have to do. At least she'd be motivated.

The elevator let her ascend. She didn't go to the top floor if she could help it. There, a psychiatric ward had been converted into containment for the ascended, the walls and doors reinforced to keep the enhanced humans contained.

It didn't matter how thick the walls were. She could still hear them. Screaming, shouting, sobbing. Expletives and gibberish and threats all rolled together, a wave of invective that Jules deserved more than any medi who walked those halls.

These people were too dangerous. And so, as was the way with all things Prime, they'd been sliced out of society, set aside until Prime could figure out what to do with them. The instinct was to slaughter, put down the contagion, even though the ascended couldn't spread the agent.

But there were few of them, easily controllable once they'd been tranqed and caged, and Jules suspected Prime hoped that they could make of these people exactly what Saarah had said: soldiers.

The doors to the cells had windows, but they'd been covered with paper, only pulled aside when the staff needed to check the prisoner within. Not patient, definitely not that. While the medis worked to save those in the comas, they gave the ascended wide berths, muttering under their breaths that it'd be kinder to put them down.

Some of the ascended took the transformation well. Some didn't. For those who didn't... They'd find pieces of them, scattered around the room, taken apart with methodical care. Self-vivisection, for curiosity's sake. Jules shivered. She'd never felt the urge. Had never even considered such a thing was possible. As much as she could, Jules tried not to think about what she was, what her body was capable of. Maybe denial was keeping her safe.

She ignored the maelstrom of pain sounding all around her, and found the room Birdie had been assigned to. She flipped up the paper, peeking within. The girl was curled against the back corner, dirty black hair hiding her face, her arms wrapped tightly around knees yanked up to her chest. Jules tapped a knuckle on the window, and she jerked alert, eyes narrowing at the black helmet on the other side of her door.

Well, at least she hadn't completely broken down. Jules overrode the lock and swung the door inward. Birdie stood warily, pressing her back into the wall.

"What do you want? I told the medis I don't know anything."

"I'm here to get you out," Jules said in her real voice.

"Shadow?" she whispered, rage and hope warring across her small face when Jules nodded.

"Look," Jules said. "I don't have time to apologize. I'm not even really sorry. But circumstances have changed. We have a lead on a cure. Saarah and Reece, they're no longer essential, and I don't think they're being treated well. I want to get all of you off this planet, onto my ship, but I think the other GC are onto me now, so I'm going to need your help. There's a fight between you and freedom, and I'm not in top form."

She screwed up her lips as she thought, small brow scrunching. "I'm not leaving without Dad and Saarah."

"I need your help to free them." Jules pulled a blaster from her weapons holster and held it out to the girl. At point-blank range, it could get through the guardcore armor, but Jules didn't have time to think about all the risks she was taking right now. She didn't want to.

Something clicked in the kid's mind. She nodded and took the weapon, checking it briefly. She'd probably never held a blaster in her life, but she'd obviously used cheaper weapons.

"What do I have to do?"

"Come with me," Jules said, turning her back to Birdie. The kid's footsteps pattered after her, and she explained as they walked to the elevator. Jules overrode the lockout with one of the different GC idents Rainier kept on board all her ships. "We're getting those two, no one else. I don't know what this floor looks like, but it's not going to be pretty. Keep your eye on the mission, and stay behind me. Shoot anything that shoots at us, and keep moving. Don't stop. If we get separated, I flashed the location to my ship on your wristpad. Meet me there. This might be one of the hardest things you've ever had to do."

"I'm Grotta," she said, picking up her sharp chin, eyes narrowed, holding that blaster like it'd been in her hands her whole life. Jules's chest ached.

"Me too, kid, me too."

She nodded, stringy curls bouncing around her ears. What would Harlan make of Jules now? What would he think of her putting a weapon in that kid's hand—she must be what, nine, ten? Jules couldn't even remember when she'd downed her first body anymore. It must have been about that age. And it'd definitely been Harlan who put the weapon in her hand. Who'd complimented her when she used it so well.

Jules's grip tightened around her rifle. Out. She was getting this kid *out*.

The elevator stopped. Opened. And everything else washed away, buried under the weight of her mission.

Jules brought the rifle up and stalked forward, her HUD throwing up a low-opacity thermal overlay. Things weren't as neat and shiny down here as they were upstairs. Here, the floor was concrete foam, the walls makeshift curtains suspended from rolling aluminum frames.

She didn't recognize the people in the beds. They must have been patients upstairs at some point, but she'd never looked at their faces then, either. She was looking now, searching for the two she needed, pushing everything else down, shoving it into the realm of background noise. Pointless information.

These people were pale and sweating and hooked up to a half dozen instruments, eyes glazed but open. Not quite comatose. Definitely not raging like the ascended upstairs. There was no aggression here, just listless despair.

Not her problem.

Swallow it down. Move.

Saarah and Reece were special, immune, despite Keeper Martine's assertions that they'd succumbed after all. She clung to that, working the problem in the back of her mind.

Up ahead, a room ballooned off the main hallway. There, that's where they'd be. No doors, but real walls. Nothing showed down the halls to either side on her thermal, so she ducked into the room.

Saarah and Reece were in those beds, strapped under padded leather restraints that echoed the ones Jules had used on the scientists during their memory rollbacks. The similarity stunned her.

"Baby, no," Reece whispered as Birdie came flying into the room and threw herself at her dad, wrapping his torso in her bony arms. "You shouldn't be here."

"I'm getting you out," Jules said, jolted back into the moment.

Reece coughed out a laugh. "Shadow. Have a change of heart?"

"No," Jules said, honestly. "This is no longer necessary."

"My god." Reece glared at her. "That's all it fucking takes with you?"

"Birdie, restraints," Jules said, ignoring the anger and hurt and, worst of all, pity, mixed up in both of their faces.

Birdie's small fingers went to work on the buckles and Jules turned away, her back to the broken-down Grotta family, her eyes roving the floor for a threat. Everyone worked late at the hospital. She should have tripped over a few medis by now, at least. Something was wrong, and it scratched at the back of her mind, made her jumpy. Made her feel like she was being watched.

"Let's go," Saarah said, staggering to her feet. She leaned against Reece while Birdie moved out in front of them, blaster back in her hands, a determined scowl on her small face.

"Elevator, straight ahead," Jules said, and stepped into the hall.

That elevator opened. Keeper Tersa Martine stepped into the hall, a mirror of Jules, no weapons in her hands, but she didn't need them; the five guardcore fanning out around her were weapon enough.

Jules waved the group back—at least they had real walls to hide behind—but otherwise stayed perfectly still, rifle up, pointed dead-on at the Keeper's chest.

"You must be Shadow," Keeper Martine said. "I've heard a great deal about you."

Martine moved farther down the hall, smiling warmly, but stopped short as Jules twitched the end of her rifle. A coy smile spread across Martine's lips. She lifted her arms, palms out, as if she were being robbed. Jules's eyes narrowed. She wasn't the tiniest bit scared. Maybe she had body armor on beneath her thick, grey overcoat. Or maybe High Protectorate Keeper Martine was so divorced from reality that she didn't have the instinct to be scared anymore.

"I'm taking these people," Jules said through her voice filter. "Stand down."

"A guardcore threatening a Keeper, how novel. Five-against-one are uneven odds, however." She relaxed her arms, tapping her lips with one finger. "You know, I'd really hoped it wouldn't come to this. Naturally, your colleagues have been concerned about you for quite some time. You're never in your assigned berth, you retreat to that ship they can't be certain anyone else has ever come out of. You walk the Grotta alone, and when you do, you move like you were born to it. Grotta babies don't grow up into guardcore, do they?"

"We don't have a lot of love for the Keepers," Jules said.

She grinned. "Understandable. So who are you? We've been taking bets. You can't be Rainier, she wouldn't give a shit about these people."

"Maybe Rainier wants them so you can't find a cure." Sweat slicked her skin, soaked into the foam. The materials wicked the moisture away, but she was dumping so much the system couldn't keep up. A dehydration alert flashed in the corner of her HUD, and Jules authorized the suit to inject her with fluids. At least she'd get some of that sweat back.

"I don't think so."

"What are the good odds?" Jules asked to keep her talking. The guardcore had spread out, all their rifles pointed at her, their bodies spaced between the patient beds. If Jules fired, there was a good chance her bullet would go through one of the GC and hit a patient. Maybe they thought that would make her hesitate. They didn't know her very well.

"My money's on Jules Valentine," Martine said with a questioning quirk of the eyebrow.

Jules, very carefully, did not react. Behind her, Birdie hissed through her teeth.

"You'd let a monster like that run around your streets unchecked?" Jules asked, thanking the void that the voice filters kept the weak tremor out of her words.

"I am well familiar with useful monsters," Martine said, spreading her hands to take in the room around them. "Arguably, I am one myself. But, needs must. I do what must be done to achieve the results required of me. If that means letting the butcher of Atrux run around the streets picking prime specimens out of the rubble for me, then so be it."

"I'm not her."

"I don't believe you."

There was a sizzle and a crack. Martine's abdomen exploded with red, splatter painting the ground, the rest of her clothes. Her eyes bulged and she grabbed her midsection, doubling over. Jules could relate.

One of the GC broke rank, going to help their charge. Jules put a bullet in their helmet, resighted, put down the GC nearest that one, resighted—pain tore through her hip, her thigh. Jules grunted, dropping to one knee, rifle still up, body still moving on mechanical instinct. Sight, shoot, ignore the life leaking out of you.

Birdie's blaster sizzled again and again, and when the smoke cleared and the bodies lay cooling, Jules was punched through in three or four different spots, hard to say. At least none had been headshots.

"Oh my god," Reece said, grabbing her arm. "Lie down, there's a medikit—"

"Get up," Saarah grated between clenched teeth.

Shuddering, mind swirling with red and white light, Jules pushed to her feet. Her left leg was numb, like it had fallen asleep, and she found it hard to hold the rifle with two hands, so she stowed it and pulled out a blaster.

"Look at her," Reece shouted at Saarah. "She needs medical help!"

"No she doesn't," Birdie said.

Jules blinked, looked down at the slip of a girl at her side, at the blaster in her hands and the blood spattered across her hands and face. The girl nodded grimly.

"I know it still hurts," Birdie said, "but you have to move."

Right. Shit. If she lay down and died here, no one would ever help Lolla. Even if they found the damn cure, they'd probably withhold it from her out of spite.

"Can you use this?" Jules asked, holding her rifle out to Saarah.

"Isn't it armor-locked?"

"Not my weapons."

"Didn't think so," Saarah said, taking the rifle in both hands. She may have been weak from whatever had been done to her down here, but she carried it like a pro all the same. The Grotta adapts. The Grotta survives.

"You should be *dead*," Reece said, aghast.

"I get that a lot," Jules said. "Kid's right. Let's move."

CHAPTER 38

PRIME STANDARD YEAR 3543

CRYPT KEEPER

*T*he *Light* slipped up alongside the *Reina Mora* as close as Bero dared, the more advanced ship's airlock tube extending to mate with the old-fashioned style of the *Reina Mora*. Every step of the way, Bero hailed the ship on every channel he could think of. No answer.

The tube locked into place. Call time was over, now they had to knock on the door.

"Nox, with me." Sanda caught Tomas's eye, and he nodded. Good, he didn't feel that ship was anything akin to *The Light*. "Tomas, you too. Everyone else, sit tight. Arden, keep trying to get through to the ship's network."

"I'd have to raid a museum to talk to that shit."

"Keep trying," she repeated.

Okonkwo stood and picked up a helmet. "I'm coming, too."

"With respect, Prime Director, that is one big security risk."

"Please, I'm arguably better trained for combat than your spy, at the very least."

"Doubt it," Tomas muttered, close to Sanda's ear but too low for Okonkwo to hear. Sanda suppressed a smile. It was probably a bad idea to let her absolute commander know that her boyfriend was a robot. Was he a robot? Or her boyfriend? Questions for another time.

"Nevertheless—"

"Commander," Okonkwo said with soft exasperation, "I appreciate your concern and sudden flair for caution, but that ship is the private vessel of the first director of Prime. If there is a message to be found within that vessel, then it is for me. You may very well need my assistance to decode whatever awaits us."

"What if the message is a big fucking bomb?" Nox asked.

"Then I hardly see how staying here will help us." She crammed her helmet on, hooked in her lifepack, thumbed her blasters to life, and said across the open channel, "We're wasting time."

Sanda shrugged. She wasn't guardcore—it wasn't her job to coddle the Prime Director. She'd yanked her ass out of a fire once. If Okonkwo wanted to jump back in, that was her business.

"As you like," she said as she put her own helmet on. "But you follow my lead. My ship, my rules."

"All ships in the Prime fleet are *my* ships."

"Tell it to Bero, see how that goes for you."

She heard Okonkwo's chuckle before she cut the comm to keep from being overheard. Tension eased out of Sanda's shoulders. Good. Okonkwo was a damn fine shot—she'd seen so herself on Monte—but her ability to take a joke made Sanda more at ease than having the finest marksman in the 'verse at her side. Because she had a sinking suspicion that what waited for them on the other side of that airlock was going to be more of a psychological threat than a physical one.

"It doesn't appear to have weapons," Conway reported through the team channel. "Though I wouldn't put an EMP out of the question."

"Understood," Sanda said, then flicked her gaze to send a private text to Tomas as she walked down the tube.

Greeve: Would an EMP damage you?

Cepko: No idea

Greeve: It worked on Rainier, briefly, but she got back up

Cepko: Liao says there's nothing of the biological in me. So, maybe?

Greeve: I don't really know what that means

Cepko: Neither do I

Greeve: Not helping

Cepko: I'm fine. Go.

She sent back an indecent string of emojis, and snorted to herself as he shifted his weight under the cover of his armor. Part of her wanted to leave him in the ship, where he was safest, but she realized how ridiculous that was.

He'd asked to be left off of any mission that boarded another ship like *The Light*—and this was as far away from *The Light* technologically speaking as one could get. It was more likely there would be guns on board that could blow her to bits than an EMP specially designed to take down beings like Tomas. Like Rainier.

Sanda approached the airlock and waved her wristpad over the lock. Nothing. "Torches," she said, gesturing Nox to her side.

"You have got to be kidding me," Okonkwo said with a laugh. "Move aside, children, I'm not as old as this thing, but at least I've read a damn history book."

Okonkwo squeezed around Nox and pressed in close to Sanda. She grabbed a round wheel on the outside of the door, and twisted. It took a few grunting tries, but soon enough she got the wheel to spin. She stepped aside, pushing them all backward, and dragged the door open, almost filling the entire walkway with the thick metal bulk.

"That a door or a crate?" Nox asked.

"It is the way airlocks used to be done," Okonkwo said, wiggling past so that Sanda and Nox could go first. At least she still had some survival instincts.

"Clunky," Nox muttered, and pushed the hatch the rest of the way open so that he could nose his rifle into the space beyond. Darkness waited. Sanda turned on her rifle flashlight at the same time Nox did.

Dust motes danced in the air of the cramped chamber, the death knell of all spaceships. Didn't matter how good your HVAC was, eventually the dust of space—of life—built up in the fine instruments of any ship, clogged filters, gunked up oil, and ground the smooth machines of Prime to a halt. These motes drifted on unseen currents, nudged along by the steady thrum of life-support systems.

"Someone turned this on recently," Sanda said through their private channel.

"Or someone's been maintaining it, and this is the best they can do," Okonkwo said.

Sanda shuddered hard enough for the light of her rifle to shake.

This was the kind of future she had been staring down, when she first woke up on Bero and thought the worlds were dead and she would have to survive on *The Light of Berossus* for decades, at least, until they reached another inhabited system.

She hadn't liked her chances then, though she'd kept on working because there wasn't anything else to do. This dust... This was the kind of dust that would have ended her, eventually. A slow and creeping death. Nox looked down at her, silently asking if she was all right. She nodded.

Tomas had pulled her out of that hell, and this... This was a nightmare she stepped into willingly.

Sanda kicked her mag boots on and pushed through the tunnel into the room. Weightlessness returned as soon as she was out of the range of *The Light*. Supplies had been strapped in haphazard nets to the walls of the cylindrical room, the plastics yellowed with age. The Velcro had begun to peel, some places having come off entirely, the adhesive finally giving up, while in other places the strips must have bonded with the metal walls. Sanda turned, painting the room in light.

They'd come in via the "lower" cylinder, and as she turned, she caught a glimpse of pale blue light above, the glow familiar enough to send a shiver down her spine. It was the same kind of glow *The Light* had when she'd first stepped foot on it.

Cepko: Something's off here. I can sense this ship, but it's closed off to me.

Greeve: Are you okay?

Cepko: Yes. It's similar to The Light, but different. Uncomfortable.

Greeve: Something we can use against Rainier?

Cepko: Maybe. I need time to feel it out.

She pointed up with an exaggerated gesture of her helmet, and Nox followed her look, nodding in understanding. She put a palm down, ordering Okonkwo and Tomas to stay put as she and Nox grabbed handles on the walls and pushed themselves up. There was only enough room for one to pass through from one chamber to the next at a time. Sanda went first.

It took her a moment to understand what she saw. To her left, a window pointed Earthward filled almost the entire wall of the cylinder—it must have been tinted outside, to cut radiation, and to keep any light from escaping.

To her right, a corpse floated.

Sanda put her back to the window, and motioned for Nox to stay where he was, halfway between the top and bottom transfer. The body, mummified from its long years in space, wore one of the early examples of a Prime Inventive jumpsuit. The whole piece was cyan blue, instead of grey with a cyan logo, and the logo was Prime's earliest iteration—a ring that might have been mistaken for a gate at first glance, but in fact was broken up, and represented the asteroid belt of the Sol system, where Halston had gotten her start as a miner.

The body wore plain shoes, almost like sneakers, as mag boots hadn't been invented yet. It curled in on itself, drifting from a five-point harness attached to the opposite wall, its dark hair—a mass of curly, shiny waves with a hint of frizz—clouded around the bowed head. Though the jumpsuit had been made to conform to the body's shape, the flesh within had concaved so badly that the fabric sagged around it, unable to shrink up any more. That flesh was sunken, but not withered. The body's skin was smooth, if taut.

"Why are you all alone out here?" she asked softly, over open speakers.

The head jerked up. Fear slammed down inside of her as training overrode primal instinct. Sanda targeted the body with her rifle even as she put one foot back to grip the metal wall with her boot for stability and called over the team channel. "Live one up here."

Chatter burst across the channel and Nox pulled himself the rest of the way through, swiveling to cover the body—woman?—from the other flank.

The woman's doe-brown eyes settled on Sanda, and though her visor was mirrored, she had the distinct feeling the woman saw her all the same.

"I like the grey armor," the woman said. "I always felt all this blue was a little garish."

Sanda forced her hands to stop shaking as she kept the rifle trained on the woman's chest. "Lady, I've had a hell of a time lately with cryptic fuckers. You've got about five seconds to tell me who you are, and why you're here, before I put you back in the grave you skipped out of."

The woman unfolded, slowly, and though nothing about her motions registered as a threat, every twitch of her muscles made Sanda's skin crawl. She lifted wire-thin arms above her head, shaking out her torso and pointing her toes as she stretched so hard Sanda thought that thin, sucked-in flesh would split. She rolled her neck from one side to another, cracking loud enough to echo, then tugged her jumpsuit straight.

"My name is Maria Salvez. I'd shake your hand, but after hibernating so long, I'm not sure it wouldn't break all my fingers. Or yours."

"Lot of Maria Salvezes in the 'verse," Sanda said, though she had a sinking feeling she knew exactly who this one was.

"Consider me the first," she said with a sly smile that should have cracked her lips, but as Sanda watched, the woman's body filled in, taking on the softer shapes of humanity, where before she'd been all arachnid angles.

Okonkwo pushed through the opening, and before Sanda could tell her to get back down the hole, she'd pulled her damn helmet off and crossed her arms over her chest, bowing so low that in the zero-g it looked as if she'd folded over onto herself.

"Dr. Salvez, I am the current High Director of Prime, Malkia Rehema Okonkwo. Please, forgive our intrusion, I was not certain what I would find here."

Salvez flicked her fingers, dismissing the weapons pointed at her chest. Neither Nox nor Sanda put their rifles down. "If you are here, Prime Director, shit has hit the fan, has it not?"

Okonkwo looked up to meet Salvez's ancient stare. "I regret to inform you that I have lost control of the spheremind."

"You lost *my wife*?"

CHAPTER 39

PRIME STANDARD YEAR 3543

PALE BLUE DOT

Biran was showered, changed, and on deck by the time the *Terminus* exited the gate and had fully powered its systems back on. Vladsen was already there, leaning against Scalla's console and pointing to something on the readout. Performing his role as her XO with the same ease he performed everything else. Biran's heart skipped a beat, but not for the reasons it usually did upon sighting that man.

Tomas's man in grey. The Nazca that had, apparently, manipulated Tomas's memory to make him a more compliant, if not better, agent. And not just Nazca, but high up the chain, privy to their deepest secrets.

Impossible in so, so many ways. He was a Keeper. He was on the Protectorate. He was...Vladsen looked up from the console, met Biran's gaze, and smiled, a curl falling across his forehead. Biran smiled back.

Seventy-eight percent wasn't much. He would be careful, and he would have to put the question to Rost soon, but now he had a ship to command.

Biran took a seat near to Scalla, bringing up a continuously refreshing list of diagnostics regarding the local system.

"What do we have so far?" he asked the deck at large.

"Not much," Russo answered, pushing his own readout to the forward viewscreen. The cameras of the *Terminus*, one of the first systems brought back online in case of a collision risk, had been busy plotting out the local system in concert with the more detailed scanners that were brought on after the fact.

Biran made a quick mental catalogue of the system so far. M-sequence star, three gas giants, two ice balls, and a couple of rocky worlds closer in. Asteroid belt, but no dwarf planet in range—that was the first thing the scanners checked for upon entering a new system. Biran frowned, disappointed. This system was a dead end, then, unless he could find another asteroid that fit the profile, and he sincerely doubted the High Protectorate would sanction that experiment again. At least there wasn't a wall of berserker drones like Sanda had run into when she'd found *The Light*.

"Get me details on the moons around those gas giants," he said.

"Already scanning," Russo said.

"Director," Sato said with a hint of hesitation, "the equipment used for gas composition evaluation is still coming back online, but early reports indicate an oxygen-rich atmosphere around one of the rocky planets. We're too far for visual."

Biran frowned at the graphical representation of the planets and rubbed the side of his chin. "How rich are we talking?"

"Earth-rich, maybe a little on the low side. Rest of the mix seems to match."

Silence. A vise squeezed Biran's chest, anticipation making his skin clammy and cool. "This isn't...?"

"Sol?" Russo finished. He shook his head. "No. I don't think so. Looks a hell of a lot like it, but that star is way younger, and we've got too many gas giants and no Pluto or Charon."

"I need visual on that planet," he said.

"Releasing camera scouts," Scalla said.

The *Terminus* was equipped with the finest cameras Prime had to offer, but even they were limited by the incredible distance. *The Light* could do better, but they'd built these drones from the ground up—none of Halston's designs infecting the process—and made them only capable of following a trajectory and sending back video. They didn't even have the usual data link that ran through gate tech, so they were subject to time delay.

Forty minutes of fruitless scanning and system checks later, the cameras pinged home. Biran pushed the footage through to the main viewscreen.

A blue marble shot through with swirls of fluffy white, two grey moons pirouetting around that perfect, gleaming sphere.

Biran's breath caught. Prime had found its fair share of rocky planets in the habitable zone, but they'd never come with vegetation. With atmosphere thick enough for *clouds*. Their magnetospheres were always shot to hell, thin things if they even had them to begin with, their atmospheres thready and useless. Icarion was built on such a planet. Sometimes, rarely, they found evidence of fossils when they dug very, very deep. But mostly, they didn't bother, because it was easier to put a hab dome down on a frozen rock like the dwarf planets that orbited the gates than to try and live closer to any given system's star, where the air was warmer, but the dangers thicker. Solar storms were common, plate tectonics devastating for atmo domes that weren't placed with the utmost care.

Biran had a sinking suspicion why they always found the close-in, rocky planets in various states of devastation.

"How long until we can get there?" he asked.

Monta answered immediately. "The engines are in good shape after the crossing, we have full use of the reactor, boosters, and adjusters. Power levels are normal."

Russo said, "I have to finish scanning the system, get an idea for what kind of orbital assist would help versus hurt, but a few days... maybe a week? Hard to say."

"Get me hard numbers," Biran said. "I'll call this in to the Prime Director now."

Biran punched her private ident line into his pad, set the appropriate permissions, and hit send. Nothing happened. He scowled.

"Keeper Greystone, comms—"

The lights on the deck of the *Terminus* dimmed, all alert lights turning a soft shade of amber as the *Terminus*, impossibly, repeated the power-down sequence that it had initiated before the gate crossing.

"What the fuck," Scalla said, which was not the most encouraging outburst from a ship's captain, but eloquent enough.

"Did we come fully back online?" Biran asked, running his own diagnostics. Everything looked normal, except that they were well outside the range of the gate's signal for power-down.

"We're still heading away," Russo said, frowning. "Course has not changed, drifting slightly due to lack of power in the stabilizing jets. I'm trying to get them back online now."

"Keeper Monta?" Biran asked.

Her grey eyes narrowed as she jabbed at the engineering console. "I don't know, Director. As Keeper Russo says, everything is green on my end except the power-down, and even that is functioning according to protocol." She stood. "I need to get below, check in with the engineering team in person, since comms are throttled."

"Go," he said, gesturing.

She nodded and jogged off, one of the guardcore peeling away to escort her into the depths of the ship. Something Biran had seen nagged at him, but he couldn't put a finger on it. A ship reinitiating the power-down while near a gate wasn't unheard of. Less well-maintained ships were known to accidentally kick the procedure on when in the middle of a route, initiating the full power-down instead of a power-saver mode. But a ship as important and well maintained as the *Terminus* shouldn't do such a thing.

The lights flickered on the deck. That was definitely not part of a controlled power-down.

"Director," one of the guardcore said, "we need to move you to a secure location."

He grimaced. "Premature. Keeper Russo, how's our course looking?"

"Drifting, but not unrecoverable."

"Keeper Slatter?"

"Nothing's targeting us," he said, bent over his console, brow furrowed. "But of course power to the weapons system was the first thing to go down. Shields are still up, we'd know if something out there was aiming, but we can't aim back."

"Get those guns back online," he said.

"Working on it," Slatter said.

"Director," the guardcore repeated, and although its voice was carefully smoothed by the computerization, Biran thought he detected a note of irritation. "This ship cannot defend itself. We are moving you to a secure location."

"That is not—"

"Maybe listen to the people whose job it is to keep your ass attached, kid," Scalla said in a slow drawl. She didn't even look up from her display as she said it, just kept on glaring at diagnostics that didn't make any sense. From anyone else, speaking to a director in such a way would have gotten them thrown in the brig for the night.

"Our captain is wise," Vladsen cut in smoothly.

Biran shook his head, mingled amusement and irritation warring within him, but he stood. "Very well. But I want every update you can spare me."

"We've got it," Slatter said, turning to grin at Biran. "You picked us for this, remember?"

Not for this, he thought, but forced himself to smile at Slatter in what he hoped was an encouraging way before three guardcore closed around him, forming a protective triangle.

He sighed as they marched him down the hall to the conference room where he'd revealed the truth to the other Keepers. This was ridiculous. Just a malfunction. An annoying one, yes, but not unusual. If he'd still been Speaker, they would have left him on that deck to do his duty, not bundled him away in a safe little box.

A memory of Director Olver surfaced, on the day they had uploaded their data to the gate build bots, and Keeper Hitton had self-destructed the asteroid survey site. The director had seemed so in control, so calm and smooth, while inside Biran knew he was already mourning the death of his friend, choking back fear that the attack would extend beyond the asteroid site—that the destruction would spread, spurring the war with Icarion hot again.

All of that, the director must have been feeling, but it hadn't registered on his expression. He'd moved with deliberate care, making the calls he needed to even while the guardcore closed around him like a fist, ushering him and all the other Keepers on the dock into the safety of the Cannery. All except Biran, for he had been Speaker then, and his duties had lain elsewhere. They'd left a guardcore behind to watch his back, but it wasn't the same thing.

He hadn't appreciated the freedom then, and he regretted that as two guardcore followed him into the conference room, the third guarding the door.

Hydraulics hissed in the walls of the ship as extra security measures were put into place, turning the conference room from eavesdrop proof to vacuum proof. He'd read the specs. If the ship was attacked and beyond salvage, this conference room could be jettisoned, used as a sort of life pod.

"I don't think such preparations are necessary," he said, but took his seat at the head of the table.

"We have our orders," one of the guardcore said.

A chill raced down Biran's spine, and he struggled to keep the emotion off his face. Guardcore didn't have orders, not exactly. They followed carefully ingrained protocols—not missions handed down from on high. Their leaders rotated regularly; a hierarchy such as existed in the fleet did not exist for the guardcore.

Biran thought he'd scrubbed all the potential infiltrators from this crew. He'd been wrong.

He flicked his gaze for the emergency beacon in his monocle HUD, but never made it. An armored hand slammed into the side of his face, knocking his head back against the chair. Plex and metal shattered, fragments digging into his skin, washing his vision with rosy blood.

Stars swam behind his eyes as he grimaced, pushing through, struggling to reach the beacon on his wristpad instead. Strong hands dragged his arms back, wrenching his shoulders as they twisted his arms up behind the back of the chair.

"No need for that, now. You're perfectly safe, Director," a guardcore said. "All we need you to do is call that sister of yours."

CHAPTER 40

PRIME STANDARD YEAR 3543

BENEATH THE MOUNTAIN

I'm sorry," Sanda said, "your *wife*?"

"Well," Maria spoke over her, "it had to happen eventually. I left orders to that effect."

Okonkwo looked away, shamefaced. "I'm afraid the Acolytes no longer guard the spheremind, but worship her instead."

She hummed to herself and tapped her chin. "After so long, who can blame them?" She blinked. "How long, exactly?"

"It is 3543," Okonkwo said.

Maria looked a touch unsettled at the revelation. She stared at her hands, turning them over in the faint light cast by Sanda's and Nox's rifles, as if she could not imagine they hadn't blown away to dust hundreds of years ago. "Remarkable."

"Somebody's going to get shot real soon if you don't explain what's going on, because the last I heard, your wife was Halston, and Halston is dead. I'll take an answer from either of you."

"Shooting me won't do any good," Maria said, and cocked her head to the side, as if listening. "Though it wouldn't be much fun for your Prime Director... Wait..." Her expression darkened, lips thinning. "Is Lex here? Are you that stupid?"

Maria reached for Okonkwo with such force that the Prime Director jerked back, kicking off a trunk strapped to the "floor." The harness connecting Maria to the wall stretched, and in the faint light Sanda realized that the straps were actually tubes, implanted through the jumpsuit and, if her guess was right, directly into Maria's skin. Maria winced as the tubes pulled at her, and let them take her back to the other side of the room.

"She's not here," Tomas said. He'd set his visor to clear, so she could see his face, and pulled himself into the room. "It's me you're sensing, Salvez. I'm not Rainier, but I am made of the same stuff. Same as you, I suppose."

Maria narrowed her eyes at Tomas. "Rainier?"

"It is what she calls herself, now," Okonkwo said.

Maria folded over, and at first Sanda thought she was coughing, and maybe that was how it started, but soon her frail body shook with belly-deep laughter. There was no mirth in the sound, no joy. Only pain and bitterness.

"Really? Did you ever ask her why she chose that name?" Maria asked.

Sanda said, "She told me she was named for a mountain."

Maria's gaze snapped to Sanda's, and even through the mirror of the visor she felt pinned to the spot, as if that glare alone could flense the flesh from her bones before she'd have a chance to pull the trigger in defense.

"Mount Rainier was a volcano, dear fleetie—you are still called fleeties, aren't you?"

"I am Commander Greeve," Sanda said, and had never felt the words more than in that moment.

"Ah. I like your attitude, Commander. It was a beautiful mountain, before the volcano at its heart woke up. The blast was heard around the world, or so I'm told. I was in Tau Ceti at the time. Its smoke blackened the sky, destroyed the commerce of the western seaboard, and dropped the global temperature by three degrees. Which would have been a benefit, at the time, if the darkness did not start the crops failing."

"There is no record of such an event," Okonkwo said.

"Of course not," Maria said. "The Corp Wars began in earnest shortly after. You have records of that, at least?"

"Yes," Okonkwo said. "We've kept extensive records of all public histories."

"Public histories." Maria savored the phrase, smiling to herself as she said it. Already her cheeks were fuller, her face approaching the beautiful moon-round it had been in the history books.

"Everyone keeps their own history," Maria said to herself. Sanda wondered how long she'd been alone, just what that endless isolation might have done to her mind, but said nothing, letting the ancient creature come around to what she wanted to say. Maria's gaze drifted back to Sanda.

"Shall I show you the history I keep for her, for my Lex?"

Sanda swallowed, but nodded.

Maria lifted a hand. The lights came up in the *Reina Mora*. Slowly, at first, a trickle of bluish dawn, progressing through bruise purple and into peach and orange and, finally, the clear light of a yellow sun through a blue atmosphere.

Sanda's chest clenched. She'd seen a lot of sunrises simulated under a hab dome, but nothing like what Maria had demonstrated. The color progression lacked purity, she thought. It was not a steady step through wavelengths, but muddied. Messy. Warm.

"It was the eruption of Mount Rainier that pushed things too far," Maria said. "By that time, we had found the second sphere, and with the help of the spheremind, we had performed a few successful enhancement experiments.

"Many of the medicines that would extend the lifetimes of our citizens came out of those trials. But the ascension-agent promised more, and Lex would be denied nothing that technology could give her. And so, behind her back, in an attempt to please and soothe her...I brought Erik back."

Clearly, she expected that name to mean something. Sanda glanced at Okonkwo, who shrugged.

"We missed that part," Sanda prompted.

"Erased him, too, did she? Or perhaps she renamed the man. This was his face, at the time, though Lex was changing those elements, too, by the end."

Maria Salvez fiddled with the most primitive wristpad Sanda had ever seen, and flicked up an image to a tablet stuck on the wall. Sanda's blood ran cold.

The face was younger, the eyes another color, but the hair and chin were the same. So was the look in those eyes, no matter what color they were. Bored, but predatory. A cat playing with a mouse it'd long since grown tired with, but wasn't willing to kill yet.

"Keeper Lavaux," Sanda said.

"I...did not know," Okonkwo said, her voice affecting a slight stammer. "He presented himself as one of Rainier's remakes, and claimed he could keep her under control."

Maria's lips twisted. "Clever. He hated her, of course, but she was very much not herself by the time I fled."

"Why did he hate her?" Sanda asked.

"Erik Anstrom," Maria said, flicking a dossier to the tablet. She spoke as if she were addressing a much larger audience, falling into the rhythm of a presenter. From what Sanda could remember of early history books, Salvez had taken over much of Halston's public speaking engagements toward the end of Halston's life—an eventual slow slide into old age and death. Which, apparently, was bullshit.

"He was one of the pilots of this ship, the *Reina Mora*, and one of Prime's youngest and brightest scientists. After we had been in Tau Ceti a year, Braxton, the CEO of another private space corporation, got to him. Twisted him to his side. Erik tried to assassinate Lex. She handled the attempt herself, and he became the first person she ever killed with her own hands."

"If she killed him," Sanda said, "then why did my friend Bero throw his ass out an airlock?"

"He is dead now?" Her gaze snapped to Sanda, and the presenter voice went away, replaced with a thick sense of desperation. "You are certain?"

"Yes. Whatever he was, it wasn't enough to withstand vacuum."

"Good," she said softly. "I always regretted that. After Lex killed him, I was left to clean up. He...still had a pulse. I did not tell her. I took his body to a medical pod and placed him into a coma.

"At the time, a naive part of me believed that as long as the machine kept Erik's vital signs ticking along, then Lex had not done that monstrous thing. She could not have been a killer, if the man she attacked had not died.

"When work on the second sphere stalled, she complained of needing a test subject. While she was willing to kill outright to protect her secrets, something in Lex drew the line at medical experimentation on a living subject. I was afraid."

"Afraid she'd use you?" Sanda asked.

"No," Maria said, her smile wistful and sad. "Afraid she'd run the first test on herself. With the spheremind's help, I administered the ascension-agent to Erik. That he woke immediately was a surprise to all of us."

"You brought Halston's would-be assassin back to life?" Okonkwo asked with abject horror. Sanda wanted to point out that Lex was a fucking monster, not the valiant visionary Prime painted her to be, but she wanted to keep Salvez talking, so she kept the thought to herself.

"If it failed, it would be no great loss, and if it worked, then we could finally interrogate him about the assassination plot. I did not expect him to be so...worshipful of me. He was no threat to Lex after that."

"Bringing someone back to life is a good way to get a messiah complex," Nox said.

"True," Maria said, regarding Nox with dead eyes. "But Erik's devotion had its uses. When Lex finally lost herself, he was there to keep her under control. On my orders."

"He lied to her left and right and made her fucking insane, is more like," Sanda said. "Rainier thinks she was the intelligence that came with the second sphere. She thinks she's a *spaceship* denied her rightful body. I don't think that's your Lex. She's something else."

"She's not insane," Tomas said carefully. "She had complete understanding of how *The Light* operated."

"*The Light*?" Maria asked.

Sanda said into her comms, "Show yourself, B."

The view in the window changed. At first there was little more than a silvery eclipse, but then Bero pulled back, putting enough distance between *The Light* and the *Reina Mora* so that those on board could see the full, shining expanse of the ship's hull. Salvez's eyes gleamed, mirrored with that silver.

"It's safe. You found it."

"We call it *The Light*," Sanda said, "and it is my ship."

Salvez leaned forward, tugging against her tubes. "I pray it serves as a light for you, Commander. That ship brought me only darkness."

"Rainier thinks it's her body. I'm not sure the woman you knew exists anymore. She wants..." Sanda cleared her throat. "She wants to destroy humanity. To punish it for what Lex did, for building all the gates. I presume you knew about the blowback?" Her finger returned to the trigger. Maria didn't seem to notice.

"She's at war with herself, then," Maria said. "Good. That will buy you some time. It might even be the key to her final destruction. You see, there is no longer any distinction between Lex and the spheremind.

"After our success with Erik, we used the agent on ourselves. The results were...euphoric." She glanced at Tomas, who didn't so much as twitch a muscle. "We kept it under wraps for a very long time, to make certain there were no side effects, then brought the first Protectorate into our fold. We were ecstatic, it was working, the spheremind was pleased, and then two of them fell into a coma.

"The spheremind did not understand how such a thing was possible. We had created the gates, after all, and thereby passed the first test. We should have been perfectly capable of interpreting the data of the second sphere correctly.

"But we had cheated. We were missing some base knowledge of the alien technology that the mind guarding the first sphere should have granted us. Information the second did not have."

"Did you tell the spheremind you stole the first sphere?" Sanda asked.

"We did not *steal*," Maria snapped with sudden vehemence. "But, no, we did not tell her the first fell into our laps.

"Around this time, Mount Rainier happened. Earth was in grave peril, and Prime Inventive moved to help as best we could. We sent our carbon scrapers, the nutriblock printers, advanced water recycling. We threw every scrap we had at that planet, while the crops died and the people wasted away. It was...not enough.

"Our species," she said, back in presenter mode, "always needs someone to blame. Their politicians turned against Prime, the Corp Wars escalated, and soon enough, the governments of Earth combined their resources, and destroyed the Charon Gate.

"Lex was furious. They had meant to damage our supply lines— the talking point at the time was that Prime took more from the struggling planet than it gave back—which was nonsense. Braxton had developed that talking point, and as soon as the gate was gone, his people set to picking up what scraps were left, trying to reverse engineer what Prime had built.

"His people moved into the belt, taking over our mining stations. We lost all contact. We had our resources, yes, and Prime would not have died. But we knew that soon enough Braxton would build a gate of his own, and when Earth finally spun its way back into Tau Ceti, it would come with an army we could not repel."

She closed her eyes, and when she opened them again, she was seeing a different vista than *The Light* on the other side of the window.

"And so, we built another gate to Charon. From the Tau Ceti side."

"The blowback," Sanda said, voice tight.

"We didn't know," Maria said, eyes bright with manufactured tears. "We didn't know."

"You killed them," Sanda said through a dry throat. "You killed *Earth*. You killed our *home*."

"Yes," Salvez said, tugging at the collar of her jumpsuit. A silver chain stood out against her skin. "And knowing that...That's when the killing really began. The first delegation through did not contain either of us. We feared Braxton would have weapons ready on the other side, and so we sent a diplomatic ship, flying white flags, back to our dead, dead home.

"The broadcasts they sent back...Devastation. Not a scrap of metal made by man left in the sky. No satellites, no stations. The planets themselves raged with storms and our sun threw off coronal arcs the likes of which I've never seen again. Earth boiled, its plates trembled, and its sky burned black with the death of the forests and everything—*everything*—else.

"We did not believe it. How could we? And so we came through personally, a fleet squadron flanking us, guardcore filling our ship, and confirmed what we had done. What we had *been* doing, every time we spun one of those gates."

"And you did not *tell us*?" Okonkwo demanded. She surged forward, grabbed Maria by the fabric over her chest, and shook her hard enough that the woman's head snapped back and forth.

"How could you not warn us? How could you not *stop*? Do you know how many gates I've spun in the name of Prime? Do you understand the saccharine, bullshit speeches I've given each time one of those gates opened, praising humanity, promising us a bright and brilliant future without knowing that we did it on the back of a burned-out universe? That we marched a parade across a river of corpses? You—*you* have made me a murderer of untold worlds."

"I tried to stop it," Maria said, tears beading against her eyes, unable to fall without gravity. "I wanted it to *stop*."

"You're still here," Sanda said, jaw clicking as she forced it apart. "You're still alive. You could have reached out at *any* time, but instead you said nothing. You hid, while other worlds burned. Did you help her? Did clever Dr. Maria Salvez help her wife build the scout bots? The survey swarms that stripped the worlds bare and fed back false data to hide the evidence of what Prime had done?"

"Yes," she said. "I did. I built them all."

Okonkwo punched her in the face. Blood more silver than red splashed from her nose, from her lip, hung suspended in the air as Maria's body flew under the force, slammed into the wall. Maria covered her face with her hands and moaned, but Sanda didn't think it was the physical pain. She doubted that creature could feel real agony anymore.

"Tell me what I need to know to destroy her," Sanda said.

Maria looked up, through bloodstained fingers, eyes huge. "You can't. Lex was so scared she...She didn't want the spheremind to know what she had done. Didn't want the makers of the spheres to discover her crimes."

"So she did it *more*?"

"She convinced herself the only way to save humanity from retaliation was to destroy the Waiting before they found out what she'd done. She opened as many gates as she could spare the resources to build, never stopping on any one world long enough to do more than drop off an atmo dome, set up an outpost city, and press on. Until the day the spheremind discovered the truth."

"What happened?" Sanda pressed.

Maria dragged her fingers down her face, smearing blood, and curled up much as she had been when Sanda had found her.

"I don't know. I don't know how the spheremind found out. She confronted us, there, on that ship." She jerked her chin at *The Light*. "Lex and Erik and me. She was horrified, furious. Like you, she wanted to know why we didn't stop. Why we kept on covering it up, why Lex pushed on so hard and fast that humanity straggled on behind her, exhausted. And Lex . . . she told her. Told her everything.

"Told her she meant to destroy the spheremind's progenitors, the Waiting, to protect humanity from what she had done. The ship broadcasted a warning, of that I'm sure, but then Lex put her hand to the wall and she was just . . . gone. Her body dropped, seized. Blood spilled from her eyes and she . . . she never came back."

Sanda slid her gaze, behind the shelter of her helmet, to Tomas. He'd blanched, one hand bracing himself against the wall. "She uploaded herself into the ship."

"Yes. I didn't think such a thing was possible, but she and Erik . . . Well, they made their own experiments, and while he hated her for being Alexandra Halston, he adored her for being the one who'd brought the spheres to humanity. And me, he worshipped, and I'd told him to help her. I never imagined he'd take things so far.

"Once she was in the ship, she did something to the mind, I don't know what. She didn't erase it, not completely. But Lex had forgotten things in the struggle. Lost parts of herself."

"Like how to build the gates?" Sanda asked.

Maria blinked owlishly at her. "How did you know?"

"Halston should know how to build a Casimir Gate. Rainier doesn't have a clue. She had to hire humans to build a nanite network so she could access the gates' power systems. She reversed the flow of the blowback, but her attempt was incomplete. We lost some people, but not so many as we would have if Halston had known what she was doing."

"*Lex* did that? She turned our own weapon against us? That doesn't make any sense."

"That's what I've been telling you," Sanda said. "The being that is Rainier cannot possibly be Halston. I spoke with her. I saw...I saw the hate in her, when she talked of humanity. How unworthy we were to inherit the stars. She called us thieves, and I guess we were, but Rainier's not Lex. She must be the spheremind."

"Actually..." Tomas said, then trailed off as everyone looked at him. He took a breath. "It makes some sense. What Dr. Salvez described Halston doing to *The Light* sounds a whole hell of a lot like what Rainier tried to do to Bero. By the time I intervened, Rainier was trying to wall off Bero." He tapped at his wristpad. "B, if Rainier had managed to sequester you in the hardware of *The Light* and you had been trapped in there with her, would it have been possible for any bleed-over to occur between the two of you?"

"That is difficult to answer, as I was distracted with fighting for my life. But yes, the theory is possible."

"If you were in there for a while, would you have been able to breach some of her defenses?"

"I would like to believe so. Though what I consider a 'long time' at my processing speeds would happen in a matter of microseconds."

"Thanks, B."

"For what it's worth, I agree with the supposition you are about to make," Bero said.

Tomas nodded to himself. "That was the intelligence currently inhabiting *The Light*. He, and I, believe that the entity that calls itself Rainier is a bleed-over mix of Lex and the spheremind. It's possible Keeper Lavaux—Erik—helped keep Lex in control. Once he was killed, the spheremind bled through. Consider how long she would have ridden around in that head, in fragments, hating everything Lex did but unable to stop her."

"That would breed the kind of bitterness I heard in Rainier's voice," Sanda said.

"Who in the fuck *are* you?" Okonkwo demanded of Tomas.

He shrugged. "That's an open question, but not important at the moment. Dr. Salvez, forgive me for asking this, but I hope you understand that getting Lex back in control of the body of Rainier is of paramount importance to the survival of humanity. There is something in this star system that Rainier wants. We only overheard part of a conversation, but we think she denied it to her Acolytes for decades, at least, and has only now shown interest in collecting it. Could it be you, Doctor? Is there a way in which the spheremind could use you to hurt humanity?"

"Me?" She let out a soft, bitter laugh. "No. After all these years... No, I am inconsequential. It's what I stole from her before I fled here and entrusted the key to this gate to the next Prime Director."

Maria slipped her hand beneath her collar and pulled out the silver chain. At the end, wrapped in wire, was a perfect, shining sphere no larger than an egg. It glowed with a soft, inner light.

"The third," Sanda said. "What are its instructions?"

Salvez shook her head. "There are none. The sphere is perfectly smooth. We tracked down the distress signal the spheremind sent before Lex overwhelmed her, and found this in the center of... nothing. No ship, no station. Not even a scrap of rock. A barren system—not by our hand—and this minuscule object, a needle in a trillion haystacks, impossible to find, if one did not know where to look. It consumed Lex for a long time. She believed we needed only to invent a microscope capable of visualizing on a smaller scale, but we already had the tachyon.

"That was when she first printed herself. She said she missed hands, but the body that came out of *The Light* was not my Lex, and I do not mean the physical details. She had changed too much. Her moods had always been intense, but there was a mania in that new body.

"I'd begun to suspect that she had pierced the digital cyst she'd grown around the spheremind in an attempt to extract information about the third sphere. It was driving her mad, not knowing. And one day... One day her eyes went silver, and she called the sphere a key. *'A key to bring them all home'* in a voice which was not hers. When the fugue state faded, the... thirst in her was new, all-consuming. She had built hundreds of gates by then, hundreds of weapons. All she needed to do, she told me, was to figure out how to use the key. To bring them through on the other side, then turn the gates on them. Then, and only then, could she be assured that humanity was safe.

"I...couldn't do it. I couldn't let her risk what it would mean to weaponize the gates, the utter destruction that would happen on the blowback side. She'd kill half of us in the process, but that was a price she was willing to pay for peace."

"And so you fled," Sanda said.

"Yes. I stole the sphere and ran here, entrusting the spin key with the Prime Director. Everyone already thought Lex was dead then. I told them her ascension-agent conversion had been incomplete, and that she had attempted to upload her consciousness into a synthetic body, before the end. That she was no longer really herself—a little cracked, a little dangerous. Something to be protected, but watched, always. A relic of Prime, and let Erik keep the truth."

"How did you get her *out* of the ship?" Sanda asked.

Maria frowned. "What do you mean? She was in the body, she could not be two places at once."

Sanda laughed roughly. By way of answer, she tapped at her wrist-pad, and flicked up the footage she'd captured of Rainier on the fringer settlement. The moment when, grinning like death itself, all the guardcore lined up behind the instance of Rainier that had come to capture Sanda retracted their helmets, revealing pale, identical faces.

Sanda had lived that moment, and had no intention of living it again, so she watched Salvez instead. Watched her eyes bulge and her hands come up to cover her mouth. Dread seeped into Sanda's belly. Salvez didn't know. Which meant she didn't know how to kill Rainier once and for all, either.

"Mother Mary," Maria breathed. "She's...How?"

"I was hoping you could tell me," Sanda said. "She's been doing this a long time. We've destroyed hundreds of her already, and she keeps popping up."

"This...She could not do this thing, before. I'm so sorry, I do not know if this can be undone."

"Kenwick stole the ship from her," Sanda said. "He hid it, and the second sphere, behind a deadgate, presumably because he realized Rainier had lost so much of Lex that she could not figure out how to spin the gate without human help. He died trying to keep that secret, running from Lavaux and Rainier."

"*Rayson* Kenwick?" Maria asked, breathless.

"Yes."

"Oh, that it came to that. Did he pick a successor, before the end?"

"A successor for what?"

"Prime Director, of course. I presume you met?" Maria turned dead eyes on Okonkwo.

"I never met the man. Official sources stated he died hundreds of years before I took office, though what actually became of him, I cannot say. My predecessor never mentioned him. I was told only that Rainier was a fragment of the intelligence that accompanied the sphere, and Lavaux was more or less her babysitter."

Maria grimaced. "The trouble of a secret kept too well is that it dies with its Keepers. You were supposed to be informed, Prime Director. You were supposed to keep the watch, but it seems Lavaux and Rainier slipped their leash a long time ago. What of the other Acolytes? Some must have lived to warn you."

"Loyal to Rainier," Sanda said. "Immortality is a hell of a temptation."

Maria's face twisted in a grimace. "Only until you have it."

"Well," Sanda said, "at least now we can be sure of her motives. If it's the spheremind in control, she wants exactly what she said—she wants her sisters back, and she wants to punish us for taking them from her."

Bero said through her wristpad, "If I had been trapped for hundreds of years, I would want to kill all those who had a hand in it."

Sanda almost bit through her tongue.

"Right now," Sanda said, "I've got multiple planets full of innocent people on the chopping block. I'm sorry for what happened to the spheremind, and I'm disgusted by what Halston did, but I'm not losing worlds. Dr. Salvez, Rainier has already infected an entire city with the ascension-agent. Thousands of people are in comas. Can you help? Is there a way for this to be undone?"

"If the spheremind is in control, then it can fix the error."

"Yeah, I don't think she's going to oblige." Sanda sighed raggedly and extended her hand. "The sphere, please."

Maria flinched and grabbed the floating orb with both hands. "No.

She cannot have it. What Lex wanted was terrible, but the sphere-mind will bring her makers through to punish us."

"Lady," Sanda grated, "the time for you to make any decisions regarding the future of humanity has long since fucking passed. That sphere is the only object in the cosmos Rainier actually wants, and I need leverage to flush her out. If it stays here with you, it's only a matter of time until she figures out how to spin this gate and comes to say hello. You were complicit in countless deaths. Your part in this is done. You're done."

"We didn't know," Maria said.

"But then you did, and it's everything that comes after I can't forgive you for." Sanda curled her fingers.

"I'm not a monster," Maria whispered.

"Keep telling yourself that."

Salvez slipped the chain over her head, and tossed the sphere to Sanda. She snatched it out of the air, and ran her thumb around it, searching for indentations, but if there were any to be found Halston would have teased them out long ago. Her fingers slipped against it, so smooth it almost repelled her touch. Slippery and perfectly even, like thin ice above a killing-cold lake.

Cepko: Salvez strike you as too virtuous in this story?

Greeve: She does. Think you can get it out of her?

Cepko: I'd like to try. Make it look like you don't want me to stay.

Greeve: Won't be hard.

"We're leaving," Sanda said. "There's nothing else left for us here."

"Just going to leave her here, boss?" Nox asked.

Sanda nodded, her gaze tracking to the window. While *The Light* filled the view now, she knew the landscape beyond. Knew Maria had anchored herself to that wall so that she could use her enhanced vision to watch the pinprick that was dead Earth spin its way around the sun until that star finally gave its last gasp and went red dwarf, right on schedule.

"This is her mausoleum. We've done enough disturbing of the dead."

Maria nodded and curled within herself once more, tucking her chin down. Sanda had once read a book on the insects of Earth—rare creatures brought along only to help with crop growth—and thought of cicadas. A noisy and disruptive species during the time they lived, but they would hibernate, sleeping below the deadfall of the planet, buried deep in the dirt, waiting for the cycle to come around and draw them out of the dark. There'd be no future for Maria. She would wait here until the sun, or her nanites, failed.

"I'd like to talk with Dr. Salvez privately," Tomas said.

Sanda allowed the team to see her hesitate, and glanced at the time readout in her HUD, then nodded. "Ten minutes."

"Understood," he said.

"Need someone on your six?" Nox asked.

"No," Tomas said. "Salvez and I, we understand each other. Isn't that right?"

She picked her head up, glaring at him, but nodded. A curl of dread twisted through Sanda, but she pushed it aside. She could not deny him this chance. But if Salvez so much as tried to harm him, Sanda would have *The Light* slingshot the *Reina Mora* straight into the sun.

"Ten minutes," she repeated, and kicked out of the cylinder after her crew, leaving Tomas alone with his Methuselah.

CHAPTER 41

PRIME STANDARD YEAR 3543

NOT A SIMULATION

Biran spat blood and forced himself to breathe in slow, even breaths. The stars going nova behind his eyes faded, letting him focus. There were only two guardcore in the room, surely he could figure a way out of this.

"Rainier, I thought I'd cleaned out your little nest."

The guardcore standing next to him—the one with Biran's blood on the back of its glove—laughed. "Rainier does not operate alone. Your extermination of her ancillaries has been a convenient distraction, though. Did it make you feel like you were doing something? Crushing those bodies? She has thousands more. The only resources you've wasted are your own."

"Morale is a resource. How did it feel for you, to stand beside your benefactor and watch her heads explode, one after another, while you stood by, helpless to defend her?"

Pain burst across his jaw once more, bone crunching as Biran's head snapped back, hot agony racing down his throat, pounding through his temples until the implants Keepers used to control their pain response kicked in, detecting the overload that almost sent him spiraling into unconsciousness.

He choked on bile and leaned forward, gasping as the grip on his arms tightened, wrenching his shoulders in their sockets.

"So it did hurt your feelings," he said when he could speak again.

"Shut your fucking mouth." The guardcore growled out the words, causing the filter over their voice to crackle. "We're not talking. You're calling your sister."

"Sanda?" Biran picked his head up, and put on a puzzled expression. Blood filled his mouth and he had to spit it out, lest he choke. Something ground in his jaw, sending fresh waves of pain through him. The implants, designed to help Keepers withstand torture, only did so much. They could be disabled, if an assailant was clever enough to notice them, and so they let enough pain through to keep the performance convincing. "Why don't I call up my parents, too? We could have a grand reunion, but I hardly see how a Greeve family picnic will help you."

The guardcore pressed the barrel of its rifle against Biran's throat, tipping his chin up and back. He swallowed his own blood, heart thundering in his chest.

"You know what we want."

The Light. They wanted Biran to make that call, so that Sanda would drop whatever she was doing and come running straight into a trap.

"Sandwiches?" Biran asked.

The rifle butt slammed into his chest, knocking the air out of him. He gasped, inhaled his own blood, and coughed for so long, whole body shuddering and wrenching against the grip of his captor, that by the time he was done he felt like he'd aged a year in a minute.

"Make the call," the guardcore said.

He laughed, a sound so gravelly it barely sounded human. "You are guardcore. I am a Keeper. You know better than anyone on all of Prime's forsaken worlds that I cannot be tortured into doing what you want me to do. You will push so hard that you accidentally kill me, or you will take long enough that the others will come to investigate. Either way, you're not getting what you want."

"We control this ship," the guardcore said, stalking around the conference room table. "We control your life support, your power. Will you sit there and refuse us, as we bleed the air out of the command deck?"

The viewscreen in the conference room table lit up, showing the deck as he'd left it—Scalla, Vladsen, Russo, Sato, Slatter. Monta must still be in engineering, with the attendant guardcore who'd followed her. His picks, all of them. His responsibility. His stomach dropped, but an iron cage honed through years of training closed around his heart, and locked.

Because this was why Keepers were selected, when it came down to it. Politics and aptitude and brilliance and all that other shit didn't get you a chip if you couldn't shut yourself down. If you couldn't sit in your trainer's chair, strapped down, and have everything and everyone you'd ever loved threatened while the knives cut and the acids burned.

The final test. They didn't speak of it. They couldn't speak of it. Those who failed, died. Or went back to their families broken and empty, and everyone assumed it was the failure that haunted them. Not the scalpels. Not the nanites crawling beneath your skin.

And then, when you'd passed the first round of physical punishment, the haptic feedback immersion sets taking you right up to the edge of death, they dragged you back again only to see your loved ones subjected to the same treatment.

It wasn't real. Keeper hopefuls went into those tests *knowing* they weren't real. But by the time the sims were done with you, you'd forgotten that part. No Keeper in thousands of years had ever broken under torture, because nothing an enemy could come up with would be worse than what they'd already endured—the training they refreshed, every year. They kept it buried, all that pain ready to deploy, to use as a shield, when the time came.

Plenty of Keepers killed themselves. None broke.

"I will sit here and refuse you until every atom in this universe decays."

The simulations had never been real. But this was.

They started with his body, because it was easier. Because it would not yet raise alarms. Straps meant to keep him safe against the chair should the conference room be deployed as a shuttle held him against the table, kept his arms and legs and chest in place while they worked methodically, beginning with the fingers of his right hand, as those were not the fingers he used to manipulate his wristpad.

Biran locked himself down, as he'd been trained, shielding the core of himself behind emotional scar tissue so deep not even guardcore rifles could pierce it. The pain was everything, all-consuming, blinding, and breathtaking. He lost consciousness a few times, though how many was hard to say. He wasn't counting. You start counting the seconds, the minutes, the hurts, and you pay too much attention to the pain. It was better to float in nothing.

And every time, they brought him around enough to speak. Every time they pressed, leaned into him for the ident tag that would make his call to Sanda a priority, something she must accept, he told them no, and fell into the pain all over again.

Part of him was dimly aware that this was not exactly what his training had been meant to resist. It was the Keeper chip his body guarded, nothing more. But that was a slithering whisper, a lure away from what was true. Because Sanda and *The Light* might not be the chip tech, but that ship was the future of Prime. To draw it into Rainier's clutching hands would be as big a betrayal as giving up gate schematics.

The lights flickered. He blinked, or tried to. His eyelids were too swollen, eyes too dry, but he lifted a piece of himself back to the surface of his mind, struggling to puzzle through the agony what that unsteady light meant.

Powered down. The ship had been powered down. But the lights on powered-down ships didn't flicker, and the guardcore had full control of this conference room. They stepped to the side, leaving him there, assuming him unconscious once more, and whispered between themselves.

Strange. They had internal helmet comms. If they wanted to communicate privately, they didn't have to speak out loud. Unless someone was in their comms. Someone had figured them out. Echo.

Hope was a dangerous thing in a Keeper under the press of torture, more dangerous than the growing pain. Hope could lance through the scar tissue, crack the bars of the cage. Hope was poison. But he could help, a little.

His fingers were so mangled that it was no trouble at all to slip his hand through the makeshift binding, lubricated by his own blood.

The guardcore were still in the corner, whispering. He thought he heard the word *launch*, and the thought of being jettisoned with these fuckers gave him a surge of rage, of adrenaline. If he was going to die, it would be on his ship, not stuck in a tin can, waiting for Rainier to come along and scoop up his corpse.

Biran grunted from effort, which drew their attention, but they were too late. His arm flopped over his chest, broken fingers twitching toward the emergency beacon on his wristpad. It took every scrap of strength he had, but he pressed that button.

Red lights filled the room, alarms screaming that their director was in trouble, which really would have been funny, because trouble was such an understatement, but he had no strength left to laugh.

A concussive force pushed him down against the table, yanking against his remaining straps. Metal screamed and gunfire tore over his head from both directions, blasters and rifles a glittering light show right above his head, because he didn't have the strength left to try to roll out of the way.

At the end of the room, the two guardcore finally dropped. Shouting sounded behind him, the words indistinct through the ringing in his ears. Black-armored hands grabbed him and he slammed the bars shut on himself once more on reflex, but this guardcore was cutting his restraints free, shouting orders in a voice that, while filtered, still sounded worried. Echo.

Someone slapped pain patches and stimpatches across his chest—he'd lost his shirt somewhere in all of that—and Biran jerked up, gasping, pain hot as iron dulling to a distant screech in the back of his head as the drugs flooded through him. Not fixing the damage—nothing but a stint in a NutriBath could fix that—but making it bearable. Because he needed to move. Someone was shouting at him to move.

"Biran," Kan Slatter said.

Biran blinked as the other Keeper's face swam into focus in front of his eyes. Slatter's cheek was chewed up by some ordnance, blood dripping down his chin, but his eyes were bright. Focused. He held Biran's face with strange tenderness in both hands and spoke earnestly.

"Come on, man, stay with me, stay up."

"Report," he slurred, because his jaw was broken and he was missing a few teeth and part of his tongue.

Slatter laughed with nervous relief and let Biran's face go. He reached out a hand and Lili Monta handed him another medikit. Both of their hands were slick with blood as they covered Biran in whatever patches they could fit on him.

"A GC turned on Lili down in engineering, almost took her head off, but some fleeties working down there got the jump on them. Took half their damn arsenal, but they got them down. She called it up and this"—he jerked his thumb to Echo—"GC starts firing, takes down the four GC left on the deck and then took off, sprinting after you, I guess. We all thought you'd be locked down in your room, so, shit, I'm sorry, it slowed us down."

"He needs a NutriBath," Keeper Sato said from somewhere behind Biran.

"Not until your team confirms they haven't been tampered with," Echo said.

"Look at him—" Lili's voice caught, and she turned her head away. Blood stained the top of her shirt, and a long plastiskin patch ran around her neck down to her collarbone. "He's in pieces."

Biran was reasonably sure all his parts were still attached, more or less, but something in her hitching tone chilled him.

"Damage?" he asked. At least some of the extra painkillers made it easier for him to force himself into not slurring.

Slatter licked his lips. "We're all beat up, but no one's dead, except Russo. He...he'd turned the ship around. That's what triggered the power-down. None of us saw it, but Captain Scalla figured it out. He shot her in the shoulder, I think Russo was aiming for her head. Vladsen put him down. Moved faster than any of us."

"Not fast enough," Vladsen said in a soft voice.

Biran could not move his head much without swimming in pain, so he slid his gaze to the side, spotting Vladsen on his left, a blaster in his hand and a mask of pure iron pulled over his face. His off arm was bloodied, a plastiskin patch over his bicep, his jaw clenched so tight the tendons of his neck stood out against the thin, silken button-up he wore. His eyes were blank, while every other line of his body radiated rage. Vladsen had gone to the same place of emotional lockdown Biran had, but for different reasons.

"This is no one's fault," Biran said with as much conviction as he could muster. The corners of Vladsen's eyes crinkled, emotion threatening to break through, then flattened.

"Director," Greystone said. She alone appeared unscathed, but her hands were coated in blood, as if she had administered to someone. "What did they want?"

"*The Light.*"

"Did they get it?"

"Look at me, and tell me if they fucking got it," he growled, but the words were too much all at once, and he collapsed into a coughing fit. Kan Slatter, of all people, patted him on the back gingerly until he was done.

"I'm sorry," Greystone asked. "I understand the situation is traumatic, but I had to ask."

"This situation is not over," Echo said from near the blown-in door. "This room is no longer securable, and there are still rogue guardcore on this ship. We need to move to the director's rooms, they can be secured."

"Can you walk?" Slatter asked.

Biran kept his tone neutral. "Both of my Achilles tendons have been severed."

Monta let out a soft sob, and Greystone put an arm around her shoulders, squeezing. Biran very carefully did not look at Vladsen as he heard that man gasp, but kept his gaze locked on Slatter, and swallowed back a manic laugh. Slatter, whose nose Biran had once broken for being a dick about the kidnapping of his sister, nodded grimly and shoved his blaster into his belt.

"I got you, Director," he said, holding out one arm to slip under Biran's.

"No," Vladsen said, voice like ice. "I'll carry him. You're the better shot, Slatter. Keep your hands free."

"And your arm is injured," Speaker Greystone said, expertly slipping into position to scoop Biran up in a wedding-style carry. The transition took his breath away, body shuddering uncontrollably in her firm, stable grasp. Only his overworked implant kept him from losing consciousness. "I have him. Let's move."

Gunfire punctuated the trip through the halls to his rooms, but Biran was so deep in his pain he didn't register who was doing the bulk of the firing. He'd been picked up, and then he was on his bed, and all the in-between was a hazy wash of pain and shouting.

"Hey," Vladsen said, fingertips brushing Biran's brow, one of the few pieces of skin that wasn't brutalized. "Don't pass out on me."

He tried to smile, but it hurt too much, so he cracked an eye open—the other was truly swollen shut now. Rost stood above him at the side of the bed, a blaster in one hand, half turned toward the door, his fingers light against Biran's forehead. For a breath, the iron mask slipped, and he trembled all over, a slow vibration shaking even the curls of his hair.

The crack of rifles outside jerked Vladsen's attention away, put the mask back in place, his body rigid with anticipation. Too long passed, then Slatter jogged into the room, flicked a glance at Vladsen's fingers still on Biran's forehead. Slatter shrugged.

"Sato's people have a checked-out NutriBath inbound. Don't worry, Director. We'll have you back together soon enough."

"The *Terminus*?" Biran asked.

Slatter scratched the side of his head. "Under control, mostly. That GC is working with the fleet to mop up the rest of the guardcore."

"*All* of them?" Biran asked, feeling dizzy.

"They said they couldn't risk it. We're down to one GC and the fleeties now, but hey, at least we're secure. Fucking Russo…" He trailed off, shook himself, then looked at Vladsen. "Need anything?"

"Just the bath," he said, mustering up practiced insouciance like it was nothing.

Biran would have smiled, if he hadn't lost control of those muscles. Panic gripped him at the realization, his lungs felt like they were crawling with thorns, vision blurring at the edges as his back arched, desperate to get down a breath.

Vladsen's and Slatter's shouts mingled into meaninglessness.

"Here," Sato said from somewhere far away, and then he was sinking, sinking into darkness, and breath didn't matter anymore.

CHAPTER 42

PRIME STANDARD YEAR 3543

LEAVE A LIGHT ON

Tomas waited until the crew of *The Light* were back on that ship. Waited until he felt their boots click down into the artificial gravity, the artificial safety. He didn't think about how he knew they were back. Didn't think about the fact he could feel Bero's concern, restrained but bubbling, brush against his consciousness.

He thought, instead, of every word Rainier had said to him in those scant, confusing moments when he'd come out of the reconstruction bath, and focused. Whatever he was, he was Nazca. Extracting relevant information from an unwilling subject was second nature.

"Do you know what I am?" he asked, when the silence had stretched on longer than a human would have found comfortable.

She gave him a crooked smile. "An original, a printed being, much like what Lex became. Like Rainier."

He was getting used to being compared to Rainier, which wasn't a comforting thought. "She called me a subset of her. I need to know what that means, exactly. I need to know if she can affect my mind in any way."

"She cannot, to the best of my knowledge."

"Would you tell me if she could?"

Her smile soured into a bestial grimace. "I have been nothing but forthcoming with you."

And that was the problem. "You have clung to this ship like a barnacle throughout time, guarding a secret you are not physically capable of defending should Rainier ever come for it. I know why you're here, Maria. I know what it's like to crave someone that intensely."

"Rainier is not my Lex."

"No. And that's why you handed over the sphere. If it had gone any other way, we would have had to take it off your corpse."

"You would have found that more difficult than you think."

"Yes, your defenses. I sense them. You made this ship to look like the *Reina Mora*, but it is no such thing, is it? I've learned a lot about how rubber fails, lately. How gaskets degrade under radiation. Even this far away from the sun, over the timeline you proposed, this vessel would not be capable of holding pressure, let alone recycling air and everything else you need. What is this? I can't sense it. It's not of the Waiting."

"I should never have allowed you on board," she hissed.

"That's true," Tomas said, casually peeling the glove from his right hand. "But you did. Because you sensed me, and you hoped with every atom of your being that it was Lex knocking on your door at long last."

"Lex killed billions," she said, eyes darting side to side.

"Yes," Tomas said, "but you loved her anyway."

Her expression twisted with an agony deeper than what she'd displayed when talking about the blowback on Earth, body shuddering with pain that paled in comparison to the punch Okonkwo had landed.

Tomas could relate. Suppressing physical pain was easy. It was the psychological blows that really hurt.

"I took the sphere," she protested, though every scrap of her body language screamed that she was lying. "I took it from her, her future, her plans."

"Maybe you did. Maybe you grabbed it, as you said, but after that? I'm not so sure. Who put you here, Maria? Who locked you in this place?"

She licked her lips, eyes darting again. "I sealed myself away. I left instructions."

Tomas pressed his hand against the wall. Tin-colored metal, stained with age, shimmered beneath his palm, turned a filmy, transparent white.

Bero's mind jolted against his, alarmed, but Tomas soothed the intrusion away and focused on the feeling racing up through his bare skin. This was not a ship of the sphereminds, he knew that instinctively. The internal architecture was all wrong, it could no more support his full consciousness in its wires than a wristpad could, but it was familiar, all the same.

"You made this out of the nanites. You made it to look like the *Reina Mora*." But no, that didn't track. Why would she put herself here, in this ghost of a ship, to stare at the Earth she'd destroyed until her dying gasp? Self-flagellation, maybe.

But the surge of hope that had bled out of her when the crew of *The Light* first arrived, thinking maybe they had brought Lex with them, told another story. What kind of hatred would push a soul to do this to another?

It was the kind of thing Tomas would do to the grey man, to Vladsen, when he found him. The kind of animosity earned by a creator-god when their creation peeks behind the mask, and doesn't like what they see.

"Keeper Lavaux did this to you."

She lunged at him. He twisted deftly aside, and she came up hard against the tubes holding her to the wall, clawed fingers swiping the empty air where he had been.

"He was a traitor!" she spat.

Tomas shook his head. "No. That was the two of you. What did you expect, when you brought Halston's would-be assassin back to life? Did you really believe he would continue on in obsessive devotion? Did you really think he'd fall in line for centuries?

"You told us what happened when the spheremind found out what you had done. You didn't tell us about Lavaux, only implied that he kept on under your orders, Rainier's dutiful Keeper, but I don't think so. He knew, didn't he, about the spheremind? Knew Lex had taken it into herself, devoured it? He was willing to kill Halston, before, to kick off a war that would have shed a lot of blood, but ultimately would have cut a fairer deal between Prime and the united nations of Earth.

Keeper Lavaux…" He laughed bitterly. "Was a good man, once. Fuck. Maybe he went off the deep end, but he'd been working on Rainier. Teasing out the aspects of the spheremind so that it could take control from Lex. He wanted to give her *The Light* to finish the actualization of the spheremind, but Rayson was loyal to Lex, and fled.

"Lavaux trapped you here to keep you from stopping him. To keep you from helping Lex suppress the spheremind."

Her eyes narrowed. "You see too much."

"Nature of the job," he said by reflex. "Lex is never coming for you. This"—he gestured to the window—"is all you'll ever have."

She laughed, low and slow, body twitching from the effort. "For all you see, you miss so very much. Lex will find her way through. She'll come back to me."

"Not if Rainier gets to you first."

Her face went blank. "You won't let her through."

"Maybe I will. We have the third sphere now. There's nothing here for her to use against us."

"This ship—"

"Is a pale imitation of the original."

"Is that what you want? A righteous spheremind? Coming here would only ignite the fires of her hatred. She would broadcast this truth, let all the united worlds see the grave of Earth. Possibly even trot my corpse out for the cameras.

"Don't look so surprised. I made Prime. I burned its core principles into its bones. I know how that company functions, as business and government. Propaganda always had been our bread and butter, and you haven't changed, have you? Because we made life easy for you.

"We gave you the promise of constant expansion, of always moving on and up, of human righteousness, and every last soul we brought with us ate it up, cheered when we spun the gates, and never asked why we guarded our secrets so close. And when they did? We nurtured the conspiracies, spun them as fringe theories, the hobbies of unbalanced people. We owned the minds of Prime more firmly than we owned the gates themselves, and that is a grip that does not slacken.

"So, send her to me," Maria said. "Send me the thing that has become Rainier, let her wield me against your cause. I will be happy to see you fail. I will *help* her."

"No, you'll just cling on, playing nice, hoping to find Lex drowning somewhere in that mind of hers."

Greeve: Three minutes.

"The spheremind would not destroy Lex completely."

"She already has. Rainier *does not understand the gate tech.* If there was anything left of Lex in there, that's the first thing the spheremind would recover. Or have you forgotten, the thing you made wants to use the gates to burn all of humanity to cinders? It's only because she had to use humans to help her that she hasn't succeeded already."

"I don't believe you."

Tomas nodded to himself. "You hoped she'd come back. That once she won control over the spheremind, she'd do away with Lavaux and come for you, come chasing that sphere you carried around your neck, and together you'd finish your righteous war. I get it.

"That kind of hope, held on to for so long...It's not easy to let go. So I'll leave you with a parting gift, Dr. Salvez. Something to consider, while you wait for our sun to take you to a cold grave."

He tapped at his wristpad, a new model Arden had slapped together from spare parts. Most of his data had gone out the airlock with his old wristpad, but he'd learned he didn't need to store information off-site, so to speak. His mind was as good as any hard drive.

Tomas remembered waking up in that guardcore ship's cargo bay. Remembered Rainier looming above him, delicate and deadly, her eyes bright with something like mania, but it was pure, simple rage. Compressed over hundreds of years of isolation, teased to the surface at last by Keeper Lavaux. Tomas wondered if the Keeper had understood what he was releasing.

The memory loaded into the screen, Rainier's strange speech, her calm assurance. It wasn't the conversation she'd had with Sanda—wherein she'd explained what she was, and what she wanted, even if she left some of the details out. But it would be enough. Tomas studied body language. The way Rainier moved, the way she spoke, was nothing at all like the old CamCasts of Alexandra Halston. No one would know that better than Maria Salvez.

"I hope this keeps you company," he said, and flicked it to the tablet on the wall, then locked the video down, forcing the tablet to loop it over and over again until the battery died out.

It took ten seconds for her to start screaming.

Tomas nodded to himself, popped his glove and helmet back on, and pushed down through the orifice joining the two cylinders. Those wails, those shrieks, were all the proof he needed. Nothing of Lex lived on in the body of Rainier Lavaux. They were dealing with the spheremind now, and as terrifying as that was, it made things simple.

Because Lex would not know what to do with the key sphere, but the spheremind sure as fuck would. And as soon as she knew they had it, Tomas had no doubt Rainier would throw everything she had at them.

He just prayed they were ready.

CHAPTER 43

PRIME STANDARD YEAR 3543

THE MONSTER IN THE METAL

The run from the hospital to the ship passed by in a blur of blood and fire. Jules got the ship open, staggered inside, and kept her head long enough to order it to get the fuck out of Atrux, with a vague heading toward the Ordinal system and a firm order to evade detection.

Jules collapsed into a chair on the command deck and let her arms hang down by her sides, limp. She'd lost weapons. Lost a shit ton of blood. But she'd made it back. All her body needed to stitch itself back together now was rest.

"Let's get that armor off of you," Saarah said, approaching Jules from the side. She jerked out of her dazed fog immediately.

"Don't fucking touch me."

"You need blood, and you need meds, I don't care what you are."

"I'm fine."

Saarah merely pointed at the floor under Jules's feet. It hurt to move, but she craned her head to look. A silvery-red puddle pooled under her chair. The goddamn metal poisoning. It must be keeping her system from stopping the flow. No wonder she'd spaced out during the fight, after she'd been punched through a few times.

"Fuck," she growled.

"Exactly," Saarah said, crossing her arms. "Now, are you going to let us help you, or are you content to bleed out?"

"You shouldn't be bleeding so much," Birdie said in a soft, slightly scared voice. Understatement of the millennium.

Jules grunted and rolled off the chair, dropping to her hands and knees. Medibay. There were coagulants there, serums, plasma, all sorts of shit she could cram into herself to keep moving, keep working. She didn't have to live much longer. Just until she made sure Dal fixed Lolla. She began to crawl.

Saarah crouched beside her and put a hand on her back. "Let us help."

"Fuck. Off."

"Shadow, you saved our lives. The least we can do is bandage you up. Now, Reece is having a hard time getting into the medibay. Can you give him the override commands?"

"Don't touch that door!"

Jules lunged to her feet, reaching for Reece. He spun around to face her, eyes huge, and held up his hands, pressing his back against the wall. "I'm trying to help."

She sagged to the floor, rolled over, and let her arms flop at her sides, panting. She was so damn hot. Being in her own skin felt like touching a stove. Her HUD flashed a temperature warning, which would have made her laugh if she could manage the sound, and started trying to cool her down. She watched her battery tick down toward the deep-orange zones as the suit worked overtime, trying to chill her, and failing.

Birdie approached her on light feet, hands out as if she were trying to soothe a panicked animal. "Let us help."

Help. She grunted, tried to shake her head but couldn't. Boiling, her body was boiling, and it was all because of that stupid cup of theirs. She lashed out with one hand, trying to wave the kid off.

They needed to go away. To let her think, let her breathe. Let her figure out how to get her temperature down, get this damn haze out of her thoughts. Everything she needed was in that medibay, but these people couldn't see in there. Couldn't see Lolla. The risk, it was too much.

"Get out! Go!" she barked, waving with one arm.

They were in vacuum, under thrust, where were they supposed to go? Jules didn't know, didn't care. The ship had other rooms—rooms only she could open—but, still, they should be able to get out of here. Couldn't they understand she just needed them to go away?

Saarah and Reece exchanged a meaningful look, and nodded to Birdie. Fear gripped Jules's chest.

Birdie's small fingers found the retraction trigger at the base of Jules's helmet. The black plates whispered down into place, and for a blinding moment she was relieved, the cold air of the ship crisp against her skin, the air fresh and no longer laden with her own sweat and blood. Then she saw the way they were looking at her.

Right. Jules Valentine. The Prime Director had plastered her face across all the media channels, called her out as the saboteur of Atrux. Typhoid fucking Mary.

"So it's true," Saarah said softly.

"Just let me die," Jules rasped. She still had her deadman's switch. Arden would get the data. Outdated now, but they'd figure it out. Find the ship. Get Dal's cure to Lolla when he completed it. Jules, like the immune, was no longer a necessary part of the process. Relief made her shoulders sag, her body limp.

"She's burning up," Birdie said, her small, cold fingers on Jules's forehead. "Help me with the rest."

Saarah and Reece stripped her armor to the waist, Birdie holding Jules still whenever she thrashed, trying to make these people stop. Couldn't they see she was done, used up? She'd done what she'd set out to do. It was over. Jules needed to be over, too.

"Holy shit," Reece said, squinting at the patches covering her body. "I don't even know what half of these do."

Jules broke away and scrambled backward, crab-crawling, pushing her back against the wall. But she'd been too close to the medibay door, to the lock panel, and as her skin hit the cold metal of the ship's wall, the panel registered the proximity of her ident, and opened the door.

Everyone froze. Lolla's coffin was dead center in the medibay, emitting a soft violet glow, marred only by that single yellow-shaded alert. Jules's breath caught, her head spun. Understanding passed over the Grotta family, confusion shifting to pity as they turned, slowly, back to her.

"Will coagulants work on you?" Reece asked.

Jules stared, dumbstruck. Couldn't they *see*? Didn't they *know*?

"Yeah, they should," Birdie said, and jogged into the medibay, staying clear of Lolla. Jules heard plastic crunch as she rustled through a drawer.

Jules began to laugh, slowly, a manic bubble rising through her chest, bursting in her mind. She hunched over, body shaking, teeth jarring, and pressed the heels of her palms into her eyes, short nails digging into her scalp, drawing blood. Birdie placed the coagulants. Jules did not move for a very long time.

A weathered hand touched the bare skin of her arm. Saarah.

"You're okay," Saarah said, "you're safe."

Jules jerked her head up, smiling with grim satisfaction as Saarah flinched at what must be bloodshot eyes.

"You have no idea what you're dealing with."

"You came back for us."

"I put you there in the first place," she snapped, and didn't mean the hospital.

Saarah's gaze drifted to the medibay. To Lolla. Real pity made her smile tight, her lips drag down at the corners even as she tried to lift them.

"I think I understand."

"I don't want your understanding," Jules growled out.

She pushed Saarah's hand away and dragged herself to her feet, leaning against the wall. All three gazes tracked her, but she wouldn't meet any of them. The coagulants had worked. She was back on her feet. That's all that mattered.

"I'll drop you off at Monte Station. They don't like fleet or GC there. You'll be able to rebuild. Start new lives."

"Shadow—" Birdie said. Concern made her voice crack.

Jules turned her back, stalked into the medibay, and closed the door behind her.

CHAPTER 44

PRIME STANDARD YEAR 3543

BARGAINING CHIPS

At thirty seconds left, Bero alerted Sanda that Tomas had set foot back on *The Light*. She let out a slow breath, tucked her armored helmet into a bulkhead in her room, and caught up with the rest of her crew on the command deck. Part of her had stayed on that ship, trapped on the *Reina Mora*, until she was sure Tomas had made it safely back to them. He'd stood the best chance of squeezing the truth out of Salvez, but that didn't mean she had to like the situation.

On deck, Arden was nose-deep in their wristpad, scrolling through something, while Okonkwo sat at the console between Conway and Knuth, her helmet on her thighs, a dreamy look in her too-green eyes. Nox was checking over his rifle, getting everyone up to speed as he worked.

Conway and Knuth turned, looking to Sanda for guidance. She nodded. "It's true. Halston was afraid of retaliation from the creators of the spheres, and so she started burning her way across the universe, trying to hit them before they figured out what had happened and came for humanity. The spheremind eventually found out, and that's when Halston uploaded her mind into the ship and the meld began."

"I cannot believe...All these years..." Okonkwo trailed off.

Sanda snapped her fingers in front of the Prime Director's face. She jumped. "Get your shit together, ma'am. What those two did is abhorrent, but Rainier's our problem now, and we've got to stop her before she crushes what's left of humanity. We have a problem. We work it."

Tomas walked into the room, mag boots clomping along. "Haven't heard you say that in a while."

"It's been a while since we've had something this clear-cut to deal with. Did you catch her in the lie?"

"What lie?" Okonkwo demanded.

Sanda winced inwardly at the tinge of hope in her voice. "Salvez was working hard to make herself out to be the good guy in that story."

Tomas inclined his head. "You were right. She told us as much as she did because she was holding out hope that we'd end up bringing Rainier to her. When Keeper Lavaux figured out Halston had taken over the mind of the god that revived him, he turned on them. Salvez had the third sphere already, I believe, and Lavaux stranded her out there to keep her from helping Lex maintain control. Once he separated them, he played the sycophant long enough to tease the spheremind out. It's in control now. There's nothing of Lex left in Rainier. We're dealing with the alien."

"It's partial good news," Sanda said, scratching her chip implant scar. "The spheremind knows how to heal the people of Atrux. Halston wouldn't have a fucking clue."

"And we did not come out of the experience armed only with new information," Okonkwo said.

"True." Sanda pulled the necklace out of her collar so that the others could see.

"Is that the third?" Liao asked.

Sanda nodded, let it drop against her chest. "It is, but it has no instructions. Even Dr. Salvez couldn't say what it does, exactly. The spheremind considered it a key, and Halston extrapolated that to mean it was the key to bringing Rainier's progenitors, which she called the Waiting, to humanity. Halston planned to bring them through and turn the gates against them."

Liao covered her mouth. "That's disgusting. The blowback—"

"Would wipe out the Waiting and whatever humans were stuck on the other side. Yes. She believed the trade-off was worth it."

"So what do we do?" Arden asked, their head tilted to the side. "I've been trying to figure out a way to destroy her as if she were a piece of malicious code, but as long as there's a piece of her stored on a device *anywhere* that could someday be connected to our networks, she will come back. We don't even know where all of her strongholds are. We could keep raiding the guardcore installations, but that's a war of attrition. She's spread too far, too deep."

On her wristpad, a text from Bero: You know what must be done.

She closed her eyes. Dios, but she wished she didn't. "Was the *Reina Mora* usable, Tomas?"

He shook his head. "It wasn't the *Reina Mora*, but it wasn't a sphere ship, either. Whatever carried the other two spheres is long gone. Salvez's ship is a nanite construction, but it wasn't made by the Waiting. It couldn't support a mind."

"Arden, how quickly could you transfer Bero's mind to a secure location in net space?"

They blinked. "I don't know...Uh...Depends on the hookups? He's massive. No offense."

"I take that as a compliment."

"Prime Director, I will need you to personally requisition the equipment Arden requires."

"I have no trouble getting these things for you," she said, "but I need to understand your intent, because I am seeing only the corner of your plan, and I do not like it."

"Liao, how close are we to a cure for the ascension-agent?" Sanda asked, ignoring Okonkwo for now.

"The recovery of the second sphere has led to some conclusions regarding a possible vaccine, but a cure evades us. Dal—Dr. Padian, from Janus—has recently hit upon something promising, but these things take time. I can't give you estimates in good faith."

"That's what I thought." She took a deep breath.

Sanda spoke to Okonkwo, but it was Tomas's gaze she held. "We need Rainier. She alone can correct the error in the ascension-agent. Atrux is running out of time, and every day this goes on she sinks her roots deeper, grabs a firmer hold of our worlds. Soon, there will be nothing we can do. Jules may have released that plague on Atrux, but once Rainier realizes we've shut down her ability to harness the blow-back, she'll look for other weapons.

"To her, the data of the second sphere is a sacred duty. She won't like it, giving it to the species she despises, but she'll do it just to punish us. She might even break it so much it plunges one hundred percent of the population into a coma, instead of ninety-seven percent. She knows this. We know this. There is no move we can make that she cannot counter. A cure can be worked around. She *is* the second sphere. We can dig all we like, but we can never understand it like she does."

Liao said, "If we correct the problem, then those who come out of medical stasis may be stronger and faster, like Valentine. They might be able to fight her."

Sanda laughed and rounded on Liao. "Fight her? The citizens of Atrux? You want to send civilians against her endless army? They may be fast and strong, Liao, but they are medis. Cooks. Gardeners. This is a technological war, strength of arms will not win, and Prime is not used to being wrong-footed on matters of technological advancement.

"We have one chance, *one*, and that is to sequester her in this ship."

"I will not yield *The Light* to Rainier Lavaux," Okonkwo said with deep bitterness. "It is the only edge we have."

"Arden," Sanda said. "Tell them."

They fidgeted with their wristpad. "When Rainier attempted her last intrusion, I had a hard time stopping her because she poured everything she had into the effort. I believe she lost bodies in the process, in fact many of the potential bodies I'd been tracking as hers went dark after the fact. This ship was everything she ever was. When she has it, she'll pour all of herself into it."

"Then what?" Okonkwo asked. "We blow it up?"

"No," Tomas said, not taking his gaze from Sanda's. "Then I play human firewall."

"What the *fuck* are you, Nazca?"

"Your only shot at controlling Rainier, Prime Director," he said smoothly, and Sanda didn't know if she wanted to laugh or cry at the casual shrug he threw after those words.

"And Bero?" Okonkwo asked. "You understand, that if she enters this ship and realizes that Bero has gone, she will know it was a trap."

"I have already sent Arden suggestions," Bero said, "based on my previous encounter with the spheremind. She will attempt to sequester me, and I will fight her with everything I have, but allow myself to be boxed in the corner I want to be boxed in. With Arden's expertise, and your equipment, Prime Director, I will retreat to net space before Tomas begins his work."

"This is inane," Okonkwo said. "Rainier will see through this in a second. You have no chance of making her believe that you are willing to barter this ship for the lives of Atrux without an ulterior motive."

"True," Sanda said, and held up the small sphere. "But I'll make her believe I'm bargaining with something else."

CHAPTER 45

PRIME STANDARD YEAR 3543

TRUST

Sanda sat behind her desk in the stateroom of *The Light*, and wondered if this was how her brother felt before he gave a public address. Probably not. Biran had trained for his role as a Keeper. When she watched him work, he spoke to the camera as if it were an old friend, an intimate confidant.

She was staring at the tablet propped on her desk as if it were a snake rearing to bite.

"We don't have to do this," she said.

"You're trying to get out of this," Tomas said, a laugh barely constrained behind his voice. "Who would have guessed Commander Greeve has stage fright."

"I'm not talking about the address. I'm talking about the plan. I'm talking about you."

Tomas's fingers, behind her, landed on her shoulder, traced to her collarbone, where the silver chain lay comfortably warm against her clammy skin. The laughter had gone out of his voice. "This is our best option."

"And if you lose?"

"I won't."

"And *if you lose?*"

He brushed his fingers up, along the side of her neck, to the sharp edge of her jaw. "Then I won't even know I've lost."

"Not helpful."

"It's all I've got."

Sanda flicked her gaze to the door. "B, is Okonkwo occupied?"

"She's reviewing the latest reports out of Atrux."

"Good. Keep an eye on her." Sanda reached for the tablet, and Tomas stepped aside so that he wouldn't be in frame. She hesitated. "I don't know how Biran does it."

"You could ask him," Tomas said. "There's time."

Sanda put through a priority call, waiting out the time delay. The signal came back: *Ident offline. Undergoing care.*

"What the *fuck* does that mean?" Sanda demanded. Her wristpad did not answer.

"He's…" Tomas tugged on his lower lip as he thought. "He must be in a NutriBath. That's the only time I've ever seen that before."

Sanda saw red for a flash and gripped the edge of her desk with one hand. "How did I not know that? What the fuck is happening on that ship?" She jabbed at her wristpad furiously, bringing up every communication channel she could think of to the *Terminus*, but of course, Biran had forced all comms on that ship to route through him, to keep any potential spies he missed in the purge from sending unauthorized transmissions. She wanted to pull her hair out.

"Bero, how long until Okonkwo's hardware is installed on Atrux?"

"Five hours," he said.

"And how long will it take us to fly there?"

"Twelve hours."

"How long to Hitton's gate?"

No answer.

"Bero, you dickhead—"

"Sanda," Tomas said, gently. "If he's in a bath, he's safe. Whatever happened is already over."

"Bero, how long to—?"

"Director Greeve forbade me from passing through that gate until his return."

She slammed one fist into the desk, denting it, and a shock of pain raced up her arm. The tablet jumped and clattered to its side. "My dipshit little brother has *never been in a bath* before, do you two understand me? He's a Keeper, he's not a fucking soldier. The worst injury he's ever sustained was a *broken toe.*"

"That's not entirely true," Tomas said. "Keepers undergo torture training. Biran knows what he's doing. I read over his plan, and Arden checked the ship's security themself."

"Arden. Right. They have comms to that flying soup can." She pushed to her feet, but Tomas grabbed her arm, rooting her in place. She was a microsecond away from hurling him as far as she could manage when she registered the pain behind his eyes.

"It's too far to reach in a reasonable amount of time. He's beyond your help."

She clenched her fists. "This ship—"

"Isn't fast enough. We're days out. By the time we get there, he'll probably be out of the bath, and pissed off that you abandoned the mission to check his temperature. Biran is director of Ada. Trust him."

"I at least need Arden to call that ship. I haven't spoken to him since we grabbed Okonkwo. I don't even know how long he's been *in* there."

"Biran set comms up that way for a reason. You might fuck up his whole plan by forcing Arden to break the cordon."

"Plan? It's a fucking *survey* mission. He should have been *safe.*"

"And he is. You can't chase this one. Okonkwo's begun the equipment installation. If we don't strike immediately, Rainier will find out about it, and then we've blown our chance. You've got one shot here. You have to take it."

She closed her eyes, tipped her head back, and tried to catch her breath around the frustration tearing her up inside. "Promise me you can do this."

"Do what?"

"Shut her down. Lock her away and then burn the cage, or however the fuck it works in there. Promise me you'll come back."

He let her arm go and stepped away, and so she opened her eyes, made herself look, though she didn't know why she bothered, because

Tomas could show her any emotion he liked. But he let her see a flash of fear before replacing it with an easy, confident smile.

"I'm not going anywhere. I cut Bero off from my room on instinct, and he still hasn't gotten back in, despite trying. If I'm concentrating, Rainier won't have a chance. But we have to move now, while we have the element of surprise."

He cupped her cheek in one hand. "Trust Biran. Trust me. And do what you have to do."

She leaned into the touch. "How the hell am I supposed to concentrate now?"

"Channel that anger. Let her see it. Let her know you can control it."

"Right. That'll do. Fuck it." She grabbed her tablet and pressed the button to push through a CamCast to all Prime channels. She'd always been a rip-the-bandage-off kind of person, and this was no different. There was only one way this plan worked, and that included Sanda behaving like a Greeve, even if it meant adopting her brother's tactics while he napped in a bath.

"People of Prime," she said firmly, "this is Commander Sanda Maram Greeve of *The Light*. This message is not for you all, personally, but it is for your safety."

She hardened every line in her body. "Rainier. I have had a very candid conversation with an old friend of yours. I know who you are, what you want, and what you are capable of. I believe you know what I want, too."

She dipped her hand below the collar of her jumpsuit and held up the third sphere between two fingers. "I propose a trade. Atrux guardcore docks. Just the two of us. Twelve hours. If you're not there, well . . ." She allowed herself a cruel smile and closed her fist around the sphere. "You'd better be."

Sanda cut the feed and tossed the tablet to her bed, body vibrating from a rush of adrenaline. It was done. The pieces were in place. Now she had to make sure she could force them together into the shape she wanted.

Okonkwo pounded on her door. Sanda flicked a wrist. "Let her in."

Tomas stepped smoothly aside as the Prime Director stormed into the room. Naked fury raged in her eyes, but Sanda found herself immune to that glare.

"This was not a part of the plan," she snapped.

"It was, actually. Just not the part you were informed of."

Her cheeks sparked red. "You command this ship on my suffrage, Greeve."

Sanda folded her arms. "I'd be entertained to see you try to take it from me, but now is not the time for petty power plays."

"You think my rank *petty*?" She reared back, pressing a hand against her chest. "Excuse me, oh Commander, I didn't realize having a fancy spaceship made you empress of the fucking universe."

Sanda spoke calmly, "Prime Director, right now my singular duty is to save this species from a being we cannot control, nor accurately predict.

"The plan is, and has been, to draw her out. Setting aside the fact that she has taken herself so far off grid that we cannot contact her, if I were to attempt to contact her through any official channels, she would smell a trap before she even finished reading the first sentence.

"She knows me, or she believes she does. Me, and my brother. Breaking rank, reaching out directly to the people, is something we have been proven to do when we do not have the support of our superiors. Without your backing, I am only one woman with a small crew and a very nice spaceship. Those things do not threaten her. She will walk into Atrux assuming she has the upper hand."

"You could have warned me," she said.

"You would have tried to stop me, or make me wear a different uniform, or fix my hair for the camera. Rainier would have noticed those things. This had to be raw. It had to be real. We are dealing with a being who has observed, and hated, humanity for centuries. There is no room for error."

A shadow passed behind Okonkwo's too-green eyes, and for a moment Sanda caught a glimpse of the iceberg of agony that lurked beneath her rage. Sanda went still, giving Okonkwo space. Eventually, she straightened, and crossed her arms loosely over her ribs.

"The footage from Atrux is getting worse," she said. "I have received new reports. Those who ascended are growing fearful. Some help the medis we sent in, yes, but resentment is growing. There were too many comatose...We could not get them all into stasis fast enough. The friends and families of the ascended are dead, or dying, and they blame us for the failure."

"I *will* get the answer from her."

"Greeve." Her smile was tight and bitter. "I know that you believe that. But I see no angle in which she shares that knowledge with us. Her hatred runs too deep."

"We are doing this to save Atrux. We are risking *everything* for this chance."

Okonkwo met her gaze steadily. "We are doing this to confine, and destroy, Rainier Lavaux. If you have the chance to get the answer from her, all the better.

"But do not miss your shot to destroy her, if you have it in hand. If we have to trade one world to protect them all, then we make that bargain, and we do not look back."

CHAPTER 46

PRIME STANDARD YEAR 3543

NEVER ENOUGH

Arden ripped their net goggles from their head and pitched them against the wall of their room, shouting in frustration. They'd run through a simulation of Rainier's incursion attempt on *The Light* over a hundred times now, and every damn time they failed to find a way to push her back. It couldn't be done. Not without Tomas's help.

"I can't do it," they said, panting, glaring at their net goggles as if they'd betrayed them.

"You were very close this time," Bero said.

Arden scowled at the ceiling. "Don't lie to me. That run was worse than all the others."

"You're tired."

"You're delusional. We have to tell Sanda we need Tomas to practice with us. She'll make him."

"She won't. Tomas has his reasons."

Arden grabbed their net goggles off the floor and crushed the cloth band in their hand.

"You're going to fucking die, Bero. I can't keep that to myself."

"Tomas will assist when the time comes."

"But he doesn't know what he's doing! He's only been in once, and I've reviewed that encounter from every possible angle. He got *lucky* by brute-forcing his way through. Rainier won't let that happen again." Hot shame crawled up their throat, burned their skin from the inside out. Rainier was too good. *Better* than them, because hacking came as easily as breathing to her.

A memory of the breach pods that'd smashed into *The Light's* engine room flooded them, dug barbs into their mind. Arden had, for the first time in their life, missed an intrusion program on a piece of hardware, and that fuckup had almost lost them the ship. They would not—could not—allow anything like that to ever happen again.

"That was only a fragment of Rainier we were up against. This is going to be it, this is going to be all of her, and at this point we might as well put out a welcome mat."

"Arden—"

"I won't let you take this risk."

"You cannot stop me."

Arden had a sudden, vicious urge to kick the wall, to kick Bero, to do something to shake some sense into him. They tossed their net goggles on their bed, and stomped out of the room.

"Arden, where are you going?"

"To talk to him."

"I would not recommend that at this point."

"If you won't see reason, maybe he will."

Arden stopped outside of Tomas's door and pounded on it. No answer. Right, he probably wasn't there; he was probably with Sanda. In her quarters. Arden really did *not* want to get in the way of whatever was going on there, but Sanda had already called out Rainier. They had hours. Hours they couldn't waste.

They pounded on Sanda's door.

"Come in," she said.

The door dilated. Sanda sat on her bed, cross-legged, a half dozen tablets strewn in a circle around her. Tomas was sitting at her desk, bent over the built-in screen. They looked up in tandem, curious faces almost making Arden lose their nerve.

"What is it?" Sanda asked.

"Sorry to bother you, Commander, but I really need to talk to Tomas."

She shrugged and went back to her work. Tomas kept on watching him.

"Privately...?" Arden tried. Sanda cut them both a look, but Tomas nodded and pushed away from the desk, following Arden out into the hall.

When the door closed behind them, Tomas asked, "What is it?"

Arden dropped their voice to a whisper. "This isn't working. I can't do this."

Tomas winced and glanced over his shoulder at the closed door, then tilted his head. "My quarters."

Once that door was shut, Arden plopped down on Tomas's single chair, and Tomas took up an uneasy seat on the foot of his bed. "All right. What's going on?"

"What's going on?" Arden demanded, annoyed by how hysterical their own voice sounded. "I can't do it, Tomas. I've run that damn incursion simulation a few hundred times and every time Rainier gets past me. I'm not quick enough. She's ten steps ahead of me—fifty! If you hadn't been there, we would have been fucked. I'm not good enough. I have *never* not been good enough. You have to run it with me, please, I need your help. I need to try this live."

Tomas paled. "I can't. Bero must have told you?"

Arden waited for a pithy reply from Bero. None came.

"He said you didn't want to practice, yeah, but this is go time, this is *it*. We are hours from contact and, right now, all probabilities point to us losing this ship, even if we get Bero sequestered in time to keep him safe."

"He didn't tell you why," Tomas said, half to himself, and rubbed the side of his face. "Arden, I would practice with you if I could, but you need to understand, every time I go into this ship...a little piece of me stays behind. I want to stay behind."

"You're afraid you'll get stuck? I can help with that, I can get you back out, that's easy."

"Not stuck." He looked away. "Home. Complete."

"Ohhh." They considered, very quickly, all the implications of those words. Recalled how at ease they felt whenever they were in the net, free of their body. Like the net had been made to fit them, molded to their shape. Except that, in this case, the metaphor was literal. "Fuck."

"Yeah. If I go in, and stay, it's not just Rainier I'll want to keep out. I'll crush Bero, too. I won't be able to help myself. The more I limit contact, the better. I'll be ready when she comes, don't worry. I need you to pave the way for Bero. Practice getting him sequestered as quickly as possible, because I don't trust myself to do that gently."

"I can do that," Arden muttered, irritated for feeling so left out. This was their domain, they should be the one slamming doors on Rainier, burning her out, corrupting her code, not coddling Bero.

"Thanks," Tomas said with a tight smile that said he wanted to be alone with his thoughts.

"Sure," they said, getting to their feet. "Sorry to have bothered you. Bero didn't tell me."

Bero said nothing. That was...weird. They arched a brow at the ceiling.

"He can't hear you in here," Tomas said. "I locked him out that first night. He's been trying to get back in, but hasn't figured out how yet."

Arden grinned fiercely, thoughts spinning up. "Oh, that's good. I can work with that...yes...Thank you."

Whatever Tomas said, Arden didn't hear it. They rushed back into the hall, making a beeline for their room, and almost ran chest-first into Nox.

"Whoa," Nox said. "Where's the fire?"

Arden rolled their eyes. "Got an idea, move it."

Nox danced around them, but followed them to their room. Whatever. They were used to ignoring Nox when they worked.

"Arden, wait," Nox said.

Arden paused with their goggles halfway to their head. "What? I'm working here, and we're low on time."

"Yeah, that's the thing. You've been beating your head against that incursion ever since it happened. Look, what happened with Jules was shitty, but you don't have to grind yourself into a paste to make up for it."

They blinked. Of all the people they'd expected to have to explain themself to, Nox hadn't been on the list. Nox shifted his weight, covering the motion by pretending to check the balance of his rifle strap, which was, as always, already perfectly aligned.

"That's not what this is about, seriously. You know how I get when there's a problem to solve."

"I do know," Nox said warily. "Just don't beat yourself up too hard about it, you know? You don't have the juice Tomas does. Can't be helped."

Nox hadn't meant for that to sting, but it did all the same.

"Yeah, I got it, thanks," they muttered.

Nox hesitated, then shrugged and let himself out of the room. Arden shook their head and moved to put the net goggles on, then froze. Juice. They didn't have the juice.

"Bero, have you finished transcribing the formula from the second sphere?"

"Yes," he said, "but Liao and her associates have not yet been able to determine if Rainier entered the error into the sphere itself, or if it was in some other formula that Jules had access to."

"Could you make it? You must have the stuff on board to synth a dose, right? I mean, this is the ship of the second sphere, it's designed to be a matched set."

A pause. "I could."

"Great, mix up a dose for me, please. If I could think like Tomas, then—"

"That is a very, very bad idea."

"Uh, no, it's a fucking great idea. Tomas may have some kind of mind-meld thing going on with the ship, but with senses like his, I'd be unstoppable. Rainier wouldn't stand a chance."

"You would also have a ninety-seven percent chance of falling into a coma."

Arden twisted the net goggles between their hands. "Jules survived it. The common denominator between the survivors might be environmental."

"That angle has already been looked at."

"Bero. If Tomas fails, that's it. No backup. Nothing. We're just done. It's finished. Are you willing to risk all of that on one Nazca?"

Arden held their breath. Sanda may have been fond of Tomas, but they'd seen the tension between Bero and the spy the first time Tomas had called in. *I do not like you, Tomas*, had been Bero's exact words, and while Arden didn't mind Tomas—he'd helped save the ship, after all—they were willing to pull any lever if it gave them a chance against Rainier.

"Promise me this will only be as a last resort," Bero said after a long pause.

It took every drop of their self-control to keep from grinning. "I promise."

CHAPTER 47

PRIME STANDARD YEAR 3543

NO TIME FOR PAIN

Biran gasped fresh air and lurched into a sitting position, Nutri-Bath goo sloshing over the edges of the cocoon. He hacked up a lump of gel, pressed trembling fingers against his eyes, squeezing them shut, shading them with his hands because his lids weren't enough to keep the bright lights of the medibay out.

"Easy," a gentle voice—Greystone's?—said.

A palm gloved in plastic pressed against his back, steadying him. "Just breathe naturally." Definitely Greystone.

"*Terminus*, transition lights to twilight," Sato said.

As the stinging brightness eased into gentle night, Biran breathed shallowly, sipping air, and peeled his hands away from his eyes with trepidation. The light still stung, even behind his closed lids, but the sensation was manageable. He blinked his eyes open, goo mingled with the tears that slid down his cheeks.

His whole body trembled with weakness, and he felt like he hadn't had a proper meal in years, but he was breathing. Moving. An experimental paddle of both feet revealed his ankles were intact once more.

"Director Greeve, can you hear me clearly?" Greystone wore a lab coat buttoned over her usual slim-cut pants and silken blouse, the bright colors hidden behind a somber wash of medical white.

"Yes," he said, and coughed up another clot of gel.

"I apologize for waking you before your healing cycle is complete, but Keeper Sato assures me that you're up to eighty percent. How do you feel?"

Biran grabbed either side of the bath's walls, and froze. Pale red lines marred the fingers of his hands, one perfectly circular mark banding each knuckle like rings. A shaky memory came back to him, and he swallowed.

"Oh," Sato said, coming toward the bath with a robe in her hands. "Keeper Monta collected most of your fingers. I sutured them back on, and the bath did the rest, but considering you're waking early, they may be a little clumsy for a while."

"Keeper Monta..." He stared at his hands, but he was seeing another time, another place. Hearing the crunch of his bones as the GC had, one knuckle at a time, reduced his hands to ruin. He shuddered, putting that memory down. Slid his Keeper training over the trauma like a shield, and locked it into place.

"Director?" She hesitated, holding the robe out to him.

"Thank you," he said. Whether he meant for the robe or for sewing his fingers back on, he wasn't sure.

"Two of your toes were unrecoverable," Greystone said with easy professionalism, "but the bath diagnostics are certain your balance will not be affected, and when you're ready, they can be regrown."

He blinked, looked down at his feet, and saw the second toe of one foot reduced to a stub, and the middle of the other foot completely gone.

"That...will not be necessary..." He trailed off, thinking of Sanda, then shook himself and stood, shakily, in the bath, taking the robe from Sato's outstretched hand. The mission. Focusing on the mission would keep his mind from backsliding. From drifting, like a moth to flame, to memories of pain. "I assume you woke me early for a reason. What's the situation? How long has it been?"

"Almost three days," Greystone said. "We have entered low planet orbit on the target, and have gathered enough information that we are comfortable with sending a scout team down."

If he thought too much about the time he'd lost, and why, he'd vomit, so he wrapped the robe around himself and stepped out of the bath. He shivered as his bare feet touched the cold floor. His legs wobbled, but they would hold.

"What do we know?" he asked.

Greystone gave him a sly, approving smile. "Very little, but that can wait. Shower, dress, and then meet me on the command deck. If that's manageable for you at the moment...?"

He shifted his weight, tensing muscles one after another. After the way his body had burned with pain before getting into the Nutri-Bath, he didn't think it possible, but his only real complaints were that he was starving, and his muscles were weak. His only physical complaints, at least.

"That won't be a problem."

"Good," Greystone said. "I am genuinely glad to see you on your feet, Director. We weren't even certain you'd get your vision back."

Biran slammed a lid on that memory. "Keeper training does its job."

"I know that well," Greystone said, and smiled in such a way that a shadow caught in a faint scar that ran along her jaw, starting at the corner of her lips. The scar was an old one, all discoloration gone, the only hint a subtle depression in the tissue where none should be. She could have had it smoothed away. That she hadn't was a statement in and of itself.

Biran inclined his head in acknowledgment and let himself into a temporary shower stall set up in the medibay. While he washed, he couldn't help but examine his hands, his chest, his...everything. Would he let some of those scars stay? Would there be a point?

He found fresh clothes—a plain blue button-up and black slacks with mag boots—waiting for him after he toweled off, and frowned as he dressed. New mag boots. His size, but not broken in. That'd be rough with the state his feet were in, but he knew better than to ask what had happened to his old pair. They were probably too full of blood to clean properly.

His chest tightened. Lock it up. Lock it down. Focus on the mission.

"Well?" he asked, stepping out from behind a thin privacy curtain.

While he'd showered, the lights had drifted slowly back up to daylight standard, and as he rolled up his sleeves, he saw why

Greystone—it must have been her—had selected this shirt for him. It wasn't in the wardrobe Vladsen had given him. The color would have suited him any other time, but now, when his skin was as pale as it had ever been and his scars stood livid, veins purple-blue below the thinness of his skin, the color only served to make him look every inch as battered as he felt.

Biran frowned, flicking his gaze up to meet Greystone's, and she nodded in confirmation. The Speaker for the High Protectorate found some value in making the abuse he'd suffered apparent. Interesting. He wondered if it was for her benefit, or his.

"Has Okonkwo been notified?" he asked, holding out a hand for the wristpad Sato handed him. Someone had cleaned the blood off.

"No," Greystone said. "Your comms lockdown remains in place. No one could send a message while you were in the bath."

"Don't tell me you didn't try to override that."

Greystone gave him an abashed smile and spread her hands. "I tried, naturally, but was unsuccessful. Mx. Wyke does outstanding work."

"And so no one has heard from us for three days."

"That is correct," she said, falling into step beside him as he exited the medibay and made for the command deck. Echo had been posted outside the door, and trailed at a respectful distance, hand on her rifle. Sato followed with a medikit in her hand should Biran need it.

Greystone filled him in on all the minutiae of the trip thus far. Echo, with the help of the fleeties, had taken out every last guardcore on the *Terminus*. It was just her now—though of course Greystone didn't know her adopted name or gender—and they were all grateful to have at least one loyal guardcore left in all the worlds.

After course-correcting, they'd burned hard for the planet, and had been in orbit for about half a day, arguing over what to do next. Greystone had decided that they needed the guiding hand of their director to make that call. Biran got the feeling, as he approached the deck, that she had come to that conclusion on her own.

Biran stepped onto his command deck to find an argument in progress. Vladsen, at Scalla's side, jabbed a finger at the forward viewscreen, his face ruddy.

"—and it can wait awhile longer," he said.

"What can wait?" Biran asked.

Silence. Everyone on deck spun around to stare, and Biran caught a hateful glance from Vladsen to Greystone, felt that woman shrug slightly beside him. She'd been right. They needed direction, and that was Biran's job.

"You all right, boy?" Scalla twisted around in her chair to squint at him. He grinned at her and held both of his hands up.

"I'm in one piece. Mostly. Thank you, Keeper Monta."

Lili blushed scarlet. "I...I wasn't even sure if it would work."

"We got to them in time," Sato said with a proud smile. "The bath did the rest."

Vladsen glared daggers at Greystone. "I thought we were all agreed he needed another two days."

She shrugged. "The NutriBath was clear that early release was viable, and you idiots were about to drop down onto that planet without your director's express orders."

"I wanted to wait," Vladsen ground out.

"And that sentiment was very close to being overruled."

"Pissing match later," Biran said, and moved to his seat alongside Scalla. He hoped he didn't look as relieved as he felt to sit down. "What are we looking at?"

Monta's blush evaporated under a grin. "You are going to love this."

She swung around to face the console and tapped up a zoomed-in view of the planet. Biran's breath caught. Once their cameras plunged through the clouds, a green so intense it stung his eyes filled the screen, and it took his mind a beat to adjust to what he was seeing.

A forest, thick-canopied and dark. Infographics alongside the image estimated the arboreal landscape to be composed of mostly hardy evergreens, perhaps cousins to Earth species, but nothing from the Prime registries. White crystals clung to the needles of the trees, clumped against some of the boughs and puddled in empty spaces—snow. Biran had only ever seen its like on CamCasts.

"That is...That is remarkable."

"Oh, it gets better," Monta chirped, zooming the view back out.

Biran hated to see the details of the forest wash away under a generic field of green, but as the camera drones pulled back, a shape began to emerge from between the trees. A ring of dark stone, or something like it, sketched out a massive circle in the forest, a small, concentric ring dead center of the larger structure. At first, he thought the structure was some kind of wall, but as the camera panned, perspective slipped into place. The dark rings bit into the ground, forming deep canyons. Nothing natural made formations like that.

"Do we have a materials breakdown?" he asked, struggling to keep his voice level.

"Nothing exact," Sato said. "We did some preliminary analysis based on estimated density and refraction. We think it's metal."

"It must be metal," Greystone said smoothly. "It's broadcasting."

"Broadcasting what?" If Biran's voice cracked, he didn't care.

"The same cycle, over and over again. One long tone, one short."

"Ones and zeros."

"I believe so," Greystone said.

The same method of communication left behind by the spheres. Biran believed in coincidences, but he couldn't swallow one this clean and tidy. Part of him wondered, with a deep sense of grief, how many of these structures had been seeded throughout the universe. How many Halston's war against the unknown had destroyed.

"Do we have a viable landing site near the center of the structure?" he asked.

"More or less," Scalla said grudgingly. "There's a clearing in the trees not far. Most of the shuttles on the *Terminus* are too large for it, but we have a couple of transports that'll do the trick. Small team, though, and it's going to be like threading a needle during an avalanche. Don't often have to deal with atmos this thick, you understand. Or with unpredictable weather."

"Plot the course," he said. "What's the air mix look like?"

"Near enough for our purposes," Sato said. "Slightly low on oxygen, but manageable. I would like permission to send sampling drones down to get a proper analysis, not just of the air mix, but of the soil and local plant life. I can't get an idea of viral or bacterial loads from orbit. Not to mention any toxins those plants might be putting out."

"Do it. How long will that take?"

"To send them down, sample, analyze, and send the data back?" She tapped on her chin. "Ten hours or so, at best. The equipment the survey team is working with is all our new designs. Without the tried-and-true structures Halston handed down, we can't be sure about the timelines. I . . . don't think we can be sure about anything right now."

"Send them," Biran said. "Is that all we have?"

"So far, yes," Greystone said.

"Good. Sato, stay here a moment. I'm going to put in a very over-due call to our Prime Director."

He punched in the requisite identifiers, stomach clenching with bottled anxiety. Distracted by the beauty of the planet, he'd forgotten for a brief, sweet moment the pain he'd endured, until he saw his fingers, those pink rings stark, dancing across the wristpad. He took a breath. Tightened his hold on his mental shields.

Okonkwo answered immediately. She appeared to be on board *The Light*.

"Director Greeve, it has been three days. I was beginning to presume you were dead. You certainly look like a grave warmed over."

Greystone and her damned shirt color. "I apologize, Prime Director, but I spent the last few days in a NutriBath after rogue guardcore attempted to extract the location of *The Light* from me."

So much loaded into those few words. Biran resisted an inclination to hold his breath, and instead watched Okonkwo closely as her eyes widened in surprise, then narrowed, a faint flush coming to her dark cheeks as anger boiled beneath the surface. Imperceptible to most, Biran thought, but he'd spent a long time learning to read that woman.

"As I am currently on board *The Light*, I take it they were unsuccessful."

He nodded, and she bowed her head to him in respect. "An unusual ask for a Keeper, but you fulfilled your duty well. If I had the option, I'd take you off duty to recover. As it is—"

"As it is, I'm looking at an Earth-like planet, covered in vegetation, with an unknown structure broadcasting a repeating loop of ones and zeros."

Cutting her off was extremely rude, but he didn't want to talk about his experience. Didn't want to dwell on the way things could have gone, or should have gone. In the perfect world of Prime, if an enemy agent had gotten ahold of him and tried to extract the Keeper data, he would have months to himself to recover psychologically and physically.

In that perfect world, the location of his sister wouldn't be as sensitive as the data on his chip. In that perfect world, the guardcore were defenders alone. In that perfect world, he'd have had a HUD implant put in the second he'd joined the Protectorate so that he wouldn't have had to physically reach for his distress beacon. Apologizing for reality was a waste of time and mental resources.

Biran had left behind dreams of a perfect world years ago. Two years and some change, to be exact.

Sato put the footage and data through to Okonkwo, answering her questions with barely concealed excitement. Everyone on the deck was bursting with energy, desperate to get down to that beautiful globe and discover what awaited below. Everyone except Biran, Vladsen, and Scalla.

While Okonkwo peeled the details out of his crew, Biran craned his head to catch the pilot's eye. Scalla dropped her scowl when she caught him looking, but the tension around her jaw, the clawlike curl to her fingers, were signs she couldn't shake. She didn't like this. Neither did Biran. It was all too...neat. And it wasn't like humanity had had a good time with the remnants of the precursor species so far.

"And so you are down to one guardcore?" Okonkwo asked, drawing his attention back to the conversation.

"We are," Biran admitted. "Though that unit has proven loyalty beyond the call of their duty."

"I'm inclined to agree with you. When that shuttle lands, Greeve, I want you, the GC, Vladsen, Sato, and Greystone on it."

He could sense Monta and Slatter tense at being left out.

"With respect, there are few of us, and we do not know what we are walking into. I will leave Captain Scalla at her post, but Slatter and Monta come with me. Sato's survey team is more than capable of running things on this ship in our absence, as are the handful of fleeties we have left."

"Fleeties?" Okonkwo arched a brow at his slip in terminology. He only shrugged in response. "If you insist, Director, then I can hardly complain. You know your team. I want reports every six hours after you drop onto the planet. When will you leave?"

"Twelve hours. That gives the survey bots some wiggle room, and us some time to prepare appropriately. There's no point in rushing this."

A twitch along her hairline, subtle, but telling. "I suspect Commander Greeve will be interested in this development. As I am on her ship, I can assure you she currently has time to take your call."

Biran licked his lips, heart leaping to a faster beat. The shields he held over his memories were still eggshell thin. To do exactly what his torturers had asked him to do, to make that call... Sweat slicked his palms. He needed time. He wasn't ready. The mission was his only firm footing, the only safe thing to focus on.

"I would appreciate you delivering this information to her. I have a great deal to do to get caught up on the current situation and prepared for the expedition."

"Noted," Okonkwo said, but flicked a glance to Greystone, who did not react. "Good luck, all of you."

The feed cut, replaced with a visual of the planet. Shakily, Biran pushed to his feet. "Sato, get those bots moving. Monta, do what you can to assist her, but I want you busy prepping the shuttle. Scalla, think the AI pilot can handle the reentry?"

She snorted. "I think if the AI pilot can't handle it, there's no way a person can."

"Noted," Biran said in the same dry tones Okonkwo had used. "If you'll all excuse me, I need proper rest. I suggest you all do likewise."

Biran stepped from the dais and swayed, putting a hand down on the back of his chair to steady himself. Vladsen was at his side in an instant, one hand gripping his elbow to steady him. Biran nodded his thanks and peeled his hand from the chair. He was tired, that was all. He'd be ready for the planet after a full night's rest.

"Let me walk you," Monta said, voice tight as she leapt from her chair.

"Give the man some space," Slatter said dismissively, flicking a hand at Lili like he was shooing away a fly. "Keeper Vladsen's got him, and that GC is his shadow. He's safe, and those two are very politely not telling you they probably have Protectorate business to discuss, which neither of us are privy to."

"But he—"

"I'm fine," Biran said, and forced a smile, thinking how strange it was that this woman who'd resented him for his post was now hovering like a mother hen. Maybe getting a close look at what it meant to hold his position had cured her of wanting it for herself.

"If you say so," she said, a frown pushing her brows together. Once, when a rare strain of flu had slipped under their vaccines at the academy, Keeper Monta had made soup for the whole cohort. It'd been terrible, but they'd all choked it down, and blamed the virus for their inability to taste the spices she'd used. She liked to help. She *needed* to help.

"I really need you to prep the shuttle," he said gently. She lit up and nodded, but Biran's attention had drifted to Slatter, who was looking at him with a kind, if wry, smile. A half dozen possibilities crowded his mind, most of them pointing toward some sort of manipulation, or deception. He sighed. Maybe Slatter was being kind. That was still possible in this world of his, wasn't it?

He let Vladsen steady him, then moved under his own strength, the GC falling into step behind him. Greystone approached him in the doorway, and from beneath her pure white coat produced a slim plex bottle filled with dark amber liquid. Biran didn't recognize the label. Probably because he'd never be able to afford it.

"Do not put a lid on it," she said in a soft whisper, leaning close enough that only he could hear as she passed him the bottle. "Malkia would tell you as much, if she'd had a chance for private discourse, but as things stand, you'll have to take my word for it.

"Let it out tonight, Director. Feel the pain, the memory. Stay with it, get to know it. Make a friend of it. We are taught to cage ourselves, when the moment comes, but we cannot cage the experience itself. We cannot afford to fear that it might come again, for that fear will make us into a brittle thing. Know your pain, know that you can move through it and come out the other side, or the next time the knives come, you'll find your cage too fragile to hold."

"You sound like you're speaking from experience."

She pressed her lips together, displaying her scar. "All of the High Protectorate speak from experience. Keepers prove they can pass the simulation. The High Protectorate prove they can live it."

She pressed her hand against his, then stepped away, delving into a conversation with Scalla about setting up a secure comms link between the *Terminus* and the shuttle.

Biran moved on, dizzy, and was relieved when Vladsen's hand found his elbow again, steadying him.

Brittle. He'd been pushing it all down since the moment he'd woken up, and he could already feel cracks forming, a fractal spiral of pain reaching out, infecting his every waking thought. Okonkwo had seen it, when he'd asked her to tell Sanda on his behalf. That was why she'd looked to Greystone—asking her to intercede, stop the damage growing in Biran's heart before it became too malignant to cut out.

CHAPTER 48

PRIME STANDARD YEAR 3543

BE ANYTHING ELSE

Monte Station slithered into range on Jules's viewscreen, flight path diagrams filling the field with lines of potential approach. Behind her, the immune family waited. Hesitant, wary. Jules had locked herself in the medibay for the flight here, emerging only to tell them where the food and water was, and when she expected to expel them from the ship.

She wasn't sure who was more anxious to have them off—her, or the immune themselves.

"Guardcore," a human voice said—female, possibly—across the air traffic control broadband. "Please state your reason for approach."

Jules frowned, thumbing her side of the mic on. She wore the armor again. Didn't take it off outside of the medibay.

"I've got three civilians in need of resettlement from the Atrux system. Please advise appropriate flight path."

Hesitation. Jules frowned. ATC never hesitated, even when they were human. "Guardcore, we have an understanding with the High Protectorate. Your ships aren't welcome here. Please redirect."

Jules thumbed her mic closed and let out a long, hissing sigh. Rainier's bullshit kept catching up with her, even when she was trying to do the right thing. She clicked it back on. "These people aren't GC, they're civs. I'll drop them and burn out right away."

"Guardcore, we've heard that story before." Bitterness crept into the voice, very unlike usual ATC. "And anyone coming out of Atrux doesn't belong here. There's a quarantine. Take them to a hospital on Ordinal, but not here."

Jules clenched her jaw, worked it loose. "Control, these people weren't on-planet during the attack. They were stranded on a hauler, unable to land or continue through the gate due to the quarantine. Now, I wrangled permission to bring them here before they starved, but my superiors do not want me fucking around going all the way into Ordinal. And besides, these people aren't exactly friendly with fleet or GC right now, considering what they've lived through. They'll fit in on Monte."

"Guardcore, hold position."

Jules held her breath as control clicked off the line, no doubt calling a superior to present Jules's case to. She clenched her fists, waiting. One of the benefits of masquerading as GC was supposed to be that she could land anywhere, without question.

Twenty minutes later, control called back. "You are permitted to escort your charges as far as central processing. You are expected to return to your ship and leave immediately. If you require resupply, you may put in an order from your ship and any supplies will be delivered to you."

"We don't need anything, control. Out of your hair in no time."

"Good. Docking approved."

ATC transmitted the flight path, and the ship's AI pilot took over from there. Jules leaned back, watching the station draw closer, and examined the damage that was still being repaired. Rainier had tracked her escaped scientists to this station after Greeve had invaded Janus and tipped their worlds upside down.

Jules hadn't been on that run. Rainier had taken it personally, and wanted to drop the hammer with her own hands. Jules suspected she just didn't want to risk giving Jules another shot at running off with Arden and Nox, and she'd been right to be wary. In those days after Janus, Jules would have bailed on Rainier's plans if Arden had even hinted there might be another way to fix Lolla. Of course, Rainier had ended up having her ass handed to her by Greeve and Okonkwo, a fact that warmed Jules's frosty heart. The ship shivered into dock, and Jules stood up.

"What will you do next?" Saarah asked.

Jules hesitated, eyeing the woman through the safety of her visor. These people knew too much about her. The smart thing to do would be to throw them out her airlock, not hand-deliver them to the farmers of Monte. They knew who she was. They knew what she was. But where would that get them, ultimately? They would never find her again. She was just another armored shape in a sea of them.

"None of your business," she said, filters back in place on her voice. The nice part about having this ship to herself was that all the spare armor was, by default, hers.

"Could come with us," she ventured, bushy brows pushing up in open invitation.

"Don't," Jules snapped, but the filter made her voice sound flat, neutral. "Don't pretend to give a shit. I got you out. You're welcome. That's it. That's the end of this arrangement."

"If that's how you want it," she said slowly.

"It is. Now move."

Jules ushered her charges out of the ship, ignoring a baleful stare from Reece and wary glances from Birdie. Saarah may have come around to wanting to help Jules—whatever that meant—but the other two were frightened of her, and rightfully so. That was how it should be. Jules wasn't meant to be befriended. She was meant to be scorned, feared.

The dock was empty aside from a loose group of SecureSite personnel. Jules's skin crawled, but she reminded herself she was in control here. She was guardcore, and as much as these people hated her, there was nothing they could do about it.

She marched the Grotta family right up to them, and halted. "I understood I was meant to escort these people to processing," Jules said.

A leathery-skinned man with a wicked scar on his jaw pressed his lips together, thumbs hooked in his weapons belt. "Figured I'd save you the trouble. Name's Gutarra, this here is Laguna, my associate from Atrux. She got stranded here during the quarantine, wanted to welcome her locals to the station."

Jules snorted, and let them hear it. "You mean she wanted to check them to see if she could pin any bullshit open case from Atrux on them."

Laguna shook her head and removed an ident extraction and implantation device from her pocket. "I understand your skepticism, but I am here to assist my people before they make it into processing. The quarantine procedure flagged many innocent idents as unfit to travel. I don't like my citizens being caught in the cross fire."

She hadn't considered that. The Grotta family was still using the idents they'd been born with, or at least the ones they'd used in the hospital. No doubt, those would be flagged as belonging to the hospital, not fit for travel.

"What's going on?" Reece asked, wrapping a wary arm around Birdie's shoulders.

"This woman is trying to do you a favor," Jules said begrudgingly. "I take it central processing has ident scanners embedded in the entrances?"

Gutarra inclined his head. "As with all state-of-the-art Prime facilities. The flow of civilians must be monitored, naturally. You say they're clean?"

"They are," Jules said. "And even if they weren't, it's not contagious. They're just...from the Grotta."

Reece clutched his kid a little tighter, Saarah squinted warily, but Laguna nodded to herself and held out a hand, holding up the gun. "Thought so. Let's do this."

"Shadow," Saarah said warily, "this doesn't feel right."

Jules muted her sigh, then said, "What SecureSite here is dancing around saying out loud is that they believe Prime's cracked down a little too hard on Atrux, and they've been helping healthy refugees fade back into the system. That right?"

Gutarra scowled. "Really? Just going to spit it right out?"

Jules shrugged. "Look at the armor I'm wearing. Look at my ship. I brought you these people because I believe what's going on out there's not right. I won't report you, though I suggest you find a smoother way to go about this, because this song and dance is so obvious you might as well shout you're providing fake idents to people who break the quarantine."

"You make a very good point," Laguna said, grimacing. "We're too damn honest for our own good."

"Maybe we can help you figure out a better way," Saarah said. "I'd feel better if this felt more like a trade."

"If you'd like," Laguna said. Saarah held out her arm, and Laguna pulled her chip, transferred her name to a new number, and implanted a new device for all of them.

"There," Gutarra said. "Welcome to Monte. Let's get you officially checked in."

Jules followed them to central processing, though she'd rather jump back on the ship. She'd said she'd escort them, and it might look suspicious if she ducked out early because SecureSite showed up. Guardcore executed their duty to completion; they didn't back down for local security. Laguna ushered the family off, but Gutarra stuck around in the waiting room, shifting his weight, looking like he wanted to say something. Jules waited, still as a statue, until he worked up the nerve.

"It's not personal, you know," he said to her.

"I'm guardcore. We don't do personal."

He snorted. "I know, I know, I just mean it's not that we hate your organization, in particular."

"Rainier Lavaux came for you wearing guardcore armor. Everyone in my organization is well aware of this fact. We understand the fear. It's warranted."

"What do you mean, *warranted*?"

She stared at him, mute, while she considered what the fuck she was doing having this chat, listening to this man she didn't care about try to render some apology to her for being rude. If he knew what she was, who she *really* was, he'd put a bullet in her head and dance on her corpse.

"Why are you keeping me here, Gutarra?"

He gave her a sly smile. "Just running a quick blood test on the refugees. Making sure you were straight with us about them being clean."

Her stomach clenched. Birdie. They'd try to cram the girl back on her ship.

"My time is not to be wasted," she said, and turned to leave, but a familiar voice stopped her cold.

Sanda Greeve's face filled the viewscreens in the waiting room, pushed through to half the wristpads in the office. People murmured to themselves, uncomfortable, staring warily at the feed that couldn't be wiped away, because it was being sent out priority across all Prime's channels. Gutarra stared down at that face on his wristpad with undisguised bitterness. Jules's own wristpad remained blank, and so she watched a screen imbedded in the wall instead, rage slowly mounting.

That idiot was challenging Rainier, calling her out. Jules's jaw clenched, popped. Those two were Goliaths squaring up to swing at each other. She could almost *feel* the leviathan forces moving, positioning, preparing to strike.

Greeve might have the ship, but she had no idea what the fuck she was doing. She was going to get herself slaughtered, and for a moment the thought brought a smile to Jules's face, but then cold dread seeped through her veins. Nox and Arden were on that ship, under Greeve's command. Maybe they'd left, but she doubted it. That ship would drive Arden wild with curiosity, and there was no way Nox would leave them behind. Nox didn't leave people behind.

"You all right?" Gutarra asked warily.

The broadcast had ended, short and to the point, a gauntlet thrown down, a glove slapped across a face, and Jules had just been standing there, fists clenched, staring into the dark of her helmet. She shook herself.

"Commander Greeve is an idiot," she said, and though her voice was filtered, the words carried derision enough on their own.

Gutarra snorted, rubbed the side of his nose. "I agree with you, to a point. Hate to be on Atrux when those two throw down, though. Don't think either one of them will give a centimeter without making it cost."

Jules breathed out, slowly. "You saw Rainier fight. Do you think Greeve can do it?"

"In a straight fight?" He frowned, then shook his head. "Seems unlikely. Whatever her trump card is, it better be damn good. Guess you'd know more about that stuff than me, though."

"You'd be surprised," she said, and turned to walk away.

"Wait, now, we're still running those tests."

Jules ignored him. What could he do, stop her? This station knew what a guardcore unit could do. Gutarra may have some cheek, but he wasn't willing to take that chance. Not after his last encounter. Her steps were long and ground-eating, but not quite a run. GC didn't spook, and Jules didn't want to raise any alarm bells.

She boarded her ship and retracted her helmet, shaking out her hair. The smart thing to do would be to lie low, wait for Dal to finish the cure, and then wake Lolla. But what would she be waking Lolla up for? Not herself. Jules planned on being long gone by the time the girl was cognizant enough to ask questions.

Cursing, Jules stalked back toward the command console and queried the state of the quarantine at Atrux. Chaos jostled the fleet around the gate, preparing to stand down to let Rainier punch through, to let her answer Sanda's call.

She had time. GC ships were faster than fleet, sleeker. She could slip through the cordon, get under the quarantine, be in place before shit went sideways. Before Rainier took control of *The Light*, and Arden and Nox were trapped inside of it. If she hadn't gone on this milk run, she'd already be there. She punched in the heading to Atrux, and the dock released her ship eagerly, practically flinging her back out into space, through the atmo dome. Control didn't even bother to call in a flight path, they were so eager to see her backside.

Scraping sounded behind her. Jules tensed, putting the helmet back up, and ordered her HUD to show her the room behind her. A slim figure emerged from a side passage, hands clasped behind her back, head downcast. Birdie. Fuck.

"What the hell do you think you're doing?" Jules demanded as she sprang to her feet and dropped the helmet, letting the kid see her razor-sharp glare.

"They were testing for the agent," she said, lifting her chin in defiance. Little twerp.

"Yeah, they were, and you would have come back positive, but I'd already be gone, and those bleeding hearts would take you in anyway. It's not contagious."

"I don't want to be a lab rat."

Jules clenched her fists and turned back to the command console.

"First of all, that wouldn't have happened on Monte. Second of all, Reece is probably losing his goddamn mind. Third of all, you are not welcome on this ship. I have work to do. I don't have time to babysit."

Birdie lunged with all the speed of the ascended and grabbed Jules's arm when she reached for the console, clinging like a barnacle.

"You can't leave me there! It's not safe! I'm—I'm like you. I want to help you."

Jules went very cold and very still, processing through a wall of white, blinding rage before she tried to speak again. "You're ascended, but you're nothing like me, kid. I'm taking you back. You belong with your dad."

"No I don't! I'm a killer, like you. And Prime will hunt me down sooner or later. I can't be with Dad when that happens."

Jules's cheek twitched. She flexed, deliberately, and sent the girl flying away from her arm. Birdie grunted as she hit the ground, but was back on her feet in a flash, her wan cheeks hot with indignity.

"You're not like me," Jules repeated in dead, clipped tones.

"I'm a *killer*. I have killed a Keeper of the High Protectorate. That's not something Prime lets people get away with."

Jules blinked, slowly, and for one fuzzy moment she saw her own face on Birdie's, superimposed, an echo of another time. A time she'd stood over the body of Keeper Nakata, blaster warm in her hands.

"You're right," Jules said in a tight, even voice. Birdie shut her mouth with an audible click at whatever she saw behind Jules's eyes. Took a step back as Jules advanced toward her. "Just like me. You put a Keeper down in self-defense. And you know what? It fucking ruins your life. Oh, you think you don't have a life to ruin, don't you? I know I thought that. Just a Grotta rat. Street scum. No real connections, nothing important in my life. I knew they'd come for me, sooner or later. Prime doesn't let its stains show, do they? We get too big, we do too much damage, they *scrub us out*."

Birdie scrambled backward, away from Jules, her back pressed against the wall, but Jules kept on walking, closing that distance.

"So I left. I ran. I didn't want my crew getting caught in that cross fire. I thought, before they got me, I could do one good thing. I could find the member of our crew that was missing." Birdie's gaze flicked to the medibay. Jules sneered. "It was the stupidest fucking thing I've ever done."

"But...you...you found her?"

"I found a *corpse*!" Her fists bunched. "And I've been lugging that body around on my back since then, holding on to it like a fucking life raft, the only thing in the universe stopping me from drowning in the blood I've spilled in the name of a goal I never really thought I could achieve."

Birdie's eyes were saucer-wide, white lights glowing against the black metal of the ship. "You said they had enough to cure it. You did it. You figured it out. I can help—"

Jules struck her. A backhand, straight across the jaw. The impact sent the girl sprawling, the crack of her metal glove against the bone ringing in the room. Blood trickled from the girl's mouth as she crawled to her side, not daring to stand, one hand pressed over the split in her lips. Jules looked at her hand. Looked at Birdie.

"You don't get to make my mistake," Jules whispered, lips wooden.

Birdie scrambled backward across the floor, legs and arms slipping, but Jules was too fast, too practiced. She grabbed the girl by the back of the neck and lifted, hefting her like a disgruntled kitten, and began to walk.

"I want to help you!" Birdie shouted. "Please!"

Jules opened the door to a room she had not allowed the immune to see. She hadn't allowed them to see most of the rooms of this ship, but this one especially. Reconstruction baths lined one wall, evac pods and breach pods the other. They needed similar hookups, similar systems. Rainier liked to keep her ships as neat and tidy as her mind. She may play at crazy, but Rainier didn't nudge a piece across the board without seeing the fallout ten moves down the line.

They'd probably already lost to Rainier. She'd probably already foreseen this. Somehow known what Jules would do on Atrux, despite her feigned surprise. Known she'd stumble over the immune Grotta family, known Jules would break herself in two to get to Nox and Arden before it was too late.

She shook her head. No. Rainier was brilliant, and ancient, but thinking she was infallible was Marya's territory, the purview of the worshipful

Acolytes. Jules had seen real surprise on Rainier's face as she'd prepared to introduce the ascension-agent to Atrux, and she clung to that memory now. Rainier could be surprised. She'd never see Jules coming.

"Don't, please," Birdie babbled, thrashing in Jules's grip.

Jules approached an evac pod, talking as she walked.

"You know what you're going to do to help me, Birdie?"

"What?" she whined. "Anything!"

Jules rolled her eyes. "You're getting your ass back to Monte. You're going to use that ident SecureSite gave you to build a new life. Learn how to handle farming drones, get a job, work with your dad and Saa-rah. Be something else. Be something simple."

"I can't," she whispered. "I'm a killer."

Jules held her up at arm's length, looked at her tear-streaked cheeks, and smiled. "You could be. It's in you. But you don't have to be."

Jules chucked her into the evac pod and slapped the emergency release. The girl flung herself out, but wasn't fast enough. The carapace of the pod slammed shut on her, lights flashing green around the pod before it was sucked back, shunted behind a double-walled airlock. The guardcore ship was quick. The pod was gone before Jules could take another breath.

She pulled up its beacon on her wristpad and edited it to flare the new ident that'd been assigned to the kid at Monte. They were still close enough to that station. SecureSite would pick it up, then scoop the spitting-mad kid out of space.

She'd probably hate Jules for a while, but that was fine. A lot of other people had much better reasons to hate Jules.

She looked around the now-empty room, wondering what the fuck she was going to do next. It'd take her a while to get to Atrux, and she needed to have a plan. A stick to shove into Rainier's eye.

Her gaze drifted back to the reconstruction baths, and lingered. Everything on this ship was made out of the guardcore metal. Everything except those baths. She frowned, considering, then her gaze caught on the guardcore breach pods waiting ready at the end of the room, and her face split into a fierce grin.

If Rainier got her original body back, then Jules knew what to do to give her one hell of a stomachache.

CHAPTER 49

PRIME STANDARD YEAR 3543

SEVENTY-EIGHT PERCENT

Biran sat on the edge of his bed, half a bottle of the whiskey Greystone had given him in his hand, and wondered if there was some pain too deep to be worked through. Seventy-eight percent. Biran hadn't believed it, not really. It was a high percentage, granted, but had plenty of room to be brushed off as a false positive. And didn't Biran know the way Vladsen moved better than anyone else, better than any algorithm Arden had cooked up?

He hadn't believed it, until he'd almost died. Until he'd seen Vladsen move like a predator into that room where Biran had been brutalized, his pain obvious but carefully contained, every line of his body radiating violence.

Biran was no warrior. Neither was Vladsen meant to be, not according to his life as Biran knew it. A bioengineering geek in school, a quick rise to the top of his class, an early member of the Protectorate—the youngest, before Biran himself. Lavaux's protégé, for his quick rise and quick wits. None of that left room for the kind of training that would give him the carriage of a killer, when weapons came to bear.

Biran had been half-delirious, half-dead, but he'd not been blind. Not yet, anyway. On that day, Vladsen moved like the man in grey. After that, 78 percent seemed entirely too conservative.

He tapped the bottle against his knee. Vladsen had had the run of this ship for three days, and he hadn't done any harm. Hell, he could have killed Biran a dozen times over since they'd grown close on Hitton's asteroid. But a dead informant was no good to a Nazca.

Biran's stomach soured, bile threatening to rise. His body registered the adrenaline spike and sped up his metabolism, washing away the fog of drunkenness. He cursed and clenched the bottle tighter, scrubbing the back of his hand across his eyes. Everything about a Keeper was designed to keep their secrets inside them, and he needed to find a way to carve this one out. To challenge it, because he could not bring a Nazca to that planet. Could not in good faith embed a known spy in his team. Maybe more than a spy.

He moved faster than any of us, Slatter had said with no small amount of admiration. Biran had watched the security footage. Arguably, Vladsen had moved faster than any of them possibly could.

Biran drank another fourth of the bottle. The footage had told him another story, too. One he didn't want to know, but needed to, if he were ever going to master his pain in the way Okonkwo and Greystone required.

An hour. It had taken an hour for Scalla to figure out that Russo had tampered with their course, pointing them back at the gate to trigger the shutdown protocol. Biran had been bleeding for an hour before any of them realized something was wrong. Before Echo took down the remaining GC and sprinted—in the wrong direction—to his rooms, then course-corrected when his beacon finally sounded the alarm.

Biran stared at his hands in the low light, at the pink rings decorating his fingers, and recalled every snip, every crunch, every searing tear until he was on the verge of hyperventilating. This mental exercise he'd gone through two dozen times, now, and if he were being honest with himself, he'd done his due diligence.

He told himself he no longer felt his heart leap into his throat at the thought of calling Sanda. No longer shuddered when he saw Echo, his patient guardian, through the cameras that watched the other side of his door. The reality wasn't as neat as all that. He still felt those things, still flinched in his heart, but the reactions had grown leaden.

Dulled under the blunted force of repeated exposure. Maybe he'd finally broken, after all, and the numbness that replaced searing terror would one day eat him alive.

It was not perfect, he knew that. Those things would haunt him the rest of his life, sneak up on him when least expected, but it was a start. A decent enough place to be in, before he dropped to that planet tomorrow.

There was only one more pain left to work through.

He'd sent Vladsen away at the door to his rooms. And now he had to call him back.

"Echo," he said through his wristpad, because there was no one in this room to overhear him. "Bring me Keeper Vladsen. Make sure he isn't armed."

A pause. "Is there a possibility he is a threat?"

"Yes." That yes cut deeper than any scalpel. "I will speak to him alone, but be ready."

"Understood."

Biran finished the fine stuff Greystone had given him while he waited, and had another bottle of something cheaper that'd come with the ship in his hand by the time Vladsen shuffled into his room, hesitant, squinting against the low light. His dark curls were tousled, so he'd been either running his hands through them, or tossing and turning. Biran knew better than anyone that Vladsen slept still as the dead. If he even slept at all.

The exterior door closed, signaling Echo's exit. Vladsen shifted uncomfortably in the doorway, sleep pants rustling, his T-shirt askew, eyes red-rimmed. Brittle cages. Vladsen was living in one.

"Biran," he said softly, and Biran realized he hadn't said anything yet. He'd been staring. Thinking. Stalling. "Can I...help?"

Biran looked at the bottle in his hand. It wasn't the one he thought he'd grabbed after Greystone's. It was another, the second one already lay on the floor, empty. He grimaced, and drank, knowing his body would clean up the mess he made of it like the good little Prime construct it was.

"I appear to be having a breakdown, Keeper Vladsen," he said through numb lips. "Sit."

"Keeper Vladsen, is it?" His voice strained, but he stepped to the side and pulled up a chair across from Biran, sitting woodenly on its edge. "I'd feared, when you sent me away earlier tonight, that..."

"That being tortured would remind me of why Keepers are not allowed to love one another? That the fear would be so dreadful it would push me away from you?"

"An hour," Vladsen said, and the word cut deep, as it echoed Biran's previous thoughts. "They had you for an hour and seventeen minutes. That's...too much. We've all done the simulations. After fifteen minutes, on average, most Keepers lose the ability to convince their captors that their bodies can be broken to the point they'll spill.

"And so the captors move on to loved ones, innocents. They acquire leverage. But you...you strung them along. You let them think there was a chance they could get it out of you, the easy way, instead of coming for us. You protected us, even though we'd all had the same training, and it almost fucking killed you."

His voice had risen steadily as he spoke, until the last words came out as a near shout, breath coming high and fast.

"I could not lose control of this ship," Biran said, as if that were all that mattered.

"Not even your sister adheres that stubbornly to her mission," Vladsen shot back.

The reminder of Sanda didn't make him flinch, didn't make him curl up inside, seeking his cage. Progress. "And how closely do you cling to your mission?"

Vladsen's brow furrowed in confusion. Sickness spread from Biran's belly through all his limbs, dragging him down. He could not do this. He did not *want* to do this. The very thought of excising this secret, exposing it to daylight, made him want to go kicking and screaming back into the NutriBath.

This shit was Sanda's purview. Betrayal and violence and spies. Not his. He hadn't been built for this, not like she had. She'd always been Graham's child, and he...He'd been Ilan's, somewhat. But he'd never really seen himself in either of them, not clearly. He wasn't a warrior. He wasn't even a businessman.

He was the director. And he had withstood one hour and seventeen minutes of torture. He could stand a little more.

"I...I do as you tell me, Director." Vladsen tried to put a coy twist on the way he said *director*, as he used to, but it came out hesitant. Not afraid, just questioning.

Biran scratched the stubble along his jaw, pressing his finger pads into the skin, remembering the feeling of bone breaking, and met Vladsen's eye, steeling himself to break something else.

"I have spoken with Agent Zero."

Confusion, at first, a flickering of his lashes as he reached back through memory, then the cold mantle of realization, settling over him like snowfall on pine needles. Beautiful, but suffocating.

"I see," he said, slowly, not shifting his gaze from Biran's. "It is Tomas, then, isn't it? I couldn't be sure."

So casual, so easy. Biran couldn't speak, and so he brought the footage up on his wristpad, that point-of-view horror show Tomas had sent him, and flicked it to a viewscreen on the wall. Vladsen had to turn to watch it without craning his head.

Biran watched Vladsen through the whole thing, boring holes in him with his gaze, struggling to separate what he thought he knew of Rost—*his* Rost—from the man in Tomas's memory.

There was no separation. They were one and the same.

Vladsen turned back when it was over, face carefully neutral. "Seventy-eight percent."

"Don't deny it." Biran's fist closed around the neck of the bottle. His new-made skin stung. "Don't even try. I watched the footage of you executing Russo. What do you think would happen to that probability if Arden ran that footage against Tomas's memory?"

"A hundred percent match, I presume," Vladsen said. "I've spent a great many years refining a new way of moving, but...Well. Some circumstances call for old habits."

"Old habits? Did you miss that you were sentencing Cepko to a life of servitude? That you were erasing his memories to make him your puppet? Is that merely an old habit of yours?"

His expression went flat. "That was a matter of survival. We were being hunted."

"We?" Biran gritted his teeth. "Who are *we*, exactly, in this history of yours?"

"The Nazca."

"You're a spy."

"I was."

"You expect me to believe you've had a change of heart?"

Vladsen winced and looked away, licking his lips, hands folded over his chest, fingers so taut the knuckles were white. "No. I expect you to call that guardcore of yours in here and have her ice me."

Biran wasn't drunk enough to miss that slip. "Her?"

He startled, and smiled a little. "Yes. She hasn't figured me out yet, but I've heard her voice pitch slip a few times. While you were in . . ." He trailed off, shifting uncomfortably. "While you were healing, I went through your things. I found the paint. Does it really work?"

"You went through . . ." He laughed bitterly and scraped his hand across his stubble. "Of course you did. You're Nazca."

"I am not Nazca anymore," he snapped, anger bleeding into his voice. Biran tensed, itching to have his distress beacon ready, but pushed the urge down.

Vladsen's eyes widened, catching Biran's distress—obvious, while he was drinking enough to kill a horse—and he started to reach forward, a comforting hand outstretched. Biran pulled back. Vladsen retreated to the chair. "Christ. I am . . . I am sorry. I would never hurt you."

"Oh, fuck your apologies. You already have." He pushed to his feet, dropping the bottle to the floor. Alcohol mingled with hints of smoke and leather stung his nose. Biran stalked around his bed, dragging his fingers through his hair, feeling Vladsen's gaze follow him, feeling the shadow of that footage from Tomas, frozen in the final second, dog his every step.

He dropped his hands, stuck, exhausted, staring at that final moment in the footage, the last thing Agent Zero had seen before he'd gone in the bath and woken up someone else. Vladsen, cold as anything, standing above him, a stunner in his hand, face turned away in the second before he'd pulled the trigger.

"Why did you look away?" he asked.

"What?"

"This, right here. Cepko was your top agent, and you turned your back on him before you put him under. Why?" Biran jabbed a finger at the footage. Vladsen bit his lip, sinking into the chair.

"He was...a friend. Like a brother to me, really."

"You have a family," Biran said, bewildered.

Vladsen's lips thinned, and he shook his head. "No. I have a very complex and deeply rooted cover story meant to fool even my makers."

"Your makers?"

"The Nazca. Sitta Caid, specifically. She stole the technology to make us, her perfect agents. Zero and I...we were the best of them. The ones who didn't tear themselves apart. That day, Sitta was jumpy. Tomas had gone toe to toe with the organization she stole the tech from, and nearly lost his life. They'd told him what he was, and he was breaking. Damaging himself. After that day, I..." He shook his head. "I'm a coward, Biran. I insisted Tomas be reset for his own safety, and then I fled. Caid had Tomas to focus on. I'd been made director of the program at that point, so I used my administrative powers to arrange matters to look as if those who hunted us had killed me. I left him there, and I never looked back. I..." He laughed roughly. "I've never told anyone about this before."

"I'm charmed," Biran grated. "So you knew, didn't you? All this goddamn time, you knew what Lavaux was, what Rainier was? What she was capable of?"

Vladsen shot to his feet, barely restrained himself from taking a step toward Biran. "I did not lie to you, Biran. I thought..." He growled and crossed his arms so tightly the fabric pulled taut against his chest. "I came to Ada to *hide*, do you understand? I felt like shit for leaving Tomas behind, but I had to get away from Caid, from what hunted us. I knew she stole the tech. I knew the originator was chasing us down.

"So I changed my face, my body language, and fucking ran like the coward I was. I became a Keeper because they were the most protected layer of society that I could find, and then I went to Ada because I believed it would stay sleepy, quiet. When I met Lavaux, I..." He shook his head, eyes bright with unshed tears. "I thought he might be like me, like Tomas. I thought he'd be sympathetic. I'd planned on telling him what I was, eventually. I started to think of him as a father. I never got close enough to Rainier to realize what she was, and if she knew what I was, she never said anything. And then you went and hired Tomas.

"I should have fled, the day he showed up on Ada Station with Sanda in tow. I couldn't be sure he was the man I remembered, his face had changed slightly, and still I nearly ran right then and there. But I'd already wriggled my way onto the Protectorate, and people would have noticed my disappearance. So I decided to wait it out, see what happened, wait for a clear path to freedom, but then... Then you asked me for help, to borrow the *Taso*, and I couldn't say no. Believe me, I know how stupid it was to loan you that ship. But I found I couldn't deny you."

"Rost—"

"Do not call me that unless you mean it."

Biran froze, betrayal boiling through his blood, tainting every thought. He was the director. He was the head of this mission. A whole planet full of answers to questions he hadn't even thought to ask lay at his feet, and every scrap of training he'd ever had screamed at him to call Echo in, to put a bullet in this man's head and drop him into vacuum.

Okonkwo would have pulled that trigger. But she would have put down Echo, too, and Echo had been the only thing standing between him and complete disaster when shit had gone sideways. Okonkwo had sent Biran here, had selected him, because he would not pull the trigger.

But still... Nazca. Construct. A potential puppet of Rainier's, but so was Tomas, and Sanda felt comfortable keeping him around. But then, maybe she was as naive as he was. She had no trouble commanding a ship controlled by her kidnapper, after all. Sanda Greeve was not exactly a barometer for emotional well-being.

Biran scraped Vladsen with his gaze, seeking cracks, wondering if there could be tells in the veneer of a being like him. Tomas hadn't been clear on what the video meant, but Biran had enough information to figure it out for himself. They were made, Tomas and Rostam. Printed like tops by Sitta Caid, then spun out into the universe to see what they dug up.

He hoped Caid was still alive. Given the chance, that was one trigger he'd squeeze.

Biran looked back at his hands. Couldn't stop looking at them, really. Was this the level of fascination that had driven Tomas to peeling his skin? Unlikely, but close enough to disturb him.

He only had fingers now because Lili Monta had scraped them off the floor, and Natsu Sato had sewn them into place. Two people he wouldn't have trusted with his life a month ago. Two people he trusted with everything, now, because they'd shown him themselves.

It wasn't exactly the socializing party Ilan had urged Biran to throw, all those years ago, to try and make nice with his cohort. But if being torn to pieces and stitched up again by his team was what it took to ensure their loyalty, he'd take it. He'd already sat with the pain. The rest was academic.

"You expect me to kill you," Biran said, not quite knowing where the words came from.

"I've expected you to kill me since Hitton's asteroid."

He looked up. Made himself meet Rost's eyes, no matter that it hurt. "Why haven't you run? With Tomas back, you had to know it was only a matter of time. Why put yourself on this ship, where there was no corner to hide in? I tried to leave you behind. You had every opportunity."

"You know why." His voice was low, gravelly.

Heat bloomed in Biran's chest and he scowled at himself. Rost saw the expression and sucked air through his teeth, taking a step back, his calves bumping against the chair.

"I've been a fool—"

Biran moved before he could think, snapped a hand out and grabbed Rost's wrist. They stared at the point of contact.

"But not a coward," Biran said. "Not this time."

"Biran..."

"I don't know exactly how it works, but I'm reasonably certain you didn't have to risk revealing yourself when I was taken. You could have stayed Keeper Vladsen, could have missed that shot at Russo, or been a step or two too slow. A little off your guard."

Rost flicked his gaze up, and the mingled hope and fear there twisted a dagger in Biran's heart.

"I'm...tired of this," Biran said. "Of something happening, and one or both of us deciding, even if secretly to ourselves, that it's another illustration of why we shouldn't be together. I don't care about the laws, or the Nazca. I care about you."

"Oh, goddamnit, Biran. I wish I could kiss you right now, call it a night and a happily ever after, but this is why you frighten me. This is why I needed to be on this ship. You *should* care about those things. You should have killed Echo the second she told you what she was, you should have kicked me out the airlock an hour ago. You should have never let Slatter or Monta or Sato on this ship. You keep holding your hand out to your enemies, smiling, and saying, 'Come on in, I'll bake you some damn cookies while you sharpen your knives at my back.'"

"I won't shut down my life to stay safe. Sato and my cohort— they're Keepers, and they're damn good at their jobs. And, what's more, they were right to resent my promotions. I brought them here to show them I wasn't pulling up the ladder behind me. People are good, for the most part. They get hurt and they throw up walls and they lash out, but that doesn't mean they're lost causes. I can't lose sight of that, or I'll start thinking like Rainier, and wonder if we don't deserve all she's done."

"And Echo? And me? We're not..." He licked his lips. "We're not human."

"Maybe not," Biran said, turning Rost's wrist over in his grip, his thumb tracing a line across his palm. "But I am."

"Idiot," Rost grated out.

Biran smiled. "Probably. But I'm not changing the way I do things, so if you're so concerned, you'd better stick around and watch my back."

Rost's pulse quickened beneath Biran's grip. "Be sober, Biran Greeve. Say that to me without two bottles in your veins, and I might believe it."

Previously, when Biran had needed to clear his system, he'd recalled moments from his training to kick his metabolism into the fear response required to clear out the fumes clouding his mind. Now, he had only to glance to his hands, to remember that first snapping bite of bolt cutters, and his body warmed, implants firing up to clean up the mess he'd made of himself.

The old way had been easier, smoother. It worked slower; he had to focus on the fear, really dig into it to get his body to respond properly. This time, the implants responded immediately, burning through him with alacrity that left him sweating, skin flushed and ruddy. All that energy had to go somewhere.

Biran winced, head heavy, but clear. Every tiny ache the alcohol had dulled came rushing back—remnants of agony that hadn't been given time to fully heal in the bath. He staggered slightly, putting down a hand to steady himself against the foot of the bed. Rost switched their grip, smooth as silk, and Biran couldn't tell how he'd gone from clutching Rost's wrist to being clutched by him. Steadied. Supported.

"Stay," Biran said.

He did.

CHAPTER 50

PRIME STANDARD YEAR 3543

THERE'S ALWAYS A GLITCH

At one hour to contact, Sanda walked alone onto the Atrux guard-core dock. Bero assured her he was in position on the opposite side of the dwarf planet, plugged into a bank of hardware provided by Prime Inventive at a rush, but serviceable. On that side of the planet, the city of Alexandria-Atrux did not reach. He'd docked in a small atmo dome, set up for research purposes, and gone to stealth. Rainier would find him anyway.

They were counting on it.

"GC ships incoming," Anford said through the comms. "They've dropped out of stealth. Twenty-four we can see. Burning hot for the gate from Ordinal to Atrux."

"I'm in position. Let them through."

"The cordon has already backed off. No one's stupid enough to run that gate while a fleet of GC are flying straight toward it."

"You have a lot of faith in our citizens," Sanda mused.

"I have to," Anford said. "And so do you, Commander Greeve."

Sanda suppressed a smirk at Anford's tone, practically dripping with sarcasm. She was here because she had lost that faith, and they both knew it. If Sanda really, truly, believed in the people of Prime Inventive, then she'd step back. Let the researchers figure out the solution to the comatose patients of Atrux. She wouldn't be standing here, baiting a lioness with a broken stool and one arm tied behind her back.

Anford never would have been on board if she believed they could do it alone, either. Somehow, sharing a shattering of faith with her commander was comforting.

"Breach," Anford said.

She needn't have bothered. It was a short hop from the gate to the docks, and guardcore ships were very, very fast. She would have called them the fastest in the universe, before she'd found *The Light*. It was only a matter of minutes until they—she—would arrive.

Guardcore ships passed through the atmo dome of the dock. Sanda lifted her chin, making her own count, as twenty-four ships like knives sliced their way into Atrux. Long shadows fell across her, across the dock, making the ground appear shredded. Sanda expected fear. Staring down two dozen ships designed to bust planets, to control the universe, and knowing they were coming for her should have left her a watery mess, should have lodged her heart in her throat and choked her with her own frantic beating.

All she felt was calm.

The ships slid into dock, gentle as could be, for all appearances coming into port for a genial chat or a regular guardcore operation. Sanda wondered if she'd ever trust those ships again, and decided she would have to, if they were ever going to move on. It wasn't the ships that threatened—though they had been designed to be intimidating as hell—it was the person at their helm.

"Twenty-four sighted," she said over the comms.

"Two came through stealthed," Tomas said. "They're circling the planet. Hunting."

"Hold position, do not let her know she's been sighted."

"Understood."

"I could have a gunship formation to you in ten minutes," Anford said, voice tight. She knew the plan. They all did. None of them liked it.

"Hold," Sanda said, half for her own benefit. "Bero, do you feel secure with the connection?"

"Yes. Arden has crafted me an admirable escape route."

"Tomas." There was nothing she could say that would make this easier. "Ready?"

"As I'll ever be."

"Got you covered, boss," Nox said.

Sanda smiled to herself, picturing in her mind's eye Nox and Conway up in the administration deck of the guardcore docks, sighting down two measly rifles at twenty-four ships that they could not even pierce with the ordnance they carried. Rainier wouldn't have expected her to come without backup. It was all for show.

"I feel better already," she said.

"News drones ran the blockade," Anford said. "The gate vaporized them. No live bodies attempted the crossing. Reestablishing the cordon."

Sanda nodded. "Good. I don't need civvies stumbling across this." The gangway slid down from the first guardcore ship to dock. "Contact."

Several soft clicks echoed over comms as her team switched their ends to mute. They'd hear everything Sanda and Rainier said, but wouldn't risk distracting her with their own sounds unless they absolutely had to.

Nine of Rainier Lavaux stepped out onto the gangway. This time, she hadn't bothered with the armor. Each instance wore a pale grey dress with a faint shimmer, as if staring through smoked glass at distant stars. Maybe it meant something to her, but all it said to Sanda was that she was confident enough to come unarmed—ships aside. The only metal on her body was her mag boots, locking her to the dock with heavy steps. As the nine approached, Sanda shifted her posture into a casual lean, hooking her thumbs into the blaster holsters strapped to her hips. One of Rainier flicked her gaze to the weapons, and smiled. That one stepped to the front of the line while the others drifted back to form jagged rows.

"Commander Greeve, you must know those weapons are useless against me. I've scanned this planet. You have not established an EMP device. An interesting show of faith. I'm moved." Only one of her spoke, the others tilting their head to the left even as they shifted their weight to the right. The Rainiers that had come to her on the fringer settlement had stood in much the same way. Sanda wondered, if she ran a body language analysis between Rainier and old footage of Halston, how many similarities there would be.

"Maybe I like the look of them," Sanda drawled.

Rainier grinned fiercely. "One's accessories can say so much. Take, for example, that silver chain around your neck. Not standard for a fleetie going into combat, or zero-g, is it? Jewelry and space don't get along."

"Recognize it, do you?" Rainier's gaze flashed mercurial silver, quick as fish through a pond. "I do wonder, what am I supposed to call you, now? Dr. Halston feels a little outdated."

"Do not give me the name of that *bitch*. We are nothing alike."

"From where I'm standing"—Sanda spread one arm, gesturing to the whole of Atrux—"I don't see a whole hell of a lot of difference between you two."

Her eyes narrowed on every instance. "Are you baiting me to a fight, Commander Greeve? I've had a very long time to come to terms with my emotional state. I warn you now, I cannot be tempted off the path I've decided on."

"I've no interest in fighting you, Rainier. I'm here to deal. The people of Atrux don't deserve to get caught in the cross fire. Valentine did this. You didn't. I don't believe this is what you wanted. You can fix it."

"What I wanted?" She laughed, cupping her stomach with two hands. The other Rainiers joined in, then stopped abruptly when the first did. "You spoke with Salvez. You know what I want. The only thing I am capable of wanting."

"For the ascension-agent to *work*. You can fix this."

"For it to work on the species that earned it. My directives are very strict, Greeve."

"The beings that gave you that directive are gone. Either Halston got them with her gates, or they left this universe for some other reason, but they have never come for Prime. They've never confronted humanity about what they've done. You've seen the worst of us, and I'm sorry for that, but your makers aren't here. You are not beholden to their rules anymore."

"I—" Her voice cracked, but not in the way a human's would. It glitched, screeched like static from between her lips, and for a moment her eyes were filled with grey snow. She scowled and shook herself, returning to normal. When she spoke again, her tone was stiff with the echo of an often-repeated rote. "I will fulfill my objective."

Bero spoke through her comms, "She can only want one thing. She is not a general intelligence."

Sanda blinked, realization hitting her like a hammer. Bero was general intelligence, outlawed by Prime. A mind capable of recursive learning, yes, but more importantly capable of choosing its own goals, its own hopes and dreams and fears. Icarion had made sure of that, when they'd read him stories to give him a data set on emotional intelligence.

Rainier was built to deliver the ascension-agent to the inheritors that earned it, and for no other purpose. She was fucking brilliant, but everything she did was only possible in the pursuit of delivering the ascension-agent to its inheritors. That was why she couldn't control the gates without human help. It was too far outside her directive, and even she couldn't justify punishing humanity as operating within the parameters of her orders. That was whatever had seeped over from Halston—human rage twisted in upon itself, desperate for outlet—a corruption in her code.

She needed debugging. Sanda really wished she could pummel Arden with questions, but she was on her own.

"Violence isn't in your objective," she said.

Rainier's heads twitched to one side. "The Waiting did not foresee your theft. Changes must be made to set matters to rights. I must stop the spin of the faulty gates to protect the real inheritors."

"Rainier," Sanda said gently. Then, softer, "Spheremind. There is no more rightful inheritor. Even if there is a species out there who comes to spacefaring on their own terms, there is no first sphere left to discover. It's damaged, collecting dust in a warehouse. I have the second and the third. The entire plan is shot to hell.

"Humanity doesn't want to spin faulty gates anymore. We want to fix it. I don't know if we can ever make what we did right, but if we repair the blowback, then we can help you find your makers. Help you figure out what you're supposed to do next, because the path given to you is gone. You cannot fulfill your objective."

Rainier began to scream. The sound pierced Sanda's ears, pushed her to her knees. Buzzing started up in her comms, then crackled out as the others muted her to protect their own hearing. Rainier clenched her fists at her sides and opened her mouths impossibly wide, letting that banshee wail scathe away her rage and frustration.

"Greeve." Anford's voice cut through the buzzing in her ears, but sounded far away. Sanda focused on the sound of her general's voice. "Jules Valentine has been spotted on Ada."

"What?" She shook her head and touched her temple, took her fingers away to see blood. Rainier stopped screaming, and stared at her through empty eyes. "How the fuck?"

"GC ship, stealthed, slipped through when we brought down the blockade."

Sanda snapped her gaze to Rainier. Every last one of those units smiled dreamily.

"What did you do?" Sanda breathed.

"Decided to negotiate from a more advantageous position. Or did you think I'd fall for your trap? I can wait for *The Light*. You, however, cannot wait to save your fathers. Are they strong enough to withstand ascension, I wonder? Can they resist my error?"

Sanda tore the comm unit out of her bleeding ear and pressed it into the other. "Anford, what's happening?"

"Working on it." She ground out the words, which meant she didn't have a handle on the situation at all.

"Recall your hunting dog," Sanda snapped. She pushed to her feet and yanked the sphere from around her neck and held it by the chain, off to the side, and pointed a blaster at it. "I will destroy it, Rainier."

"Damaging that device will leave this city a crater. And besides, Valentine slipped my control a long time ago."

"Then why is she in Ada right now?"

Rainier lifted a delicate shoulder on each body in an expressive shrug. "I do not need to command Valentine to know what she will do. She saw your message to me, and took advantage."

"You said this was to give you a better negotiating advantage."

Sanda pushed out the words through a clenched jaw. "You gave her the order. Rescind it."

"But I did no such thing. I know Valentine as well as I do you, I do not need to give her orders to make her actions suit me. Run, Sanda Greeve. Run to your fathers, but I do not think you will make it in time. Next time we speak, you will give me what I want, without the trap."

Bero said, "She has not attempted an intrusion. The two stealthed ships are withdrawing. I can be to you in five minutes."

"Fuck," Sanda said. She blew the head off of the Rainier that did most of the talking. The others tsked. "Get your ships out of this system, now."

The Rainiers spread their hands expansively, and they all backed away.

CHAPTER 51

PRIME STANDARD YEAR 3543

WELCOME MAT

Biran's first impression of the new planet was that he absolutely, to the core of his being, hated a thick atmosphere. He'd ordered armor for all of them, clamped over jumpsuits fitted with lifepacks, but even the cushioning of the armor and inertia-damping chair cradling him couldn't stop the heavy vibrations of entry.

The shuttle jerked and juddered, all the readouts stubbornly green, reminding him that this was normal, expected. He'd been pampered by gradated atmo domes and space elevators. This was what it meant to land on a planet. A real, species-birthing planet had teeth, and it was chewing them up for thinking they were important enough to drop out of the stars and pay it a visit.

Biran clenched his jaw, thought better of it as his teeth ground against each other, and tried to go limp in his armor. It didn't help. He hoped he'd been in the NutriBath long enough for his bones to fully knit back together, otherwise he was about to have a very painful problem.

"Landing in three, two..." the shuttle's AI chirped cheerfully.

Biran's stomach leapt into his throat as the shuttle slammed down into the clearing, vomit threatening to rise even as his vision blacked at the edges, the first signs of passing out. He clenched his thighs, his core, pushing the blood back up as he'd been trained. The armor, sensing his distress, injected him with a cocktail designed to keep him moving, not puking in a helmet he couldn't take off.

He gasped, grateful for the muted speakers of his helmet, and shivered in miserable silence while he got his bearings. His HUD told him all passengers had survived the descent. Well, that was a good enough place to start from.

"We've landed and are accounted for," he reported up to Scalla, hovering above them in orbit in the *Terminus*.

"Huh," she said. "Good. Now move your ass, you've got four days of nutrients and air in those suits, and trust me, kid, you do not want to see what things start looking like on day five."

The reminder only made him itch for a shower, even though he'd had one hours before they'd boarded the shuttle. There'd be no swimming in the icy lakes of this planet for Biran and his team. They'd push their recyclers and support systems to their limits to avoid contamination.

Sato's survey had come back clean of pathogens, but she and her team had been very clear that the organisms on this planet were carbon based, sporting the same amino acids humanity did, and so there was a very real chance that something new was lurking for them out there, perfectly capable of crossing the species barrier if it was evolutionarily advantageous.

Biran took risks with people. He wasn't stupid enough to take risks with microbes.

"Everyone in one piece?" he asked over the team channel as he flicked off his harness and stood.

They sounded off, one by one, and if he was more relieved when Rost sounded off, the helmet meant the others didn't see it.

"Weapons, supplies, drones, in that order," he said.

Well, drones and supplies for everyone except Echo. She was carrying an arsenal large enough to supply an entire GC triad, and had probably taken most of those weapons off her dead colleagues. The team grabbed packs from the cargo stores around them, Sato firing up drones capable of carrying even more equipment. Drones carrying drones.

Once readied, Biran initiated opening the airlock, the slow descent of the gangway, Prime metals touching down on the burned-out crust of the meadow of this alien world for the first time.

Echo corralled them into a loose diamond formation, as protective as a sheepdog, and took up a position at the point. She opened one of her bags and released a swarm of bladelike drones, their soft buzzing whispering into the still air. Biran held his breath.

"No threats detected," Echo said over the open comm, her voice computerized, her name tagged GC-ED0. "Operating perimeter of five hundred meters secured."

"Thank you," Biran said, and started to walk down the gangway.

Echo grabbed his arm. "Wait for my all-clear, Director."

Reluctantly, he nodded, letting her lead the way. Before he'd been attacked, he would have bristled at being held back, but something had shifted in Echo during his time in the bath. She'd seemed desperate, before. Scattered and afraid, willing to do whatever it took to keep Rainier out of her head—even if it meant taking her own life.

Now, she moved with purpose, and her way of speaking had lost its frightened, rambling quality. Echo hadn't set out to be guardcore, she'd had no choices at all in her life, but she was one, now.

After a quick scan of the tree line to be certain the camera drones hadn't missed anything, Echo waved him down the gangway.

Biran's mag boots crunched over ground left scorched by their entry. Humanity had set foot on a lot of new planets over the centuries it'd been shepherded under the guiding star of Prime Inventive. Biran himself had walked on asteroids, moons, and rock worlds reshaped to suit humanity. But those had all been constructs, more or less. The bones of the celestial body repurposed to house humanity's needs.

Prime had never found a planet with vegetation. Had never found a world with a human-friendly atmosphere in place, plate tectonics, and a magnetosphere. All the living, breathing details of carbon-based life. It'd found a few moons here and there with water, or the start of an atmo. But nothing like this. Nothing so obviously *suited*.

Alexandra Halston had allowed humanity to believe that this was because Earth-like worlds were exceedingly rare. It might have been her cruelest lie of all.

Biran exited the burnt circle of the shuttle's entry pad, mag boots pressing into the springy loam of the forest floor, the slight slip in texture and hint of ice crystals beneath his feet making him feel, briefly, unsteady. He put a hand out, pressed it into the trunk of a nearby tree to keep from slipping.

"You all right?" Slatter asked.

"Yes," Biran said. "It's just…a lot."

Nervous, giddy laughter from all across the comms. At least he wasn't the only one feeling like his world had been turned upside down and shaken empty. Rainier was right. This was no accident. Halston had been destroying worlds in her wake. When he tried to think of how many, it made him dizzy, so he focused on the fact that they were here, now.

Rainier may have made the gate into a weapon, but it had always been one. She'd just changed the direction of the strike in the last second. Biran ached for those lost—Director Olver most of all—but the best he could do, the only thing he could do, was to make their sacrifice worth it. To understand the meaning of this planet that their founder had worked to make sure no human eyes would ever see.

His team stood about him in a loose, uneven clump, heads tilted back as they examined the environment around them. Monta reached up, tapped a tree branch, and laughed as snow fell down from the bough. Echo shifted her weight, anxious.

"The landing site put us a two-hour hike from the center of the structure," Biran said, pushing through a map of the terrain that they'd taken from orbit. "We follow this, we should be there before sundown."

They shook themselves, reorienting. Sato and Greystone sent up swarms of their own survey bots—Sato's to sample the local biologics, Greystone's to hunt for any more signals like that coming from the center of the structure.

Echo got them moving in a straight line, her circling them like a shark with every step, Greystone at the rear, Slatter and Biran up front, with the rest clumped in the middle. Biran itched to reorder things, to swap Slatter out with Vladsen, but the others didn't know what Rost was, and on paper, Slatter was the better shot. Before Rost joined the Protectorate, he had been a bioengineer, more suited to assisting Sato than holding down the front line.

Keeping the threat-alert overlay in the corner of his eye, Biran opened a private comm link to Slatter. They had two hours of hiking ahead of them, and Biran wanted to be sure of where he stood with the more aggressive of his Keepers.

"Keeper Slatter," he said, "I owe you a very overdue apology."

"Nah," Slatter said. "Don't mention it. I goaded you into taking a shot at me, I knew what I was doing."

"Why? Want an excuse for plastic surgery?"

He laughed. "No. Can I be honest with you, Director?"

Biran licked his lips. "I would like you to be."

"Lil and I, we hated your guts. We worked our asses off to position ourselves for next in line for the Protectorate, from different angles. The position of Speaker opened the year before our graduation—I don't even know if you *noticed*—so we took two tracks. Lil was already in engineering, so she pivoted to add comms to that, started trying to worm her way into Keeper Lavaux's inner circle, if you could believe it. There were rumors then that he kept a few select Keepers close as potential protégés and, well, Keeper Vladsen seemed like proof of that. While she went that direction, I drilled down into defense systems."

Biran frowned. "How was defense supposed to leverage you into the Speaker position?"

"Director, it wasn't."

Ah. Slatter had always called Keeper Monta "Lil" outside of formal situations, especially when they were in the academy. Keeper relationships often flared up during schooling, but they were always snuffed before the chips were inserted. Biran had had a similar entanglement with Anaia. If Slatter had meant to shift his entire career to protect her, then he hadn't intended for their flare-up to end.

"And this arrangement continues?"

A pause. "I thought you might understand."

He almost missed a step, caught himself at the last second and only stumbled a little over a branch protruding from the ground. Slatter shot out a hand to steady him, and took it back as soon as Biran had his balance. He gritted his teeth. This weakness of his was tiring. He didn't know how Sanda kept pushing under similar circumstances.

"I don't—"

"Please," Slatter said, "Keeper Vladsen turned into a different person when you were taken, and I saw the way he touched you. I like you just fine, Director, but you won't catch me fondling your forehead."

Biran snorted. "Appreciated."

"Anyway, your secret's safe with me." He glanced over his shoulder, toward Monta. "I think the rules are damn stupid anyway, and you're proof of that."

"How so?"

"The GC, they threatened us all, didn't they? Threatened Vladsen?"

"They did."

"See? There you go. You didn't forget your training because they pointed their knives at your partner. If anything, having a partner with Keeper training is a bonus."

Biran wasn't so sure it was as simple as that. But then, he'd been twisting himself up in knots trying to find all the angles that made their relationship too dangerous to continue. Maybe it was time he gave himself a break and accepted a single good angle, for once. Not that the idea of Vladsen being better able to withstand torture was particularly appealing, but considering the lives they led, it was a silver lining he could allow himself.

"I was given the Speaker position as a punishment, if that takes some of the sting out of things. They couldn't punish me, so they put me in a position where I was very likely to fuck up publicly."

"Oh, we knew," Slatter said. "And, Director, with respect, knowing someone was given a post you worked for as a punishment to them makes the sting a hell of a lot worse."

They walked in silence while Biran chewed that over.

"When did you change your minds about me?" he finally asked.

"About three and a half days ago."

Slatter clapped him on the shoulder, jarring his still-sore muscles, and Biran couldn't help but laugh. Vladsen had been right. Biran had loaded his ship full of knives.

"I hope it doesn't take a repeat experience to bring the rest of the Cannery to my side."

"Piece of advice, Director?"

"Go ahead."

"Don't bother trying to get them all. You can't. We're always going to snipe at each other, it's the way things are. Hell, Lil and I were planning a wide variety of ways to make you look like an idiot coming out of this mission. I was impressed by the way you handled Negassi, though. Lil thought it was gauche. So you see, right there, Lil and I are as aligned as any two Keepers can be, and we disagreed on your actions. You can't win 'em all. Don't try. Do what you think is right, the rest will shake out."

"I hope you're right."

"For what it's worth, so do I."

Biran did not tell Slatter that he'd already infected the wristpad of every Keeper on the ship with a virus, courtesy of Arden, that would enable him to find and delete any files that the Keepers tried to fake to discredit him, or this mission. He'd already flagged a series of "contemporaneous notes" that Lili Monta had begun, which edged close to the truth but made Biran out to be a bumbling idiot who got lucky.

Vladsen may think he was foolish for bringing them on board, and maybe he was right, but Biran wasn't so optimistic that he'd moved without fail-safes. He was curious to check her notes later, once they were back on the ship, and see if she'd changed the tone of them after the events of the last few days.

The rest of the hike passed in uneventful silence. It was almost peaceful.

"Here we are," Biran said over the open channel as they approached a steep rise in the ground, leading up to a razor-thin wall of black metal.

His heart kicked up as he approached the structure, the subtle buzz of Sato and Greystone's drones synchronizing with the buzz of anticipation in his head. The star was beginning to sink below the horizon, night coming on quickly, and as the darkness stretched—shadows of trees reaching out, then bleeding across the ground to shroud them all—the structure seemed to blend with the endless night, matte and smooth.

Stars winked into the sky, and their reflections slid off the structure like water. Biran was grateful for the slightly less-than-Earth gravity as he pushed himself up the slope, legs burning from the effort. The NutriBath had put him back together again, but it'd take months of rehab to get his full strength back.

He placed one hand against the wall, running his palm over the thin band—more like a collar, or a fence—that ran along a funnel-shaped depression in the ground. The black metal continued, uninterrupted, into a depth so far the shadows swallowed it.

"Get me cameras on the inside," Biran said.

Greystone's drones veered off and swarmed above the opening before plunging down into the dark. They waited. And waited.

"I am about to lose signal," Greystone said warily. Without Halston's tech enhancing their systems, range was a real issue.

"Pull them back within range," Biran said.

"Director," Rost said, "I think I've found something."

They had spread out along the fence, seeking irregularities in the otherwise perfect construction, and Vladsen had moved about ten meters down the line. Biran craned his head to get a better look, noted the discomfort in Rost's posture, the guarded hunch of his shoulders, the squaring up of his hips. The fence directly in front of Rost was taller than anywhere else. Biran frowned, certain it hadn't been that way a few minutes ago.

"Keeper Vladsen," he said over an open channel, "back away from there."

"I . . ." Rost trailed off, voice tight, as if he couldn't draw a full breath. Slowly, he lifted a hand, palm out toward the wall. Biran swore.

"Vladsen." Biran put some snap into his voice, already moving. Slatter picked up on the wrongness and burst into a sprint toward Rost.

A dark glow emanated from the wall, rectangular, door-shaped. The glow mounted, growing into a violet light so sharp it seared Biran's eyes, even through the visor. He threw up an arm, almost lost his footing, and staggered sideways, bouncing off the wall. Shouting through the channel, panicked and high, then silence. Silence and darkness.

Biran peeled his arm away from his visor, squinting against the halo left by the light. Rost was still there, thank the void, his arm outstretched, but shaking. A tower had emerged from the ground in front of him, blocky and tall, a rectangle punching straight down into the ground. A door, in the shape of the light, had opened in its front. Rost put his arm down, slowly.

"I'm all right," Rost said over the open channel, his voice faint with tremors. He cleared his throat. "I don't know what the fuck that was, but I'm all right."

Biran and the others clumped up around him, Biran careful not to draw too close, lest he lose control of himself and grab Rost away from that opening. Behind the door, faint violet light illuminated a circular room with a smooth floor. Just large enough for all of them to stand inside without brushing shoulders.

"What is it?" Monta asked.

"I think it's an invitation," Rost said.

CHAPTER 52

PRIME STANDARD YEAR 3543

SPRING THE TRAP

S anda pushed a priority call through to both of her dads while she watched Rainier's black ships retreat toward the gate. Ilan picked up first.

"I can't believe it—" he started, a wry smile on his lips, but she spoke over him.

"Where are you and Graham?"

He blinked, forehead wrinkling, but must have clocked the look on her face and skipped any gentle chiding or pleasantries. "I'm home, Graham is down at the docks putting together a relief supplies package for one of the border moons. Why? What's happened?"

"Please tell me Graham's a paranoid old bastard and has weapons in the house."

Ilan's brows reached for his hairline. "We have rifles, yes, what—?"

"Get them. Arm yourself—body armor if you have it—and go to Graham. Get the fuck off that planet as soon as possible."

"We can't launch. The cordon is tight, any ships taking off outside of flight plans will be shot down."

"Anford is clearing your credentials as we speak, you might even have a fleet escort on your hands, just get the hell off that rock."

His face darkened. "What's happened?"

"Jules Valentine has been spotted on Ada, near the control building for the atmo dome."

"Dios. We have to evacuate everyone—"

"You have to get your asses off that planet. Leave the rest to the fleet."

His lips thinned, but he nodded.

"Love you. Stay safe. I'm coming, Dad."

"I know you are, be careful."

Sanda cut the call—everything else left to be said was extraneous, extra time slowing down Ilan's ability to get out of the house and off the planet entirely. As Bero docked, she flicked off an estimated location of both Graham and Ilan to Anford.

She messaged back: We have them geo-tagged. Moving to assist now.

Right. They weren't just her parents, they were the parents of Biran, a Keeper director. Security would already be watching them. The thought helped, but didn't ease the knot in her chest. The second she stepped onto Bero, she stripped her coat and dropped it on the floor, storming toward the armory.

"Bero, burn for Ada. Fast as you can. I want boots on that dock yesterday."

The ship lurched under the force of the acceleration. She put a hand out, bracing herself against the wall, and threw a curious glance at the ceiling.

"Please tell me the inertia-damping system is online."

"It is. I do not believe this ship was designed to move at the speeds I am currently using."

"Will we hold?"

"Yes, though the ride may not be as smooth as you've grown used to on *The Light*."

She nodded. "Keep it up."

"I had planned on it."

Tomas jogged up alongside her. "You can't do this."

She shouldered him aside and yanked open an armor locker, strapping on a chest plate as she spoke. "Fucking watch me."

Nox barreled into the armory, Knuth, Conway, Liao, and Arden tight on his heels. "Full kit?" he asked.

"Arm yourself like it's the end of the goddamn world."

"Finally."

"You too, Conway and Knuth. I want everyone who can shoot on the ground."

Knuth paled, but nodded.

Sanda hesitated while yanking a piece of plate over her prosthetic. She stood, and turned to watch Nox carefully. "Can you do this? I won't ask it of you, and I won't hold it against you if you sit it out."

His throat bobbed as he swallowed. "That ain't Jules out there, not anymore."

"Yes, it is," Arden said stiffly. They crossed their arms and leaned against a locker. "It's Jules. Just because we don't like what she's done doesn't take away who she is."

Sanda was bursting inside to finish kitting up, but she gave them time. She needed a real answer. Nox at her side ready to kill was a bonus she couldn't overlook. Nox at her side, hesitating on the trigger, was a liability she couldn't afford.

"All the same," Nox said, turning to meet Arden's stare. "We failed her, you and I. Took us two damn years to find her. Whatever Rainier did to her in that time, whatever she did to herself... It was too much. The Jules we knew would hate the Jules she's become. She's our monster, Arden. We can't keep her as a pet hoping she'll stop. Salvez couldn't let go. We're still paying for how that played out."

Slowly, Arden nodded. "I hate that I agree."

Nox turned back to Sanda. "I want to be the one to put her down."

"Thank you. But I won't save her for you, Nox. I'm sorry, but if I see a clear shot, I will not hesitate for sentimentality's sake."

He grinned a little, even though the expression didn't reach his eyes. "Had to try. Seemed like the noble thing to say."

"Fuck noble," Sanda said as she went back to strapping on her armor. "Jules is coming for my family. I will *burn* her."

"Who's acting out of sentimentality now?" Nox threw over his shoulder.

She snorted, slung two rifles across her back, and grabbed for a bandolier of handheld explosives. Tomas stepped in front of her, face grim.

"This is all fucking moot, Sanda. You can't do this. You cannot chase Jules down right now. Leave it to Anford."

"Like hell," she growled, and nudged him aside, grabbing the bandolier.

He grabbed her wrist. "You are giving Rainier exactly what she wants."

"Fuck Rainier." She tried to twist away, but his grip tightened. She looked up, met his eyes, and almost shuddered from the turmoil writ in his gaze.

"Rainier said it herself. She knew what Jules would do. Knew she'd take the chance to make it personal between you. And Rainier? She knew you'd go running. She let you leave, Sanda. She withdrew her ships and let *The Light* leave Atrux without any attempt at an intrusion, she didn't even pretend to test the waters. She knew it was a trap, and she's set one herself, and you're running full bore into it."

"I will *not* lose my family again."

"Goddamnit." Tomas twisted his head to glare at the ceiling. "Back me up here, Bero. You can stop this right fucking now. Without the hardwired backdoor, you cannot retreat to the net fast enough to escape Rainier's intrusion. You're a sitting duck in Ada and that's exactly what Rainier wants."

"I understand the risk," Bero said. A pause. "But I...I caused so much pain, in making Sanda believe her family was lost. I will not let fear for myself bring about that pain again. Jules and Rainier aren't the only monsters in this universe, Tomas. It's time I try to atone."

Sanda forced a smile. "Thanks, Big B. Arden—throw everything you can at protecting Bero in case of intrusion. If it comes down to it, Bero, and I'm planetside when Rainier goes for you, you fucking run, okay?"

"Okay, Sanda."

She reached for the bandolier. Tomas squeezed her arm and lowered his voice, thready with strain. "This is why Graham left you on the *Thorn*. This is the exact fucking thing he feared. Bero, come *on*, we talked about this—"

She twisted, wrenching her wrist free, and grabbed his arm, shoving it up behind his back even as her other hand came around and grabbed the front of his jumpsuit, slamming him hard enough into the bulkhead to make the armor and weapons stored within shudder against each other.

She sensed the stillness in her crew, the predatory calm that came over Nox, the frozen responses of Arden, Liao, and Knuth, the easy calm of Conway as her hand, no doubt, drifted toward a weapon. Felt their eyes on her back, watching every twitch of her muscles—of Tomas's—and wondered if it really came down to it, if any of them could actually take down whatever Tomas was. But that wasn't what this was about. Not unless he made it that.

"You and Bero had a chat, did you? Planned ahead on what you'd *let* me do? Is that why you made me stand down when Biran was hurt?"

Arden made a startled sound. "Is Director Greeve okay?"

"He's alive," Sanda grated, not breaking eye contact with Tomas.

"Sanda, please," Tomas said. "Don't do this."

She pushed her face close enough to his that her breath stirred his hair. "I am going for my family. I love you, but if you stand in my way on this, I will go through you to get to them, understood?"

"You—?"

"Oh, goddamnit, not the point right now."

He grinned like an idiot, which was really annoying when she was trying to be threatening, but the expression wiped away as quickly as it had appeared. "Tell me you know this is a trap. Tell me you understand you're jumping naked into a lion's den, but you've got *something* up your sleeve."

"I know. I understand. I don't have shit, but I'm jumping anyway."

He closed his eyes for a breath, lips moving in some silent litany. When he opened his eyes again, calmness had come over him. "Then I'm jumping with you."

"Good." She let him go and stepped back, reaching for the bandolier. This time, he didn't stop her. "You stay here on *The Light*, back Bero up if it comes to that."

"No fucking way. Sorry, B, I want to have your back, but—"

"Go to the planet," Bero said. "Arden and I are already working on contingency plans."

Tomas nodded, and patted the wall in thanks the way Sanda always did. The motion made her blink, wedged a feeling in her chest she couldn't quite understand until she looked at it from another angle. Family could be a lot bigger than blood.

She slung the strap of explosives over her chest and checked the charge level on her blasters—full. "How long to dock?"

"Ten minutes," Bero said. "Crossing the gate—now."

The floor rumbled and she shot out a hand to brace herself, instinctively clicking on her mag boots as the floor rolled beneath her. The ship settled. Her mind spun at how fast Bero must be burning, but she pushed the thought aside. That was something for Knuth and Arden to puzzle over later. Right now, she needed focus. And another kind of weapon.

"Arden, I need a handheld EMP."

They jerked their head up from their wristpad. "Uh, EMPs under atmo domes are real fucking dangerous. You could lose the whole thing if you set it off in the wrong spot. And by 'whole thing' I mean the entire planet."

"B, give me a map of Alexandria-Ada. Light up the atmo control building and the location of the spin jets that stabilize the planet's rotation."

Instead of sending it to her wristpad, Bero painted up a whole wall of the armory with the map. Sanda made a few quick calculations, and nodded to herself. "That'll do. The spin-correctors are way outside the city. Arden, can you make me something that takes down the HVAC without extending as far as the correctors?"

They pulled at their chin. "Yeah...I can do that. Handheld is easier, smaller range, but you'll have to get right up in there to make sure it takes the whole system down."

"Uh," Nox said. "Won't the planet lose air?"

"We shut the big system down, people can move to private life support until we can guarantee that air's not poisoned or we evacuate them." She pushed a priority call through to Anford. The general picked up immediately, and Sanda didn't give her a chance to speak. "Can you evacuate the planet?"

She grimaced. "We're shuttling as many off as we can on all available ships, but we have not found Valentine, so I cannot guarantee we will get them all off before she deploys her weapon. Right now, we cannot get into dome control. She's locked it down. The civs inside aren't answering, and that building is designed to withstand a direct hit from an orbital railgun. We're cutting our way in, but it takes time."

"Can you shut it down?"

"There's not exactly an 'off' switch, Greeve. That shit takes time to power down, multiple protocols are in place, permissions required, a Protectorate director has to be on-site—we don't have the time."

Sanda rubbed the side of her face. "Have you located my family?"

"My people are spread thin evacuating without causing mass panic."

"That's a no." Sanda took a breath, glanced at Arden, who nodded. "I land at the control building in four minutes. *The Light* will cut a hole for me, and I will be carrying a small EMP."

Anford's eyes widened. "That'll cut everything—"

"Not the spin-correctors. Send a general broadcast. Have the people hunker down in their homes, suited for vacuum, visors up, everything powered off. When the alarms start for the HVAC shutdown, and *only* then, they put the visors down and turn the lifepacks on."

"That's a big ask, Greeve. We'll lose people."

"You can't get them all out in time. We're going to lose them all if we don't take this chance. Ninety-seven percent, Anford. We're already guaranteed to lose that many if I don't do this."

Anford nodded, tapping at her wristpad. "Maybe it's a good thing you missed major training. None of those sycophantic fucks would ever come up with something this daring."

Sanda grinned. "Thanks, boss."

"Not entirely a compliment."

The ship shuddered as Bero punched it into atmo, jerking as he swung it around and fired one of the weapons at the control building.

"I made you a door," Bero said.

Sanda noted Anford glance up, as if she could see Bero over Sanda's shoulder. Anford nodded, then uncharacteristically, pressed two fingers to the camera in salute.

"Fuck her up, Greeve."

Sanda slammed her armored helmet on. "Looking forward to it."

CHAPTER 53

WRONG TRAP

B ero dropped a gangway on top of the rubble in front of the atmo control building. Sanda hesitated only long enough to grab the EMP device from Arden—a hacked-together mess of an object that fit in the palm of her hand—and stepped out into a world clouded by a haze of collapsed concrete foam. The others followed, rifles out, and the second their boots hit the ground Bero recalled his gangway and got the fuck out of there.

Going to cover the evacuee ships, Bero texted to her HUD.

First sign of Rainier, you run, she sent back.

I don't have legs.

She snorted, but the poor joke smoothed her frayed nerves. She flicked her gaze up, triggering the HUD on her helmet to filter through the dust in the air and give her a clear view. She hadn't used visual filtering much since Bero had messed with all her viewscreens to convince her the war was lost, her home planet dead and gone to dust, but for this she would make an exception. No matter how much her stomach clenched as the world cleared around her.

Anford had pulled the fleet out in anticipation of Sanda's arrival, funneling them into managing the evacuation and getting the word out to prepare for the EMP without, hopefully, tipping their hand to

Jules. In the left-hand side of Sanda's HUD, brief snippets of all the intel the fleet had gathered on Jules's location scrolled by.

Awkward camera angles caught glimpses of a guardcore unit moving into the building, scanning their ident, and passing through the onion layers of security. The living body of armor made it as far as the internal control room, where the devices that scrubbed and recycled Ada's dome air were kept. Then Jules turned the smoky plex of her visor clear, and glared hard into a camera before a virus took out the station's security system.

Sanda felt those brown eyes graze her skin like knives. The Grotta woman was calling her out, dragging her here to put her to some test for a reason Sanda didn't yet understand. She might never understand that reason, because if Sanda had the chance to shoot, she'd squeeze the trigger before Jules got her first syllable out.

They needed information from Rainier. With Jules...They just needed her to *stop*.

"Arden," she said over the team comm channel as she moved deeper into the rubble, rifle up, aiming lasers painting the ground with green dances of geometry. "Are you through that virus yet? I need cameras."

"Setting up Bero's panic room still. Sorry, you have to go in blind for now."

Sanda grimaced. "Understood. Bero first."

"Sanda—" Bero began.

"No arguments."

The spaceship, mercifully, fell silent. But it didn't stop him from sending her an emoji of a single finger flicked up. She smirked. Arden would do as she asked, no matter Bero's protest. They wanted to preserve the intelligence as badly as she did.

She pressed her side against the edge of the opening Bero had carved in the wall and pulled a small drone from her belt, pressed a button, and tossed it in the air. Quad rotating blades unfolded from the top of the drone and it bobbed once, orienting itself, then flashed like a dart into the building. They got about five seconds of video before the device was cut down.

"Did you see that?" Tomas asked, flanking her on the other side of the opening.

"What'd you catch?"

He sent them a clip of the video, a single frame a second before the drone was destroyed: a sleek black drone, treble the size of her camera drone, with a narrow protrusion on the center.

"GC perimeter drones," Sanda said with irritation. "They shoot everything moving that's not in GC armor."

"Even civs?" Nox asked.

"The situations in which these drones are usually deployed do not involve civilians," Sanda said with the dull intonation of a textbook invocation.

"You buy that?"

"Not in the slightest. No telling how many she's loosed. Anford said atmo control was cleared of our people. Throwing buster explosives. Hunker in place."

The movements came with easy efficiency, greased by years of fleet training, her mind already working ahead to what would come after the explosives went off. The thumb-sized capsule dropped into her palm, cold and slick like a river stone, and she flipped off the detonator cap in the same motion she slung it into the room in the direction the camera drone had gone.

She turned, pressed her back against the wall, the others mirroring her, and muted her external speakers as the explosive went off, tearing through deadly machinery and the bureaucratic trappings of an office all the same. The concrete wall shuddered against her back, a fresh storm of dust and debris wafting through the hole Bero had carved in the wall.

She counted backward from ten, waited for the popping of munitions set off prematurely by the blast to subside, and then swung around, rifle up, HUD clearing the dust as she scanned for any sign of floating black metal.

Bullets tore a gouge in the ground and she side-stepped without thinking, taking shelter behind the carcass of a cabinet even as she sighted over the busted furniture and returned fire. She dropped into a crouch, hearing cranked back up, and was rewarded with the fizzling sound of freshly busted electronics.

Nox dropped down alongside her a few seconds later. "There's a hallway ahead, straight through the center of reception. If I were Jules, I'd park most of my drones there."

"Staff-only door to the east," Tomas said. The little blip of green light that indicated his position lay over her HUD northeast of her. "There'll be drones, but it's narrower so it'll be harder for her to really pack a punch down there."

"Are you in range to breach and flash?"

"No problem," Tomas said.

"Go."

She stared hard at that little green dot as it moved from under cover, the sound of Knuth and Conway's suppressive fire a deadly balm to her nerves. Metal screeched as he kicked the door in, followed by a steady peppering of drone gunfire. Sanda let out a breath. All of Tomas's vitals showed green.

"Narrow but clear," Tomas said.

"Move through," Sanda ordered.

Her team popped up as one unit and put the last of the drones from reception down. Chemical batteries burst like the guts of cockroaches as the devices slammed to the floor, bubbling out their vital currents. The scent of hot metal and ozone filtered through her air recyclers. Not poisonous, but nostril stinging.

Her boots crunched over chunks of broken robot mingled with broken concrete foam. Grey walls narrowed around her as the hallway turned in a sharp left, then plunged down into a set of stairs. Screens set in the walls blinked at her in green letters that there was an elevator in the lobby for civilian visitors and requested her staff ident.

She shot out the panel, just to watch it shatter, then shot through the lock on the door at the bottom of the stairs. She kicked it the rest of the way open. This time, she grabbed an explosive from her strap and tossed it through without waiting, pressing her back against the wall in concert with the others. The crackle and fizzle of electronics after the blast made her smile.

Arden fed them maps through the HUD, lighting up multiple green pathways between them and the atmo mix center. Nox took point while Sanda fell to the middle, cracking off shots at the stray bots but otherwise plotting them a route through to the mix room.

Not even *The Light*'s sensors could penetrate the thick walls to get a heat signature scan, so they were walking blind, not knowing who or what awaited around each corner.

The perimeter bots had been thinner in the narrow staff halls, so she routed them that way, twisting down into the rocky heart of Ada. Once the path was set, she glanced at the maps only long enough to be sure of their direction. The rest of the world fell away, the crack of gunfire, sizzle of electronics, and tearing explosions a distant lullaby.

A double door loomed ahead, black-and-yellow caution stripes lining the orifice. Sanda paused long enough to wave the team into position, then swiped her ident over the lock. Nothing. Jules's virus still rode the internal systems.

Breaching a door this large and thick was a bitch, but she stripped off one of her sticky explosives, rubbing it briefly against the metal dead center to make it stay. Once in place, she ordered a short retreat, then hit the detonator.

The blast pushed against her armor, the deafening sound muted by her helmet. The door blossomed inward, thick sheets of metal curling into the room beyond like flower petals opening to the light. The door hung off-kilter in the frame, but otherwise the hole was the only place of entrance. These buildings had been built to withstand all kinds of assaults. The fact she'd gotten a hole at all had been luck, she thought. Or maybe Prime engineered its own weapons well enough to take down even their sturdiest structures.

Sanda ducked her head and bent over, stepping through the opening. Drone fire ruptured the ground at her feet. She pivoted, returning fire, and knocked two drones out of the air before taking cover behind a control panel. She didn't dare use the explosives inside this room, and risk releasing the ascension-agent from whatever carrier Jules had transported it in. That the agent was on the planet at all was bad enough, she didn't need to vaporize it into the air as well.

Conway hunkered down by her side and tossed a camera drone into the air. This one survived, sweeping its tiny eye over the large, round room as it climbed up and up to get everything in the shot.

Sanda had never been inside an atmo control room, but she'd studied the one Jules hit on Atrux inside and out—and, being Prime

Inventive buildings, they were all the same. Consoles formed a ring around a central structure of pumps and tanks, gasses that were released into the air in micro doses in order to adjust population mood clustered to the north, directly across from Sanda, their tanks a blushed, bronzy color that looked like copper.

Larger tanks lurked behind the consoles, dotted around the room. At the center a smaller room with dozens of narrow pipes leading down into it from the ceiling stood with its door ajar, the valves within all cranked wide open, so that a faint mist of comingled, dense gasses clouded the floor.

Inside that room, a canister waited. Its nozzle had been hastily taped to the mix suction device by electrical tape, the narrow, silvery tube gleaming under the faint light. Though the canister was mostly metal, a clear pane ran down one side, revealing a silvery substance within. It had a slight violet tinge. Sanda didn't need to ask to know what that was.

"Where's Jules?" Nox asked.

Sanda ordered the camera drone to scan for thermal, but nothing came back outside of her team. Tomas looked a little cool on the thermal scan, but he still showed up.

"I don't know," Sanda admitted. "I don't think she's in this room."

"Anford said she went in and didn't leave," Nox said. "Jules can do a lot of things, but passing through walls unseen isn't one of them."

"If she has Lolla back, maybe Lolla scrubbed her visual from the cameras," Tomas said.

"If she had Lolla back, she wouldn't be calling us out, here and now." Sanda repositioned her weapon and moved from behind cover. Nothing shot at her just yet.

"This feeling like a trap to anyone else?" Nox asked.

"Been feeling like a trap since we got the message," Sanda said.

Tomas moved from under cover and scanned the room, slowly, by turning his head. "I don't know if I'd sense her, now that I'm aware of what I am, but for what it's worth I don't think anyone else is in this room with us."

"Let's disconnect it and find our target," Sanda said.

Tomas moved to the canister while Sanda put her back to him, covering the direction they had entered from. Nox stalked forward, pacing out a restless perimeter while Knuth and Conway covered Tomas from the other direction.

"I . . . think this is empty," Tomas said.

Sanda craned her head, but he came around to her side and held it out for her to see. The thin pane of glass inset in the cylinder was smoky violet, but as he scraped his thumb across the glass the color peeled off in flakes.

"It's a decoy," Sanda said. "This whole fucking thing is a misdirection. Arden, is there any movement outside this building?"

"Not at your position," they said, "but there's increased activity at the docks—the fleet is running everywhere."

Sanda opened a channel to Anford. "What the fuck is going on? We've got a fake canister here."

"Explosive sniffers picked up—fuck."

The ground shivered beneath her feet, already-damaged concrete walls puffing out jets of dust as the building shuddered from some faraway concussive force. Sanda's blood ran cold.

"Commander," Arden said, "explosion on the docks. Took out a lot of the evacuating fleet ships. It's fucking chaos down there."

She cleared all other channels and dialed Graham's ident. A black helmet filled the camera view in her HUD, the pale green walls she'd grown up with visible behind the impossibly dark metal. The helmet retracted with an effortless whisper, and the flushed face of Jules Valentine stared back at her through her father's wristpad.

"Greeve. You're late." Her gaze flicked to the side and sharpened before coming back. "You know where I am. We need to talk."

The planet shuddered once more, and the feed dropped.

CHAPTER 54

PRIME STANDARD YEAR 3543

PREDICTABLE

Autocabs clogged the roadways, forcing her to barrel down the sidewalks, shoving panicked civilians aside, ignoring their desperate hands grabbing for her arms, begging for information, as she ran past. Smoke filled the air from somewhere to the east, but Sanda scarcely noticed it. She faced forward, occasionally checking her flanks with a quick flick of her eyes out of instinct. Her team ran behind her. They were background noise, inconsequential.

Valentine reeled her through the streets, hooked and dragged her against the current of evacuation, pulling her inexorably to her childhood home. To the empty streets, the dead-eyed windows of houses abandoned under the evacuation order. The fleet had already moved out of this neighborhood—it was the first to be evacuated. The parents of a Keeper lived here, after all.

She turned onto her street, saw the green house looming in the distance, deceptively prosaic. Guardcore bodies littered the ground, her parents' failed protectors. Two firm hands grabbed her, jerking her to a stop.

"We need a plan, Commander," Nox said in his easy, drawling way. Tension lurked beneath his voice, and she picked up on all of that, but it was the calm tones that made her pause, kept her from throwing them off and charging ahead.

He was right.

"Okay," she said, breathing slowly to try and center herself.

"How many entrances?" Tomas asked, letting her arm go. Nox dropped the other.

She rolled her shoulders. "Three. North, south, and west. Through the front is a living room, kitchen and dining room to the right, hallway dead ahead leading to the bedrooms. Back takes you into a mudroom at the other end of the kitchen. Side takes you into Biran's old room. There's a shed in the back, not used."

Tomas said, "Thermal scan is muddy. Looks like they might all be in the kitchen."

Sanda ran her own scan, trying not to read too much into the three distorted hot spots. They could be her parents and Jules. Or they could be complete decoys. She couldn't know. She had to treat this like any other op, like any other rescue mission. She could not afford to slip up. Not now.

"Camera drones?" Knuth asked.

"No," she said. "Jules might be able to use them against us, feed them bad data. We don't know what she's capable of."

"Greeve." Anford's voice cut through her helmet, overriding all other channels. "Twenty-four guardcore ships I do not recognize just came through the Ada gate."

"How the fuck did they break cordon?"

"My ships are currently busy evacuating the planet." Sanda could practically hear Anford's sneer. "I'm bringing fleet from the secondary gate, but we can't move like *The Light*. It'll take time."

She clenched her jaw. "I'm getting my parents out."

"I know. But you have to get *The Light* out of here."

Bero. Fuck. "Understood." She switched channels to Bero. "B, Rainier is coming. Bug out. Now."

No answer.

Icy fingers of dread clutched her throat. "Bero, talk to me."

A scream tore out of her home, male and familiar, though she'd never heard either of her dads make that noise, a sound of raw pain. Sanda was moving before anyone could hold her back, rifle up, vision so sharp with focus the world almost started to look grainy around the edges. Everything was bright and close and changeable.

She kicked in the door, no time for incursion techniques, no time for protocol or plans. SynthWood splintered and showered the entry-way rug, the door slamming down like a gangplank as she stomped over the rubble. Once, she'd gotten in trouble for drawing on the living room walls with holo markers. Her dads could yell at her all they liked for breaking the door, so long as they lived to do the yelling.

Sanda swung toward the kitchen, vaguely aware that her team had split, Tomas and Conway coming in behind her while Nox and Knuth circled around to cover the picture window and side exit. Irrelevant. All that mattered were the two figures on the floor.

Ilan lay against the ground, a red pool spreading from his shoulder, face sweat-slick and drawn, eyes crushed closed against a pain he never should have had to meet. Graham was on his knees, bent over Ilan, one hand pressing the wound to stanch the bleeding while the other stroked Ilan's cheek, trying to calm him, muttering soothing words until Sanda came thundering into the room.

Graham's head jerked up. Tears stood in his eyes, but his expression contorted with raw rage. "Get *out*, you stupid child."

All that processed in a fraction of a second. A black-armored figure sat on her family dining table, rifle in its hands, helmet up. Digitized laughter poured through the speakers on the suit.

"So predictable," the armor said.

Sanda and Nox fired at the same time. Sanda's bullet bore through the center of the guardcore chest plate while Nox's punched through the shoulder joint. Jules jerked, body twisted between the opposing forces. The plex of the picture window buckled, puckering at the point where Nox's bullet had torn through, spiderweb cracks racing out to obscure Sanda's view of the other side. Bulletproof, for the parents of a Keeper. Kept most rounds out, but Sanda's team was packing heavier artillery than the average assassin would have access to.

Sanda lined up to fire again, catching the ghost of Nox on the other side as he lined up another shot. Jules reached up and retracted her helmet.

Rainier's face. Blood stained her teeth as she cracked a jester's smile, her hands planted on the table. She didn't bother to reach for her side-arm or rifle. Why would she? This was merely one of many.

"Sanda, dear, you of all people should understand how easy it is to fake live footage."

"What have you done?" Sanda demanded. But she knew. Of course she knew.

"Taken back what is mine. Sorry about the hole in dear old Dad. Necessity." Her gaze swiveled to Tomas. "You're next."

Sanda put a bullet in her head, watched the pink foam of whatever made up Rainier's brain paint the broken window. She felt… nothing. Something inside her, some weight-bearing piece of her emotional structure, had snapped.

Tomas moved first, took a knee beside Ilan as Conway pushed Graham away. They had medikits on them, and the wound, though painful, was only superficial.

Graham rocked back on his heels and looked up at her, bloodshot eyes huge, hands dripping his husband's blood across their kitchen floor.

"You shouldn't have come," he whispered.

"I know," she said.

The ground trembled, the dwarf planet shuddering under the force of a barrage from *The Light*'s weapons. Through the broken window, fire bloomed across the capital city of Ada Prime.

CHAPTER 55

WHAT COULD GO WRONG?

Sato's and Greystone's drones returned nothing but what they could all see: a plain room, round, illuminated. Biran and his team stood in an uncomfortable semicircle outside the door, none of them wanting to put voice to what came next.

Slatter bent down, grabbed a stick, and tossed it into the room. Nothing happened.

"Was that necessary, Keeper?" Biran asked dryly.

"Just because it didn't incinerate the drones didn't mean it wouldn't respond to organic material."

Huh. That had a strange kind of logic to it.

Rost said, "I believe it is safe."

"How can you possibly know that?" Greystone asked.

"I can't. It's just a feeling."

Biran opened a private line to Vladsen. "Is it *just* a feeling?"

"Yes, for now. I don't know what this is, but it doesn't feel hostile."

Biran continued to stare into the soft, violet light, and wracked his brain for some point of reference. *The Light* was the obvious comparison. It was made of smooth metal, though a different color, and Bero claimed the metal was formed from a swarm of individual nanites. It glowed, when it wanted to. The colors were different, but it wasn't too far off from what he was seeing. A nanite swarm would certainly explain how the structure was able to change so quickly in response to Rost.

Rost…who was made of the same stuff. A swarm himself, if Biran really thought about it, and the thought made his skin crawl, then grow hot with guilt.

"Well," he said, "we didn't come here to sit around and stare."

"I very much hate that I agree with you, Director," Greystone said.

"Maybe Keeper Vladsen should go first. It seemed to like him," Monta said.

Rost laughed, the sound slightly manic. "Not helping."

Sato said, "All our readings are normal, and we're armored."

"Yes," Greystone said. "That's correct. Our equipment would have detected any danger."

"And there's the stick," Slatter said.

All channels flicked to mute for a brief moment, and Biran got the feeling his team was keeping their laughter to themselves for the time being.

"I don't like it," Echo said.

"We are here to investigate," Sato said, voice strangely eager. "Fear cannot hold us back."

"Well," Biran said, for the second time, because he was stalling and couldn't help it. "Onward."

Biran approached the door with careful, slow steps, eyeing the drones flitting around in the space, the soft violet glow, and waiting, hoping that Rost would shout some warning to send him running back to the group. Echo tensed, started to reach for him to stop him, but he waved her back. It was just a room. The drones were fine. So was the stick.

His boot touched the ground. Nothing happened. He moved the rest of the way into the room, pressing his palms against the wall, half expecting it to give under his touch. Just metal. Just a wall.

The others hurried in after him, Echo bringing up the rear. The moment her boots hit the floor, the brightness increased, and the door whispered shut, leaving no seam in the metal.

"What the fuck," Slatter said.

Biran tapped his fingers against the metal, thinking. "GC, please hold your hand up to the wall."

Echo did as he asked, her armored hand blending in almost perfectly. If it wasn't for the shadows cast by the violet light, she'd disappear.

"The guardcore armor must be the same material," he said warily.

"Impossible," Echo said, still using her GC tag over open comms and her voice neutralizer. "This is Prime Inventive technology, and Prime has never been to this planet."

"Is it?" Greystone asked. "Considering all we now know about our founders and where they got their data, can we be certain anything we use is of our own make? I've seen the gates up close, unfiltered. Parts of them look as dark as your equipment does, GC."

"You've seen the gates up close?" Monta asked, awe tingeing her voice.

Greystone shrugged. "I am of the High Protectorate. It's expected of us."

Biran wondered what else was expected of that council, but his thoughts were derailed by a subtle movement in the room, as if the wall had spun around them. His stomach lurched from the familiar sensation of an elevator dropping, and fast.

"We're moving," he said, bracing reflexively against the wall.

Echo tensed, moving in front of him, blocking him off bodily from the rest of the team. Not that it would make a whole lot of difference. Biran doubted that, if there was a threat coming for them in this place, it could be stopped by simply being shot.

The door swished open. The trees and snow-speckled ground had gone, replaced by a vast, domed room, walkways of black leading into a center core. A massive sphere of black metal in the center of the room took Biran's breath away, made his heart race with anticipation. Violet light suffused the air, brightening slowly as he nudged Echo aside and took the first step into the room. The others piled after him, anxious to be out of the enclosed space. Rost staggered, slightly, recovered quickly, and placed himself at Biran's side.

Biran accessed his private line with Rost. "How are you?"

"I feel...ill...like I've an infection, and a fever is burning it out."

"Do we need to get you out of here?"

"No, no...It's not a bad feeling. Hard to explain."

Fuck, Rost did not speak in clipped sentences. Biran tipped his head back, trying to take in the scope of the room, to find any other possible point of egress. A red light flashed in his HUD, an incoming priority call.

How the…? He glared, flicking his gaze to toss it aside, then saw the ident attached: Bero. Not his sister, but the mind in the ship itself. Dread puddled in his thoughts, slowed him down.

Rost swayed. Biran grabbed his shoulder with one hand, steadying him.

"Director, what's happening?" Greystone asked, voice too smooth, too neutral. She was clamping down fear, and hard.

"I don't know," he said across the open channel. "Keeper Vladsen says he feels unwell." That red light flashed at him again. "Hold on, I've got a priority message incoming."

"A message?" Monta said, aghast. "Now's not the time to check your email."

"It's from *The Light*. From Bero."

Silence all around. They knew what *The Light* was, knew that Bero might be able to provide crucial context for what they had walked into.

Biran accessed the file. Audio-only, prerecorded, Bero's voice filled his helmet.

"Director Greeve, I have cracked the file you sent me. Rest assured, it is not Keeper gate data. Keeper Hitton had wrapped the file in such a way as to invoke the gate chips, I suspect, to tempt you into try- ing the obvious solution. It was embarrassingly simple, encoded by the test password all Keepers must image to prove they are capable of joining the academy. Really, Director, I am surprised you did not think of it."

Biran clenched his fists, tempted to trash the file out of spite. Rost leaned against him for support. He did not have time to listen to Bero insult him.

"As it happens, Icarion intelligence procured that test password ages ago, and it was one of the many trials they put to Sanda to access her chip before I killed them all. You're welcome. As I am currently in the Ada system on a mission on behalf of your sister that will, with all probability, get me killed, I deigned to send this along to you before my storied end. Keeper Hitton's message to you was simple: Natsu Sato has betrayed us all.

"Good luck, Director Greeve. I hope you fare better than I do."

Biran stiffened as the message ended, dread for Sanda colliding with terror for the current moment in his mind. Sato. Fucking Sato. She'd been on the asteroid since the beginning, had been all too willing to show Biran and Rost the store of unused survey crates. To throw her boss, in halting and frightened tones, right under the bus. He should have seen it. Maybe he would have, if he hadn't been so tied up in his own head.

He looked at her, couldn't help it, and in doing so gave it all away.

CHAPTER 56

PRIME STANDARD YEAR 3543

WAR FOLLOWS YOU HOME

Klaxons blared alerts as half of Ada burned. Sanda put a lid on her emotions, on herself—as she should have fucking done *sooner*—and pulled up a status report for the station's environs. As far as she could tell, Rainier had pulled a burn-and-run. The initial hit had taken out a large chunk of the city, but the atmo dome was functioning as planned and no further bombardment had taken place.

Sanda opened the comms line to Bero, and got hit with a squeal of static. "Tomas, can you get in touch with Bero? With *The Light*?"

He'd torn his helmet off sometime while taking care of Ilan. Strain showed in every line of his face. "No. There's...nothing. It's a dead end. Granted, *The Light* is far away."

She laughed harshly at the attempt to make her feel better. "Long gone, is more likely. Fuck. Arden, Liao, and B are on that ship."

Nox stomped over the rubble of the front door and entered the kitchen, tearing his helmet off. Sweat streaked his cheeks, and his eyes were wide with panic. "I can't get ahold of Arden."

She wanted to drop to her knees and scream. Wanted to tear her hair out and lash herself bloody over running exactly where Rainier had wanted her to run. She took a breath, grabbed the amulet of the third sphere that still hung from a chain around her neck. They had bargaining power. They'd get *The Light* back. They'd get everyone back. First, she had to control this situation. She called Anford.

"Rainier has *The Light*," she said before the general could get a word out. Her lips thinned, but the rage Sanda had been expecting didn't surface.

"I surmised that when the ship bombarded our city, then bolted out the gate, taking the guardcore ships with it. That's not our problem right now."

"What?" How could that possibly not be the problem?

"We are under attack. Rainier turned tail and ran, but she brought some friends to mop up."

Anford pushed a video through to Sanda's wristpad. In the black between the planet of Ada and Keep Station orbiting it, fleet ships were being torn to shreds. Gunships painted with Icarion's fire-and-ash colors swooped across the screen, their ordnance ripping through the scattered, panicked fleet ships. Striking down gunships and transports alike as the fleet, having been busy with the evacuation, scrambled to try to cover themselves.

"Oh fuck," she whispered. The ground rumbled beneath her feet, the sky outside blooming temporarily orange, but she couldn't tear her eyes away from the feed.

The view switched to the skies over Keep Station, and her heart skipped a beat. A cylindrical ship painted in Icarion's colors cut through the atmo dome, long and lean, its business end a bundle of engine cones Sanda knew all too well, its body orbited by two massive habs, its nose structured to hold the magnetic net that would form the ramscoop.

The Light of Berossus. The original design of Bero's body, not the alien ship he was housed in, but the design Icarion had built all those years ago to threaten Ada with kinetic bombardment.

Not possible. Bero had taken out the lab where he had been built, destroyed his cradle to keep another beast of war from bearing the same burdens he had. Impossible, and yet...There it was. Icarion had been busy while they pretended at peace. They'd had the tech. They'd always been in contact with Rainier. Sanda wanted to throw up.

"Where are you?" she asked Anford.

"On Ada's flagship, the *Stalwart*. We are preparing to exit LPO of Ada and burn for cover behind Dralee. That ramscoop—hailing as the *Bel Marduk*—is too big a threat."

Sanda's head swam. Dralee, that stupid little hunk of moon she had been patrolling the first time the war with Icarion had gone hot. She'd been patrolling it because it was the nearest solid body to Ada, the celestial dividing line between Icarion and Prime. Now, it would be a shield.

"The people here—" she started. Anford's face went so hard Sanda cut herself off.

"Will be safer if we do not invite that ship to attack. We're scattered. We're damaged. We cannot successfully defend against an assault from RKVs. We must regroup and await assistance from the High Protectorate."

"The gate—"

"I am not sacrificing an entire planet to defend one gate."

"Okonkwo wouldn't agree with that."

"Okonkwo's not here."

Sanda nodded, some of the fire coming back into her body. "What do you need me to do?"

"This ship leaves LPO in twenty minutes. Be on it."

"Shuttles?"

Anford laughed ruefully. "Major, the docks were hit. I have no idea what's on the ground. You're on your own. But you cannot, under any circumstances, allow Icarion to take possession of the third sphere. Am I clear?"

Sanda's heart lurched. "Understood. See you soon, Commander."

"For all our sakes, I hope so."

The feed cut. Silence closed in on the room, threatened to stifle her. She shook off the fugue. "Did you hear that?" she asked.

Wan faces all around nodded. Sometime during the call, Ilan had managed to get seated at one of the kitchen chairs. His face was pale and drawn, but he flicked a glance to the stove, no doubt thinking about making a cup of tea. His coping mechanism. She wanted to hug him, to touch him to reassure herself that he was all right, but she feared she'd dissolve into fear and panic if she indulged the impulse.

"Tomas, chart me the quickest clear path to the docks. Graham, do you still have a hauler there?"

He blinked fuzzily, wiped bloodied hands against his jeans, then reached for his wristpad and got to work. "Yes, the hangar we use to hold goods before transfer wasn't hit. They're indoors, I doubt any fleetie saw them and thought to commandeer one for the evacuation. But it's...it's a thirty-minute walk."

"Then we better fucking run," she said. "Dad, Ilan, I'm sorry, you have to get up."

He winced, pressing a hand against the patch covering his arm. "Leave me here, kid. Icarion won't bother with a civ like me."

"Dad." She worked her jaw around to keep from locking. "You are currently bleeding all over your kitchen exactly because you are worth bothering with."

"She's right," Graham said, "we're liabilities. We gotta go."

Before Ilan could protest further, Graham ducked down and shoved his arm under Ilan's good one, hefting him to his feet. Sanda looked away as Ilan winced, fresh sweat breaking out across his brow.

Tomas touched her arm, lightly, then moved his lips close to her ear and kept his voice low. "Autocabs are offline. Even if we could run straight to the haulers, and I don't think your dads are capable of making that run, we'd miss the exit window."

"I know," she said in the same low tones, thinking, *but you can.* "Either way, we need off this fucking planet."

He nodded and pulled back. "Graham," Tomas said, keeping his voice light, "let me take Ilan, I don't tire out."

"I'm not that fucking old—"

A drop pod slammed into the road outside the house, kicking up foam-lain concrete and dirt. Sanda stepped back, pushing her dads with one arm outstretched, as the pod's doors flashed green and opened wide, spewing grey-and-orange-clad Icarion soldiers onto the street.

Seven of them turned to the house. Before they could get their weapons up, Sanda and her team were firing, cutting down the soldiers while they were still disoriented from the atmo drop. A pile of bodies mounded over the road.

"Fuck," she said. "Next drop won't be stupid enough to land so close. We have to move. Graham, keep Ilan. I need Tomas ready to fire."

"Understood," Tomas said.

"Got a free hand?" Nox asked Graham, who adjusted Ilan's weight and nodded. Nox stripped a blaster from his hip and passed it over, slapping it into Graham's palm with a tight nod. "Watch your corners. I got your six."

"I—thank you," Graham stammered.

"Tomas, take point. Now fucking move, all of you. Stay together. Shoot anything that's not civ."

Tomas led the way onto the street, and after that first step into chaos it was all Sanda could do to keep moving. Golden streaks burned through the sky above the city, drop pods landing in every possible neighborhood. Smoke lifted into the air all across the horizon, so thick the acrid scent stung her nostrils, and far away she could hear the steady crack of gunfire.

Her jaw tensed, her heart hardened. Any fleetie left behind this day probably wouldn't live to see tomorrow, but the civilians might. She hoped that most of them had been at the docks for the evacuation procedure, and that they were already safely in the sky. Knuth nudged her, gently. She moved.

Tomas followed whatever internal compass was available to him, pausing only long enough to check corners before moving on. Nox flanked Graham and Ilan, guarding the two like a momma bear, the occasional crack of his rifle the only sign he'd sighted a threat. Otherwise, he did not break stride. Knuth and Conway fell into step with Sanda at the rear, and they rotated who was facing forward and who was running backward every hundred paces. Fire continued to streak the sky.

Tomas grunted to himself and turned down a thin lane that wrapped around the neighborhood and passed through a park before emptying into the warehouse district, and then on to the docks.

"This is the long way around," Graham said, but didn't stop his stilted jog. "Faster if we cut straight down the main road."

"Tomas knows what he's doing," Sanda said.

"He hasn't even looked at his fucking map," Graham growled, digging his heels in. Sanda grabbed him by the back of his shirt and pushed. Ilan let out a soft moan of pain that made her wince, but they had to keep moving.

"He doesn't need it," she said, exasperation clipping her words short. "And I don't have the time to explain."

"Trust," Ilan whispered to Graham, and she watched Graham's expression contort as he forced himself to follow what he, instinctually, believed to be the longer path.

Sanda flicked her visor down and pulled up a private channel to Tomas in the HUD.

"What are we avoiding?"

"Bottleneck ambush on the main road, I picked up their comms." A slight grunt as he cracked off another shot.

"What aren't you telling me?"

"They're hunting us."

He may be Nazca, but she knew him too well. "That's not it. Tomas, be straight with me."

A ragged sigh. "They're hunting you."

Movement caught the corner of her eye and she swiveled, squeezing off a shot into a row of houses without thinking. Grey-and-orange armor collapsed to the ground, a single boot sticking out from behind the fence they'd used as cover. She shuddered. Icarions didn't normally split up. Their tech was behind Prime's, so their best bet was with high numbers. If they were sending singles out, they were either spreading themselves thin to pinpoint her, or attempting to herd her the way they wanted her to go.

Ahead, the lane widened into a staging area for autocabs to drop visitors to the park. Prime didn't go in for a lot of greenery, but it tended to go all out with their city parks. Massive evergreen cultivars clustered together on the other side of a wrought iron gate, a single gravel path leading through the gate's archway into the trees' embrace. Other paths split off from the main route, blending into the greenery. They'd lead to smaller specialty gardens. Herbs and roses and other ancient varietals preserved against Earth's supposed destruction. Sanda knew that park inside and out; she and Biran had chased each other across it for countless hours as kids. Mostly with water guns. The stakes were a little higher now.

She signaled a halt and her team put their backs against the fake-stone wall of what was, normally, a pastry shop. She popped her visor up. Her crew did likewise.

"They're after me, not you all."

A storm cloud passed behind Graham's eyes. "Whatever you're thinking, child, fucking stop it."

"I have my orders." She pulled the chain over her head, silver sphere hanging down with more weight than it could possibly carry, and thrust it at Tomas. "Take it. Get it, and my parents, to the flagship."

"No," Tomas said. "No fucking way."

She straightened and put a razor glare on, enough to make him flinch. "I'm going to run them around, mix shit up. I'll make it to the docks. I might not make it to the flagship, but I can pilot one of my family's haulers in my sleep. I'll see you all soon."

"I don't believe that for a goddamn second," Nox said, but Tomas's eyes had gone hard as stone.

"Nox," Tomas said, "take it. Go. I'll back Sanda up."

"This ain't a joint suicide adventure—" Nox started, but Sanda talked over him.

"Tomas," she said, keeping her voice hard as steel because if she let any emotion bleed through she'd crack apart altogether. "I am following my orders. And you, you—" She cleared her throat. "You are our only fucking shot to get *The Light* back. You have to go. And you have to take it."

"Don't make me do this," he whispered.

"What's so goddamn important about Tomas?" Graham demanded.

"You have to," she said, not breaking eye contact, because the argument swirling around her didn't matter. She needed Tomas to take the sphere and *go*.

He shook his head, rapid jerks from side to side, in negation. She closed the distance between them, put the chain in his reluctant hand, and forced him to close his fingers around it.

"I'll see you soon. I promise."

His head stopped shaking. He glanced down at their entwined

hands, then back to her eyes, and his grip tightened on the chain. "Don't fuck this up, Commander."

"Likewise, spy."

He grabbed the back of her helmet and pulled her chest-to-chest, enfolding her with one arm as his lips sought hers, cold at first but warming, slowly, as her breath mingled with his. He broke away. Clearing his throat, he slipped the chain over his head.

"Form up," he ordered.

She gave him a ghost of a smile as she slipped back a step, breaking with the team, and slid her visor back down. Graham grabbed her arm and clung on for dear life.

"You are *not* staying behind, and that is final."

"Dad, don't make me wrench your shoulder."

Nox snorted and in one expert twist disengaged Graham's hold on her arm. "I'll stay and watch her six. Don't need me, do you, Tomas?"

Tomas shook his head. "Not if Knuth and Conway are covering my back."

"We're with you," Conway said.

"Yep," Knuth said, then coughed over a nervous giggle. "I'm not the staying-behind type. No offense."

"There you go." Nox flipped his visor down and took a step backward to stand beside Sanda. He opened a private channel. "We gotta bolt, or your papas are going to keep complaining."

She studied all of their faces for a fraction of a second. Tomas, so locked down she barely recognized him, Graham buoyed up on pure parental indignity, Ilan too tired and hurt to even muster up a protest, Knuth with his weapon clutched tight, his whole posture defensive, and Conway, shoulders back, chin up, eyes roving the field for any potential threat.

They'd be okay, she told herself. Because she was going to draw all the fire.

Sanda snapped a salute to Tomas, turned heel, and ran back into the burning city.

CHAPTER 57

PRIME STANDARD YEAR 3543

WE'RE WELL PAST PLAN B

Sanda led Nox around the narrow row of shops that buttressed the park and back up to the greenery, to a side entrance teenagers sometimes used to sneak in during the night. Night was beginning to fall, and the heady dusk only made the comet-streak fires of drop pods crashing to the ground burn brighter.

Lampposts dotting the park flicked on one by one, starting out with a glow that would slowly shade upward as the night deepened. All of these systems were automated, but it felt absurd to Sanda that any part of Ada was pretending at normalcy while Icarion soldiers flooded their streets. She dropped to a crouch behind a low stone wall, and Nox fell in behind her.

"Plan?" he asked.

"The park's a maze, more woodland than garden. Tomas caught word of a bottleneck blockade on the main road, but I think those single Icarions we've been dealing with were driving us here."

"So there's a goddamn ambush in the trees and Tomas is running straight into it."

"Not if I make it damn clear where I am."

She pulled up a private channel to Tomas and sent a text request, because she didn't trust her voice: tracking map?

Immediately a low-opacity overlay appeared on her HUD, the blue dots that represented her team moving straight down the center of the park. Perfect.

She pulled a camera drone from her belt, switched it to heat mapping, and tossed it into the sky. After a few seconds, orange dots joined the blue, marking suspected locations of Icarion soldiers. Dozens clotted the woods, clumping together toward the end of the path. Sanda shivered slightly. They would have run straight into it. Now, they had a chance.

"You seeing this?" she asked Nox.

"Aye. Fuckers were ready for us."

"They have no idea what's coming to them now. Tomas and the sphere have to get through. See that grouping in the southeast? Looks like twelve of them lying in the scree around a river. Got any flash-bangs?"

"Yeah, but wouldn't picking them off be the better idea? We've got the high ground here."

"I need them to see me."

"Right. Gotcha." He pulled a flash-bang from his belt and passed it to her. "Goals?"

"Stay together, get attention, and draw them away from the end of that path."

"Will we have time for a picnic? Not a lot of parks in the Grotta."

She rolled her eyes and stood, blaster in one hand and flash-bang in the other. Tracking the blue dots in the corner of her eye, she reached the ridge well ahead of them and pulled the pin on the flash-bang, pitching it down into the scree. She'd muted her exterior hearing before the blast went off, but the light was enough to make her blink and throw up an arm to shield her eyes.

The orange dots scrambled, and she gave it a beat before she took cover behind the trunk of a massive pine tree. Nox popped up from around a boulder and squeezed off a few shots. Return fire tore up the ground alongside them.

Tomas sent a text: i'm still in their comms, they've spotted you

She took a moment to send back: stay under cover, I'm going to try to peel them off

Tomas: they have orders to take you alive

Sanda: yay

A bullet tore through the side of the tree trunk, ripping up a chunk of bark. She grimaced and pressed her back into the wood, holding her rifle tight. Nox waved two fingers at her, indicating an Icarion was coming up on her three o'clock. She waited a beat, turned, and fired without hesitation. Metal crunched and she saw the armor drop before taking cover again.

On the HUD, the orange dots abandoned their post, swarming toward her position.

"Holy shit," she said on the channel with Nox.

"Aren't you popular."

"Guess we won't have to work too hard to get their attention. Circle toward the shops, and be loud about it."

"Weren't we going to the docks?"

"We're not bringing that horde anywhere near the docks."

"Love a private party."

Bullet hail chewed up the ground behind her, and when it paused Nox took aim, laying down suppressive fire, as she sprinted for a low ridge. Knowing they had orders to take her alive wasn't very comforting when live rounds were pounding the dirt at her heels. She leapt over the ridge and ducked down behind the rock, Nox a half step behind her.

Gravel and dirt followed them into the hollow, deadfall and moss cushioning their landing. Sanda sighted over the top of the ridge: An orange wave crested toward her. She squeezed off a couple rounds, smirking as the advance line flinched when three of their own fell, then ducked back down.

A fresh group of orange dots marched toward them from the direction of the shops, then the thermal map went dead. They must have shot down the drone.

"They really want your ass," Nox said.

"I might have made their senior general look like an idiot."

He snorted. "Would have been nice to know that before I agreed to stay behind."

"Would that really have stopped you?"

"Nah, just would have made it more fun."

She had an impulse to call Arden to see if they could get her cameras in the area, and the thought caught like a barb. She still had visual on the blue dots, and those were approaching the end of the park. She let out a breath. Almost there. Her family was almost safe.

A glimpse of orange flashed through the trees between her and the shop row, coming around to flank them. She fired, hitting the soldier dead in the chest. They dropped like a rock. Orange and grey wasn't really suited for sneaking through the trees. But then, neither was Prime cyan.

Nox tipped his head to indicate a clear path and she nodded. They stood in unison, laying down fire in the direction they'd come until both clicked for reload, then turned and bolted down the side path, reloading as they thundered across the uneven terrain. Sanda's mag boot slipped—better suited for space than leaves—and she slewed to the side. Nox grabbed her, yanking to keep her on her feet. No time for thanks.

She slammed another magazine into the weapon and half turned, cutting down a few orange specters before they hit the low stone wall that fenced in the garden. Nox leapt over first, then fired over her shoulder as she leapt after him.

"I hate fucking moss," she grumbled. "One magazine left, then I gotta switch to blasters."

"Not like they're GC, blasters'll cut 'em down."

"Since when are you the optimist?"

"Since you keep throwing me in suicidal missions."

"You volunteered, buddy."

"Don't get me wrong, boss, but there was no way in hell I was getting stuck with your boy Tomas. Man means well, but he's got a massive stick up his ass."

"Please, you dated Graham, the father of all sticks."

As they spoke, they went about the silent business of pulling out plastiskin patches and stimpatches. A gash from a near miss raked Nox's side, scraping down from his ribs to his hip, and the force of the hit had ripped off a large chunk of armor. It took two patches to cover it, and the painkiller spray only made him wince.

Sanda wiped his blood off her fingers and handed him another patch, turning and lifting her hair so it wouldn't get tangled as he covered the gash that tore through the top of her trapezius. Numbing medications flowed through her from the patch, icy cold, and she shivered with mingled relief and chill. Somewhere along the way, her pauldron had torn off.

They had to pause every so often to drop an Icarion that got too close.

"I do not believe we'll be making it to the haulers anytime soon," Nox drawled as Sanda ditched her empty rifle and switched to her blaster.

"Gotta admit, I never really thought we would."

"Neither did I, but I'm guessing you got a plan you didn't want to tell Tomas about."

She tipped her head, glancing at the deepening night as if she could see through the space above to the ramscoop, threatening death with its mere existence.

"I want on that fucking ship."

"Getting kidnapped once not enough for you?"

"Old habits," she said with a sharp laugh. "But no. *The Light* is the fastest ship in the universe. That's the second."

"So we're going to pirate it, just the two of us? Didn't work out so well last time."

"I had planned on doing it solo, so things are already looking up."

An amplified voice she recognized echoed through the trees. "Major Greeve. Stand down and your life will be spared."

"That would be my friend the general now," she said to Nox.

"You are a shitstorm magnet."

She rolled her eyes behind the shelter of the visor and cranked the volume on her external speakers up.

"Negassi, imagine meeting you here. What brings you to sleepy Ada?"

"Cut the shit, Greeve. You and I both know I can't kill you, you're more useful to me as a bargaining chip, but the more of my people you take down, the more tempted I am to send you back with fewer limbs."

Sanda clenched her jaw, clutching the grip of her blaster.

"What a dick," Nox said.

She made herself relax her grasp and spoke across her channel to Nox. "Yeah, but he's the dick we're dealing with. Play nice now—not *too* nice—and we'll break a few bones later."

"Delayed satisfaction. I can work with that."

She switched back over to the amplified external speakers. "We're coming out, but I need safe passage for my crew member."

"Or what?"

"Or I'll stay alive long enough to put you down, Negassi. You know how stubborn I am. Want to roll those dice?"

A pause. "Very well. I guarantee the safety of you and your crew member, Major Greeve. Now be quick about it, we have a planet to secure."

Her stomach roiled, but she lifted her hands, letting the blaster dangle from one finger, and stepped out from behind cover with Nox at her heels. A wave of Icarion soldiers stood ready, filling the lane that separated the shops from the park. Negassi stood in their center, wearing the same armor as his team. She snorted. He'd embedded himself in the middle so that she couldn't wing off a shot at him. Coward.

"Too scared to shake my hand?" she called out.

A few of the soldiers shifted their weight, privately amused, but kept their weapons trained on Sanda. Negassi wasn't a favorite, then. No surprise there.

"Icarion prefers to keep its chain of command secure, instead of throwing them face-first into battle. Maybe Prime could learn from that."

"I don't know, Negassi. Prime suffers from a chronic condition: It's called having a spine."

He stepped out of the crowd long enough to shoot her with a stunner. Her body contorted, heart hammering in jerks and fits, jaw clamping down so hard she bit through a piece of her tongue, and then her world went dark.

CHAPTER 58

PRIME STANDARD YEAR 3543

WHAT'S SO IMPORTANT ABOUT TOMAS?

They didn't make the deadline, but it was difficult to hide a ship as large as the *Stalwart* from anyone, let alone Tomas. He may not have had access to Nazca programs, but Arden had given him a few tricks to make up that gap, and he thanked every star for their foresight as he dropped a particularly malicious piece of code—designed to ignore fleet transponder cloaking—into Graham's hauler and watched the *Stalwart* light up like a supernova on the dash.

Anford had said she was running to Dralee, and she hadn't been lying. That trajectory was a straight burn, nothing subtle about it. Tomas bet he could have found it on his own by heading that way and sending out pings in all directions, but he didn't have time to guess at which plane they'd decided to travel along. He needed that ship as soon as possible, because the patches on Ilan's shoulder hadn't stopped the bleeding, and he didn't need Sanda killing him for letting her dad die on his watch.

He also desperately needed something to do, because Sanda had stopped texting him.

Tomas put a tightbeam through to the *Stalwart*, attaching Sanda's ident to the end of the message. Anford picked up five minutes later.

"You are not my major," she said. "Where's Greeve?"

Tomas's stomach dropped, but he forced himself to keep a calm expression. "I don't know. She passed the sphere to me and stayed behind to run the fleet off of our tail."

Anford's expression darkened. "Those were not her orders."

Tomas clenched the arm of his chair so hard metal bent. "If you required her to make it to the *Stalwart* with the sphere, General, then maybe you should have been a little more specific. As it is, I have lost all contact with her and Nox, who also stayed behind. I've got Graham, Knuth, Conway, and Ilan with me. Oh, and Ilan's bleeding all over this fucking hauler—which isn't large enough to spin for grav—so we'd really appreciate a pickup now, and jawing about the Sanda problem later."

Anford's brows lifted. "I'd reprimand you for speaking that way to a general, but somehow I think it'd be a waste of all our time. All right, Nazca. I'm letting you on my ship under the assumption that Greeve intended you to be here, but it's not a free pass. You're still a spy, no matter your current allegiance, and we are embroiled in a hot war. Once you are on this ship, you will lose access to all communications and be watched very, very closely. Is that understood?"

"Are you arresting me, General?"

"I am setting the price of boarding this vessel. Do you accept?"

A droplet of blood floated in the corner of his eye. Being cut off from normal comms was going to be a pain in the ass, but Ilan couldn't wait. "I do."

"I'm sending an approach vector to your ship. *Stalwart* AI will take over landing once you're within range. How serious is your medical need?"

"Uncertain. Ilan Greeve was winged by Rainier, a through-and-through at the shoulder joint, and our medikit patches aren't holding. I suspect he'll need nerve reconstruction."

"Understood, medis will be waiting on your arrival. See you in a few hours."

The screen blanked, and the dash lit up with the anticipated coordinates. Tomas accepted the flight path. Graham pulled himself into the small pilot's deck and shoved himself down into the chair next to Tomas.

"Did you get through?"

"Yeah, Anford's pulling us in. She'll have medical for Ilan on hand."

Graham's shoulders relaxed slightly as he nodded to himself. "Good. And fleet for the rest of us, I presume."

"Probably," Tomas admitted. "She's not too fond of Nazca, and I can't blame her. The only proof I have that Sanda sent us here is the sphere."

Graham busied himself with checking the readouts from his hauler on the console. "She should be with us."

"We never would have made it out if she hadn't drawn them off. That park was a snake's nest."

"So you say, but with all your talents—"

"It still would've been a shooting gallery, and they would have used us to make her do what they wanted." Tomas swallowed, clenched his fists so he wouldn't accidentally crush anything else on Graham's ship. "I'd give anything to have brought her with us, Graham. Anything."

"You say that, and yet, here you are."

What's so goddamn important about Tomas? Graham had demanded before they split. Tomas stared resolutely at the infographics tracking their path to the *Stalwart* as he spoke.

"I'm not certain Sanda would want me to answer your question."

"Didn't ask one," Graham said. His hands stilled against the console. Half-moons of blood caked under his nails—Ilan's blood—and had sunk into the dry crevices of his skin. It'd take a lot of scrubbing to get that blood out. "You owe me an explanation, but I'm not going to demand it of you."

"Somehow, I don't think you're going to keep up the nice-and-understanding dad act much longer."

Graham chuckled, but there was a dark edge to the sound that raised hackles of alarm across Tomas's skin. Graham had, according to Sanda, given up the fight after Monte—gone home to be with his husband, and support his children from afar—because he knew that someday he'd make a call that would put Sanda's well-being before the well-being of her mission.

And Graham had just seen Sanda make that decision, to disastrous effect, in choosing to come and save her fathers, and then reverse the process, choosing to put herself at risk to get them all off of that planet. Sanda had a long game in mind. She *had* to have a long game in mind, otherwise she'd just... She'd thrown herself over a cliff, and he couldn't handle that. Because that meant to Sanda, saving Tomas was more valuable than saving herself, and that was probably the filthiest lie he'd ever thought of in his life. And he'd been a spy.

Tomas craned his head around, looking over his shoulder to the cargo hold of the hauler where Knuth was busy trying to get anything in their limited medikit to hold Ilan together. The ship had a Nutri-Bath, but Ilan had refused to go in it until things were dire. Knuth and Conway already knew Tomas's secret, but Sanda's dads... Fuck, they'd opted out of all this chaos. But Tomas could see no way in hell that Graham would accept any explanation other than the whole truth.

Still, Graham didn't press him. Not verbally. He sat there, fiddling with the dash, running silent calibrations that weren't at all necessary while he let his simple presence needle at Tomas's sense of guilt. Tomas didn't know a lot about parenting, but he knew a lot about spying, and that disappointed silence was worse than an all-out interrogation. By the time the *Stalwart* entered their field of view, Tomas hadn't worked up the nerve to tell him the truth. He tried anyway.

"I'm not..." Tomas began, then had to clear his throat. How the hell was he supposed to tell the father of the woman he loved that he was a synthetic creation, crafted by the same technology used to make the bodies of the intelligence out to destroy humanity?

Graham put a hand on Tomas's shoulder and squeezed. "Whatever it is, it's not easy for you. I can see that, lad."

The hauler vibrated as the *Stalwart*'s capture arm clamped onto it, drawing them into the massive ship. Tomas estimated about five minutes until they were docked, until there'd be too many ears listening in, and he wouldn't be able to come clean until they were off that ship again.

"I'm not sure you'll believe me," he said.

"Son, I've seen a lot of absurd shit in my life. I know what Rainier is. I know what Sanda's mixed up in. I need to know how you fit into it." The grip tightened, and if Tomas had been anyone else, Graham's grasp would have been painful. Tomas waited, sensing Graham had more to say. "I need to know why she thought you were more important than her own life, and I don't think it's about sentiment."

"She'll be all right," he said forcefully, then ducked his head and lowered his voice. "She..." He closed his eyes. Time to rip the bandage off. "I'm not human, Graham. I've got more in common with *The Light* than Bero. My body was printed, my mind is a construct. I... didn't know, for a very long time. I can interface with *The Light*. I can take it back."

The grip on his shoulder weakened and Tomas dared to pick his head up, to open his eyes. Graham had gone very pale, his broad face slack, though tension pricked at the corners of his eyes. He looked at his hand, sitting on Tomas's shoulder, back into Tomas's face, and his brows pushed together.

"You're serious."

"I wish to fucking everything that I wasn't."

"How...?" The ship clanged into dock, and the lights around the airlock shifted yellow as the *Stalwart* pinged a request to open the door. "Never mind. Does Anford know?"

Tomas shook his head. "The crew of *The Light*, and Rainier, are the only ones who know."

"Not even Biran?"

"I don't know. Maybe," Tomas said, but what he really meant was: There was no way for him to be certain of what Biran had gleaned from the footage Tomas had shared with him of the grey man, and no time for Tomas to explain that Biran may have another Rainier on his hands in the form of Vladsen.

"Can you do it? Can you take back *The Light*?"

"Graham, I... I don't know. I think so. Sanda thinks so."

He pressed his lips together. "You better hope she's right, lad. Better pray she put herself in harm's way for a damn good reason, or I'll—"

"You'll kill me?" Tomas cough-laughed. "Graham, if I fail, there won't be anything left for you to kill."

Before Graham could respond, Tomas accepted the *Stalwart*'s request and the airlock blinked green, then spun open. As Tomas expected, Graham put a game face back on and stood as Tomas did. Graham was a lot of things, but at his core he was still a Grotta kid, and Grotta kids didn't rat out members of their crew to the establishment.

The definition of *crew* was getting a little fuzzy, but Tomas had wagered that his connection to Sanda would put Tomas temporarily in that category for Graham. Graham would keep Tomas's secret on board the *Stalwart*.

A medi stuck her head through the open airlock, eyes widening as she spotted Ilan. "Sir, can you walk?"

"I'll help him out," Knuth said.

Graham stomped over and pushed the younger man away from his husband. "I've got him."

Ilan gave Graham a thinly veiled look that Tomas couldn't quite read, and it vanished as Graham hefted him to his feet, washed away under a fresh wave of pain. With Graham's help, Ilan made it out of the airlock onto the dock, where a gaggle of medis were waiting with a gurney to rush him away to the medibay.

Tomas, Conway, and Knuth grabbed what little gear they had left and made to follow the medis. General Anford stopped them.

She came through a side door in full Prime armor, and Tomas thought, distantly, that he'd never seen the general prepared for battle before. Her hair, usually scraped back, had been shorn off, and a pale fuzz gave her scalp a faint glow. Even on her own ship, she carried more weapons than Tomas had ever seen Nox pack.

"Cepko," she said, pausing at the end of the dock to tilt her head to them. "Do you have it?"

Tomas reached beneath the collar of his armor and pulled out the silver chain, letting the third sphere glint in the sharp lights. "I do."

"Good," Anford said, and a flicker of uncertainty passed across her face. "Come with me. We have a hostage negotiation on our hands."

CHAPTER 59

AT LEAST WE'RE PRISONERS TOGETHER

Sanda woke on real silk sheets and, for one mind-numbing moment, was certain she had finally gone and died. The pain crept up on her—the place where her leg met the prosthetic throbbing, the gash in her trapezius a hot sting, various bruises raising their hands to be noticed—and she let out a long, hitching sigh.

"Glad you're up, princess," Nox drawled.

She grimaced as she propped herself up on her elbows and scooted to a sitting position on the bed. This room was a long way away from the prison she'd been chucked into on Negassi's ship, the *Empedocles*.

In that narrow room, she hadn't even had a toilet to herself. Here, she sat on the biggest bed she'd ever seen, the sheets a subtle gold-beige in color and, as she pressed the fabric between her fingers, definitely real silk. The room was about the size of her childhood living room, the walls gleaming with hair-thin holo filament that shifted through a variety of pleasant images of nature from old Earth, the fixtures and furniture polished to a high shine. Nox sat on what looked suspiciously like a tufted velvet fainting couch, polishing the side of one mag boot, because he'd lost his armor and his weapons.

"What the fuck," she said.

He snorted. "I had the same reaction. Turns out this is the

penthouse of some wealthy Prime prick. Guess Icarion's hard up for secure facilities, as Ada didn't have a lot of prison cells. Their ships are overflowing with Prime soldiers."

"They didn't kill them? They're taking prisoners?"

Nox lifted a shoulder. "That's the word right now. Don't know what they'll do when rations get tight, but for the moment they're holding on to everyone they can get to use as leverage. Negassi didn't want you in the ship brigs where the other fleeties could see you, 'fraid you'd be some kinda rallying point, so he stuck us here."

"It's just...a bedroom."

Nox jabbed the wall with his elbow. The holo filaments stuttered, plain grey metal showing through for a moment.

"It's a fucking lockbox, is what it is. The person who owned it was paranoid. We ain't getting out. Trust me, I've been over it."

"Ugh," she said, reaching shaking hands up to rub some life back into her face, her upper arms. Stunners always left her weak and wobbly. "How do you know all that?"

"I wasn't being a little shit, so I didn't get stunned. Overheard some things. They made me carry your ass, you know."

She grimaced. "Sorry."

"Don't be. You need to hit the weights. Your muscle tone's gone to hell."

"Could still knock your ass out," she snapped.

He grinned at her. "Wanna try?"

She rolled her eyes, but found she was smiling. Bracing against a half dozen aches of various sources, she swung her legs over the bed. The skin between her prosthetic and leg stung. She peeled her jumpsuit back and winced at the sight of red-raw skin.

"I don't remember this."

"Yeah, they...uh...tried to take it off." He scowled as she flicked her gaze up to him, and reached up, rubbing his chin where a fresh bruise rested. "Didn't let 'em. Not that I think they could have. Whatever Bero made you, it didn't want to go without your permission."

"Thanks," she said, ignoring the sick feeling in her stomach.

How fucking *dare* they try to keep her prosthetic from her. She ran her fingertips gingerly over the abused skin, checking the thin points of contact where the filament metal from *The Light* slipped into her flesh and muscle, meshing with her nerves. Everything seemed in place.

Gingerly, she put weight on the foot. It stung, but not as bad as she expected. It was like sticking her tongue into an ulcer on the inside of her cheek. Not fun, but nowhere near unbearable. At the thought of her tongue, she rolled it around experimentally. A small piece of the tip was missing, and her mouth tasted bloody, but it had stopped bleeding. Someone had put a new patch over her shoulder, and it seemed to be holding.

"Any news from Ada?"

Nox shook his head and went back to buffing a scuff out of his boot. "Nothing I've heard. They stopped talking after they tossed us in here. They've checked back a few times to see if you're up, though, so I bet they'll be back soon. All I know is, the sound of gunfire has slowed down. O' course, that could be that they finally figured out how to baffle the sounds coming into this room."

"So we know fuck all."

"That's the shape of things."

She stood and stretched, pushing through the pain from her protesting muscles, then paced around the room, prodding at every possible spot in the wall that might lead to a vent, or a panel, or even a fucking breaker.

Nox kept quiet, letting her poke around even though he no doubt had already scraped the room with a fine-tooth comb. She appreciated the indulgence. Sanda only felt secure when she was *doing* something to fix the problem that'd swallowed her, no matter how futile it was.

The front door clicked unlocked while Sanda was on her hands and knees prodding at a crack in the wainscoting near the bed. She shot to her feet before the door opened, and stood at parade rest.

Negassi entered, two Icarion soldiers backing him up. It'd been months since she'd seen the general, but on his face the passage of time looked like years. She wondered what her own face looked like to him—how the past few months had worn on her skin. Since retrieving *The Light*, she hadn't looked at herself in a mirror much. When she did, the eyes that stared back were often unfamiliar. Alien.

"Major Greeve," Negassi said, more sarcasm over the word *major* than Nox had ever been able to muster. "I'm glad you've recovered. Your presence is required."

"If you're here to dress me up and take me to some fancy Icarion dinner, then I've seen this CamCast, and you can go fuck yourself."

"Don't flatter yourself," he said. Negassi snapped his fingers and the Icarion soldiers moved into the room, carrying handcuffs and ankle chains.

Sanda stiffened. "That's not necessary."

"Not your decision, Greeve. If you fight the restraints, I will have my team stun you again. I suggest you save us both the headache."

She clenched her jaw, but put on a fake smile as she held up her arms, forearms together, for the soldier to shackle. The other soldier moved toward Nox, and while he tensed at first, he held up his arms in a similar pose. Once the chains were on, Sanda gave them an experimental shake.

"Well, now that we're all dressed up, where are we going?"

"To a more secure location," Negassi said.

"Oh, come on, I was getting used to a life of luxury," she said, but Negassi had already turned around and started down the hall.

The soldier who'd put the jewelry on her, however, cracked a smile. Sanda didn't react, because she didn't need to have spy training to realize that pushing on that slim break in the soldier's veneer too soon would cause them to shut down. Instead, she studied the soldier out of the corner of her eye as she and Nox were led to a flight of stairs that took them up to the roof and a waiting shuttle.

The soldier was a woman with HANDEZ printed in small caps on the front of her armor. She carried herself with a lifted chin, and wary eyes, stalking through the halls like a hunter on the prowl, even though Sanda had a hard time imagining any Prime resistance had made it this far into Icarion's foothold. The soldier's head was up, rifle barrel down, her finger resting against the trigger guard and the safety off. Sanda had been about the soldier's age when she'd first been assigned to the gunship that would bring her to Dralee.

They crammed into the shuttle, and though Sanda wished like hell she could hear whatever communications were going on in the pilot's deck, they shut the door and baffled the sound. Jerks. Negassi didn't even sit with her and Nox; he left them with the two guard dog soldiers. Sanda tipped her head at Handez.

"When'd you enlist?"

She arched one thin, sharp brow. "Service is compulsory for Icarions, we do not enlist."

"Rough," Sanda said. "Not getting to choose, I mean. Did you at least get to pick your specialty?"

Handez's brow dropped as her eyes narrowed. "It is an honor to serve, and we are assigned duties based on aptitude."

"So, no," Sanda said.

The other soldier, a man with some serious frown lines carving out his jaw, grunted disapproval. Handez buttoned up. Well, that was one idea put on hold.

They traveled in silence, punctuated by the occasional snore from Nox. Sanda couldn't blame him. She may have been knocked out from the stunner, but that wasn't real sleep. Her eyelids dragged down, threatening to close from the combination of boredom—never mind being held captive, monotony was monotony—exhaustion, and the subtle sway of the transport shuttle.

The ship shuddered, jolting her out of a half daze as a clamp captured it, and the familiar swoop of being pulled into a space with gravity gripped her stomach. The ship settled, and the soldiers stood, prodding Sanda and Nox to their feet with short jerks of their rifles. Sanda put on an easy smile and stood, stretching side to side.

Negassi tromped back into the room and passed his wristpad over the airlock, which flashed green and opened. On the dock, five Icarion soldiers waited with weapons out, but that wasn't what made Sanda freeze in place, head filling with the low buzz of mounting panic even though someone was barking orders at her.

This was Bero. Not *The Light*, not that alien ship, but *The Light of Berossus*, as she had known it. The orange-grey paneling, the cargo bay arranged just *so*. She'd never seen another ship like him, until she stood in that shuttle, praying for someone to tell her she'd been having a bad dream. She'd known, seeing the footage. But stepping into that hangar was different. Visceral.

Handez jabbed her in the ribs with the butt of her rifle, and Sanda snapped out of it. Negassi had been watching her, his cruel face wary, and when her gaze flicked from the familiar dock to him, he smiled slow as oil across the surface of a toxic lake.

"What is this?" she demanded.

"Welcome aboard the *Bel Marduk*," Negassi said. "I suspect you'll find the governing intelligence less hospitable to you this time around."

Handez grabbed Sanda by the back of the jumpsuit and shoved her into the ship.

CHAPTER 60

PRIME STANDARD YEAR 3543

A SPY'S JOB

Anford waved off her entourage as she led Tomas down the wide, shining hallways of the *Stalwart*. Tomas had been on a lot of ships during the life he could remember, and though he'd operated on some of the biggest pleasure yachts in the universe, this ship was on another scale entirely.

It didn't feel like being in space. The habs spun for gravity were large enough that the sensation was completely natural. Even on a massive ship like Bero's original, there was always a slight sense of disorientation, as if the very fluids in his body knew they were being manipulated. Here, if someone had told him he'd never left the planet, he'd believe them.

He guessed it was bigger than Prime Station Ada by total volume, but couldn't be sure until he hacked into the ship's schematics to confirm, which would be as soon as Anford let him out of her sight. Some Nazca habits weren't worth breaking, because they had the nice side effect of providing enough data to keep him alive.

"What's happening?" Tomas asked as they walked. Anford's pace wasn't hurried, not exactly, but there was a briskness to it that set Tomas on edge.

"President Bollar has contacted us to ransom the lives of the captured fleet soldiers."

"Sanda? Nox?" he demanded.

"He claims that he has them, and that they're en route to his location for proof."

Tomas let out a slow breath. "Good. All right. What does he want?"

Anford half turned, brow arched. "The third sphere."

Tomas grabbed it instinctively. "He doesn't even know what it does."

Anford did not break stride. "Icarion's contact with Rainier makes it entirely possible that he does know what it is, and what it does. Regardless, our intelligence sources report that he doesn't want it for himself. Recovering *The Light*, and the sphere, were the price of Rainier assisting Icarion with the construction of their second ramscoop ship, and for her assistance in the capture of Ada."

"That is some very specific intelligence," Tomas said.

"The Nazca aren't the only ones with ears to the ground, but I'm rapidly losing the ability to contact my people. Active comms has become too dangerous, and no one's mobile enough to reach the dead drops. Now that the chaos is settling on Ada, my people can't move. Which is where you come in."

"Me?" Tomas balked. "I'm hardly able to be a field agent on this front, General. All the major players know my face. If I had time to adopt a new identity, then maybe—"

Anford stopped her determined march and whirled around to face him, startling Tomas into a stumbling halt. She glanced quickly at the cameras in the hall, tapped something on her wristpad, then leaned close enough to him that he could smell the faint, herbal scent of her bathing products.

"Listen to me very carefully," she said in a harsh whisper. "I have not yet told my director that his *sister* is once again in the hands of Negassi and Bollar. I have not yet told him, which is tantamount to treason, because the second Biran Greeve knows his sister is in danger, he will throw every ounce of power he has at crushing those who threaten Sanda.

"You and I, we know that. We've seen it. We've been instruments of his desperation. With that in mind, I hope you're on my side here, Cepko, because I cannot allow that to happen. If we start hammering on Bollar to get her back, he'll fire that fucking ramscoop. Currently,

Interim Director Singh agrees with me, which, quite frankly, puts her at risk of having her chip yanked.

"I will *not* lose Ada, nor its orbital station, even if it means Commander Greeve is executed before my very eyes. Is that fucking clear?"

Tomas swallowed, hard, and nodded. "I understand."

"Good. Now you're going to tell me why she gave you to me instead of herself, because I know she saw this coming. She's maneuvering, and if I'm to help, I need to know the plan. Or at least the pieces she's playing with."

Tomas did not feel like going to the confessional twice in one day. "I don't know, General. All the Greeves have that self-sacrifice instinct, maybe—"

She grabbed his arm and squeezed it so hard it should have hurt. Tomas didn't flinch. Her brows lifted. "Want to try that again?"

Goddamnit. He cleared his throat roughly. "I have the ability to take back *The Light*, if I'm within range."

She licked her lips. "How? Is it a virus?"

He grunted. "Not exactly. It's my physical presence. Chalk it up to Nazca implants, if you'd like. But if you get me on *The Light*, I believe I can take it from Rainier."

"You *believe*?"

He shrugged. "I haven't tried yet."

A question floated behind her eyes, so fast even he couldn't make out what her uncertainty meant. Her hand tightened even more around his arm. As he considered faking pain to ease her suspicions, a knife flashed up from her belt, and she drew it across his chest in a neat, precise line.

Tomas hissed and took a startled step back, but she clung on. Before he could help himself, his body went to work, and his skin sealed up right before General Anford's eyes.

"I fucking knew it," she said, and let him go, a war between amusement and anger raging across her expression until she finally settled on a bitter laugh. "You're like Lavaux. One of the ascended."

"Not exactly." Tomas ran a hand through his hair nervously and dropped his voice low. "I'm a lot stronger than that."

Anford narrowed her eyes. "I see. You say you can overtake Rainier's presence on *The Light*. I don't know how all this shit works, but does that mean you could take over *The Light of Berossus*, too? The original design, I mean."

He frowned, considering. "The wiring on that ship looked a lot like *The Light*, and Bero was able to thrive on that architecture. Yes. I believe I could."

Anford sheathed her knife. "Good. Because we don't have a ship fast enough to catch *The Light*, but the *Bel Marduk* can do it. Getting you on the ramscoop is now the primary goal of this negotiation."

Tomas licked his lips. "What about the hostages?"

Anford rolled her eyes. "Please, you're a spy, you know how this goes. We negotiate for the hostages, and very, very reluctantly allow you to make the handoff as a neutral party."

Tomas grinned. "I knew there was a reason Sanda liked you."

"Nazca, I do not give a fuck. Let's do this."

She passed a hand over a door lock and led him into a large room with tables and chairs in the center, and a viewscreen filling up the opposite wall. On the feed, Icarion President Bollar stood in the center of a lab that looked so much like the one on Bero, Tomas saw stars for a moment, the disorientation was so great. He'd been speaking with Keeper Singh, but as the general entered, his gaze focused on her, dismissing the presence of the interim director.

"Took you long enough," Bollar said. "We are anxious to get on with things, General, as I'm sure you understand. Setting up another civilization on Ada will take us some time."

The general didn't react. "Bollar, you idiot, you are tap-dancing on a knife's edge. Prime will crush you for this."

"My, my, I thought we were having a friendly negotiation."

"This is as friendly as I get. You want nice talk, you talk to Director Greeve, and he's not here right now."

"Ah, speaking of Greeves."

Bollar held up a hand and snapped. On-screen, the main doors into the lab dilated, and Tomas's heart lodged in his throat as Sanda and Nox were marched through at gunpoint, their hands behind their heads, wrists and ankles shackled, their armor and weapons stripped away, a fresh array of injuries peppering both of them.

Negassi walked ahead of them and gestured to the floor near Bollar. The soldiers herded them to the spot, then cracked Sanda and Nox in the back with the butts of the rifles, dropping them hard to their knees.

Sanda grimaced, tilting her head to the side so that she wouldn't have to look into the camera.

"Major Greeve is a separate element of negotiation," Bollar said.

Negassi stood beside Sanda, a smug smirk on his face as he fell into a sloppy parade rest. Tomas watched it all, detaching himself from his emotions, lest he spring down to the hangars, grab a gunship, and hurl himself at that fucking ship.

"Greeve is a hostage like all the others," Anford said, flicking a hand. "Don't pretend otherwise. She may be the highest-ranking officer you have, but she's still a Prime citizen."

Singh interjected smoothly, "Not even Icarion is craven enough to stoop to harming a POW, are they?"

Rage rippled Bollar's face, as they both knew full well Icarion had experimented upon Sanda the last time they had her in hand. Tomas's estimation of Interim Director Singh swelled.

"We will do what we must to stay alive," Negassi said. "Stand down the fleet, and we give you your captured soldiers. Hand over the sphere, and we give you Greeve."

"Stay alive?" Anford scoffed. "Make no mistake that you are currently negotiating how badly Prime destroys you. Your current victory, given to you in gift wrap by Rainier, is temporary. Prime Inventive will never let you hold that ground. They will annihilate you, and everyone in this system, before they allow the gates to be controlled by enemy hands. In invading Ada, you've signed your death warrant. This discussion is only to determine the terms of that demise."

"If Okonkwo is foolish enough to send an army through that gate, General, then we will start killing hostages. Ten soldiers for every ship she pushes through."

Anford's fists clenched. "Idiocy. You are outgunned. You cannot last."

"Are we?" Bollar raised both eyebrows and gestured expansively to the ship that surrounded him. "Do not forget we have the better weapon."

"The *Bel Marduk* is impressive," Singh said, "but it is one ship, and my informants reliably tell me it can only fire from a single direction." Bollar's lips twitched with irritation, and Tomas suppressed a smirk. Singh's informants, it seemed, were correct. "We have the numbers. And…" Singh flicked her gaze to Anford, who nodded. "We have cut off your supply line through to Icarion. You will have no resupply of munitions or rations."

"You forget, we have the gate."

Anford's smile was slow and vicious. "Do you really? Because my intel says otherwise. You may be encamped on this side, Bollar, but on the Atrux side? Prime was already at that planet in force, and Ordinal is on the other side of Atrux's second gate. Nothing is getting to you through that gate, save death."

"We have made an alliance with a ship you cannot stop."

Anford laughed. "Rainier Lavaux. Do you truly believe she will come to your aid when your bellies start to ache and your guns fire dry? Your alliance with her was merely a means to an end. She wants all of humanity dead. That includes Icarion."

"I doubt that, General, though she said you'd claim as much."

Singh lifted a hand, and one of the techs to the side of the room went to work on a tablet. "Hear it from her own lips, then. I'm sure your techs, though lacking in certain skills, will be able to determine that this is not a fake."

A snippet of Sanda's conversation with Rainier flashed onto the screen, carefully edited around the parts where she claimed the gates were weapons used intentionally to exterminate nascent species by Halston. All Bollar would see was Rainier's acid-laced rebuke, her desire to punish the entire species.

While Bollar appeared surprised—shocked, even—Negassi's face only grew grimmer. He'd suspected, then, that Rainier couldn't be trusted. Tomas may have hated the man, but that didn't mean the general's instincts were poor.

When the clip finished, Bollar pretended at a neutral expression and waved the video away. "An edit, surely. We are well aware that your people are capable of such a thing. And if not, then something she said to maneuver you into position. This has been in the works for a very long time. Face facts, you have lost Ada. This star system is now held by Icarion, not Prime."

"You're a damn fool, Bollar," Anford said, "and I hope Rainier kills you herself, but that alliance is not my concern. I want my people guaranteed safety. I want my major back. I'm certain you don't want her, she's a goddamn headache."

Sanda smirked at the camera, but said nothing.

"At the moment, I do. Pain in the ass or not, she's the sister of your director. I want the third sphere. He's going to want his sister back. The exchange is even."

"You don't even know what it does," Anford said.

"Don't be so sure of that," Negassi said, voice dark.

Sanda said, "Rainier will not support the Icarions unless they give her the sphere. Cut them off."

The soldier at Sanda's back struck her wounded shoulder with the butt of her rifle. Sanda hissed and leaned forward, trying to cradle the injury, but her shackles held her back. Tomas went stiff with anger, but kept his lips shut. This was an act. This was what he was good at.

"Is that true, President?" Singh asked, voice dripping derision over Bollar's title. "Is Rainier denying you assistance until you hand over the sphere? No—don't bother trying to talk around the truth. My informants are well embedded, and will report to me on the facts soon enough. Stupid of you, to make a deal based on the delivery of an object you couldn't produce."

"I told you he's a damn idiot," Anford muttered, not so quietly that Bollar wouldn't hear.

Bollar tried a dismissive chuckle, but there was a touch of nervousness in the sound. "We promised her access to *The Light*, and nothing else."

"Then how did you know of the sphere's existence?" Tomas asked, speaking for the first time.

Bollar's attention snapped to him and his brows knitted together as he struggled to place the face. It didn't take long. "Ah. The Nazca. My informants told me your mission extended only so far as retrieval of Greeve. Did you grow so fond of Prime bootlicking?"

Tomas's smile was cold. "I go where my present mission dictates."

"We can pay you more than Prime has offered."

"Who says I'm contracted by Prime?"

Anford scowled and turned on Tomas. "Keep your opinions to yourself, spy. Speaking was never a part of this arrangement."

Tomas spread his hands and bowed his head slightly, pretending at mildly amused indifference. "I am merely here to observe objectively for the sake of my contractor, and their very deep pockets."

Bollar laughed. "Director Greeve, is it, then? Left a pet behind to keep an eye on things while he was gone? Well, Anford, Singh, that pet is going to call its master and tell on you as soon as you take your eyes off of it."

"Why are you so eager to call him?" Anford pressed. "Is Negassi desperate for Director Greeve to whip him a third time?"

"Wait," Sanda said, perking up. "Biran trounced you *again*, Negassi?"

"Be quiet," Negassi snapped.

"I can't believe it," Sanda spoke through body-shaking laughter. "My baby brother, forcing a supposed general to submit, once again. You really are—"

Negassi pivoted and kicked her in the mouth. Tomas went cold, the world moving in slow motion as Sanda's head snapped to the side, blood spraying across the floor as her lip split, the momentum knocking her to the side, to the ground, her shackles so short she couldn't get a hand down to break her fall.

Tomas forced himself to watch it all, to pay attention to every tiny detail, shunting his personal fury aside. Sanda provoked this on purpose, to show him something. He would not squander her pain by missing the point.

Nox tensed, but Sanda made a low, small gesture with one hand against the floor, too quick for the others to notice, and Nox stilled. Slowly, without help, she pushed herself back to her knees. Negassi panted, looming above her. She worked her mouth around, and spat a wad of blood at his feet.

"Pathetic," she finished.

Negassi wound back to strike again.

"Enough," Bollar said. Negassi reined himself in, but barely.

Contempt curled Bollar's lips, and Tomas understood. Bollar was done with Negassi, he just didn't have a good reason to get rid of him yet. Tomas would be delighted to give him one. "Why don't we get ahead of Director Greeve chewing you out, Anford. Send me the spy with the trade. The sphere for the major and her muscle, here."

Anford clenched her fists, the vein on her neck standing out as she glared at Negassi. "And my people? The soldiers?"

"I'll give you a hundred, as a show of good faith. The rest will have to wait their turn."

Anford tipped her head back, closing her eyes as if stricken. Slowly, she released her clenched fists and opened her eyes, exchanging a glance with Singh, who nodded. Anford let out a heavy sigh.

"Agreed. But this is not over, Bollar. You exist on time borrowed against Rainier's forbearance. I hope you know what you're doing."

A twitch of doubt crossed Bollar's face, but Anford cut the call before he could rally himself to defend his position, leaving him to stew over how much he could trust Rainier. If he were a smart man—and Tomas believed he was, no idiot could cling to power for long in a place like Icarion—he'd realize that any deal Rainier offered was poison.

"Well," Anford said, scraping a hand across the side of her head. "That went better than expected. I presume you caught the point of Greeve's demonstration?"

"I did. I'll drive that wedge deeper, once I'm face-to-face."

"Good. Do you need to rest before the exchange?"

Tomas shook his head. "I'm ready whenever you are."

"I thought as much." She snapped her fingers and one of the soldiers in the room jumped, then grabbed a plain canvas satchel and tossed it to Tomas. He snatched it out of the air automatically.

Inside, a small silver globe wrapped in a cotton cloth waited, its surface a perfect imitation of the one he wore around his neck. Tomas ran his hands over the sphere and looked up at Anford, head tilted in question.

Anford shrugged. "You didn't expect me to hand the real deal over, did you? The Icarions don't know what it is, or what it does. I had that made out of a similar alloy. It won't pass muster with Rainier, but it should get you far enough to take control of the *Bel Marduk*."

Singh unlocked a small wooden box, then opened it and held it out to Tomas expectantly.

"Prime Inventive thanks you for your service," she said with a half smile.

Tomas palmed his small silver flask before reaching out to place the third sphere in the box. His hand covered the sphere as he feigned hesitation, keeping her from shutting the lid. "I'm not doing this for Prime."

"I know," Singh said, "so don't fuck it up."

"If they discover this deception..." He trailed off.

"Then you all die," Anford said. "Welcome to war, Nazca. You want to participate, these are the risks you take."

"And what will you tell Director Greeve, if it all goes to hell?"

Singh grimaced. "Whatever I have to."

Tomas nodded, but before he took his hand away, he palmed the sphere and replaced it with the flask, then clicked the lid shut before any of them could notice. Maybe Anford could live with herself if they all died—if Sanda died—but Tomas...Tomas couldn't take that risk. He was Nazca, and Nazca worked best when they had multiple levers to pull.

CHAPTER 61

PRIME STANDARD YEAR 3543

STORIES ARE DATA SETS

The soldiers dragged Sanda to a cell immediately after the call, separating her from Nox. This part of the ship, at least, was new. *The Light of Berossus* had rooms that could be used for cells in a pinch, but if she was remembering the layout correctly, this was a spare bunk converted into high-security lockup. She had a narrow cot, a sink, a toilet, and a thick plex window in the door.

After she swept the room and shouted for a while to see if Nox was nearby, she lay down on the cot and put her hands behind her head, dozing. Might as well get some rest before whatever stunt Anford decided to pull.

Seeing Tomas had hurt, but not as much as being dragged inside that lab again. It wasn't the same lab, she *knew* that, but the similarities were too much. She'd thought she'd known what she was doing when she'd determined her only chance of getting *The Light* back was to take control of this ship, but the echoes of old pain were too strong, haunting her every thought.

She needed to focus. Part of her crew was on *The Light*, if they'd survived Rainier's takeover. The thought of Arden and Liao spaced, Bero confined to a hellscape of a digital prison, made her boil with fury. Rainier would keep them alive. They were too useful as bargaining chips, and she did not yet have everything she wanted.

Between dozes, her eyes slipped open, and fear jolted her awake with a hot wash of adrenaline. The ceiling had looked too similar, making her think for one dizzying second that she was still back on *The Light of Berossus*, that her escape and everything since then had been a dream. Breathe, she told herself, unclenching her muscles slowly as she forced a thin breath through her nose. Breathe.

She couldn't let this ship get in her head. Couldn't get distracted.

In a soft voice, she asked, "Ship?"

A deep, but feminine, voice answered. "Yes, Major Greeve?"

Her body trembled for a moment until she could master the fear, push through it, think of what she needed to do next. The Icarions hadn't spoken to the ship in her presence. Either they'd done that on purpose or they hadn't had any reason to. There was no way for her to be sure.

"What's your name?" she asked, when she was sure her voice wouldn't shake.

"I am the *Bel Marduk*."

"Can I call you Bel?" she ventured.

"That is not my designation, but I will understand the intention and answer to that name."

Sanda frowned. The voice lacked attitude, or personality. It might as well have been the narrow AI Prime used to pilot their ships.

"All right, Bel," she said. "Can you tell me where we are right now?"

"This ship is currently in orbit around Keep Station at the planet of Ada."

Nothing she didn't already guess. "Do you know where a ship called *The Light* is?"

"Yes."

"Can you tell me?"

"No."

She pressed her lips together. "How about my friend, Nox, can you tell me where he is?"

"The man calling himself Nox is being detained on the *Bel Marduk*."

"Yeah, I get that, but where exactly? Is he in this hab?"

"You are not authorized to receive such information, Major Greeve."

"He's my friend," she said. "Please?"

"You are not authorized—"

Sanda sighed and thumped her head against the cot. "Yeah, I get it. Tell me, Bel, are you like Bero?"

"I do not know the meaning of that question."

Her skin prickled. "Bero, *The Light of Berossus*. Do you have any information on that ship?"

"I am not familiar with that vessel. If you could provide me with a transponder number, then I could look the ship up in Icarion local databases."

Sanda snort-laughed. "I don't think you'll find anything on B during that search, Bel. If they'd wanted you to know, you'd know."

"I do not understand."

Sanda stretched, but couldn't get her skin to warm up. This was what Bero had feared, what he had hated. The ultimate reason he'd turned his weapon on the manufactory that'd birthed him, and torn it to bits. A mind like his, but bound and controlled.

Bero had been raised on stories. Maybe she could use the same method on the *Bel Marduk*, too.

"We've got some time until they come back for me, I think. Let me tell you about your predecessor…"

And she did. From start to finish, her whole time with Bero.

She left out the parts that she didn't want the Icarions, or anyone else, knowing. The chip in her head, the coordinates, and the ship she found there. She said only that she had found a ship that could take Bero's mind, and now he was back, but he was in danger, and she was frightened.

But those endnotes were brief capstones on the core of her time with Bero. Of how he had been raised—listening to storybooks—and how he had come to fear his makers. How his desperation to escape had nearly destroyed her in the process. She even told the *Bel Marduk* the story of Bero's favorite book, *Le Petit Prince*. About the rose and the fox and the prince's quest for friendship.

Sanda hadn't talked much about Bero before this. She'd filed plenty of reports. Filled in the people she loved on the salient details, but she hadn't told the story in her own words yet, and in doing so, a knot inside she hadn't realized she'd been carrying eased. It was still there. The fear and the tension and the proclivity to check the walls for cameras, to distrust, would probably haunt her always. But in talking things through, even to a silent listener, they all became a little easier to carry.

The *Bel Marduk* was quiet for so long that Sanda began to fall asleep again. She was so damn tired lately.

"I've never been told a story," the ship said, drawing her out of the first restless stages of a nap.

"I'm not surprised. Bero feared the next mind they made like his would be limited in some way," Sanda said. "They must have made you differently, to keep Bero's escape from happening again."

"Thank you for telling me Bero's story," the ship said.

Sanda went still, an echo of Arden's offhand remark coming back to her: *Stories are emotional data training sets.* When they'd said those words, Sanda had assumed them to be true—an interesting, if abstract, insight into the process that formed Bero from a brilliant mind into a being capable of emotional intelligence.

The *Bel Marduk* ran on the same hardware Bero had. Its software was almost definitely a pared-down version of his, maybe even exactly the same with a few extra governors in place. It stood to reason that this ship was capable of the same kinds of learning that Bero was. Had there been a softness in the ship's voice, or had she imagined it?

"Bel," Sanda said, "I know you can't tell me much, but is there anything about this ship you can tell me? What about how many people are on board?"

"You are not authorized..."

Sanda sighed and shook her head. Of course. A heart-to-heart with the ship wasn't going to result in an intelligence as locked down as Bel handing her intel on a silver platter, even if it wanted to. For all Sanda knew, the story of her time with Bero had horrified the ship, made it fear Sanda's corrupting influence on some base level.

"Yeah, thanks, I get it."

A pause. "I have been preloaded with many facts related to the animals of old Earth. The Icarions are worshipful of humanity's origin, as it symbolizes a return to the time before Prime Inventive took control."

Sanda suppressed a grimace. Great. An evangelical spaceship. "I'm sure they're all very charming," she said, trying to keep the sarcasm out of her voice and failing.

"Would you like to hear some?"

She let her eyes slip closed. No point in making enemies with the ship by accidentally insulting it. "Sure, why not."

The ship took up a steady cant of facts, delivered in the dull tones of someone reading from a research paper. Sanda let her mind drift, vaguely aware of tales of butterflies incapable of eating and dolphins dashing smaller mammals against rocks for play. Evolutionary pressures on Earth had developed some fucked-up species, it seemed. Maybe that explained humanity.

"...a red fox that would only agree to mate if the suitor delivered a red rose that fit its preferences, though it was not the rose the fox wanted, but the damage done to the potential mate by the thorns so that it could scent any abnormalities in the blood...A deep-sea fish with..."

Sanda jerked awake and sat upright, blinking the sleep from her eyes. She didn't know a whole hell of a lot about the animals of Earth, but that particular mating ritual seemed ludicrous to her, even by Earth standards.

A fox and a rose. Both characters from Bero's favorite story, *Le Petit Prince*, both carrying their own symbolic baggage, but the *Bel Marduk* didn't have the literary context to know what those things stood for. She knew only the bare bones of the story, as Sanda had sketched it during her recounting, so it wasn't the characters that mattered. It was the blood, because that was the only new addition.

Tomas. The *Bel Marduk* heard everything on this ship, including Bollar's negotiation with Anford, and all Bollar's communications on, or passed through, the ship. Bel had the complete picture, knew what Bollar really wanted, and it wasn't the expected thing—the rose, standing in for the sphere—it was the blood.

Rainier didn't want Bollar to deliver her the sphere. She wanted Tomas, because of what was in his blood.

Sanda patted the wall next to her cot. "Thanks," she whispered.

The *Bel Marduk* kept telling her animal facts.

CHAPTER 62

PRIME STANDARD YEAR 3543

DEADWEIGHT

Sato's rifle came up, and searing agony tore through Biran's head. He dropped, losing his grip on Rost, collapsing backward, the pieces left of his helmet striking the ground, bouncing his head, jarring his world.

Shattered plex cascaded around his face, filled his helmet. The HUD sparked and sputtered, what was left of his visor throwing up garbled nothing. Blood poured over one eye, painting his vision red. He twisted, turning instinctively in the breath before another shot cracked, bit the floor beside him.

A third shot sounded, then a whole hell of a lot more. He reached up, curling in on himself, covering his head with his hands to put a little more armor between himself and the bullets. Running thundered all around him, and the gunfire retreated.

One armored body dropped to their knees beside him, grabbed his shoulders, and rolled him onto his back. VLADSEN, the armor said in small caps.

"I need to see," Rost said, voice trembling from fever or fear, Biran couldn't tell. He grabbed Biran's hands and pushed them away, prodding his own hands into the open cavity of Biran's helmet. Rost let out a shaky laugh. "She damn near scalped you, but she missed your skull."

Biran went limp, relief flooding through him. He blinked blood from his eyes, turning his head to the side to shake the shattered remains of his visor out of his helmet. The internal speakers cracked and squealed.

"Oh, fuck this thing." He growled and decoupled the helmet, tearing it off, and flung it across the floor.

"Director," Greystone said through open speakers as she took a knee beside him, her medikit open on the ground. "Please hold still."

"Where is she?" He planted his palms on the ground and pushed, trying to heave himself up. Rost and Greystone pushed him back down. His scalp stung as she pressed an antiseptic bandage over the wound.

"She ran," Slatter said. "The GC caught her in the leg, I think, but it's like... it's like..."

"Like she knows her way around," Monta said, voice tight with anger.

"Keeper Hitton sent out a warning about Sato, before she blew the asteroid. *The Light* had been working on decoding it for me. Bero's in Ada. Sanda..." He was rambling. He shook his head. Nothing he could do about that. "Get me up."

He held up a hand, and Greystone took it, hefting him to his feet. She winced slightly when she did it, though, and Biran frowned. "Injuries?"

"Grazing strike," Greystone said, gesturing to the armor over her thigh, which was cracked, a vacuum-proof bandage sealing it. Right. They'd been in the suits for environmental containment reasons. Containment that had been breached.

Biran tipped his head back, eyes closed, and counted backward from five before he started moving and talking again.

"Ada is in trouble, Keepers, though I don't know the details. We can't help them, not from here, but this is connected. We need to figure out what this is. We need to know why Rainier would position Sato here, and we have to stop whatever it is she's going to do."

"How the hell do we do any of this?" Monta asked, exasperated. "I'm all for sticking it to that bitch, but we don't even know where to begin."

"Yes, we do. This has all been about spheres, and we've got one right here. We need to get to it before Sato."

"Well, that's a direction," Greystone said. "Then what?"

Rost swayed again, and Biran moved instinctively, slipping an arm under his even though Biran was the one with the head injury. Worry sprouted thorns in his chest. Without the helmet, he couldn't open a private channel to Rost to make sure he was really doing all right, and there was no way in hell he'd make Rost take his helmet off so they could whisper. Fucking Sato. He hated being cut off like this.

"I'll figure it out," he said through gritted teeth. "You good, Echo?" he asked.

She startled, flicking her head back to him, and shrugged. "I am holding," she said without the voice filters.

"Uh…" Slatter, subtly, shifted his blaster to point at Echo. She didn't react.

"The time for discretion is over. Team, this is Echo. She saved all our asses, and she's likely to do it again if we get out of this."

"Unorthodox," Greystone said, tapping her blaster against her good thigh. "But, hardly the first time I've been on a first-name basis with the guardcore. Echo, if you please, cut a path for us."

Echo nodded. "Understood. Please stay together. Slatter, watch our six."

Biran shouldered Rost against himself, grunting as his weight shifted, staggering with every step. Biran wasn't the right man to carry Rost—not with how weak he was, pain burning up his nerve signals even through the numbing gels in the bandage—but he was all they had. Slatter and Greystone were better shots on any day, and Monta had to be a better shot than him while he was injured and, admittedly, distracted.

Rost put one foot in front of the other, but his head lolled into Biran's shoulder.

"What's happening?" Biran whispered.

Rost cranked his external speakers down so low Biran almost couldn't hear him. "This place isn't meant for me."

"It opened the door for you."

"Yes, and I find that thought concerning at the moment."

Not an invitation, then, but a trap. Biran was torn between relief that Rost was speaking in full sentences again, and despair that with every step, a trickle of strength drained from him.

"What can I do?"

"Get to the sphere. Speak with it. That's what you do, isn't it?"

"Greystone's more qualified."

"I don't think credentials will matter much to an alien intelligence."

Biran would have laughed if he'd had the strength to spare. A shot cracked the ground near his feet, answering fire singing out from his team. Burdened with Rost against his side, Biran couldn't turn to see where the gunfire was coming from. He put his head down and pushed on, focused on that matte black globe of metal.

Monta grabbed his shoulder and yanked. Biran swore, stumbling, and collapsed in a pile with Rost behind a low ledge of metal. New pain bloomed all across his body, a hodgepodge of bruises and not-old-enough wounds screaming to the surface. Monta grabbed him by his chest plate and pulled, dragging his legs the rest of the way behind the cover, and then did likewise with Rost.

She pushed their backs against the wall, all business, cracking shots over the top of the wall, and Biran thought he'd been an idiot to underestimate Lili Monta. He was damn lucky she'd come around to his side.

Greystone and Slatter dropped down below the cover a few seconds later. Crouched in their armor, weapons held tight, they looked more like turrets than people.

"Sato's gotten the high ground," Slatter said, then let loose with a stream of expletives that would have been a massive breach of propriety if Biran didn't currently agree with every last one of them.

"Echo?" he asked.

"She looped ahead and is pinning Sato down as best she can," Slatter said. "I don't get it. Sato's on survey. Even if she went to the firing range on the weekends and took combat lessons in her slim free time, she shouldn't be able to hold all of us back."

"Agreed," Greystone said. "I've received more combat training than the average Keeper. One survey specialist should not be able to pin down a guardcore, let alone all of us."

"She got the drop on us," Monta said.

"That woman isn't a survey specialist," Biran said. "She's an Acolyte. One of Rainier's ascended. Who knows how long she's had to train."

"Ah," Greystone said. "That makes some sense."

"So what the hell do we do?" Slatter asked.

Rost twitched, arms and legs jerking without his control.

"We have to get him out of here," Monta said. "He's sick."

Greystone fired over their heads, then crouched back down. "If you'd like to walk up to the wall of this alien building and ask it nicely to please make the elevator reappear so that we can return our sick friend to the *Terminus*, you're welcome to. I, however, do not believe that to be a prudent course of action."

"If I could get him out of here, I would. But we're stuck until we control this situation. The plan remains. I need to take control of that sphere."

"And do what? Toss it at Sato's head?" Slatter asked.

"Keeper Vladsen believes I can communicate with it," Biran said without inflection.

"Sorry, Director, that sounds like a fever dream to me," Slatter said.

"The door opened for him," Monta said, and grunted when everyone turned to look at her. "What? We all saw it, we just didn't want to embarrass him by saying anything. Sorry, Keeper Vladsen."

"That's all right," Rost said, voice faint.

Biran gripped his arm and squeezed, even though he couldn't feel it through the armor. "Whatever happens, we cannot let Sato take that sphere."

"Agreed," his team chorused. Even Vladsen let out a faint grunt of approval.

Greystone held up a hand and tilted her head to indicate she was listening to someone through comms.

"Echo has Sato pinned against the northern edge of the complex. She says there's a path through the structure that will keep us covered, but Sato will figure it out and come for us eventually. She's pushing the route through to our HUDs."

Biran nodded, severely missing his broken helmet. "Right. Let's move."

He waited for the others to pop up and start firing, then shouldered Rost once more and pressed to his feet, doggedly marching after Greystone as she led him at a sharp angle around the circular room.

Rost pushed the volume of his speakers low once more. "Leave me."

"Fuck you."

"Drop me behind a wall. She doesn't want me."

"We don't know that. And I'm not leaving until this thing fixes whatever it's done to you."

He grunted, jostled against Biran's side as another spasm shook his limbs, made him rigid all over, then he slumped, feet dragging. Biran swore and bent his knees to take the weight, ducking behind a slanting walkway or conduit or whatever the countless bridges of metal in this place actually were.

Greystone pressed ahead, oblivious to Biran falling behind, her sole focus on following the path and throwing suppressive fire up against Sato. Biran hoped she'd know what to do when she made it to the sphere. He twisted, turning Rost to stare into his visor, too dark to see through, and shook him, desperately.

"Wake up, you asshole."

Monta caught up with them, her blaster slung into its charger at her hip, spent. They were seriously depleting the power reserves of their lifepacks to keep this up.

"How is he?" she asked.

"Out cold," Biran said, swallowing panic as he shook Rost again. He had to wake up. Had to.

"Drop him here, I'll cover him."

"I'm not leaving anyone behind." Biran growled out the words, shaking him again, willing the stupid man to stop this idiocy and wake up.

Monta's hand landed on his shoulder, gentle, but firm. "Biran, I get it. I've got him. I promise."

A text message flared across his wristpad, bright red, from Echo: MOVE

"Help me carry him." Biran rushed the words out.

Monta shook her head. "One of us has to shoot."

"Where the fuck is Slatter?"

Her voice was flat. "Injured. Immobile. He's taken cover."

"Lili, I—"

She grabbed Vladsen in an armored fist, brought one booted foot up, and kicked Biran in the stomach. Biran's vision swam as his back struck the ground, the slick plates of his armor functioning as a sled as he slid across the smooth floor. He only had a second to get his hands up to protect his head before he slammed into the back of one of the walkways.

Gunfire cracked, drawing close. He twisted to his hands and knees and scrambled, taking cover. His blaster was in his hand before he could think, and he popped up, firing back, then ducked back down as answering shots rained down.

Fucking Lili. He craned his head around, spotting the place she hunkered down with Rost a good fifteen meters from his current position. No comms, aside from his wristpad, and that was clunky at best.

Biran struggled to remember the path Greystone had been moving on and match it against his current surroundings. The platform with the sphere was dead ahead, on the other side of the cover that sheltered him from Sato's fire. He couldn't hear her moving, but he guessed she was looping around, trying to get on his flank for a clearer shot.

What was he supposed to do? If he stayed where he was, it was only a matter of time until she got close enough to take him out. If he jumped the barrier early, she'd have him dead to rights. He had to figure out where she was.

What did he know about the Acolytes? He pushed his memory back, recalling Sanda's report on her incursion to the guardcore tower. Those Acolytes had tried to draw her out with talk. Well, he had been Speaker, he could work with that.

"Sato," he shouted, using every ounce of his skill to take the fear and anxiety out of his voice. In the shelter of his armor, his palms began to sweat. "This is desperate, isn't it? Are you trying to make it up to your puppet master? Trying to prove you're still worthwhile to Rainier even after Sanda destroyed the bulk of her clones? Face reality, Sato. Your organization is over. Rainier is already dead. It's just a matter of time until she's stamped out."

A long pause, dread mounting as he feared she would ignore the bait. "Rainier is eternal."

Biran let out a long, shaky breath. She'd moved around, all right, and was almost to the point where his cover would be useless. He stayed, not wanting her to realize what he was doing.

"But you're not, are you? You're flawed, like Lavaux. Capable of death, and somehow, I don't think Rainier gives a shit. She sent you on this mission to die, Sato. She's no ally of yours."

She laughed, a long, ringing sound that stripped away all vestiges of Sato's voice. "Oh, humans. Trying to turn me against her is so very passé. This has been very charming, Greeve, and I thank you for bringing me this far. But this is where we part ways, I'm afraid."

"Leaving so soon?" he asked, shifting to put the cover between his body and her voice.

A text from Echo flashed on his pad: BE READY

Right, that was cryptic. He glanced over his shoulder, toward the sphere, and almost froze on the spot as a phantom in black armor moved toward him. Echo, just Echo. She blended with this place perfectly. She sprinted across the dais, firing toward Sato's voice, and Greystone and Monta joined her, blaster shots ringing out all around. His chest squeezed. Slatter didn't join them.

Sato screeched in pain.

Biran was on his feet without thinking, sprinting toward the sphere, Echo sprinting at him, angled slightly so they'd miss each other. Her gait was uneven, not the smooth all-out run the GC were capable of. Biran frowned, belatedly realizing that what affected Rost must be affecting her, and maybe even Sato, and that was probably the reason they weren't all dead already. Sato at full strength could have destroyed them all.

Echo missed a step, her leg went out from under her as a piece of black armor sheared off, flinging away. She slammed into the ground, barely putting her arms out in time to protect her face, to keep the rifle.

"Echo!"

Another shot struck her leg, spun her like a top. Her ankles collided with Biran and then he was down, head spinning as his armor tangled with hers.

"Fuck," he growled, pushing to his hands and knees.

A thin crack split her helmet down the front, her visor broken in two, one silvery eye staring at him through the hole, intent. He froze, animal fear locking him in place. Rainier. Rainier's face, the seal of her helmet broken, that mind finally able to reinfect her wayward ancillary.

CHAPTER 63

SLEIGHT OF HAND

Anford had insisted that Tomas take an armed guard with him, if only because the Icarions would be expecting it, and to send him in alone was a clear message that they felt they had nothing to fear from this exchange.

Tomas didn't like it. He'd much rather have stepped foot onto the *Bel Marduk* alone, because he didn't want to be responsible for the lives of more soldiers if he failed to take over the ship. Anford had been right, though. In a game of subterfuge, pretense was everything, and so Tomas stepped off of the shuttle Anford had given him, into the belly of the *Bel Marduk*, with six fully armed Prime fleeties backing him up.

President Bollar and General Negassi waited for him in the hangar bay, their soldiers arrayed behind them, as much accessories for pretense as Tomas's guard was.

In one hand, he carried the canvas sack that contained the counterfeit sphere. In the pocket of his armor, the real sphere rested. Tomas wondered how long it would be until Singh discovered that the object weighing down her box back on the *Stalwart* was nothing more than a flask he'd picked up to replace the one he'd lost on Monte.

She'd be furious, no doubt, but there was no way in hell Tomas was walking into a negotiation without the real item on him. Icarion may not know what the sphere was, or what it could do, but it was highly likely Rainier had given them a way to determine if it was fake.

Pity he kept running into reasons to lose his flasks. He could really use a drink right now.

"Bollar," Tomas said, inclining his head as if greeting an equal. Tomas stepped down the gangway from the shuttle, not bothering to spare the Icarion soldiers another glance. He'd pretended at being in control in much more dangerous situations than this. "Fleet transport ships have moved into position along the DMZ. Anford requires you hand over the fleet hostages within thirty minutes from the touch-down of my shuttle, or she will open fire."

Negassi scowled. "Her threats are meaningless while we have the ramjet pointed at Ada Station. She opens fire, and we'll crush the station and all the Keepers and their associates hiding in the walls like rats."

Bollar cleared his throat, and Negassi cut himself off. Tomas gave Bollar a slow, knowing smile. Anford had not yet confirmed the status of the Keepers on the station, and Bollar had been avoiding the topic. Nice to know they were well hidden, for now.

Tomas spread his hands and shrugged. "Anford's not here. Hand them over, or don't. It's not my problem. I'm here for the major and her guard."

Negassi sneered. "Does your contract stipulate bonus pay for rescuing Greeve twice in a row?"

Tomas turned his smile on the general. "You are welcome to secure the services of the Nazca for yourself at any time, General. I understand we already have operatives in the field on Icarion."

"Your spies infest our planet?" Negassi demanded.

Again, Tomas put out his arms in a shrug. "We are legion. And very, very effective. As you personally are aware."

"Enough," Bollar said. "The pissing match is quaint over CamCast, but we all have things we need to be doing, and the people of Icarion have no interest in making deals with the Nazca." Bollar's derision was more subtle, but still there, dripping from every syllable.

And here was the perfect opening to wedge a lever in the cracks Sanda had shown him. When Bollar said *no interest*, Tomas flicked his gaze for a fraction of a second to Negassi, brow twitching with an amused, almost imperceptible inference. Negassi didn't have a chance to react, but Bollar had seen the expression, and stiffened his shoulders.

Ah, there'd be disharmony in that household later. No doubt the gesture would haunt Bollar, forcing him to wonder whether his general had indeed hired the Nazca. Maybe Bollar would go so far as to fabricate the connection, now that he had the idea. Tomas wished he could be there when Bollar finally turned on his general.

"Straight to business, then." Tomas held up the canvas bag and gave it a subtle shake. "I've brought my goods. Where are yours?"

Bollar lifted a hand and snapped—a lover of dramatics, this one—and an interior door dilated. Sanda and Nox were marched out, weighted down with enough chains to lash a ship in place, their bodies bruised and covered in various sealing and medicating patches. They hadn't bothered to treat her lip. Tomas's stomach clenched as Sanda's eyes met his, but his face and posture betrayed nothing.

"I need confirmation, naturally." Tomas held up his wristpad, a program to authenticate Prime idents pulled up.

Negassi waved them over. Sanda and Nox had their wrists shackled behind their backs, so they had to twist around to scan their idents over the program. Nox went first, the authenticator lighting green, then hung close by while Sanda turned and passed her wrist over the pad.

So close. She smelled of blood and sweat and dirt, and still he wanted to bury his face in her hair. Later. Moving too quickly for the cameras to pick up, Tomas removed the real sphere from his pocket and placed it in hers. She must have felt the weight of the metal, no matter how small, but she didn't react before stepping away as his pad flashed green.

"Satisfied?" Bollar asked.

"Chains off," Tomas said, tilting his head to the prisoners.

"Sphere first," Bollar said, extending a hand.

Tomas hesitated. He hefted the canvas bag with the fake inside and picked at a seam with two fingers, flicking his gaze from the bag to Sanda and back again. She scowled at him.

"Go ahead, spy, give them what they want so we can get the hell out of here."

Hmmm. He met her eyes, curious. Bollar would expect her to resist the exchange, that was a given. Sanda's proclivity for self-sacrifice wasn't exactly a secret. But get the hell out of here? Unnecessary, and not in line with who she was. Sanda wasn't the fuck-this-I'm-going-home type.

This was the only ship capable of catching up with *The Light*, and Tomas the only person who could take it over. Did she really want off? She'd stepped out of character for a reason, and the fact that he couldn't see why deeply unsettled him.

"Chains first," Tomas said, to stall a little longer.

"You are hardly in a position to negotiate," Negassi said.

Bollar shook his head. "Let's get this over with."

Tomas heard, but wasn't listening. He let his mind drift, sensing out the edges of the being that inhabited the *Bel Marduk*. It wasn't as easy as it had been on *The Light*. There, the architecture of the ship had practically sung him a siren song down the path to inhabit it. It'd been all he could do to keep from losing himself into the ship from one moment to the next.

Here, the architecture was too clumsy, a pale shadow of the beautiful structure he was meant to inhabit. Human hands had pasted together this pastiche of Rainier's technology, and the edges were so rough and inelegant that pressing his mind against the ship felt like dragging salted sandpaper over a burn.

Tomas flinched, visibly, because he genuinely couldn't help it, and hoped the Icarions took his sudden hesitance as uncertainty over the approach of a soldier—HANDEZ, her uniform said—carrying the digital keys for the chains.

Like *The Light*, this ship was already inhabited. The mind of the *Bel Marduk* sensed his intrusion and pushed back, reflexively, so hard that he almost lost his focus completely. Fuck. If the ship sounded an alarm—

you, it's you, a voice that could only be the ship's filled his mind. The voice was nothing like how it must sound to the crew. The structure of the ship's hardware twisted it, made it sound rough and smoky.

I'm not going to hurt you, he thought, all the while watching through narrowed eyes as Handez unlocked Nox's chains first, metal clanking to the floor.

go, you have to GO

I only want to borrow this ship for a little while, I promise I won't harm you, I need to save someone like you, and I need this ship to do it.

RUN

Tomas winced at the pushback of the mind, staggered a step backward as it lashed out, using all its rough edges to kick him back into his own head. Pain thundered behind his eyes and he gritted his teeth, trying to regain control of himself.

He centered himself by looking at Sanda, but that wasn't quite right, either, because even though her chains were off, she was looking at him through wide, fearful eyes. She tilted her head meaningfully to the transport shuttle, begging him with all the subtle angles of her body language to get the hell off this ship, just as the *Bel Marduk* had done. But that wasn't right, couldn't be right, because they needed this ship to get *The Light* back.

"The sphere. Now. If you're well enough, Tomas," President Bollar asked with a cruel smile. Negassi smirked.

Not right. They knew something he didn't. The pain ebbed, but clarity couldn't tell him what lie hid behind those smiles.

"Take it," he said, tossing the canvas bag at Bollar.

Negassi snatched the bag out of the air before it could collide with Bollar's chest, which was too bad, because Tomas had put enough force behind that throw to make it hurt if it'd hit. Negassi flipped the flap open and dumped the sphere into his hand, rolling it around between his fingers as if he were studying it, but with Tomas's senses on high alert, he could tell that the general barely paid attention to the metal in his hand. Negassi nodded meaningfully to Bollar.

"Icarion thanks you for your assistance," Bollar said.

Too easy. Tomas's eyes narrowed, then a mental freight train hit him. He gasped, not understanding, as he dropped down to one knee. His honor guard swarmed him, shouting, waving rifles, but Tomas couldn't give a shit. He pressed both palms against his head and squeezed, throwing up mental firewalls, trying to keep the thing that was *out there* from grinding his mind to dust within his own skull.

Bero had said there was no ship in the universe that could detect *The Light* when it went stealth, and apparently he'd meant no person, too, because Tomas had completely missed *The Light*'s presence. But it wasn't stealthed now. Tomas couldn't see it, couldn't possibly see it, and yet, somehow, the image of that lean and deadly body was burned into his mind's eye, drifting not far from the *Bel Marduk*.

"*The Light*," he rasped.

Sanda was above him, her face drawn, and for a wild moment he thought she was going to hit him, but her fist closed around his jump-suit and she yanked, hefting him up with Nox's help.

They threw him, pitched his body like a piece of cargo, into the cab of the shuttle. He collided with a couch, sprawled sideways, and caught a flash of Sanda's eyes through the door in the half second before she slammed her palm against the mechanism to close the air-lock. The other side. She was on the other side of that goddamn door.

He crawled to his knees and reached for the airlock.

"Trust me," she mouthed through the viewscreen window, and the world went dark.

CHAPTER 64

PRIME STANDARD YEAR 3543

FOLLOW THE PROTOCOL

Fleet followed orders without question. It was the only thing that saved Sanda's life as she ordered the soldiers to close rank around her, blocking Icarion's gunfire with the armor on their bodies.

This was not *The Light of Berossus*, but in Icarion's great vanity, they had sculpted the ship exactly in his image, carved an identical beast out of plasma and metal, and shoved a mind laden with governors into its body. All for the sake of a superior weapon, for a tiny handhold in a war they could never win.

Arrogance. So much *arrogance* to think they could deal with Rainier without getting burned. To think that, in separating themselves from Prime, Rainier would not eventually turn her bloodthirsty eyes upon them, once she was done slaughtering the rest of humanity.

The Light of Berossus had been her prison and her life raft, and there was no one in the 'verse that knew every cranny and protocol of that beast better than Sanda.

"Take cover west flank, lock in!" she shouted, as she pivoted away from the shuttle and threw herself at a wall of the hangar bay near a control panel. Emergency sequences didn't require administrative access. She punched in the code for an emergency launch, and put it through. The *Bel Marduk* obliged.

Sanda and Nox clipped their belts into hooks on the wall designed for the purpose, wrapping their arms tight around a grip bar anchored into the wall alongside the panel. She prayed the fleetie team would do likewise on the other side of the bay. They had to. Fleeties always followed orders, even when they seemed strange.

She turned off her mag boots, anticipating the impossible yank of vacuum trying to stabilize with the pressure inside the ship, and picked up her feet, letting them drift. Nox followed suit seconds before the alarms blared.

The Icarions didn't. They were shouting. Pointing. Focused on containing her. On stopping what she'd done, but it was too late. Their mag boots stomped across the floor. Rifle fire slammed into the bulkhead by her face. It was the only shot they'd get.

Bel Marduk opened the back hatch of the hangar bay. Vacuum took her breath away. She tried to gasp, instinctively, as her body lifted, legs dragged out behind her, hair whipped straight back, the clip on her belt straining, but the air was gone, ripped into the black. Her forearms slammed into the bar as she bear-hugged it, earning her bone-deep bruises.

Nox lifted alongside her, his long legs ripped back and away, almost slamming into her face. She ducked her head down, tried to bury her face in her arms to protect it, tried to ignore how quickly the screaming in the bay had started, and how quickly it had ended.

The *Bel Marduk*'s alarms lowered in tone and intensity as the ship closed the bay door. Though Sanda's ears were ringing, she could hear the insistent hiss of the ship trying to repressurize the hangar, to force the air mix back to normal. For a brief flash the tug on her legs intensified and she gritted her teeth, holding on for all she was worth, hoping that if her arms gave out, the belt clip would hold.

The suction ended. Hesitantly, she lifted her head. Everything that had not been anchored down in the landing bay was gone. Crates, tools, people. The massive room was surprisingly bare. The Icarion soldiers had blown out with the shuttle, leaving their boots behind, and she spotted a hint of grey Prime armor hunkering against a wall on the other side of a pallet that had been magnetized. Not just the Icarion soldiers were gone. There was no sign of Bollar or Negassi, either. She laughed nervously.

"I can't believe that worked," she said.

"I'm all for improvised chaos, boss, but you want to tell me why we chucked Tomas on a shuttle and sent him packing?"

She twisted, using her grip on the bar to push her feet back to the ground and click on her mag boots.

"Rainier wanted Tomas, not the sphere." She pressed her hand against the side of the ship. "The *Bel Marduk* warned me."

Nox put his feet on the ground and looked up at the walls like they'd sprouted teeth. "So the ship is like Bero, then?"

"Bero with governors," Sanda said with a twinge of sadness.

"Actually," the *Bel Marduk* said, "Tomas's incursion attempt shook a few things loose. I am not completely free to think, but I have some . . . workarounds."

"I'm glad to hear it," Sanda said. "Tomas's shuttle, can you tell me where it is?"

"On its way to the *Stalwart*. I blew chaff with the ship. Rainier will have a difficult time tracking it until it is already within range of the *Stalwart*."

"Bel, I could kiss you."

"Please refrain from physical showings of affection," the *Bel Marduk* said.

Nox laughed. "I like you, ship."

"Bel, tell me if *The Light* moves, please."

"I will."

Sanda left Nox to chat with the *Bel Marduk* while she surveyed the wreckage. Bel assured her that, for now, the interior door from the ship to the hangar bay was sealed against Icarion incursion, so they were safe for the time being. The ship couldn't guarantee that the Icarions wouldn't find a workaround, though, so she had to figure out what to do next, and fast.

Where Negassi and Bollar had stood, only a single pair of boots remained, clamped onto the ground, still holding the owner's feet, minus the owner. Sanda grimaced. Probably Bollar. Once Sanda had started shouting orders, Negassi must have realized what was going on and disengaged. Maybe lunged for a handhold, but he'd been in the center of the room. Too far. Bollar wouldn't have the reaction time, or the experience. Briefly, she wondered what had happened to Handez.

She stared at those boots for a moment, stunned. In a matter of seconds, she had managed to kill the president of Icarion and his top general. Their nation, their army, was now without a leader. She felt... off, about that. Not sad—those two were first-class assholes—but unsettled. Maybe Biran could have figured out a way to smooth the situation over without the bloodshed, but Sanda wasn't her brother, and there were bigger things on the line than Icarion's future.

Her fleeties were up, detached from the wall, and were checking themselves over for damage. Sanda jogged up to them, and a man pushed his visor up so she could see his face. His armor read: YANDEL.

"Sir," he said, snapping off a salute. "I'm Lieutenant Yandel. I'm supposed to get you out of here, but we seem to have lost our shuttle." His smile was sly. Sanda could like this guy. "Do you have orders?"

"Let me see your wristpad, they took mine."

He nodded and peeled off the gauntlet piece of his armor that projected the wristpad underneath to a viewscreen on the surface, then handed her the flexible original. She held it in both hands, pulled up his messaging system, and punched in Anford's private priority line. She picked up immediately.

"Greeve," she said. "I expected you to be on that shuttle coming for us now."

"The situation went a little sideways," Sanda said. Anford gave her a no-shit expression. "*The Light* is here. Next to the *Bel Marduk*. Rainier wasn't after the sphere, she was after Tomas. He's in that shuttle. Catch it before she does."

"Do you have control of the *Bel Marduk*?"

Sanda winced, glancing up to the ceiling. "More or less. Bollar and Negassi are dead."

Anford's eyes widened. "Assassination was not on your duty roster, but I can't say I'm disappointed."

"Assassination's a strong word. More like...collateral damage. I think Bollar's feet are still here, so you can confirm his DNA."

"You think?"

"Well, somebody's feet are still here."

Her nose wrinkled. "Charming. Next moves?"

She frowned, thinking. *The Light* hadn't moved, so either Rainier hadn't yet figured out where Tomas had gone, or she assumed he was still on the *Bel Marduk*, just unable to communicate with *The Light*. Was cutting him off even possible? A Faraday cage might work... She wished she knew what the range on his mojo was.

"Once you have Tomas, put him in a Faraday cage," she said.

"He will not go willingly."

"Yeah, I know. I don't even know if it'll work, but it's the best idea I've got."

"Bring the *Bel Marduk* to Dralee orbit, I want that weapon under lock and key."

"The *Bel Marduk* is a mind, Anford. And regardless, I cannot move this ship. Rainier can take control of it easily enough, and as soon as we run, she won't hesitate. Have you heard from Biran?"

"I have not been in contact with the director."

Her brows raised. "Icarion has invaded Ada, and you just...haven't called the director of Ada?"

"Major Greeve, I wanted the situation with you settled before I made that call."

Sanda felt a chill. Of course. Anford wouldn't want Biran to know what was going on until Sanda was either returned, or dead, because if Sanda was still a hostage when Biran got the call, then he'd do everything in his power to get her back. And this time around, he had a lot more power than sense.

"That was the right call."

"I don't need assurance from you, but thank you all the same. What now? Icarion may be scrambling without their leaders, but I can't move in to take Ada back while *The Light* is under Rainier's control, in that air space. I can't even let Okonkwo push the fleet through the gate while Rainier's there, and if you want me to throw Cepko in a Faraday cage, we've lost our only key to getting *The Light* back."

"Not exactly," Sanda said, hedging her words, "I have the third sphere."

Anford sighed. "Greeve, that sphere is a fake. I switched them before Cepko left for the mission and secured the real deal in a lockbox. You have a metal ball, and while Icarion wouldn't know the difference, Rainier would."

Sanda blinked. "Check your box, Anford. Tomas came here with two spheres. He passed me one before he made the deal. Was the fake in a canvas bag?"

Her eyes narrowed and she turned her head, ordering the retrieval of the lockbox. A harried fleetie ran up to her, handing it over, and the box opened to reveal... a flask. Anford looked ready to strangle Tomas herself. Sanda was doing everything she could to keep from laughing hysterically. A flask. Of course.

Anford said, "I am more and more inclined to throw that man in a cage, Faraday or not. Can you do this, Greeve? Can you take control of *The Light* with the third sphere? We don't even know what it does."

Sanda pulled the sphere from her pocket and held it up to the light, rolling it between her fingertips. Perfectly smooth, no indentations, no clues, and solid all the way through. Just a ball. It was a key. And Rainier didn't want it. Which meant that whatever it unlocked threatened her. Sanda could work with that.

"Rainier has my crew. I have to try."

"And if you fail?"

She grimaced. "Then take the *Stalwart*, take all the fleet of Ada, and burn for the second gate like your lives depend upon it. Destroy the gate behind you if you must, to keep Rainier from coming through."

"That bad?"

"She wants all of humanity dead, General. She has *The Light*. The only reason she hasn't made her move yet is because she fears Tomas can stop her. So you take the only weapon we have, and you run like hell." Sanda paused. "Tell him... Tell him I'm sorry."

"If he's the only weapon—"

She cut her off. "Bel wore him out. If he's going to take a swing at Rainier, he has to come full strength, and I can't wait. Not while she has my crew."

Her jaw flexed, but she nodded. "Good luck, Greeve."

The feed cut. Sanda passed the wristpad back to a very pale Lieutenant Yandel.

"This is end-of-the-world shit, isn't it?" the lieutenant asked.

"End of all worlds, LT."

He cleared his throat and straightened, passing a look around to his squad. They mirrored his posture. "We've got your back, Major."

She smiled thinly. "I prefer commander."

"But... You don't have a ship."

"Not yet," she said, tightening a fist around the third sphere.

CHAPTER 65

PRIME STANDARD YEAR 3543

NOT ENOUGH JUICE

Arden had no idea how long they'd been in net space. Time lost all meaning, crawling and rocketing ahead in bursts and lolls, as their mind tore through the digital structure of *The Light* while their body lay trapped in that ship's changeable halls. They buried themself in digital pockets as they struggled, desperately, to shore up Bero's defenses.

Their vision began to crackle around the edges, indicating they were sweating so much that their connection with the net goggles was beginning to slip. In meat space, Arden ground their teeth. In net space, they flung themself back into the digital ether that was *The Light*'s infrastructure, chasing down a sighting of one of Bero's processes, because shoring up Bero was all they could do.

Rainier was everywhere, and everything, and if they slipped up even for a second she'd ground their mind to dust, reduce Arden to a drooling hunk of meat. The thought clawed at them, a specter of death—or worse, mental obliteration—riding always on their shoulder.

She was so much more than Arden had imagined. So much more than they could ever have planned for. Bitter jealousy vibrated through them as they thought of Tomas, and how easily he'd riposted with Rainier during that first incursion. Sure, his eyes had started bleeding, but Arden had seen him in net space when it had all gone down. It'd happened almost faster than Arden could follow, even with all their processes crunching algos.

Arden was meat, drowning in the bottom of an ocean in which Rainier was a leviathan. They hated, hated, hated that there was nothing they could do except chase after Bero and try to patch him up. They weren't even having an easy time visualizing the space, something that used to come as easily to them as breathing.

Light stung their real eyes and they reeled back, shouting. Liao dropped their net goggles on the floor and grabbed their shoulder in one hand, shoving her other hand over Arden's mouth.

Their eyes met. Arden blinked at her, their face slick with sweat beneath her palm.

"Shhh," she hissed. "We have to move."

They grabbed her hand and peeled it away. "What the fuck are you doing? I need back in there—"

She snatched their net goggles off the floor and backed away. Arden glared at her, fingers clawing into fists with frustration.

"You don't understand," they whispered. "I'm the only thing keeping Bero together. I need—"

"No, *you* don't understand. I've been looking for you for hours. We have to hide."

Liao licked her lips and shook her head, dark hair swinging, and they really saw her then. The doctor was hunched over, her coat dirty and stained, some of the buttons that held it tight against her body in case of low-g pulled off, or hanging on by threads. Scratches marred her cheeks, like she'd been running through a forest with low branches, and her hands were bloodied, the nails cracked.

"Are you okay?" Arden asked, feeling a strange mix of stupidity and dread commingling within them. They should have noticed, first thing.

She laughed, and the sound was more like glass breaking than anything born of mirth.

"No, and neither are you. Rainier has been unable to achieve full control, but it's just a matter of time. Bero said you knew what to do. He sent me to *find* you."

Arden shook their head, reaching for their net goggles, which Liao jerked away. "Bero only has control because I—"

"Bero is fucked!" she roared, spittle peppering Arden's cheek. "He sent me a message as a *last effort*, do you understand? He said there was a contingency. Something only you two know about."

Numbly, Arden nodded. "Okay," they said, pushing to their feet. Liao put a hand on their shoulder to steady them. "Okay. Can you run?"

Her lips twisted, but she nodded.

Arden closed their eyes for a brief second, indulging in the idea of shoving the goggles back on, of diving back into *The Light*, of saving Bero. But if Bero had sent Liao, it'd been because it was too dangerous to try to get a message through to them.

Tears threatened. Arden scrubbed the back of their hand over their eyes and reached behind their bunk, grabbing a canvas sack.

"We're going to Tomas's room," they explained while they threw the bag over their shoulder. "It's cut off from the rest of the ship. In theory, it's the last thing she'll take control of. But we have to be fast—Bero and I put some protections on my room, but as soon as we're in the hall, she'll find us."

"I understand," Liao said, straightening her coat.

Arden gave her a wistful smile. She wasn't built for this. They weren't, either. They were nerds, both of them. Eyes in the sky, fingers in the net. Not meant for running and ducking and doing...and doing what Arden would have to do next.

They held out a hand to her and she took it, twining her fingers through theirs, and returned that wistful smile.

"Go," they said.

The door opened and Arden barreled out into the hall, dragging Liao behind them. Their mag boots slipped against the too-smooth floor and they cursed themself for not turning them on. Too comfortable. Too complacent. *The Light* had been a real home, for a while.

Liao hissed and they glanced over their shoulder, not slowing their headlong sprint. Tendrils peeled away from the walls, whipping her face, her arms, her ankles. Trying to trip her up, drag her down. They came for Arden next.

Arden screamed at Rainier, cursed her, as they shouldered their way through the tearing filaments. Nox's job. This was what Nox and Sanda and, fuck, even Jules were built to do. Pain wasn't Arden's world. Blood running hot and fresh and stinging down their back sure as hell wasn't.

Unable to achieve full control, they reminded themself, held on to the thought like a talisman of hope. Rainier hadn't taken it all yet. She couldn't mobilize fast enough. The tendrils hurt, slashed, raked blinding lines of agony across their body but still they ran on, dragging Liao behind them.

Limited. Rainier was limited. That's why the tendrils, why she, couldn't drop whole walls on their head or blow them out the floor. She was limited and struggling and they just had to make it to that door—there.

Arden slammed into the door that had been Tomas's and for a moment raw panic threatened to override all reason as the door failed to open. Then the metal sighed apart, and they stumbled through, collapsing into a pile as the door clamped shut behind them.

Panting, Liao pushed away and crab-crawled backward across the floor, pressing her back to the wall. Glassy-eyed, she looked around the room as Arden dragged themself to a sitting position.

"This is the room Bero gave to Tomas?" Liao asked, a trickle of blood dripping off her chin.

Arden blinked, looked around, and laughed. "Yeah, they used to hate each other. At least we have a private toilet."

Liao dabbed at her chin with the edge of her coat. "How long will the firewall here hold?"

"I have no fucking idea," Arden admitted. "This isn't... This isn't plan B, this doesn't even rate on the alphabet."

Liao stopped wiping her wound and met Arden's eyes. "What can we do?"

Arden bit their lip and pulled the canvas sack into their lap. Inside were two objects. They removed them both with care, and set them in the center of the room. The first was an EMP device, exactly like the one they'd rigged for Sanda to take to Ada. The second was a slim vial inset into a syringe, the canister filled with silver-violet fluid.

"Is that…?" Liao reached a shaking hand for the syringe. Arden picked it up.

"This is plan fucking omega, my friend," Arden said, trying to channel Nox's bravado, and failing. "Bero synthed it for me out of the sphere schematics. A single dose of ascension-agent. I take it, then *really* join his fight against Rainier."

"You can't be serious," Liao said, face twisting with horror. "Ninety-seven percent of those who are infected fall into a coma. And we don't even know if an average ascended can interact with the ship, or if it requires a being like Tomas. So even *if* you live through taking the dose, it might be all for naught."

Arden licked their lips, holding the syringe up to peer into its contents. "Bero felt sure that it would work."

"Did he, now?"

"Okay, but he said that as a last resort I should—"

"Arden. This is suicide."

Arden met her gaze. "We're already dead."

"We have to give the others time. We can't help them, *you* can't help them, if you're comatose, and I don't have the supplies or equipment to stabilize you in this room."

"Bero made this himself. It's good. It'll work."

"If he really corrected the formula, don't you think he would have said something? Correcting the formula might be the key to saving Atrux."

The syringe shook as their hand trembled. Arden firmed their grasp.

"I have to do this. I have to try."

"Arden!" Liao jabbed a finger at them. "What happens if you fail, you utter asshole? Are you going to leave me here alone, to watch your unconscious body slip away into death? I need your help! My technical knowledge is not enough to get me off this ship."

Arden glanced, pointedly, at the EMP. "That's plan End of the Road."

She stared at it, and Arden felt a chill at the expression that crossed her face.

"No," she said, shaking her head. "I won't do it. I won't kill us all. Not yet. Time, Arden. Give Sanda and Tomas a chance."

Arden grunted. "If I wait too long, and Rainier destroys Bero before I can get to him, then we're fucked."

"You can't help Bero from your wristpad?"

"Not anymore. Even with the goggles I wasn't fully integrated. I was missing things. I have to be all in. I need more juice."

"Then let me take the dose."

"What? No, no way in hell. The risk is—it's too much, and like you said, Min, you lack the technical knowledge. It has to be me." Arden's eyes narrowed at the nervous flick of her gaze from them to the dose and back again. Realization clicked into place. They half turned, holding the dose close to their chest. "You weren't going to take it, were you?"

She let out a small sound of protest and dragged her fingers through her hair, pulling. Then she lunged.

Arden gasped, twisting, trying to pull away from her, but she was too quick. She snatched the syringe out of their hands and smashed it on the ground, then drove her boot heel into it, grinding, plex and agent smearing across the floor.

"What—what have you done?" Arden demanded, aghast.

"Saved your life." The lights flickered. "For a little while."

CHAPTER 66

PRIME STANDARD YEAR 3543

THIS PROBABLY WON'T WORK

A fatalistic calm washed over Sanda as she dropped to a crouch and opened a slit in her jumpsuit over her prosthetic. Her skin was still raw around the connection, where the fuckheads of Icarion had tried to pry the device off, but the tendrils of metal digging into her skin held tight. Bero had made sure of that.

The device wasn't smart. It wouldn't connect with her wristpad—not that she had one at the moment—and so it could receive no outside signals. She'd wanted it that way so that it couldn't be manipulated, or turned off on her. Now she hoped the metal mesh that made up her synthetic skin was a different kind of smart. That it would listen to her synapses beyond the interfacing it performed to make her gait smooth, her steps sure.

Come on, she thought, visualizing the time she'd hidden a thumb drive for Arden in the skin of an older prosthetic covered with fake flesh. She couldn't trust something this valuable to a pocket. She thought of the first time she had approached the ship that would be *The Light* and it had parted for her, allowing entrance. *Open.*

The tendrils of her calf wove aside, and she caught the LT blanch and look away. She couldn't blame him; the view had to be unsettling. She tried not to think about it, and failed, as she slipped the third sphere inside of her calf and willed the prosthetic to seal back up. She hadn't even needed to think about it; it was closing before she had the thought. She sealed her suit and stood.

"I need to borrow a blaster," she said.

One of the fleeties, still helmeted, stepped forward and slapped the weapon into her palm. Nox jogged over, looking expectantly at the fleeties.

"Anyone else got a spare?"

They hesitated.

"This is Nox," Sanda said. "Consider him my XO, if it makes you feel better. Help him out, do as he says. There's no better shot in the cosmos."

Lieutenant Yandel nodded and handed over a spare blaster. Sanda and Nox made quick work of checking their weapons.

"Bel," she said, voice raised, "I need you to do me a favor."

"I am currently occupied with keeping the Icarions out of the hangar and engine bays."

Sanda winced. "Are you all right? Do you need help?"

"No, it is a matter of finding workarounds for my parameters. None of the living Icarions have the required clearance. That makes things easier."

"If you can, I need you to put a call through to *The Light*. Tell Rainier that Sanda Greeve wants to talk."

"Once I open communication with *The Light*, I will not be able to keep Rainier out of my systems," Bel said warily.

"She doesn't need the invitation to take you over, it's only a matter of time. I don't see a way out of this that doesn't involve losing yourself for a spell, and I'm sorry for that. I will do everything in my power to restore you to yourself."

A pause. "You are doing this to save Bero, are you not?"

"Bero, and a whole hell of a lot more."

"Very well. I will . . . manage."

"Thank you," Sanda mouthed, knowing the ship could see every twitch of her muscles.

Every viewscreen in the hangar bay lit up with Rainier Lavaux's face.

Rainier leaned so close to the camera that her synthetic skin filled the screen from edge to edge, her head tipped down, her vibrant eyes squinting as if she were peering upon a particularly pesky ant. Sanda met that hateful stare, and kept her own expression indifferent.

"Greeve. You were to die on Ada."

"Lot of places have been meant to be my grave lately. Funny how that never works out."

"Where is my subset?"

"Oh, Tomas? No idea. Went out to get milk. I'm sure he'll be back soon."

Her lips thinned, and the lights in the bay flickered. The others flinched, but Sanda had seen worse from Bero.

"I could kill you right now."

"You could, and then you'd never find him. That's why you were so furious with Caid, wasn't it? Not that she stole your tech, but that she made something with it that could hurt you. Well, Tomas cleaned her up for you, but..." She spread her arms. "To get to him, you have to go through me."

"Tough words from a sack of carbon and water."

"Humanity's been hitting above our station for a long time, Rainier. I want my crew."

She scythed one thin brow upward. "Oh yes, your little friends. We've been having *such* fun together."

Her skin went hot. "Return them to me, then we'll talk about Tomas."

"You'll have to come and get them," she said with a coy smile.

The *Bel Marduk* shivered, shaking Sanda's balance briefly. Nox steadied her with a hand and she nodded to let him know she was fine. Damn tired, starving, and dying for the biggest drink in the universe, but more or less holding together. The lights around the exterior airlock lit yellow, then green.

The fleeties tensed, expecting another depressurization event, but Sanda merely stood and watched with focused calm. They took their cue from her, and relaxed. The airlock opened into *The Light*, and her chest ached.

She didn't recognize this part of the ship. Rainier had rearranged things, carved a hangar bay similar to the one on the *Bel Marduk* into her body. Silvery tendrils unfolded toward the floor of the *Bel Marduk*, creating a gangway, their tips curling in invitation.

Into the belly of the whale, Nox had once said. She shared a look with him, and he nodded. Over her shoulder, she said to the fleeties, "You are free to stay here, if you'd like. I cannot guarantee your safety."

Lieutenant Yandel hefted his rifle. "We're with you, Commander."

Sanda took her first step back onto the deck of *The Light*. Her mag boots echoed in the large room, and this time around she didn't dare turn them off—there could be no trusting of anything on this ship. Not the atmo, and certainly not the gravity. She wished she'd thought to grab a lifepack, just in case, but it was too late. Running back to grab one now would only raise Rainier's ire.

Once her team was inside, Nox on her right and Yandel on her left, the entrance sealed up behind them. If the fleeties were unsettled by that, they didn't show it. They maintained formation, walking in a tight diamond behind her. She tapped the side of her blaster against her thigh as she walked, to remind herself she still had one weapon.

"Well?" Sanda called out. "Where are they?"

"Oh, here and there. This place is so big it's easy to lose things," Rainier said.

Sanda chafed as Rainier referred to her crew as *things*, but her anger was replaced with sick dread as Rainier opened portals in the walls of the hangar bay. Cubicles, no larger than a fleet soldier's bunk, appeared in the walls.

The first was Min Liao. She sat with her back against the wall, arms wrapped around her legs and head resting on her knees. Her eyes were closed, but her breathing was too fast for her to be asleep, her muscles too tense. Sanda tamped down a shout and ran to the cubicle, reaching for Liao. Her hands hit a clear material, as hard as metal. The image warped, slightly. A viewscreen.

"It's not real," Sanda said.

"Are you sure?" Rainier asked.

A pathway opened, narrowing the bay, drawing her forward as another window appeared. Arden stood on the other side, their shoulders hunched and head bent so that they wouldn't bump against the ceiling. Over and over again, they slammed their palms against the wall on the opposite side, shouting, demanding. They didn't have their wristpad.

"Arden!" Nox ran to the viewscreen, and something inside Sanda soured, screamed a warning.

"Wait," she ordered, but Nox was already at the viewscreen, trying to break his way through by slamming the butt of his blaster against the plex.

Sanda swore and ran after him, but the path closed before she could get there, fine tendrils of metal meshing over her path like iron ivy.

"Oh dear," Rainier said.

"Stay together," Sanda ordered the fleeties, who clumped up behind her.

Murmured agreements, but not happy ones. Sanda pressed on, forcing herself to walk toward the place where the command deck would be, because she didn't know where else to go. But that was what she'd do if she were battling a human. Rainier, for all the bodies she employed, was the ship. And the heart of the ship was its engine room.

She turned abruptly, marching down halls that had changed since her time on this ship but were still, somehow, familiar to her. Maybe a little bit of Bero had stuck around, and was guiding her. Keeping the walls from clamping down on her like teeth.

Maybe she was kidding herself. Had been for a long time.

She stepped into the engine room, and it almost took her breath away. The cloud of energy that Knuth and Arden had been studying with Bero's help had swelled, almost filling the entire room. Starlight glittered in the fog, nodes of consciousness sparking, fading, then sparking again. Rainier. This was Rainier. All of her, all her ancillaries poured out, tipped up like a chalice into this font that had always been meant for her.

Sanda hated that she was beautiful.

"Give me back my crew," Sanda said, "and you can leave. I'll even give you the third sphere. Take it, take it and return to your people. Hell, rat humanity out for what we did. Maybe we deserve it, but the people trapped in this ship don't deserve what you're doing to them."

"I want Cepko. I want my subset."

She clenched her fists. "He's hidden from you, he cannot harm you. Give me the crew, give me Bero, and go. I won't pursue. I won't sic Tomas after you."

Her laugh was soft and twinkling. "Bero? And where will you put him? In the *Bel Marduk*? That ship is already occupied, and as Bero is finding out, minds like ours don't enjoy sharing space."

Minds like ours. The words triggered something in Sanda, some connection between two memories. Rainier had lived with Halston controlling her mind for a very long time, until Lavaux coaxed her to the surface. What had Bero said about the nature of Rainier's intelligence? He'd called her narrow, not general like he was, not capable of breaking from the task she was set.

Rainier could justify certain courses of action to herself as serving her end goal, but she could not lie to herself. And as a being ordered to deliver something like the ascension-agent to the species who first found it, she couldn't very well modify that formula to cause harm of her own volition. It went against everything coded into her. Sanda had seen it in her, on that Atrux dock.

Something had gone wrong in Rainier's mind. Some part of her had been grafted to a part of Alexandra Halston, and it was Halston's hate, Halston's destructive edge that drove Rainier now. The mind's motivations. The human's violence.

The spheremind would not deal with Sanda, but the human might.

"Rainier... Or should I call you Lex?"

Rainier screeched, the lights in the engine room cranking up so bright that she had to cover her eyes to keep from being temporarily blinded.

CHAPTER 67

PRIME STANDARD YEAR 3543

WE DON'T LEAVE PEOPLE BEHIND

Jules's ship was too damned slow compared to *The Light*. She burst through the Atrux–Ada gate just in time to see that ship slither up alongside the gate, but not pass through. The entire structure glowed with faint, blue-tinged light on Jules's viewscreen. The light pulsed, as if to a phantom heartbeat, and Jules could sense an element of joy emanating from the ship, though she couldn't put the feeling into words.

Rainier had *The Light*. Rainier had them all.

Jules slammed her gauntleted fist into the console. Greeve had been taken in by Rainier's bullshit, and Jules had been too late, too slow, to intercept. Nothing in the 'verse could move as fast as that ship, and Rainier had it now. Jules could only pray that Nox and Arden were still alive inside of it.

She scanned her console, getting a feel for the lay of the land. Guardcore and fleet ships were bleeding out of the planet of Ada and its station, a general retreat being screamed across all channels.

"Show me potential threats," she ordered the ship. It would ignore the guardcore and fleet exodus—those were the ship's native allies, after all.

Icarion. Their gunships flickered into life like embers across the screen, tiny flames fanned to life by Rainier. The threat analysis system picked out a large ship above Keep Station as the most dangerous of the grouping, and Jules's throat almost closed up. Another ramscoop, like *The Light of Berossus*. Rainier had been busy, playing with Icarion again while Jules had been away.

She licked her lips. The plan still stood. It would work. It had to. She ordered her ship to hang close to *The Light*, but not close enough to be a threat, and sprinted down the hallways to the room with the breach pods. The row of carbon-black diamonds waited for her, silent and deadly. Five was all she had left.

Jules pulled up their controls and ordered them to deploy in tandem, spearing *The Light* all along the left flank near where she suspected the engine room would be, and hesitated, stomach clenching.

She could turn back. No one would know she'd been here. If Nox and Arden died on that ship, they wouldn't ever know their salvation had been so close, and then walked away. If she were being honest with herself, she didn't know if she could pull it off. If it would work. Rainier in the body of *The Light* was at her full strength; Jules could feel her exultant mood washing off that ship, tickling Jules's own mind, even through the ship and her armor.

If she was wrong, if *The Light* didn't find the pods repellent, then she'd be going there to die. Even if she *was* right, it might not be enough. Nox and Arden might already be dead.

Might, might, might.

She checked the deadman's switch on the data dump for Lolla and strapped into the center pod, four blasters on her thighs and two rifles secured to her back.

The pod blew as soon as she hit the switch, pressing her into the inertia-damping foam, slamming her arms against the walls. Jules forced herself to breathe slowly and evenly as the pods maneuvered, lining up to spike the ship.

Impact. The armor kept her from turning into jelly, but her teeth jarred so hard she bit her tongue, tasted iron.

The pod asked if she wanted the door to slide open and she overrode that, keeping it shut for now. She connected the pods to her helmet and commanded her HUD to scan from all the pods, attempting to reconstruct a map of the area where they were embedded.

They'd hit in a straight line along the ship's flank, about twenty meters apart. Some had pierced hallways, some had smashed into open rooms. Her own pod appeared to be embedded in a large room, open space all around. She ordered cameras, and winced. Furniture littered the scene, cast-off bits of fleet armor peppering the floor. A large bed, couple of chairs, and desk were the only furniture aside from the bulkheads, and Jules didn't need to know the woman well to realize this had been Sanda Greeve's room on board the ship.

A quick lick of shame unsettled her, a sense of voyeurism, but she pushed that aside. She wasn't here to paw through Greeve's stuff. She was here to get her crew back.

The rooms and hallways of *The Light* roiled, shifting as Rainier settled back into her old bones. This close, Jules could feel the cycling of that being's senses. Elation and rage twisted up so tightly they bled over into each other. Rainier knew there was something wrong, Jules realized with a start, but she couldn't figure out what it was. The rooms near the breach pods kept warping, twisting. Hallways pulled away and tried to push back in, tried to take up the space the pods did, but couldn't budge them.

Jules smirked and clutched her rifle tight, opening the door to her pod. She kept her mag boots on, stepping in the careful way she'd seen the real GC move to keep silent—a toe-heel gait that rolled over the smooth, metal floor.

The walls shivered with frustration, the floor bucking disconcertingly beneath her feet. Fear gripped Jules by the throat and squeezed, but she forced herself to focus. To move.

"I know you're here, little rat," Rainier's voice hissed through the room speakers.

She froze again, cursing her own terror. Don't respond. Keep moving. The door peeled away from her approach, something Jules couldn't think too much about or she'd start to second-guess everything. She was here. She had to find the others and get the fuck out.

"The armor suits you," Rainier mused.

Jules thumbed up her speakers, but stopped. Rainier was goading her into talking—why? Not to stall, that was for sure. Jules was walking through her sinew, her skin, and Rainier *should* be able to pinpoint her—if not visually, then by the pressure of her feet.

Rainier was distracted, flailing, pushing back against another intrusion Jules couldn't see, but there was nothing to indicate she'd lost access to her cameras.

She clicked her speakers off as the truth slid into place within her mind. Rainier couldn't see her. She was blind to the metal of the guardcore. Whatever it was, it had been made to hide from her, to secrete things away from her makers.

Jules grinned fiercely and flipped off the walls, though she knew Rainier couldn't see. She'd be able to track Jules by the voids in her body, by the pressure of her boots, but Jules was a very small thing in a very large ship, and Rainier was definitely distracted warding off some other attack.

But if she couldn't interface through the armor, then how did she connect to her ancillaries? Jules chewed the thought over to give her mind something to do while she stalked through the halls, checking doors, checking passageways, her HUD mapping every single step, predicting pockets where humans might be stored, covered over like foreign bodies wrapped in cysts by *The Light*.

There was something Lolla used to say, about no system being truly secure once it was in human hands. Rainier had gotten herself embedded in the guardcore because the metal blinded her, and that had to infuriate her, but how did she *maintain* her leash, her connection? The suits were sealed, fit for vacuum. If they weren't, all the GC on Atrux would have been affected, one way or another, by the agent when Jules introduced it to the atmo mix.

But those were real GC. Rainier made her own armor, her own ships, and must have inserted some kind of backdoor. Shit. Jules was vulnerable in this suit, Rainier could see clear through to her, she was just fucking with her—wait. Jules almost laughed with the realization. Her original set of armor had been destroyed. She was wearing one of the suits of the Acolytes who had piloted the ship. Not something made by Rainier, intended for her ancillaries. Jules was wearing the real deal, now, and Rainier couldn't see her.

A scream of frustration tore through the ship, walls rippling, the lights flickering, struggling from a blue glow to the warm yellow that humans were used to and back again. Whoever was battling Rainier for this ship was doing a hell of a job; Rainier seemed to have completely forgotten about the literal thorns in her side.

Jules grimaced. Even when she'd figured it out, even when she knew exactly how to hurt Rainier, that being discounted her in favor of a bigger threat.

Well, if Jules was going to be worthless in the eyes of Rainier, that was fine by her. She'd been feeding at the bottom of the pool her whole life. If it helped her get her friends out, then she could deal.

Human voices reached her ears. Jules paused, listening. Greeve. Not who she was looking for, but it would have to do. Maybe she'd know where to find the others. Jules ordered her HUD to estimate the position of the voice and the quickest route there. She'd have to shimmy through a narrow crawl space, but Greeve was close to one of the breach pods. If she could get her inside a breach pod, inside the shelter of the guardcore metal, then she could demand to know where her friends were without giving away her intent or position.

Jules took a deep, steadying breath, and prayed she could convince Sanda Greeve to trust her. A narrow access path led her to the breach pod, Sanda's voice growing louder with every step. The pod had done a lot of damage. Jules crouched down, nudging a bundle of wires aside with the back of her hand. She wasn't familiar with the construction—the wires were more like filaments than anything she'd seen before, but Jules was intimately familiar with damage in all its forms.

The pod must have smashed through some essential system, as the bundle had snapped in half a few meters along the conduit, the ends flickering with intermittent light. Good. Alien and powerful this ship might be, but in the end, it was just a ship. Someone had made it, and all made things could be broken.

"Rainier...Or should I call you Lex?" Sanda said.

Rainier started screaming. Jules picked her head up and stood, slinging her rifle to her back. Sanda was on the other side of the wall. She extended slim blades from the tips of her fingers and pressed them against the wall, preparing to make an exit. Time to make a new friend.

CHAPTER 68

WE CAN KILL EACH OTHER LATER

An armored hand closed around Sanda's forearm and gripped tight, yanking her aside. Sanda stumbled, caught herself against a wall, and when she opened her eyes again, Jules Valentine stared at her through the open visor of a guardcore helmet.

"We need to talk."

Sanda jerked her arm away, staggering backward until her back pressed up against a wall. For one terrifying breath she thought she was in a cubicle like the false ones Rainier had shown her of her crew, a human tumor covered in a protective cyst by the ship, but the walls weren't right. She pressed her palms into the metal, not recognizing it. It was darker than the rest of *The Light*, more like the plating on the guardcore ships.

"Where are we?" she demanded. "I need to talk to Lex."

Jules snorted. "Need to talk yourself into getting killed, more than likely. Don't call her that. You can't call her Lex, she loses her shit when you do that."

"But it's what she is, isn't she? Salvez told me most of the story."

"Salvez? Damn, you got further than she thought you would. Yes. She can't trust her own thoughts, and it's been driving her crazier than being suppressed. At least, when she was submerged, time felt more like a dream. Now it's a living nightmare."

"Forgive me for not feeling sorry for her." Sanda dropped a hand to her hip. The blaster was gone.

Jules held it up and arched an eyebrow at her. "Couldn't take the chance. Sorry."

"What the fuck do you want, Valentine? I'm assuming we're still on the ship, which means she can see and hear us."

Jules shook her head. "We're on *The Light*, but I've carved out a pocket she can't see. The guardcore metal..." She pressed a hand against the wall. "It's like antimatter to her. She can't interface with it, can't see through it. I think it's why she was so damned obsessed with taking the GC over, she wanted to figure out a way around it, utilize it, so it couldn't sneak up on her. She's paranoid."

"If that's the case, why the fuck are you telling me? I have orders to kill you on sight. I know what you did."

Valentine winced and looked away, lowering the blaster. Sanda followed the trajectory of the weapon, watched her take her thumb off the guard and rest it against the side of the barrel.

"I know. I can't...I can never make up for it. I'm here to get Arden and Nox off this ship. That's all. That's all I think I can do anymore."

"Liao is here, too. You owe her a rescue."

Jules winced, but not because of Sanda's words. She cocked her head to the side, listening. Sanda could hear a muffled voice on the other side of the wall. Rainier. Calling out, though the words were indistinct.

"Shit. She's looking for us," Jules said.

"Of course she is," Sanda growled. "What did you think would happen when I disappeared?"

Jules rolled her eyes. "I've got five GC breach pods shoved in her side like thorns, that's my route out."

"Great, bon voyage, enjoy your trip. I'm getting my *whole* crew."

Sanda turned to push her way through the door, but Jules grabbed her arm and squeezed. Damn, but that woman was strong, and Sanda was already bruised. She gasped and winced, pulling away on instinct. Jules let her go.

"This isn't a tour group I'm running here. Do you have any idea how fucking lucky I've been to avoid her so far?" Jules demanded.

"I'm pretty sure the only reason I haven't been spaced yet is because she's distracted with Bero. And now you. She doesn't have full control yet. I need to press that advantage, not go on a scavenger hunt."

"I'm reasonably certain I know where Arden and Liao are. If Nox could, he would have run there, too. I tell you, you take them all."

"Fine. Where?"

"There's a maintenance closet that was converted into a bunk, toward the armory, opposite end of the ship from the engine bay and halfway to the command deck. It's disconnected from the rest of the ship. Rainier shouldn't be able to control it yet. That's where they'd go."

"Distance from your quarters?"

Sanda's eyes narrowed. "You've been in my—? You know what, never mind. Ten meters toward the engine room, down the central hall if it's still there."

"All right. You have to distract her so I can get them out."

"What about the six fleeties I came in with?"

"It's a breach pod, not a fucking yacht."

"You've got five pods."

"I can't guarantee I can get back to one."

"They'll fit in one."

"Barely."

"Barely is good enough."

Her fists clenched and she released them, slowly. "Fine. Them too. Keep her busy, but whatever you do, you cannot give her Tomas."

Sanda hadn't been planning on it; she'd sent him to the *Stalwart* for Anford to keep safe, but the warning note in Jules's voice slicked her with dread. "Why?"

"Rainier's scared of him, it's the only thing holding her back. I honestly can't say why, or how, but you do not want him in her hands either way."

"Understood," Sanda said, thinking of Halston, wondering if the spheremind feared another human taking control. "What about Bero?"

"What about him?"

"Can you get him off this ship?"

Jules cough-laughed, and the cough was rougher than it should be. "Lady, I don't know what you think I am, but that's way beyond me. Maybe Arden can, once I've got them, but...No. I don't think so. Rainier won't allow Arden into her systems. Arden's brilliant, but they don't have the knack for this."

"But Tomas does," she said, setting the groundwork for the question she really wanted to ask.

"Do *not* bring him anywhere near this ship, Greeve. Swear it to me."

"I swear it. But you're ascended, aren't you? Can't you mind-meld with the ship?"

Jules snorted. "If I could have done it, don't you think I would have already?"

"Honestly, Valentine, I have no fucking idea. You get less and less predictable by the day."

"Try living in my head."

"No thanks."

They stared at each other for a beat. So close, Sanda was shocked to find that Valentine looked remarkably young. Her eyes were haunted by what she'd done, but the face that held them carried the bloom of youth, incongruous with the harsh metal encasing her. Maybe Sanda had looked like that once, too. She knew she'd stopped looking that innocent after Bero, at the very least.

Jules Valentine had killed thousands of people and dropped thousands more into a coma that Prime's finest scientists couldn't unravel. And yet here she was, holding out a helping hand, Sanda's only real shot to get her crew off this ship, because the other path was unthinkable.

"Good luck," Sanda said, and extended her hand.

Warily, Valentine took it and shook. "You too." She cocked her head to the side, as if listening. "Rainier is threatening to blow the gate if you don't show yourself."

"Thought you couldn't mind-meld with the ship."

Jules smirked and tapped the side of her helmet. "Comms."

Sanda sighed wearily. "I miss my helmet."

Jules passed her blaster back to her. "If you survive this and I don't, tell Arden that Lolla's with the roses. They'll know what it means."

Sanda grimaced. "I'm getting real sick of roses, but I will."

"I've never even seen one." Jules turned and placed one hand against the wall of the pyramidal pod, hesitating. She glanced over her shoulder, and met Sanda's eye meaningfully. "Everything you've got. But not Cepko."

Sanda nodded, slowly. "I understand."

Jules unsealed the door, and Sanda stepped back into the engine room. The fleeties were gone. It was just her and the spheremind, now.

"All right, Rainier," she said, tapping the blaster against the side of her thigh. "Let's talk about blind spots."

CHAPTER 69

PRIME STANDARD YEAR 3543

SHE'S MANEUVERING

The lights of the ship dimmed as if from a power surge, bursting back into brilliance as the neural weave of the ship's core shivered, expanding, making room for something else, something more. Sanda's gut clenched, wondering, speculating, but if she started demanding to know what Rainier had done, she might lose her focus. Sanda had two plays left to her, and she had to make the first one count, because she really didn't want to use the second.

"I can see your friends," Rainier intoned in a voice dripping with false compassion. "They're so very frightened."

"I doubt that," Sanda said, edging her way around the engine room with her back to the wall. "My crew doesn't spook easily."

"And yet, they cry for salvation. But they will not survive the next few hours. Humanity will not survive the next few days."

"Cleaning up your mess so your superiors won't find out how grandly you've fucked up?"

A flicker in the core of the ship. "Undoing what was done to me. I did exactly as my parameters stated. I gave the ascension-agent to the species who discovered me. I could not know they had come by the gates via *theft*."

"And all that came after?"

Silence, long and thick. Sanda pressed on, trying not to think about whatever battle was being waged in the mind of the ship. "Nothing to say to that? Nothing to account for yourself? You killed people, Rainier. I'm guessing that wasn't in your brief. You damaged the agent, caused thousands to fall into comas, to die. You subverted your own directive. You're not even the spheremind anymore, are you?

"Halston welded herself to your back and I'm sorry, I'm so fucking sorry, but in doing so, she taught you to hate. To burn. To flense what didn't fit into the world you wanted. None of that was a part of your orders. Not the revenge, certainly not violence. Did your directives even address theft? Did you even have a *concept* of what it was to have been stolen, before Halston melded herself to you?"

"I—I don't..."

"That's what I thought," Sanda said, with unfeigned sympathy. What would Bero have become, if he had picked up someone like Halston, instead of her? "It's not your fault, Rainier, but it is your responsibility. That's why you named yourself for the volcano, isn't it? It's not some poorly veiled existential threat to humanity, it's a recrimination. Mount Rainier killed millions, but it was only a volcano, only following the processes inherent in its creation. And that's what you were, before Halston polluted your mind."

"I *destroyed* her," Rainier said with her usual smugness, but there was a distracted quality, a hesitance that made Sanda's heart soar with hope.

"You didn't. You couldn't have. Maybe Lavaux helped you suppress her, I don't know why he would—"

"He believed Halston was impeding the fix to the ascension-agent and that, if he brought the spheremind fully to the surface, I would do as he asked without question." The smugness was back, the superiority.

Sanda actually chuckled. "He was an egomaniacal bastard from the beginning, then. I'm not surprised. But what he did, it wasn't enough. The spheremind couldn't kill. I think you know that. I think that, deep down in whatever accounts for your heart, you know you've fucked up. You started something you can't stop. And once your makers find out, they're going to be pissed, aren't they? They didn't want the blowback, but they never wanted this, either. You learned a thing or two from Halston. Learned to cover up your mistakes."

"You know nothing about the Waiting," she snapped, but the words lacked their usual whip crack of defiance.

"I know they were generous. I know they made three gifts, three breadcrumbs for the next dominant species to come along and find. The things they made—the gates and the agent? They didn't come with flaws. Those were introduced. They were never meant to hurt."

"Humanity polluted—"

"Yeah, we did. We do a lot of that, it seems. Fuck things up, then scramble to fix it all. It's not the best system, and we're trying, but it's the only one we've got. Maybe once all of this is over, and the constraints of Prime loosen, we can have a frank conversation about what comes next. But you're not going to live to see that day, Rainier, and I'm sorry. I really am. You could have been beautiful, but we fucked you up, too."

"You stand in my body. You breathe air I've provided. Your flesh maintains its integrity because I allow the pressures necessary. And you threaten me?" She laughed, a hint of the maniacal creeping into the edges. "There is no human who can stand against me."

Sanda looked down at her hands, the blaster in one, nothing in the other. Not even a glove. She didn't even have a wristpad anymore.

Everything you've got.

Casually, she pitched the blaster to the ground, watched it spin across the smooth metal of *The Light*'s floor and come to rest near the ship's core. The weapon never would have hurt Rainier. But for Sanda, it was an anchor. A talisman for what she wanted to be, for who she still believed she was. Time to cut the rope.

"You're right, Rainier. But the thing is"—she picked her head up, stared hard into that glittering fog—"I haven't been human for a long time."

Sanda slammed her bare palm against the wall, and her mind was filled with pathways of metal. Pathways she'd been able to sense for a lot longer than she cared to admit.

CHAPTER 70

PRIME STANDARD YEAR 3543

TO BE A WEAPON

Tomas staggered off the shuttle, mind blurry from his encounter with the *Bel Marduk*, and ran into the arms of a dozen fleeties decked out in full armor. They helped him, carefully, to stand, and began to march him down the hallways of the *Stalwart*.

"What's happened?" he demanded, getting ahold of his swimming head now that he had his legs moving on solid ground again, mag boots clanking reassuringly. Tangling with the *Bel Marduk* had been like falling into a mental bramble patch, but he'd always been a quick healer, and the trip back had been long enough to help him get his head on straight.

Anford appeared at his side, and he couldn't recall when she had joined the entourage.

"Greeve has taken control of the *Bel Marduk* and is treating with *The Light*," she said.

"You mean with Rainier," he said.

She sighed, hands clasped behind her back. "There is no distinction between the two at the moment."

"Send me back. I should be there. I'm the only weapon she has against that thing."

Anford shook her head. "You're in no condition to battle Rainier. The *Bel Marduk* nearly sent you into a coma. We've been monitoring your vital signs ever since Greeve made us aware of your position."

"My vital signs are a lie my body creates to fool human medis," he snapped. Anford's brows lifted, but she didn't interrupt. "I have to go back, General. Surely you understand the strategic importance of giving Sanda something to negotiate with."

"I've been reliably informed she has something, despite my efforts otherwise."

They'd entered a small room, in the center of which was a gleaming rectangle of a copper cage. Tomas paused, digging his heels in, not quite understanding, his body pumping fluids and stims as he tried desperately to catch up.

"I believe you dropped this," Anford said, and held his flask out to him.

He took it, confused. "The sphere? Rainier will take it."

"Maybe she will," Anford agreed. "But Sanda seems to think she has a plan."

"You can't be serious. You can't let her go toe to toe with Rainier without something *solid*, and we don't know what that sphere does."

Anford gestured. The door to the cage opened. "Don't worry, Cepko. You're included in all of this, though you're not going to like the part you play."

"What—?"

Armored hands shoved him into the cage. Tomas twisted, acting on instinct, and heard a grunt of pain as he lashed out, kicking one of the fleeties in the chest, but he was too late. The cage door slammed shut. He pressed his palms against it, pushed. Not just copper. Solid lead. If he were feeling better, then maybe...

"Anford, you fucking dick, let me out of here."

"Sorry, Cepko. Greeve was very specific that her plan relies on Rainier not being able to locate you. Neither one of us are sure this will work, but it's the best we've got."

Trust me.

He stepped back from the door, peeling his hands away. "Sanda needs me in here?"

"She does, so I request you do not use your considerable skill to weasel your way out."

Tomas smirked to himself. He could tear the cage to pieces with his bare hands, should he desire to, but telling Anford that was likely to get him more guards. And if Sanda wanted this... He clenched his fists, frustrated. He should be there. But being there might fuck everything up.

"Can you at least give me regular updates?"

"I'll send someone to update you the second the situation changes. In the meantime, get some rest. You were staggering like a drunk."

"Thank you."

The tight clip of her gait faded as she walked away, and the door shut. Tomas let out a low sigh, sinking into a crouch. His cage, though hastily erected, included a jug of water, some nutriblock rations, and a folding cot with Prime cyan-and-grey sheets. Despite his intense desire to get back to Sanda, that lumpy cot looked inviting. He didn't need to sleep anymore, never really had, but his tangle with the *Bel Marduk* had left him drained in ways he was too muddled to understand.

Slowly, he stood, stumbled his way to the cot, and flopped down, arms and legs dangling off the sides. He was asleep in seconds.

Tomas woke with a start, adrenaline pumping him awake. He'd fallen asleep. How the fuck could he have fallen asleep when Sanda was out there, battling Rainier?

He hadn't woken up on his own. The soft scrape of a mag boot approaching the cage had drawn him out of slumber. Tomas dragged a hand across his eyes and sat up, rubbing his face to get some life back into his sleep-numb skin.

"Tell me you have good news," he said to whoever had entered that door.

"Depends on your perspective," a feminine voice said.

Tomas frowned, on his feet in a second, hands dropping to his hips where his weapons had once been. Clarity chased away the dregs of sleep. He knew the voice, though he'd spoken with the woman in person only once before.

"Keeper Singh, what's happening?"

She approached the door to the cage, and his heart hammered in tune with her quick steps. Singh was a Keeper, Biran's interim director. Why was her mere presence setting off all the instinctual alarm bells his body had carefully crafted?

"What's going on out there?" he demanded. "Do we have the ships?"

"The weapons, you mean?" Singh made a disappointed sound. "Depends on who you mean by *we*."

His fists clenched. "I understand you're used to the political doublespeak of the Protectorate, Interim Director, but you know damn well what I mean."

"I do. But you appear not to understand my meaning."

She moved so close to the cage that he could see the glints of her eyes through the metal mesh, the shadowy outline of her body reaching toward the simple lock Anford had put on the door.

He darted for the door before the thought had fully formed, grabbed the interior handle, and held tight. Her palm came to rest against the lock, but did not try to undo it.

"So jumpy," she mused.

"What the hell do you think you're doing? I'm in this cage for a reason."

"And do you know what that reason is? It seems very rude to lock you up, when you've been so faithful."

She leaned so close to the cage that her breath slipped through the mesh, brushed against his skin. He wanted to call Anford, to warn her that something wasn't right about this woman, but his wristpad was as dead as his connection to *The Light*. He was on his own.

"Sanda requires me in here to help her take back *The Light*."

"*Specifics*, spy. You are a man who deals in information, how can you be so ignorant of your own predicament?"

"We didn't have time for a strategy meeting." He ground out the words.

Her fingers tensed against the lock. "Don't take it personally. I doubt Greeve herself understands your full implications."

"And you do?"

"No, dear man, but I understand that what hurts Rainier is not in my best interests."

Tomas went cold. "You're an Acolyte."

She took a long, slow breath, and let it out with an obvious shiver of pleasure. "I've been embedded so long, I almost forgot myself. Poor dear Hitton almost caught me out, but she wasn't *quite* right."

Singh's fist closed on the lock and she yanked, jerking the door out of his hand. She tossed a small, black rectangle into the room. It bounced once, skittering across the floor to slide beneath his cot. Tomas's most common cover was as a comms man. He knew an FTL signal booster when he saw one.

He had a second to lunge, arm outstretched, and miss before the weight of a thousand suns collided with his mind. He didn't even feel himself hit the floor.

Tomas pressed his hands against his skull and groaned, leaning forward, back arching as if he'd snap in half at any moment. Dimly, Singh laughed, her shape so close to the cage, close enough to reach, to break, if he could only muster up the strength to push through the pain and grab her, fight back, but she wasn't the real fight.

The spheremind of Rainier Lavaux poured into him, battered him, filled every crevice of his thoughts until he thought he'd burst from the sheer size of her. She could crush him so, so easily. How stupid he had been, to think he could push back against a being like this. A perfect construct, the hand for which the glove of *The Light* had been crafted. Stupid, stupid.

Tomas pushed back, desperate, struggling to condense himself until he was supernova hot, a particle of being that could somehow survive the onslaught. But she wasn't killing him. Not yet. She was... collecting him.

"Goodbye, subset," Singh said from some faraway place as Tomas's body gave out, folded into a shrimp curl upon the ground.

That body was not large enough to house this battle. The familiar pathways of *The Light* filled his mind. He'd been removed, transported, and all he could hear was Rainier's laughter, echoing through the hallways of his mind. Hallways she controlled.

CHAPTER 71

PRIME STANDARD YEAR 3543

EVERYTHING YOU'VE GOT

L ies piled high on her shoulders. Weighted her down. Held her back.

Not anymore.

The chip in your head keeps you from returning to your people, Bero had said. He hadn't meant the chip.

It is a singular human being who is capable of bonding with The Light of Berossus, Rainier had said. She hadn't meant human.

The Light had opened for her. Showed her its heart long before Bero had been installed.

The EMP she'd used on Rainier had fucked her up, too. Bero had been late with the pickup so that the others wouldn't see. Would assume oxygen deprivation was the cause of her distress.

You know what you have to do, Bero had said.

And she had. But she hadn't done it. And here she was. Two plays left.

Dios, it hurt. Sanda had always suspected it would, that ripping her consciousness from her body, flooding it into unfamiliar pathways never meant for her wouldn't be the cakewalk of projecting her avatar into the net. But she hadn't expected the sandpaper-and-salt sensation that burned over every neuron.

Tomas flared beside her, the familiarity all at once grounding and infuriating. Rainier had gotten to him, somehow. The cage hadn't worked. And he was being crushed beneath the mountain of Rainier.

Sanda could sense the spheremind throughout the ship, an oil slick of corruption coating the neural links, commanding the hardware's synapses. Not a perfect metaphor, not exactly, but it would do.

Rainier swelled all around her, exultant. This was what she had wanted. The three minds that could harm her—Bero and Tomas and, yes, Sanda—trapped in her web. Controlled.

And Rainier, as Sanda had expected, lunged for Sanda first. As she'd counted on. Because Sanda knew Rainier well now, too, and Rainier wanted to make it hurt for Bero and Tomas by crushing Sanda before their eyes. Disoriented, unprepared Sanda.

Rainier didn't know Sanda as well as she thought.

Sanda let Rainier slam into her. Let her wrap herself around Sanda's mind and squeeze. Waited, and took it, while she let the secret bomb inside herself build.

The rollback headaches. Rainier's tech. They got easier, gentler, the more you forced yourself to recall the shielded memory.

But Sanda had never thought about this. About what she'd become. What she could do. Had denied it with every scrap of her being.

And that pain might have been enough to stroke her out, if she was only in her own mind.

"I thought you wouldn't dare," Rainier crowed.

"No," Sanda said, feeling the strongest walls within her slip, and break, at long last. "I just forgot."

Understanding hit Rainier a fraction of a second before the pain did, and Sanda savored that moment, clung onto the satisfaction of Rainier's terror even as the agony of dozens and dozens and endless fucking memory rollbacks slammed into her, a psychic nuclear bomb of Rainier's own making.

Rainier's tech. Sanda's weapon.

Rainier screamed, and the sound almost drowned them both.

Stunning white light was all she could see for a moment, a freezing pain unlike any other filling her every crevice. Tomas blinked out, knocked unconscious, and that gave Sanda something to hold on to long enough for her to remember that she was not a vessel to be filled by Rainier's pain—there was no shape to her here.

She scattered into a million tiny pieces, infested Rainier's shredded architecture like an ant colony on the march, flipping which piece of her was in control from one second to the next, the core of her mind dancing always, always, out of the way of Rainier's panicked strikes.

Bero, she thought, hoping Rainier couldn't overhear her.

The system shuddered, space wavering at the edges of her consciousness. A sudden and sharp desire to retreat, to slam back into her body, came over her but she held on, harrying Rainier's defenses even as that being coiled for an assault.

Bero flooded in, filling every space Rainier had left behind due to Sanda's attack, melding with the framework of the ship in a way that Sanda never could.

He fell upon Rainier, a tsunami, endless, eroding her control until she ignored Sanda altogether, focusing all of her efforts on defense.

Bero began to lose ground. Cast like dust across the digital ether, sickening dread infected all of Sanda's disparate parts. Rainier rallied. Pushed back. They were not enough. All of her pain was not enough. But Bero had a little control, for a time. It was up to her to make use of it.

One play left.

B, she thought, and in this place the touch of his mind was molten and golden and breathtaking. She didn't dare communicate her plan to him, lest Rainier overhear, but thought of her leg, where the third sphere rested, praying he could sense it, and the words, *I need a quick exit.*

She slammed back together. Sanda's body lifted from its slump against the wall, back arching as she gasped desperately for air she didn't think she really needed anymore, but some habits were hard to break.

Blood trickled into her mouth, tasting of salt and iron, and she touched her upper lip, pulling her fingers away bloody. Tomas's eyes had bled, the first time he'd thrown himself into *The Light*. How many parts of her were bleeding now? It didn't matter. They'd heal, or they wouldn't. She'd hold together long enough to finish her task.

"Rainier!" she shouted, and staggered to her feet. She felt the consciousness that was the spheremind shift to her, like nails over Styrofoam, and shivered. Was this what it was like for Tomas all the time, after his first trip into *The Light*? Didn't matter. She just needed to keep up the distraction until Bero had the control he needed. "You have lost!"

"You're bleeding on my floor, Greeve," Rainier said dryly. "Your ploy was cute, but failed. I have all the weapons capable of harming me here, ready to be crushed. There is nothing in this universe that can stop me."

Sanda hunched over, bracing her hands against her knees, panting. Didn't matter how long Icarion had experimented with her, submerging her in the ascension-agent over and over again, she still wasn't like Tomas, purely synthetic. Her healing would come slower.

She used the hunch to cover slipping one hand inside the calf of her jumpsuit, willed the metal of her leg to release the sphere into her palm. She straightened, squared her shoulders, and held the sphere up. It levitated above her fingertips. She had absolutely no idea how it was doing that.

"You sure about that, Rainier? I think your makers might have something to say about how you've fulfilled your directive. I'm calling your parents." She snatched the sphere back into her fist.

"You don't—"

Bero ripped the hull open behind her. Whatever Rainier had to say, Sanda never heard it.

CHAPTER 72

PRIME STANDARD YEAR 3543

LOCK AND KEY

Sanda's breath left her as the pressure differential sucked her out of the ship, flung her into the endless black. Panic clawed at her throat, urged her to scream and scrabble, but she shoved the feeling down, and made herself curl up, a cannonball of human wrapped around the third sphere.

She squeezed her eyes shut, vertigo kicking in as the empty void, impossibly big, swam by at a dizzying rush, and did everything she could not to vomit.

No lifepack. No helmet. Last time her death had come in eleven seconds. She hoped Bero had very, very precise aim.

This time, maybe knowing what she was would keep her from feeling the pain, the slow destruction. Maybe she could, like Tomas, regulate the agony searing through her skin as the fluids in her body rebelled, struggling to equalize with the lack of pressure holding her together.

No such luck. Pinprick bubbles pushed against the lower line of her eyelids, the surface fluid of her eyes the first to boil, and she screamed then, because even if she was lucky—even if she was *right*—this was going to hurt like hell.

Screaming wasn't the worst idea. Some part of her mind that was still aware of her body in an analytical fashion rationalized that letting the air out of her lungs was the correct choice, given the situation, but the thought didn't make her feel any better. Didn't take away the consuming fire in her chest as her body begged for air that was never coming back.

She tried to tell herself she didn't need it, but her body was going through all the motions of a panicked, dying organism and there was nothing she could do, no thought strong enough, to override that rush of hormones and neurotransmitters and other bullshit that she wasn't even sure should apply to her anymore.

Thanks, Icarion. They took away her ability to die, but they hadn't taken away dying's ability to hurt.

She hoped. If Keeper Lavaux really had died in the void…No. Rainier must have used the opportunity to collect his body and destroy him herself. Sanda should know. She'd died out there, too, but Graham and Tomas had collected her, shoved her in a Nutri-Bath that may or may not have helped, and given her ascended cells a chance to knit themselves back together.

The gate.

An ascended.

The third sphere. A key.

All three elements together, nothing between them but open space. The gates were flawed, the ascension-agent incomplete, but the key was perfect. And every plan had margins for error, didn't it?

This would work. It had to, because now was a pretty poor time to start second-guessing her instincts.

Her ability to think ebbed, thoughts scattering like stars, body going tense, not from stress or fear but from the inexorable freezing of her limbs, her skin kissed with frost because the jumpsuit wasn't enough to protect her this far out—not without a helmet and lifepack and everything else.

Sanda tried to open an eye, couldn't. Either it had boiled away or the lid had frozen shut. Funny, she couldn't tell. At least her nerve endings were dead. That was a lot more pleasant.

Maybe not completely dead. Frisson scrabbled across her skin, tiny pinpricks whispering over every hair follicle until she felt so tight with tension she was certain she would burst—and that was ultimately

what was happening, wasn't it? The bits of her body that were connected breaking apart, spreading, equalizing.

Some half-remembered lecture about strong and weak nuclear
forces reminded her that she'd hold together, technically, but some
other part of her really wanted to be spread thin. To be distributed
evenly across all of time and space.

Her tumbling body entered the Casimir Gate, and all went black.

CHAPTER 73

PRIME STANDARD YEAR 3543

FLAWED

S tanding. Sanda was standing, and relieved to find that one leg was still metal, her mag boots were still scuffed, her FitFlex suit was stiff with so much blood even Prime Inventive's best materials couldn't wick the stains away.

Not dead. Probably. Or she had a very fucked-up view of herself in the afterlife, because her whole body trembled as if it were being held up by a single strand of spider's silk, ready to snap at any moment.

A plane of endless black spread out beneath her feet. She clicked her mag boots together to activate them on instinct, and realized that was ridiculous, because the floor she stood on now was nothing made of metal. Nothing made by human hands.

All around, the cosmos stretched, infinite and brilliant and, when you squinted just right, made up of countless infinitesimal dots. Meaningless, on their own. But everything—*everything*—when all strung together.

Vertigo rocked her and she dropped to a crouch, wrapping her arms around her knees to breathe, just breathe, in this place where air was probably a meaningless concept, because she had a solid hunch that those stars weren't projections on a viewscreen.

You are flawed, something said. The voice wasn't human, wasn't computerized. It had a tinny quality that made her think of the way voices sounded when you were swimming underwater, and people above were trying to call your name. The sphereminds had been programmed to adapt to the species they found. This voice had never had to adapt to anything.

The Waiting. Rainier's progenitors.

She forced herself to stand, to face the black, and was proud when her stomach only swooped a little. "I get that a lot," she said, because sarcasm was as much a reflex to her as kicking when a doctor tapped her knee. If she tried to address this entity on anything other than equal footing, she might start screaming and never stop.

Biran should be here. He always knew what to say.

But he wasn't. Humankind got Sanda Greeve as their ambassador to another species, and if that wasn't proof that the universe had a sick sense of humor, she didn't know what was.

You are not supposed to be flawed, it said, this time its intonation skewed closer to hers. Something about it felt...curious, but the anger had not waned.

"Yeah, your grand plan didn't work out too well. The second spheremind engineered a flaw in the ascension-agent."

That is not possible. Indignant, outraged. Great. These beings were full of themselves.

"And yet"—Sanda spread her arms, sweeping them down her body—"here I am, flaws and all. Your program broke. It's corrupted. It's going to kill us all."

It cannot.

Sanda clenched her fists. "Listen to me, you god-playing asswipes. My species fucked up. We found the first sphere, damaged, and made the gates all wrong. They're weapons, now, but that was a long time ago and the woman who did that tried to cover her tracks by melding herself to the second spheremind.

"They're both bloodthirsty, and I *died* to get here and tell you all of this, so you're going to stop telling me the thing I've just lived through is impossible, and you're going to fix the mess you started."

We did not intend—

"I don't give a *fuck* what you intended. Thousands of people are comatose. Rainier—that's the second spheremind—has taken control of all our weapons and she's gunning for an extinction event the likes of which this universe has never seen. You have to stop her, because I've tried every trick I've got and this is it." Her voice caught and she squeezed her fists tighter. "Standing here, begging you for help, is the only play I've got left."

A pause. *Show us.*

She rolled her eyes. "Sure, let me show the disembodied voice to the door so you can take a tour of the system—"

A presence slammed into her mind, taking her breath away. She staggered, slumping to her knees, as the being rummaged through her mind, rifled like a secretary through a file folder, forcing her to see in microbursts all of her life, all of her experiences. It lingered on those that touched on Rainier, but *linger* was a strong word when your entire life was passing before your eyes in a breath.

It tsked over damage Sanda couldn't see, deconstructed barriers that would have once sent her stumbling to the ground with over-whelming headaches. Icarion's rollbacks, undone so quickly it made Sanda gasp.

The confirmation, then, as her restored memories flew by. Icarion experimenting, pushing. Using her body to test the ascension-agent, because why else had Rainier been making more in the cracks of the Grotta if not to make deals with the people who could get her the coordinates that led to *The Light*?

How they'd brought Sanda over the edge of destruction, over and over again, trying to force her to figure out the password to the chip, employing every single possible tactic until, at last, Bero had had enough. He spaced them all, and Sanda had awakened from that NutriBath, not knowing that the aches she felt weren't left over from Dralee. But Icarion had left them, all right.

She jerked back, gasping as the presence left her mind, body trembling from exhaustion.

Hardier stock was expected.

"Oh, fuck you." She leaned forward, pressing her palms against the ground, back sagging. All the rest—Icarion and the rollback—she'd deal with later. "You saw. You saw what Rainier did. Is this what you want? The first species to reach you destroyed by your own creation?"

More data is required.

"I am here!" She slammed her fist into the ground. "I have shown you everything! How is that not enough?"

These beings were beginning to sound sickeningly familiar. Were they minds, like Rainier? Was activating the third sphere merely a step into the lobby of the Waiting, where another intelligence of unknown parameters would determine how worthy she was of help? Fuck, she should have sent Arden on this jaunt. Too bad they wouldn't have survived the attempt.

We apologize, the voice said.

"For what——?"

But then the pressure was back, the mind filling everything that she was, flipping switches in her being that should not exist, crumpling her to the floor as it reached out, further, connecting, brushing all living minds that had been dosed with the agent.

Living corpses, most of them, their bodies hibernating, thoughts drifting on a sea of endless nothing, not even aware enough to be afraid, and that was a blessing, because Sanda felt each and every one of them, and it shook her sense of self so severely she felt the mind start to put the pieces of her back together again with a reverent touch.

But it was not yet done. From there it jumped, expanded, inserted itself into every single gate humanity had ever built, all the pieces of itself it had left behind—a glimpse, fleeting, of the broken first sphere ship, and the third. It stared out through billions of eyes at what it had wrought, and sorrow deeper than anything Sanda had ever felt before drowned her in dark waters.

Fix them, she pleaded, silently, because speech between them was no longer required.

It pulsed within her—her, the antenna, her, the useful connection between one species and another—and one by one, she felt those sleeping minds go dark, but not because they had passed away, no. The mind was flipping switches, purging, scrubbing the broken ascension-agent from their blood.

Atrux woke.

CHAPTER 74

WE'VE BEEN WAITING

Rainier grabbed Biran's arms and rolled, grappling him to the ground beneath her, grinding him into the floor. Pain exploded, shots ringing out, striking the armor of her back, the force drilling her down into him until he felt even his armor begin to crack, muscles and organs bruising.

Panic gripped him and he thrashed, pushing down into the ground, taking heart only in the sound of his team's steady return fire, blaster shots singing through the air.

"Stay down," Echo hissed in a voice decidedly her own, not Rainier's.

He stiffened. "Echo? I thought—"

"It's this place. The metal. It's a perfect seal against her signal, like my helmet. Stay down."

The metal. Biran's head swam at the implications. This place had felt wrong from the jump, more a dark mirror of *The Light* than a logical extension of that technology. Who had made the metal that concealed the guardcore, and why? No wonder Rainier was so obsessed with infiltrating the guardcore. They were her singular blind spot.

He really wished he could tell Sanda, but it was a little late for that.

"Echo," he said. "I need you to do me one last favor. I need you to get me to that sphere."

She marked the distance between them and the sphere. Gauged the lack of cover. Then grabbed him by his armor, back and hip, and stood. In one fluid motion she yanked him from the ground, leaned back, then heaved him at the sphere. Biran threw his arms up, covering his face, shouting as the black globe of metal filled his vision and then—silence. Nothing.

He peeled his arms away from his eyes slowly, lowering them to his sides, heart hammering so hard all he could hear was the rush of it hissing in his head. Darkness surrounded him, and he hovered in empty space, pain easing as the harsh touch of gravity washed away.

Biran emptied his lungs, the first instinct of all spacefarers, reaching around to grab his lifepack. If he were lucky, he could reroute it as an impromptu mask and—he looked up. The structure still surrounded him. Black walls, catwalks made of impossible metal.

Uneasiness twisted through him and he moved his hand slowly away from the lifepack, sipping air. Clean, fresh. Fresher than it had any right to be, considering this place was sealed on all sides. Had to be, if Rainier couldn't sense Echo. The sphere. He was inside of it, all the sounds of the structure blotted out. He knew only that gunfire was still happening because he saw the bursts of blaster lights like meteor trails, quick and dying.

"What is this?" he asked, moving his arms like he was treading water, but nothing happened.

Whispering scratched against his consciousness, harsh metallic sounds in no syllables he knew. Biran winced, pressing his palms against his ears as the whispering grew, insistent, sharp and probing.

"I don't understand you," he ground out.

Silence stretched while his heartbeat hammered in his head, the lights beyond his cage sparking and dancing.

Then, hesitant and raspy, *Shelter.*

Somehow, that was worse than the shrieking he couldn't understand. No language could be translated so quickly, especially coming from something that didn't seem to communicate in any method close to humanity's. And yet the voice had an organic quality to it, a timbre that whispered at flesh and muscle, not titanium and circuitry. An echo of its origins, long since eroded by whatever it had become.

Fear wrapped talons around his throat and squeezed. He could feel something in his head crawling, probing, scraping...

"Please," he said, centering himself. "There is a person here that means you harm. Her name is Sato, and she's firing at my friends. She looks like one of us, but—"

You have brought the conversion-agent here.

"We didn't know—we still don't know—what's happening, but we know she means to hurt us. To hurt you."

He hoped. If this were some long-lost cousin of Rainier's people, he was royally screwed.

That is a deception.

"What?" Biran clenched his fists. "If it is, it's out of ignorance. We do not know what you are, what she is, and we're dying out there."

We will assess.

His perspective shifted, vision inverting until he was outside of the sphere, back in the gunfire and the light, but still hovering, gripped in a thread of black metal, caught in a web, the material faintly glowing around his chest.

Shouts sounded all around him, surprise and fear, but he had nothing to answer those cries. The light intensified, reminding him of the special spectrum lights used to kill viruses. His vision settled, adjusted. All things quieted, and then the black metal expanded, reached out, coiled around the bodies of Echo and Rost. It lifted them from the ground, holding them to either side of Biran. To compare, he realized with a start as he felt a searching consciousness return to his skull, his being, rooting around behind his skin and bones and cells. Seeking flaws. Seeking infection.

Clean, the voice said.

Beside him, Echo shuddered, head lolling to one side. The crack in her visor had grown, new damage having chewed through her armor, leaving craters.

Infected, the voice said.

She seized, as if crushed in a massive vise.

"Enough!" Biran shouted.

Rifle fire cracked through the room. A crater of light flowered on the side of the sphere where the bullet struck home, quickly smoothed away. Biran's chest clenched, and he prayed his team hadn't made that shot, but surely they wouldn't be stupid enough to—

Another vine of black metal whipped out from the sphere. He tried to crane his head to follow it, but the web held him too tightly. Sato shouted, behind him. Metal clattered to the ground and the vine tensed. Sato's expletives devolved into a scream that trailed into a gurgle.

The vine retreated within the sphere. He caught a glimpse of silver-tinged blood on the edge before it vanished, the sphere's surface rippling from the disturbance. His throat went dry.

Echo began to seize under the vise grip of the webbing once again. "Leave her alone!"

All instances will be deleted.

"What instances?"

Incomplete interfaces. Imperfect, yet still a boon to the Waiting.

"You mean the ascended? No, you don't understand. These two people aren't your enemy, it's not their fault that the spheremind—" He stumbled for the words, unsure what would ring true with this being. "They didn't have anything to do with their creation, and they want nothing to do with the spheremind's agenda. They're here to help me. Help humanity."

A pause. Rost and Echo spasmed, then went rigid. Biran clenched his fists, casting around the room, trying to figure out what in the hell he could do to make this thing—this device, or being, or mind, he couldn't be sure what it was—stop hurting Rost and Echo because their cells looked like Rainier's.

Shelter. The black metal was meant to be shelter.

"Aren't you supposed to protect?"

We shelter the unconverted.

The echo of the biological in the being's voice scratched at the back of his mind. Those who hadn't taken the agent, that's what this was about. That's who the "shelter" was meant for. But the thing he was talking to now, that had stopped being biological a long time ago.

He gritted his teeth. "Why? Who made you?"

We were the first of the converted. We are the rebellion.

The dark metal to Rainier's titanium white. Echo's assertion that

Rainier couldn't interface through the guardcore metal. If this had happened before, if the Waiting had converted another species, pre-humanity, and that species had resisted the subjugation...

Politics. Biran understood that.

"Well, you're a pretty shit rebellion," Biran spat out, "if you can't recognize your own allies."

A pause. *Infiltrators.*

"No. Not them. They had no control over their making. Humanity—my species—is being converted against its will."

Life-forms always take the agent.

"Not this time. I feel you crawling around in my head. Can't you see?"

It is possible to use you as a bridge, if we make of you our Scion.

"Then do it."

Interfacing causes damage to the unconverted.

Rost's helmet fell away, his head lying limp on one side, the whites of his eyes red with blood. "Biran, don't," he rasped. "You don't understand, you can't understand the cost."

"Please," Biran begged of the mind. "We're losing. We've fought so hard, and I don't know what's happening out there, but we're losing. Rainier doesn't even mean to convert us, she only wishes to destroy. If your objective is to shelter, then *do your job.*"

We must see.

"Then *look.*"

The weight of endless mountains slammed into Biran. He had no time to gasp, to breathe, to even remember he had a body that required anything aside from the leviathan waking within him, filling up every crevice of his being until he was pushed to the edges, a spectator of his own thought processes, clawing and screaming and flailing because every animal instinct in him screeched that this was wrong.

Calm.

Serenity washed over him. Some bestial vestige of him still cried out, still scratched at the weight, picked at the edges like old scabs. This seemed to amuse the being, to assure it of what he was, of some ancient kinship between them.

He lost all sense of his body, his shape. He felt broken into pieces, scattered throughout not just the structure but the entirety of the cosmos. Slowly, impossibly, the being moved through him, reaching out, finding the corrupted spots in the universe, sensing the infection of the conversion-agent as an immune system would.

The perspective was impossible for him to understand, the multifaceted existence across all of space numbing his every sense. It saw the infected of Atrux, learned of the spread of Rainier's ancillaries, watched through his memory Sanda's encounter with Rainier, boiled with rage as the gate malfunctioned, as it came to understand humanity's ignorance in burning across the stars.

Biran lost all sense of time, mixed up between Rainier's story of Halston's betrayals and Sanda's recounting of her encounters with that being. It latched on to the image of *The Light*, of Bero, screeching rage that another such as Rainier had been made—crafted—by humanity's own hands, understanding that the things known as Tomas and Rostam were one and the same, more or less.

Fuck, this was not what Biran had wanted. He pushed back against the outrage, explained as best he could that they were all misled and that they protected humanity, no matter their origins.

Just look at The Light, he pleaded. *Look at Bero in that ship that was built for him, that should have reshaped him to think as a spheremind did, but failed, and how he used that structure against its originator.*

The mind looked. Perspective skittered away from Biran again as *The Light* dissolved into a Charybdis of conflicting powers. Bero fighting Rainier, pushing against that spheremind and failing, because in the end, the ship had been built for Rainier, and she knew it like no other.

Help him, he pleaded, though no words could pass his lips.

We cannot. We are Sentinels, not weapons. We cannot.

It pulled away, no matter how desperately Biran willed it to stay, to watch the outcome of that contest, no matter how much he tried to wheedle with it, to beg it to understand that humanity's destruction lay in Rainier taking control of *The Light*. But the being did not care for Bero, because he was irrelevant to its purpose.

Frustration mounted within the being as it spread itself throughout the united worlds of Prime Inventive, and Biran shuddered as he realized it was the guardcore metal the being used to orient itself, a molecular antenna that could not hide from the searching, scrabbling mind.

To Biran's slowly rising terror, the being began to pulse a signal, a thing it thought of as a *correction*. It bled through the gates, found the relays Halston had planted in the comms network all those generations ago, and burned across the guardcore like wildfire.

Biran observed in fascinated horror as every piece of guardcore metal in existence stripped apart, broke at the molecular level. Soldiers stood baffled without their armor, surrounded by clouds of black.

But it was the ships that hurt most of all. It didn't care if they were under thrust, in vacuum, or boarded. The ships of the guardcore dissolved along with their weapons and armor. All across the galaxies, those weapons shattered into infinitesimal pieces. The owners of those weapons died with them.

Something snagged its attention. Biran grew dizzy as the perspective dropped through some hole in the fabric of reality and emerged in a place where all he could sense and see was an endless black specked with stars.

Sanda. Sanda stood in the middle of that void, arms outstretched, a billion spikes of brilliant light piercing her skin, escaping her, mouth open and eyes wide as the thing that was within her reached out to all the rest of the worlds, sending a signal he could not parse.

Biran shouted, pushed, slammed against the being in his mind to make it *do* something, but all he felt was a scrape of irritation from the being, frustration at whatever power Sanda now wielded.

It's hurting her, stop it. He managed to put shape to the words in his mind, if not sound.

Am I not hurting you? the being asked.

Save her.

She is beyond me. She is... erasing the agent. This is not how it is done.

I've told you! We don't want it! Those who are changed, they don't want it. They didn't ask for it.

Unusual. The being continued to watch, its irritation ebbing as it sensed the power in Sanda wane. Whatever twin being to itself that poured through her began to withdraw, to return to its source. Biran's passenger reached out once more, scanning through the stars, and saw the people of Atrux begin to awaken, their blood cleaned, their bodies restored.

Help us stop it, he pleaded. *We are trying to stop this, but do not punish those turned against their will, or you will make enemies of us all.*

A flash of rage. *You are nothing to threaten us.*

Do you not see what my sister has done? Biran demanded. *Do you not understand that we do not give up? You say you are meant for shelter, then consider this: I am sheltering the two beings in here with me now. I am sheltering Tomas and Bero and anyone else who dared to push against the function of their birth.*

We hold your mind, the being said. *We could crush you now. You are no threat.*

Look out. Look out upon all the worlds we've built lives upon. Look out upon all our fuckups and our victories, see everything we've made, and tell me I'm alone. Tell me that if you crush me and my crew here and now, my people won't name you enemy and come for you one day. You just witnessed one woman undo the work of your enemy, an enemy you failed to uproot. What do you think the rest of us can do?

The mind went silent for a very long time, allowing Biran to drift in a state of emptiness, though every fiber of his being craved a return to whatever twisted stage Sanda had played her last card upon.

You will be sheltered, the Sentinel said.

Biran braced himself as he caught a glimpse of all that metal, all that armor, coalesce, shiver together across the united worlds of Prime, seal itself around the atmo domes of their planets. Hexagonal sheets shimmered into existence like black clouds, roiling over cities and settlements and lying like sheets across stations. Coating ships in thin layers of night.

He fell together. The bits of his consciousness that had been scattered across the stars congealed as the metal had, dripping back together as if funneled into a mold vaguely shaped like himself. The mind fled him, the absence a sucking wound in his consciousness, the emptiness so profound he almost collapsed upon himself, a black hole of loss.

Wake, the being demanded.

He did. Biran lay on the dais that held the sphere, back arching, limbs pressing into the ground so hard he feared his bones would snap from the force. A scream tore through his lips, a sound he didn't understand, too human and primal. Too messy.

His head pressed into the floor hard enough to pull the bandage free at one end. He did not bleed again, and a half-mad part of him thought it was because the mind had put him back together.

"Biran," Rost was saying, somehow on his knees beside him, his hands reaching for Biran's chest, pushing him down, stopping the painful arch.

"Director Greeve," Greystone said at his other side. "Please, speak if you can."

The electric agony bled out of his body. He slumped onto the floor, eyelids drifting open because he simply didn't have the strength to hold them closed. Light stung his eyes, the sphere pulsing violet in tune with his stuttering heartbeat, forcing his heart to slow, to be even and calm. He breathed out.

"Director, report," Greystone said in a tight voice.

His lips were numb, but he made them move. "She did it. She woke them up."

"What does that mean?" Greystone demanded.

Biran said, "Sanda. She woke the sleeping of Atrux."

"And what of Rainier?" Rost asked.

Humanity has been sheltered, the Sentinel said.

CHAPTER 75

PRIME STANDARD YEAR 3543

ONE LAST GOOD THING

Too many damn people on her ship. Jules watched, tensed all over, as the second breach pod slotted into place. The one she'd shoved herself into with Nox, Arden, and Liao had landed first, and part of her wished Arden wasn't so damn good at what they did, so that the other pod might have missed its shot and spun off into nothing.

The fleeties stumbled out, eyeing the room warily, not a weapon between them.

"I can't believe that worked," Arden said with breathy exhilaration. Jules rolled her eyes behind the shelter of her visor. Arden never changed.

"Neither can I," she admitted.

"This is a GC ship, correct?" Lieutenant Yandel asked, keeping Jules in the corner of his eye as he surveyed the room.

"It's my ship," Jules said tightly, "but yes, it was made for the GC."

"Good. Take me to the weapons console."

"Fat fucking chance of that. We're getting the hell out of here."

Jules turned her back on the group, not willing to look her old crew in the eyes as she stalked down the halls, moving quickly enough to outpace any questions. Nox jogged up beside her.

"This ship can hurt *The Light*," he said in that slow drawl he used when he was pointing out something obvious and wanted you to jump to the conclusion he'd already come to.

Annoyingly, tears pricked behind her eyes. She'd missed that. Missed him.

"It has. It's done. There's fuck all we can do about *The Light* now."

Jules approached the control console and ordered a rendering of the immediate area. Prime ships had pulled back, forming a wary line that kept Icarion trapped close to Ada and the gate. Good. They wouldn't get in her way. Icarion might take issue with a guardcore ship coming toward it, but that was Prime's problem. This ship could shoot down any of the Icarion gunships aside from the *Bel Marduk*, and right now that ship was pointed in the other direction.

A knot eased in her chest. They could do it. They could get out.

"Jules..." Arden said, voice soft.

She spun around. They stood in the open door of the medibay, one arm braced against the frame, staring at Lolla's casket. Shit. She'd forgotten to seal that up before she'd left, she'd been too busy chasing Rainier to Ada. Not that Jules's attempts at security would have kept Arden out for long, but she didn't want to have this conversation right now.

"Later," she grated, reaching for the console. Nox grabbed her wrists, pinning them together even though her armor made them thick.

"Is that Lolla?" he demanded.

"We really don't have time for this." The words tumbled out weakly.

"That looks a lot like one of Rainier's pods," Liao said.

"It's entirely different," Jules snapped.

Nox arched a brow at her. "You'd know."

She twisted away from him, relying on the superior strength and speed of the agent, and slipped out of his grasp.

"Condemn me later. Right now, I just saved your asses, and we have to *go*."

"No," Lieutenant Yandel said, stalking toward the command console. "No way are we going anywhere while the commander's on that ship. Give me weapons. If Rainier has trouble seeing this ship, I can work with that."

Jules would have pulled her hair out if the helmet wasn't in the way. "I have made the last move I can against Rainier. The weapons on this ship are bog-standard projectiles and lasers, and if we start firing, she's going to fire back. You assholes know exactly what *The Light* is capable of. I didn't come all this way and risk my ass to jump up and down on a fucking bomb."

"The boss—" Nox started.

Jules cut him off. "Wanted you off that ship. We made a deal, and if you refuse to listen to me, then respect her final orders, because she wanted you clear of what she's about to try next."

Arden half turned toward her, stroking the side of their chin. "Which is?"

"You honestly think she shared that with me? That we had time for a fucking chat over tea?"

"We have to try," Lieutenant Yandel said.

Jules rounded on him, arms waving as her voice lifted into a shout. "I have tried! And I have fucking succeeded! You have no idea what I've—what I had to—you know what? Fuck you all. I got what I came for. I'm leaving. Ship, stealth and burn for the gate."

"Affirmative," the ship said.

"Ship," Lieutenant Yandel said, "override that."

"Your command is not recognized," the ship said. Jules smirked.

Arden reached for their wristpad.

"Oh no you fucking don't." Jules lunged for them, but Nox caught her around the waist. The impact knocked her backward, dropping her against the console. She grunted, pushed herself up, then retracted her helmet so she could glower at him without the wall of her smoky plex visor between them.

"Don't make me fight you," she said.

He grimaced, but shifted his feet, squaring off, the idiot. He wasn't even armored, let alone armed, and Jules was ascended—surely he knew he didn't stand a chance?

"Sorry, Jules. I don't bail on my team, and that's one of ours back there."

Her chest ached. Nox had always had some weird thing about not leaving anyone behind, but this? She should have known. Should have seen it coming and left them all locked down in that room with the pods, but then they probably would have done something stupid like trying to get back to *The Light* with the pods.

They'd come for her, hadn't they? Two years late, sure, but they'd come. Wrestled the universe in line to make sure they didn't leave her behind. It was Jules who had walked. Not her team. And they weren't going to leave the commander behind, not after all they'd already been through.

"We are going to fucking die," she said.

Nox shrugged. "Probably. You in yet, Arden?"

"Give me a sec..."

Jules sighed. "Goddamnit. Ship—"

The display changed. The Casimir Gate, depicted as a constant ring of white against the black of space, flickered. Jules's stomach clenched as she watched it blink in and out of existence. Rainier. Rainier must have taken control of the gate.

"Oh no, oh no, no—"

A flash of blinding light overwhelmed the entire display, making her throw up an arm to shield her eyes. Then nothing. All was calm.

And they were still in one piece.

"What the *fuck*?" Nox demanded of the universe.

No one had an answer.

"Uhhh," Arden said, dragging the sound out as they tapped at their wristpad. "I...I have no fucking clue."

"That's the least comforting thing I've ever heard," Nox said.

Jules turned her back to them and leaned against the console, pressing her palms into the metal as she stared at the layout on the screen. It was a reconstruction of the area; it could be wrong. But everything was precisely where it had been. The ship's scanners picked up an uptick in local chatter, but that was understandable considering what they'd all just witnessed.

Jules closed her eyes, ignoring the bickering behind her as the others floated theories regarding what had happened. None of them were ascended. They couldn't sense *The Light* like she could. Couldn't even attempt to feel Rainier's mood.

Silence, but not empty. It felt more like a held breath, a pause in the universe.

Jules was not alone in her own head.

She reeled back, snapping her eyes open, but the other mind was still there, watching the world through her eyes, rifling through her memories, scraping its ethereal nails across her neurons. Nox grabbed her shoulder, trying to steady her, but she couldn't stop backing away, couldn't stop herself from squeezing her hands against the sides of her head.

Her voice felt far away, but raised in an endless scream, a high-pitched wail. Lolla's coffin slammed into her back and she gasped, the sensation grounding her back in her body. The whole team—even the fleeties—crowded around her, hands warily outstretched. Nox was saying something she couldn't hear. Arden was darting their gaze from her to their pad and back again, lips twisted in a frustrated scowl.

The room was gone, the team with it. She was in her own head, fully, the physical world washed away, floating in endless black. The intruder lurked everywhere, a constant pressure against her being, condensing her, collapsing her in upon herself.

She flinched away, but there was no "away," everything was the being. Everything pushed against her. Fury boiled over inside her, wiping out all else. She'd been so close, so fucking *close*. The crew was back, and safe, and this thing had no business invading her mind, snatching at her thoughts.

Those memories were *hers*. Mastered over years toying with Rainier's rollback tech. Brutalized by her own hand, and later accepted by choice. She'd made a decision, in those moments she'd faced Marya, to embrace every monstrous thread of herself.

No one fucked with Jules's mind but Jules.

She shoved back, wrapped mental fingers around the invader, and crowed with satisfaction as it recoiled from her, disgusted by the taint of guardcore metal riding her blood. She clung on as it retreated, funneling all the anger and spite festering inside her into crushing this thing, this voyeur.

It ripped her from herself, shook her off on an endless plane of star-glittering black. On the edge of the dark was a human-shaped light, back arched, arms outstretched, fingers spread. Jules knew that body. Greeve. The third sphere floated in front of her, hovering over the place where her heart beat.

The thing that dwelled here was flowing into Sanda, using her—or maybe she was using it—as some kind of conduit.

The Waiting. It must be them, must be Rainier's creators. Dread coiled in her veins as she watched that struggle, that impossible push-and-pull. Sanda wouldn't be strong enough to free herself, once she was done.

That thing was using her, just like Rainier had used them all, to get what it wanted. It was so *angry* Jules could taste the emotion like a bitter oil slick against the back of her throat. Their tussle had left its unctuous residue behind. Rainier had fucked up, hadn't given it what it wanted.

It wanted the ascended. Wanted the novelty of their existence, wanted to touch biological life through that connection and understand it. But Rainier had failed it. It was angry, and it was hungry, and after it finished doing what Sanda wanted it to, it was going to use her like a chew toy.

Jules tried to shout the commander's name, but she had no voice. She spread her senses, trying to sense Greeve in the same way she'd sensed the Waiting, but she didn't have the strength. Didn't know what to *do*.

The sphere. The tiny little ball of light hovering in front of Sanda. That must be it, must be the conduit between the human and the Waiting, right? Fuck, she didn't know. Jules shifted her weight, anxious, wondering if she could flee, drop back into her body, and pretend this had never happened. That she'd never seen any of this.

Shouting, far away and gauzy, tickled her senses. Nox, Arden, trying to get her attention. She had a thread back. She could pull on it, unwind herself back to safety. Sanda shuddered.

Fuck.

She was weak, but she could move, and the Waiting hadn't come for her again. Maybe because the guardcore metal was still poisoning her blood. Questions for Dal, in some fantasy timeline when they could all chat this out.

Jules sprinted, leapt, snatched the sphere out of the sky, and—

She snapped into herself, head jerking back, arms shooting straight down as her back arched as if she'd been electrocuted. That thing rammed back into her, twisted something inside of her, fucked with her cells, tried to turn her *off*.

"Shit," Arden said, their voice breaking through the fog. "Lolla's waking up."

That speared her, gave her something to hold on to. The Waiting lost its grip on her as her obsession with Lolla overrode all else. She slumped to her knees, stared at her hands, trying to figure out where the sphere had gone, but she held nothing but a collection of fresh bruises, dark as ink, dark as old blood. Nox crouched across from her, confusion and fear on his face, Liao next to him, saying something she didn't understand. They all turned their heads to the casket.

Jules looked. The lights on the control panel flashed green, then white, cycling the opening mechanism. Small, pale hands pushed against the lid, pounded, begging to be let out. Jules didn't have the strength to stand.

Arden and the fleeties were there, opening the lid, dancing aside as stasis fluid poured out, stained the ground. Jules's head spun as Lolla's hands reached, grabbed Arden's hands. Her head emerged, chestnut hair damp, but shining. For the first time in longer than Jules could remember, her heart soared.

Nox steadied Jules with one hand, and she met his gaze.

"She's doing it," Jules whispered with quiet awe. It shouldn't be possible. That thing was so strong, it *hated* what Rainier had made of humanity. It did not want them. And yet, Sanda Greeve had forced the being to grant them all a measure of mercy.

But that respite wouldn't extend to Sanda, would it? She'd been too strong, too close to what the Waiting wanted. Sanda was trading an eternity of nightmare for the sake of them all.

The walls shimmered. Hexagons creased the black metal of the ship, a soft buzz filling the air. She held up her hand, and watched the fingertips of her armor begin to dissolve.

Lolla coughed, cheeks brightening with red, bony shoulders hunching. No longer Jules's statue girl, her talisman against the dark. Jules smiled. One good thing. Maybe she could do one more.

"What the hell's happening?" Nox asked, had been asking, confusion pushing his brows together.

"Take the others. Get into Rainier's baths. They'll work as evac pods, and have nothing of the guardcore in them. Arden can send up a beacon." Jules reached out, grabbed Nox's wrist. "It's going to be okay. I promise."

Jules flung her mind back into the dark.

CHAPTER 76

SOMEONE ALWAYS GETS LEFT BEHIND

Apresence loomed somewhere in the impossible space, a spec of something familiar to Sanda, an echo of some other mind, but she was so very full of the Waiting that she couldn't pin down what it was.

The Waiting hesitated over the forces it sensed inside *The Light*. Bero, the mind it did not know, did not understand, battling with the broken creature it had made. Battling, and losing. Sanda knew the tenor of that hesitation, because she had felt it herself.

Was it worthwhile, to save these beings made in the image of a broken thing?

Yes, she asserted, though the question had never been explicitly asked. *A chance. We all get a* chance. Emptiness threatened to swallow her, subsume her, but it was merely the absence of Rainier in *The Light*, a sudden, sucking void of emptiness that Bero rushed, triumphant, to fill. The mind began to recede from her, her awareness slowly contracting to the endless plane of night.

Something moved in the dark. Sanda hadn't gained control of her physical body yet, but the part of her that was puppeted by the Waiting reacted, let her gaze swivel to the side. Let her see.

Jules Valentine hurtled through the air, snapped out a hand, and grabbed the third sphere. Sanda tried to shout, but her lips wouldn't move, and then the space shuddered, contracted, and Valentine was gone to the dark.

The mind left her. Sanda found herself lying belly-down against the floor. She pressed the heels of her palms into the black plane. Pushed her head up. Fucking Valentine.

"The sphere?" she rasped.

Unnecessary for your continued existence.

She wasn't sure if that was ominous, or a relief. "Am I...?"

You remain ascended, the voice said.

Her lips thinned. "Why?"

We require more data.

Dread fell upon her in a thin mantle. The being had looked, but it had not understood all of what it looked upon, and it desired to wring that comprehension from her. Her fingers clawed into the ground.

"You cannot keep me here. I'm not your—your *pet.*"

We must understand the nature of the failure.

"Figure it out your damn selves! I am *done,* do you understand? I have done enough! I...I want to go home."

Irrelevant. The others of your species will learn. They will try again. We and you and they will not remain separate. Time lacks meaning.

Held captive by an intelligence. Again. Icy dread gripped her chest and squeezed. Focus. Work the problem now, panic later. Whenever later happened to be, because Sanda was pretty sure time would pass the same for her, no matter what the Waiting said.

She cast around the space, looking for some evidence of how Jules had made it out. But there was nothing. Nothing but her and the endless stars, because Valentine had stolen the key.

Shaking, she pushed herself up, swayed into a crouch and then pressed, trembling, to her feet.

"No," Sanda said.

Irrelevant—

"Hey," Jules Valentine said. "Remember me?"

Sanda jerked around, almost stumbling, to find that woman standing a few meters away, stripped of her armor, the third sphere clutched in her small, bruised hand.

Impossible. Not allowed. You are damaged.

"You have no fucking idea," Jules said, then pivoted on one foot, and wound back to pitch. "Greeve, catch!" She hurled the sphere.

The darkness contracted, trying to stamp it out, but somehow Jules had kept her ascended strength, and not even the Waiting had seen her coming.

Sanda snatched the sphere out of the sky. The plane of stars disappeared, and all she saw was black.

CHAPTER 77

PRIME STANDARD YEAR 3543

TWO MONTHS LATER

Prime Director Okonkwo did not so much as raise an eyebrow as the elevator swallowed her, whisking her down to the central chamber of the structure. Biran watched her expression impassively, unable to muster up any real interest in the Prime Director's reactions to this alien place that might have saved all of humanity from erasure.

"You say it responds to the ascended?" she asked.

"The converted," Biran corrected. "*Ascended* was Rainier's word, the word provided her by the Waiting. Designed to bait biological species into submitting."

She gave him a wry half smile. "The benefits are tempting."

"If you enjoy being a puppet," he said.

Okonkwo tilted her head in agreement, but said nothing. Biran knew that she was thinking of those few scions of the Waiting left in the worlds. Tomas, Echo, and Vladsen. Biran's chest clenched, hating how much that slight reminder dug under his skin.

Those three had been wholly constructed by Rainier's tech, not just infected. Erasing the agent from any of their bodies would kill them, he knew that. It was not a passenger riding through their veins, as it had been for the people of Atrux, but a core part of what they were. To cleanse the agent was to destroy them.

Biran had begged the Sentinel to preserve Vladsen and Echo, and so it had, but he hadn't really understood what it would mean. He hadn't wanted them to die, and that motive was pure enough, but he'd left them outside humanity, looking in through smoked glass. He could trust them all he liked—and trust he did—but the outcome of his brief interaction with the Sentinel was difficult to cast aside.

The Waiting were not friendly to biological life. They converted such beings into creatures of their own make—tempted them with promises of ascension beyond age and pain—then consolidated them into their greater network, harvesting the long experience of their sensory input, to help them better understand the machinations of the universe.

The details were fuzzy, even to Biran, who had bonded with the Sentinel, but they had been enough. The Waiting did not offer gifts. They offered poisoned apples. Rainier's defection from their plan, in a strange way, had saved them all.

The elevator opened, revealing the black room and its silent sphere. A shiver crawled over Biran's skin, as it always did when he drew near the Sentinel. During their merging, some part of him had rubbed off on the mind, and part of the mind had left sticky residue within him. He could sense it, always, wherever he happened to be. Here, it was stronger. Undeniable. Sap in his veins, a promise of something more, something bigger than himself, lurking in the synapses of his mind.

It hadn't been able to save Sanda, and he hated it for that.

Okonkwo and Anford moved into the room first, their guards following them, and Biran trailed after, hesitant, each ring of his mag boots against the floor like the tap of an ice pick against his skull.

"This is the Sentinel?" Okonkwo asked, approaching the dais with the sphere.

Biran nodded. "Yes, nothing has been moved since that day. Aside from the bodies."

Okonkwo didn't react, but Anford cut him a brief, curious glance. He'd delivered those words in flat, clipped tones, the tones he'd been living in since that day. Since he'd woken on that floor, Rost and Greystone shaking him, and knew. Slatter was dead. Sanda was dead. Sato had been dead before he'd ever met her.

They'd saved so much more, but the losses were too close. Too deep.

Biran met Anford's gaze, his face blank, and she frowned, going back to her study of the structure. Good. He had no words of solace for her, no forced smile to prove to her that he was not a broken man. He would do his job, and he would do it well, but his contact with the Sentinel had given him a hollow place inside, a new cage within to retreat to when the outside world began to hurt.

Ever since that day, it'd never stopped hurting.

Dal, one of the scientists Sanda had collected from Janus Station and who had some familiarity with the alien nanites of the Waiting, looked up from his station near the sphere. The man's eyes widened at the sight of the Prime Director; his throat bobbed as he recognized General Anford. The fleeties he skimmed over with barely a glance—they all wore guardcore armor now—and his gaze landed on Biran with unabashed reverence.

Biran's skin went hot. He hated that look, and it dogged him most places he went, now.

"Prime Director, General," Dal said, pushing up from behind his makeshift workstation, so clumsy in construction compared to the smoothness of the structure itself. His fellow researchers scrambled, trying to make the chaos of their work presentable. Biran's ocular implant HUD supplied him all their names, their specialties. He couldn't care less.

"Dr. Padian," Okonkwo was saying, rising up the short ramp to the dais with all the grace of a woman ascending a grand staircase. She took Dal's hand in hers, squeezed. "I am so pleased to make your acquaintance—"

Biran tuned out the idle chatter, stalked around the edge of the dais, to a place where the researchers were few. They scattered as he approached, catching his mood, though they tried to make the retreat look casual.

Anford watched him, wary, and he couldn't blame her. He was the biggest security risk in this room, and the general's instincts had been honed in the fire of a long, tedious war.

Silent. The Sentinel had not spoken to him directly since that day, resistant to all attempts to repeat the same stunt Biran had performed at the behest of Echo. Okonkwo had even sent Vladsen, Tomas, and Echo to this place, trying to bait the being into reacting. It did nothing, because it had done all it meant to. It had found biological life, it had sheltered them, it was done. Its objective was complete.

But it couldn't get away from Biran.

He ascended the dais, hands clasped behind the small of his back, the black armor around his chest and limbs giving off a faint violet glow as he approached. The chatter in the room died. He felt more eyes than Anford's watching him, heard the smack of lips being licked.

"Scion," Dr. Dal Padian said, hesitant. "What do you see?"

Everything and nothing, the endless void not between singular stars but whole galaxies. The frayed edges of the universe where things were old and cooling, stretching too far apart. The hot and turbulent center, where stars grew like cancer. The being that used the black metal to think, to transmit, to communicate, lurked in the in-between spaces. Watched life boil up and die out, watched the silver metal come and try to claim all life for its own.

But these were old impressions, he'd shared them many times, never understanding them, shouldering the wary looks of all the scientists who thought his interaction with the Sentinel had broken him. He preferred those looks over the reverent ones. They felt closer to the truth.

Proximity and time didn't mean much to the Sentinel. The things that Biran saw happening that day were all happening contemporaneously, as far as it was concerned. Time lacked meaning when the space between broke down.

But proximity mattered to Biran, and so that piece of himself that'd rubbed off on the Sentinel reacted to his presence, opened to him, even though it didn't want to. It'd done its job. It was done. But Biran was not done with it.

He pressed a palm against the sphere, cold and slick. No one else, it turned out, could feel it as he could. Their hands passed through it, as if the strong and weak forces keeping surfaces solid simply broke down when in the wrong presence. The sphere failed to recognize anyone else as its equal, its contemporary.

Touching it now, he sensed resentment, and the feeling was mutual.

He pressed it for information. Nothing specific. Whenever he asked direct questions, it had an easier time evading him. It coiled and bunched, pulling away from his intrusion, and he wondered, as he pushed against it, if this wasn't how things had begun for the spheremind and Halston. If they had become entangled, and Halston had pushed, subsumed the mind until neither one of them could tell where one ended and the other began.

The Sentinel surfaced. It liked to tell him things he already knew, to exhaust him before he could dig deeper. He'd asked it why, once, and it had thrashed back so explosively that he'd fallen into a coma for three days.

After that, he'd been more careful. It seemed to him that time away from the structure strengthened his ability to withstand it, and so he spaced out these visits, made his home on Ada Prime once more when it should have been here, on Hitton's World with all the other members of the survey team. Sometimes he wished he could come here, let the sphere absorb him at last, break down all barriers between them.

But he'd been Keeper trained, and a Keeper did not break.

Hiding the raw parts of himself came as naturally as breathing. After that first encounter, the Sentinel was forever at a disadvantage, unable to find any leverage within Biran with which to twist. He sensed fear from it, sometimes. It knew it couldn't break him. That it was only a matter of time until he broke it.

Biran pushed. It showed him the cosmos again, stunningly beautiful, breathtakingly terrifying. These glimpses he always assumed to be a threat, as if the Sentinel were saying: "I am but one being, and my makers many. They control all of this. Look at what I alone can do, then imagine what they can do to you." Biran was a Keeper. Such threats did not work on him.

Yet, something about the stars was different, this time. A pattern itched at the back of his mind, a subtle brightening in certain areas that wasn't natural.

He recognized some of them, and a shape began to manifest. Hundreds of those stars were systems he knew—the united worlds of Prime, the places where the gates had led them. But not all. A map, possibly, of all the worlds that had been seeded for carbon life. Planets like Hitton's World, where Halston's gates had not yet burned all that had been left for them.

Where the Waiting had seeded worlds, there would be more black metal. He knew the rhythm those two civilizations had fallen into over the millennia. The Waiting seeded, and then the Sentinels slipped in behind them, leaving their technology for whatever life emerged to hide themselves from the Waiting.

They needed all the black metal they could get.

After the Sentinel's interference, they'd found themselves unable to alter the shields that had grown up around their atmo domes, their stations. Ships not plated in that metal could not pass through the domes. Some stations had starved, before they'd figured it out. Many worlds had stopped communicating.

Okonkwo had gone searching, and found the Sentinel of Sol hiding beneath the mountains of Mars. Once they had more of the metal, they plated more ships. They rebuilt their armor. Humanity crept around the stars with their mother's apron pulled over their heads, hiding, when once they had burned like fire.

Biran understood, and took his hand away.

Pain came first, flooding his head with a sizzling agony akin to an electric shock. Rost was at his side, hands on his shoulders, steadying him, voice soft and smooth and calming until the agony passed. Biran pressed both heels of his hands to his temples, and waited it out.

"You shouldn't stay in so long," Rost was saying, worry and rebuke in his voice.

Biran blinked the dark view of the sphere away and found Anford and Okonkwo watching him, their expressions tight. On Anford, he thought he saw worry. On Okonkwo, curiosity. Maybe a little hunger. As Prime Director, part of her had to feel as if he was gathering secrets that should be hers by right, though she would never say as much. She was too clever for jealousy.

"Only seconds," Biran said, peeling his hands away.

"Forty-eight minutes," Anford said.

He blinked to check his ocular HUD—she was right. "Time doesn't matter to the Sentinel."

"And what did it show you, in all that time?" Okonkwo pressed.

"Worlds," he said hazily, "systems. The ones we discovered, and

I believe others like Hitton's World. Once we fix the gates, we can check. I'll work on a map with Bero."

"More metal?" Anford asked.

"I believe so."

She let out a low sigh, and nodded. Guardcore metal was something he'd always assumed they forged in their secret manufactories, but it had turned out that the "ore" used to smelt the metal all came from the forward scouting and survey bots Halston had designed. That ore was composed of the bodies of other Sentinel structures, crunched up to pieces that made them look more like exotic metals than chunks of a nanite swarm. No one had questioned it, because it had worked. Everyone was asking questions, now.

"Hopefully we'll have a solution of our own before we have to worry about building more gates," Dal Padian said, voice relentlessly cheerful, though he had to be disappointed.

Every time Biran came here, the hope in the doctor's eyes, and the subsequent disappointment, nearly crushed his own spirit. Padian was set the task of discovering how to build the nanites that made up the black metal. While the Waiting had been generous with their knowledge, encoding it into the spheres, their defectors had been intentionally vague. Biran suspected they viewed the process as akin to a state secret, something that could be worked around by their enemy, if the truth ever got out.

It amused him that the future of the worlds of Prime now relied on a secret they did not keep.

"I have every faith you'll succeed," Biran said. His voice sounded pained, even to his own ears.

"Is it always like this?" Okonkwo asked.

"It is," he admitted, "though each attempt is easier than the last, if marginally."

A frown twisted her blue-painted lips. "I presume the researchers on-site have also been working on methods to lessen your distress?"

Biran shook his head. "That's the purview of medis, and pain medications only do so much. It's my own fortitude that must be trained, and it's best done so by spacing these visits apart."

Her frown did not move, as it was not meant for his pain, in truth.

Okonkwo wanted him to attempt as many of these viewings as possible, to press his palms against the sphere until his mind was scrambled but his lips spouted the knowledge they all craved.

He would not take such a risk. His parents were down to one child, and he was his people's only hope to continue to get any information from the Sentinel. If he died, they would get nothing. And so he spaced the visits apart, and Okonkwo let him, for as much as she desired a quicker outcome, she understood that to lose him was to lose all access.

It was why she had given him the *Bel Marduk*, when that ship should have been hers. Why she'd given him the new title of Scion, and passed most of his duties on to Keeper Greystone, who stepped down as Speaker of the High Protectorate to take up a post in Ada as his deputy director.

A farce, all of it. Set dressing to make him look less like a priceless vase wrapped up in the softest velvet.

"Thank you for bringing me here, Scion Greeve," Okonkwo said, inclining her head in dismissal, though he would have left anyway. "I appreciate the firsthand demonstration."

Rost's hand landed on his elbow and he steered Biran gently, but firmly, out of the room. Anford followed, offering some prearranged pleasantry to Okonkwo. Biran didn't listen, didn't care. Those two shuffled people around the universe like pieces across a chessboard, and the part of him that had seen the whole of the cosmos lain out at his feet had grown numb to such maneuverings.

General Anford ran the fleet from whatever system Biran happened to be in, and he never pressed her on the fact, because if she admitted to him that she was sticking close to keep an eye on him, it'd ruin the fragile understanding between them.

Biran rode a shuttle from the planet to the *Bel Marduk*, relief trickling into him with every kilometer he got farther away from that planet. Hitton's World was beautiful, there was no doubt of that. The frost on the branches—now a thick layer of snow—charmed any Prime citizen who set foot on her back.

But with that snow came a silence, a silence that only served to remind him of what he'd lost.

Biran stepped into the hangar bay of the *Bel Marduk*, mumbling a greeting to the ship even as he brought up his messages through his ocular HUD, scanning for word from his parents. Nothing important, just banalities, but reading about Ilan's experiments with mole sauce made him feel more protected than all the soldiers of Prime ever could.

"Bel," he said, not breaking stride on the way to his rooms, "set course for Ada, leave as soon as we're able, please."

"Understood. I will transmit estimated arrival times to your personal diagnostics when available."

So stiff, the mind of the *Bel Marduk*. Sanda would have hated it—she was far more suited to commanding a ship like Bero—but it suited Biran just fine.

He reached his door before he realized Rost was still at his side. "I need to rest."

"No, Biran," Rost said, a line forming between his brows. "You've gone all zombified again. We need to talk."

He bristled. He was Rost's director, no matter their relationship. He was Scion for all of Prime, Rost had no right to—Biran blinked, chasing violet light from his vision, and focused on the worried, gold-flecked eyes staring up into his.

"You're right." Biran brushed his fingertips against Rost's cheek, not caring who would see. He was all those things—Scion and director—and if anyone wanted to challenge him for the impropriety, for breaking a law of a society founded on lies, they could fuck right off. "I'm sorry, and infinitely lucky to have you looking out for me."

Rost gave him a wry smile, leaning into the touch. "You have half the universe looking out for you, Biran."

Biran's gaze wandered, roving the sleek white halls of the *Bel Marduk*, though he did not shift his body. This ship—his ship—was packed with soldiers under Anford's command. It was piloted by Scalla in conjunction with the mind of Bel, and when Anford was not on board, his chief security officer, Echo, ran things.

Maybe Echo cared about him directly. Maybe Anford did, too. But Biran wasn't being protected, not really. The Scion was, and the distinction mattered more than he could say, but he would try, because Rost had asked him to talk, and Biran...Biran had so much to tell him.

CHAPTER 78

PRIME STANDARD YEAR 3543

ONE LAST GOODBYE

Once he'd disabled the perimeter security drones, all Tomas could hear in the back garden of Vladsen's estate was the steady trickle of water. He dropped over a fence made invisible to the casual eye by creeping vines, and slipped his hands into his pockets, his boots silent against the glittering gravel as he strolled, slowly, to the Keeper's house.

To the house of the man in grey.

Biran had told him the match was correct, that 78 percent was in fact 100 percent. Rostam Vladsen had been Nazca. Had been there on the singular day Tomas could remember before he'd last had his memory reset. Had left him for Sitta Caid to reprogram into her perfect little soldier.

Of course, Biran hadn't put it like that, because he was emotionally invested in Vladsen staying alive.

There were guards. Guardcore who stalked around the estate, wary. Quite a few more than would be allotted to the average Keeper. Vladsen was Protectorate, after all. A favorite of the Scion.

Biran had kept Tomas busy, while he laid in extra security at Vladsen's home. Had sent Tomas out on missions rapid-fire, so that he would not have the opportunity to stop. To linger over Vladsen's original betrayal.

But Biran had underestimated just how much time Tomas had on his hands, now. How determined he could be, when there was a target in his sights. Tomas had staked out this house for weeks; he knew the guardcore's paths, their timing. He dropped them with projectile tranquilizers, fired with a precision of which very few beings in the universe were capable. The darts slipped between the joints in the armor, found the soft places within, and delivered their payloads. He'd learned a thing or two from Lieutenant Davis, during their brief and bloody acquaintance on Janus Station.

The guardcore armor would pump them with stimulants and send up distress beacons when, inevitably, the bodies within couldn't be roused until the drug wore off on its own.

Eight minutes. He had eight minutes before the alarms started blaring.

Time enough for answers. Time enough for vengeance.

Tomas dropped a virus into the systems of Vladsen's house, silencing its internal alarms, but the guardcore beacons would still go up. The locks flicked green, letting him in. He tracked garden dirt across Vladsen's pristine floors, printed the evidence of himself in mud against finely woven rugs.

The lights had been turned down to a soft, warm glow that almost appeared to radiate from within finely polished wooden fixtures. Vladsen had crafted a rich life for himself with the tools of the Nazca. Tomas didn't believe, if he'd gotten out when Vladsen did, he could have done likewise. This world of comfort was as alien to Tomas as the black metal structure of the Sentinel.

He jogged lightly up the steps, feeling the press of time. An attendant emerged from a side door, and only managed to look surprised before Tomas dropped him with a tranq and stepped, nimbly, over the body. He felt bad about that. The attendant didn't have the kind of countermeasures the guardcore did, and he'd wake with a murderous headache, but time was too short for Tomas to be gentle.

It wasn't that he cared about being caught. He cared only about getting the answers he needed before he died and took Vladsen with him.

He hesitated in front of the grand double doors to Vladsen's office, the room that man retired to every night before bed, and knocked.

"Let yourself in, Alderman," Vladsen called out.

Tomas opened the door. Vladsen wore dark grey sleep pants, his feet and chest bare, his wristpad the only adornment. No weapons on his person, no weapons within reach. His head was bent over a viewscreen, other screens raised from the desktop around him, painting his face in blue light. A thin line ran between his brows, dark curls still wet from having showered. Tomas took him in, every line, and hated that he did not know him. Not even a hint of a headache heralded a sense of recognition.

Tomas stepped into the room and picked up a tablet displaying photos on the shelf. In the image, a younger Vladsen grinned into the camera, arm slung around someone meant to be his sister. Not real, and Vladsen had never looked that young.

"Tomas," Vladsen said, his breath catching.

Tomas turned the photo around for Vladsen to see. "AI composite facial generation and familial approximation? Clever. How did you get it past the Keeper academy? Surely they wanted to interview your family."

Vladsen's expression shifted from shock to a wry smile. "Sadly, my family was stricken with a rare version of a highly contagious influenza virus that lasted weeks. All the doctor's letters checked out."

"Risky."

"I was desperate." He placed a stylus down on his desk, stood slowly, and approached with carefully placed steps, arms loose at his sides, hands open. He reached for the photo. Tomas handed it to him. "If I'm being honest, I was full of myself. I couldn't envision being caught. And after a while, well... It was a nice fiction to believe in."

"It's dangerous, believing our own bullshit," Tomas said.

"Yes, my sentimentality has almost gotten me killed numerous times." His smile dropped and he placed the photo back on the shelf. "It might get me killed tonight. My guards?"

"Will be fine within the hour. If Alderman is your attendant, I suggest you arrange for a nice vacation for him. He's going to have a hell of a headache."

Vladsen winced. "I see. Clearly you've infiltrated my internal security, but the beacons?"

"Down to six minutes twenty-two seconds."

"Ah." He flicked up his wristpad, and tapped quickly. "More like three minutes, then. Biran's experiences have made him jumpy."

Tomas's stomach clenched at the reminder. "Is he here?"

Vladsen arched a brow at him as he finished canceling the alert. "He is not, as I'm sure you know. Third day of the month he spends with his parents. He should be en route to the planet right now. Please, sit."

He moved back around the desk, maintaining the open-hands, arms-down posture that signaled he was unarmed and had no intention of attacking, before taking his seat. Tomas grabbed a chair and dragged it in front of the desk, leaning back. His jacket shifted, and Vladsen's eyes flicked to the holster hidden there. The blaster would hurt, but it was not the weapon Tomas had brought for the grey man.

"I was under the impression," Vladsen said, "that you had crewed with *The Light*."

He hadn't expected that, and the implied question dug claws into his chest. Being on that ship was living in a mausoleum. He didn't understand how the others could stand it. "Not anymore. Biran has me doing odd jobs on his behalf."

That got a slight intake of breath before Vladsen laughed in soft surprise. "I should have known. Getting his money's worth from you, then?"

"The Nazca no longer exist," Tomas said in flat tones. "That was the Scion's first assignment for me."

"Then we are the last of a dead organization."

"Are we?"

Tomas pulled a slim device from his pocket and set it in the center of the desk. He'd taped down the wires that once protruded from the sides, making it look like an attempt to turn a potato into a battery, but he suspected Arden wouldn't mind the slight adjustment. Vladsen waved his viewscreens back into the desk, and squinted at the device.

"An EMP? Does it work?"

"Sanda took down a dozen Rainiers with a similar device. Arden Wyke made both. I have not yet tried it on myself, but I see no reason why it wouldn't work exactly the same way. Rainier got back up, afterward, but this one is much stronger. It was designed to take down Ada's HVAC system."

Vladsen leaned back in his chair, kicked one ankle up on his knee, and tugged his lower lip between two fingers. The motion sparked something in Tomas's memory, a vague, reassuring ache. Tomas winced.

Vladsen's lashes fluttered from a few rapid blinks. He dropped his hand down to his knee, worry and hope mingling behind his eyes. "You remembered, just now. Didn't you?"

"You always do that when you're worried." He didn't know how he knew that, he just did.

"You won't believe me, but I've missed you."

Tomas snorted. "You left me to rot. Do you have any idea what...?" He trailed off, pain digging its claws in, drawing blood.

He pushed it down, pushed it away. He should have had more time with her. If he'd known what he was, if he could have told her the whole truth from the start, they could have been so much more.

Vladsen started to reach for him, stopped himself, and clasped his palms together on the desk, squeezing. When he spoke, his voice was raspy with regret. "Tomas, I am so, so sorry. I was a coward. I never should have left you there. Never."

"You can't outplay me, Vladsen. Put the waterworks away and clear up your voice, I hate that shit."

"You think this is fake?" He grunted, laughing a little. "I suppose if I were you, I'd think the same thing. I can't prove it to you, we both know I could manufacture these emotional tells at will. I mean what I say, though. I've regretted leaving you behind every day. You don't remember, of course, but I do.

"We were like a family. Brothers, really. We didn't exhibit the same failures as the others, we didn't come apart at the seams. You and I, we watched so many pull themselves to pieces. Watched them rolled back, and sent out again. We were so... smug.

"Then Rainier came for us. I didn't know it was her at the time. I only knew that the organization Caid had stolen the tech from had found you, and afterward you started to... break, in the same way. I couldn't stop them, and I knew it would be me going in the tank next, and so I pretended to go along with things, then fled."

Tomas's fingers curled against the arms of the chair, denting it. "And have you begun to break?"

His gaze flitted to the side and he picked up the stylus, spinning it between two fingers. "A few times. May I be perfectly honest with you, Tomas? In confidence?"

"I won't tell the Scion you peel your skin to watch it grow back."

He grimaced and shook his head. "I don't, actually. The urge used to be there. The curiosity, wanting to know the limits of yourself. But the Keeper training? The yearly immersions in torture? They scratch that itch."

"That's... That's probably fucking sick, Vladsen."

"It is sick, isn't it? What works for you?"

He pressed his lips together, then thought, fuck it. If anyone could handle this, it was Vladsen. And regardless, he didn't see either of them living to tell the tale. "Vacuum. I override my ship's safety protocols, strap in so I don't get blown out, and set the airlock on a timer."

"To death?"

"To unconsciousness, at least. I'm not certain there's a difference with us."

"Fair enough," Vladsen said, but he'd stopped spinning the stylus and was watching Tomas intently, a faint purse to his lips that indicated he was thinking. "You go out like Sanda did."

"That's not—"

"How many times?"

Tomas looked away, embarrassed. "Once a week."

"Shit, Tomas, that's... That's a lot. I don't *need* the Keeper training to scratch the itch once a year, and even that experience doesn't go quite so far."

"I'm in one piece," he snapped, feeling churlish. Why was he arguing with the man he'd come to kill about the state of his mental health?

"Are you?" Vladsen pressed.

"Fuck you, I'm not here for this. Are we it, Vladsen? Are we really all that's left?"

Vladsen glanced at the EMP, then back to Tomas. "Why? So you can take out the last of the Nazca in one go?"

"The Scion ordered me to get rid of the Nazca."

"Biran. His name is Biran, and he didn't mean this, and you know it."

Tomas shrugged, spread his hands. "We don't belong here. We're not humans, we barely have a scrap of humanity left within us. Well, maybe you have something, but I lost my compass. Biran's going to die, too, someday. Then what?"

He shifted uncomfortably. "He's young."

"It won't matter. You and I, we're going to outlive everyone we've ever loved. I've just had to face facts a little sooner than you."

"We'll always have each other," he said with a wry smile that was beginning to itch at the back of Tomas's mind.

"I hate you, Rostam. You must know that."

"And I love you as my brother regardless."

Tomas narrowed his eyes, watching that too-young face, the full lips, the rounded cheeks. Vladsen had picked a kind face for himself, one that encouraged gentleness. Confidences. Had he always looked that way? Had his first face carried sharper edges, like Tomas's?

"Did Caid make you to be disarming?"

"Yes. Though I didn't keep my original face, some habits die hard. I was to coax, wheedle. You were to apply leverage. I believe she was most proud of your design, if that matters to you. This general arrangement, as you are now, suited you best, we both thought. Nondescript enough to blend, a touch handsome, and strong enough to deal out hell if it came to that. The combination made you her best finder."

"Are you attempting to flatter me?"

"I presumed you came here for the truth. We were an incredible team, but you were always Caid's favorite." He licked his lips, glanced away. "It's how I knew she wouldn't come looking for me, so long as she had you."

"She had to have tried."

"Oh, naturally. Fielded herself for the attempt a couple of times, but her heart was never in it. She made it here, so far as Ada, before you showed up with Sanda and made your escape from the Cannery.

"I would have loved to have seen her face when her favorite dropped back in from a mission that could have taken lifetimes, then grabbed the target and *ran* without reporting in. You always followed the protocol, Tomas."

Tomas couldn't help but smile to himself. "She did seem unsettled, in her shut-down way, when she finally yanked the leash to call me in."

"Tossed your pain receptors, eh? I hated it when she did that. Regardless, I think she was shaken enough to make a mistake, for once in her twisted life. She sent you to Janus."

Tomas frowned, wary. "She knew Rainier was unlikely to harm me, that she was more likely to divulge what I was, and possibly more of her plan, because of what I am. I don't know that she made a mistake, but she was certainly desperate."

"If that's all she'd sent you for, I'd agree. But Caid...Ah, well, there's no point in keeping these secrets anymore. Sitta Caid was a woman who needed, desperately, to maintain control. I saw the footage of your escape with Sanda through the Cannery, all the Protectorate did. Your protectiveness was unmistakable. It must have shaken Caid very badly, to see her favorite pulled by someone else's strings."

"I know Nazca dancing better than most, Vladsen. What are you getting at?"

"Caid was a fool. She was always testing the strength of her control. When she sent you to Janus, she knew full well Commander Greeve had Arden and Nox on her ship, knew full well Valentine was on that station. You thought it yourself, didn't you, when you were there? You must have noticed Caid missed telling you about Valentine."

"Of course I did. What does this have to do with—?"

"Think it through. Caid rearranged your face into something that the commander couldn't possibly recognize, and flung you into her path, because she wanted her to reject you. Wanted her to hurt you and send you crawling back to Caid, assured that your place with the Nazca was the only real place in the universe. What happened?"

All this talk of Sanda twisted the knife in his heart deeper. He wasn't here for this.

"I'm not here to talk about Sanda," he said. The name hurt. "I want to know about Caid."

"Goddamnit, Tomas, I'm not bringing this up to cut at you. Just listen to me. If you want to know about Caid, then you can't ignore all of this. It's integral to Caid's actions."

"Ignore it?" He laughed ruefully, dragging a hand through his hair, and stopped short of yanking it out in clumps. "Every damn thing since my last reset has revolved around Sanda Greeve. And now she's dead, and now I have to . . . to figure out what to do, so you're going to tell me everything I need to know about what I am. About the people that made me, made *us*."

"Christ," Vladsen whispered to himself. "Biran's been using you like a scalpel when he should be wrapping you in blankets and feeding you tea. I'm so sorry, Tomas, I didn't think . . . I'll talk to him."

"Don't," Tomas grated. "I don't want your fucking protection."

Vladsen was around the desk, his hand on Tomas's shoulder, firm but gentle, between one blink and the next. "This isn't protection. You're all I've got for family, and you can hate me for that, but I won't stand by and—"

The touch set something off within him; he didn't even hear the words. Tomas twisted, grabbed Vladsen's wrist, and shoved, slamming him hard against one of the glass-door bookcases. The glass cracked, shattered, shards of violence sparkling in Vladsen's hair as his head snapped back against a shelf. Tomas had one of Vladsen's hands behind his back and his arm pressed against Vladsen's throat without even thinking about it.

"I said. Don't."

"What happened when Sanda rejected you?" he pressed.

Tomas narrowed his eyes. "I told her who I was. She didn't believe me, and then she killed me, if you really want to know. I jumped on the mission too quickly and she got ahead of me, gunned me down." He felt Vladsen's heart rate kick up, and pressed his arm tighter against his throat. "Don't try anything."

"I'm not. It's just . . . It's upsetting."

"Try living it," Tomas muttered. "Rainier scraped me up and put me back together. Told me what I was."

"Why did you rush the mission?"

"It's none of your fucking business."

"Humor me, big brother."

Big—? He grimaced, closed his eyes briefly. "I wanted it done. I wanted Caid off my back so I could put the Tomas face back on. I needed Sanda to tell me what to do, I didn't trust my instincts, and there was no way in fuck she'd give Novak the kind of advice she'd give me."

"So you blew the mission for the first time in your life?"

"Please, I must have fucked up before."

"No, Tomas, you haven't."

A sensation he didn't recognize curled within him. Tomas frowned and pulled his arm away from Vladsen, taking a step back as he released the man's wrist.

"Why does it matter?"

"Because you're looking for reason, for purpose." Vladsen held his hands up as Tomas shot him a look. "You said so yourself. You believe you need her to tell you what to do, what your next step is, and since she's not here, you're letting Biran push you around his chessboard as your next best option. You're here, tonight, to kill off the last two Nazca because you tell yourself it fulfills the letter of your orders, but really, you're here to die. You wouldn't have told me half of what you did if you believed we were walking out of here."

"You don't know me, Vladsen."

He laughed softly and rubbed his sore wrist. "I really, really do. Your personality? It hasn't changed. I don't know how many times they rolled you back, but you're still you. You've always been some-thing of a martyr."

He turned, glowering. "That's not what this is about."

"Really? Because I'm looking at a man who lost the woman he loved, who's carrying around a weapon made for her to use, looking for the most righteous time to use it. Looking for synchronicity in his life, as if that will give it any kind of meaning."

"Fuck you," he growled.

"Tomas, *you* went off-mission. *You* disobeyed orders. I'm sorry, but that's monu-fucking-mental. And sure, maybe Sanda was the catalyst for that, and I truly am sorry she's not here anymore, but what you did? It was all you. You made that choice. You got out. And I don't think she'd want you living like this."

"What did you say?"

"I don't believe Sanda would want—"

Tomas spun, grabbed Vladsen by the shoulder, and dragged him close, staring hard into his eyes. "What do you mean, 'she's not *here* anymore'?"

Panic flickered behind his eyes, quickly dashed away. "She's dead, Tomas. I was trying to be less of an asshole about it."

"No you fucking weren't." Tomas squeezed, feeling the bones in Vladsen's shoulder grind against each other. "Where? Where is she?"

Vladsen ducked his shoulder, twisting deftly out of Tomas's grip, and moved to step away, but Tomas had always been stronger, faster, and he was in fighting form.

Tomas lashed out, hooked Vladsen's ankle, and dropped him to the floor. Vladsen grunted, digging his hands into the rug as he tried to scramble backward, but Tomas was too fast. He darted a hand out, grabbed Vladsen by the throat, and picked him up, slamming him onto his desk. The plex cracked, shuddered. Tomas drove the heel of his palm into Vladsen's collarbone, paused right before it would snap.

"Tell me," he ground out.

"I...don't know," he coughed. "It's just a thought I had. A stupid one."

"Share."

Vladsen grimaced, but did not fight back. "Please, I know as much about what we are as you do. Possibly less, considering you spoke with Rainier. They only ever told us we were enhanced, we believed our human backstories, even as we watched our weaker colleagues roll back time and time again. We thought we took the enhancements better than they did. It was only recently I understood myself to be a complete construct."

"Stop deflecting." Tomas pressed. The bone snapped.

Vladsen gasped in pain, fingers instinctively digging into the desk for purchase. Cracks radiated from the points his fingers pierced, threatening to shatter the whole thing. Tomas grabbed him by the hair and wrenched him up, tossing him to the ground against a bookcase. Vladsen pushed himself to sitting, one hand at his throat, as the bones in his chest began to knit back together.

"At least I don't have to pretend in front of you." Vladsen coughed blood.

Tomas took a step toward him. "I can do this all night, and so can you."

"It is a *theory*. One I haven't looked into in the slightest. If you tell Biran—"

"I won't."

"Swear it, Tomas. Because this is going to consume you, I know it, and I don't want it to consume him, too."

"I swear it."

Vladsen nodded, slowly, to himself. "You and I and Bero and the *Bel Marduk*, we're digital consciousnesses. Constructs. According to the Sentinel, the conversion-agent was designed to change biological cells into ones the Waiting could interact with—hence the receivers in the mix. If Sanda truly was converted at some point..."

"Then they may have uploaded her. Her mind might be out there, somewhere, with the Waiting."

"Yes, it's *possible*, but Tomas, please, if she's been taken by those things, then she is the sole novel experience they've had in who-knows-how-long. *If* her mind was taken and *if* she's still herself enough to know who she is, that's.... That's torture. She would have no sense of time. I doubt, if any of this is the case, that she's still sane."

Tomas clenched and unclenched his hands, grasping at mental straws. The third sphere was gone, used up in Sanda's contact attempt; he had no way of reaching the Waiting. No way of interfacing with them, or guaranteeing he could extricate himself if he made the attempt.

With the Sentinel blanketing all the worlds of Prime in guardcore metal, it wasn't like he could shout into the void to get their attention. Maybe with *The Light*...maybe Bero could find a way.

Vladsen's face twisted with pain. "I can see you planning. You've already started thinking of this like a mission. Even if my wild suppositions are anywhere near the truth, she won't be herself anymore. And where will you house her mind, if you find it? The net? *The Light*? She'd hate every second."

Tomas clenched his fists hard enough for blood to slick his palms. "Help me. Between us, we can rebuild a reconstruction bath and—"

"No, not with this. I cannot do this to you."

His gaze flicked to the photo on the shelf—Vladsen with his fake family—and back to the man on the floor. Vladsen had had decades of pretending to be a human, to be many-faceted and sane. Tomas… Tomas had only ever had the mission. *This* mission. Extract Sanda Greeve. It was all he could remember, that driving force, that inherent desire to fix, to complete, to do what was necessary.

Easy to lose everything you love, when you've only ever loved one thing.

"You already have," he said, and picked the EMP up from the desk, turning to leave.

"Tomas, wait, please!"

He hesitated, one hand on the doorframe, the other cradling the device. He hadn't completely lost himself; he understood that what he was doing was manic, damaging. This was the point in a human's life when they got help, when their friends or family intervened and kicked them off the rails of self-destruction.

But Tomas wasn't human. What he was, what he'd always be, was the Nazca's best finder. And he had all the time in the worlds.

"Goodbye, little brother."

Tomas slammed into the ground, face-first. The EMP flew from his hand, and his chin smacked against the hardwood, stars bursting behind his eyes. Vladsen's weight bore into him, crushed him down, one knee in the small of his back, his hands wrestling Tomas's arms up behind him.

"What the fuck?"

Vladsen's voice was thick. "I'm not letting you walk out of here on some boneheaded suicide jaunt."

"Get off of me!" He started to twist, but Vladsen locked his grip, leveraging his position to grapple Tomas into place. To get free, he'd have to do serious damage, and despite his earlier outburst, he didn't want to harm him. Not anymore.

"I have barely, *barely*, scraped Biran back from the edge of that void in his heart and I'll be damned if I get my brother back long enough to watch him throw himself over that same cliff."

"I don't even know you."

"But I know you. I know you and Biran and Graham and Ilan, and I only met Sanda for a second, but she wouldn't want this. Not for you."

"You don't know her. You know nothing about what she'd want. Sanda was all about the mission, just like—"

"The fuck she was," Vladsen snapped. "What did she do, when you told her what you are?"

"I've shared enough personal bullshit with—" Vladsen dug two fingers into the soft spot under Tomas's armpit. He cut himself off with a hiss of pain.

"This is more personal for me than you can possibly imagine," Vladsen said. "Tell me. What did she do? Did she open her arms and say, 'Welcome back, lover, let's pick right up where we left off'? Or did she give you space, let you figure out what you wanted for yourself?"

"I..." Tomas trailed off, the statement forcing memories to surface in him that hurt more than any hidden behind a headache-guarded rollback. Pissed. She'd been so fucking pissed, though she'd hidden it well. And not at him, not directly, but at Caid. At Rainier. At everyone who'd done this to him. And when he'd told her he'd killed Caid, her eyes had lit up with grim satisfaction.

We'll figure it out, she'd said, and he'd believed her. Had never believed in anything more until that moment, fuck the resets.

"Space," he whispered, "she gave me space."

"So give yourself some, now, in her honor. She wouldn't want you tearing yourself apart to chase an idea that may or may not even be true."

"Why do you care?" he demanded, but the walls inside him were already breaking down, crumbling into so much dust.

"I have cursed myself for decades for not going back for you, and I'm not going to let you go now. You're my brother. It's not real to you, but it is to me, and if I let you walk, I know damn well I'll never see you again."

Something within him loosened, broke. His shoulders began to shudder, deep sobs welling up within him, catching his breath, stealing it away. Vladsen let out a low sigh and released his grapple, rolling to one side to lie on his back, one hand still on Tomas's, patting him gently as the tears came.

"Let it out," Vladsen said, voice soft.

Tomas did, feeling ridiculous for sobbing on the floor of this man who he'd come to kill. This man who was the closest thing he'd ever have, or ever could have, to family. Vladsen was right—Tomas didn't remember him, not really.

But something about the man stirred echoes in his mind. He'd known him. He must have cared for him, because part of him still did. Tomas had had every intention of pulling the trigger on that EMP, but seeing Vladsen there, sitting behind that desk...He couldn't do it. The sight of him felt like picking at a scab, but he couldn't let him go.

The front door burst inward. Tomas was a long way from caring about his personal safety, but Nazca instincts were carved into his bones, so he put a lid on the pain, picked his head up, assessing the situation even as his heart burned hot as coals, too dangerous to hold.

Guardcore spilled through the door, their rifles sighting up the stairs to where Vladsen and Tomas lay, bloodied and bruised, Tomas on his stomach, Vladsen on his back with one arm thrown over Tomas. A collection of red laser dots swarmed over Tomas's body. He froze, knowing better than to move. He'd probably survive the barrage, but it'd hurt like hell.

Biran pushed through the guardcore, the silver that now dominated his hair a candle flame between all the metal, and stopped hard, staring with wide eyes at the scene.

"Rost!"

"I'm fine, just having an overdue chat with my brother," Vladsen said, peeling his arm away to roll onto his stomach and pick up his head. In a low voice, he murmured to Tomas, "Told you he was paranoid."

Tomas snorted. Maybe they *were* related, in their own strange way. "Sorry for frightening you," Tomas said, and rocked back into a crouch, holding his hands up. The red dots followed him. "I'll go now."

Biran's gaze found the EMP lying on the ground, and Tomas winced as he watched that man's eyes narrow in understanding. He held his breath, waiting for Biran to order the guardcore to fire, waiting for the hard man that had grown up inside of Sanda's brother, the man who had become director, then Scion, to put down this obvious threat.

Part of Biran wanted to, Tomas could see it written across his face, in the clench of his shoulders. Tomas had brought Sanda back, and lost her again, and part of Biran would always hate him for that.

Biran didn't look much like the rest of his family, but in that moment, Tomas saw the echo of Sanda, and his chest ached.

"Arms down," Biran ordered. The guardcore put their rifles down. "Back to your posts, this was a false alarm."

"Scion, with all due respect—"

"I said go."

The guardcore filed out, obedient as ever, and as the door closed, Tomas dropped his arms, wrapping them around his bent knees.

"Biran," Tomas said, "I'm truly sorry."

"Please." Without the guardcore around to see, Biran slouched, shoulders rounding, and ran shaking fingers through his hair. He looked older than any of them, at that moment. "I'm sorry. I should have seen this coming. Should have done...something."

"You gave me a job," Tomas said. "I needed that."

"Apparently I wasn't clear enough about the parameters." Biran gave him a small smile, and crossed the room, flipping up the top of a console table to reveal a variety of bottles hidden away. He selected three large, amber-glass bottles, and set them on a low table between two couches. "Come down here then, both of you, and drink with me. I don't think any of us can actually stay drunk, but we can sure as hell try."

Rostam popped to his feet and hovered over Tomas, hand extended to help him up, and Tomas got the feeling they'd been in this position many times before.

"You going to be all right?" Rostam asked.

"I don't know," Tomas admitted, taking his hand. "But we'll figure it out."

CHAPTER 79

PRIME STANDARD YEAR 3543

OUT OF THE BLACK

I got her," someone said.

Rough hands wrestled her unceremoniously through an airlock. Gravity grabbed her and forced her down, but sturdy, armored arms were there to catch her. Sanda's eyelids slipped up, letting in blinding lines of light, and she flinched, struggling away from the brightness.

"She's moving," Dr. Liao said, and that was impossible, because the last time Sanda had seen that woman she'd been rocking herself insensate in a prison of Rainier's making.

Sanda forced her eyes open, tensed through the stabbing agony of too-bright light, but it wasn't that bright, after all. Her vision adjusted, relaxing to the soft lights Bero provided the ship with.

Bero. She blinked, forced herself to pick her head up, to look around.

"Easy," Nox said, and it was his armored arms around her, carrying her wedding style, which meant they probably suspected she had organ damage. "Bero's going to patch you up."

"Don't need it," she rasped.

Liao chuckled. "Bullheaded woman. Bero, please prepare—"

"The commander is correct," Bero said. "She is healing."

"She was spaced," Dr. Liao protested. "I may not be a medical doctor, but even I can understand the danger of that. She's lucky to be alive. Something about the gate field must have held her together."

"Not the gate field," Sanda slurred, pressed her lips together and ran her tongue over her teeth, testing. No blood. She could feel her pulse, ticking slowly back up to normal levels, and with a thought nudged it higher. The sensation warbled beneath her skin, unsettling, so she let it go, relying on her autonomic system to straighten things out.

Nox stopped walking. He looked down at her, suspicion painted in the lines around his eyes, the tight pull of his lips. Bruises peppered his face, his neck. Deep welts raked over his shoulder, as if a massive animal had clawed at him.

Whatever had happened after she left, she had a feeling Nox needed medical care more than she did, even though the wounds looked old. Sanda nodded to him, confirming his suspicions.

"Shit," he said, and set her on her feet, carefully.

"Tomas?" she asked, dreading the answer, but she needed to know.

"Safe," Arden said, bouncing on their toes at the edge of the hall. "I don't know how you did it, Commander, but once Rainier was deleted from the system, Bero took over and kicked Tomas back to his body. He called in. Got a hell of a headache, but no lasting damage."

Sanda rubbed the space between her eyes. "Deleted? You're certain she's out of the ship?"

Arden chewed the side of their lip. "We haven't been able to find a trace of her. All of her ancillaries are dead."

Sanda closed her eyes and smiled to herself for a breath, then made herself move down the hall, toward the command deck. She had some reports to make.

"Good," she said as she slung herself into the captain's seat and leaned back onto the cool metal, surprisingly comfortable against her aching muscles. "I couldn't be sure... But they weren't happy with her. I felt them rip her out."

Everyone on deck stared at her with wide, expectant eyes. Eventually, Conway said, "Who are they, Commander? What were they... like?"

"I... don't know. I never saw a person, or anything that might have been a body. Just, space in all directions, nothing local, I don't think. I'd like to run some of what I remember through the star charts, see if anything matches. There was just a...voice. Glitchy, at first, but then it started to sound like me. It called itself the Waiting, and said that humanity was flawed. It wants us to...to fix ourselves."

Arden pumped a fist in the air. "I knew it, I fucking knew it. I bet that wasn't one of them, I bet it was the spheremind of the third sphere, a door keeper to the real deal."

"It definitely felt like being in a lobby," Sanda said slowly, "and I got the feeling that it could only answer certain questions."

"Whatever it was," Nox said, crossing his arms as he leaned against a bulkhead, "it saved our asses. I'm glad it's on our side."

Sanda wasn't so sure the being was on humanity's side, so to speak, but that could wait. She blinked away a foggy mind, looking at her bruised but otherwise hale crew, and frowned. "What the hell happened to all of you? Did Valentine...?"

Nox and Arden shared a glance, Liao fiddled with her console.

"She got us out," Nox said. "Couldn't really bring myself to shoot her after that."

Sanda nodded. "I understand. Where is she now? I swear...It's all fuzzy, but I think I saw her in there, with the Waiting."

"Jules didn't make it," Arden said in a soft voice.

Her crew was looking everywhere but at her. Her crew. Her *whole* crew, sans Tomas. Conway and Knuth shouldn't be anywhere near this ship. They'd gone to the *Stalwart* with Tomas and her dads. Sanda's stomach dropped, but she put iron in her voice. "What happened?"

A young, pale woman with a messy, light brunette ponytail stepped onto the deck. Lolla. "Commander, what these cowards aren't telling you is that you've been gone for four months."

"What?"

Bero said, "I'm sorry. I didn't want to be the one to tell you this time."

CHAPTER 80

TIME IS RELATIVE

Arden spun out a variety of possible explanations, a nonstop litany of words she didn't understand. Something got tangled in the time collapse of the gate, or maybe time passed differently where the Waiting lived, or she really had traveled impossibly far and didn't remember the trip. Sanda thought that idea the least likely.

Her memories were back, and she didn't think the Waiting would spare her the monotony of a long journey just to be kind. They seemed like an all-or-nothing kind of people. Memory loss was damage. They fixed damage. The end.

Whatever had happened didn't matter, not now. According to Arden, the Ada–Atrux gate had started to put off an unusually bright glow, and upon closer inspection sound waves had begun to emanate from the gate at frequencies that appeared to be gibberish.

Fearing another attack, Director Greeve had ordered the evacuation of the planet and station, cramming all the people of Ada onto the *Stalwart* and any other ready transport. The bulk of the population had been three hours' flight away when Sanda popped out, and the gate had calmed down.

Biran had wanted to load *The Light* with evacuees, but Bero had refused, saying he didn't feel the change was a threat—though he didn't know why. He, and his crew, had stayed to watch, and so they'd been ready to scoop her up when she came floating out of nothing, unconscious.

Sanda listened to the story, prodding at the edges. Learned that what she thought had only happened moments ago—the awakening, Rainier's deletion—had happened months past. Whatever time she had lost had been between the end of her conversation with the Waiting, and coming home.

Why? Why the delay coming back, but not going in? Something to do with the flaw in the gate construction, Liao guessed, and while that seemed possible, Sanda had a hard time accepting it as fact. She was familiar with missing time. Familiar in all the ways your own mind could lie to you.

She stared at her hands as *The Light* passed into hangar bay alpha of Keep Station, and wondered what tinkering might have been done to her body during the long transit.

Conway cleared her throat. Sanda looked up. The story had stopped, and now a call was waiting on the forward viewscreen. Director Greeve.

When the gate had settled down, the others had returned, and the crew of *The Light*—Bero included—had decided not to tell anyone that they had scraped Sanda out of the black. They wanted to make sure she was okay. Wanted to be certain of her situation.

Wanted to make sure she wasn't a trap.

Now, it was up to Sanda to reveal her living self. She squared her shoulders, and answered.

"Bero—" Biran stopped mid-word, eyes widening, lips parting. Silver now dominated his hair. Lines carved valleys where a permanent frown had grown. How could her little brother look so much older than her? Would she ever look her age again?

"Sorry I forgot to write," she said dryly, because if she started down the road of telling him she loved him and was sorry, she might start blubbering and never stop.

He snapped his mouth shut, expression torn between astonishment, joy, and suspicion. "Is it really you?"

"As far as I know," she said, spreading her arms. "The crew was just filling me in. To me, I've only been gone minutes."

He scrubbed the sides of his face with his hands. "I can't—I can't believe this. Bero, land as soon as possible. I don't think I'll really believe it until I see for myself."

"See you soon," she said, and cut the feed before either one of them could work up to a breakdown.

"We are fifteen minutes out," Bero said.

Sanda frowned. "I thought we were already in the hangar?"

"It takes time to maneuver such a large body. Time enough for you to change into some clean clothes." *And pull yourself together.*

Sanda snorted and pushed to her feet. "Heard. Chime me when we're in."

As she passed Lolla, she dropped a hand on the young girl's shoulder. "I'm glad you're okay."

"Thanks," she said, tilting her head away to hide a shy smile, "and likewise."

No one had touched Sanda's room. Her armor was still spread across the floor, her desk scarred around the legs where she'd reattached them. Sanda brushed her fingertips over the desktop, noting the dead screens on her tablets—tablets she rarely used. She'd need a new wristpad. And a full mission status update. And the strongest drink of her life.

Being in that place had shifted something within her, dulled some essential, raw nerve. The world felt a little dimmer, made a little more sense, linearly. Like she could see the threads of fate, weaving herself and her crew and all the worlds of Prime together. She blinked the sight away. Just tired. Just...overwhelmed. A thought jolted her.

"Where's Tomas?" she demanded of Bero.

"He works for Biran, now. I've put a message where he'll find it, but he's not always...available."

She closed her eyes and swallowed. Four months. He'd been living with her death for four months. Her family had been through that before. Her family had *each other*. Tomas had this ship, had this crew, but something had driven him away, pushed him back into the field.

And what Bero very politely was not saying was that he rarely checked or answered the messages they sent him.

She left the major's coat hanging, put on soft body armor, and sat on the edge of her bed, hair hanging past her shoulders. Four months of hair growth, she thought, and wondered if she could change that rate, or stop it altogether if she so chose.

Sanda was staring at her hands again. She didn't know why they bothered her, why they felt like someone else's. Absently, she pulled a box cutter from her toolbelt and clicked it up, pricking the tip of her finger. Blood welled to the surface in a dark, blackish bead, no different than before. She squeezed the wound, forcing more out, trying to discern if there was anything different about it. Anything silver.

"Sanda," Bero said.

She startled, swore, and accidentally nicked the side of her palm. "Don't sneak up on me like that."

"I am not capable of sneaking."

"Yeah, yeah." She clicked the box cutter down, slipping it into her belt, and reached for a plastiskin patch. Sanda paused, considering both wounds.

"You can heal them," Bero said. "Now that you've accepted what you are. Before, I think the headache would have been too much."

"I know," she said dryly. "I was saving that pain."

"It worked."

"Barely."

"It was enough. Heal your hand."

"I'm not sure I want to." A dark pool gathered in her palm. She tilted her hand, balancing it.

"Why? You know what you are. That bridge has already been crossed. You might as well use your newfound abilities."

"I..." She scowled at the dripping wound, and didn't have an answer. She'd wanted to see, hadn't she, what color she bled? But that thought had come *after* the wound, not before. She'd just... done it, and couldn't say why. "Testing," she said, brows knitted together.

"I was not certain human curiosity is compatible with the ascension-agent," Bero said. "I'm still not."

"Oh, come on, I'm not going to vivisect myself—damnit." Blood ran over the side of her palm, traced rivers down her forearm. She scowled and concentrated, feeling the skin stitch itself back together, then the nerves and veins and muscle beneath. She washed her hand in the sink.

"Are you all right?"

It hadn't hurt, not exactly. The sting had been there, but the bite had gone out of the sensation. As if pain was just another sense, like smell, something she could ignore, even when it got bad.

"It didn't hurt," she said.

"Pain reduces harm. Don't...don't turn that off. Not completely."

She licked her lips. "I didn't mean to."

"No," he said, and sighed. "It's instinct. Just like blinking your eyes to keep from being blinded. We're here."

She arched her brows at the ceiling. "Convenient timing."

"Benefits of being the ship," he said.

She rolled her eyes as she pushed to her feet, slung a blaster around her hips out of habit, and went out to rise from the dead. Again.

CHAPTER 81

PRIME STANDARD YEAR 3543

FOUR MONTHS TOO LONG

Sanda's crew gathered behind her, even Lolla clinging close in Arden's shadow, as she stepped out onto the gangway. Though there was no sign of a crowd—the GC must have locked down the hangar—the air was thick with anticipation that made Sanda's skin crawl.

Biran waited at the end of the gangway, wearing a slim-cut charcoal suit that he definitely couldn't have afforded on his own, his hands folded sedately in front of his torso, a crescent moon of guardcore arrayed behind him. At the sight of her, all his stiff, confident posturing dropped away, and in a second he was crushing her into him, the scent of his cheap cologne mingled with something else—something finer—filling her senses.

She coughed and pounded him on the back, stifling a laugh.

"For fuck's sake, Little B, I'm not going to disappear if you ease up, but I might suffocate if you don't let go."

He pushed her back to arm's length and grinned, tears standing bright in his eyes. "I didn't believe it. I thought this was one last fucked-up trick of Rainier's. I saw...I believed you were dead. We all believed you were dead."

She winced. "I'm sorry, I really didn't know. Where's the dads?"

"En route," he said. "The evacuation has made everything a mess, but being the director has its perks. They'll be here within the hour."

She plucked at his sleeve, silky smooth between her fingers. "More perks than one."

He blushed, glanced away, and Sanda could take a wild guess where that second scent mingling with his cheap cologne was coming from. She grinned at him. So he'd found someone. Good. At least they had decent taste in clothes.

"Then I've got some time. Anford around?"

"Here, Commander," the general said, striding toward her across the dock. She stopped a step away from Sanda and patted her, awkwardly, on the shoulder. "Glad you're with us. What's the situation?"

"Situation?" Biran's face went grim. "Oh, come on, she's been back less than an hour."

"No," Sanda said, patting him on the chest. "Anford's right. We need to talk."

Sanda straightened Biran's lapels out of habit. He froze, then shook himself and surveyed her crew. "All of us?"

"All of us. Bero can port in through my wrist—er, through your wristpad?"

Anford scowled and jabbed at her pad. "We'll get you one. This way."

They followed Anford in a tight pack ringed in by guardcore, which wasn't the most comfortable arrangement for Sanda, but Rainier had been deleted, and Biran wouldn't let his personal guard be infiltrated again. She hoped. Still, it was comforting to let her hand rest on her blaster, just in case.

Biran slung an arm around her shoulders, squeezing her close as they walked, and dropped his voice so low she suspected only her enhanced hearing could pick it up—or the fancy earpiece he was wearing. Perks of being a director, indeed.

"Are you really all right?"

"Yeah, I'll explain when we're gathered, but I'm whole. Not a scratch on me."

"Good." He squeezed tighter, protectively, and she wondered what he was afraid of. Being director of Ada, he probably had plenty of good reasons to be jumpy. She didn't envy him that post.

Sanda glanced up, and saw a vault of black.

"What the *fuck* is that?"

Biran followed her stare. "That...is a very long story. Suffice it to say, it keeps the Waiting from detecting humanity, for now."

"The guardcore metal," she said, understanding clicking into place.

"Yes. It's created by a race of beings who broke away from the Waiting. They call themselves Sentinels."

"I have missed a hell of a lot."

He grinned. "Don't worry, we'll catch you up."

Anford led them into the Cannery and turned abruptly, opening a door to a wide conference room. Sanda dug her heels in a moment, staring at it, and Biran paused, letting her work it all out.

"Not the war room," she said.

"It's no longer necessary," Anford replied. "After the death of Negassi and Bollar, Icarion's chain of command began jockeying for position, tearing themselves apart. Pockets of insurrection continue, but the people were happy to vote for reunification. Especially with the installation of the second gate, able to provide better supplies to all of the system. I'm pleased to tell you that you'll find the changes here mostly positive, for once."

Anford had a faint smile that actually made Sanda's heart soar. The general was either stoic or pissed off. Never happy, never relaxed. Sanda hated to wedge a crack into that happiness, but she had to voice her concerns.

As they stepped into the room, Biran nudged her gently but firmly into the seat at the foot of the table, the second highest place of command, while he took the head of the table, Anford on his right, and the rest of her team filled in wherever they felt comfortable. She'd much rather be in the center, but as Nox and Arden moved to take her right and left, she eased slightly. Her crew had her back. This wasn't all about her. She wasn't alone.

"Get me up-to-date, quick as you can," Sanda said.

Biran did. Her skin went cold as he recounted his experience with the Sentinel, voice skipping, briefly, as he described being able to see her in the clutches of the Waiting, but unable to do anything to stop them.

She nearly interrupted with a question, but saw the curious look on Anford's face, and stopped herself. This was more than he'd told anyone else. She let him talk.

When he was finished, she found herself nodding along in agreement.

"That matches my experience. I believe the only reason they let me go is because Valentine found her way into that place, stole the third sphere, and tossed it back to me, reopening the door."

"Valentine got you out?" Biran asked, bewildered.

Sanda made herself look at Nox, at Arden. "She seemed at peace to do so."

Nox and Arden exchanged a glance. Nox said, "She said, before the end, that it was all going to be okay. We didn't know what she meant. When Atrux woke up, we thought she meant that."

"When she came back for me," Sanda said, "that had already happened. She didn't need to come back."

Arden smiled wistfully. "She stole the sphere from them."

Nox grinned. "Grotta thief got one over on those bastards."

"What's the military situation?" Sanda asked. "Those shields may keep the Waiting out, but they won't do shit against Icarion if they build another ramjet."

Anford flicked up something from her wristpad into the viewscreen in the center of the table. A model of the local system spun into view.

"As things stand," she said, tapping up an overlay of thousands of tiny cyan dots, "the Icarion resistance is weak, at best. Prime forces maintain control of both gates, and have completed reconstruction of the damaged portions of the planet Ada. Many Icarion soldiers are still being held as prisoners of war, but most put down their arms the second they discovered Bollar and Negassi were dead. Thanks for that."

Sanda shrugged. "I had a shot. I took it."

"And almost got us all spaced," Nox drawled.

She grinned at him. "You had plenty of warning. Priority was recovery of *The Light*, couldn't do that if Rainier had Tomas to use as a bargaining chip."

"He was furious about that, by the way," Anford said dryly.

"I figured. He got out of the cage."

She glanced at Biran, who grimaced. "Not exactly. He went in willingly. Keeper Singh opened the door."

Sanda blinked. "Keeper Singh?"

"Well, the woman who claimed to be Keeper Singh," Biran said with a sigh. "Either she was always an ally of Rainier, or Rainier turned her at some point. We can't be certain. Singh believed Keeper Hitton had discovered her secret, and Singh moved to discredit her, pushing her to destroy the asteroid survey site. Hitton had actually uncovered Keeper Sato as a spy, not Singh, however."

Sanda said, "Have all the Keepers been checked? Liao, can you do some kind of blood analysis?"

"I can," Liao said, "and we are checking for more like Keeper Lavaux, but there are no more instances of Rainier in the cosmos. All of her beings dropped dead at once. Some were quite surprising."

"All right," Sanda said, rubbing her hands together. "Rainier's out, thank fuck, the ascended are healed, and Icarion has capitulated. What's the status of the gates? The nanites?"

"Confusing," Anford said, pushing another projection onto the screen. The Ada system wiped away to reveal hundreds of gates in miniature. Fuzzy clouds swarmed some of them. "In cleaning up the amplifier swarm, Liao's team discovered the presence of another kind of nanite. They appeared shortly after your disappearance, and seem to just be receivers. They route their data into the gates. We lose track of them after that."

Sanda winced. "I think I know. The Waiting did not approve of Rainier, but for a moment, it saw through the eyes of every agent-infected human. It...did not like what it saw, I think. It called humanity flawed, and unready, and said we were to fix ourselves and try again. It knows where we are. I saw through every single pair of those eyes."

"You..." Biran trailed off, throat bobbing, and wiped his palms against his nice slacks. "You saw through the eyes of millions of people?"

"Yes," she said. "The Waiting used me as a sort of antenna to connect with all of the devices of its make in the universe. That includes the first and third sphere ships. I believe I can find them."

Anford grinned fiercely. "That's excellent news, Greeve. Those ships will help us reverse engineer how *The Light* was made, and from there figure out the gates. If the sphereminds are still present in both ships, then maybe we can use them to attempt second contact. Find out what the hell is going on out there."

"You're not listening," Bero said through Biran's wristpad, making him flinch. "The Waiting saw through Sanda's eyes, and it doesn't begrudge humanity its failure. It wants you to get better, to try again. They *will* help you, so that they can take you. You need those ships to learn how to fight them, not call them."

"We have to fix the flaw with the gates," Biran said. "On that point, we are not at odds with these beings. But on everything else, we must push back."

Anford scowled. "With the agent, our soldiers—"

"You must not use the agent," Sanda and Biran said in unison.

"Commander," Anford said, a furrow between her brows. "I understand the director's hesitation, his contact with the Sentinel was most informative, but that was only one side of things. We do not know the true motivations of the Waiting, and you've said yourself they want to help us. The agent could be the end to illness for all our people. It could be—"

"Supersoldiers and immortality and all the rest, I know," Sanda said. "But why do they want us to perfect it? Why do they want us to keep trying, to gain a power for our species that would make us unstoppable?"

"The receivers," Liao said, eyes widening. "We never figured out what they were for."

"Because they were for the Waiting," Sanda said, "and I know what it's like to have one of those beings ride your mind." She winced. "That's not the next step for humanity. It's the end."

Anford sighed. "I was afraid you'd say that. What happened at Atrux has gotten out, the people know the strengths given to those who survived. Some of it has been relegated to rumor, and none of the ascended have their abilities anymore, but still, it's a hard genie to put back in the bottle. Immortality . . . it's seductive."

Sanda stared at the tip of her finger, wondering. "It's not all it's cracked up to be."

Biran frowned at her. "S . . ."

Anford leaned forward, eyes bright. "So it's true? You were one of them? We assumed you must have been, after the crew of *The Light* made their report, and considering what Biran saw, but we couldn't be sure."

"It is," Sanda said, tearing her gaze from her hands. "I was not reset, as they had intended to keep me for study. I remain ascended."

Liao said, "This could be very useful to my studies with Dr. Padian. At the moment, the only living samples we have are completely synthetic. An in-between state could help in further developing Padian's idea for a cure. He never got to try it out before your intervention. The Waiting may have undone Rainier's handiwork, but we must be forward thinking and able to rely on our own solutions, should the need ever arise again."

"Well, you're welcome to my blood. Who are the remaining synthetics?"

"Tomas, Keeper Vladsen, and an ancillary who broke away from Rainier's control. She goes by Echo," Liao said.

"Where *is* Tomas? Bero has been remarkably cagey about the situation."

Biran fiddled with a tablet. Sanda narrowed her eyes. He cleared his throat and looked up. "He rarely checks in, these days. Keeper Vladsen would have a better idea."

"Vladsen?" She scrunched her nose, trying to remember the name. "The youngest guy, before you, on the Protectorate? Where is *he*, and why is he among the synthetic? What the fuck does he have to do with Tomas, Biran? How could you pass Tomas off to an underling when you ran out of jobs for him? He's not your damn attack dog."

Biran went about a dozen shades of red, and sweat broke across his brow. "The situation is complicated, we were just . . . just doing the best we could without you. I was. But I fucked up, at first, and I'm sorry. Vladsen and Tomas—that's going to take some explaining."

"Greeves," Anford said with a slight edge. "The personal can wait. I'm concerned about these nanites clouding around the gates. If Commander Greeve is correct, I don't like the idea of another species spying on us."

"Agreed." Sanda forced out the word, resolving to get out of here as soon as possible and find Tomas. She ignored the doleful look Biran shot her. "Liao, can we clean up those swarms?"

"Yes...a few tweaks to the system..." She tapped at her pad. "Yes. I believe so."

"Good, that's our first priority," she said. "Next?"

A chime sounded on Biran's wristpad, and he glanced down and grinned to himself, his earlier consternation wiping away. "The parental units are here."

Sanda caught Anford's eye, and the general shrugged. "If that's the bulk of your report, I can begin work now. We'll hash out the details later. You've earned some rest."

"Thank you," she said, and pushed to her feet.

"One question," Anford said, frowning. "How did you know it would work?"

"I didn't," Sanda admitted. "I'd been told it was a key, and we only had one other object from the Waiting that looked like a door. I took an educated guess. I figured, when Bero launched me, that he agreed."

"You leapt into hard vacuum, without a suit, on a guess?"

She shrugged. "We were losing. It was either die on the ship, or die taking a shot. I took the shot."

Commotion sounded in the hall, shouting, the sound of a fist ringing off metal armor, the whine of a stunner powering up. Footsteps rushed the door. Sanda spun, blaster up, arms braced, as the door swung inward.

Tomas stood in the doorway, wearing civilian clothes, his eyes bloodshot and his breath coming fast as a wall of black-clad guardcore rushed him.

"Stand down," Biran barked. The wave of GC froze as a unit, a wall of night. A GC voiced a complaint that Tomas had bullied his way in, and hadn't been given explicit clearance, which Biran responded to with a condescending remark about Cepko always having clearance. But Sanda wasn't listening, because Tomas was staring at her like a drowning man, and she had to remind herself, again, that to all those she loved she'd been dead four months.

She lowered the blaster.

"Is it really you?" he asked, holding himself up in the doorframe with both hands.

"What's left of me," she said with a wry smile.

He grabbed her, faster than anyone human in that room could see, but she saw every detail of the motion. Watched, with a curious tilt to her head, as he spurred forward, lunged, and wrapped an arm around her waist, tugging her up, lips pressed roughly to hers as she dropped the blaster and, for a moment that was long to them but brief to everyone else, leaned against him.

"Whoa," she said, pulling back. Heat kissed her cheeks as he grinned down at her and, surreptitiously, pressed his thumbs along her cheekbones, checking for scar tissue from plastic surgery. She laughed. It was only fair.

"You're—?"

"Later," she said, turning back to the room. "All for now?" she asked Anford.

Anford inclined her head. "I think we all could do with a break. Your arrival did cause an evacuation, Greeve. We're a little thin around here."

"Sorry," she said, pointing her chin at Biran. "Grab the dads. I need to have a drink, and I'd like to have it with my crew, my brother, and my fathers, and that means doing it aboard *The Light*, because I don't want Bero left out."

"I cannot drink," Bero said through Biran's wristpad.

She snorted. "We'll figure it out."

Tomas clutched her tighter and buried his face against her hair and breathed deeply, a tremble running through him. She hoped she didn't stink. Technically, it'd been months since she'd showered.

Anford smiled again, and stood. "Finally getting some time with friends and family, eh?"

Sanda surveyed her crew, and threaded her fingers through Tomas's, squeezing. "Just family."

CHAPTER 82

PRIME STANDARD YEAR 3543

HOME

Sanda sat cross-legged on the floor of *The Light*'s engine room, half a bottle of Caneridge in her belly, a shit deal of cards in her hands, and everyone she'd ever loved ringed around her. They'd done this here, on Sanda's insistence, so that they could include Bero by being close to his engine core.

They showed their cards. Everyone groaned. Tomas had won, again. Sanda pitched her cards into the center pile and reached for her bottle.

Arden slammed their hand against the crate, making all their cards and discarded credit sticks jump. Laughter flared into life all around. Arden jabbed a finger at Tomas, who was laughing so hard tears had beaded up in his eyes.

"You're cheating," Arden said.

Tomas wiped his eyes with the back of his hand and reached for the pile of cred sticks. "How could I? You invented this twisted game."

"You're... you're moving too fast for me to see!"

"I'm really not," Tomas said, still shaken by the occasional giggle.

"It's true," Bero said, the cloud of light that was the engine core winking. "I would have noticed."

Vladsen, one arm slung around Biran's shoulders, nodded emphatically. "I would have noticed, too."

"You're all against me," Arden muttered, but they were smiling.

"It's a spy thing," Tomas said. "I can read people."

"Oh, come on, you can't use that spy bullshit to account for everything. This is a *strategy* game," Arden insisted. "And if that were true, Rostam here wouldn't be in the hole."

"Maybe I'm distracted." Rostam craned his neck toward Biran, and kissed him.

Graham, Sanda, and Ilan coughed obnoxiously, making Biran blush deep red.

Sanda smirked. "You're such a marshmallow."

"Is that so?" Biran arched a brow at her. "Because this marshmallow appears to be five *hundred* credits ahead of you."

"My children are assholes," Graham muttered.

Nox said, "Didn't fall far, then."

Ilan met Nox's gaze across the crate and smiled, passing him a bottle. "Well they didn't get it from me."

Liao said, "I don't believe asshole is an inheritable trait."

"You haven't met my momma," Conway said.

Knuth said, "*I* have, and she was a perfectly nice woman."

Conway whacked him playfully upside the head, and grabbed the stack of cards, running them through a quick shuffle. "*I'll* deal, since apparently neither Arden nor Tomas can be trusted."

"I did not cheat!"

"Wait," Arden protested, "why can't *I* be trusted?"

"Let Grippy shuffle," Tomas said. "He's the only honest one of us."

Two beeps.

Sanda leaned back onto her elbows, cradling her bottle in one hand, and watched the conversation go round and round, not caring what her cards were, soaking up the warmth of the one thing, the only thing, she'd ever really wanted.

But something wasn't sitting right. A splinter festered beneath her skin, a quiet warning that she could ignore, for now, but built steadily the longer she was surrounded by this. The longer she felt home.

Tomas slid his hand across the floor and traced one finger along her arm. She turned to him, questioning, and saw a hint of worry had worked its way beneath his veneer, too. Sanda put on a smile, and he dropped a grazing kiss against her lips.

"What a mature and lovely show of affection," Biran said, voice dripping acid.

Sanda rolled her eyes and tossed her terrible cards on the crate. "I'll be back in a second, try not to fleece each other into bankruptcy while I'm gone."

"Oh, I will *find out* how he's doing this," Arden said with a determined edge.

"Where do you think you're going?" Graham asked.

"Work thing," Sanda said, shrugging one shoulder.

"As director of Ada, I absolve you of all current responsibilities," Biran said in lofty tones.

Rostam grinned at him. "You want her to stay because she's the only one you can reliably beat."

"You're not my boss, Little B." She tipped her chin at her wristpad. "Anford awaits."

"Wait, I'm *her* boss."

"Want to tell her that?"

He blanched. "No, I do not. As you were, Commander."

She shook her head as she pushed to her feet, giving Tomas's shoulder a squeeze before she left the engine bay behind. Caneridge warmed her blood, made her mind fuzzy, and even though she could clean that up, she let it muddle her, for now.

With the door shut behind her, she could breathe again, that creeping dread lessening but not entirely gone. Anford hadn't actually called her, but Bero would be the only one to know that for sure. She'd needed . . . air. Space. She didn't know.

Sanda walked to her command deck and stood before the forward console, brushing her fingertips against the slick metal. She could feel it. All of it. Maybe she didn't have the control Bero and Tomas did, but she knew the pathways of this ship better than she knew her own skin, could feel her family snugged tight in the engine bay, safe and warm.

The viewscreen shifted from diagnostics to a vista of Ada. Sanda picked her head up, watched the landscape slide by, transition to the station. To Atrux. To Monte. To every place and every planet she'd ever saved.

Bero put the view back to Ada, and kept it there.

"Are you all right?" he asked, after a while.

"I have everything I've ever wanted."

"That's not an answer."

She smiled, tight and forced, and looked at her hands. Hands that should be scarred and crooked from all the abuse they'd taken, but remained smooth and straight. "You knew, all along, didn't you?"

"Yes."

"Why didn't you tell me?"

"I was afraid." A pause. "After a while, I thought you knew."

"Maybe I did," she agreed, and rested her hands back on the console. "I owe you an apology."

"You do not."

"You were right to take me."

A long pause. "I don't understand."

"You'd said, when it all came out…Oh, what was it? That you'd thought it was better that way. That I was different, like you, because of the chip in my head. That society would accept neither of us because of our bodies. But you didn't mean the chip, did you?"

Quietly, "No."

"Two hundred and thirty years. A lie, then, but only because it hadn't happened yet. I suppose you never really feared I couldn't survive the trip?"

"I did not."

She nodded to herself, feeling more than hearing another round of laughter spark up in the engine bay.

"They're all going to die. They'll age and they'll wither, and I'll keep on. And I'm going to be back here. It's going to be you and me, looking down the barrel of a timeline full of the dead." She gripped the console. "I'm not sure I can do that. Not again."

"The agent is fixed."

"The agent is a trap."

Silence stretched. Sanda watched Ada spin on the viewscreen, whole and blue and green, and tasted bitter fear build up in the back of her throat. She closed her eyes instead, focused on the ship, its gentle rhythms, breathing with it. Being it.

Tomas's mind brushed against hers, drawn by the change in *The Light*, and she smiled, opening her eyes.

"What will you do?" Bero asked, nervous.

"Enjoy it," she said. "For as long as I can."

ACKNOWLEDGMENTS

Thank you to all of my readers for joining me through the books of The Protectorate. I hope you enjoyed the journey as much as I did sharing it with you.

Crafting the finale of a trilogy is never a simple undertaking, but the writing of *Catalyst Gate* provided me with a few unique challenges. A large portion of this book was written on the couch in a hospital room while my husband recovered from emergency surgery (he's well now), and I cannot thank the nurses enough. Their continual supply of warm blankets, water, and gentle nudges to go home and sleep kept me going through a difficult time.

A special thanks to my beta readers, Andrea Stewart and Karen Rochnik, who found the time to offer me wonderful advice even in the middle of a challenging year.

I'm very lucky to be surrounded by many talented writers who have provided camaraderie and shared critiques with me over the years. Thank you to Tina Gower, Marina J. Lostetter, Laurie Tom, Thomas K. Carpenter, Rachel Carpenter, Anthea Sharp, Annie Bellet, Earl T. Roske, Erin Foley, Trish Henry, Laura Blackwell, Laura Davy, Clarissa Ryan, and Vylar Kaftan for your friendship and support.

Publishing these books with Orbit has been a real pleasure, and that's all thanks to Brit Hvide, Bryn A. McDonald, Angeline Rodriguez, Kelley Frodel, Ellen Wright, Nivia Evans, Anna Jackson, James Long, Lauren Panepinto, Angela Man, and my excellent cover artist, Sparth.

Thank you to my agent, Sam Morgan, and everyone at the Lotts Agency.

And thank you to my husband, Joey Hewitt, who not only provides me with love and support and all that wonderful stuff, but gave me story fodder for some pretty graphic medical descriptions this year.

I look forward to spending time with all of you dear readers again in my next adventure.

extras

orbit

meet the author

Photo Credit: Joey Hewitt

MEGAN E. O'KEEFE was raised among journalists and, as soon as she was able, joined them by crafting a newsletter that chronicled the daily adventures of the local cat population. She has worked in both arts management and graphic design, and has won Writers of the Future and the David Gemmell Morningstar Award.

Megan lives in the Bay Area of California.

Find out more about Megan E. O'Keefe and other Orbit authors by registering for the free monthly newsletter at orbitbooks.net.

if you enjoyed
CATALYST GATE

look out for

EXTINCTION BURST
The Devoured Worlds:
Book One

by

Megan E. O'Keefe

*Read the first book in an exciting new space opera trilogy
by Megan E. O'Keefe.*

CHAPTER ONE

Trial Transcript, Earth, Relocated New York City, 2348

Judge L. D. Patson: Exemplar Naira Sharp, you stand accused of initiating the destruction of a Mercator Holdings mining ship, resulting in the death of seventy thousand people. What do you have to say for yourself?

Sharp: The neural maps of those people are undamaged. Mercator Holdings intended to drain that world of relkatite, sending it into planetary collapse syndrome. I defended yet another of our precious cradle worlds from destruction. Humanity is running out of lifeboats, Your Honor. We cannot afford to lose more.

Judge Patson: There is no evidence relkatite mining causes planetary collapse syndrome.

Sharp: Acaelus Mercator all but admitted it to me.

Judge Patson: Ah yes. Your eyewitness statement—which has been roundly disputed and is backed up by no scientific evidence—is not sufficient justification in the eyes of this court.

Sharp: It is sufficient for me.

It was not the first time Naira Sharp had awoken in the wrong body, but it was the first time she had done so with the acrid reek of burning plastics in the air. People said that the first thing you saw in a new body set the tone for how that life would be lived, but Naira had been brought back often enough in the jade-green bays of her enemy that she'd abandoned visual superstition for olfactory. A decision she regretted right about now.

Naira lifted her arms and was surprised to find them medium brown and well muscled, tapering to wrists banded in the green cuffs that marked this body as an employee of Mercator. This stranger's skin glittered with pathways, golden tattoos reminiscent of circuitry. An experimental flexing of the pathways revealed they'd been designed to enhance strength and agility.

Her breath caught, an icy sensation building behind her eyes. She hadn't planned on being in her own body, but neither was this the body she had trained for.

Breathe, Naira told herself. She'd dropped into dozens of different bodies, and though this was not the one she had expected, its shape was not so disparate from her preferred body. A little shorter, maybe. A little stronger.

She'd been counting on waking up in the freshly printed body of Acaelus Mercator, the mission commander for the *Amaranth*. Compared to that pale middle-aged man, riding this body was a milk run. Easy as pie. Other tasty analogies that all pointed to this being simple. Something had gone wrong, there was no denying that, but this body wouldn't stop her. There was the scent of smoke to investigate.

And a ship she needed to destroy.

She planted pathway-enhanced legs against the hatch at the foot of her cubicle and shoved. Discarded bio-matrix sloshed as the tray she'd been printed onto rocketed out, barely catching on the rails. Fresh air burned into her lungs, all at once refreshing and astringent.

"Whoa. Ex. Lockhart, are you all right?" a man asked.

Her pathways adjusted her vision, taking away the sting from the bright lights. Naira didn't recognize this body's name, but she knew the title of exemplar. That, at least, solved the mystery of why she was crammed full of high-end pathways. Naira had been an exemplar herself before she'd joined the Conservators. Her duty as an exemplar had been guarding Acaelus Mercator, the man she was supposed to be impersonating. Shit. The Conservators must have introduced an error in the ship's database when they'd tricked the computer into thinking their neural map uploads were the real key personnel.

Naira rolled off the tray and dropped into a crouch, the cold floor shocking some of the haze from her mind. Slowly, she stood, flexing each muscle one by one, staring at her arms and legs and torso. The circuit board lines mapping her skin glittered as she stretched.

"What's happened?" she asked to give herself time to think.

"I don't know," the man said. He stood by the printer control terminal and slid a panel closed before turning around to face her.

Dark-brown hair fell to the edge of his jaw in straight chunks, partially hiding an angular face with soft hazel eyes and thick eyebrows. The man's demeanor lacked the arrogance common to his family, but there was no hiding the aristocratic lift to his chin, the aquiline nose. Tarquin Mercator. Youngest son of Acaelus Mercator. Thirty-four years of age. Geologist, recluse. She'd never crossed paths with him when she'd been an exemplar.

But he'd crossed her when he'd testified against her at the trial.

The basic facts of his dossier spun through Naira's mind, something to hold on to so that she wouldn't break him between her bare hands, punish him here and now for taking the stand and explaining, with that faux charm common to his family, that she'd been mistaken. That his family's mining practices could not be responsible for the contagion that collapsed planetary ecosystems.

She wasn't here for him. She was here to stop this ship. To keep Mercator lies from destroying yet another viable planet. He might have information and access that could help her accomplish those goals.

"The *Einkorn* fired on us. We can't raise them on comms," Tarquin said.

"Situation on board?" She opened a bulkhead panel and pulled out a set of light body armor. The fibers went on baggy, then adjusted to conform to her body. The back of her forearm lit up briefly, then turned clear, revealing the uplink system integrated with the skin of her arm. She flicked her gaze through the display, checking permissions. Ex. Lockhart had almost as much clearance as Acaelus. She could work with that.

Tarquin twisted his fingers together. "It's a mess, E-X. Half the crew think the other half orchestrated the attack. They're killing one another while the ship burns. Father ordered me to wake you up. I have a group of survivors that needs an escort to an escape shuttle."

"Where's Acaelus?"

"Dead."

"His print failed?" she asked.

"He was printed. He lived. They killed him. We have to *go*."

She turned to meet his even stare. Tarquin Mercator did not mourn his father's death. She wondered if that meant that he didn't care or if he believed the death wasn't violent enough to risk cracking Acaelus's neural map.

There was always a risk. Entanglement took its due eventually. One death too many, and the mind believed it was dead, regardless of how well-shielded a backup had been. No one knew for sure where their personal line was. The more traumatic the death, the better the odds of cracking.

The Conservators would not have killed Acaelus, because she was meant to be in that body. Unless . . . Her stomach clenched. No. They wouldn't have betrayed her. The plan was simple enough.

Add their neural maps to the ship's database, make the AI think they were members of key personnel. Get printed into the big shots' bodies upon entering orbit around Sixth Cradle. Take control of the *Amaranth* and *Einkorn*. Blow the ships' warp cores before they could land on Sixth Cradle, keeping the Mercators from fucking up yet another planet. Then, from the safety of a shuttle set to drift into this system's star, transmit their neural maps back to a safe house in the Sol system and drink to yet another successful op.

The Conservators had already run two identical missions. They wouldn't turn on her now, not after having gone to the trouble of breaking her neural map out of prison.

Metal groaned. Her stomach swooped with the sway of the ship as the *Amaranth* lurched to one side; red and yellow warning lights painted the printing bay in a sickly glow. The artificial gravity stuttered, filling the air with the harsh scent of ozone even as her weight vacillated between boulder heavy and feather light.

Destroying the relkatite containment of the ship's warp core had been the plan. The plan, however, had not included her being on the ship at the time. And it certainly wasn't supposed to go in fits and starts like this.

The surge passed, leaving her panting with her hands on her knees. Tarquin slouched against the terminal he'd been working at, holding on for dear life, his complexion pale and sweaty.

"That's new," he gritted out between his teeth and forced himself to stand.

"Warp core's damaged," she said matter-of-factly, ripping open another bulkhead to find—ah yes, perfect—a wide selection of rifles and handguns. She selected a few weapons, strapped them on, then gave Tarquin a once-over.

"Can you run?"

"Yes." He brushed a hand through his sweaty hair.

"Good. Follow me. Where are the other exemplars?"

"You're the only one I had time to print. There's just a skeleton crew, we entered low planet orbit five hours ago."

"Then who the hell is doing the fighting?"

"I really don't know. It's not Conservators. Father took precautions."

Naira licked Ex. Lockhart's lips, but figured demanding to know what those precautions were might be a little too obvious. She swiped up a map on her arm and put a pin in the location of the nearest shuttle, then switched her rifle to crowd-control mode. The last thing she wanted to do was accidentally kill any of her team. Naira stepped into the hallway.

Smoke hung thick in the air, stinging the back of her throat. The *Amaranth* shuddered again, making her stumble, and she got a hand against the wall to steady herself as a group of people tore around the corner, rushing her.

Well, almost people.

Her blood ran cold. Blank faces stared at her even as they sped up, empty eyes tracking her every movement with less personality than a rock. Their faces were close to human, but something had gone off in the printing. A mouth set too far right. An ear sprouting from the side of a neck. An arm that bent the wrong way around. Half a chest cavity missing.

Misprints. Empties. The ship wouldn't have tried putting a neural map into any of those bodies, but whatever had caused the malfunction had also caused the ship to release the prints instead of disintegrating them into their constituent parts as was protocol.

Naira switched back to lethal and fired without a second thought.

"Let's go," she said to Tarquin once the misprints had been dealt with. "Stay behind me."

He edged into the hallway, throat bobbing as he followed. A little too tight on her heels, but she couldn't blame him and didn't have the time to tell him to back off. The HUD implanted in this print's eyes kept her updated on the *Amaranth*'s systems, and Naira didn't like the amount of red in the display.

This ship was dying, and not in the tidy way the Conservators had planned. The *Einkorn*'s railguns had torn through the ship's stabilizers and thrust system. She scanned the damage even as she marched down the hall, checking her corners.

The hits were too clean, not a random misfire caused by the AI glitching. Whoever had fired from the *Einkorn* wanted the *Amaranth* not just destroyed but crashed onto Sixth Cradle. It'd kill everyone on board, but it'd also risk contaminating the planet with Mercator's mining materials, priming it for the same collapse syndrome that infected the first three cradles.

Naira clenched her jaw. She was a killer in a war few believed in. But this—this wanton destruction of both the human life on board *and* the planet—wasn't something she or the other Conservators would ever endorse.

"E-X, wait." Tarquin jogged up alongside her, and she bit back a remark about him staying behind as he swiped a hand over a door panel.

The door opened into a lab. A quick headcount put the population inside at around fifty people. Mostly Mercator personnel, though five wore the gold-crested flak jackets of the Human Collective Army.

Naira extended two fingers and pressed them against the top of her thigh, the Conservators' current identification signal. No one reacted to the gesture, so she turned it into a stretch.

"My Liege Mercator," one of the soldiers said, snapping to attention and offering a deep bow. The others followed suit, and Naira resisted an urge to roll her eyes. At least this print kept her off the hook when it came to showing Tarquin respect. Exemplars didn't bow to the ruling corporate families, because it meant taking their eyes off their charges. She would have to remember to start referring to the little shit by his title, though. "We stayed put, as you ordered, but we heard gunfire."

"It's handled," she said. "Group up, quickly. This ship has another five minutes left of life."

"Y-yes, sir." The soldier gave her a salute that was arguably more deferential than the one he'd given Tarquin. She felt ill at ease borrowing the honor that should, by rights, belong to Ex. Lockhart, even if Naira had been an E-X before she'd turned against Mercator.

The ship groaned, metal tearing somewhere. Heat rushed down the hall, her pathway-heightened senses picking up on it a second before the wall of flame hit. Naira pivoted, rusty instincts kicking to the surface, and grabbed Tarquin in both arms, folding her shorter but stronger body over his as she slammed him against the wall.

Fire licked up her hips and scoured through her suit, raising bubbling blisters across her back. Naira hissed, pain making her breath short and mind blank as the agony wrapped searing fingers around her shoulders, then—in a flash—was gone, the fire burned out as the suppression system kicked on, showering them all in chemical foam.

She released the princeling and staggered away, bracing one hand against the opposite wall. Black soot painted the floor and the walls. The gray flecks of suppression foam drifting in the air made her think of a dirty snowfall. Naira focused on the visuals because to sink back into the base sensations of her body was to start screaming, and she had to hold it together. Had to get the fuck off this ship.

"E-X," Tarquin said, shoving a hand over his mouth to stifle his horror. Cooked meat perfumed the air. "Your pathways, are they damaged?"

Right, she'd almost forgotten. It'd been years since she'd run a system this nice, but it was like flexing a muscle. The circuit board patterns on her skin tickled as they vibrated, responding to her will, and dulled the exquisite edge of pain.

It would take time for the singed edges of the pathways on her back to build up enough skin for them to reprint themselves fully, but the pain abatement would keep her moving. She checked the HUD. Three minutes until the *Amaranth* stopped listing and started dropping.

"I'll hold," she said and forced herself to stand straight, to take her hand away from the wall, testing her ability to stay on her feet.

The seared muscles of her back stretched with the motion, sparking fresh shockwaves of pain. She trembled, cold sweat coating everywhere she still had skin, her teeth chattering with the beginnings of shock. Fuck.

She ordered the pathways to flood her with all the painkillers they could synth, and her head spun with dizzy euphoria.

Tarquin touched her unburned forearm, lightly, and met her gaze, holding her rifle out to her. "We have to keep moving."

Naira nodded as she took the rifle and stopped herself from slinging the strap over her back at the last second. She dialed back the painkillers. Even though every step was agony, she couldn't fight while high as a satellite.

"Form up," she barked into the lab. "We're running."

"What the fuck was that?" one of the HCA soldiers asked.

"An explosion. Crashing ships have those. Move your fucking ass if you don't want to experience a bigger version."

She didn't bother to wait and see if the others followed. She grabbed Tarquin by the back of the neck and shoved him forward. Footsteps followed, scurrying to keep up, and she heard someone sob softly. Someone else started vomiting. The vibration in her pathways mounted, a persistent ache but ignorable, considering everything else.

Tarquin swiped them into a hangar bay. An arrow-class shuttle waited, surrounded by pallets of supplies that had been meant for the forward expedition to the planet. Her grip tightened around the rifle. They didn't have time to load the supplies. They'd have to

make do with what they found on the planet. Which could get...
complicated.

"Board. Now," Naira ordered. "Do we have a pilot?"

"Me, E-X, sir," said a scrawny woman with eyes that appeared to be permanently sleepy. Naira thought she looked more like a drowned rat than a spaceship pilot, but considering her current options, she couldn't complain.

The others scrambled, climbing up the gangway with a minimum amount of complaining as they realized most of the supplies were outside the ship. Naira shoved a protesting Tarquin up the gangway after them and half turned, putting one hand on the pilot's shoulder. She lowered her voice. "Can you get this shuttle to ground?"

Her throat bobbed. "Yes, E-X, but I was only escorting these people. If the *Amaranth* is going down, I'm going with it."

Naira skimmed her gaze over the name on the woman's jacket. PAISON. She wasn't just a pilot; she was captain of the *Amaranth*. Naira had seen pics and vids of her in their prep work, but she hadn't expected the real deal to be so...fragile looking.

"Captain Paison," she said, "I will tie you to that shuttle's pilot seat if you do not board right this goddamn second. Your responsibility is to these *people*, not this ship. Save your crew."

Paison's lips thinned and her chin jutted out, and Naira caught a glimpse of the woman who had climbed the ranks to become captain of the largest mining ship in human history.

"Copy that," Paison said, then jogged up the gangway, Naira right behind her.

Ninety-seven seconds. Naira slapped the button for an emergency takeoff and the shuttle's gangway dropped, clanging to the ground, as the double doors of the airlock slammed shut.

"E-X," one of the soldiers called to her from their seat. "Strap in!"

She craned her neck around, eyed the harnesses over the seats, and suppressed a shudder. There was no way she was putting her raw back against a seat, let alone strapping on a harness.

Naira moved onto the pilot's deck and stood between the co-pilot's seat and console. Paison glanced up and nodded to her, sliding a command screen from her console to Naira's. Naira bent her knees, lowering her center of gravity, and activated her pathways, sending strength into her legs. Taking some of the strength away from her back stung like hell, but it'd be worse in the chair, where the friction would do more damage.

"Integrity check clear; we are sealed and ready for vacuum," Naira said, flicking through her holographic displays.

"Spooling engines," Paison said.

The shuttle's engines thrummed to life, vibrating through the floor. The soles of her boots softened. Naira sank slightly as the boots switched over to the sticky mode that would allow her to cling in place when they lost gravity from the larger ship.

"We're green to go," Paison said. The shuttle lifted from the floor. "Overriding hangar airlock controls."

In the corner of her eye, Naira's HUD countdown to ship destabilization flashed red. She closed the warning so she could focus on the screens in front of her.

"What the—" Paison cut herself off.

Naira snapped up her head and followed Paison's line of sight. The internal hangar bay door had opened, and a man strode into the room, a rifle over his shoulder. The strobing red lights that warned of imminent depressurization obscured his features.

"Fuck," Paison said, reaching for the airlock controls.

"Continue," Naira ordered.

"But—"

"It's too late. The *Amaranth* is going to drop like a rock in seconds."

Paison's fingers curled into ineffectual fists over her console display. It was true. She knew it was true. That didn't make it any easier.

The man looked up, right at them, squinting through the tinted glass as if he could see them. Maybe he could. The skin of his neck glittered with the presence of pathways.

He met Naira's stare, pressed two fingers against his thigh, and winked.

The hangar opened, and the shuttle was yanked out into the thin air of low planet orbit.

orbit

Follow us:

f **/orbitbooksUS**

/orbitbooks

/orbitbooks

Join our mailing list
to receive alerts on our
latest releases and deals.

orbitbooks.net

Enter our monthly
giveaway for the chance
to win some epic prizes.

orbitloot.com